more detail the faith of the average Roman than do most authors.”

“I can't remember the last time that a book stirred so many emotions! I laughed, cried and cheered my way through this book and can't wait to meet again this wonderful family of characters. Roll on to the next book!”

Awards for *The Etrurian Players* and Praise for the Author...

5 Stars and the 2022 'Highly Recommended' Award of Excellence! - The Historical Fiction Company

2023 Historical Fiction 'Distinguished Favourite' Award - NYC Big Book Award

2023 Finalist - Chaucer Award for Early Historical Fiction - Chanticleer International Book Awards

"...Haviaras handles it all with smooth skill. The world of third-century Rome...is colourfully vivid here, and Haviaras manages to invest even his secondary and tertiary characters with believable, three-dimensional humanity." - The Historic Novel Society

"With vivid descriptions and real dialogue... The author's skill in fusing vivid storytelling with historical detail is astounding, resulting in an engaging and educational story." - The Historical Fiction Company

Reader Reviews...

"So far these are the best books about ancient Rome. Keep them coming!"

"...another home run for this incredibly talented and knowledgeable author. This is one series of books that I look forward to more than any other that I read. The characters and it have become like family to me. I heartily recommend this book and the entire series to anyone who enjoys reading about life in Roman times."

"New author to me but ranks alongside Ben Kane and Simon Scarrow. The attention to detail and all the gory details are inspiring and the author doesn't invite you into the book he drags you by the nasal hairs into the world of Roman life… Well worth a night's reading because once started it's hard to put down."

"Historical fiction at its best! … if you like your historical fiction to be an education as well as a fun read, this is the book for you!"

"Loved this book! I'm an avid fan of Ancient Rome and this story is, perhaps, one of the best I've ever read."

"An outstanding and compelling novel!"

"I would add this author to some of the great historical writers such as Conn Iggulden, Simon Scarrow and David Gemmell. The characters were described in such a way that it was easy to picture them as if they were real and have lived in the past, the book flowed with an ease that any reader, novice to advanced can enjoy and become fully immersed…"

"One in a series of tales which would rank them alongside Bernard Cornwell, Simon Scarrow, Robert Ludlum, James Boschert and others of their ilk. The story and character development…are superb and edge of your seat! The historical environment and settings have been well researched to make the storylines so very believable! I can hardly wait for what I hope will be many sequels! If you enjoy Roman historical fiction, you do not want to miss this series!"

"… a very entertaining read; Haviaras has both a fluid writing style, and a good eye for historical detail, and explores in far

AN ALTAR OF INDIGNITIES

A Dramatic and Romantic Comedy of Ancient Rome and Athens

THE ETRURIAN PLAYERS
BOOK II

ADAM ALEXANDER HAVIARAS

Sign-up for the Eagles and Dragons Publishing Newsletter and get a FREE BOOK today.

Subscribers get first access to new releases, special offers, and much more.

Go to:
www.eaglesanddragonspublishing.com

For Lena and Costis Diassiti,
My love and gratitude for welcoming me into the beautiful chaos of family
life in Athens…and for adopting interesting dogs.

AN ALTAR OF INDIGNITIES

A Dramatic and Romantic Comedy of Ancient Rome and Athens

DRAMATIS PERSONAE

Felix Modestus - leader of The Etrurian Players and, perhaps, the greatest actor and theatre director in the Empire. At least, he thinks so. Once again, he is responsible for much of what follows.

Electra - leading lady of The Etrurian Players, and wife of Felix Modestus. She is figuring out how to deal with an additional child on top of everything else.

Thespis - newborn son of Felix and Electra. Prolific to no end and very needy. He does not like it when others try to sleep.

Rufio Pagano - Etrurian farmer, would-be playwright, and husband of Clara Probita. Surprisingly adept at parenthood, but can not escape mischief. He hates fish, and sees dead people.

Clara Probita - the brains and the money behind her and Rufio's successful farm operation. New mother who does it all, including trying to keep her husband out of trouble. She loves to travel.

Felicia - boisterous newborn daughter of Rufio and Clara. Also prolific, but has a soothing effect on animals and other children.

Errol - aged steward of Rufio and Clara's farm. He keeps things running. He has a soft spot for Clara and Felicia. He also cares for Rufio, but tries not to let it show.

Julius - still the veteran actor of the company. He's finding time for pleasure in his old age. He's earned it!

Fausto - the young, handsome member of The Etrurian Players. Likes to party, especially with friendly prostitutes.

Castor and Pollux - two brothers who have come into their own on stage. They still build and drink a lot, but they are ready for theatrical greatness.

Damon - the mute, flute-playing member of the company. His skill dazzles and mesmerizes the audience. His is the music between scenes.

Beatrice - the company's youngest female member. Somewhat jealous. She acts, she sews, she does the makeup. She also tries to keep her male colleagues in check.

Domela - newest member of the company. No one is quite sure of her past, but she can act and mother with the best of them. She likes older men.

Sextus Annius Sabinus - wealthy Roman praetor and patron of The Etrurian Players. He has become good friends with Felix, but does not always know how to manage him.

Martia Annia Sabina - wife of Sextus and keen to help Electra and Clara every chance she gets. She is dealing with a deep sadness which she does not impose on others.

Captain Memnon - grizzled sea captain of the Hippocampus. Has no patience for landlubbers, and less for dogs, but he can get you where you want to go.

Icthius - the flustered harbourmaster at the port of Pisae. He dislikes Captain Memnon almost as much as errant dogs.

Cassius Cantor - leader of The Rome Antics, a low-brow pantomime troupe. He never misses a promotional opportunity. His work is not to everyone's liking.

Atticus - steward of the villa playing host to The Etrurian Players. He loves theatre and art, and aims to please the guests in his care.

Arcas - grouchy guard at the Porta Hadriana of Athenae. You don't want to get on his bad side.

Cosmo - the grumpy caretaker of the odeon of Herodes Atticus in the heart of Athenae.

Publius Leander Antoninus and Delphina - a Roman magistrate and his wife who live in Athenae. A kind couple with three daughters. They have a thing or two to teach new parents.

The Shade - has a pivotal role to play in this. The less you know, the better.

Boreas and Circe - burly owner of the Taberna Thesias, and his buxom wife who runs the House of the Nymphs. They are all about good food and good times, but no fighting!

Calypso, Amazonia, and Medusa - three friendly prostitutes with a penchant for actors.

Phemius - an intelligent man and librarian of Athenae. He knows his way around the stacks of papyri. If you have a question, he's the man with the answer.

Aegisthus, Cadmus, Zotikos, and Telephus - three actors and their playwright friend. They are the shining, snobbish lights of Athenae's theatre scene. They do not have a high opinion of Romans.

Zonas and Philemon - stoic and epicurean philosophers who can be found in the agora of Athenae. They enjoy watching life go by, and commenting on all of it!

Melampus - an Athenian seer with an aversion to clothing.

Peli - Rufio and Clara's adoptive dog. He's protective of his familia and won't be without them…unless he's enjoying himself. He should be kept on a leash!

Nicodemus - a territorial goat with an attitude. He doesn't like Peli.

Momo - a monkey and member of The Rome Antics. Peli doesn't like him.

Sometimes you have to lose your mind before you come to your senses.

— SOCRATES

PROLOGUS

It is believed by many that, despite the torments of this life, the Gods do indeed love mortals. However, like stern parents who want only the best for their children, they must allow their offspring to suffer and learn, to better themselves through adversity. In so doing, mortal triumphs are so much more wonderful, are they not?

But mortals are a strange lot. They constantly question the blessings that are set before them and are tempted by self-inflicted misery and despair rather than a calm moment, a breath, or a smile.

The Gods try to encourage their mortal delinquents to linger longer in moments of happiness and beauty. Some days Helios' chariot falls slightly slower and more brilliant over the edge of the world, and some nights the stars' fires burn that much more brightly to tempt a lingering look in the dark of night.

The Gods are expert creators, and no wonder, for they have their own purpose to fulfill, as do their children.

Mortals too create…oh yes…

Their art and deeds can inspire the Gods themselves at times, and so admiring gazes can travel both ways along the pathways of the skies between the heights of Olympus and the world below.

Some mortals may claim that the creation of art and life are mutually exclusive, that one cannot co-exist with the other. But the Gods have made these inherently symbiotic. Though the melding of the two may contain something of life's torment, it is indeed possible to reconcile art and life with the joy that is family. Is not the creation of art like to the creation and nurturing of a life? Is the latter not the ultimate form of creation and beauty?

Some mortals believe so and achieve the dance with wondrous grace, while others manage with as little dignity as possible.

Either way, the Gods cannot help but watch their children dance or stumble through their gifted lives. They smile and chide them, and send them back upon the path.

This is a story of mortals prone to tormenting themselves for the sake of the act they love most: Creating.

IT WAS A WINTER DAY UNLIKE ANY OTHER IN THE MIDDLE OF Aegeus' sea, for the roiling waves had been still for days, and the sun's warmth shone full upon the expanse of Neptune's realm. At the Cycladic heart of this sea, blessed Delos lay peacefully where it had finally moored itself to provide succour to Leto and all others who set foot upon its shore.

Upon that island jewel, by the shores of the Sacred Lake, Felix Modestus, the leader of The Etrurian Players, stood contemplating the play of the wind upon the surface of the water about the towering palm where Leto had finally given birth to Apollo, safe at last from Python's menace. In that brilliant Delian light, the fronds of that palm sang of the past, the present, and the future with each breezy kiss.

At the shore of the lake, Felix's wife, Electra, heavily pregnant and exhausted, stood in the water praying for something of the courage shown by Phoebus' mother in her own trials. She caressed her swollen belly and muttered prayers to the Gods, her long black hair falling about her shoulders like a veil in the warm wind.

Felix sighed as he watched, and turned to look at the row of guardian lions behind them, watching him to make sure he did not defile the birthplace of Apollo. Felix breathed deeply, his mind in turmoil, and rolled his muscled shoulders which were still stiff from the previous night's victorious performance in the theatre district of the island.

The tragedy of *The Children of Herakles* may not have been the best choice as he stood upon the brink of parenthood, but it had certainly pleased the crowd. The streets of Delos echoed with the company's praises, and the rest of The Etrurian Players still enjoyed the tributes of the Delians by way of free food and drink wherever they went.

Normally, Felix would have joined in the celebrations and public adoration - he never passed up such opportunities - but Electra had fervently expressed her desire to visit the sacred lake after making offerings to Leto, Artemis, and Apollo that morning. She was driven to do so by some unseen force and would not be deterred, though she was supposed to be resting.

Felix had learned not to try and dissuade her once her mind was set upon a path, especially in the last eight months.

There was, however, another reason why Felix had acquiesced to his wife's desire to visit that sacred spot. The previous night, as the warm glow of wine and revels had worn away and Felix's lids had grown too heavy to fight where he lay beside his wife, a dream had come to him from Apollo himself. And as Felix knew well, when Apollo, God of Art, Music, Prophecy, and Light, turned his gaze upon you, it was one's duty to obey.

"Isn't it a wonder to be standing here?" Electra said over her shoulder to Felix.

"But how?" Felix asked himself aloud as he contemplated all that he had seen under Hypnos' spell.

"What do you mean, 'how?'" Electra turned to see her husband before the lions, as if they were ready to pounce upon him for not listening. "Are you still obsessing over your dream? Felix!"

Felix tore his gaze from the palm and looked to his wife, so beautiful, and yet so ready to engage in battle. He shook his head and walked to her side. "I can't stop thinking about it. To be given such a dream, in this place of *all* places… I need to write to them to tell them."

"We don't have time for that, my love," Electra said, leaning against Felix's bulk. "Our child will be coming soon."

"I know, but this can't be ignored, Electra. Apollo has spoken to me here, on sacred Delos. I know what I need to do. It's no coincidence that just last night we were asked to come to Athenae for this year's Panathenaea."

Electra shook her head. "I can't think of performing anymore until our child is safely born."

"All will be well," Felix reassured her. "Tomorrow, we return to Ephesus and you will give birth to our son."

"You're sure it's a son, are you?" Electra smiled, her hands and his upon her belly. "What if it's a girl? How then would the great Felix Modestus stand against the adoring eyes of his daughter?" She laughed.

"It will be a son, of that I am certain," Felix retorted. "But if it is a girl, I shall stand before her like the lions at our backs to keep her safe."

"I should hope so," Electra sighed as they began to walk around to the eastern edge of the lake. She suddenly felt very tired. "I need to rest now. Let's get back to the inn. Then you can join the others while I sleep."

"Very well," he said, taking her hand. They both turned to look at the great palm one more time, and Felix fell to his knees before Electra, parted her cloak and kissed her belly beneath the dark blue of her stola.

"Apollo, Leto, and Artemis, please bless our child…"

Electra smiled at that, for she had witnessed the slow change in Felix the larger her belly had become. Wonder had a way of changing a man, even one so filled with confidence as Felix. She stroked his thick dark hair and placed her hands upon his bearded cheeks as he looked up at her. "Let's go."

Felix got to his feet and they began to walk.

They had only got a few feet from the shore of the lake when Electra squealed loudly and stood rooted to the spot, her body unable to move another step.

"Felix!" she cried.

"What is it?" he turned to her, suddenly very alert, and then afraid as her eyes locked onto his. "What?"

"My waters have broken!" she hissed, pain echoing in her voice and lacerating her body from womb to foot. "Our child is coming."

Felix was frozen for a moment. "What? It can't! It's not permitted! Not here!" He looked down at Electra's belly and the pool of water soaking the ground at her feet. "You must wait!" he said as if to the baby.

Electra's hand gripped his shoulder tightly as a wave of pain came. "If this child is yours, it will not obey!" She groaned. "So typical!"

"Electra," Felix said, his mind whirling. "Keep it in! It's forbidden to give birth on Delos."

"Then we had better get to the harbour... NOW!"

"Let's go then!" he said, taking her hand and pulling her.

"I can't move!" Electra cried, sweat beading upon her brow. "It hurts too much!"

Felix looked about for a litter, but there were none. There were only the crowds of people going in and out of the nearby Italian agora. Then, without another thought, he tossed his cloak to the ground, scooped his wife up in his thick arms, and charged into the crowds. *Apollo, guide me*! "Everyone out of the way!" Felix Modestus roared.

The crowds were think as they passed the walls of the Italian agora and Felix was red with rage. "Move!" he yelled. "Out of the way!"

"Dominus!" someone called out, and Felix recognized Fausto, the youngest of his players, coming out of the agora.

"Dominus? What's happening?" The young man came running, his long hair still dishevelled from the night of frolic.

"The baby's coming, Fausto!" Felix roared, and several people about them gasped and moved away from them. "We need to get to the harbour! Clear a path for us!"

Fausto gasped when he saw Electra's contorted face.

"Move, Fausto!" Electra yelled, spurring him into action.

Fausto whirled around, his arms waving wildly as he ran ahead. "Make way for the baby of Felix Modestus!" he shrieked.

The three of them barrelled along the street only to be met with either applause and cheers of encouragement, or occasional chiding and reminders of the consequences should the birth occur on the island.

"Let us through!" Fausto shouted again as they passed the temple of Dionysus and the monument of the famed actor, Carystius, with its twin phalluses pointing to the sky.

Electra looked up at those soaring, erect knobs and, reminded of Felix's attentions, proceeded to punch him as he carried her through the crowds of the sanctuary of Apollo. "You did this to me! You couldn't help yourself!"

"Stop it, woman! I can't see where I'm going!" Felix roared.

"Get that woman off the island!" a passing priest of Apollo cried as he exited the great temple in the middle of the sanctuary.

"Then get out of our way, priest!" Felix shouted back as they followed Fausto between two temples and past the colossus of Apollo who seemed to smile down at them.

Electra cried out louder this time, and the sound of pain in her voice made Felix move even faster, though exhaustion was beginning to grip his every limb.

"MOVE!" Felix barked as they came onto the Sacred Way flanked by the two stoas filled with shoppers.

Ahead, Fausto squealed and jumped as a black and white serpent darted across his path.

Felix swerved precariously to avoid the asp before a stray dog grabbed it and bolted.

"Don't drop me!" Electra cried.

"I've got you!" Felix grunted as they reached the next agora and the harbour came into view. "Fausto!" he shouted. "Go and fetch the others from the theatre district! Tell them what's happening!"

Fausto stopped, breathless. "Yes, Dominus! It'll be fine, Electra!" he said as he watched them charge for the harbour.

"Shut up, Fausto!" Electra shouted back.

"She'll be fine," Fausto smiled and muttered. "It'll be fine." He then turned and ran up the street to find the rest of the company.

As they came to the ancient harbour, Felix bellowed orders. "A boat! Quickly!" he shouted. "We need to get to Rheneia!" They went straight for the area where several small vessels were moored, bobbing up and down in the brilliant turquoise water.

Without waiting for the sailors lazing about in that strange winter sun to move, Felix picked the sturdiest-looking vessel and stepped in from off the pier, just barely keeping upright with Electra in his arms.

"Now, or I'll have you flogged!" Felix shouted at the sailors who stood slowly.

"Hey, that's Felix Modestus!" one of the men said to the others. "I saw him as Herakles last night! He was fantastic!"

"We need to get across the straight to Rheneia right away!" Felix ordered.

This time, three men jumped to, all smiles and quick about

their work as they untied the boat and unfurled the small, triangular sail.

Electra screamed as the boat pulled out of the harbour. She looked at the distant island where people went to give birth and to die, and it seemed an impossible distance. "Felix…my love…" She shook her head. "I can't do it! It's no use! Something is wrong!"

Felix knelt beside her in the bottom of the boat near the prow. He shifted ropes and a couple sacks of grain to try and make her as comfortable as possible as the boat rose and fell over the increasingly tumultuous sea toward the island. "I've got you. I won't let anything happen to you." He removed his tunica, folded it, and placed it behind her sweating head.

"Having a baby, are we?" one of the sailors suddenly said from over Felix's shoulder, looking down at Electra.

"What do you think?" Electra shouted.

"Step back," Felix warned the man.

But the sailor persisted. "Don't worry, lady. It happens all the time. That's why we have these boats ready to go."

"Shut up!" Electra howled as another wave of pain spun through her body.

While the other two sailors manned the rudder and sail, the third one persisted. "Can I just say… I saw your performance last night…and it was one of the best I've seen in a long while!"

Felix turned to look at the man, incredulous at the poor timing.

"You were magnificent as Herakles!"

"That's enough!" Electra screeched, and before Felix knew it, her hand had reached over his shoulder to grab the sailor by the tunic and pull him overboard with a great splash. "Swim back, cretin!"

The two other sailors laughed at the sight. "What's that?" asked the one. "Second time?"

"Third," the other replied.

"Sail on!" Felix roared, standing in the boat to face them.

"Do not worry, Felix Modestus! The midwives of the shore are always ready. As we said, this happens all the time!"

"Not to us, it doesn't!" Felix said, before turning back to Electra. It was then that the look in her eyes told him she was not exaggerating.

"Felix..." she breathed rapidly, shaking her head. "Our child is here! We're...we're not going to make it!" This time, she cried so loudly that the gulls above were silenced and her voice seemed to echo over the sea.

Felix breathed and stood to look up at the sun where it hovered over sacred Delos. He thought of that swaying palm where Apollo had been born, and of the dream the god had sent to him the previous night. *This is meant to be...* he thought.

"The baby's here!" Electra wailed.

"And so am I, my love!" Felix said, kneeling before her. He began to gather the hem of her stola and hoist it up.

"What are you doing?" she asked.

"I will deliver our child!" he declared.

"Oh no!" Electra pushed at her dress to cover up. "Look away you!" she shouted at the sailors who gazed skyward, whistling. "Felix stop!"

"It is time!" he said. "I can do this!"

Electra screamed again, her legs widening with the pressure, as Felix hoisted her stola again and set her cloak in the floor of the boat beneath her.

"I see our child's head!" Felix suddenly said. "Push, my love! PUSH!"

Electra pushed with all of her might, her nails digging into the wood edges of the boat, her voice carrying over the water such that the midwives of Rheneia began to gather upon the shore.

"Again!" Felix said. "Push!"

Electra braced herself against his shoulders and did as he commanded in that moment.

"Again!" he yelled.

She wept then. "I can't! It hurts too much!"

"The Gods are watching, Electra! Our child wants to come to us! Now! PUSH!"

From deep within, Electra found the strength she needed, and she pushed with all of her might, long, and lingering, and painful. But she did it, unaware of the spray of the sea upon her head, of the applause of the sailors, and of Felix's victorious shouts.

Then she heard the wailing of a child in all of that chaos, and she looked down to see Felix holding their baby, his face all smiles and pride as he looked up at her.

"We have a son!" he shouted. "You did it, Electra!" he said as he wrapped the child in her cloak and handed it to her.

"A son?" Electra said, her voice shuddering with exhaustion, her eyes blurry with joyous tears.

"We're almost there!" one of the sailors said.

"Fetch a litter!" the other yelled to those on the shore.

Felix sat beside Electra as the boat bobbed toward the shore, and together they looked at the child they had brought into the world.

"He's beautiful," she said, exhausted as she leaned her head against her husband.

"Yes he is," Felix replied, gently stroking the child's cheek. "And so are you." He kissed her cheek just as they felt the bottom of the boat grinding on the pebbled shore of Rheneia.

"Quickly!" one of the midwives shouted, directing the litter-bearers to the boat, while she and several others reached out to help Electra.

"Get her to the first hut!" the midwife commanded her servants. "The after birth is coming!"

"Will she be all right?" Felix asked, jumping from the boat to walk alongside the litter.

"She'll be fine!" the midwife said. "Well done!"

"Felix don't leave me!" Electra said, clutching her child to her breast.

"I'm coming my love!" he called back to her, noting the row of birthing huts at the top of the beach.

He turned back to look at the sea and the distance they had just travelled from Delos.

A cool wind was picking up and, despite the fact that he only wore breeches, he felt flushed and warm with all that had just happened.

Felix Modestus strode into the sea then to wash his hands and face. He stood there, looking at the place where Apollo had been born, and felt the magnitude of what had just happened. He raised his hands to the sun above.

"Oh mighty Apollo... Bless our child the length of his days. He has made his entrance onto this stage most boldly. May he live his entire life in such a way!"

Felix lowered his arms and breathed deeply of the sea air, the Delian light reaching out to him from across the straight to fill his eyes.

He then remembered his dream of the previous night, and nodded. "I hear you, Lord Apollo. It shall be so." He turned to go to Electra and their child. "I'll wager you haven't seen a crossing like that before!" he said to the two sailors who were washing out the bottom of their boat.

"Happens all the time!" the one said.

But Felix ignored him and strode up the beach toward the huts.

"Someone bring me a stylus, ink, and paper! I have letters to write!"

ACT I

HAPPINESS AND WINE

I

NOT AGAIN!

2 05 CE

THE GODS WERE SMILING DOWN ON ETRURIA THAT LOVELY morning in Aprilis when the sun shone brightly and the birds sang their joyous songs of life and renewal. All over the countryside, flowers had begun to assert themselves in lively bursts of purple, red, and yellow to adorn rocks and roadways. In the forests upon the hills, deer and boar roamed the damp, scented pathways, their eyes and ears keen to the presence of the men and women toiling in the neighbouring fields.

In one corner of that lush and lively world, the small latifundium of Rufio Pagano and Clara Probita lay peacefully in the shadow of an ancient tomb upon a hill, crowned with whispering cypresses. The land was full of promise for the coming season with healthy orchards of plum, apple, and pear, and the olive groves and vines had remained strong through the winter months, weathering the frosts with aplomb.

The labourers on the farm had started early that morning, each happy to make a contribution to the familia they had all so recently been welcomed into. Not all latifundia were as kind and thriving and so, for those who tilled that happy bit of land, there was rarely anything to complain about.

That said, there seemed to be something of a fuss in the air that day, for the dominus had been forced to abandon his labours due to the arrival of the impatient courier who now stood by the well with a bucket of water, wiping at his riding breeches which were stained with canine urine.

"You should be happy of that bit of piss!" said Errol, the ancient foreman of the farm, as he passed the flustered messenger. "That means Peli likes you."

"Likes me?" the man said, rubbing at the deep canary yellow splatters. "Your dog's a menace!"

"Ach! You're Fortuna's favourite today, my son," Errol chuckled. "If Peli doesn't like you, he'll have your figs clasped tight between his jaws in a second. Then you'd be wiping up a fair bit more!" The old man continued on his way back up to the domus leaving the courier staring after him.

"Tell your dominus I need an answer!"

Errol waved as if at a fly and carried on.

"'WHEN YOU ARISE IN THE MORNING, THINK OF WHAT A precious privilege it is to be alive - to breathe, to think, to enjoy, to love…' Remember that beautiful quote you read to me last week, Rufio?"

Clara Probita lay back upon a couch, feeding her baby daughter, Felicia, beneath the loggia at the back of the domus. She watched her flustered husband pace back and forth with the papyrus scroll still clutched in his hand.

Rufio stopped suddenly to wag the scroll at her. "Yes, well… Marcus Aurelius didn't have his best friend sending sudden summonses from across the sea, demanding an answer on the spot." He began to pace once more. "A matter of life and death? Again?"

"It's been some time since we last saw Felix and Electra," Clara said, trying to soothe him. "It's been so long since Rome."

"Not long enough!" Rufio coughed, paused to take a sip of watered wine from the cup upon the table where ientaculum had been laid out, and then continued to wear a path of worry into the tiles at his feet.

"Rufio," Clara sighed. "Just the other day you were saying how much you missed them."

"I know... It's just...things have settled so nicely now." He came to sit beside his wife and daughter, shoulders hunched and exhausted from his self-inflicted worries. "Felicia has only just begun to sleep through the night, the farm is thriving with more orders for oil and wine than we can handle-"

"You forget what a good quartermaster I am!" Clara interjected. "All the orders are going to be met."

"I'm sorry. Yes," Rufio acknowledged, taking a moment to breathe and look her in those bright grey eyes. "You're a wonder, my love, and I couldn't manage without you... But still!"

Just then, Errol came through the domus and sat across from them feeding Peli a piece of cheese from off the table.

"Errol, don't give him cheese," Rufio pleaded. "The smells that waft from him afterward are intolerable."

"It's all right," Errol responded. "I can't smell much anyway since the horse kicked me last year."

Rufio shook his head.

"By the way," Errol continued, "that there messenger is anxious for a reply. What do you intend to tell him?"

"I don't know!" Rufio barked, and Peli echoed the sentiment, his mismatched eyes scowling at Rufio.

"Oh, just eat your cheese," Rufio muttered at Peli.

Clara finished feeding Felicia, and pat her back a couple of times before settling her on her lap. "Rufio, read the letter again, slower this time so we can take it all in."

They all looked at Rufio - his wife, his baby, his servant, and his dog - each with strange and expectant looks upon their features.

"Fine." Rufio stood to face them, took another drink of the watered wine, and unrolled the papyrus.

"To Rufio Pagano and Clara Probita
From The Felix Modestus"

Rufio shook his head. "Really? *The* Felix Modestus?"

"Just read, Rufio," Clara urged, making every attempt not to laugh.

Rufio continued.

"I am writing to you from the island of Delos where my son was almost born. We just made it off of the island which is good, for if we had not, The Etrurian Players would never have been allowed to perform in this sacred place again."

"You see?" Rufio stopped reading. "He just mentions a baby in passing!" He turned his eyes back to the missive, rubbing his beard with his right hand as he found his place again.

"But there are much more urgent matters I am writing to you about. I had a dream last night as I slept fitfully beneath a Delian moon. Apollo himself sent me this dream. He appeared to me, shining and resplendent, his star-whirling eyes intense and adamant."

Rufio's voice faded away, for a tingle had spun up his spine and it was most unnerving.

"Out loud, Rufio," Clara said.

"Sorry, yes," he said before starting again.

"…intense and adamant… For the first time in my life, I was nervous…"

Rufio shook his head. "First time!" he scoffed.

"… After a moment, Apollo spoke of a trial The Etrurian Players must undertake. He spoke of all members of the troupe, 'both near and far', and even as I listened to the shining god, at those words, your faces appeared to me."

Rufio sat down now, as if his legs were ready to buckle from frustration, though fear was no small part of his momentary distractedness.

"Apollo commanded that we perform a specific play at the Panathenaea this very year. He said to me that it was a matter of life and death for a 'very great artist and Roman'. I immediately thought of myself - that much was obvious - but then I remembered that the previous night, after my performance as Herakles, I received an invitation to perform as part of the Panathenaea!"

Rufio looked closely at the papyrus here and noted some tiny droplets. "I think he's wept upon the paper here."

"Felix?" Clara asked. "He must be quite shaken if Apollo has appeared to him!"

Rufio peered more closely, and then sniffed, wrinkling his nose a little as he did so. "Never mind. It's Theran wine." He carried on, trying to decipher Felix's hasty scrawl.

"I will write to Sextus so that he may set things up…he has friends in Athenae. But you must prepare to come as soon as possible to the Goddess Athena's city and join us. And remember to leave the dog, and bring the baby. We should love to meet her at last!"

Rufio looked down at Peli, who sighed from where his head lay flat upon the tiled floor.

"I tell you both, I feel like a god after all that has happened here. There is much to tell."

"I see that he still drips with sacrilege," Errol added as he chewed upon a crust of bread. "Always naughty that one, ever since you three were young!"

Clara smiled and nodded to Rufio to finish.

"I pray, my friends, that you will come to my aid as you did before. Matters of life and death are nothing to be trifled with."

"There he goes again! Life and death…" Rufio rubbed the top his ginger head rapidly as if he were faint from frustration.

"Electra and my son are both well. We cannot wait to see you… Felix."

Rufio tossed the papyrus onto the table between he and Clara.

"It's a terribly written letter!" Rufio said, leaning back, his arms crossed.

"What are you angry about?" Clara asked as she stood with Felicia in her arms, stepping into the morning sunlight at the edge of the loggia. "His hubris?"

"No. He's always been like that. '*The* Felix Modestus' is a bit much, but no, that's not it."

"Then what, Rufio?" Clara asked. "It's been almost three years since we last saw them. Wouldn't it be nice to be together again? And you've never been to Athenae. It's where theatre was created!"

Rufio stood and turned to step onto the grassy verge where he looked out over the olive groves to the distant vines beyond. He loved his home, what he and Clara had done with it. He ached when he was away from it, and so was loathe to even consider time away. He could feel Clara and Errol staring at his back, but he did not turn. He straightened his deep blue tunica with the embroidered meander borders and remembered when Felix gave it to him in Rome when they had last performed together. He closed his eyes.

Another performance? "The messenger said he came from Ephesus!" Rufio suddenly declared.

"So?" Clara said.

"But Felix says he wrote this from Delos, not Ephesus. There's a continuity problem there!"

"I think you're missing the point, my love."

"Am I? He speaks of urgency and making haste, and yet he waits to send the letter?"

"Rufio…" Now it was Clara's turn to shake her head.

"It's just another one of his ploys to lure us to do his bidding."

"Apollo's bidding, it seems," Errol chimed in with raised, bushy eyebrows.

"Don't you have some workers to oversee?" Rufio said, and not kindly, but the old man chuckled and ignored the jibe.

"Rufio, was it a ploy last time we were in Rome?" Clara asked. "Do you even remember the men who tried to kill Felix *during* our performance?"

Rufio was silent.

"Had you not been there, Felix would not be alive today."

Rufio began his pacing again. "I doubt we can do it. I worry about leaving the latifundium when things are so busy."

"What is there to worry about? Errol is here and the workers know what they are doing." Clara came to stand in his way and make him look at her.

"The planting isn't finished," he said.

"One more week, and it will be," she answered. "Everything is on time."

"The groves and vines need pruning."

"We finished that weeks ago." Clara smiled and tickled Felicia's chin.

"The animals will miss me too much. What about Peli and Stella?"

"They'll survive, Rufio."

Peli barked in protest to that.

"Oh stop," Clara chided, and the dog sat pleadingly at her feet.

"You see?" Rufio presented the sad canine.

"You men will stick together, won't you?"

"I also don't want to leave Stella alone with that new field hand. He thinks they're wedded to each other!"

As if on cue, Stella came trotting up from the olive grove with a flower crown ringing her furry ears. Behind her, walked her intended.

"Get back to work!" Rufio shouted at the young man who turned, head down, and went in the opposite direction, the very image of sadness.

"He's a good lad," Errol said, "a strong worker."

"I'm afraid he'll try and consumate his made-up marriage!"

"Don't be ridiculous!" Clara tried to keep a straight face.

"Oh, I wouldn't worry about that," Errol added. "I heard it straight from one of the maids that he's no longer able to be lustful after the mare kicked him last year."

"I always liked that mare," Rufio said.

"Listen, Rufio," Clara began, her hand reaching out to rest on his shoulder. "They are our chosen family, and we haven't seen them in a long time. I would like to see Electra too, and meet their son. I already feel time slipping by."

"But what about all there is to do here?"

"The Panathenaea takes place in Augustus. We'll be back here in time for the harvests. Also, the oil and wine shipments from last year's crop are set to be delivered next week. The timing is, when you think about it, perfect. We could use a change of scenery as well."

"Not me. I like it here," Rufio crossed his arms and tried to pull away, but she held him fast.

"Don't pout. That doesn't work with me, you know it. One

of the shipments of wine is set to leave for Graecia next week. We can go with it!"

Rufio found it difficult to argue with Clara. He noted how fervently she wanted to go. In truth, he had heard the excitement in her voice the first time they had read the letter. If he was honest with himself, he did miss Felix and the others. *Perhaps an adventure will help me with my own work?* he wondered. But the uncertainty was still there.

That is, until Errol stood and came to Rufio's side.

"I know you think me an old dotard, Rufio, so what I have to say may not sway you."

"What is it, Errol?" Rufio forced himself not to dismiss the old man, for he had truly come around after the death of Pagano Pater. "Please, tell me what's on your mind."

"I remember the last time Felix Modestus sent you a letter… You were at the bottom of life's barrel then, I don't mind saying. But even then, you were ass-stubborn about leaving this place, about going anywhere."

"What is your point?"

"My point is…look at how much good came of that letter!" He looked directly at Clara and Felicia. "How different would your life be had you not listened to Felix, no matter his sacrilege. Perhaps the Gods *do* speak through him in some mysterious way?" Errol shrugged. "I don't pretend to know the ways of Apollo - he's too lofty a god for my prayers - but when it comes to the things you love, the path you both and Felix have walked together, it seems that he's the one to listen to."

Clara stood beside Errol and together they looked at Rufio who was struck by the old man's sudden wisdom.

Rufio sighed as he began to lean toward going to Athenae, though he was frustrated that he did not know what play they were to perform. *Felix and his great reveals!* He looked down at Peli then.

"You'll have to stay here. You can't come this time."

Peli whined.

"Do you people have an answer for me, or no?" The courier whom Peli had irrigated earlier that morning came around the corner of the domus to find them, impatient as he was to get going. "The sender of that letter spared no expense. He paid for the fastest service!"

"Of course he did," Rufio grumbled.

"Do you have an answer?" the man asked again.

"Tell him 'The Rufio Pagano' and 'The Clara Probita' will meet him in Athenae."

Just then, Peli began to growl and charged after the messenger who ran screaming back around the way he had come.

"You had better write something to send with him," Clara said, a broad smile gracing her lips. "That messenger won't remember anything after Peli bites him."

"You're right," Rufio said, watching jealously as Stella nuzzled Errol.

"I'll start packing," Clara said. "Here, take Felicia. She needs to be changed." She handed their daughter to Rufio who held the child aloft to look at her flawless face.

Rufio couldn't help but smile when he looked upon his daughter, and thought that Errol's wisdom was greater than he could ever have imagined. "Looks like we're going on an adventure, Felicia!"

Beside them, Errol sighed and spoke to Stella. "Come on girl… Let's go find your husband."

Rufio turned to watch the old man and his ass walk off, but his gaze returned to his daughter as the sound of a surging squirt erupted within her tiny bracae.

"You pleased with yourself?"

Felicia smiled.

II

SEEKING JOY

It was early evening upon the Esquiline, that lofty, peaceful, hilltop neighbourhood that overlooked the much seedier maze of the Suburra of Rome. Safe behind the high walls of their urban compounds, the elite of Roman society roamed their gardens where the air was scented with lemon and jasmine, and dined upon plush couches within the adorned triclinia of their vast villas.

In the gardens surrounding the domus of Praetor Sextus Annius Sabinus, the scattered cries of roving peacocks accented the cool evening calm while he and his wife, Martia Annia, dined together at the end of the long row of low tables.

As he sipped his wine and ate, Sextus' eyes were drawn to the theatrical mural that adorned one of the walls, the fresco that had been painted in the wake of the Ludi Apollinaris a couple of years previously by members of The Etrurian Players. He smiled as he thought of that heady victory in which he and Felix Modestus had thrilled Rome with their production of Plautus' *Menaechmi*. The success of those games, which Sextus had overseen, had ensured his promotion from aedile to praetor and the joy he and Martia had felt in the wake of that success had been palpable.

In recent months, however, a pall had been cast over their

home, and his wife's usually cheerful demeanour was greatly dampened.

That morning, Sextus had sensed that something was amiss as he departed for the Forum Romanum, but he had been rushed and had not wanted to press Martia. Now, however, as they ate in silence, gazing longingly at the happy fresco before them, he knew he should ask.

"Is everything all right, my love?" He reached out to take her hand.

It had always been in Martia's nature to lean toward happiness and gratitude, and a refusal to burden him with her own worries had been a big part of that.

Martia's slender neck turned as she tore her eyes from the fresco to look upon her husband, her bright eyes painfully sad, lined with more kohl than she habitually used. She had not wanted to disappoint him again, believed she could just keep it to herself, but the pain was too great.

"Please, Martia," Sextus said softly. "You can tell me anything, you know that."

"I don't want to upset you."

He smiled and shook his head slowly. "You could never upset me. You are my world." He stroked her cheek. "I know something has upset you. Why do you think I returned early?"

"A lack of clients, perhaps?" she tried to joke.

"I do wish that were the case, but no," Sextus answered. "Tell me. I'm your husband. You can unburden yourself to me."

Martia nodded and turned upon the couch to look directly at him. "I got my menses today."

Sextus felt his heart plummet, but he did not let on. There were moments when his political acumen proved useful. This was one of them. "That is why you have not been yourself." He stroked her hand.

"Yes." Martia's lip trembled, but she rallied as he kissed her forehead. "I'm so sorry, Sextus. I-"

"You what? You think you have disappointed me?" He smiled as sincerely and compassionately as he could, knowing that it was what she needed. "My love… Don't you know me by now? Surely you know that in my eyes you can do no wrong."

"But we've been trying for a child for so long. I know how important it is to you, to both of us."

Sextus breathed deeply and put his arm about her, nodding to the servants to leave the triclinium from where they hovered in the darkened corners. When they were gone he kissed her forehead and cheek. "You are right. It is something we have both wanted. But…perhaps it is the will of the Gods that we do not have children?"

"You don't know that. Perhaps you are meant to have a child with some other wife? Perhaps this is your punishment for marrying a freedwoman and not a noble like your family wished you to?"

Sextus ran his hand over his short hair and smiled again. "That is nonsense, and you know it. I'll tell you what *I* know. I know that it *is* the Gods' will that we should be together, and I knew it from the first moment we met. Yes, it may be that we are not meant to have children of our own. So be it. I still enjoy the trying!" He winked.

Martia smiled, despite herself, and her eyes brightened once again with the love she felt for that kind and honourable man.

"Besides," he continued, "in a way, you have children. Think of all those you help through your charitable work in the Suburra! You have improved the lives of so many children there. You're the only woman that I know of who walks through that wretched neighbourhood to help others with her own hands. I am so proud of you!"

And he was, for while other politicians' wives shunned such work, Sextus was constantly amazed by Martia's kindness and grace in helping the less fortunate people of Rome. She handed out money, bread, and clothing from a fund they had set aside for just that purpose. And it was not for votes for her husband, but out of the kindness of her own heart. When she visited overwhelmed mothers whose husbands were away at war, to give them aid and help care for their young ones, some of the noblewomen whispered that it was undignified. But Sextus argued that it was the complete opposite, that his wife was the most dignified and noble woman he had ever known.

"I cannot imagine a life with anyone but you, my love. Please know that."

"Nor can I." She started to feel a little cheered, if not relieved at his reaction, and she chided herself inwardly for having doubted him. She sniffed once, sighed, and took up her golden wine cup to sip. "Tell me of the day's business. What happened?"

"Oh, nothing of great import. Just a long line of clients seeking favours. I don't want to bore you with that. But! The messenger that Felix Modestus sent to Etruria stopped in Rome on his way to Ostia. Seems he wanted to update me, but also he needed the help of a medicus. Some kind of animal bite…" Sextus shook his head. "Anyway, he told me that Rufio and Clara have accepted the invitation to come to Athenae for the Panathenaea."

"Really?" Martia's face lit up at that news.

"Truly," Sextus confirmed. "They will take a ship from Pisae. Apparently they have a wine shipment bound for Piraeus anyway."

"They do make good wine!" Martia winked, raising her cup again.

"That they do!" Sextus laughed, appreciative of the shipments of wine and olives which Rufio and Clara had sent them. "But it will be good to see them again, will it not?"

"It will be wonderful," Martia agreed.

"But if seeing them with their children will upset you, Martia, we don't have to go. I can make excuses-"

"Absolutely not!" she said quickly. "What sort of person would I be if I were not happy for our friends?"

"You would be an ordinary human with feelings."

"Well, thankfully, I'm not *ordinary*!"

Sextus laughed at her jest. "Quite right! You're a goddess among us!"

She blushed and waived the compliment off.

When they had first received their letter from Felix with news of their newborn child - secondary to the proposed performance in Athenae, of course - Martia's eyes had gone quite glassy, but it seemed that she was now at ease with the news.

"I really cannot wait to see them!" Martia said.

"Nor I. Not only have I missed our friends, but we've also missed so many of their wonderful performances. There was Leptis Magna, Alexandria, Caesarea, many more in Ephesus, and then the last one on Delos!... I can't wait to see them."

At first, Martia had been worried what friendships with actors might do to her husband's political career, that in being known to associate with common players his noble peers would ostracize him. However, after Felix had been crowned by Emperor Serverus before all of Rome at the Ludi Apollinaris, other opinions mattered little. The emperor approved, and the games had been a tremendous success. Besides, she had seen that Sextus felt lighter, happier. It was a wonderful relief that even the thought of spending time with that raucous troupe seemed to blow away the fog of sadness that had so recently hovered about them.

Sextus popped one of the Etrurian olives into his mouth. "I was thinking…"

"Yes?" Martia asked.

"I think I'll take up the offer of that magistrate, the grandson of Herodes Atticus, the former imperial magistrate…"

"The grandson…" Martia tried to remember. "You mean the man we met at the imperial banquet last month?"

"Yes! That's him. We spoke at length about Athenae then, and about theatre. He had been told about the games we put on, and wanted to speak with me." Sextus shook his head to gather his thoughts. "At any rate, he invited us to use his villa in Athenae if we ever needed it. It is a city villa which his grandfather built, but the family rarely uses now. Herodes Atticus preferred his villa near the sea at Kephissia when he was not at his home in Marathon, or the other place in…what was it?"

"Eva, in the Peloponnese," Martia remembered.

"That's right! But the timing works well for my work too as I've been meaning to connect with my fellow magistrate, Antoninus, in Athenae on some building and improvement projects for the city. Some imperial funds have become available. He has a villa near that of Atticus, on the slopes of Hymettos."

Martia smiled and began to eat her food rather than pick at it as she had been doing so precisely before.

After some discussion of the details of the journey, they began to reminisce about that magnificent performance in the theatre of Pompey at the now-famous Ludi Apollinaris. They remembered the colour, the chaos, and the cheer of the crowds as The Etrurian Players had taken their bows. They were indeed memories the two of them revisited as often as they could and, when they did, it never failed to put a smile upon their faces.

"Does Felix require much for this production?" Martia

asked. Ever since the performance in Rome, Sextus had been a funding partner for the company who had enjoyed success after success around the Middle Sea.

Sextus shook his head. "He said he didn't need much apart from a place to stay and rehearse. The villa is large enough to accommodate all of us."

"We'll all stay together in the same villa?" Martia asked, more surprised that her husband would want to.

"Why not? It will be fun!"

"I agree!" Martia clapped. "Maybe a little chaos will be good for us?"

"Absolutely, my love!"

She was quiet again, and for a moment Sextus feared that her thoughts had turned back to children, that she was perhaps dreading being around Rufio and Felix's offspring.

"Do you think the Athenian theatre crowds will warm to The Etrurian Players? From what I've heard you say, the audiences there are quite different from our Roman ones. If the play is not well-received, it could harm your reputation."

Sextus nodded. "You're right, of course. But I'm not worried!" He clapped his hands and pulled his wife to her feet to kiss her. "I'm not worried at all! We shall go to Athenae, and we will enjoy that magnificent cultured city together with our friends! The Panathenaea is one of the greatest festivals in the Empire! You'll see!"

"I'm silly to worry." Martia laughed as Sextus spun her around. "The Etrurian Players can win over anyone!"

"Indeed they can!" Sextus agreed.

"I'll start packing tomorrow," Martia said before planting a lingering kiss on her husband's lips.

III

THE WINE-DARK SEA

In the midst of those Etrurian, springtime days of sun and rain, cool nights and misty mornings, the customary peace of the routines on Rufio and Clara's latifundium was interrupted by moments of chaos as the day of their departure for Pisae, and thence to Athenae, approached.

When the day of their departure finally arrived, Rufio stood at the front of their domus holding Felicia in his arms as the spring breeze toyed with her blonde curls. He watched the workers load up the seven large wagons with amphorae of their wine which they were to accompany to Athenae aboard their ship, the Hippocampus.

Normally he would have been helping load and secure the cargo in the wagons, but he had become so flustered in his anticipation of the great journey ahead that Clara had asked him - No, commanded him! - to take care of Felicia while she oversaw the work, a task which she had learned when she had lived in Syracusae years before.

Rufio was happy to oblige, for he wanted to savour the sounds of his home before he left it for several months. He enjoyed the dripping of last night's rain from the new leaves on the chestnut trees nearby, and the constant chatter of birdsong by an avian chorus, or a sole sunrise performer. His eyes gazed over the steep green hillsides that surrounded their home, and the lanes lined with sentry cypresses. He sighed.

The truth was that he had not really left Etruria since he had last been to Rome, and now that they were to bring their child along with them, there seemed to be an added dimension of anxiety. He looked down at Peli who still sulked in the dirt at his feet, and never seemed to leave Felicia's side.

"I'm even going to miss you," Rufio said to the dog, kneeling down so that Felicia's little hand could reach out to grab a tuft of Peli's black and white fur.

Peli whined and rolled over, his tongue lolling out the side of his jaws.

Rufio laughed. "Who do you think you're fooling? Poor, innocent you, being left behind. I feel for that messenger whose groin you clasped onto. Frankly, I don't know how the man could ride."

Rufio yawned and stood up, and Felicia did the same, her soft head leaning into his neck as she did so. He smiled at that, and suddenly, his exhaustion did not matter. Not that she had kept them awake. No. His most recently sleepless nights were of his mind's own making as he mulled over the greatness of the journey before them. It would take a couple of days by road to Pisae, and then at least thirteen from Pisae's port to Piraeus, the great port of Athenae. And that's if the seas were relatively calm.

Memnon, the captain of the Hippocampus, insisted that the corbita was a sturdy vessel, and adequate enough to safely transport Rufio and his family. The grizzled seaman had dined with them two nights before to discuss the journey and cargo before heading back to Pisae to prepare the ship for their imminent departure.

The thought of all of it made Rufio's stomach churn, and he held Felicia closer as if she were a talisman against his growing discomfort. He looked down the path from his hiding place among the curls of his daughter's hair to see Clara coming up with Errol, laughing with the old man as they walked together.

How did I get so lucky? Rufio wondered as he watched his wife come toward him, her face happy, flushed, and full of life. It was then that he was reminded of Errol's shocking bit of wisdom which had finally convinced Rufio to accept Felix's invitation and take the journey. *If so much came of my trip to Rome, the Gods only know what will come out of this adventure.*

He wasn't quite sure he believed his own optimism, but yielded to it anyway.

The truth was that Clara wanted to go on this journey more than anything. She had been beaming ever since they had taken the decision to go, and talked of little else than of seeing Felix and Electra, meeting their child, and setting off on another creative endeavour.

"Doesn't it matter that you don't know what that endeavour is to be?" Rufio had asked her, for it certainly bothered him.

"No. It doesn't!" Clara had insisted. "It will be a thrill to discover along the way!"

Rufio shook his head as he remembered her saying that.

"Why are you shaking your head?" Clara asked as she and Errol arrived. She reached out to take Clara from Rufio.

"I'm not," he answered.

"Yes, you were," she replied.

"I saw it too," Errol said. "You've got that look about you, Rufio." Errol looked at Clara, his furry eyebrows arched most knowingly.

Clara nodded her agreement.

"I don't now what you two are talking about," Rufio insisted.

"That look," Errol continued. "Ever since you was a child, when there was something you didn't want to do, you would have a sulky, brooding look on your face. It was like you were mulling over all the bad things that could happen but never would."

"He does that, Errol," Clara said kissing Rufio's cheek. "Come on. Are you all packed yet? I've got a couple more of Felicia's things to put in the trunk."

"More?" Rufio said, following her into the domus. "She's bringing more than I am!"

"A lady never travels light!" Clara laughed as she nuzzled her daughter's nose.

"Be happy, damnit!" Errol barked after Rufio.

"You're one to talk!" Rufio turned to shout back.

"I'm old! I don't have to be!" Errol said before turning and going back to the wagons.

THE MORNING WAS WEARING ON, AND WHILE CLARA WAS feeding Felicia and packing the rest of whatever accessories babies required for a journey - it was all still a bit of a mystery to him - Rufio stood in his tablinum and stared at his shelf of scrolls, worrying over which ones he should bring. Had he known the play they would be performing, he could have brought that and begun studying it, but as it was, he was plagued with guesswork.

"Mundus stercoris!" he cursed. Then he spied his leather satchel on a nearby table. He had packed and unpacked it several times over the last few days, wavering as to whether he should bring it or not, wondering if he would have time to write. "Who am I kidding?" he said to himself. "When will I have any time for such things?"

The truth was that since Felicia had been born, parenting, in addition to the operations of the thriving latifundium, took up all of his time and energy. Daily, he tried to find a crack of time in which he could set down his ideas, but all he ended up doing most days was scratching out a few words on the stock of papyrus he carried around in his satchel, jotting whatever thoughts came to him so that he would not forget.

Some months ago, when Clara had seen that Rufio had begun making an attempt at writing, she had purchased a small, cedar writing desk for him that fit nicely into his satchel.

Now, as they were about to set off on a very long journey for whatever humiliating tasks the Gods had in store for him, Rufio began to shove his few pages of notes, three lead ink pots, two bronze styli, three blank papyrus scrolls, and a copy of Plautus' plays in case Felix wanted to relive the glory of two years before.

"Rufio!" Clara called from down the corridor outside his tablinum. "We need to leave!"

Panicked, Rufio's eyes scanned the shelves as he struggled with the weighty decision of which scrolls to bring.

"What are you doing in here?" Clara appeared in the doorway with Felicia in her arms, her eyes heavy-lidded after her feeding. "The wagons are waiting."

"I'm trying to pick some scrolls to bring with us. I may have time to read."

"You know, they do have some decent libraries in Athenae."

Rufio huffed. "I know. But I prefer to read in Latin."

Clara smiled to herself. "Why don't you bring Aristophanes? Felix may wish to do a Greek play this time for the Athenian crowd."

"Good idea." Rufio nodded and bent down to pull out one of the scrolls which he promptly dropped. As he bent to pick it up, another came tumbling down from off of the shelf and landed on his head with a thump.

"You all right, my love?" Clara asked, feeling badly for him. She knew he hated travelling, that he even muttered about it in his sleep. "We'll have a perfectly safe journey, you'll see! The

Hippocampus is a sturdy vessel, and Memnon a skilled captain."

Rufio rubbed his head and picked up the aggressive scroll. "Terence…" he muttered. "Fine." He shoved it into his satchel and turned to her. "I'm ready."

"Good," Clara said as he approached her, sweat on his brow, his eyes wide with anticipation and panic. "We're together. It will be fine."

"I know." *I most certainly do not!* "I just love our home."

"It will be wonderful to see our friends again. You'll see," Clara reassured him with a kiss. As they walked down the corridor, she asked, "Did you pack your clothes?"

"Clothes?" *Futuo!* "No…I…"

She laughed. "That's why I did it for you, Rufio. We're all set. Let's go."

"What would I do with out you?" he said as they made their way outside.

"You'd probably end up like one of those philosophers in the forum of Saena Iulia, wearing the same old rags every day of your life."

The image was not a pretty one.

Rufio stopped to take a last look at their land, the verdant hills, the groves, the new farm buildings…his still-new life! He did not want to leave it behind, for many reasons.

Clara turned to come back to him and Felicia, awake again, reached out to touch his beard with her tiny fingers. "But you are not a poor philosopher, Rufio. You are my husband, and Felicia's pater, and we are so proud of that."

Clara's grey eyes glinted with sunlight and he could not help but smile as she did.

"We'd better get going," he said, kissing them both on their foreheads as the two trunks with their belongings were loaded onto the last wagon down the hill.

Together, they walked to where Errol stood with Stella and Peli, waiting to say goodbye.

Peli shivered and whined as they approached, while Stella's long furry ears swivelled atop her head like the antennae of a summer grasshopper.

Errol stood between the two beasts with a strangely watery look in his eyes as the heads of his familia stepped up to say goodbye.

"We'll be back well before the harvest, Errol. Don't worry about us," Clara said, kissing the old man on the cheek and holding Felicia up for him.

"You take care of these two, Domina. They need it." The old man winked.

"I will," Clara replied before bending down to pat Peli who licked her hands vigorously, pleading. "Oh, you'll be fine." She then climbed up into the back of that last wagon to sit among scattered sheepskins and straw, with Felicia cradled in her lap.

Rufio was rubbing Stella's large head and her eyes closed slightly at his touch. "You going to be all right, girl?" he asked, unable to stop thinking of his favourite ass having to deal with her harasser while he was away. He turned instinctively to see the farm hand hovering in the orchard, watching the farewells. He then turned to Peli who stood, tail wagging, tongue lolling, hopeful of the invitation to jump aboard.

"Sorry, Peli. You're staying." Rufio ruffled the canine's neck. "It'll go quickly, you'll see."

"Graecia is a long way away," Errol muttered.

Rufio stood and faced the elderly man. "You're the one who told us we should go!"

"Yes, I did," Errol replied.

"So? We're going. Aren't you happy?" Rufio could see the redness in Errol's eyes, the tears at their departure.

"Of course I am!" Errol said.

"Then why are you crying?"

"Pah! I'm not crying! One of the hogs flung shit in my eyes this morning."

"Oh. All right then," Rufio answered, trying not to smile. "Well, we'd better get going." He could see the first wagon begin rolling on down the lane to the main road. Then, without warning, he hugged the old man.

Errol stiffened at first, and then awkwardly slapped Rufio's back. "Go," he croaked, "before your father's shade climbs out of his grave to chide us both!"

Rufio pulled back, nodding. "All will be well."

"It will," Errol answered, patting Stella's head beside him.

Rufio removed his satchel and set it in the back of the wagon and, before climbing onto the driver's bench, he turned to look at Peli. "Stay!"

Peli barked but fell onto his haunches to sit in the dirt.

"Good boy," Rufio said before taking a last look at the domus, a last breath of the air he loved, a last glimpse of the light and the way it hung about his land. He sighed and looked back at Clara and Felicia. "Ready?"

"Yes, my love," she replied from her position among the straw-strewn fleeces.

Rufio smiled, for seeing Clara there with their daughter tucked in her arms, smiling in the angling light, he suddenly felt a great optimism about the journey ahead. "Let's go then! To Athenae!" Rufio called out and flicked the reins so that the cart horse lurched forward after the train of wine-laden wagons.

"Don't get into trouble!" Errol called after them, now allowing his old, salty tears to fall freely.

Rufio and Clara waved as the wagons turned onto the road and disappeared.

For some time, Errol stood there, between the donkey and the dog, until all that could be heard was the sound the birds, and the distant chatter of the workers in the fields.

"Come on, you," he said to Peli. "You stay with me."

Peli fell into step with Errol as he plod back up to the domus, the two of them stopping occasionally to crane their necks to look toward the road.

"Maybe this time, they'll bring you back a girlfriend?" Errol said to Peli as they went inside, and Stella's strange husband emerged from the orchard to kiss her forehead.

THE TRIP FROM THE LATIFUNDIUM TO PISAE WAS A PLEASANT, three-day journey that passed without incident. Spring in Etruria was idyllic. One could not help but feel hopeful about the days ahead as the warm wind rustled the grass and wild-flowers that lined the road, and as the salutations of birds upon fenceposts and milestones met their ears. The two inns where they spent the night were clean and pleasant and happy to serve a fellow farmer, and fortunately no wine was stolen from the wagons in the night.

At last, as the hills fell away and the Arnus River made its final sprint toward the sea, Pisae lay spread out in a grid before them, nestled among the river's tributaries. The wagons by-passed the city and crossed the river on the southwestern edge where the road led directly through the gates to the port.

After Rufio explained to the guards where they were headed - and after he slipped them a small jug of wine - the harbourmaster directed them to the location of the Hippocampus at the far end where it bobbed up and down in the orange, evening light.

The wagons came to a stop where the corbita was berthed and the workers immediately began to unload the myriad amphorae, grunting and sweating as they carried them one by one onto the ship to be secured in the hold by Captain Memnon's crew.

"Good evening, Captain!" Clara called out as she slid from

the back of the wagon with Felicia in her arms. "Permission to come aboard?"

"Permission granted, Domina Clara!"

Rufio looked up to see the grizzled captain smiling down at his wife from beneath his sea-foam white beard. He waved, but as soon as he did that, Captain Memnon's leathery face scowled as he nodded curtly in Rufio's general direction. "How come he's always pleasant with you, but when I try to say anything, he looks as though he smells something?" Rufio cast a discreet sniff in the general direction of his underarms, and was satisfied.

"Oh, he's not that bad!" Clara laughed as she bounced Clara up and down. "The captain has just known me longer. He helped me a lot with the trade from Syracusae after Aeson passed. Made sure that none of the merchants took advantage."

"I guess I should be grateful to him," Rufio muttered. "At least he's happy with the ship we purchased."

"He is," Clara confirmed as she directed two of the dock workers to the trunks in the back of the wagon.

The men heaved and carried the one aboard before coming back for the second a few moments later.

"We should make our offerings," Clara said once the trunks were taken aboard.

Together Rufio, Clara and Felicia went to one of the stone altars lining the port, beside which was a burning bronze brazier. Rufio reached into his satchel and pulled out a piece of cedar incense he had brought for the occasion. It was, after all, bad luck to begin a sea voyage without asking for the Gods' blessing.

Rufio lit the incense in the brazier's fire, trying not to curse as he burned his fingers. Once the incense caught and began to smoke, he blew on it and then placed it in the bowl of the altar, raising his hands to the sea where the sun was dipping quickly beneath the horizon.

"Mighty Neptune…" Rufio prayed. "Look favourably on our journey over your watery realm. Bring us safely through the straights and across the sea to Athenae. We honour you… and we are grateful for your protection. Please accept our offerings."

Clara then tossed a small bough of olive woven with jasmine from their land into the water so that it bobbed gently upon the surface and then toward the open sea.

"Nicely done, Domina Clara!" Memnon called down from where he and the crew had been standing, heads bowed during the offering.

"Ready, Felicia?" Clara said as she cast an eye over the evening skyline of Pisae behind them. "We should get aboard."

"I quite agree," Rufio said as he looked suspiciously at the roving groups of sailors and lone cut purses about the harbour, all making their way to the various tabernae and brothels. Daytime in the port was one thing, but the dark hours were quite something else. Rufio then turned back to the altar and his smoking offering. "Oh Neptune, if it isn't too much trouble, please also make it so that the sea is calm for us. My stomach can't handle it otherwise. Thank you," he said hastily before hoisting his satchel and checking the back of the wagon one more time to make sure he had everything. He then waved down the harbourmaster he recognized from previous dealings. "Salve, Icthius!"

A large, clean-shaven and frazzled man turned at the utterance of his name and spotted Rufio. He smiled and headed straight for him.

"At least *he's* happy to see me," Rufio said to himself.

"Rufio Pagano!" Icthius said, clutching a large wax tablet. "Is the Hippocampus ready to sail?"

"Very soon," Rufio said. "Captain Memnon wants to sail before dark."

"Good luck with that one!" Icthius said, looking warily up at the captain where he stood in the stern above the cabin, his hands gripping the smooth wood of the steering paddles. The harbourmaster shook his head. "What is it with these Greeks of Sicilia? They think they're better than everyone!"

"I know!" Rufio said. "I can't do anything right by him," he whispered.

"Don't bother. Memnon's always telling me how to do my own job. Never makes berth where I tell him, but where he thinks he should go."

"I'm not surprised."

As if on cue, like a cutting line from the mouth of a Pseudolus, Memnon barked at them from on high. "If you two ladies wish to stay on land together, that's fine. But I'm leaving!"

Icthius turned on Memnon and roared. "Just you wait, Captain! You don't have leave to go yet. The fleet from Carthage is leaving first!"

"Yes, *harbourmaster*!" Memnon replied, most sarcastically, making the whole crew on deck laugh out loud.

"I tell you, Rufio, if he wasn't your captain, I'd ban him from Pisae for good."

"I appreciate that," Rufio said, laying a hand upon the bigger man's shoulder. "We'll be leaving as soon as he says."

Icthius checked his wax tablet. "You're sailing for Athenae?"

"Yes. Shipment of wine, and then we're staying for the Panathenaea to perform."

Icthius snapped his tablet shut. "I'll have to see you perform someday!" he said. "If I can ever get away from this fly-infested port!"

"Maybe some day," Rufio replied, his hands clutching his satchel. "Can I trust you to have someone drive the last wagon back to the farm with the others?" Rufio fished in the scrip at his waist for a denarius and placed it in Icthius' hand.

"Will do, as usual. My cousin will be happy of the journey. I'd do it myself if I could get away from here. Anyway, good luck with all those Greeks, and may Neptune bless your journey, Rufio Pagano."

"Thank you," Rufio said. "See you in a few months."

"Farewell!" And with that, the flustered harbourmaster went to check if the Carthaginian ships had passed out of the port. "Now, you may leave my port, Captain Memnon!" Icthius yelled over his shoulder as he walked away, narrowly missed by the thick rope that landed at his feet.

Though not a sea-loving kind of person, Rufio could not help but admire the design of the corbita they owned. It was a work of art in some respects. As he mounted the gang plank and stepped onto the deck, his eyes took in the intricate network of rigging that was woven between the main mast and sail, to the smaller sail at the prow. His favourite part, however, was the enormous winged hippocampus that curled up from the stern and over the cabin and quarterdeck, its wings providing some shade.

"That's it, little boy!" Captain Memnon laughed. "It is a beautiful horsey. Now get out of the way while we cast off!"

The crew around Rufio laughed, but he forced himself to stare them all down as best he could. "As your employer, I expect more respect!"

It was then that Clara emerged from the cabin to look over the scene. "What is happening here?" she demanded.

"We're just readying to set sail, Domina!" Memnon said.

"Good," Clara looked at Rufio who stood in the middle of the deck, red-faced and seething.

Captain Memnon spoke again to Rufio. "Dominus, if you would please get settled in the cabin, we'll cast off now."

Rufio eyed the old man, who had a scar running down the

side of his face, and thought better of the insulting retort he had been chewing on. "Will do, Captain."

Rufio followed Clara into the cabin where the trunks had been secured against two walls and their sleeping pallets already made with clean sheets which they had brought.

"I can't believe we're leaving Etruria for so long," Rufio mused a little sadly.

"I know," Clara agreed, reaching out to pick up Felicia from the bed. "It does feel strange. But I'm excited to go on this adventure with you…with both of you!"

Rufio smiled. "Come. Let's show Felicia the coastline as we leave." He accepted his daughter from Clara and together the three of them stepped out to stand just in front of the cabin door to watch as the Hippocampus began to pull away from its berth. "Look Felicia… Etruria. That's where home is. We're leaving for a while, but we'll be back. Don't worry."

Clara smiled and leaned against Rufio, kissing his cheek.

Just then, on the shore, there were scattered shouts as some people in the crowd jumped out of the way for something.

"What's going on there?" Clara wondered.

Then there was a loud, wild and irrepressible barking, the originator of which was a black and white blur running at full tilt toward the harbourmaster.

"Oh, no…" Clara muttered.

"Oh, Gods…" Rufio seconded. "PELI STOP!"

But it was too late. The determined canine ploughed through the harbourmaster, knocking him into the murky water, and then paddled wildly in the direction of the Hippocampus.

Rufio handed Felicia to Clara and rushed to the port side of the corbita. "What are you doing, you mad dog?" he shouted.

Peli choked as he swam and attempted to continue his barking.

"Captain, stop the ship!" Rufio shouted up to the quarter-deck. "That's my dog!"

"It's not a wagon, Pagano!" Captain Memnon bit back. "We can't just stop it moving! Your dog's done for!"

"Captain please!" Clara called up. "Bring him aboard!"

"Ach!" Frustrated, Memnon looked to some of his crew. "Grab a net and fish that hound out of the water!"

"Yes, sir!" they shouted back.

Rufio was leaning far over the side of the ship, hanging on for dear life with one hand and reaching for Peli who seemed to be tiring rapidly. "Come on, Peli! You can do it!"

Just then, a hemp net soared over Rufio's head to land in the water beside Peli. As the sailors dragged it along, it caught the accidental sea creature who was promptly hoisted up, flailing against the hull of the ship.

Once the net reached the top, Rufio pulled Peli aboard, and together they fell in a heap on the deck.

"Don't you bite me!" Rufio said as he tried to disentangle the small leviathan whilst avoiding his snapping jaws. "I'll throw you back!"

At last Rufio got Peli out of the net and the barking and snapping turned to frantic licking of his face and a joyous whipping of his tail as the climbed all over Rufio.

"Well that's a first for the Hippocampus!" Captain Memnon said, shaking his head and focussing again on making his way safely out of the port.

"Thank you, Captain," Clara called up to him.

Memnon smiled at her and then turned to look back at the distant harbourmaster who cursed as he climbed out of the sea. "Maybe that dog's not so bad after all," he chuckled. "For Athenae!" he called out to the crew.

Clara and Felicia joined Rufio and Peli, the latter whining as he licked the baby's feet and nuzzled Clara.

"He must have run the whole way from the farm!" Rufio

said in amazement. "You're a mad dog!" he said, but no matter how angry he tried to be with Peli, he could not sustain it. At last he rubbed his muzzle and kissed him on the head. "Just you behave, all right?"

Peli barked, and Felicia laughed at that.

"Well, I guess it's the four of us now." Clara hugged Rufio and kissed his cheek before turning to go into the cabin as the sun disappeared.

"I'll be in soon," Rufio said to her, before turning his eyes to the darkening Etrurian coast. It felt strange to be leaving, but with Clara and Felicia in the cabin behind him, it did not feel quite as lonely as last time. He turned to look up at Captain Memnon. "Captain, how long did you say the journey to Athenae would be?"

"If the weather holds, about fourteen days. We've got a lot of supplies on board so we won't need to stop often. If we sail through the nights, we can do it in ten or eleven days. But you may want to take breaks on land occasionally. I can see you're not a seafaring sort, Pagano."

Rufio rolled his eyes. "I'll manage just fine," he said. "The sooner we arrive in Athenae, the better."

"Aye," Captain Memnon muttered.

Rufio looked out to sea once more, and as he did so, he felt water on his leg. He looked down to see Peli urinating upon his calf. "If we run out of food, we might have to eat you."

Peli barked once at him and then strode into the cabin to lie down beside Clara and Felicia who were already asleep beneath the blankets.

"Sooner the better," Rufio grumbled as he rinsed his leg with water from a bucket. "Good night, Captain," Rufio said before going into the cabin and securing the door.

Captain Memnon muttered something incoherent and settled himself on the quarterdeck with the steering paddles in hand, his eyes searching for the first stars of the night.

· · ·

THE HIPPOCAMPUS SAILED ON DAY AND NIGHT, HUGGING THE coastline of Italy for the first five days of the voyage. They were beautiful spring days during which the corbita was expertly manoeuvred through the sea traffic coming and going from Ostia, the port of Rome, and on south toward the narrow strait between Regium and Messana.

Neptune seemed to have accepted their offerings before their departure, for the turquoise waters were still and brilliant beneath a bright spring sun during the day, and deep and dark and calm during the nights, blanketed with the stars' fires.

Occasionally, usually in the mornings, one of the crew could be heard cursing after having set foot in one of Peli's steaming deposits upon the deck of the ship. It seemed the sea did not agree with the canine whose guts had become quite fluid.

This frustrated Captain Memnon no end as his crew were now watching where they set foot rather than being fully aware of the swinging and shifting of the rigging. So, he assigned the greenest member of the crew to scour the deck throughout the day to check for the soft caltrops.

Even though the captain and crew harangued Rufio about his prolific cur, he was, nevertheless, enjoying the voyage, lazing upon the deck of the ship and occasionally scribbling at his writing desk where he leaned against the wall of the cabin. To the crew's delight, as a peace offering, Rufio even opened one of the amphorae of wine, most of which he began to consume to pass the time, obsessing over the quality of the vintage they were bringing to Athenae for their customers.

"Don't drink it all!" Clara chided him at one point. "It belongs to our customers!"

"Not to worry, my love," Rufio answered easily. "I've brought several extra amphorae to share with the rest of the company and our hosts in Athenae. There's plenty!" he laughed.

Clara raised an eyebrow and looked at Captain Memnon.

"We're almost at the straits, Domina Clara," he said.

"That's what I'm afraid of," Clara answered, looking over her husband's drunken form.

"We'll be coming up on Regium and Messana in about an hour," Captain Memnon added. "Best get everything - and everyone - into the cabin. Secure your belongings."

"I remember it well, Captain!" Clara answered. She then turned to Rufio who had suddenly dozed off with the small wine jug in his lap. "Rufio, wake up! We need to get inside the cabin now!"

"Huh? What?" Rufio held up his hand to shield his eyes from the sun. "What's wrong?" His sudden alertness caused him to tip the last of the contents of the small jug upon the deck and Peli, who had been lying beside him, immediately licked it up. "Are we there?"

Clara shook her head and bounced Felicia who was getting restless and hungry in her arms. "By Bacchus, Rufio! How much have you drunk?"

"Just a jug," he said, as he stuffed his writing desk into the satchel. "Are we going inside now?"

"Yes. Captain says it's time."

"But it's such a nice day!"

Just then the ship began to bob a little more dramatically, and the coastline appeared to pass more quickly as the sails and rigging snapped more tightly.

"Get inside!" Captain Memnon shouted down now as his crew ran about the deck securing anything that was loose.

Clara turned and went into the cabin with Felicia, followed by Peli, and then Rufio who climbed to his feet only to sway a little to one side, and then to the other before bouncing off of the cabin doorframe and tumbling onto the sleeping pallet.

"Why is the sea so rough now?" Rufio asked as he placed his satchel beneath his cloak in the corner. "It was such a nice day! I was rather enjoying it!"

"There's some rough water ahead," Clara said, setting Felicia between her legs and turning to the wall at the back of the cabin to take up one of the ropes that were tethered there.

"What are you doing?" Rufio asked, seeing her place the rope around her waist and tighten it before picking up Felicia once more. "Those ropes are for the baggage."

"They're also for us," she replied.

"What?" Now there was panic in his voice.

"I didn't want to worry you, but things are going to get pretty bumpy now."

"Bumpy?"

Just then, it felt like the floor fell away from Rufio and he landed about a foot from where he had been sitting.

"Tie yourself up quickly!" Clara said.

Rufio did as she ordered, and then beckoned for Peli to come to him.

However, the stubborn canine remained hunkered in an opposite corner of the cabin, eyes wide and ears back.

"What's happening, Clara?"

A howling started outside as the wind picked up and the corbita creaked and strained.

"We're heading into the straits between Regium and Messana."

"So? Is the water rougher?"

"You could say that."

Rufio felt his stomach lurch. "What aren't you telling me?"

"You've read the *Odyssey*."

"Of course. You know I have," Rufio replied.

"You know the part with Scylla and Charybdis?"

"Ye...yes?"

"Well, some people believe - the sailors, that is - that those two monsters still dwell in the straits."

"WHAT?" Rufio strained at his rope as if wanting to escape. "The straits we're passing into right now?"

"Yes. But don't worry, it will be fine," Clara reassured. "Captain Memnon has never had an issue passing through. It will just get a bit rough and loud."

Rufio was shaking his head now, wishing more than anything that they were back in Etruria with a cup of wine in hand and watching the sun set over their lands. "Ugh, no wine," he mumbled, putting his fist over his mouth.

"It might have been better if you had not drunk so much," Clara added, casting a wary eye over her husband's increasingly hunched form. She turned to her right with one hand and grabbled hold of the newly rinsed bucket they usually used for a privy. "Take this."

Rufio grabbed it and clung to it. "How many times did you make this journey with Aeson?" Though Clara's deceased former husband had never touched her, had treated her more like a daughter, he still cringed at the thought of her having been married to another. He tried to picture the old man braving the waves which the corbita now rolled up and over, and it made him feel distinctly lacking.

"Several times, but the first was the worst," Clara added, relieved to see that Felicia was laughing and smiling. "Yes, you like it don't you?" she cooed at her daughter.

"I've married a sea nymph."

"Hold on, Rufio. Now it's going to start," Clara said.

"Start?" Rufio was about to ask more but then the ship suddenly shifted sideways, back and forth, before riding up what felt like a titanic swell to fall down the other side. "Ahh!"

In that moment, Rufio spotted Peli as he appeared to be suspended in mid-air in the middle of the cabin, like some strange hanging ornament above a child's cot.

Peli looked just as confused, but then plummeted down onto the pallet at Rufio's feet before lunging for his master's side.

"Hang on!" they heard Captain Memnon's voice from above.

There was a loud cracking and snapping that slapped Rufio with no small amount of terror. He looked immediately to his wife and daughter who both seemed fine. Reassured that they were all right, he shut his eyes tight, wishing for it to be over as he clutched the bucket with his right arm, and his whining dog with his left.

Peli was the first to vomit his stomach's contents, but as he did so it landed in the crook of Rufio's groin.

Horrified, Rufio looked down. "Not my favourite tunicaaaaaaa!" Immediately, Rufio followed suit and purged his wine-filled guts into the bucket.

Clara did not know how long the chorus of sick went on for. She had turned away, holding Felicia, inhaling the sweet scent of her baby's hair as best she could while the boys' world went to chaos.

The spinning, howling, creaking, racing and retching went on for some time. Rufio felt as if he had been caught in an undertow from which he could not escape, and from beneath his tightly shut and watering eyes, he believed he was done for. Then, as if spat out by some great sea creature, he felt as though he had broken the surface and came out into calm and sunlight once more.

The howling and bobbing stopped, and the ship seemed to sail calmly on once more.

Rufio opened his eyes slowly to see the form of Captain Memnon outlined in the doorway of the cabin, the sun bright behind him.

"We're safely through the straits," he said gruffly. "Are you all right, Domina Clara?"

"I'm fine, Captain. Thank you," Clara said as she undid the rope and stood up with Felicia. "Would you mind holding her while I clean up my husband?"

Captain Memnon reluctantly accepted the child. He watched as Rufio swayed from his moorings against the wall. "His first time?"

"Yes," Clara held back her own bile now. "Oh, Rufio…"

"I'm fine," Rufio muttered. "I…" He passed out before he could utter another word.

"I'll have the men bring a spare pallet up from the hold," Memnon said. "That one's done for."

"Thank you, Captain," Clara replied as she set about extricating Peli from the side of Rufio's sick-covered tunica. "Well, he won't be drinking for a while now," she said as she went about her grisly work.

As the Hippocampus sailed on over Neptune's deep, Rufio continued to sleep, and sleep, and sleep. It was not the exhausted slumber of a man who rarely had the chance to walk the dark pathways of Morpheus' realm. When Felicia was sleeping, Rufio had no problems when it came to dozing off.

This was something else.

Clara worried over him, dabbing his sweaty brow, wondering if he had hit his head against the cabin wall when they had passed through the straits. *Please Gods…let him be well,* she prayed every time she looked at him.

Peli had recovered from his own ordeal and had once more taken to decorating the corbita's deck with faecal ornaments.

Not even Captain Memnon's shouts of displeasure could wake Rufio, and as Clara sat beside her husband, singing to their daughter, she wondered where he was, and what the Gods had in store for him.

· · ·

ON THE OTHER SIDE OF THAT VEIL, RUFIO PAGANO WONDERED too what the Gods had in store for him. He fell in and out of consciousness like a man tossed on the angry waves of Neptune's sea for days, exhausted, spinning, desperate. He could hear a sweet singing on the air, and wondered if the Sirens were luring him to his death, to shatter his body on the rocks at their clawed feet.

Longing for land and unsure if he could stay afloat much longer, he swam as best he could toward the sound. But the sea grew vengeful once more and the waves rose and fell even more in foamy precipices the closer he came to shore. Beneath the surface he caught glimpses of maenads swimming alongside titanic beasts, the slither of sea serpents at the bottom, and even palaces of coral and pearl. When he managed to break the surface, he spied trees upon a near shore, swaying in the hot breeze, and a brilliant sun orbited by black clouds. At last, he could no longer swim, and allowed the waves to carry him toward that sweet sound.

He felt himself thrown through the air until he landed upon a pink and white pebbled shore. Rufio waited for the Sirens to do their worst, to tear into his flesh or abuse his body, but nothing of the sort happened. Rather, the howling of the sea stopped in his ears, and all he heard was the gentle lapping of water upon the shore.

The singing that had been his guide had stopped also, and its cessation brought panic to his heart.

"No!" he cried out, sitting up quickly, only to see a vast and lonely shore backed by shapely pines. He rubbed his eyes and looked around. "Where am I?" he asked himself, though it was another who answered.

"You're on the other side," a voice said.

Rufio turned quickly to his right to see a young man with a scraggly beard and long dishevelled hair sitting beneath one of the pine trees.

The stranger wore a long stained tunica of brown home-spun, and was barefoot. He did not rise to meet Rufio, nor did he even look at him right away. What was curious about him - and the thing that Rufio noticed immediately - was that he was writing furiously upon a ridiculously long scroll of papyrus. It was impossibly long, and gathered in heaps about his feet and yet, as Rufio looked upon it, the scroll was not blank, or dotted with sketches and ideas the same as his own, it was completely filled with text.

And the man continued to write, dipping his stylus continuously into the ink pot at his side, one of hundreds that sat in a pile nearby.

"Who are you?" Rufio asked.

"Isn't that *the* question?" the man retorted, still writing.

Rufio stood and brushed the seaweed from his hair and tunica. He stomped his sandalled feet to get feeling back in his tired legs. "Where am I?"

"Surely you know."

"No. I don't." Rufio found the man exhausting already, not least rude, for he had not even deigned to look upon him. "Where are we?"

"You are where the Gods have placed you," the man said.

Upon closer inspection, Rufio decided this was a ship-wrecked man who had finally lost his mind. "All right then. Why did the Gods place you here?"

The man looked frustrated then, and for the first time, his stylus hesitated above the papyrus, a few drops of ink falling into the rough shape of a person. He still did not look at Rufio. "I'm here because I got sick. I'm here because I have to finish writing."

"What are you writing? Seems like an awful lot." Rufio looked at the piles of papyrus. "How on earth did you get such a long scroll?"

"I am writing life. I am writing truth," the man replied.

"I guess you would need a long scroll for that," Rufio joked. "I prefer something a bit shorter. Comedy."

"This is a comedy. Life is a comedy."

"You think so?" Rufio was puzzled now. *Who is this guy? He's so odd!*

"Why aren't you writing?" The question was sudden. Somehow detached from the feeling of the conversation thus far.

"I…uhm… I am, just not at this moment." Rufio looked around for his satchel, and began to feel panic. *My notes! My styli! My desk!*

"I never stop writing. If I stop, I'll die."

"Pfft! That's daft! You need to stop to eat, to relieve yourself, to make love to your woman…all manner of things."

"Not Terentius."

"Who in Hades is Terentius?" Rufio asked, though he felt he knew the name quite well.

The man stopped writing this time and looked directly at Rufio.

And Rufio wished he had not. Those blue eyes were disconcerting, wild even beneath the long hair that surrounded his face like a mangy lion's mane.

"Is he a writer?" Rufio asked, taking a step back.

The man stood up then, and walked toward Rufio, dragging the scroll with him. "You're the one the Far-Shooter spoke of."

"I'm sure I don't know what you're talking about, friend. I'm just a farmer who writes, and is now wrecked."

"Not yet. But…" He stepped closer to Rufio and the latter backed up even more until he tripped over a log to flail on the beach. "You can help me!"

"With what?"

"You must help me! You must make them *see* me!" He pursued Rufio who began to run toward the sea.

"I'm sorry! I don't know what you mean!" Rufio dove into the water and he immediately heard the soft sound of that familiar singing.

"FREE ME!" the strange man suddenly screamed at Rufio who was swimming out into the water now.

The screaming from the shore pushed and pulled with the singing in Rufio's ears, and his head began to spin wildly until he felt something clawing at his leg.

He panicked and looked down to see the deranged writer beneath the surface, wild eyes gazing up at him as he screamed at Rufio who felt himself pulled under into darkness…

"AAAH!" Rufio howled as he sat up on his pallet and Peli, who had been licking at his foot, jumped into the corner, distraught by the sudden outburst. "Clara! Clara!" Rufio sprang from the cabin and burst into the blinding light outside. He did not see the recent deposit upon the deck and a moment later was sliding through it until his legs got ahead of him and he fell flat upon his back.

Rufio groaned and looked up to see the rigging and sails of a ship against the brilliant blue backdrop of the sky.

Clara's face appeared in the frame of his vision, and then Felicia, Captain Memnon, and some of the sailors.

"Are you alive, Pagano?" the captain asked.

"I think so… I don't know."

Captain Memnon sniffed and wrinkled his nose. "Cacare." He turned to some of his crew. "Pull up some buckets of sea water for Dominus Rufio! He stinks!"

Rufio looked at Clara's concerned face. "What happened?"

"You've been asleep for days," she said. "Your fever broke this morning."

Rufio sat up, waiting until the spinning in his head stopped, and then pushed himself to his feet. It was then that the smell clinging to him assailed his nostrils and he ran for the railing to vomit, though nothing happened.

"Let's get you cleaned up," Clara said.

"I don't think I like sea travel," Rufio grumbled.

"I think we've established that," Clara laughed, more out of relief then sheer amusement.

"Where are we?

"We're just entering the Saronic Gulf now," Captain Memnon put in from his perch above the deck. "You slept through much of the voyage!"

Rufio could not tell whether the captain was making fun of him or just being observant. It did not matter one iota to him what the grumpy old seaman thought. As far as Rufio was concerned he was an employee, and a well-paid one at that. From where he leaned against the railing, he looked at Clara and could tell that she had bottled up her worries for many days.

"I'm so sorry," Rufio said to her, wanting to hug her but keenly aware of the reeking state he was in. "I must have had you so worried."

Clara forced a smile and nuzzled Felicia whose little hands toyed with her hair. "You were fine for the crossing, but when we came near to Tainaron and Cape Malea, you seemed to worsen. You were talking in your sleep quite a bit, and I worried the fever was getting worse."

"I was just having some very strange dreams," Rufio said, though the image of that stranded man still unnerved him. He shook his head. "Right! I need to get cleaned up and then eat something!"

"Do you need help?" Clara asked.

Rufio shook his head. "It sounds like you've cleaned me up a few times. I'll do it myself this time." He frowned and looked to Peli who stood a few feet from him, watching him curiously. "Maybe *you* should help clean me since I'm wearing *your* mess!"

Peli tilted his head and promptly ran back inside the cabin.

"Thought so," Rufio muttered.

Clara laughed. "I'll get you a fresh tunica."

"Thank you," Rufio said as he removed the soiled one he wore and stood only in his bracae on the deck.

Several of the sailors whistled playfully at his leanly muscled build, and he pointed to them and shouted. "Back to work, you scum!" Then an idea hit upon him. "A cup of wine to the first man who spies land!"

In an instant, they were all pointing to the other side of the ship where the Peloponnesian coastline rose up to the mountains of Arcadia. "Land!" they all shouted gleefully.

"All right, all right!" Rufio shouted back. "I'll break open another amphora!" *Rufio, just look before you speak!* he thought.

They all cheered, and the captain laughed. "Ha, ha! You're all right, Pagano!"

Rufio looked up to the quarter deck to see Captain Memnon smiling to himself. He then took the bucket that was tied to the ship's rail by a long rope, dropped the bucket into the sea and hauled it up. He dumped it over his head and the cold hit him like a gladiator's punch. He repeated the process several times until he was clean, scrubbing with a sea sponge each time. Rufio sniffed himself afterward, but was still not satisfied that he was any better than the farmhand who minded the hogs.

"Going to take more than a little sea water to get that smell off of you!" one of the sailors joked.

Rufio sighed.

THAT EVENING, AFTER RUFIO HAD HAD A MEAL THAT CONSISTED mostly of bread and water, and after he had doused himself in Clara's clove oil, they stood at the prow of the ship watching the sun dip behind the Arcadian mountains. The sea had gone from brilliant turquoise, to purple, and then to indigo in the space of a couple of hours. As the valleys and mountains darkened in the distance, an ominous feeling came over Rufio as he held his daughter, humming to her while the sailors on deck sipped their cups of wine and diced away their coin.

"It feels different here," he said to Clara.

"How so?"

"I don't know…more ancient maybe? I can't find the words."

"Shouldn't be problem for a writer." Clara nudged him.

"I deal in feelings before words, my love." His eyes ranged along the distant coastline. It was strange, but he could swear that his mind and his sight were clearer than they had ever been.

Clara could tell that Rufio was apprehensive about their journey to Athenae, but she could also see a resoluteness in him that was not there before. She leaned against him, one hand stroking their daughter's still face, and looked up at the first stars that appeared in the night sky. "I'm just so relieved you're feeling better."

"Me too," he said as he kissed her temple. "We should get some sleep. We'll be there in the morning."

Together they turned to go back inside the cabin. "Good night, Captain," Rufio called up to the quarterdeck.

"Good night, Dominus," Memnon replied.

Rufio smiled to himself as he went into the cabin, whistling to Peli who ran to join them.

As they lay down that last night at sea, Rufio stared up at the ceiling. He felt Peli settle himself beside him, and he pat him gently. "I wonder what awaits us in Athenae…" Rufio muttered, trying even then to shake the images of his fevered dreams.

ACT II

THE CITY OF THE GODDESS ATHENA

IV

BABES UP IN ARMS

I t was the month of Maius in the ancient city of Athenae, or 'Thargelion' as many stubborn Attic Greeks still insisted on referring to those beautiful late spring days between mid-Maius and mid-Junius. This was the halcyon period of the year, the time before the great heat when the city boiled and baked, and the whirr of cicadas resonated both day and night. Now, in that moment, the city of the Goddess Athena was at its most glorious.

Everywhere one went, the brilliant Pentelic marble of temples, arcades, and myriad monuments and porticoes still shone after their spring scrubbing. In beautiful contrast to man's creations were the soft greens of ivy, fern and fig, pine and palm. Laneways and gardens were splashed with the whites and fuchsias of jasmine and bougainvillaea coming to life again, and the blossoms of bitter orange and citron trees sweetened the air, greatly emboldened by their coming fruit.

And above it all, the sky, a permanently cloudless expanse of blue, stretched over the city from sea to mountains across Attica. There was, truly, no other time so alluring. In Athenae, when the Sun's chariot drove into the distant west, and Selene's lovely visage brightened the night sky, any mortal still not abed cast furtive looks around corners or into moonlit gardens, not wanting to surprise any of the gods who came to enjoy that beauteous space and time.

It was thought by many, and quietly so by any Roman, that if Rome was a monument to the Gods, Athenae was their very home.

ON THAT PARTICULARLY BRIGHT DAY, THE STREETS OF ATHENAE were host to crowds of revellers who yet lingered in that beautiful polis after the Thargelia, the festival in honour of Apollo. The stoas were packed and the agorae bustling with commerce and conversation. Smoke wafted from the temples of the city to create a rose-coloured haze through which to view the world.

"You seem happy," Felix said to Electra as they rode in the curtained litter that belonged to the owners of the villa that Sextus Annius Sabinus had arranged for them. It was not very long, but was broader than many Roman litters, with sheer, creamy curtains that filtered the sunlight. Felix stroked his wife's hair and she lay back smiling as they rode down the Panathenaic Way into the ancient agora.

"I am happy," Electra responded, her eyes closed as she breathed in the warm air. "Very much so." She opened her dark, sunlit eyes, and smiled. "It feels good to be back."

Felix could not help but smile back at her. He could feel it too, and to see Electra so happy, so calm...the world just seemed perfect. "It does feel good," he said, his voice low as their litter turned off the street to go down the length of the Stoa of Attalus. "I am sorry we didn't get to go inside the temple of the goddess today though."

Electra nodded. "I had been looking forward to making an offering for our son in the Goddess Athena's great temple...but we'll come back."

"Indeed we will, my love," Felix said as the litter came to a stop. "I'm sorry I didn't realize that today was the day of the Callynteria."

"Even the goddess' house needs a spring cleaning," Electra said, her hand on his shoulder. "When we do go back with our little Thespis, the interior will sparkle like the halls of Olympus itself."

Felix smiled. "I can't wait."

"We're at the scribes', sir," the head litter-bearer said from outside.

"I won't be a moment," Felix said as he kissed Electra. "Keep the curtains closed. This is Athenae, after all." Felix pulled aside the curtain on his side of the litter and slid out. "Don't let anyone approach," he said to the bearers. "I don't want any of these Greeks hooting at my woman."

"We won't, sir," the leader replied, happy to be in such close proximity to the great Felix Modestus and the much-lauded archimima, Electra. They had carried many a famous actor in their work at the domus of the family of Herodes Atticus, but playing host to The Etrurian Players and their leader certainly was the highlight.

Electra watched Felix mount the steps of the stoa and go into the offices of the scribes and copyists. She sighed to herself, not without pain, for the pressure in her full breasts was becoming unbearable. "I'll see you soon, my son," she whispered to herself. *Divine Athena…protect him always…*

A few minutes later, Felix emerged from the stoa, stepping lightly down the marble steps carrying a large leather satchel brimming with papyrus scrolls.

"Is that it, sir? The play?" the head litter-bearer asked as Felix rounded the litter with his cargo.

"Yes, it is!" Felix said.

"Any chance of you telling us what play it is?" the man asked cheekily.

Felix knew that the man was a great admirer of the theatre,

so he did not mind the question. "Absolutely not!" he laughed. "After the company knows, you may know, but not before!"

"Thought I'd try anyway," the man laughed as he pulled aside the curtain for Felix to get in. "Where to now, sir?"

Felix looked to Electra. "Do you want to go to one of the tabernae to eat in the shade?"

She shook her head. "We should get back to the villa. My breasts are going to explode, and I'm sure our son is starving."

"Come now. He fed just before we left," Felix said. "I'm sure he's quietly dozing in the shade of an olive tree. Domela is quite good with him, you know."

Electra knew that the newest member of the company did have a knack with children, but she could feel that her son needed her. "Please. Can we go home now?"

Felix nodded. He had thought to have some time alone with Electra, to linger longer in the sunny disposition brought on by Athenae. But he did not mind. If he was honest with himself, he was somewhat nervous whenever they were away from their baby, though he would not admit as much to anyone. Felix smiled. "Very well," he said before turning to the curtain. "Back to the villa!"

"Yes, sir!" the litter-bearer called back. The litter rose, and they began to move slowly into the crowds.

"So?" Electra then asked, her hand stroking Felix's leg.

"So, what?" he replied with a mischievous glint in his eye.

"Are those the scrolls of the play?" She began to reach for one of them but he tapped her hand as if she were a naughty child reaching into a honey pot.

"Yes. Yes, they are!" he said, grasping the satchel to his chest.

Electra's lips pouted and she grasped him hard beneath the bucket, hoping the coercion would work. "How about you tell me what play we are to perform now? You always tell me first. Why keep it a secret this time?"

"I did not want to cause you undue stress. You need to focus on our child. You've been through much."

Electra leaned closer to him, squeezed harder. "I'll be the judge of that. If you tell me, I will…" she leaned very close and whispered in his year.

Felix's eyebrows rose up in pleasant surprise. "Really?"

Electra nodded. "Just tell me what play Apollo has commanded us to perform."

Felix looked down at the satchel stuffed with scrolls. It was a gamble, to be sure, but one commanded by Apollo himself. The dreams the Gods had sent him previously had changed his life, and ever since Delos he had wondered what they had in store for him this time.

"Whatever it is, I'm sure it will win over the Hellenes in a grand way," she said, her lips brushing his cheek.

Felix hoped it would, for the reception the company had received upon arriving in Athenae had been lukewarm at best. It was not like when they had entered Rome like a victorious army. In Athenae, there had been no hint of fanfare, no shower of rose petals, no cries of adulation. In fact, the Athenians had pretended not to know them at all as their three theatrical wagons had passed through the streets with Felix upon horseback at the front. They had passed the theatres more like thieves in the night rather than returning heroes marching through the city. It all struck him as odd, and the reception had caused him to temper his enthusiasm in a most unusual way.

"Tell me, my love," Electra said before the tip of her tongue gently tickled the side of his mouth.

"Very well," he said, before turning to her, one hand clasping the satchel while the other caressed her hip. He put his mouth to her ear and whispered.

Electra's eyes shot wide and she pulled away. "You're not

serious?" she shouted as the litter moved on through the Roman agora.

It took an inordinate amount of time for the litter to cut its way through the streets of Athenae, something Felix regretted deeply, for the chorus of Electra's complaining rang in his ears as the litter-bearers plodded along. The confines of the street of Tripodon acted like a sort of echo chamber for her haranguing until they made the sharp turn at the monument of Lysicrates, the one-time patron of musical performances in the city.

"Turn here!" Felix shouted from the confines of the litter, his patience nearing its end, for Electra had moved on from her dislike of the play to her worries about their son and what was happening back at the villa. "I'm sure he's just sleeping, my dear." Felix tried to calm her stormy disposition but it was no use.

"I still can't believe you want to perform that play!"

"You're back on that?" Felix roared, not completely ignorant of the sniggers of the pedestrians beyond their curtained world. "I told you, the Gods demand it!"

"Perhaps you misunderstood your dream's meaning?" she said, her arms firmly crossed now, the amorous advances long forgotten. "You're no oracle!"

A part of Felix knew that Electra's ongoing outburst was largely due to the poor reception they had already received in Athenae, but still, he regretted telling her before the others. *Now, she'll stew on it!* With a great sigh, he turned to his wife, brushed back the hair from her face, and placed his hand on her flushed cheek. "I need to walk."

With that, Felix slid deftly from the moving litter, trying not to listen to Electra's grumbling from inside. "It's not funny…"

As Felix's weight was lifted from the litter, it was the turn of the litter-bearers to sigh with relief. They hoisted the litter higher and walked on along the road to the quarter of Novae Athenae.

Felix followed on foot, keeping apace with the litter-bearers as he walked along with his precious satchel of scrolls. *She'll see!* he thought. *It will be a magnificent success!* Though, he was already doubting himself. "Listen to the Gods, Felix," he mumbled.

Electra's voice eventually faded to quiet in the litter, and Felix wondered if she had complained herself to sleep. He realized that was not fair, however, for they had not slept well for some nights as their son maintained his nocturnal existence. If he was honest with himself, Felix had to admit that their mute entrance into Athenae had unnerved him as well. He understood Electra's worries, but he needed to maintain his hope, something which became easier as they broke the confines of the older neighbourhood and walked past the soaring columns of temples and arcades, monuments and newer domi of the Roman quarter that lined the broad avenue.

To his right, as they turned again, the roof of the great temple of Olympian Zeus hovered over the city, vast and imposing with its forest of mighty columns. The smoke from the Roman bath complex rose up in contrast to the pure blue of the sky, a thing that seemed out of place in that city of gods.

Let us not be just smoke and air to these Athenians, Felix prayed, angry at his lack of optimism.

Felix followed the litter-bearers across the plaza adorned with a high equestrian statue of Emperor Hadrianus, the city's greatest Roman patron. A part of him wished to slip into the bath complex on his right, but then he needed to get the scrolls safely home, for he had spared no expense on the best papyrus and the skills of the most talented copyist in Athenae. It would not do for them to be stolen while he soaked himself, or for the moisture to get at them.

Once the litter-bearers passed beneath the enormous guard tower that comprised the Porta Hadriana, Felix asked them to stop.

Grateful for the repose, the bearers set the litter down in front of a small temple on their right.

Felix went around to Electra's side and parted the curtains to see her sleeping soundly within. "You're so beautiful," he said in a low voice, her rantings now forgotten. He turned to the head bearer. "I'll get back in now."

"Yes, sir," the man said, not managing to hide the disappointment in his voice very well. The climb up the Hill of Ardittos at the foot of Mount Hymettos was not an easy one. Together, all eight men hoisted the litter with a grunt and they were on their way again.

Felix parted the curtains on the other side as well and, with Electra nestled in the crook of his muscled arm, he watched and listened as they crossed the bridge over the River Ilissos, its crystal waters gurgling happily along the forested riverbank. As they crossed the white marble bridge, Felix looked up to see the soaring statue of Nike, Goddess of Victory, seemingly waving down at him with a corona in her lithe hand. "We'll endeavour to earn that crown, divine goddess," he whispered as they moved on to the sound of birdsong and their sweating servants.

Ahead, the great expanse of the Panathenaic stadium stretched before them, signalling the outer reaches of the polis and the start of their uphill climb. The road, now a hard-packed track of earth, wound its way around the front of the stadium and up to its left. The trees thickened and the scent of mountain pine sweetened the air as they followed the road uphill, passing the temple of Artemis Agrotera, which stood nestled in the thicket somewhere to their right.

Felix strained his neck to try and see the lone temple set back amongst the trees. Though he was aware that Artemis Agrotera was the guardian of the hunt on the mountainside, he still prayed to the goddess whenever he passed that place that she protect his infant son, for Artemis was also a protector of young children.

Even as the thought came to him, there was a wailing on the wind that plucked at Felix's heartstrings.

Electra woke at the sound and sat up in the litter. "Thespis!"

"He's fine," Felix tried to get her to settle. "He's probably just woken up is all."

But the wailing became louder and louder, like the crescendo of a chorus of Bacchic revellers.

Electra began to grasp at her chest, the need to feed her son most urgent now. "I knew we should have brought him with us! We were gone far too long. We're not doing that again!"

"Yes, my love. If that is your wish." Felix saw no other option but to aquiesce. "Just remember that you are the one who thought we should leave him because it is still somewhat frowned on for women to be out and about in Athenae, worse still with their children."

"Those are old ideas!" Electra bit back, her worry clearly visible on her features. "If anyone says anything about me being out with my child, I'll put out their eyes!"

"I believe you."

Felix sighed and settled in for the final stretch of road leading to their accommodation. The villa that Sextus had secured for them was a ways out of the city, but it was quiet - if not in that moment - and much closer than Piraeus, the port of Athenae, where the warehouses were located. It was also much quieter than the tenements within the city walls where it would be too loud all the time. The baby would never have been able to sleep, and as a result, neither would they. And they needed sleep in a most desperate fashion.

The outer walls of the vast villa finally came into view, and the crying that emanated from within was most frantic, such that if one did not know there was a ravenous child inside, one might have thought that the place was under siege.

"Open the gates!" the head litter-bearer shouted as they turned down a short cypress-lined path and passed through the wide arch where the double gates opened.

The crying got even louder then.

Felix sighed. "Here I was hoping you and I could honour Aphrodite before our parental duties kicked in."

"Are you joking?" Electra snapped, her pained expression morphing into a theatre mask of sorts. "You'd drown in all the milk I'm carrying!"

The litter was set down in the great circular courtyard beside the central fountain, and a second later, Electra burst from the curtains to rush through another archway into the villa to find her son.

Felix waited a moment before gathering the scrolls and going after her. A quick glance around the courtyard revealed several of the servants sitting, perhaps hiding, beneath the five olive trees that provided shade. "How long has he been crying?" he asked one of them.

"So long," one of the servants said with bowed head.

"Wonderful…" Felix rushed after Electra, more worried about what she might do to one of his cast members. "Electra!" He found her in the peristylium garden beyond the atrium, amidst the couches and another fountain, spinning on the black and white mosaic floor calling out.

"Where is my son?" Electra said, her eyes scanning the upper floor corridor as well, her ears cocked like a mother lion searching for her cub.

Felix finally caught up with her. "It sounds like they're at the back of the domus."

Electra rushed across the manicured pathways lined with flowers and shrubs, through the archways that flanked the enormous triclinium, to the back of the house where a small odeon sat surrounded by high walls. "There you are!"

There, in the seating of the odeon, the child was surrounded by The Etrurian Players, all of them dancing and singing, holding and shaking various toys, their faces comically contorted, all in an effort to get the child to stop wailing.

Felix stopped in his tracks and, were it not for his wife's state of frantic worry, he would have laughed at the scene.

"Mama is here, my little Thespis!" Electra said as she took her son from Beatrice, whose turn it had been to cradle him.

Without a word to anyone, Electra rushed to the apodyterium of the bathhouse at the back of that courtyard, and within moments, the wailing stopped. Electra sighed painfully then as the pressure in her chest, and her worry, began to slowly dissipate.

The Etrurian Players all collapsed about the seating of the small odeon and Felix turned in the orchestra in front of the small stage to look at them.

Beatrice stood in front of the seating, her body still performing the rocking motion she had locked herself into. In the front row, Damon, the mute player among them sat cleaning all of the spit from his flute which he had been playing non-stop for what felt like hours.

In the middle, Fausto, the youngest player among them, sat wiping the sweat from his brow and brushing back his long hair, wondering why on earth anyone would want a child in the first place. Beside him, the brothers, Castor and Pollux, lay collapsed, surrounded by an array of rattles, tambourines, masks, and wooden horses, all of which had been completely ineffective in calming the raging infant.

Julius, the veteran among them, sat with his head hung, rubbing his temples to soothe the unbearable headache that was splitting his tired skull.

It was Domela, the newest member of the cast, who came

forward to speak to Felix. Her red hair was plastered against her flushed cheeks and her tunica was stained with a little vomit which the child had launched at her. "I'm sorry, Dominus," Domela shook her head. "I know I told you that I'd taken care of children plenty of times before, but this time I could just not manage it. Young Thespis wants only for his mother."

Felix could see that the poor woman was out of breath, shaking even, and most likely not a little afraid of Electra's wrath. "Don't worry Domela," Felix said, placing a hand on her shoulder to calm her. "We won't do that to you again. Thank you for trying."

"He started out just fine. I played with him, and sang. He drank a little water, and then went to sleep. But when he woke up…"

Felix nodded. "Oh, I know. Trust me."

"If Damon hadn't farted and hooted so loudly, he might have slept longer!" Castor said, rising up from his prostrate position to accuse his mute colleague.

Damon made an obscene gesture in return but was too tired to do much else.

Felix looked at all of them. "Are you all right?"

They just looked at him like his question was born of madness.

"Very well." Felix sat down on the small stage with the satchel beside him.

"Don't people usually get nursemaids for this sort of thing?" Fausto asked, still unbelieving of the lungs on the child.

"Fausto," Felix warned. "Unless you want Electra to put your head on a spear outside the gates, I suggest you keep that to yourself."

"Yeah, shut up, Fausto!" Pollux laughed. "You've heard about Greek mothers."

Felix looked to where Domela now sat beside Julius. "Julius?"

"Yes?" the older man looked up.

"Maybe Atticus has some opium to help you with that headache?" Felix suggested.

"If you can find him!" Beatrice laughed, her smile returning. "Our house steward went into hiding some time ago."

"Poor man," Felix smiled. "He didn't know what he was in for when his master offered us the villa." Felix tilted his head upward. "Atticus!"

A few moments later, a short, portly man in a dark green tunica with a studded brown cingulum emerged from the triclinium doors. His brown hair was dishevelled, despite his efforts to tame it, and he rubbed his beard in worry. He scowled, though he did not mean to, unused as he was to the presence of so loud a guest as the child.

"I am here, Felix Modestus," the house steward bowed. He was, of course, a great fan of the theatre, and his position there afforded him the opportunity to meet many a famed performer, but for the last hour or so he had been wondering whether he would be able to handle The Etrurian Players. "What may I do for you, sir?"

"I apologize for the afternoon you have endured, Atticus," Felix said. "Rest assured, we will not leave the child alone again."

"Alone?" Pollux said.

"You know what I mean," Felix said, before turning back to Atticus. "Please set out some wine and food and, if you have any, a little opium for poor Julius' cracked head would be much appreciated."

"It shall be done, Felix Modestus." With a bow, Atticus turned and strode back into the triclinium to call on the other servants to help.

"Now," Felix said to the group, "tell me what you've been up to today. Did you get *any* work done?"

Beatrice began to speak, but it was Domela who started

from where she sat beside Julius, the latter staring into nothing as his head pounded. "As you directed, Beatrice and I have been working away on the costumes. And-"

Now it was Beatrice's turn to jump in. "And we've kept the costumes much more simple for our Athenian audience, as you asked, Dominus." Beatrice shot a fierce look at Domela who crossed her thick arms and looked up at the younger woman.

Felix held up his hands. "First of all… Beatrice, how many times do I need to say it? I freed you all a long time ago. You don't need to keep calling me 'Dominus'."

"I don't mind," Beatrice said. "Honestly! It's much easier anyway and, besides, you're still our leader, aren't you?"

"Yes, but-" *How many times do we have to have this conversation?* Felix thought.

"Yeah, Beatrice!" Fausto teased. "You can call him 'The Felix Modestus'!"

"Or, 'The Magnificent'?" Castor added with a laugh. "If the Greeks' Alexander - whom they talk about constantly, by the way - could be 'The Great', I think Felix can be 'The Magnificent'!"

"All right, shut up, the lot of you!" Felix said, wanting the curtain to fall on this once and for all. "Fine then! Just call me 'Dominus', but only in reference to being the leader of the company. Satisfied?"

"Yes, Dominus," Domela said, before Beatrice could answer.

Felix shook his head. Domela had been with them for about a year after they found that they needed another player and accountant to replace the parasitical Silas. She had joined them in Caesarea and was, apparently, a Roman widow who had done the accounts for her merchant husband who had died mysteriously one day in Judaea. She loved theatre and everything about it. She was also a decent actress when it came to minor roles. Sadly, she and Beatrice did not get along.

Felix sighed and turned to see Electra emerge at last from the bathhouse. "Are you all right my lo-"

"Shhh!" Electra hissed as she carried their sleeping son across the courtyard to go to the second level where their cubiculum was.

Felix nodded, and the others fell silent, happy at the thought of the child sleeping at last.

When Electra had gone, Felix cleared his throat. "What else? What about the sets? Castor, Pollux?"

Pollux stood up and stretched. "We've been busy building the set pieces you asked for - a broad olive tree with a driftwood trunk, and slots for fitted branches from a real tree when the time comes."

"Have you started on the fountain?"

"No." Pollux looked at Castor and Damon and back to Felix. "We're not sure about the design as we don't know what play we're doing. If you can give us a hint, we can do it more accurately."

Every member of the company stared up at Felix most expectantly, but he simply smiled and stared back. "Nice try, you lot." They all slumped, having been certain he would break this time.

"Why are we not allowed to know?" Domela asked, looking around at the others as if she missed something.

Beatrice rolled her eyes, but stopped when she saw Felix's stern look.

"On the occasions that Rufio and Clara join our company," Pollux began, "Felix the Magnificent prefers to reveal the play at the latest possible moment."

"Just stick with 'Dominus', Pollux," Felix added. "And remember that Rufio and Clara are founding members of The Etrurian Players."

"Wonderful!" Domela said, her face lighting up, for she did

truly enjoy the company of players, even pouty ones like Beatrice. "How often do they perform with us?"

"This will be the second time," Castor added with a smile.

Domela's eyes widened. "Only the second?"

"Gaws com-an nt!" Damon hooted.

"What?" Domela asked.

"The Gods command it," Julius whispered as he leaned closer to her.

"Ah." Domela stopped talking, clearly having missed much, or been left out of many a conversation since Delos.

Julius pat her knee and smiled. He then turned to Felix. "Do we know when Rufio and Clara will be arriving? It will be nice to see them again."

The others began to talk excitedly, for the last time they had all been together in Rome was one of the most momentous performances of their careers.

"Will they be here soon?" Beatrice asked.

"Any day now, I hope," Felix answered. "We'll finally get to meet their infant daughter."

"Then you can be 'Uncle Felix the Magnificent'!" Castor laughed.

Felix could not help but smile, already imagining the full company rehearsing in that small odeon at the heart of the villa.

"Another baby?" Fausto asked, his expression one of terror and disgust.

"That's right, Fausto!" Felix clapped. "And then there were two!"

"I need a drink," Fausto murmured.

"Me too!" Pollux agreed. "Can we go into the city for the afternoon, Dominus?"

Felix thought about it, thought about reminding them that as freedmen, they were able to make their own decisions about where to go. "Of course you can. But don't get into trouble in the brothels!"

"We swear, we won't!" Castor said with a wink.

"Beatrice, you coming?" Fausto asked.

Beatrice looked at Domela who was handing Julius the opium water which Atticus had just given her. "Yes, I will!" she said, jumping up to join Fausto.

Felix was already daydreaming of sleeping in the small odeon, beneath that brilliant blue sky after they were all gone, when Pollux stuck his head back through the archway.

"Dominus?"

"Yes?"

"What play was it you said we were going to do?"

"Nice try!" Felix barked. "Get out of here!"

Pollux laughed and ran to join the others.

"Dominus," Domela said then. "Julius and I are going to go for a walk in the forest outside the villa. It might help to clear his head."

"Good idea, Domela. You can work on the accounts tomorrow."

She helped Julius up and together they walked out, leaving Felix alone at last.

He set down the satchel of scrolls and lay himself on the small orchestra to look up at the sky. The spring sunshine felt good on his face and the sound of the birds floated into his hearing like music from Apollo's cythara.

Soon enough, his eyes began to grow heavy as he settled in for his long-awaited nap.

"Felix!" Electra's voice broke the silence like a cornu in the night. "Felix come quickly! I need your help cleaning up the baby! It's a bad one this time!"

Felix Modestus sighed and pushed himself to his knees, and then to his feet.

"I bet Rufio never has to deal with this sort of thing," he

grumbled as he left the courtyard with the scrolls under his arm.

A moment later, Atticus emerged smiling from the triclinium doors. "Dominus, the food and wine are…" he noted the empty odeon, "…ready."

V

A WORLD OF FOOLS AND HEROES

The entirety of the sea voyage from Pisae to Piraeus, the port of Athenae, was something of a blur for Rufio. The last couple of days sailing across the Saronic Gulf had been pleasant enough, but he had no recollection of much prior to that except for the echoes of storm and sick.

So, when the vast port of Piraeus finally came into view and their destination was called out by Captain Memnon, the relief Rufio felt was great.

Clara was relieved as well, for however much she enjoyed the beauty of a sea voyage, she yearned for a long walk on land, and the reassuring solidity of a tree's trunk. She was extremely grateful that Felicia had her tolerance for sailing, rather than Rufio's constitutional defiance of sea travel. She could handle one child's sick, but not two, though Peli and Rufio had a somewhat similar experience. Her gorge rose as some of the more gruesome interludes came into her mind, and so she focussed on the beauty of the sun's sparkle on the surface of the sea as they joined the traffic headed for the northern harbour of Cantharos.

Captain Memnon was well acquainted with the harbour, and Rufio marvelled at his skill in manoeuvring the Hippocampus in amongst the forest of hulls and masts of ships from across the middle sea, including Iberia, Massilia, Mauretania, Carthage, Aegyptus, Cyprus, and even Britannia.

"Did you come here often in the past?" Rufio asked Clara as he stood beside her, his hands gripping the rail at the prow of the ship where they stood.

Clara smiled at him and his awkwardness whenever he spoke of her previous life with Aeson. "I've been a couple of times. Athenae is beautiful. You'll love it, Rufio."

"What about the port?" Rufio nodded ahead of them where the broad and crowded curve of the harbour of Cantharos stretched out before them.

"We should probably get out as quickly as we can," Clara said.

Rufio's eyes widened in panic.

"Felix will be expecting us," she added hastily.

"It will be good to see him," Rufio smiled, allowing himself to be excited about their reunion with Felix and the company, now that the sea voyage was behind them. "I should probably go and hire a wagon right away to take us into the city." Rufio scanned the harbour.

"Captain Memnon will take care of the cargo. He has his instructions," Clara added.

"Why is he taking us so far away from all the activity?" Rufio noted that the ship was turning to the starboard and heading for a berth near the place where several ships were out of the water being repaired or having pitch reapplied to their hulls. "Where is he going?" Rufio looked to the stern where Captain Memnon was giving commands to the crew from the quarterdeck. "We'll have to go so much farther to the main thoroughfare this way!" He went to speak with the captain.

"Rufio, wait!" Clara said, but he was already marching down the deck, stepping over another gift of Peli's on his way.

"Captain!" Rufio called up as the sailors rushed all around

him, securing the sail and getting the ropes ready to toss to the slaves on shore. "Captain!"

"Not now!" Captain Memnon bit back.

"Yes, now!" Rufio was not to be deterred. "Why are we making berth so far from the unloading areas?"

"It's safer!"

"Safer? How so?" Rufio climbed the steep stairs to stand beside the captain, further annoying the old seaman.

"It's safer for you, Dominus."

"I can deal with a little crowd," Rufio lied.

Memnon shook his head, his eyes still on the crew. "Now!"

The crew tossed ropes to the slaves on shore, and then three of them jumped like panthers over the closing gap between the ship and shore while those onboard tossed them sacks filled with sheep's wool to cushion the approach.

"Why are we here, Captain?" Rufio shouted, thoroughly frustrated at being ignored yet again.

Captain Memnon turned to Rufio, his leathery arms crossed over his chest, his white beard shuddering as he worked his jaw. "It is true, we could make berth over there."

"Then why didn't we?"

The Captain sighed. "Listen, Dominus. You are Roman."

"Etrurian," Rufio corrected.

"To them…to Greeks…you're Roman. Your ship is Roman."

"So? This is part of Rome's empire, no?"

"Yes, but… Not all Greeks appreciate Romans," Memnon tried explaining. "Especially here. When Sulla was campaigning in Graecia, he destroyed Piraeus and Athenae."

"That was hundreds of years ago!" Rufio protested.

Now Clara was standing below the quarterdeck with Felicia and Peli looking up at them, waiting to gather their things in the cabin. "Rufio? Captain Memnon knows what he's doing. Let's get going."

Rufio held up his hand and turned back to the captain. "What about all that Hadrianus has done for the city, and that was less than a hundred years ago? Surely they remember that?"

"It's easier for people to remember brutality than generosity," Captain Memnon said, his hand on Rufio's shoulder. "The Hellenes remember the deep wounds left by Sulla more than the shining marble left by Hadrianus. You, and your ship, are safer on this end of the harbour, the Roman end." He tried smiling at Rufio, an act that did not quite suit his sea dog face. "I'll send a runner to get the wagons. For now, you can gather your things. I'll see that the amphorae you've set aside for yourselves are placed in your wagon for you."

Rufio was silent, thoughtful. He nodded absently, a little saddened and worried at what the captain had told him. Now, he was nervous about driving through the great port! He climbed down and stood on the deck beside Clara to look out over Piraeus.

"I tried to tell you," she said as she handed Felicia to him.

"I had no idea. I just hope it's better in the city."

Clara did not say anything, just stroked his salty hair and kissed his cheek. "It's far bigger than Pisae, isn't it?"

"Gods… It's enormous," Rufio answered, finally taking in the great commercial harbour of Athenae.

From their distant viewpoint they could see myriad ships of varying sizes docked all along the harbour from one end to the other, their masts like a swaying forest. The sailors and slaves everywhere were like ants going to and from their hills, loading and unloading cargoes from around the world, including timber, incense, spices, wine, oil, garum, wool and other everyday items that carried a great price in quantities such as those. In amongst the dock workers there were also exotic animals such as zebras, camels, and elephants whose occasional trumpeting would be heard above the general murmur of activity that echoed throughout the harbour.

At the back of the harbour, the cracked, tiled rooftops of the vast customs building could be seen alongside tabernae and brothels where hetaerae and lupae hung out of second storey windows waving to the wealthier looking men in the crowd.

Beyond that general chaos, the pediments of the temples of Zeus, Poseidon, Aphrodite, and Athena peeked above the rest, halos of smoke resting about their crowns. These structures had evidently been given more care and restoration compared to the rest of Piraeus' buildings which, upon closer inspection, still carried the scars of Roman aggression.

Felicia pointed up at the sky where the gulls circled in their hundreds, their screeching song by far the loudest refrain in the great harbour.

Peli barked at the sky, amusing Felicia such that she giggled in her father's arms.

"You like the birds, my girl?" Rufio said and he kissed her rosy cheek.

Clara rejoined them, having packed up the rest of their belongings. "Sometimes I think all the gulls in the world congregate at harbours and nowhere else." She remembered that every port she had ever sailed to with the aged Aeson had been the same.

"It's like we're in Aristophanes' *The Birds*," Rufio said, remembering the dreamy play of the comic master.

"And you're Pisthetaerus?" Clara said, smiling.

"Yes!" Rufio declared.

"Really? He replaced Zeus in the play, did he not?" Clara arched a blonde eyebrow.

"All right. Maybe not," Rufio acceded. "But I'm still reminded of the play."

Clara did not remind him that there were no gulls in the chorus of *The Birds*, for he and Felicia were enjoying them too much. "My gods, would you look at that!" Clara suddenly burst out, pointing to a large, gaudy wagon in the harbour. It was drawn by two thickly-muscled horses pulling and draped with brilliant yellow and purple hangings. At each corner of the wagon's pillars sprouted bunches of peacock feathers that twitched and danced in the sea breeze. People stared and pointed at the wagon as it cut a swathe through the sweaty masses followed by a row of other cargo wagons.

"That's hideous!" Rufio joked.

"Unbelievable," Clara agreed. "Let's hope that we can find something a little less…attention getting."

"Agreed." Rufio chuckled. "It probably belongs to some fat Bithynian merchant. So tasteless!

"Here, I can take Felicia," Clara said reaching out for her daughter.

"I can do it," Rufio protested, but Clara insisted. "She'll need to eat again soon… Actually…" Clara sniffed. "Well-timed as ever, my love." She turned to Rufio. "I'll be back."

Rufio nodded and pat Peli's head as the dog set his forelegs on the corbita's railing beside him. "I hope you'll behave in Athenae. These Greeks are somewhat more conservative than we are." Rufio gazed over the rooftops to the Acropolis of the destroyed fortress of Piraeus and then to the distant rocky mountains that loomed above Athenae. "Captain!"

"Yes?" Memnon said as he came down from the quarterdeck.

"How far is it to Athenae from here?"

"About five or six miles," he replied. "Shouldn't take you too long by wagon."

"I see." Rufio looked out again. "Has your man returned with the wagons yet?"

"No. I was just going to check. I'll be back." The captain went down the broad gang plank and spoke with some of his men on shore, two of them pointing animatedly down the harbour. A few moments later, Captain Memnon returned, just as Clara rejoined Rufio. "The wagons are here… As is yours."

"Ours?" Rufio asked. "But I haven't negotiated one yet. How much?"

Captain Memnon smiled. "It's been paid for already by your friend, Felix Modestus. It seems…" the captain stifled a chuckle, "…according to the driver, that he spared no expense for you. The man has been waiting for three days."

"Where?" Clara asked.

"There, Domina." It was then that Captain Memnon pointed at the purple and yellow, peacock-bedecked transport that drew the eyes of every sailor in the harbour. The crew burst out laughing.

"Oh, no," Clara muttered. "Rufio…"

"I…um… We'll just ask the driver to go quickly."

Captain Memnon pat Rufio on the shoulder. "I'll have your things loaded onto the wagon for you. Be careful walking down," he said over his shoulder.

"Oh, dear," Clara said, wrapping her cloak about her and Felicia before making her way down the gang plank.

Rufio hoisted his writing satchel, which he preferred to carry himself, and walked to the plank, still taken aback by Felix's very loud mode of transportation. He looked down at Peli who barked at the thing as it came to a halt.

"Be careful when you come off, Rufio!" Clara called up, her voice barely audible over the screech of the gulls.

"I can walk just fine!" Rufio snapped, wondering why the crewmen on shore were gawping at him and Peli. He did not notice Captain Memnon and the others behind him, lining up to watch.

Rufio and Peli made their way down the bobbing gang plank, but as soon as they took three steps on solid ground, Peli crouched immediately while Rufio swayed upon his feet, lurching once, twice, then a third time before he stumbled several paces to his left, slammed into the side of the colourful wagon, and fell upon the ground. "What in Hades?"

The crew laughed and applauded, and then set about unloading the cargo.

Clara looked down at him, her face and Felicia's ringed by sunlight. "You all right?"

"What was that?" Rufio shook his head.

"You need to get your land legs back. You've been at sea for a long time and aren't used to it," Clara said.

"And you are?"

She shrugged. "I've actually never had that problem before. But I thought you might, especially since you were lying down most of the time." She looked to where Peli was crawling toward them. "Peli's had the same trouble."

Just then, a particularly irksome gull dropped a white load upon Rufio's forehead.

"Ahh!" he cried, squinting and wiping at his face.

Clara smiled to herself. "Come on, Pisthetaerus. Let's get you in the wagon."

While Rufio dragged himself to his feet and tested his legs, two crewmen loaded the three amphorae of wine and their two trunks into the very back of the enormous wagon and secured them with rope. The objects looked strangely at odds with the interior of plush cushions.

"At least we'll be comfortable," Rufio said as he walked round to the front of the wagon to address the driver. "Salve!"

"Huh?" the Greek answered gruffly.

"Kalimera!" Clara added as she joined Rufio.

The driver smiled then and began to babble and gesture in a version of Greek Rufio could not quite wrap his head around.

"What's he saying?" Rufio asked.

"He's begging us to leave as soon as possible," Clara

smiled. "He says he's had enough embarrassment for a lifetime waiting here for us."

"Well, I'm sure Felix is paying him well enough." Rufio frowned up at the driver who was gesturing to the back of the wagon. "Just hold on, you! We're not ready!" He turned to Clara. "You want to check with Captain Memnon that everything is in order before we go?"

"Yes. You get in first and I'll hand you Felicia."

Rufio climbed up into the bed of the wagon, careful not to fall off it from a height, set his writing satchel down, and knelt at the edge to take Felicia's babbling, kicking form. "Come on, my girl. Time to visit the goddess' city!" Rufio turned and noted baskets of food and drink that had been set out for them, including what looked like goat's cheese. "How old is this stuff?" he asked the driver.

The driver, who had been making faces at Felicia, turned to Rufio and shrugged. "Today. Bought today."

"That's all I wanted to know." Rufio held Felicia closely and looked over the small feast. "I'm famished." He then noted a few nibbles out of one of the pieces of meat and looked at the driver's back. "Of course." He shook his head. "Peli!" he called without looking, lobbing the small leg of meat over the edge so that the dog caught it.

Clara met Captain Memnon to the side of the gangplank.

"Do you have everything, Domina?" the captain asked.

Clara smiled. "I do. Thank you, Captain. I know we…we made the crossing a little difficult."

Captain Memnon smiled and shook his head. "Not at all. It was entertaining, to say the least." He looked at the wagon to see Rufio holding Felicia and singing to her. "He's a strange one your man, but he's good and kind to you. Master Aeson would have been happy for you, as I am."

"I appreciate that, Captain." Clara looked over the men who continued to carry amphorae of their wine off the ship and place them into the wagons. "You have enough coin for the taxes?"

Captain Memnon's voice was back to business. "Yes, Domina. We have plenty. I'll take care of it at the customs office as soon as the ship is unloaded."

"Thank you. And you know where the shipments are going?" Clara asked.

The captain smiled and put a fatherly hand on her shoulder. "I do. Just as we reviewed. Worry not, Domina. Everything is in hand. I'll make sure of it personally, and I won't accept less than the agreed upon payment from each of the buyers."

"Excellent." Clara nodded and looked at the wagon.

At that moment, Peli came running up to stand beside her.

Captain Memnon ignored the canine and smiled fleetingly at Clara. "All will be well here. You just go and enjoy whatever it is you are going to do in Athenae."

"Who knows what will happen!" Clara laughed.

"Just be careful, Domina."

"We will." She pat Peli's head and he nuzzled her leg. "If you can be back here in the first week of September, that will be perfect. We want to be back in Etruria for the harvest."

"You can count on me, Domina. I'll send word when we make berth again in Piraeus. The Hippocampus will be here in this spot, waiting for you."

"Errol will have instructions for the next shipments when you get back."

"Domina…"

"Yes?" Clara stopped talking.

"You should get going." Without looking, Captain Memnon nodded downward.

"Yes… I, uh… Peli, no!" Clara looked to see Peli lifting his leg to piss upon the captain's boots. "Oh, I'm so sorry, Captain." She turned to Peli. "Bad dog! Go get in the wagon!"

Peli shot off, most fortunate that the Captain did not retaliate with an attack of his own.

"I'm so sorry, Captain! It means he likes you."

"Afraid the feeling is not mutual, Domina. If he were not your dog I'd-"

"I'm sure!" Clara said. "I guess we'd better be off."

"I think that would be best." Captain Memnon sighed, looking down at his wet boots before watching Clara hoist the naughty hound and then climb up into the wagon herself. "Domina!"

"Yes, Captain?"

"May Fortuna and Apollo win the days for you!"

Clara smiled as the wagon began to roll. "Thank you, Captain!"

Captain Memnon watched as they rolled away, the Roman sailors working on the ships' hulls nearby hooting and whistling at the bedecked wagon. "Back to work!" he shouted at his crew as he turned. "The Domina is counting on us!"

"Well this is nice," Clara said as she settled in the cushions with Rufio, Felicia, and Peli who was growling at the driver's back. "That's enough, Peli. Don't worry," she said to the driver. "He's harmless."

Rufio raised an eyebrow.

"Hey girlie! Nice ride!" One of the Roman sailors called out from where he and others were applying fresh pitch to a hull. "Can we join you!"

"How dare you speak to my wife like that! Futuere, the lot of you!" Rufio shouted, his face red.

"We weren't talking to her, ginger knob!" another shouted back.

"This is going to be a long ride, isn't it?" Rufio said as the wagon paraded itself through the thickening crowd of traffic and pedestrians from around the empire.

"Maybe that's the worst of it?" Clara mused, taking a piece of bread for herself and dipping it in some honey. "Hmm. Attic honey is the best!"

"Not Attic wine though!" Rufio said. "Felix will be thrilled at the taste of home we've brought."

"You used to the idea of Athenae now?" Clara asked, leaning back against a large cushion.

"Yes. Yes I am!" Rufio smiled and tickled Felicia before handing her to Clara. Sadly, his level of discomfort rose quite rapidly as their wagon was swallowed by the crowd making its way to the main thoroughfare out of Piraeus and straight for Athenae. "I hope this crowd thins out."

All around them, people were pointing and laughing, and there were not a few stray comments about uncouth and loud Romans.

"I'll get Felix for this!" Rufio growled as he looked up at the buildings rising up beyond the temples, tabernae on the ground floor and lupanaria above.

"Hey beautiful!" one of the lupae shouted and waved as she and another leaned out of a second storey window, her breasts sunning themselves like pigeons upon a window sill.

Rufio smiled and puffed out his chest. "Well, that's better!" he said, leaning back against his own cushion. "Hello ladies!" he waved back.

"Not you!" one of the lupae shouted back and pointed. "Her!" She winked and blew a kiss to Clara.

Clara laughed and nodded, waving back with Felicia's tiny hand. "Well, I do look good today," Clara said, smiling at Rufio.

He smiled back. "Yes, you do!"

Finally, the wagon was rolling along between the ruins of Athenae's long walls from Piraeus. The sun was high and bright in the blue sky, and the squawk of gulls was fading away as they drove off into that ancient land of rock and olive toward the goddess' polis.

THE JOURNEY WAS A MOST PLEASANT ONE, FOR THE SPRING sunshine was brilliant and warm and perfect for travel.

While Clara sat back, feeding Felicia in the privacy of the wagon - for which they were very grateful - Rufio sat looking out, enjoying their passage through that ancient landscape.

The remains of Athens' ruined 'long walls', that stretched all the way from Piraeus to the city itself, lent a feeling of antiquity that was far greater than one felt in Rome. In the dry, thyme-scented air, among the crumbled rock of the long-dead walls, wild flowers burst forth with shouts of purple, red, and yellow. Even the light seemed brighter, and colours more vivid, as if the Gods and other numina lurked in the surrounding hills, watching humanity's daily performance.

Rufio thought about all the great playwrights he admired, and how many of them must have walked this very road between the harbour and the city where their art was born. He shook his head in amazement and popped another olive into his mouth.

"What is it?" Clara asked him as she lay Felicia down among the cushions to sleep. She leaned against Rufio who put his arm about her.

"Just think of the men who have been here... Euripides, Aristophanes, Sophocles, Menander, Aeschylus..."

"What about them?" Clara yawned, tired from her feeding, but thoroughly enjoying the ride now that they were far out of the port.

"They walked here. Lived here. They were inspired by this place!" Rufio's eyes were wide in amazement.

Clara could feel his heart race with excitement where her

hand was placed upon his chest. "It's not like many people of renown haven't walked the streets of Rome." Clara loved to challenge Rufio's grand observations at times as he had told her once that it helped to make him think through ideas.

"That's different!" he exclaimed, quickly quieting his voice so as not to wake their dozing daughter. "It's different if it's warring generals. The men who wrote those plays created something that inspired others, that lifted people up, that still do! Their work was revered."

Clara noted a hint of sadness or desperation in Rufio's voice in that moment. She sat up to look at him. "What is bothering you? Are you getting nervous about the performance of whatever play Felix has in store?"

Rufio looked down. "No. But trust me, I'll do that later." He sighed and looked up at the cloudless sky. "I suppose that thinking of all the great playwrights who were here makes me feel quite small." He paused. "I already feel like, to me at least, this is a world of heroes…my heroes, at any rate… And I'm a fool among them."

"You are no fool, Rufio."

"My father certainly thought so." Rufio could not help but remember his father's wretched clapping whenever he entered a room, mocking his love of theatre. *Strange, I haven't thought of that in a long time,* he thought.

"Your father was a bully, and certainly no hero," she replied, her voice stern for a moment. "To me…to us…" She reached out to gently touch Felicia's arm. "*You* are the hero." Clara turned his head to face her and kissed him. She felt his body relax. She looked him in the eye then. "You can't put so much pressure on yourself. Whatever it is you're working on - and don't think I can't see how you clutch that writing satchel to your breast wherever you go! - it will be *your* work, uniquely so. Each of those great, creative men you spoke of had their own hardships on their creative journey, no doubt, just as you do. Be *inspired* by them and their world, my love, not defeated."

"I know you're right. Who knows what might happen when a Roman comes to Athenae?" He thought then of what Captain Memnon had said to him about how the Greeks viewed Romans.

"Rufio, don't worry," Clara said, knowing full well the judgment he feared from the people of Athenae. "You're not going into Athenae as a Roman general, but rather as an Etrurian playwright and player."

He smiled. "I understand you," he kissed her forehead. "Surely the Athenians will see that no harm could ever come of that?"

"Ee polis!" the driver suddenly said to them over his left shoulder from where he sat at the front.

"What?" Rufio replied.

"Athenae! Ee polis ine etho!" The driver was pointing ahead.

"He says the city is there," Clara said, though Rufio's Greek was good enough to understand that.

They both knelt and looked past the driver to see Athenae at last, the Goddess' city.

"My Gods," Rufio muttered. "It's beautiful!"

Clara smiled. "It certainly is...so much more than I remember..."

Their lavish wagon slowed as it rolled along into the thickening traffic entering the city. This afforded Clara and Rufio the chance to look at the world around them.

Beyond the Piraean gate, the Pnyx rose up to their left, that place where Athenian democracy was born and where so many great political performances were carried out in ages past. To their right, the Hill of the Muses bubbled up from the ground, topped by the recent monument to the Syrian-Roman Consul, Philopappus. It seemed strangely out of place beside the ancient Pnyx, but then, so was their mode of transport among all those pedestrians.

It was difficult to see much before they passed through the gate, but the primary wonder to fill Rufio Pagano's eyes in that moment was the ancient Acropolis crowned by the great temple of Athena Parthenos. The high pediments supported by a forest of thick columns, along with the brilliant Propylaea, the long Temenos of Artemis Brauronia, the Temple of Athena Nike, and other structures, hovered like a city in the clouds.

"Maybe this *is* Mount Olympus," Rufio mused, his heart beating faster with anticipation. "I can't wait to see the rest!" He turned to Clara with a big smile on his bearded face. "You said before that the theatre district is on the south slope of the Acropolis?"

"Yes," Clara said. "We should see them once we pass through the gate and the Pnyx."

Just then, Felicia awoke and started her usual post-nap chorus.

Clara turned to pick her up to try and quieten her. "Surely you need to sleep longer than that, my beautiful girl?" she asked the child. But the chorus turned to a frenzied wail.

All around them, people who had been pointing at their wagon already began to murmur and shout, as if the crying of a child were some abnormality out in public.

"Shut that child up!" someone yelled.

Rufio turned in a fury to stare at the sea of faces turned in his direction. "Futuere landicae!" he burst out, making a gesture.

"Oh, great!" another person said. "More Romans!"

Rufio tried to ignore the inane babble projected at him, but it was no easy task.

"I need to change her," Clara said, rummaging through their belongings. "Rufio, hand me that satchel."

Rufio handed it to her and muttered. "Maybe the Athenians gave Sulla the same reception."

Suddenly, before they reached the gate, the wagon turned right off of the Piraean road and onto a smaller track that led around the outside of the walls.

"Oi, where are you going?" Rufio tapped the driver on the shoulder, his hands out questioningly.

"No wagons in the city!" the man said.

"But I want to *see* the city!" Rufio protested.

"I guess it's like Rome in that way. The streets are narrower here," Clara pointed out. "It makes sense."

"But where are we going?" Rufio asked as the wagon rolled on, past the Hill of the Muses and then past the Itonian and Phaleron gates. "I guess we'll just by-pass the entire city then! So long, Athenae! Nice to see you!"

"Rufio," Clara said, as she settled down to feed Felicia again. "Be calm. He's probably taking us straight to the villa. Look around." She pointed to where the wagon was rolling into a forested area between the city walls and the River Ilissos. "It's beautiful here."

Rufio had been so engulfed by his annoyance that he had failed to notice the absence of shouting Athenians and the grind of wagon wheels on cobblestones. All about them, ancient cypresses, broad plane trees, fragrant pine, and silver-leafed olive made up an ancient sanctuary where few people ventured.

"Panhellenion," the wagon driver said as he pulled up beneath a tall pine, pointing at a building that appeared to be an ancient law court but which had, clearly, seen better days. A couple of men stood speaking on the steps of this structure, their gazes momentarily drawn by the bright wagon. The driver turned then to point to a large and very ancient temple, the roof of which was supported by thick Doric columns.

"Apollon Delphinios," he said as he brought the wagon to a halt.

On hearing the god's name, Rufio turned quickly to look, his eyes wide as he gazed upon the image of Apollo upon the pediment, sitting upon a mountainside with his cythara in hand. "We should make an offering for our safe arrival," he said beneath his breath as he slid off the wagon.

"Good idea," Clara returned as she finished feeding Felicia and arranged her stola so that she could descend from the wagon. "Here, take her," she said, handing him their daughter before getting out.

The driver was already laying himself against the bole of a tree nearby.

Once Clara was down, she and Rufio took a few steps away from the wagon to properly look around. "Well, I never came to this part of the city," she said.

"Seems like few people do," Rufio answered, watching as the two men who had been standing on the steps of the old law court departed up a staircase. "What is that?" Rufio pointed above the retaining wall beyond the temple of Apollo to a soaring rooftop set upon a forest of titanic columns.

"That, I know," Clara said. "It's the Temple of Olympian Zeus. Aeson told me before that Emperor Hadrianus finished it for the city. Apparently he loved Athenae."

"Who, Aeson?"

"No, Emperor Hadrianus." She looked back up at the temple. "We'll go see it."

Rufio looked back down at their immediate surroundings. "I think I prefer it here. It's so quiet."

In amongst the trees about the temple of Apollo were scattered altars and statues dedicated to various gods and goddesses. They stood like silent sentries in that ancient place where the loudest sounds were mourning doves in the trees above them, and the gurgling of the crystalline river Ilissos.

Farther down were smaller temples dedicated to Chronos and Rhea which sat in a darker part of the sanctuary.

"Where's Peli?" Rufio felt a sudden panic.

"Over there," Clara said, pointing toward the temple steps. "He jumped down as soon as the wagon slowed. Maybe you should get him, Rufio. We don't want him making a mess of Apollo's doorstep."

"No. That wouldn't do. Here," Rufio handed Felicia back to Clara. "You two can sit by the river. I'll get Peli."

Clara smiled at her daughter as she carried her in the shade of the trees to the riverside.

Eyeing Peli, Rufio reached into the wagon to get his satchel. When he turned to walk back toward the temple, Peli was bouncing from side to side, and he thought that his hound had finally lost it. "What are you doing, you mad dog?"

As he got closer, Rufio noticed that Peli was dancing about as he faced off with a rather large serpent upon the cracked marble of the temple steps. "Peli, leave it alone!" Rufio shouted, his voice rather louder than he would have liked in that idyllic place. "Come here!" he hissed.

The serpent, which was no doubt the temple resident, intended to keep the vermin in check, was loosing patience with its dodgy-eyed harasser, and so launched itself at Peli's behind.

The dog yelped and ran past Rufio to join Clara and Felicia with its tail between its legs.

"Fine then," Rufio grumbled as he came to a stop in front of the temple, a comfortable distance from the aggravated reptile. "I apologize for my dog," he said, unsure if the serpent was in fact a local numina. *Better safe than sorry,* he thought.

The deep quiet of the place settled over him again, and Rufio felt a calm he had not felt in many days. The calm gave him hope, and it infused all of his senses as he gazed up at the temple pediment.

He reached into his satchel and pulled out the small olive bough he had brought from Etruria. He then formed it into a small wreath and set it upon a nearby altar which stood before the temple.

"Oh, Apollo… Thank you for bringing us safely to Athenae… Please guide my thoughts…my writing hands… Let our play - whatever it is - win over these Greeks…"

Rufio wanted to go into the temple, but it appeared to be locked, and so he turned to go and rejoin Clara and Felicia by the river. As he walked, he looked down the shore among the other shrines and statuary in the thicket. There, he noticed a dishevelled man in a tunica sitting beneath an olive tree. He appeared to be writing. For a moment, Rufio thought he recognized the man. From where, he did not know, but it gave him a chill to look upon him. "I'm just tired," he said to himself. For a second, he thought to go and offer a greeting. However, as the man appeared to be muttering to himself, Rufio thought it best not to disturb him.

"I've got a good feeling about this place," Rufio said. He sat himself upon a large boulder beside Clara who was holding Felicia upright so that her tiny feet danced in the tickling grass of the riverbank. "Looks like you do too!" he bent down to make a face at his daughter.

Felicia giggled, and her joy was like a water nymph's laughter beside that ancient river.

"Did you make an offering?" Clara asked as she sat Felicia in her lap again.

"Yes." Rufio was silent for a moment.

"What is it?"

"This place feels very different. Not in a bad way. Quite the opposite actually."

Clara observed her husband for a moment. He had always been out of sorts when he left home. But this time, he seemed different, as if he were at last opening up to the larger world.

She smiled and reached for his hand to press it to her cheek. "It will be good to perform again, I think."

Then, Rufio's face darkened. "I wasn't thinking so much about that. In fact, I'd rather not just now."

"Aren't you excited to see the others? It's been so long since Rome."

Rufio looked around and nodded, his smile returning. "Yes. I am. I wonder how much they've changed."

"I guess we'll find out." Clara looked to where the driver was snoring beneath a tree. "We'd better wake him so we can get going. Felix will be worried."

"Will he though?"

"All right. Maybe not. But I'd like to get to this villa before Felicia wants to eat again."

"I'll go and wake the driver."

While Clara stood and went to the wagon with Felicia, Rufio wandered though the grass to where the driver was snoring into the Ilissian peace.

"Erm… Excuse me," Rufio said, attempting to rouse the driver. "We're ready to go."

"Wha? What happened? Non iocari!" the driver said, a panicked look in his eyes as he was pulled from his deep afternoon sleep.

"I'm not making fun of you! We just want to -" Rufio stared at the man as he grumbled. "Just a moment. You speak Latin?"

"Of course I do!" the driver proclaimed. "Our dominus insists on it."

"Why did you pretend not to know much?" Rufio asked.

The man shrugged and smiled. "For the Roman tourists. They seem to think it quaint. I can also listen in on their conversations."

"You sneaky man!" *Here's a parasite for a play!* Rufio thought.

"Ready, then?" the driver asked, watching Rufio as he stared off into the trees.

"Oh, ah, yes. Yes, let's go!"

They walked back to the wagon and Rufio helped Clara and Felicia while the driver took his place on his seat, taking up the reins of his horses who were happily cropping at the thick grass.

"Peli!" Rufio whistled, and the hound came running up from where he had been drinking at the river. "I hope you didn't drink too much!" Rufio asked their panting companion as he lifted him into the wagon.

"Did you know our driver speaks Latin?" Rufio whispered to Clara.

"He does?" She looked at the man's back and smiled to herself. "I think we're in for an interesting adventure, my love."

"Seems that way," Rufio said as he took Felicia to give Clara's arms a rest. "How long to the villa?" Rufio asked the driver.

"Not long. It's but a mile up the Hill of Ardittos."

"The hill of what?" Rufio cocked his ear.

"Ardittos," the driver repeated more slowly.

Rufio settled back to enjoy the rest of the journey with Clara leaning against him and Felicia already sleeping against his chest. Peli was curled at his feet.

The overly resplendent wagon rolled through the shrines along the Ilissos river like a thief in hiding outside the walls of Athenae. Rufio looked again for the man whom he had seen, but he was nowhere to be found.

"We're in the birthplace of theatre," Rufio reminded himself, awed by the fact.

"What's that?" Clara asked.

"Nothing. Just musing."

Soon, the sounds of the city returned as they drove up a

small hill to make a sharp right onto a paved road before a small temple outside one of the main city gates.

"This is Hadrianus' Gate," the driver pointed. "This road leads up to the villa."

Rufio looked around, amazed at all of the new structures he saw. "Is this part of Athenae new?"

"Yes. It is Novae Athenae," the man answered, waving his arm in a broad arch to their left. "Also called 'Hadrianopolis'."

Rufio caught sight of several domed rooftops clustered inside the city walls. "Are those the public baths?"

"Yes. The new baths."

Rufio did long for a visit to the baths. He secretly hoped that the place where they were staying was not so small that it would be lacking baths. He was not sure how clean the Greeks where when it came to such things. *Here's hoping.*

They came to a tripled-arched bridge over the River Ilissos, adorned with statues of heroes and an arch on top of which soared a statue of Nike, the Goddess of Victory. Marble shrines lined the road on either side, and Rufio noted several of them with Latin names. They were all well-kept and clean, some painted with brilliant colours to rival their wagon, while others were of purest white marble from the Attic quarries.

The wagon rolled directly toward what appeared to be a massive stadium.

Clara sat herself up to look around. "Are we almost there?" she asked.

The driver shook his head and continued. "That is the stadium where the games are held."

"What games?" Rufio asked. "The Panathenaea?"

"Of course! And others!"

The closer they got to the stadium, the more dizzying it became in Rufio's eyes. True, it was not the Circus Maximus, but there was something about it that drew one in. "Do they ever perform plays here?"

The driver grunted. "The arts of Apollo are performed in the Odeon of Pericles, the Theatre of Dionysus, and the Herodeon."

"The Herodeon?" Rufio asked.

"My dominus' family theatre," the driver said, now clearly confusing Rufio who gave Clara a quizzical look.

"Is he joking?" he whispered to her. "Do they perform in the streets as well?" Rufio asked.

The driver turned with a shocked look upon his face. "Why would you do such a thing?" he demanded.

Rufio shrugged stiffly, trying not to wake Felicia.

"Romans…" the driver muttered.

Clara looked around and far up the hill to their right she saw a temple set back in among the trees. "What temple is that?" she asked the driver.

"That is the sanctuary of Artemis Agrotera," the man said. "Very old. And beyond that is the ancient necropolis."

Rufio had thought that the forest was quiet enough, but now, knowing there was a necropolis just steps away, he wondered what lemurs roamed the darkened paths about that place.

Soon the temple became hidden from view and the wagon continued on its way.

Just then, they made a sharp right and began to drive around the side of the stadium and then uphill from there. "Now we go up Ardittos."

Suddenly, with the high walls of the stadium rising up on their right, they had left Athenae behind them and were cutting their way up through a pine forest track. Their wagon, like a splash of bright paint in the midst of a dark canvas, creaked and groaned as it climbed.

A few scattered shrines dotted the roadside, some newer than others, and the prevailing sound was of the wind in the pine branches and the sound of birds flitting in amongst them.

The air smelled sweetly, and a new calm fell all around them. It began to lull them, and weigh on their eyelids.

"We are almost at the villa!" the driver suddenly declared.

Rufio and Clara's eyes shot wide.

The pine forest had suddenly given way to an olive grove that sprang from an endless bed of wildflowers where apiaries were scattered about. Soon, a long, high wall came into view, set back a ways from the dirt track.

Peli awoke suddenly, and stood immediately with his head over the edge of the wagon, his snout sniffing at the fresh air, his ears alert to the wild sounds of nature about them.

"I hope it's not a goat shed," Rufio said to Clara.

"Somehow I doubt it," she replied as she spotted a broad, arched gate set in the middle of the wall.

"If it is, I'm leaving."

The wagon slowed on cue, turned sharply to the right, and proceeded down a short gravel drive.

Gathered outside the gate were several servants, more than were needed to man a gate. They were all dressed in clean tunicae, well-turned out in fact, but the pained look upon their faces told of something more.

"What are you all doing outside the gates like this?" the driver asked them. "Atticus is going to have a fit!"

"He already is!" one of the men replied before they all stepped aside for the wagon. They looked up to see Rufio and Clara, yet another baby, and a dog who eyed them suspiciously and growled at them.

"So what's the problem?" the driver asked.

"You'll see!" another of the men said.

"*Hear*, rather!" a third offered, rubbing his temples. He and another proceeded to open the double-wide gates and the moment they did, a wave of wailing rushed from out of the villa.

Rufio and Clara looked at each other, all too familiar with

that sound. "The baby," they said to each other in unison, unable to withhold their smiling.

Rufio rubbed Peli's head to calm him. "Oh, Peli! You're in for it!"

Clara watched Felicia who was already beginning to rouse, aware of the increasingly high volume of another child nearby.

The wagon was through the gate now and pulled into a large square courtyard with a perimeter arcade. Five large olive trees orbited the path and a central fountain sang with a pleasant splashing. Several litters were parked in the shade of the trees, ready for use.

The wagon rounded the fountain and came to a stop on the other side, at which point the wailing grew louder.

"At last! You've arrived!"

Rufio turned to see a rather heavy, short, bearded man in a neatly pressed tunica embroidered with a meander pattern about the hem and sleeves. He smiled uncomfortably as he approached, his hair slightly dishevelled, though it was obvious he had started his day quite neat indeed. His brow was creased in worry as he rushed up to greet the newcomers in the unmistakable wagon. "Salvete!" he said, rallying himself for the greeting he always prided himself on.

Rufio noted that the man's Latin was impeccable, at least to his Etrurian ears. "Salvete!" Rufio said as he descended first and then helped Clara down with Felicia.

"Rufio Pagano and Clara Probita!" He stopped and inclined his head politely to them. "I am Atticus, the steward of this domus. I am here to ensure that you have everything you require while you are here, and that all runs smoothly."

"And how is that going for you?" Rufio could not help but ask as the wailing reached a painful crescendo.

Clara hushed Felicia as she too began to grow upset.

Atticus' eyes looked at the second baby most desperately, and he was about to speak when a mad-looking dog leapt from the wagon to stand between him and the newly-arrived couple and child. He eyed the canine warily. "I...um... All is well. Lady Electra's child is warming up his vocal chords."

"That is a kind way of putting it, Atticus," Clara said, her smile putting the steward at ease.

"I will have the servants unload the wagon for you," he looked to the amphorae in the back of the wagon, "and bring your belongings to your cubiculum on the second floor."

"May we see the others?" Clara asked. "Are they all here?"

"Yes, of course," Atticus replied. "I shall let them know you have arrived immediately." He began to go and get them, turning one last time. "I bid you welcome to the Villa Atticus."

"Wait," Rufio stepped forward. "That's your name. Is this your domus?"

Atticus shook his head. "No, no, no. I am named for my dominus' family. This great domus is named after my dominus' father, Herodes Atticus, who was an imperial magistrate at Athenae, and a great patron of Apollo's arts. I shall return momentarily."

As Atticus left, Rufio turned to Clara. "Did he just say, Herodes Atticus?"

"I believe he did," Clara said, kissing Felicia's forehead, willing her not to join the approaching chorus.

"Where is everyone?" Rufio asked, gazing toward the arch on the opposite side of the courtyard that led into the villa itself.

Just as he was about to turn away to begin unloading their things himself, the doors were flung open.

"Clara! Rufio!"

The bright if not somewhat distraught faces of the members of The Etrurian Players came rushing out of the doors to greet them.

In the lead was Fausto who did a line of tumbles to land before them. "I'm so glad you're here!" he said, embracing both Rufio and Clara, though he was taken aback by the second child she held in her arms, and quickly bent down to ruffle Peli's collar as the dog's tail whipped round with extreme excitement.

Beatrice followed, all smiles as she rushed up to them, exuding an air much more confident now than she had done when last in Rome. "I'm so happy you're here!" she said to Clara, whom she kissed upon the cheek before tickling Felicia's chin. "She's beautiful!"

"And quiet!" Pollux declared as he and his brother Castor walked up to Rufio. "Salve, Rufio!"

"Lads," Rufio returned, squinting at the distant crying and argumentative voices of the still unseen Felix and Electra. "Are you all right here?"

"No!" Castor said, unable to stifle his mad laughter. "The young god is berating us all endlessly!"

"Aaaahoooo!" Damon howled to mimic the child as he too bounded up, his flute in hand.

"Damon!" Rufio slapped him on the back and the mute musician smiled and whirled his eyes as if to tell Rufio he was certainly in for a wild time. Then he spied Julius approaching and walked forward to meet him and some other woman who remained close by his side.

"Julius!" Rufio said as the others greeted Peli who tore around them all in a great circle, intermittently marking every olive tree in the courtyard.

"Rufio, Clara!" the older man greeted them with a broad, warm smile, his thin blond hair awhirl atop his head. "Our company is now complete!" He took Rufio's hand and then turned to greet Clara. "You look lovely, my dear."

"Thank you, Julius," Clara said. "And so do you! Athenae agrees with you, it seems!"

"Well…yes, I suppose it does. And who is this lovely young lady?" he asked, leaning in with all of the others to look upon

Felicia whose eyes were now wide open and gazing upon all the roundheads staring her way.

"This is our daughter, Felicia," Clara said.

"She's beautiful!" the woman who had come out with Julius said above the others.

"I don't believe we've met," Rufio stepped up, uneasy about this total stranger touching his child. "Rufio Pagano," he introduced himself.

"Oh, I know who you are, deary. I've heard all the stories." She looked at the rest of the company.

Rufio noted the guilty looks upon their faces. "Not everything, I hope!"

"Only the colourful bits!" Fausto said, putting his arm about Rufio and squeezing.

Julius cleared his throat. "Rufio and Clara, this is Domela. She is the newest member of our company, and a wonderful actress to boot!"

"That's debatable," Beatrice muttered in Clara's ear.

Clara recovered quickly and smiled warmly at Domela. "It's very nice to meet you, Domela."

"Likewise," the latter said before turning to Rufio and straightening his tunica for him. "I'm the new mother of the company, I suppose."

Rufio looked around, slightly confused at this attention to his appearance.

Domela then licked her finger and was about to clean a bit of dirt from Rufio's cheek, but he managed to sidestep it.

"MY FRIENDS!" Felix Modestus' booming voice suddenly burst from the interior of the villa, momentarily drowning out the sound of crying that followed in his wake. "You're here at last!" Felix rushed up to greet them, taking Rufio in a great crushing hug that lifted him off of the ground, and then turning to Clara to kiss her upon both cheeks before turning his attention to the infant in her arms. "And here she is! The offspring of your genii!" He bent over the child in awe, his eyes actually a little glassy.

"This is Felicia," Clara said.

"I never would have thought… She's a true wonder!" Felix said, wiping his eye quickly.

"Where are Electra and your son?" Clara said.

Felix closed his eyes at the approach of the riotous sound. "Three, two, one…curtain!"

Just then, a wild-eyed Electra in a red stola came bursting into the courtyard with her wailing son held tightly in her arms, rocking him like a tiny boat on a storm-tossed sea.

Felicia began to cry just then, and everyone about them stepped back.

"Electra!" Clara said as she walked straight for the distraught woman. "You look beautiful!"

"I know dear!" Electra responded. "I wish I felt like it!" She then looked at Rufio who came to stand beside Clara. "Rufio," she nodded.

"Are you all right, Electra?" he asked, and the question got him a fiery look that would have been suited to a gorgon. He pinched himself to make sure he was not turning to stone in that instant, just to be safe. "I mean, I could hear the crying and-"

"Of course I'm not all right," she said, her voice loud so that she could be heard above her son.

"And who is this strong-lunged young man?" Clara said, turning so that she could better see Electra's son.

"This is Thespis!" Felix declared.

"Thespis?" Rufio said. "As in, the first ever actor?" He tried not to smile.

"Of course!" Felix said. "But what in Hades does that-"

In that moment, the entire courtyard - the company, the servants, and even the dog - stopped what they were doing to enjoy the sudden and wonderful sound of silence.

They looked to the children whose eyes and tiny fingers had locked onto each other.

Felix put his arm about Rufio then. "Look! They're fast friends already!"

For a moment, Clara thought Electra would weep at the sudden, unexpected quiet, but she just sighed, and the sentiment was echoed by the entire company.

"My friends," Felix said. "This is a sign from the Gods. All will be well."

"Extraordinary," Julius said as the two infants giggled and smiled as they looked at each other.

"I never thought to enjoy quiet again," Fausto laughed.

"Careful, you!" Electra hissed. "I can remove your ears if you want quiet so desperately."

Clara leaned in against Electra then, spotting the very familiar feeling of desperation and exhaustion in her friend's voice. "Come, let's sit together. Tell me how you are."

Electra's eyes closed and opened slowly and she nodded. "I would like that."

"That's a wonderful idea!" Felix said. "Atticus?"

"Yes, Felix Modestus?" the steward said as he came around from the other side of the wagon. "Will you see my friend's belongings brought to their quarters?"

"I am already about it."

"Good man." Felix looked at the wagon. "Rufio, is that Etrurian wine I see in the back of your gorgeous wagon?"

"You are right about the wine, my friend," Rufio said. "But the wagon?" he laughed.

"Too much?" Felix poked him.

"For these Athenians?" Rufio replied. "Absolutely!"

Felix laughed. "Atticus, ensure the wine our friend has brought is at our disposal. There will be many a celebration!"

"Yes, Felix Modestus!"

"It's wonderful to see you again, Rufio!" Fausto said as he and the others began to disperse.

"You as well!" Rufio replied, smiling at the lot of them.

Just then there was a loud squeal of displeasure and everyone turned to see Domela wiping at her tunica where Peli had, it seemed, watered her even more than the surrounding trees. "You cur!"

"I wouldn't worry about it, Domela," Rufio said. "It means he likes you."

Beatrice passed Rufio then. "Come on, Peli!" she said, a smile on her face as the dog fell into step to follow her into the villa.

Felix let all the others go into the villa, enjoying the quiet moment with Rufio. He looked to where Clara and Electra sat with the children upon a bench beneath one of the olive trees. "It's so good to see you, my friend," he said, hugging Rufio again.

Rufio looked up at him, slightly quizzically. "You all right?"

"I'm absolutely fine!" Felix replied. "Couldn't be better now that you're both here."

"Good."

"How was the crossing? No trouble?"

Rufio shook his head. "Smooth sailing the whole way. No trouble at all," Rufio said, trying to ignore the look Clara gave him when she overheard.

"Glad to hear it." Felix looked up at the blue expanse of the sky and filled his lungs. "It is beautiful here."

"Did I hear Atticus correctly? Does this villa belong to the family of Herodes Atticus?"

Felix nodded. "It does! Sextus knows the family and he arranged it for us, good man!"

"Has he arrived yet?" Rufio, of course, did not know Sextus Annius Sabinus as well as Felix did, but he remembered him as a kind and helpful fellow who also loved the theatrical arts, and that was enough for Rufio to feel an affinity toward him.

"Sextus and Martia should be arriving any day," Felix said. "It will be good for you to get to know him better. They are wonderful people with no pretension at all. They're honorary members of the company now too."

"Like me and Clara?"

Felix shook his head. "Nobody could be like you and Clara are to me."

"I can't believe we're fathers now," Rufio said.

"Nor can I, my friend." Felix looked at Electra and Clara. "Aren't they beautiful?"

Rufio smiled at Clara. "They certainly are."

"Such beautiful babies!" Felix said.

Rufio looked sidelong at him. "Of course, the children too."

They walked over to Electra and Clara.

"Now that Felicia has tamed our little Thespis," Felix said to Electra, "shall we show them the rest of the villa, my dear?"

Electra sighed and nodded with a smile. "Yes. Let's." She led the way with Clara while Felix and Rufio followed.

"What's in the satchel?" Felix asked.

"Oh, just…ah…just my scrolls," Rufio replied, clutching at it.

"Hmm. Always studious!" Felix pat him on the back. "I'm glad you're still a performer first, and a farmer second!"

"I'm a husband and father first," Rufio corrected with a smile as he watched Clara walk around the mosaic impluvium of the atrium before stepping into a vast sunlit peristyle garden beyond.

"I have to tell you about how I delivered our little Thespis upon the sea!" Felix suddenly said.

"What?" Clara turned to look at Felix, and Electra shook

her head and rolled her eyes. "You delivered the child yourself?"

"I did!" Felix confirmed. "And I tell you, I felt like a god doing so with my own two hands!"

"Why upon the sea?" Rufio asked.

"We were on the island of Delos and-" Felix began.

"Do we really need to go over all of this again?" Electra asked.

"The Gods were with us, that day," Felix continued, immune to her protestations.

"No childbirth is permitted on Delos though!" Rufio said.

"Exactly!" Felix agreed. "We were at the sacred lake when Apollo decided that it was time. As soon as Electra touched the waters, our child began his descent and-"

"Felix, no!" Electra protested.

"Her waters broke, and so I scooped her up, and carried her to the port where we took a boat to the island of Rheneia where births are permitted and-"

"I hurled one of the boatmen from the craft," Electra added, not to be outdone by her husband.

Felix continued, backing through the manicured garden set with couches, describing the great occasion. "I could see the Gods wanted me to do it, to deliver our child, for the shore was still far off and Electra's cries echoed above the roar of the sea."

"You exaggerate," Electra said. "But there was no time. Thespis was coming quickly. Eager for his mother's arms!"

"And his father's voice!" Felix added. "I helped my son into this beautiful world with my own hands and…and…"

"And what, Felix?" Electra said, her gaze as of fire.

Felix stopped and looked at her calmly, lovingly. "And she was like a goddess giving birth to her son."

Electra smiled. "And he was like a god, bringing our son into Apollo's light."

"Amazing," Rufio said, his eyes meeting Clara's.

"What about when Felicia was born?" Felix asked. "Were you there, Rufio?"

"Oh, he was there all right!" Clara chuckled.

Rufio shook his head, but she smiled.

"Upon the couch beside me where he had passed out."

"You didn't!" Electra looked at Rufio most accusingly.

Rufio shrugged.

"That's what happens to mortals in the presence of gods, they say," Felix added, most unhelpfully.

"Well," Rufio said, "Clara is a goddess to me, and Felicia is our joy. So yes, this mortal fainted."

Felix pat him on the shoulder again. "And you are the very best among them, my friend! Come. We'll show you the rest of the villa, your room, and the rehearsal space!"

"The rehearsal space is here?" Clara asked.

Felix smiled. "Just wait till you see it." He looked up at the second storey of the villa where the upper cubicula looked down on the peristylium. "The Etrurian Players are together again!"

There was distant applause from the rest of the company, followed by a resonant squirt.

They all looked at the two children, trying to discern which was the guilty party.

"Here you go, Divine Felix," Electra said as she handed Thespis to him. "Use your powers to clean your son. I'll show Clara the rehearsal space." With that, she threaded her arm through Clara's and walked with her and Felicia the rest of the way through the courtyard.

Felix wrinkled his nose and held up his son.

In that moment, Thespis began to wail once more.

"Come help me, Rufio. We can talk of theatre and fatherhood and the future."

Rufio gagged as he tasted the air about Thespis' kicking

legs, and he shook his head. "I'm good, my friend. This mortal will follow his goddess for the moment. You join us when you're finished your divine duties!"

Rufio all but ran after the two women and his daughter, leaving Felix standing alone with his son.

"You certainly know how to clear a room, my son," he said with a grin. "But one day, you'll fill entire theatres!"

VI

PROCREATIVE DIFFERENCES

It felt strange not to wake up to the sound of waves and shouting sailors. The broad bed in which Rufio and Clara found themselves was soft and still, absent the rocking which they had endured for the two weeks of their crossing.

As it was, the Gods granted Rufio and Clara a long and peaceful rest that first night, until Apollo's light crested the peaks of Mount Hymettos to awaken the forests and groves sweeping down to Athena's beautiful polis.

Their eyes opening slowly, Rufio and Clara looked at each other in comfortable silence, as if that quiet time of the new day were for gratitude, their hands and bodies slowly reaching out to each other beneath the soft sheets as the first birds in the surrounding hills saluted the rosy-fingered dawn.

After luxuriating in the villa's private baths and then dining upon salads, fresh breads, goat's cheese, fresh fish, and roasted lamb in the enormous triclinium with the rest of the company the previous night, they had decided to retire early due to the acute nature of their exhaustion. As much as they wished to hear about the adventures of the past couple of years, Rufio and Clara had been far too tired to be of good company. It was agreed then that they would catch up properly the following day.

The tour of the villa alone had been enough to sap their

strength, for it was a surprisingly vast domus at the heart of a rugged and rural latifundium.

Beyond the first courtyard where the litters and wagon had been parked, the peristyle garden was adorned with statues of gods, flowerbeds, and topiaries radiating about a central fountain surrounded by six couches which were reached by manicured pathways. To either side of the atrium that led onto this garden was a room reserved for women and children - a most traditional portion of the Greek domus - and a lararium where the household gods, mainly Zeus, Athena, Artemis, and Apollo, were worshiped alongside Hestia.

Around the peristylium were also the numerous cubicula for guests, a well-stocked library filled with copies of every play imaginable, and a study where Felix and Domela had already been at work on the accounts for the coming production. At the far end of the peristylium, almost equal to the width of the villa itself, was the triclinium, the walls of which were adorned with forest scenes with nymphs and satyrs peering out from behind the trunks of trees. At the centre of this vast space were several long, low tables surrounded by couches which the army of villa servants served from the kitchens at one end of the room. The kitchens were also accessed through the outer courtyard on the east side of the villa where wagons, a large workshop, the food stores, and servants' quarters were located.

The second floor of the villa soared over the central peristylium and consisted of four spacious suites for honoured guests. These included sitting areas beside high windows that looked onto the surrounding olive groves and wood beyond, as well as a large table for writing, and cedar closets filled with men's and women's clothing, some more suited to the emperor and empress than to farmers and players.

Rufio suspected that Felix had had a hand in stocking the closets. The expense was telling.

The greatest surprise of the wondrous villa, however, had

been the large court between the triclinium and the far bath-house that contained not gardens or statuary, but rather a small odeon with a circular orchestra and a small stage.

While beneath the tiled rooftops of Herodes Atticus' Athenian villa, they would be living and breathing theatre, something which, Felix was certain, would inspire their production like no other.

"The birthplace of theatre," Rufio whispered beneath the sheets.

Clara gripped his face playfully. "Not right now, my farmer. You have a different performance to focus on at the moment."

Rufio smiled and continued his joyous explorations in a rare occasion of quiet when the early morning duties of the latifundium were absent and their child yet slept in the crib several feet away.

As the birdsong outside in the boughs of the pine and olive trees grew louder, Clara made every effort to stifle her own exclamations to the morning. Evidently, it was not quiet enough for Peli whose furry face appeared on the edge of the bed and proceeded to nudge the engaged couple.

"Peli, no!" Clara hissed.

The dog then whined in his increasing panic.

"I knew we should have left him outside," Rufio muttered.

"Rufio, focus!" Clara said.

"I'm trying!"

"Oh…ah…yes, my love…"

And then Peli barked, and the sound was as if Zeus himself had hurled a lightning bolt at that very spot.

"No!" Rufio said.

"Yes!" Clara replied. "Don't stop!"

Then Felicia began to stir.

"Peli, go see the baby!" Rufio ordered, and the hound ran to circle the crib as if he were herding sheep back at the farm, his claws scritch scratching on the tiled floor.

Clara and Rufio reached their quick but muffled pleasure just as Felicia added her voice to the dawn chorus. Hiding beneath the sheets, breathless and relieved, they smiled at each other and kissed one more time.

"Ready to start the day?" Rufio asked.

"I am now. But this is to be continued."

Rufio brushed aside her blonde hair to look one more time at her reddened cheeks. "Thank you, Venus!"

And with that, they flung back the sheets and rose from the bed.

Peli came rushing over to Rufio then.

"I'm considering tying you out in the wood next time."

Peli tilted his head and looked up at Rufio with his mismatched eyes.

Rufio pat him and went to open the cubiculum door. "Go on. No barking."

Peli ran out of the door and through the villa to find a spot.

A moment later, there was a loud bark, and a servant's squeal.

"He pissed on me!" the servant yelled.

Rufio looked at Clara, and sheepishly closed the door. "I thought he would use the garden."

He slid a grey tunica with an embroidered wave border over his head while Clara began to feed Felicia in a fur-covered chair that sat before a large, frescoed wall. He then made his way over to the south-facing window.

The world outside felt completely different to the one to which he was accustomed, more wild and mysterious. Even the olive trees looked different to those that graced their own lands in Etruria, for those below him now were thicker and more gnarled. He wondered for a moment what sort of numina inhabited those groves.

But no matter where he looked as the warm pine air filled his nostrils, Rufio's eye was constantly drawn to the distant skyline of Athenae and the Acropolis that hovered over the world. The temple of Athenae Parthenos glinted in the morning light like a beacon over all of Attica.

"I still can't get over that view," he said over his shoulder. "A home for the Gods," he whispered to himself.

"It is lovely," Clara replied with a smile as she dabbed Felicia's cheek with a cloth before moving her to the other breast. "It seems different than the other two times I was here."

"Better, you mean." Rufio turned to look at her. "Now that you're here with me."

"Of course, my love."

Rufio was silent for a moment as he belted his black cingulum about his waist and tied up his caligae. He remained sitting on the edge of the bed and looked at her. "Do you feel strange being with everyone again?"

It was Clara's turn to be silent. "I suppose I do. A little, anyway. I think it's normal. We're a little preoccupied with the children, and there's a new member of the company whom we don't really know."

"I was so tired at the cena last night…" Rufio shook his head. "Felix probably thought I was rude."

"At least you didn't urinate on him like Peli did to Domela," Clara laughed.

"Yes…well… That would be rude." Rufio rubbed his eyes and wondered what the canine was getting up to. "I should probably find him."

"Felix?"

"No. Peli."

Just then, a loud crying could be heard from the suite on the other side of the second storey.

"Sounds like Thespis is awake," Clara said to Felicia who had begun to suckle more rigorously the moment the wailing had begun. "You like your new friend, don't you?" She held her up and pat her back until the child belched.

Rufio shook his head. "I'm still amazed that such a small child can make such a big sound."

"She just ate, Rufio."

"No, I mean Thespis."

"He has Felix's voice, that's for certain."

"And Electra's stubbornness." Rufio raised his eyebrows.

"You need to be kind to Electra. She's been having a difficult time and, from what she told me last night, Felix seems to be having some trouble adjusting to fatherhood."

"Really?" Rufio stood, confused by the sudden scratching at the door. "Didn't seem like it from the way he was speaking."

"You know Felix," Clara added as she placed Felicia on the bed to change her bracae.

Rufio opened the door and Peli burst into the room to hide beneath the large bed. "Had enough of Thespis?" he laughed. "Or have you upset Atticus?"

Peli whined.

"I'd better go down and see what damage he's done." He kissed Clara and tickled Felicia's foot. "You want me to help with this? She's moving all the time now!"

"We're fine. You go ahead," Clara said, blowing strands of her hair out of her face as she changed the child.

"See you down there then." Rufio went to the door and opened it so that the sound of crying filled the room. "Peli, you coming?"

The dog whined again and remained firmly ensconced beneath the bed.

"Have it your way," Rufio said, going out into the corridor and closing the door behind him. He walked to the wooden railing to look down into the peristylium, expecting to see some of the players lounging by the fountain, but the place was empty. He heard some muttered curses in Greek and looked straight down to see one of the household servants scraping at the bottom of his sandal.

"You do it, woman!" Felix suddenly shouted as he opened their cubiculum door on the other side of the domus and slammed it shut. He strode barefoot to the stairs and went down.

Rufio walked slowly after his friend, slightly unnerved as he had never seen Felix in such a state. He was usually more confident, at least outwardly.

At that moment, some of the cubicula doors about the lower level began to open, and a few of the others emerged, no doubt on their way to the latrina which was located at the back of the villa, behind the baths.

Beatrice emerged from her room first, a long, wrinkled tunica dragging on the ground about her feet.

Then Damon emerged, stark naked, and seemingly still asleep.

"Damon!" Rufio called down.

The mute looked up at Rufio and waved, a groggy smiled upon his face. "Woofio!" he called up.

"You forgot to dress!" Rufio said, pointing at him, just as the steward, Atticus, passed by, doing his utmost not to look at the strange guest.

Damon looked down at himself in surprise and nodded before going back to his cubiculum.

Rufio made his way downstairs where he bumped into Domela slinking out of a cubiculum.

"Oh! Good morning…ah…"

"Rufio," he said. "Good morning, Domela."

"Rufio, yes!" she said, some clothes bundled beneath her arms, her cheeks flushed. "Did you and your lovely wife sleep well?"

"Yes, we did. I'm sorry we quit the gathering so early. We

were exhausted last night. We'll be better company from now on."

"Oh, no, no… Not to worry. You didn't miss much," she said. "The usual bout of drinking between Castor, Pollux, and Damon… Fausto and Beatrice singing Catullus… The usual antics."

"Do you sing?" Rufio asked, not quite comfortable enough with the newcomer to make small talk.

"Yes, yes I do. But not as much as little Thespis." Domela looked around hurriedly for a moment. "Speaking of which, I had better see if Electra needs my help."

"Please, do," Rufio said. "I'll go and find Felix."

Domela nodded and went around the peristylium to the other side of the corridor into a cubiculum opposite.

Rufio looked at the door and then to the upper level where Electra and Felix's rooms were located. "Strange," he said to himself before shrugging and moving on.

Just then, behind him, the previous cubiculum door opened and out came Julius, humming to himself and straightening his dark red tunica.

"Salve, Julius," Rufio said.

The older man looked up, taken aback for a moment, but then he smiled broadly. "Rufio! I can't say how wonderful it is to see you and Clara again!"

"It's good to see you too," Rufio replied. And he meant it, for Julius had always been welcoming and encouraging when they had joined the company in Rome. "Did I just see…" Rufio was going to ask, but thought better of it.

"Yes?"

"Nothing. I'm just tired."

"Young Thespis will do that," Julius laughed. "Are you coming to ientaculum? Atticus does ensure a wondrous array of food every time. The yoghurt and Hymettos honey are especially good!"

"I'll meet you in there," Rufio said, letting Julius pass him. Once the older man had gone, Rufio took a deep breath but the scent that met him was not a pleasant one. "What is that stench?"

Rufio continued down the corridor and passed the servant he had seen from above still scraping at his sandal, his face red beneath his crown of curly black hair. He walked past him, holding his breath even as the servant gagged, gave up, and rushed the other way.

"Ah, there you are! Rufio Pagano, may I speak with you?"

Rufio looked to see Atticus coming out of the triclinium toward him. "Good morning, Atticus. Yes, of course." Rufio stopped, ready to meet the frazzled steward of the domus.

"I'm afraid I must speak with you about your…your dog!" Atticus stopped before Rufio, a little breathless, but whether from running, anger, or shear frustration, one could not tell.

"Yes, I'm sorry about him," Rufio said preemptively, his hands out in apology. "I saw one of the servants just now had stepped in it."

"If by 'it' you are referring to the sacrilegious pile of cacare he dropped on the mosaic of the Goddess Athena, then that is only one of myriad offences."

"Offences? He was only out of the room for a few minutes."

"Yes, well… In that time he managed to also urinate upon the plinth of the statue of Menander…" Atticus turned to point to where another servant was scrubbing at said statue on the other side of the garden. "…he bit poor Laius, the goatherd, who had come to the kitchens for his meagre breakfast, and he stole a leg of lamb from off the table in the triclinium!"

"Surely not, Atticus," Rufio protested. "Peli does not bite. He pisses." At that precise moment, Rufio remembered Peli chomping on a thug's figs at the end of their last performance. *Then there was the messenger at the farm…* "Well, he doesn't usually bite…" *By Cerberus, he was only gone a few minutes!*

"Well, he did." Atticus stopped his tirade, unused to being so flustered. He took a deep breath, eyes closed, and when he opened them again, he was calm. "I am sorry. We are, of course, thrilled to be host to The Etrurian Players, and their guests as well-"

"Actually," Rufio butt in. "Clara and I are the founding members along with Felix. We just don't act that much."

"Really?" Atticus was clearly taken aback. "I have never heard of or seen either of you."

"Unless you were in Rome two years ago, you wouldn't have."

"I see."

The steward had suddenly warmed a great deal, and Rufio wondered if the man truly did have a great appreciation of the theatrical arts, living in that place and working for a family of artistic patrons as great as that of Herodes Atticus.

"I also write," Rufio added, a bit quietly.

"You do?" Atticus' eyes lit up. "What are you working on now? Will you be undertaking a great work whilst beneath my dominus' roof? How exciting!"

"Well, maybe not a great work…not just yet." Rufio looked at the ground and then up at Atticus. "I'm in the early stages of a new play."

"Say no more!" Atticus clapped his hands and at that, Thespis, who had taken a respite from his wailing, burst out again.

"Who did that?" Electra shouted from the upper storey.

Atticus looked terrified for a moment, but before leaving, he turned to Rufio. "If you require any materials, you may use the domus library on the other side of the peristylium. It has copies of all known plays and histories."

"Thank you, Atticus. I appreciate that." *Anything to divert attention from Peli!*

"I must go now, but do enjoy the ientaculum that has been set out. Much of the company is already there."

"I will. Thank you," Rufio replied as he turned and left before Atticus remembered what he had wanted to speak to him about. He broke free of the peristylium and entered the triclinium where Julius, Beatrice, Castor and Pollux were already reclined upon the couches.

The long low table was set with meat - though no longer any lamb - cheeses, fruit, yoghurt, pots of Hymettos honey, bowls of almonds and pistachios, pitchers of heavily-watered wine, dishes of olive oil, several loaves of fresh bread, and honeyed pastries.

"By Ceres, Atticus wasn't joking!" Rufio said as he entered the room. "This is a ientaculum!" He looked about the room and saw that Julius was the only one who appeared fresh. "Did you stay up drinking all night?" Rufio smiled as he looked at Castor, Pollux, and Beatrice.

The players' hair was all askew, and their eyes were half shut with dark circles beneath them.

"No," Beatrice replied, her face lighting up for a brief moment to greet Rufio. "We barely drank anything at all."

"We didn't even touch your Etrurian wine!" Castor said, his disappointment evident.

"Then why do you all look so bedraggled?" Rufio asked.

"Young Thespis serenaded us all night long, that's why!" Pollux said, casting a quick glance at the doors beyond to make sure Felix was not there.

"That's funny. I must be accustomed to babies crying. I didn't hear him at all," Rufio said.

"Nor I," Julius added.

Beatrice shot Julius a look. "You were too busy, weren't you?"

Julius turned red and looked at the table. "This cheese is a wonder! Would you like some, Rufio? There is still time for such things before we perform."

"Just bread and water for me, for now," Rufio said. "My stomach is still recovering from the sea journey." He poured himself some water from a black and orange ware pitcher into a silver cup, and then tore a hunk of bread from a steaming loaf. "Where is Felix?"

"He went to the baths," Pollux replied.

"I've never seen him so frustrated," Rufio said. "Is he all right?"

The group was silent.

"I'll go see." Rufio made his way out one of the two arches that led from the triclinium to the vast, grassy courtyard where the odeon was located. There, at the front row of seating, in front of the small orchestra, Felix sat with his wet head in his hands, shoulders slumped such that he looked three times smaller than he actually was. "Good morning." Rufio made his way down the slope to sit beside his friend. "How is *The* Felix Modestus this fine day?"

For a moment, Felix did not seem to register the words Rufio had spoken, nor even his presence, but then he turned slowly to look at Rufio. His face was contorted with exhaustion and frustration, his eyes bloodshot, his brow more creased than ever it had been before. There were even faint traces of grey in his once dark head of hair.

"Tell me," Rufio said, sipping his water.

That was all the permission Felix needed.

Felix sat up straight and turned to straddle the seat so he could face Rufio. "I'm in a mundus stercoris, Rufio, and I don't believe I can extricate myself."

Concern gripped Rufio, and he leaned forward. "What's wrong? Have you lost all of your money? Don't tell me you went to more loan sharks. I mean that thing with Leno in Rome was such a mistake and-"

"No, of course not!" Felix looked aghast at the mere suggestion of financial ruin. "I have more coin than Midas!"

"Then why are you saying you're in a universe of shit? Seems to me Fortuna favours you. She always has!" The smile returned to Rufio's face but Felix did not reciprocate.

"How can you even ask that? Isn't it obvious?" Felix held his hands out.

Rufio tried to decipher what was going through his friend's mind, but to no avail. He shrugged.

"You're impossible." Felix slouched again.

"Felix," Rufio said, tempted to walk away if not for the fact that he had been looking forward so very much to Felix's company. "I'm not a forum fortune-teller out of Aegyptus. Help me to understand."

Felix looked around and cocked his head to listen for the faint sound of crying. "There it is." He shook his head.

"Young Thespis?" Rufio asked. "Your son?"

"I thought it would be a complete and utter joy to be a father at last. I felt that I was ready for it. Electra was so overjoyed when she discovered she was with child... I had never seen her so happy and beautiful."

"It's a wonderful thing, is it not?"

Felix shook his head. "Yes, until the child actually arrives!"

"Babies cry, Felix. I wouldn't worry about it. Felicia cried all the time in her first couple of months."

"There is crying, and then there is my son. It's like we live permanently in the temple of Cybele during the castration rites."

"Gods forbid it!"

"It's true! Thespis screams and wails, except for when he is suckling. And then, there's the shitting! By the Gods! I don't know where it comes from. He shits day and night. I'm up to my elbows in shit!"

"It's normal. It means he is functioning properly," Rufio said.

"How do you know? You a medicus all of a sudden?"

Rufio ignored Felix's tone. "No. But Clara and I had the same worry about Felicia. Our children are healthy, and so they eat a lot. Thankfully, our wives can produce enough milk. The more they eat, the more they shit…and piss, for that matter!" Rufio laughed alone. "The medicus we saw in Saena Iulia said as much."

"Then there's Electra!" Felix stood now and paced in the middle of the orchestra. "She's always concerned with the child. I tried getting her to use a wet-nurse but she wouldn't have it. She wanted to suckle Thespis on her own and wouldn't trust anyone else with him. The one time we went out recently, it was a disaster. The child simply cannot be without his mother."

"He's still an infant. It will pass."

"Will it though?"

"It will," Rufio reassured. "And don't be so hard on Electra. It is new to her as well. From what Clara says, it can be quite draining on a woman to feed a child constantly."

"Tell me about it! It's all Electra has time or energy for! I can't remember the last time we made love. We lay side by side every night, but we're so exhausted that our eyes are shut within seconds, and then that's just so that we can steal a few minutes of sleep until the child cries again!" Felix raised his fists to the sky as if pleading for the Gods' help. He turned back to Rufio. "I swear, I'm walking around like Priapus all the time. It's most uncomfortable!"

Rufio thought about telling Felix that would get better soon as well, that he and Clara had, that very morning, enjoyed each other's delights, but he thought better of it. He nodded. "That too will improve."

"Right now I don't feel like anything will be good ever again!" Felix sat beside Rufio.

"Have you talked about this with Electra? She's probably quite desperate as well, no?"

"She only shouts at me."

"You're both exhausted. In two people as passionate as you are, it is to be expected."

"Rufio…there's 'exhausted' and then there's mad with weeks and weeks of sleeplessness. I'm talking about madness on a Medean level!"

Rufio was starting to grow impatient with Felix. Of course he knew his friend to be a complete Narcissus incarnate at times, but he was also a good and loyal man. He tried his utmost to remember what it was like not to sleep for weeks on end and, in remembering, he found a measure of sympathy for Felix who was now in the middle of the storm.

"Listen, Felix." He put his hand on his friend's shoulder. "It will get better, I promise you. You need to be there for Electra and Thespis. You are the paterfamilias now. It won't do to rage and shout at them. The child will sense it and get upset even more. I promise, it will get better, and soon. Just be patient."

"That is not my strong suit."

"Don't I know it! But Thespis doesn't. He is a small child suddenly thrown into an enormous world. It's terrifying! He needs his father to be calm. His parents to be caring toward each other and toward him."

"You didn't have that," Felix noted.

"And look what happened to me!" Rufio rebutted. "Until a couple years ago, I couldn't even leave Etruria, let alone my domus. Now Felicia and Clara give me the strength to face whatever comes. Even a sea voyage." Rufio shook his head.

"That bad, was it?"

"You have no idea." Rufio could smile now, but even the thought of it gave him a taste of bile in his throat. "My point is, the Gods have blessed you. You have a child who is healthy and obviously strong, whom you delivered yourself! Your wife survived childbirth, *and* is able to feed him. You just have to set your own needs aside for a time."

"For how long?" Felix asked, and the question was most sincere.

Rufio shrugged again. "I don't know. I guess we'll find out!" he laughed, and this time Felix joined him.

"Thank you, my friend. I am calm again."

"We've missed you all."

"I do apologize for last night," Felix said. "With all the wailing, and my lack of sleep, I didn't even fully register that we are all together again. The Etrurian Players!" He clapped loudly.

"It's a new day!" Rufio said.

"And we're finally in Athenae together!" Felix put his arm about Rufio.

"Remember how we always used to wonder what this place was like? The birthplace of theatre!"

"I know. I still don't quite believe it. I can't wait to see the city."

"There will be plenty of time for that and-" Felix stopped suddenly.

"What is it?" Rufio asked.

"Silence… It's silence!" Felix looked around, clearly confused and struck by the absence of crying. "What if something's happened?"

"He's just stopped crying, is all. Don't panic, Felix."

But Felix turned and walked briskly through the odeon court to the triclinium doors where he burst in upon the full gathering. "What's happened?"

Rufio arrived at his shoulder and the two of them spotted

Clara and Electra seated on neighbouring couches with the children upon their laps, cooing and giggling at each other as their mothers shook tiny rattles between them.

Peli was huddled and dozing beneath Clara's couch, looking calm after his previous feast and ablutions.

Electra looked up with an enormous smile at Felix. "They get along so well!"

Felix was stunned and shook his head. "I'm dreaming."

Electra laughed and therein he spotted the woman he loved. Felix walked over to her and leaned down to kiss her before sitting beside her.

Rufio could see the relief all about the table and the smiles that spanned everyone's faces.

"Maybe you two should arrange the marriage now!" Castor joked, and everyone chuckled at that.

"Felicia certainly has a calming effect upon him, does't she?" Felix said to Electra.

"She does." Electra looked at the children and smiled at Clara. "She's a little muse come amongst us."

Felix put his hand on Electra's shoulder and brushed her hair aside. "Maybe we should have another one?"

The rest of the company gasped at that.

Electra whirled on Felix, a Chimera look in her wild eyes. "I have a better idea! Why don't I just cut off your testicles and then we won't have to do this again?"

Damon howled in mock pain at the far end of the table.

Felix smiled, which further infuriated his wife. "There she is," he said before kissing her cheek.

Clara leaned close to Rufio and whispered. "And there *he* is."

Rufio smiled at her and stroked her shoulder.

Electra shook her head and, to the great relief of the others, her smile returned. "*The* Felix Modestus!"

Felix grinned and stood with a full wine cup in hand.

"That's correct! And as such, now that the madness had dwindled, I feel that I should make a proper acknowledgement of the fact that The Etrurian Players are all together again, thank the Gods!"

"Thank the Gods!" everyone echoed and poured a bit of watered wine upon the floor before drinking together.

"I say all together again," Felix added, "but really, there are two more honorary members of our company still missing."

"So you won't tell us what play we're performing?" Pollux asked.

"Not yet!" Felix laughed.

"This is really too much, Felix Modestus!" Domela said, her exasperation of weeks finally breaking out.

"That's *The* Felix Modestus," Fausto said as he laughed, his wine clearly less watered than the others'.

"Thank you, Fausto!" Felix bowed. "But have no worries, my friends, for the play will be our greatest yet. That, I promise you!"

Electra looked up at him doubtfully, but her smile, though thin, was still there.

"It's a shame Sextus and Martia are still not here," Clara said. "We've been looking forward to seeing them as well."

"I hope the Gods have blessed their voyage," Beatrice said.

"And so it seems the Gods have heard your prayers, Beatrice!"

Everyone turned to see Sextus Annius Sabinus and Martia Annia appear at the far door to the triclinium.

There was a round of applause from the players that made each of them blush and smile.

"Sextus, Martia…you've arrived on cue!" Felix bellowed, marching around the room to greet them.

"Yes, indeed!" Sextus replied, removing his bright blue cloak and handing it to the steward. "Thank you, Atticus."

"Your rooms have been prepared, Praetor," Atticus said, all

smiles for this dominus' friend. "And cubicula have been set aside for your servants as well."

"Thank you, Atticus," Sextus said, "but please, here, among my friends and fellow theatre-lovers, I am simply Sextus."

"Yes, Praetor," Atticus replied, squinting at the immediate slip. "I'll have the servants take yours and lady Martia's belongings to your rooms."

"Thank you, Atticus," Martia said, smiling broadly. Her eyes sparkled with delight as Electra and Clara came around to greet her.

Sextus watched as the two women approached his wife with their babes in their arms, but was reassured when Martia's smile remained. He turned to Felix. "We would have arrived yesterday, but we were invited to stay a night with a fellow magistrate in the city." He sighed. "It does get quite raucous in Athenae at night. I hope these accommodations are much more conducive to the magic of your production."

"This place is a wonder!" Rufio said, taking Sextus' hand. "Thank you for arranging it."

"Think nothing of it, my friend," Sextus grabbed his shoulder.

"So this is the home of Herodes Atticus?" Rufio had to ask.

"Yes." Sextus nodded. "I am acquainted with his son who is a great theatre-lover. He was more than happy to allow us all to stay here to prepare for the Panathenaea."

"They don't require it for their own use?" Julius asked.

Sextus shook his head. "The family prefers their villa at Marathon when they are in Attica."

"And we're glad they do,' Felix said. "Come, sit. Eat and drink with us."

"Just a cup of water for me. I already had ientaculum. But first, I would like to greet these charming ladies and their children." Sextus walked around the table to where his wife stood with Electra and Clara.

Rufio followed, but Felix went back to his couch to settle himself.

"It is good to see you again, good ladies," Sextus inclined his head politely to Electra and Clara. "Martia has told me of how young Thespis came into the world at Sacred Delos."

"Almost *on* Delos!" Felix piped up.

"We'll have to add the title of 'medicus' to your many talents, Felix Modestus!" Martia said.

Sextus noticed her smile was a bit tightly-fixed at the corners of her mouth, though she made a heroic effort to be happy for their friends. He looked down with his wife as the two infants reached for each other and babbled back and forth, their mothers smiling as they did so.

"Are they sleeping very well?" Martia asked as she held Electra's son, whom his mother had thrust into her arms. "I've heard that newborns are slow to adjust to the world without their mothers' wombs.

There was a collective sigh about the table at that.

"My son will be the greatest singer in the empire with all the practice he gets!" Felix laughed, though he was the only one.

"And what a name he has!" Sextus said. "A wonderful homage to the very first known player!" He looked at Martia who seemed genuinely happy for Electra and Clara.

Martia had already written to Electra of their misfortune in conceiving, and the latter had informed Clara that morning.

"Now that I am here," Martia said, "I will be happy to watch over the children while you are all rehearsing."

"Oh, my lady," Domela said from down the table, "young Thespis is inconsolable without his mother. Believe you me, I've tried!"

Martia smiled at the only person there with whom she was not acquainted.

"He certainly seems calm with Martia," Electra added, as she placed her arm about the latter and tickled her son's cheek.

Thespis looked up at Martia quite calmly, his little hand placed upon her high cheekbone.

"Thespis and Felicia are already good friends," Electra said.

"Oh, Clara, she is *so* beautiful!" Martia exclaimed, marvelling at the young girl's bright eyes.

"My dear," Sextus said, so that only Martia, Electra, and Clara could hear. "Are you all right?"

She nodded and smiled, willing the tears waiting in the wings not to fall. "I'm quite well, Sextus. Do not worry." She looked side to side at Clara and Electra. "I'm among friends now."

"You are," Electra said. "And we're so happy you're here."

"I can't believe I haven't seen more of you both over the last couple of years, especially you, Clara. We live so near to each other." Martia sighed and gave Thespis back to Electra.

"I know," Clara answered. "Running the latifundium takes up all of our time, and now with Felicia, it is all a whirlwind!"

"And how have Felix and Rufio taken to fatherhood?" Martia asked, smiling at Rufio who stood silently in thought behind Clara.

At the utterance of his name, he looked up and smiled.

"Rufio helps a great deal. He is always concerned for Felicia's safety and makes sure I have everything I need. Especially in the beginning when she was much more demanding." Clara looked at her husband. "He's always striving to be the opposite of his own father. He's obsessed about it, really."

Sextus and the three women looked at Rufio. Even the babies seemed to focus on him then too.

"I just want to encourage my daughter in whatever she wants to do!" Rufio protested.

"My love," Clara smiled. "She is not even a year old."

"It makes no matter," he replied, before heading back to his couch, beneath which Peli snoozed, his snout jutting from underneath.

"And Felix?" Sextus asked.

Electra sighed. "Felix is Felix. Since his dream on Delos, and since he delivered our son, he has been an island unto himself. An island I cannot possibly swim out to."

Martia leaned in to kiss her cheek. "Then we shall find you a boat."

Electra's eyes grew watery at that.

"Help is here. You are surrounded by friends now," Martia said. "And I must say, you look stunning, both of you. Motherhood obviously agrees with…with you." Martia finally broke a little, but Clara and Electra were right beside her, lending her strength. She breathed deeply and found her smile again. "I must admit," she whispered to them as conversation around the table picked up again, "it has not been easy to have our hopes dashed over and over again."

Sextus reached out to take her hand and squeezed.

"Thank the Gods that Sextus has been wonderfully understanding that I will never be able to have children. That's what the medici and priestesses have said. I have accepted that." Martia's stoicism was quite humbling to the two other women. "We *are* blessed in each other, and in friends such as you," Martia nodded. "Besides, I am helping many other children in my own way."

"Yes, tell us how the charitable work in the Suburra is going?" Clara asked, and the three of them made their way to couches on the other side of the table.

Sextus, now relieved to see that his wife had overcome the initial obstacle of meeting the children, settled himself on a couch in the middle of the long table, beside Julius, so that he could speak with everyone. "It's so good to be back among you all," he smiled, and his easy manner made them all forget they were sitting with a newly-made Praetor.

A servant handed Sextus a cup of water.

"I believe you remember everyone," Felix said, "except for Domela Fabiana, perhaps?"

"Ah, yes. Domela? It is a pleasure to meet you at last," Sextus said. "Felix had written to me about your joining the company." He turned to Felix. "In Caesarea was it?"

"That's correct," Felix answered.

"Felix Modestus was kind enough to take me into the company. He knows how to spot a theatre-lover."

"And a wonderful actress as well!" Julius added quickly.

Peli growled momentarily beneath Rufio's couch, and Beatrice smiled and whispered to Fausto beside her. "It's good to see Peli again too."

Fausto stifled his laughter and shook his head.

Sextus smiled. "Well, if Julius endorses you in such a way, then I look forward to watching you perform, lady Domela!"

"Speaking of performing," Rufio said, his voice louder than he intended, "now that we're all here, are we going to learn which play we're to perform?"

All chatter and chewing ceased. All cups were set down. And all eyes about the triclinium turned to Felix Modestus. Even the servants at the room's periphery listened and watched, for they too had been looking forward to learning of the production to which they would bear witness to the preparations.

Felix rubbed his hands and sat up to address them. "I suppose you're right, Rufio. The time is ripe, and-"

At that precise moment, Thespis chose his moment of flatulence, and the sound reverberated about the table.

"Thespis has your timing, Dominus!" Castor laughed.

Felix was not amused. He turned to Electra who was rocking their child. "Did you train him to that?"

Electra scowled at him. "Of course not. He's not like that wretched monkey you bought me. Thank the Gods we left Nero in Ephesus!"

Clara turned to Felix. "You bought your wife a monkey? Why?"

"There was an incident in Alexandria…" Felix grumbled.

"You named him Nero?" Sextus blurted.

Electra turned to Clara. "It was so hot, *The* Felix Modestus thought it would be a good idea to purchase the creature to fan me wherever we went."

"They can be trained to do that?" Rufio's eyes bulged.

"No," Electra answered. "Nor does he play the fiddle! Instead, the hideous animal tries to rip off my stola at every opportunity!"

"Gods, I love that monkey," Pollux whispered to his brother beside him.

Martia squealed in surprise.

"Did you train him to *that*?" Rufio asked Felix, unable to stop himself.

"I heard they eat monkeys in Alexandria Eschate!" Domela said to Julius.

Electra's face lit up and she looked back at Felix, hope in her eyes.

"You wouldn't!" he said.

"If he fiddles in my wardrobe or burns down our domus while we're away, I will!"

Propping Felicia on her knees, Clara leaned in to Electra. "I thought he didn't play the fiddle?"

"Not that kind," Electra said in disgust.

"Oh no!" It was Clara's turn to be shocked.

"Surely we digress from the matter at hand!" Felix bellowed, his face reddening by the second.

"Felix is right!" Sextus came to his rescue. "I think we can all agree that it is time to learn of the play!"

"Here, here!" Julius cried out with a surprising amount of verve.

The room fell silent again, and they looked to Felix, their leader in all things theatrical.

Felix looked about the gathering, but though he wanted to speak, he was distracted by the space. "Not here. Everyone, to the odeon!" he said, before turning and going out the door behind him.

It took a moment for everyone to register what was happening, but when Peli shot off after Felix, Rufio followed, and so did the rest of the company, one by one.

They found Felix pacing the small stage of the odeon beneath the midday sun, and gradually, they all took their seats in the small cavia, Clara and Electra sure to sit beside each other so that the children were together.

When everyone was seated, Felix stopped pacing and turned to them. "This is not something to be announced over a hasty meal and talk of monkeys! We are about to set out on a journey demanded by Apollo himself! I think a bit of formality is required, don't you?" Felix looked about, his eyes resting on Sextus. "Praetor, would you like to say a few words before I tell you all what the God of Art and Music commanded of me?"

"Oh! Yes! Of course, Felix." Sextus rose from his seat and stepped onto the stage to look at the full host of The Etrurian Players with Martia seated amongst them. He smiled and felt the ease that he had trained himself to in recent months when speaking to a crowd. The only difference was that he was most comfortable with those before him in that moment. *What a wonderful troupe!* he thought before clearing his throat and addressing them. "My friends...welcome. Welcome to Athenae, the place where the theatrical arts, which we all love so very much, were truly born."

From the outset, Sextus had their attention, for his command of speech had greatly improved.

"It warms my heart to see you all again, and to meet the newest members of this joyous family." He smiled as he looked to Electra and Clara who held their children.

Martia watched him with great pride.

"It has been my honour to help fund your wondrous productions these last two years, and though I have not seen most of them due to the hectic nature of my new position, I have been with you in spirit each and every time. For I am proud to be your patron and, I hope, your friend."

"A very dear friend!" Julius called out from the back.

This made Sextus smile even more. "I thank you for making Martia and I honorary members." He looked to the back of the odeon court to see Atticus and the servants lined up, watching and listening as well. "I must also thank our gracious hosts, the familia of that great patron of Athenae, Herodes Atticus, for inviting us to stay in this beautiful place for so lengthy a period of time. The legacy of your dominus' family and his generosity to Athena's great city was equaled only by Emperor Hadrianus himself. Thanks to Herodes Atticus, this city was gifted the magnificently restored stadium down the hill, and the great odeon that graces the southern slope of the Acropolis of Athenae."

At the back of the court Atticus, who was touched by the words, clasped his hands in thanks and bowed to Sextus where he stood.

"The thanks are mine to give, for it is wonderful to be back in Athenae. Emperor Hadrianus, a great philhellene, loved this city, perhaps as much as he did Rome itself. And while we are here, we carry on the emperor's legacy of love and respect for this wondrous place. I know that our late emperor, Herodes Atticus, and others will be watching us from the other side of the dark river."

Everyone grew silent at that, for in invoking the shades of the dead, Sextus had added a severity to their mission in Athenae.

"While we are here, not only will we have the great pleasure of experiencing the delights of Athenae, we will also have the honour of participating in the great Panathenaea, that ancient festival in honour of Athena." He paused and took a deep, calm breath. "My friends…in this city of the goddess, the birthplace of theatre, may you make Rome proud."

Sextus then turned to Felix.

"Thank you, Sextus." Felix rose from his seat and Sextus went back to sit between Martia and Rufio. "Your words have inspired us and we are, as ever, grateful for your friendship. We are also grateful to our hosts who have, I am well aware, put up with a great deal of noise."

At the back, Atticus shook his head and waved his hands. "Not all all, Felix Modestus!"

Felix ignored the surprised looks on the other servants' faces, and carried on.

"Tell us about your dream and the play!" Fausto burst out.

"Yeah!" Castor echoed. "Tell us!"

"We've waited long enough!" Pollux added, and a general murmur went up.

"Very well!" Felix said, his hands up for silence. "The night before our son was born on the waters that hug sacred Delos, the birthplace of Apollo…the night before I brought Thespis into this world with my own hands…" Felix held up his hands as if they were oracular tools. "Apollo himself appeared to me in a dream. He told me that 'at theatre's womb, in the shadow of Athena's sacred house,' we would 'perform the work of a son of Rome'. Felix looked up at the sky, and nodded as if in converse with Apollo in that very moment.

"What's he doing?" Fausto asked Beatrice, but Domela shushed him.

"Apollo approached me," Felix continued, "and I looked into his star-whirling eyes… He said 'perform the work of a son of Rome…and the sons of Rome will be freed'."

"What does that mean?" Castor asked.

Electra turned to shoot him a look that flayed. "What does it matter? Apollo has spoken!"

Castor put up his hands.

Felix stopped and then looked at all of them, each face, each pair of wide eyes gazing up at him, their leader. He nodded.

"I felt that my heart would burst, being so near to an Olympian, but then a supreme sense of calm came over me. Apollo reached out and touched my forehead, and I saw our production in full, the costumes, the props, the place…"

"Did the Far-Shooter say anything else?" Sextus could not help but ask.

Felix nodded very slowly. "He did."

"Whaaa?" Damon hooted, clutching his flute.

"The name of the play…"

Every person there leaned forward.

"*Heautontimorumenos.*" Felix raised his arms to the sky. *Lord Apollo, it is done. And it has begun…*

"Are you sure you understood Apollo correctly?" Pollux asked.

Felix looked back down to earth and the array of strange looks his players cast his way. "Of course I did."

"*Heautontimorumenos…*" Pollux repeated. "The Self-Tormentor?"

"That is the play Apollo commanded us to perform, yes." Felix sat on the edge of the stage.

"The one by Terentius?" Domela asked, shrinking under Felix's withering look.

"Do you know of another?" Felix asked his newest company member.

"No."

"Have we ever done that one?" Beatrice asked, looking at all of the others for confirmation.

"No, we haven't," Julius added, his previously jovial manner more muted now as he crossed his arms in thought. "Felix, *The Self-Tormentor* is not an easy play to pull off."

"Yes, I'm aware of that, Julius," Felix said, "but Apollo has spoken."

"Why is it not an easy play?" Castor asked. "I don't think I've seen it."

Fausto stood up then, his eyes clearly displaying his worry. "Well, I've seen it! I'll tell you why it's not easy. It's *not* funny! That's why!"

Suddenly the company members were on their feet, arguing about the merits of Terentius' play, putting the pieces together with regards to the costumes and set designs they had been working on in ignorance of the performance they were to adorn.

Felix was clearly deflated by the opposition and lack of enthusiasm, and made eye contact with Rufio and Sextus who were silent in thought, despite the raucous debate about them.

Felicia and Thespis were now wide awake and growing more upset by the second at what was happening, and Martia went over to them to see if she could help as the babes added their own voices of displeasure to the scene.

At that moment, Electra began to feed Thespis, not having the time to leave the gathering.

The men turned away from her to give her privacy, all except for Fausto.

"I saw Electra's nipple!" Fausto hissed into Beatrice's ear.

"Shhh!" Beatrice hit him. "Forget what you saw or she'll put out your eyes!"

Fausto averted his gaze as if he were Perseus in Medusa's lair. There had been a time when Electra had not cared if the world saw her breasts, but since her child, she was most secretive. He went back to debating the play's lack of merit.

Rufio felt his head ready to explode with frustration for Felix. He loved the *Heautontimorumenos*, and always had. When Felix had uttered the title given to him by Apollo, it made perfect sense. It seemed right, even as the hairs on the back of his neck had tickled his senses. He leaned over to Sextus. "I had been thinking of Terentius for some reason."

Sextus nodded, his hand on his shaved chin. "It's a wonderful play, to be sure. But how will the Athenians take it? That is my worry." He looked across at Felix, whose face was growing angrier and angrier.

It was then that Felix's Vesuvial reaction burst forth. "Everybody shut up!"

The bickerers fell silent and sat, and the children continued suckling to the side. At the back of the odeon court, one of the servants squealed as Peli, unnoticed by the others, had slinked up to him and blessed his leg with an arching stream.

"Shhh!" Atticus, who was clearly interested in the conversation to come, quieted the man.

Felix was standing again, this time in the orchestra, looking down on his company. "Since when do The Etrurian Players shun the will of the Gods? Apollo himself has given us this play to perform! True, it does not have the hilarity of Plautus, but it is funny, heartwarming, and thoughtful. Are we so unsure of our merit and talent that we go in for easy laughs alone?"

"Felix is right," Julius said, standing up and turning to look at his colleagues. "Are we now above hard work? We've not been given coronae across the Middle Sea for our lack of effort." He turned to look at Felix. "In fact, the more I think about it, the more I think that the *Heautontimorumenos* is more suited to our Athenian audience."

Sextus rose to stand in the orchestra now. "Julius is correct. I may not be a player like all of you, but I do know theatre."

The group was quiet, ready to listen to the praetor, their primary funder.

"Athenian crowds are different to the ones back in Rome. True, the more lewd and buffoonish the material the better, when it comes to Rome. But here, they are more serious about their theatre. Terentius' work - especially the *Heautontimorumenos* - is more complex. I have faith in all of you, and in Felix Modestus. You can do this!"

"Thank you, Sextus!" Felix said, his hand on the praetor's shoulder. "Atticus!" he called to the back of the court. "Please bring the satchel of scrolls from the tablinum!"

"Right away, Felix Modestus!" Atticus said, thrilled to have been entrusted with such a precious, and secret cargo.

"I think this is a good time to announce something else, if I may, Felix?" Sextus asked.

Felix nodded and smiled. "Please do."

Sextus turned to look at everyone, comfortable now to look at Electra who was finished feeding Thespis. "I have bad news, and good news."

"Better give us the bad news first, Praetor," Julius muttered.

"Very well. I discovered yesterday that as non-Greeks, The Etrurian Players cannot compete in the theatrical competitions at the beginning of the Panathenaea."

"What?" Fausto exclaimed.

"I am sorry. The rules are quite clear," Sextus added quickly. "However, you will be a part of the procession to launch the great festival."

"Wonderful!" Pollux blurted. "We get to go for a walk!"

Sextus laughed. "It is much more than a walk, Pollux. To take part in the procession of the Panathenaea is a great honour!"

"When will the performance take place?" Felix asked, trying to hide his disappointment about the competition.

"The performance will take place at the end of the festival in the Roman odeon built by Herodes Atticus!"

"But then no one will see it!" Fausto said.

"On the contrary," Sextus said, his hands up, "everyone will see it. Including the other theatre companies, playwrights, judges…everyone!"

"And we'll make sure they know about it!" Felix bellowed. He then turned to accept the satchel of scrolls from Atticus. "Now, everyone come and get your copies of the play! I want you to spend the afternoon reading it and then, after the cena this evening, I will assign your parts."

"Can't you tell us now?" Fausto asked.

"I think you should stop being so plaintive, Fausto." Felix stared him down. "I want you to read it first without analyzing your own part. I want you all to feel it on the first reading."

Each of the players came to take a scroll from the satchel and when they had all taken one, Felix handed the last copies to Rufio and Clara who stood with him, Electra, Sextus, and Martia.

"Well?" Felix asked when the rest of the company had melted back into the domus' gardens. "What do you think?"

"It will be a challenge," Sextus said, "but I'm confident you will make it a wonder!"

"I agree," Martia said. "I love that play."

"I don't," Electra said, "but as the Gods demand it, we will make it work."

Felix pursed his lips and turned to Clara and Rufio. "You two have been pretty quiet. Thoughts?"

"Sextus is right," Clara said. "This is more suited to an Athenian audience. I saw it once in Syracusae, and the Greeks there loved it. But we have to get the tone just right."

"I agree," Felix nodded. "I have some thoughts on that. Rufio?"

They all looked at him expectantly.

Rufio rubbed his bearded chin. He was highly aware of the odeon behind him, the blueness of the sky, and the growing heat of the sun above. "Like I said... I like that play. Terentius..." He said it more to himself and the others looked from one to another. Rufio turned the scroll over in his hands as if trying to decipher the words through osmosis.

"Take some time. Read it," Felix said.

Rufio nodded absently.

"Felix," Sextus said. "Martia and I are going to get settled in our rooms. When you are ready, I need to speak to you about the finances and what else you need for the production."

"Very well. I'll bring Domela too," Felix said. "She's our new accountant. Excellent with an abacus."

Sextus turned to Martia. "Come my dear."

Martia smiled at Clara and Electra and went off arm-in-arm with her husband.

"It's good to see them again," Clara said.

"I feel sorry for poor Martia," Electra added. "See how she loves children?"

"I bet they sleep well," Felix muttered.

Electra looked at him, clearly appalled, and stormed off, Thespis beginning to cry as he went farther and farther from Felicia.

"What's the matter with you?" Clara chided him. She looked at Rufio and went after Electra.

"No sleep," Felix said to Rufio when they were alone. He shook his head. "So why didn't you back me up more before?"

"I was thinking."

"About what? Your navel?"

Rufio shook his head. "No. I was thinking about how wonderful a play it is."

"Are you teasing me now?"

"Not at all. I'm serious. This play has been on my mind." Rufio looked up at the sky where two swallows were diving in the wind above the courtyard. He couldn't help but recall his fevered-dreams on the crossing over. "Perhaps Apollo has a plan after all?"

"I hope so," Felix sighed. "I'll make sure the Far-Shooter doesn't lack for offerings, that's for certain."

"Are you going to play the lead?" Rufio asked. To his surprise, Felix shook his head.

"Apollo was actually vague about the roles. Between you and me, Rufio, I had thought to, but I'm too exhausted."

"Then who will play the Self-Tormentor?"

Felix put his finger to his lips. "Shhh. Later." He looked around, a little like a lost child. "I…I'd better go and see what Sextus wants to discuss. We need the coin to make this happen! I'll see you soon." Felix began to walk away, but then turned back to Rufio. "I'm so glad you're here, my friend."

"Me too," Rufio smiled, but as Felix left, his smile faded. He had never seen Felix so unconfident. It worried him. He sat on the edge of the stage, and Peli strode up to sit before him. "Where have you been?"

Just then, one of the servants cursed somewhere in the back of the domus. "Gods, that dog!"

Rufio sighed and looked at Peli. "Why can't you do it outside?"

Peli barked once at him.

"They're going to cook you if you keep shitting everywhere."

Peli whimpered and placed a pleading paw on Rufio's knee.

"Come on," Rufio said. "Time to read."

ACT III

ROMANS IN ATHENS

VII

LAUGHLESS

An eerie silence fell over the villa over the next few hours as every member of The Etrurian Players settled down to read the script of the play they had been anticipating ever since they had discovered they were going to Athenae.

After days of Thespis' crying, and the inebriated comings and goings of the theatrical troupe, Atticus, the steward, began to grow uneasy. He knew he should have enjoyed the calm that the moment afforded him, but it was such a shock to be suddenly thrown into utter silence, that he wondered if Earth-Shaking Poseidon were readying himself to level the city and its surrounds. Even the goats and birds in the woods and groves were silent.

"Do a round of the property to make sure all is well," Atticus told one of the servants. "It's far too quiet. I feel as though the Gods are toying with us."

The servant walked off, intent on finding a shady spot in which he could doze and enjoy the peace.

"I wonder if infants grow silent when an earthquake is imminent?" Atticus said to himself as he went to the kitchens to go over the menu for the cena.

.   .   .

WHILE MOST OF THE COMPANY WERE SCATTERED ABOUT THE villa and grounds, reading the tale they were to bring to life for the people of Athenae, Clara and Electra sat with the children in the calm heart of the house, upon lush blankets set down about the fountain in the peristyle garden. They were joined by Martia who settled herself upon the ground with them to admire the children who reached out to each other to clasp hands, giggle, and sputter their incomprehensible babble.

While Felix and Sextus went over accounts and planning in the tablinum of the villa, Rufio reclined on a couch across from the women, in the shadow of a statue of Aristophanes, to read the play. As his eyes raked over the script of the excellent copies Felix had procured, he could feel Clara looking at him. He turned to smile at her, and went back to it.

He's in his element, Clara thought to herself, before turning back to Electra and Martia.

Martia tickled Thespis' feet, giving Electra a moment to enjoy a cup of water and the echoing calm that now seemed so foreign to her. "They are both so beautiful," Martia said to the other two women. "The Gods have really blessed you."

Electra glanced at Clara, a sad look in her eyes. She tried to fight down the urge to make a sign against the evil eye, not wanting to insult Martia who was, by far, one of the kindest people she had ever met. She made the sign discreetly as her arm dropped behind the couch on which she sat.

Clara turned to Martia. "Are you sure it's not upsetting for you? To see the children, I mean."

"We would understand if it was," Electra added.

Martia looked up and smiled at each of them, shaking her head. "No. Perhaps at first, it was a bit of a shock, but I've made my peace with the fact that the Gods do not intend for me to have children. I am blessed that Sextus still loves me, and for that I thank Venus."

"Oh, he is as smitten as ever with you!" Electra said.

"I know." Martia turned to her. "I promise you both, I am nothing but happy for you. Truly." She stared at each of them, waiting for them to register understanding of her earnestness. When they smiled back at her, Martia nodded, a playful look upon her face. "If you want to make me an honorary matertera, I won't complain." She leaned over to tickle both infants' tummies.

"Oh, I think you're already their favourite, Martia!" Clara laughed as Felicia's eyes looked up at the other woman.

"I'm just relieved you're all here at last," Electra said. "Thespis has been inconsolable since we arrived." She looked down at her son and could not help but smile. "You want to sing, don't you?"

Thespis grinned and drooled back at her, his little legs kicking as if he had no control over them, a thing which seemed to surprise him.

"Apart from how quiet our children are, does anyone notice the silence in the domus?" Clara asked.

"Yes, isn't it wonderful?" Electra commented, tilting her head to feel the sun upon her face.

"Yes, but the rest of the company is off reading the play, and I don't hear any laughter. Do you?" Clara asked.

Electra and Martia cocked their ears and shook their heads.

"You're right," Martia said. "Perhaps they are just very focussed upon their task?"

"Should we be worried?" Electra asked. "I mean, I never really laugh when I'm reading. Even if it is a comedy."

"I seem to remember hearing at least some laughter when we did our first reading of Plautus in Rome."

"Terentius *is* different," Martia added. "I wouldn't worry. It's a wonderful play."

"But *Heautontimorumenos* is very different from his other

works," Electra added, shaking her head. "I do hope Apollo is not toying with us."

Martia looked up to see Rufio smiling to himself, stifling an easy laugh. "It looks as though Rufio is enjoying the play. Rufio? What do you think of it?"

Rufio finished reading a line and then sat up to look at them. "I think it's a wonderful play! A perfect choice!"

"You do?" Electra asked.

Rufio nodded. "It has always been one of my favourites, even though I didn't fully understand it." He looked down at Felicia. "Now, however, being a father… I feel as though I have a new perspective. It's funny, but not overly so. More than that, however, it's truthful and heartwarming."

"Let's hope the audience feels the same way!" Felix said as he and Sextus entered the courtyard, each holding a cup of wine.

Felix settled himself on the couch beside Rufio, and Sextus sat behind his wife, kissing her head as he leaned over to look down at the children.

"What did you do to them?" Felix asked Electra and Clara when the quiet registered.

"Nothing," Electra said. "They're just happy. And Martia has such a way with them!"

"I'm glad of it." Felix leaned back. "That way, everyone can read in peace."

Electra glowered at him, but he took no notice.

Rufio looked at Felix and Sextus. "Is everything in hand? Are we set for a grand production again?"

"The accounts are well in order," Sextus replied. "But this production - especially as it is being held in Athenae - will not require much."

"We're keeping it simple," Felix added. He looked at Rufio who was clutching the scroll. "Have you read it already?"

Rufio nodded and smiled. "I have. It's wonderful."

"You don't think it too sedate?" Sextus asked him.

Rufio shook his head. "No, I do not. It has all the makings of a wonderful play."

"Felix, are you going to tell us what our roles will be?" Clara asked.

Felix put up a hand. "I will…just not now. Later."

"You do like to draw things out, don't you?" she said.

Felix nodded. "Yes. I do." He downed his wine and reclined to look up at the sky and enjoy the faint trickle of the fountain in their midst. Within a matter of seconds, he was sleeping.

While Sextus and Martia fell into discussing the children with Clara and Electra, Rufio reclined upon his couch again to ponder the play. It was indeed a perfect choice, and fitting, considering his recent state of mind. In truth, for the last several months, he had been pondering the type of father he wanted to be, the type of father he had had, and how he was determined not to be the same as that.

It was moments like that when he could feel the Gods' eyes fixed directly on him, and it was both thrilling and terrifying.

"I had been thinking of this play recently…and now we're doing it!" Rufio whispered to himself.

"What's that, my love?" Clara asked.

He realized he had spoken aloud, looked over at her, and shook his head. "Nothing… Just musing."

It had been a glorious few hours in the villa. While The Etrurian Players silently read through the play which they had been anticipating for weeks, the servants in that expansive domus went about their duties as if in a glorious daze. Their ears were no longer ringing, and their jaws were no longer clenched from the high pitch that had, for days, resonated off the walls and swirled in every corner.

In their cubiculum on the second storey, Felix and Electra slept soundly with Thespis nestled between them upon the broad bed. Their chests rose and fell in concert as they dozed, the East-facing room darker now that the sun had long passed its zenith.

Lying there, Felix felt his mind begin to wander, but he refused to open his eyes, for that would mean the first solid sleep he had had in a while would be at an end.

In that moment, that was unthinkable.

It wasn't long, however, before Thespis' legs began to kick, and his little arms began to flail.

Felix breathed deeply before turning onto his elbow to look at his son. *He is handsome!* he thought. *You have your mother's eyes too.* He leaned closer and made a face not dissimilar to the comedic masks they used to use on stage.

It was then that Thespis' dark eyes widened in horror and his little balled fists jerked and walloped Felix in the eye.

"Ahh!" Felix grunted, a little too loudly, and thus was the oil of Thespis' displeasure set alight.

"No…no…no!" Felix hissed, looking at Thespis through one eye. "You've been so good. Don't start that now!!"

"Why…are…you…shouting?" Electra mumbled from beneath the waves of her long hair.

"He just took out my eye!" Felix grumbled.

"Then you have one less with which to ogle other women."

Felix shook his head, the crying from his son's seemingly massive lungs getting louder and louder.

There were voices from without the door and Felix realized that the rest of the domus was astir again.

"Looks like it's time to assign everyone their roles!" Felix said, swinging his legs off of the bed.

"Oh no you don't!" Electra was wide awake now. "I'll feed him, but you're going to burp and change him after. Stay where you are!" Electra took her screaming son and directed him to the nearest breast which he fastened onto most eagerly.

"You're fine. I need to go. You can handle the changing," Felix said as he slid his tunica over his head.

Electra growled. "Until you can squeeze milk from your own nipples, *you* are going to do the changing! You've escaped your duties too often."

"I have a play to put on!"

"We all do," she retorted. "So sit yourself by the window and drink some wine while you wait for the suckling to be finished."

For a moment, Felix thought about storming from the room. He eyed the door hopefully, but then he thought on the consequences of such a rebellion. He went over to a wide table where a wine pitcher stood with four cups, poured himself some wine, and sat by the window to gaze beyond the pine wood to the high slopes of Mount Hymettos.

On the other side of the villa, in their own set of rooms, Rufio and Clara had slept fitfully for a couple of hours while Felicia had dozed on and off in silence in her crib a few feet away.

From time to time, Rufio, who had slept less than Clara, had listened to his daughter's gentle murmurs as she observed her hands and feet, those appendages which, to her surprise, seemed to follow her everywhere. When she began to babble more, Rufio rose to pick her up.

"Let's let your mama sleep a bit longer," he whispered to her. He held her up then and observed how much longer she was. *How is she growing so quickly?*

In the bed, Clara turned over on her side to watch as Rufio carried Felicia to the window to look out at the trees and the distant brilliance of the Parthenon with the late afternoon sun above it. He hugged her close and felt her little fingers grasp his beard. Those moments when she was newly-woken were his absolute favourite. He felt calmer than at any other time, and thanked the Gods for it. "I love you, little one. Always remember that."

Clara smiled to herself as she spied upon them. There had been a time, she remembered, when she had wondered whether Rufio would be up to the task of fatherhood. He had surprised her from the outset, and her heart seemed to swell with pride daily.

Felicia began to whine and Rufio began to bounce her more quickly in an attempt to quiet her.

"It's all right. I'm awake," Clara spoke up. "Bring her here. I'll feed her."

Rufio turned to look across the room at Clara and he marvelled at how lovely she was where the sunlight streaked across the bed and lit her blonde hair. He walked over to her and laid Felicia down beside her. "There is something about this place…the light…the colour…"

"The play," Clara finished.

Rufio looked at her and smiled. "I can't stop thinking about it."

"It's a strange choice."

"I wonder what roles the Gods have assigned us?" Rufio wondered.

"You mean which ones they inspired Felix to give us?"

"That's *The* Felix Modestus," Rufio joked.

They heard the crying break out from across the upper level of the peristylium.

"I think he has his hands full," Clara said. "Electra said that he's having some difficulty adjusting to putting someone else ahead of himself."

"Really? He's always been so good at everything." Rufio knew that Felix was having some trouble, but he had put it down to the lack of sleep. "I'm surprised."

"Maybe you can help…inspire him. Give him a different perspective."

"Me?"

Clara looked up at him as if it were obvious. "Of course, you. You're his best friend!"

"A best friend who rarely sees him. As are you, by the way!" He shook his head. "Felix has friends all across the Middle Sea. He won't listen to me."

"Sycophants and men with whom he has business dealings are not friends. You know that. Just try."

Rufio shrugged. "I'll try." He then walked over to the table where he had laid the play's scroll and his eyes raked over the words scrawled across the papyrus. "It's just so strange that Apollo should choose this play…and for the Panathenaea!"

"Not really *for* it," Clara corrected.

"No," Rufio agreed. "Not *for* it, but to be performed in Athenae."

"I'm sure it will all come together."

Rufio looked at his satchel and reached across the table to remove his wax tablets, styli, and ink pots. He opened the largest of the tablets and was about to write down some thoughts he had when Clara called him.

"Can you help me for a moment?"

He looked over and quickly set down his stylus before going to the bed.

"I just need to get her some fresh bracae."

"I can do that." Rufio knew he was not going to be writing anything anytime soon. "How about you get yourself ready and go down to join the others? I'll be along shortly."

"Are you sure?"

He nodded and smiled as he took Felicia. "Positive."

"All right then." She placed a towel over Rufio's shoulder and he adjusted Felicia so that he could burp her properly. "I'll just change." Clara went to the other end of the long room where the wardrobe was set up and chose an olive green peplos which she slid over her head and fastened at the shoulders with knotted gold clasps. "These things are more complicated than tunicae, but I do love to wear them!"

"What?" Rufio said from the other end of the room just as Felicia let out a strangely enormous belch which was followed by a splatter upon the floor. "There you go!"

In a moment, Peli was licking at the mess at Rufio's feet.

"Gods, Peli! Don't we feed you enough?" Rufio wrinkled his nose as he walked with his daughter to get fresh bracae from their belongings. That done, he laid her on the bed upon the blanket to clean her up and change her.

"What do you think?" Clara asked as she emerged from the wardrobe, her hair newly-brushed. The peplos' pleats hugged her body in such a way that Rufio could see her curves from her shoulders to the floor.

"You look like you would be at home on Olympus!" he gasped.

Clara smiled. "I'm quite happy being here with you two." She looked at Peli. "Shall I take him with me?"

Rufio eyed the dog. "No. Leave him here. He's helping me. Besides, he'll just piss on poor Atticus again."

Clara nodded. "See you down there." She kissed his cheek, tickled Felicia's chin, and opened the door to leave.

"All right my girl," Rufio was saying, "let's get you cleaned up. Aaah! You didn't? Not again!"

Clara paused outside the door to listen. She was about to go back in when she heard more shouting and crying from across the courtyard. It was coming from Felix and Electra's rooms. Below in the garden, she could see the servants scatter to get as far as they could.

"Woman, stay here and help me!" Felix roared, but soon after, their door burst open and Electra stormed out like a red tempest racing down a mountainside. Her hair was wild and her eyes searched about as if looking for something, or someone, to throttle.

No wonder the servants are running! Clara thought, though she immediately regretted it and went after Electra who had already gone downstairs and disappeared toward the back of the villa.

A FEW MINUTES AND A LOT OF FRUSTRATION LATER, RUFIO AND Felix emerged simultaneously from their respective cubicula. They stared at each other from across the peristylium.

Felix shook his head as he gripped his son, and Rufio walked with Felicia, Peli in tow, around the gallery to see him. "You all right?"

Felix glowered at him. "Do I look all right to you?"

Rufio observed the remnants of splattered spit on the shoulder of Felix's tunica, his wild hair, and the pleading look of desperation in his eyes. "You look great."

Felix shook his head. "How am I going to put this production together with all that's going on? Electra seems to think it's also my job to care for the child, even though she'll have very little in the way of a role in the play!"

Rufio was about to speak when Felicia's hand gripped his lower jaw. He extricated her little fingers from his mouth. "Maybe just do what she asks and don't protest too much. For now at least."

Felix seemed to rise in height, his face a slightly darker shade of red.

"It's like this in the beginning. She's mad with exhaustion and just needs to know you are her ally."

"I'm exhausted as well, Rufio!"

"I know. Trust me. I know. But the feeding of the children is draining. Or at least that's what Clara says."

"But it was her choice! I offered to get a nursemaid for Thespis, but she refused."

Rufio nodded to Felix's son, his eyebrows arched. "Would you offer a god anything other than nectar and ambrosia? You want the best for him, do you not?"

Thespis reached out to Felicia then and Rufio stepped closer so that they could clasp their little fingers together.

"Putting a production together in Athenae is also draining," Felix mumbled. "But you're right, I suppose. Only the best for this one." He held his son up as though he were a prized piece of fruit at a market stall.

"Shall we go down to join the others?" Rufio suggested.

"Yes," Felix said. "I want some of the wine you brought."

"It's good isn't it?" Rufio said as they walked.

"Tastes just like home."

Felix and Rufio found everyone gathered not in the triclinium but rather outside in the odeon at the back of the villa.

"And here they are!" Sextus said as he saw them enter. "The Etrurian Players are complete!"

"And half-mad!" Felix added, shooting a look at Electra who remained calm and sipped her wine, her lips lingering on the rim of the cup as she looked back unflinchingly.

Clara came over to take Felicia from Rufio. "Weren't you wearing the blue tunica?" she said, noticing the grey one he now wore.

"She got me again," he muttered.

"Ah."

Martia walked over to Felix. "May I hold him for you, Felix?" she asked.

It was as if the sun had alighted upon his face, for Felix smiled broadly and presented her with his son. "The Gods love you, Martia! Yes, please do so that I can finally get down to the business of assigning roles."

Martia took Thespis, cradling him carefully in her arms, and seated herself beside Clara and Felicia.

Electra watched the other woman with her child and, most annoyingly, felt a pang of jealously, even though she had been wishing to be away from him for a time. These feelings were quickly dispelled when she saw the smile upon Martia's face. *Help her, my son,* Electra thought.

All about the odeon, the members of The Etrurian Players sat, drinking and waiting, scrolls in hand as Felix mounted the stage to address them.

Sextus and Rufio sat front and centre with Electra to their left and Clara and Martia to the right with the children. In the second row, Domela and Julius watched and waited for Felix to begin. Behind them, Fausto and Beatrice laughed at something one of the servants had told them related to Peli who was, Gods knew, up to some new mischief somewhere in the villa.

Farther back, Damon lay upon the seats twirling a few soft notes on his flute as he gazed up at the purpled-hued sky. Near to him, Castor and Pollux both shook their heads as they pointed at the scroll, clearly upset with the choice of play.

Felix Modestus looked on his company with some hesitation and, for the first time in a long while, he felt doubtful about the journey they were about to undertake. He downed his wine and set the cup upon the stage before running his hands through his hair.

The murmur of chatter continued until Felix clapped his hands loudly and a silence fell over the group but for the flutter of Damon's flute.

"Damon!" Felix shouted. "Are you with us?"

Damon sat up quickly and nodded. "Yeeaaahh!"

"Good," Felix continued. "It's time to assign roles, but first, I take it you've all had a chance to read *Heautontimorumenos?*"

"Yes!" Fausto stood up, gripping his scroll. "It's not funny, Dominus!"

Beatrice nodded her agreement beside Fausto. "I agree. I laughed maybe once the whole time."

Rufio was on his feet. "I disagree." He held up his copy. "This play is Terentius' most brilliant. It's smart-funny."

"'Smart-funny'? Are we inventing words to describe this?" Castor asked. "The audience won't be so lenient with us."

"My brother's right, Felix," Pollux now stood. "What Rufio calls 'smart-funny' won't win over an audience. In Rome they would riot at this if they were expecting a comedy."

"Except, we're not in Rome!" Rufio said, more forcefully than anyone would have expected.

Clara looked up at that.

"Rufio's right," Julius added. "We're not in Rome. We're in Athenae, and here the audience is more sophisticated. They expect a more intelligent form of comedy. This play is heart-warming and thoughtful."

Domela nodded beside Julius.

"Julius makes a good point," Sextus stood now. "I agree with Pollux in that if this were Rome, it might not be the best choice. But here, in Athenae, it is different to anywhere else. There is no room for crassness."

"Are we sure about that?" Castor said. "I mean, what would any performance of Lysistrata be without the men and their engorged bollocks on stage?"

"Good gods!" Martia squealed, and Electra shot Castor a look.

"I take your point, Castor," Sextus said.

"Or rather, the knob!" Fausto blurted.

"All right, all right!" Felix bellowed. "That's enough. So you *have* read it!"

"Ye…yes!" some of them answered.

Felix looked at Domela, Fausto, and Beatrice who had not

given him an affirmative response. "You three. Did you not read the play?"

"Well, Dominus…" Fausto began.

"It was such a nice afternoon, we thought we would walk up the mountain," Beatrice added.

"But we did peruse it!" Fausto said.

"Really." Felix was clearly not impressed. "And Domela?"

"I had a fitful sleep, Dominus. I am sorry. It's just that with young Thespis up all night, I couldn't-"

"Enough!" Felix barked, shaking his head. "I expect you all to read it through. Got it?"

"Yes, Dominus," Fausto and Beatrice replied, looking down at the ground.

"I can't really assign you your roles unless you understand the story," Felix said. "I'll summarize the plot first."

Everyone settled back to listen as Felix paced the stage a couple times before beginning.

"The play takes place in Attica…over the course of two days…" Felix stopped to clear his throat and make sure they were all listening. He had never seen them so distracted. It was as if the Athenian light had bedazzled and befuddled them. *Tell the story, Felix,* he told himself. *Hook them!*

"There is an Athenian farmer by the name of Chremes. A successful man, to his mind. One day, he finds his neighbour, Menedemus, toiling away all day on his farm. The man - this 'self-tormentor' - does this everyday and-"

"That's the title of the play!" Beatrice said a little too loudly to Fausto beside her.

"Shh!" Fausto tutted.

"Yes, Beatrice. It is," Felix said, trying not to lose his temper.

"Let *The* Felix Modestus speak, Beatrice!" Castor chided playfully behind her.

"As I was saying…" Felix pressed on, determined to pierce

the fog that seemed to be engulfing his audience. "Chremes asks Menedemus why he toils so hard at his work when he could have his servants do it for him, and Menedemus says that he is punishing himself for having forced his son, Clinia, to go to war in Asia."

"Why did he force him?" Domela asked.

"He didn't," Felix responded. "Clinia was in love with a young woman named Antiphila, whom his father did not deem suitable."

"So he left?" Fausto asked, unable to stopper his lips. "He went to war over a girl?"

"He was in love!" Felix bit back. "At any rate. That is in the past. After this conversation, Chremes finds that his own son, Clitipho, who is in love with a lupa named Bacchis, had just brought home his good friend, Clinia, that same son of Menedemus, who has recently returned from Asia."

"I'm already confused," Fausto blurted.

Felix ignored him and continued. "Now, the wily slave of Clitipho, Syrus, had planned to bring Antiphila to his master's domus along with his master's lupa, Bacchis. The girl is posing as one of Bacchis' servants in her large entourage. But, to conceal Clitipho's affair with the lupa, they pretend to Chremes, Clitipho's father, that Bacchis is actually Clinia's mistress, so that she may stay beneath the roof of Chremes. Meanwhile, Clinia asks that his presence back home not yet be revealed to his father for fear of what his father may do or say."

"Are Clinia and Antiphila reunited?" Beatrice asked, leaning forward more eagerly now.

Rufio smiled to himself.

"Yes!" Felix said. "They are, and they are overjoyed to see one another."

"Is that it then?" Fausto asked.

"No, Fausto, that is not it. This only takes us up to the second act." Felix rubbed his beard roughly.

"How many acts are there?" Fausto could not help himself.

"There are five. Now will you shut up?" Felix bellowed.

Beatrice's hand was up.

"What is it Beatrice?"

"Sorry, Dominus, but where did this Antiphila come from?"

"In a brilliant fashion, Terentius has made her the child of Chremes and his wife Sostrata. When she was born, Chremes had asked her to expose the child, and Sostrata had done as he commanded."

"What a brute!" Electra burst out.

"Yes. But the old weaving woman to whom Sostrata had given the task of exposing the child, ignored the command and raised the child as her own."

"Is the weaving woman in the lupa's entourage?" Beatrice asked.

"No. She has recently died and young Antiphila is mourning her."

"How tragic!" Beatrice burst out.

"No, it's funny!" Felix added.

"If you say so, Dominus," Beatrice added, shaking her head. "Please continue."

"Why thank you, Beatrice!" Felix bowed sarcastically. "In the third act, Chremes reveals to his neighbour, Menedemus, that his son, Clinia, has in fact returned, but also tells him that he has brought a haughty and demanding mistress, Bacchis. Meanwhile, the slave, Syrus, has advised his master that he had a plan, but the plan is actually designed to get money from Chremes for Clinia to pay Bacchis… Sorry," Felix paused, "to get money from Menedemus to pay off his son Clinia's pretend mistress, Bacchis." He shook his head.

"To get money from both, in a way," Rufio added.

Felix nodded. "Yes! At any rate, it isn't so important. What is important is that the slave, Syrus, is plotting to get money from one of them, and then the other, at different points in the play."

"This is so confusing," Beatrice said.

Felix sat on the edge of the stage, stared for a moment at his empty wine cup, and carried on. "Syrus has also told Chremes that Antiphila had been pawned off to Bacchis by the weaving woman and that Bacchis wishes to sell the girl. Syrus tells Chremes to tell Menedemus that he should buy her as she is a good bargain because her family in Caria will pay a handsome reward for her."

"Caria?" Fausto said. "I thought this takes place in Attica?"

"It'll take place up your arse, Fausto, if you don't shut up!" Pollux growled.

"I do apologize for my players, Lady Martia," Felix said.

Martia smiled back at him, seemingly incapable of being dismayed with young Thespis upon her lap. "Carry on, Felix Modestus," she said. "The story is fascinating."

Felix inclined his head and continued once more. "Syrus is plotting… Then, in the fourth act, Sostrata, the wife of Chremes, upon seeing the ring of the girl, Antiphila, realizes that the girl is in fact her long lost daughter whom she had asked to be exposed."

"What?" Domela burst out.

"Yes!" Felix turned to her. "You see, the ring is the self-same ring which she had hung around her baby's neck so that the child would not go into the Underworld with out anything. Meanwhile, Syrus the slave begins to panic because this upends all of his plans, and Clinia, the son of Menedemus, is overjoyed because the revelation means that Antiphila is a suitable wife. Syrus tells Clinia he may tell his father the truth, but wishes to keep up the pretence for Chremes a bit longer so that it is not discovered that the lupa is actually his own son's mistress and not Clinia's. The lupa, Bacchis, threatens to tell all and get Syrus in trouble."

"Never trust a lupa, eh Pollux?" Castor teased his brother.

"I don't want to talk about Alexandria ever again!" Pollux bit back.

Felix stood staring at them. "Are you finished?"

"Yes, Dominus," they said in concert.

"While Syrus continues with his desperate plots, Menedemus and Clinia are reunited, but then Chremes convinces Menedemus that his son is lying about wanting to marry his newly-discovered daughter, Antiphila, because he actually wants the money to pay his mistress, Bacchis. The two old men plan a way to entrap Clinia."

"How unfair! He loves the girl!" Domela cried out.

"Yes, but Syrus' plots have twisted everything, when in reality, Clinia will get exactly want he wants."

"Which is?" Domela could not help herself.

Julius smiled. "The hand of Antiphila." He looked to Felix to carry on toward the end.

"In the fifth and final act, Menedemus confirms to Clinia that his marriage to Antiphila is agreed with Chremes, and the latter is puzzled that the youth agrees so willingly, for he thought that Clinia actually loved Bacchis, the lupa. Chremes realizes that he had been played, and that Bacchis is actually his own son's mistress. He is determined to punish his son and puts it out that he is giving his entire estate to his new-found daughter, Antiphila, as a dowry for her marriage to Clinia. Menedemus advises Chremes to forgive his son and bring him round to his way of thinking - this is the same advice that Chremes gave to Menedemus at the start of the play. Clitipho, Chremes' son, at Syrus' urging, asks his mother, Sostrata if he is even her son, and this prompts Sostrata and Chremes to quarrel. Clitipho begs his father to reconsider, and Chremes does so on the condition that Clitipho give up Bacchis and marry someone respectable. Clitipho, rather than be destitute and hungry, agrees to his father's terms, and at the very end, convinces his father to forgive Syrus for all his trickery."

Felix stopped, a little breathless after all of it, and waited for a reaction.

There was none that he could hear, but rather a round of twisted faces upon his players. Rufio and Sextus smiled to themselves, clearly fans of the play, but the others, besides those with babies in their laps, seemed confused.

"Is that it then?" Fausto asked.

"Yes," Felix answered. "That is how the play ends."

"Syrus gets away with all of it?" Beatrice demanded. "Just like that?"

"Yes, Beatrice," Felix said, waving to Atticus for more wine which the steward brought immediately.

"You'd think he'd be sold or something!" Fausto added.

Felix downed another cup of wine and breathed deeply. "Does everyone now understand the plot?" he asked, his look stern.

"Yes, Dominus!" the entire company replied.

He could tell that some of them were lying, but he ignored it. "Good. That's a start!" Felix sighed. "Though this might be a tough play to put on in Rome, let's not forget that Terentius was Roman, and one of our greatest playwrights."

"But why this play, Felix?" Pollux asked. "I mean, of all Terentius' works, why this one?"

"Because Apollo commanded it to be this one!" Felix shouted.

Everyone was silent again.

Felix rubbed his face vigorously. His company had never before complained so much about the choice of play. They had always met a challenge head-on, been excited by it. Now, he was confounded by their reticence, their fear.

"I think there is a misconception here that the choice of

play is up for debate." Felix slid off the stage to stand in the orchestra. "It is not. We are performing this play, as Apollo commands."

"We are with you, Dominus," Julius said, standing again and casting a chastising look over his fellow players.

They all nodded and mumbled their agreement.

"Sorry, Dominus," Beatrice said. "I'm sure once we start rehearsals, we'll all feel better about it."

"That's better," Felix said. "Now, do you want to know who will play what role?"

"Yes!" they answered, and Damon played a few quick notes.

"Good. Now this play has a smaller cast, to be sure," Felix began, "but we will add background action as well. However, based on what the Gods have shown me, these are your roles…"

Felix looked over them all for a few seconds. *Apollo, I pray you are right about this.*

Felix cleared his throat and began. "Beatrice, you will play two roles. Sostrata's servant, and Phrygia, the slave of Bacchis."

"Thank you, Dominus," Beatrice said before whispering to Fausto. "But who's playing Bacchis?"

Fausto shrugged and leaned in to listen to Felix.

"Domela," Felix continued. "You shall play Sostrata, the wife of Chremes."

"And who shall play my husband?" Domela asked.

This got her an angry look from Beatrice. "Let him finish!"

Domela looked at the younger girl and showed her the palm of her hand as if she were threatening an errant child.

"Electra will play Bacchis, the wealthy courtesan and lover of Clitipho." Felix looked to Electra and she nodded.

"Clara," Felix smiled. "You will play Antiphila, the beloved of Clinia."

"I can do that," Clara said, bouncing Felicia on her knee.

"I know it's not a big role, but you can make it your own." Felix continued. "Castor."

"Yes, Dominus!"

"You'll play Dromo, Clinia's slave."

"The slave?" Castor asked. "You didn't even mention him in your summary!"

Felix ignored this. Castor was right, he had forgotten to mention Dromo.

"Yes, but he's a good slave!" Fausto said, laughing over his shoulder.

Felix eyed the younger man. "Fausto, you'll play Syrus, the naughty slave."

Everyone laughed at that, though secretly Fausto was happy as it was one of the larger roles in the play from what he could tell.

"Rufio, my friend," Felix carried on, "you shall play Clitipho, the son of Chremes and friend of Clinia."

"The one who is the lover of Bacchis?" Rufio asked, his eyes straying to Electra who would play the courtesan.

"Is that a problem?" Felix asked, his eye catching his wife's.

"Pfft! Of course not!" He looked to Electra. "We'll have them howling in the aisles, won't we?"

Electra simply stared back at him.

"Who plays Clinia then?" Rufio asked, happy to look away from her.

"I will play Clinia," Felix said.

"Maybe we should switch?" Rufio added. "It might be more believable, no?" He did not want to say it aloud, but he would much rather have kissed his wife than Electra who, after so long, still frightened some part of him.

"It's as Apollo demands, Rufio. Sorry."

Clara smiled at her husband, trying not to laugh at his discomfort.

"That leaves the two main roles then!" Fausto said.

"Yes, it does," Felix answered and looked to the last two. "Julius, you will play Chremes, the father of Clitipho."

"Thank you, Dominus." The older actor smiled and nodded. He loved that role.

Felix's eyes finally rested on Pollux who looked behind him, genuinely surprised that he was left for last. "Pollux?"

"Yes, Dominus?"

"You will play Menedemus, Terentius' 'self-tormentor'."

"Me, Dominus?" Pollux asked, still clearly confused.

"Yes. I know you can do it and so, it seems, does Apollo himself."

Castor slapped his brother on the back.

"Don't trim your beard," Felix added. "We need you to look older."

"Heyoooo!" Damon was on his feet, his hands indicating himself as he smacked his chest.

"Yes, Damon!" Felix said. "Don't worry. I haven't forgotten you. You are in charge of the music. There won't be songs in this production, but I want a constant reflection of the countryside. The play takes place in Attica, so I want you to wander about the villa and listen to how this world sounds. I want the audience to feel as though they are actually in the fields and forests of this land. Understand?"

Damon nodded and saluted sharply.

"Excellent. And some of you will be part of Bacchis' entourage in some way. I just haven't worked that out yet."

Everyone began talking, and it was then that Sextus stood to walk over to Felix.

"Felix, I would not question you *or* Apollo, but should you not at least play the lead? Is Pollux up to it?"

"It's as Apollo commands, Sextus."

"I really don't mean to be insulting, but what if you misinterpreted your dream? I mean…" Sextus wiped the sweat from his brow. "…people misinterpret Apollo's messages all the time, don't they? Perhaps we should consult an oneirocritica?"

"I don't need a dream manual to know this, Sextus. The dream Apollo sent me on Delos was as clear as a glass of spring water."

"All right. I believe in you, and this company. Apollo knows all."

"He does," Felix agreed. *Including how exhausted I am!* Felix had thought about it, and he was grateful to be given a smaller role.

"You all right?" Clara asked Rufio as she came to his side. "It will be fine."

"I like the role," he answered. "I just wish I was opposite you."

"Just have fun with it. Bacchis isn't even in the play that much."

"I suppose." Rufio looked at Electra who was, it seemed, chiding Felix for something. "This will be interesting." He noted how exhausted both Felix and Electra looked, how it added fuel to their every conversation, and he felt for them. He and Clara had both lived with a similar weariness, one that dug deep into the body and mind in a most unrelenting way.

Felicia had, at least, been kind to them and not lingered long in that state of sleeplessness babes are partial to.

Thespis, however, he seemed to be a most unwilling participant in sleep, and the pain and frustration of that showed upon his parents' faces.

Felix and Electra seemed to relax a little, the former having soothed her worries, whatever they were.

"Felix Modestus," Atticus came up to them then, having been waiting for an opportune moment to approach.

"Yes, Atticus?" Felix turned to the steward.

"The cena will be served in the triclinium in three hours."

"Very well. Thank you."

Atticus bowed quickly and left to go back to his work, but not before the echoing sound of barking grew louder and louder and Peli burst onto the scene at the back of the odeon. "Aaah!" Atticus shouted, almost bowled over by the racing hound.

"Peli, stop!" Rufio shouted, but the miscreant canine ignored Rufio and continued on, pursued by a white goat with curling horns.

"Nicodemus, heel!" Atticus shouted.

"Is he talking to the goat?" Fausto laughed as they all watched the livid livestock chase Peli, attempting to ram him with his horns.

Rufio and Clara watched, and Felicia pointed and giggled at the scene.

"I am sorry, Felix Modestus, Praetor…" The steward ran after the goat, joining the pursuit along with two other of the house slaves before they all disappeared into the domus.

"Now *that's* funny!" Castor cheered.

Clara looked to Rufio who shook his head. "I don't want to know."

"Me neither," she responded before smiling at Felicia.

As the rest of the company began to discuss their ideas about how they could insert more humour into the play, Felix stopped as though in the eye of a great storm to observe and listen. He shook his head and cleared his throat. "There are a few hours until the cena. You may all do as you wish and contemplate your roles. Tomorrow morning, we'll have our first rehearsal!"

"Yes, Dominus!" the players responded.

"Castor and I are heading into the city if anyone wants to join us!" Pollux declared.

Beatrice and Fausto consulted. "We'll join you!" Fausto replied.

"Damon, you coming?" Beatrice asked.

"Ahooo!" Damon howled.

"Domela and I are going to search for the sanctuary of Artemis we've heard about," Julius told Felix. "We'll be back soon."

"Make an offering to the goddess for us all," Electra said.

Julius nodded and went out with Domela, Beatrice's gaze following them.

The odeon was suddenly very quiet and Felix and Electra sat down beside each other, seemingly unaware of the others.

Martia, who had been rocking Thespis the entire time, looked at Clara and nodded toward the two exhausted parents.

Clara smiled and nodded. "Electra, Felix... Why don't you both go and rest? Martia and I can entertain the children for a while."

Electra looked up from her waking slumber. "Are you certain?"

"Of course, dear," Martia said. "With Felicia here, your son will be quite entertained."

"Especially with goats and dogs racing about!" Rufio joked, but Felix took no notice.

"Sextus," Felix said as he rose to follow Electra who was already on her way to their cubiculum, "perhaps you can describe the set pieces we discussed to Rufio and Clara."

"Worry not, Felix. Just you rest and be free of cares."

They watched Felix and Electra go and then Martia turned to Clara. "Shall we take the children to the garden? They seem to like the splash of the fountain."

"Good idea," Clara replied.

Sextus and Rufio followed them.

"I do hope we get a chance to explore Athenae more fully while we're here," Rufio said to Sextus. "This polis intrigues me."

"Oh, I'm sure you'll have a moment or two to make some

memories," Sextus replied. "Athenae has a way of drawing one in."

For the next while, the entire domus was strangely quiet, apart from the occasional bark of Peli's without the villa walls.

WHILE THE PRAETOR AND HIS WIFE SAT IN THE GARDEN WITH the couple newly-arrived from Etruria, Atticus thanked the Gods that the children were now quietly entertained in the garden. He was also pleased that the dog that had come to stay had been kept at bay by Nicodemus. Atticus had to admit that he was not often a fan of the goat that had taken to roaming about the villa and stealing food from off of the set tables, but his harassment of the dog had won him some favour in Atticus' eyes.

As the staff finished setting the tables in the triclinium for the cena, Atticus walked around to make sure that all was in order. He knew he was likely exaggerating, for the company of players were hardly the most demanding bunch when it came to the formalities of dining. Still, a praetor of Rome - as well as a great artistic patron - was beneath their roof, and Atticus had wanted to make his own dominus proud with the reception he proffered their guests. And then there was The Felix Modestus, onc of the greatest players around the Middle Sea. Atticus still pinched himself that he was receiving the great man himself. Even in Athenae, the news of what had happened on Delos had reached their ears. He was truly touched by Apollo, as was his lady-wife, the archimima, Electra. Atticus saw it as his sacred duty to make them as comfortable as he possibly could so that they could bring their greatness to Athenae's stage.

Admittedly, it had been a shock to see them in a less-than-immortal light, exhausted, angry, and as bedraggled as any common young family. It had certainly dimmed the lustre that had at first blinded him so, but at the same time it gave him some hope for everyone, hope for finding greatness in his own purpose, that is, running the best domus and household staff in all of Athenae.

Just as Atticus finished checking each place setting, Felix Modestus walked into the triclinium looking rested and resplendent in a tailored indigo tunica that showed off his strong stature. Atticus bowed and smiled, his arms wide to present the tables. There were silver knives and spoons, silver wine cups, and polished silver plates which reflected the fire-light from the lamps burning about the room so that the ceiling sparkled as though the sun were reflected off of a still sea.

"The Felix Modestus," Atticus said. "I hope you will enjoy this evening's feast."

"I'm sure I will, Atticus," Felix said. "I am well rested and famished! And the children are sleeping!"

"The Gods love you," Atticus added, a little shyly. "Erm… Will the others be along soon? I don't want the food to grow cold by bringing it out too soon."

"They are trickling in. The children needed tending, and I believe the Praetor and his wife are freshening up after minding the little ones with Rufio and Clara."

"Ah, Felix, there you are!" Julius said as he came in, followed by Domela. "We ran into the others on our way back. They are going to eat in the city and apologize for not being here."

Felix shook his head and sighed. "I suppose that will be better for our first rehearsal tomorrow. Let them get it out of their systems."

Atticus stepped up. "Does that mean you will not require all of the place settings?"

"I'm afraid not, Atticus," Felix said, placing his hand on the man's shoulder. You can clear away…five of the settings. All the more room for us!"

"More room?" Rufio said as he and Clara walked in.

"Seems the lure of Athenae's delights was too much to resist for our younger players!" Felix said. "They'll not be eating with us."

"More food then as well!" Rufio laughed. "I'm starving. What smells so delicious, Atticus?"

Atticus bowed before launching into his description of the meal. "We'll begin with olives, cheese, and salads, and for the main courses, I have brought in various fish from the harbour at Piraeus, including sea bass, squid, and sardines, all of which have been prepared in different ways."

"Sounds lovely," Clara added.

Atticus inclined his head, and smiled when Sextus and Martia entered the triclinium.

Rufio moved to recline beside Clara, opposite Sextus and Martia and beside Julius. "Atticus, do you happen to have fresh bread and some game available?"

Clara slapped his shoulder.

"What?" he said.

"You can try them!" Clara hissed. After her time at Syracusae, she had grown accustomed to fish and, rarely eating any in Etruria, she was already looking forward to it.

"You know I can't stomach fish."

"You'll be fine," Clara added before turning to Electra who had come into the triclinium last. "You look beautiful, my dear."

Electra smiled and sighed. "I feel it. It's amazing what a bit of sleep will do for the complexion!"

"Oh, I understand all too well," Clara said.

Sextus' hand reached out to touch Martia's most subtly, but Rufio noticed and took the opportunity to squeeze Clara beneath the edge of the table.

"Is the rest of the company not joining us?" Sextus asked.

"They are at leisure within the city walls," Julius commented.

"Ah, I understand," Sextus said, smiling. "I mean, when I was a young man visiting Athenae I used to go to the-" He stopped suddenly, Martia eyeing him suspiciously. "…the…the library!"

"Yes, I'm quite sure, Sextus," Martia laughed as she lifted her wine cup to her lips. "I do not presume that you did not live before we were wed."

"I was living, my dear, but I was not truly alive until we were wed."

There was a momentary silence, but before it grew uncomfortable, Felix raised his cup for a toast. "To living!"

"To living!" everyone echoed, pouring some wine onto the floor before drinking.

Clara smiled. "Well, I for one am relieved that we can trust our men to behave themselves now. Am I right, ladies?"

"They'd better," Electra growled, but then laughed along with Martia and Clara.

The men stared at each other, but none offered a retort.

"Erm… Julius, Domela… How was you walk?" Rufio asked. "Did you find the sanctuary of Artemis?"

"We walked about the hill of Ardittos, but the sanctuary of Artemis eluded us," Domela said as she reached out for a piece of cheese from a large platter before her. "There were pathways all over the hill, and we thought that one of them would eventually lead us to the temple, but it was as if the goddess did not wish us to find it."

"We will find it next time," Julius added. "It was a beautiful walk nonetheless with the comforting presence of Athena's temple atop the Acropolis always visible. There is a magic in the air, certainly."

Domela continued. "It's as if it is another world of pine trees, olive, cypress, eucalyptus, carob, almond, and pepper trees. There were some grazing goats with no hint of a herder, and we supposed that the god Pan may be sitting nearby, keeping a watchful eye. The giant agave plants are especially haunting!"

"Haunting?" Rufio looked up.

"You know, I have heard that the Athenians call those plants 'immortals'," Sextus added. "Perhaps the goddess was leading you down pathways of her choosing?"

"We'll have to bring a proper offering next time," Domela said.

"That would be wise," Atticus suddenly said from where he was setting bowls of fresh greens drizzled with oil and lemon.

"What do you mean, Atticus?" Julius asked.

"Oh, ah, forgive me. I did not mean to speak out of turn."

"We are not emperors, Atticus!" Felix said, refilling his wine cup. "Speak freely!"

"Well, I do know that the goats are our own herd, and I shall have words with our sleepy goatherd as soon as possible. They should not be up there."

"Why?" Rufio asked, unable to stop himself.

"We do not normally roam the wooded slopes of Ardittos, for between the temples of Tyche and of Artemis, the ground belongs to the goddesses, muses, and nymphs. The dead were also buried in that soil. Some are said to roam the wood at night."

Rufio gulped.

"I would much rather recommend you walk the slopes of the hill of Agras on the other side of the stadium. There, our master, Herodes Atticus, commissioned the great platform for the ship that carries Athena's handwoven peplos for the Great Panathenaea. They are cleaning it now in preparation for the festival."

"Your dominus' family has indeed done much for this city, Atticus," Sextus said, raising his cup. "To our hosts and their forebears!"

"Here, here!" Felix echoed.

Rufio drank, but his mind was stuck on the idea of the dead roaming the slopes of the hill that was very near to where they were currently staying.

Conversation flowed into talk of the city and the upcoming festival, of which they were to be a part, and as they spoke, course after course of food was brought out - salads, fruits, breads, cheeses, and fish, fish, and more fish. Everyone seemed to be enjoying the fresh fare gifted to them from Neptune's realm.

Rufio, however, not wanting to insult their hosts, ate as much salad, fruit, bread and cheese as he could before he attempted to choke down some fish. When he had had enough, he focused on his wine cup and bread, and secretly hoped that that would be the only meal of fish to grace the table during their stay.

The wine and food had done their job warming the somewhat smaller than expected gathering, and conversation eventually turned to the play.

"What do you think, Felix?" Julius asked. "Will we pull this off? I mean, the others had trouble following it. And I, admittedly, only followed the plot because I have watched it a few times over the years of my career."

"And how were those performances received?" Martia asked, keenly aware of how much her husband had invested in the imminent production.

"Not well… I'm sorry to say. Come to think of it, the performances ended up being those companies' final ones." Julius looked into his wine cup and swirled the dregs. "Every time, the production was either confused, or attempted to insert humour where Terentius did not intend any."

"But these previous productions did not have The Etrurian Players!" Felix boasted.

Rufio looked at Felix and then to Julius. "I think the key with this play is to remain true to its purpose."

"What purpose do you think that would be, Rufio?" Sextus asked.

Everyone turned to Rufio, including Clara who craned her neck to look at her husband.

Rufio did not speak for a moment, trying to organize his thoughts. "Terentius' purpose with this play was, I believe, to paint a picture true to life, especially when it comes to the relationships between fathers and sons. And in remaining true to life, there cannot only be humour, but it must also be accompanied by outrage and sadness, perhaps some regret. But it must avoid falling over the cliff's edge into the realm of tragedy. All ends well, though for a time it seems that it may not."

Domela shook her head. "You've already lost me. I don't see it."

"What do you see then, Domela?" Clara asked.

"I see two old men who cannot keep up with the whims of their sons. They are fools, at the end of the day, and it takes a wily slave to reveal that, to unveil their hypocrisy."

"I think that's an oversimplification!" Rufio snapped, sitting up straighter as he turned to address Domela. "I think Terentius was delving much deeper that we know and-" Rufio found his thoughts swirling in his mind and chided himself for having drunk so much.

"And what, Rufio?" Felix asked.

"I don't know! I just think that if everyone let themselves feel the play more, they would understand."

"But that is our job, my friend!" Felix said. "It's up to us as players to help our audience to feel what Terentius intended, to liken it to their own lives and relationships."

"But how will we do that if half of us don't understand the plot?" Julius said.

Felix sat up on the edge of the couch and raised his cup to his lips. "We'll figure it out as we go!"

"That sounds like a solid plan," Electra scoffed. "Apollo will surely be pleased!"

"Don't start with the sacrilege, woman!" Felix growled at his wife. "The Gods are listening in this place."

They all quieted and looked about as if expecting an immortal to come in a the door at any moment.

"May I serve the sweet course now?" Atticus suddenly said from the other end of the triclinium.

"Yes, Atticus," Sextus said. "By all means. I think now would be a good time to cheer ourselves with some delectables."

Atticus bowed and snapped his fingers and several servants filed into the triclinium to clear away the dirty plates, platters, and bowls. Four other servants entered with platters of fruit, honeyed pastries, and goat's cheese drizzled with Hymettos honey, as well as pitchers of golden wine from Samos.

Electra was about to help herself to some of the sweets when there erupted a loud wailing from within the bowels of the domus. She closed her eyes slowly, as if not seeing would make the crying stop.

But it did not.

"I suppose that is the end of the cena for me," she said, brushing back her dark hair and sighing. "It was lovely while it lasted." She rose from her couch and just in that moment a tiny soprano voice joined that of her son.

"They are in concert," Clara sighed. "Don't worry, I'll go," she said to Rufio. "You can continue your discussion." She turned to the others. "Please excuse me."

"I'll help," Martia said, "if that is all right with you, of course."

Electra smiled at her. "Of course, my dear. We can talk as my baby sucks the life from my breasts."

"Oh dear!" Sextus gasped.

But Felix laughed at Electra's inebriated humour. "And what fine breasts they are, my love!"

Electra looked at him and winked. "You may wake me later," she whispered, but not low enough to avoid the others hearing.

Domela blushed and fanned herself.

Felix eyed his wife and looked to Rufio. "She says that to tease me. The truth is that when I do try to wake her, she will smack me upside the head and turn her back to me."

Clara, Electra, and Martia floated out of the lamp-lit triclinium like three nymphs in a wood at dusk, leaving their husbands, Julius, and Domela sitting in silence as a servant refilled their wine cups. When that was done, they each picked up their cups and drank.

"Julius," Felix said suddenly. "I don't think you've ever told me about your parents."

"What would you like to know?" the older man replied, brushing back his pale, wispy hair.

"What did they think of you wanting to be a player? Did they chide you for it? Mock you, as Rufio's father did him?" Felix looked to Rufio who raised his cup to acknowledge the still-fresh fact as if it were a stinking pile of manure on a winter morning.

Julius was silent a moment before speaking, his mind reaching back into the distant past to recall the faces of his parents which had, long since, begun to fade and waver like a desert mirage. Then, he smiled to himself, his eyes focused on the table and the memories that returned to him, before looking up at the others. "As you know, we were not a wealthy family by any means. My mother and father worked very hard. I had no siblings, for they had lost three children before I was born. As a result, I felt that they always appreciated me, though I could be quite a handful."

"I can't believe it!" Sextus said in a most affectionate way, for he had always admired the elder player.

Julius nodded. "Yes, I was quite the disturber of the peace in our village!"

"Well, I never…" Domela began but stopped herself so he could continue, her hand touching his shoulder.

"I was! That is, until a travelling mime troupe came through our village. They stayed at the inn there and put on a free performance for the farmworkers." Julius lit up at that, the divine memory of when his purpose had come to light for himself. "I was just ten years old at the time. Gangly, and rather unfit for farm labour, though I did try. At any rate, that night when the players performed a few comedic skits for the village, I saw my neighbours' faces light up in a way that I had *never* seen before. My parents' as well. They laughed until tears poured out from beneath their lids."

"They must have been an excellent troupe?" Felix asked.

"Not really. But to me, they had achieved the greatest thing in the world: they brought joy to a normally tired and dour group of people." Julius set his cup upon the table and turned his palms upward as if to express his thanks. "It was in that very moment that I knew what my purpose in this life was, what I wanted to do. What I was meant to do!"

"And your parents? Your father?" Rufio asked. "Did they accept that?"

Julius nodded. "Just as I had seen the joy in their faces while watching the performance, they had seen the change in me, the excitement, the hope, the…the…divine spark, if you will, that had engulfed my person then." His eyes turned glossy as they all listened, moved by what he was telling them. "When I told them, my mother hugged me like she had never done before, and my father said that Apollo and his Muses had sent those players to our village that night - something which had never happened before - and that I was meant to see them. He said that if I was in that much earnest about my new-found love of theatre, and if I worked hard at it, he could foresee that I would be one of the greatest players in the empire."

Sextus smiled. "How prophetic he was, Julius. Like the leaves of Jupiter's oak tree at Dodona."

"I wish my father had been so supportive," Rufio mumbled.

"At least you knew your parents," Felix added.

Rufio smiled sadly back at Felix. "True." Rufio turned back to Julius. "Your parents sound wonderful."

"They had their flaws like any other mortal, but they did their utmost. They were supportive, and they believed in me, even though they did not understand the theatre. What they did understand was that I had made an unwavering decision, one that brought me joy. That is all they could ask, really, no?"

"And you have brought joy to thousands since," Domela said, her heart moved by the tale he had just told.

"I pray so," Julius said as he began to fidget and sit up to leave. "Now, I'm afraid the wine has got to my head and I must retire for the night." He got to his feet.

After an awkward moment, Domela followed suit. "I too am quite exhausted from our walk today. I will retire also."

"Good night to both of you, friends," Felix said, his voice low and quiet, as though he still contemplated Julius' tale.

When Julius and Domela were gone, Rufio, Sextus, and Felix sat looking at each other.

"How long have Julius and Domela been…uhm…" Rufio nodded in the direction they had departed.

"Since Delos, I think," Felix said, a smile returning to his lips. "They think they are hiding it, but we all know. Beatrice is especially annoyed." He laughed and the others joined in, having all seen Beatrice's interactions with the older woman.

Once the laughing faded into the wine cups, Sextus' voice grew thoughtful. "It is interesting what Julius said, though, is it not?"

"How do you mean?" Rufio asked.

"Well, his parents, by all accounts were poor and simple, presumably uneducated…and yet, they had the wisdom to see what lay within their son at an early age."

"Perhaps the Gods did intervene?" Rufio said.

"Perhaps," Sextus mused. "Or perhaps their belief in Julius from so very early on is what really set his flame alight, so that it was ready to burn brightly at the right moment in his life. I wish my own parents had had such a belief in me. They do now, of course, but early on they were so focussed on my older siblings that, well, I was like a dry leaf skittering around the peristylium for most of my childhood before they took notice."

"Maybe going unnoticed is not so bad?" Rufio ventured. "There were times I wished I was invisible to my father…the beatings I received!"

"And the clapping!" Felix laughed.

Rufio smirked. "There was that." He reached out to pat Peli who had curled up beside him.

After a pause, and another sip of wine, Felix shook his head. "At this moment in time, I can't even begin to think of my son as a young man with a purpose in his heart. All he does is piss, shit, eat, and wail like a piglet."

"Felix," Rufio said. "Thespis is still a babe-in-arms. Be patient."

Felix shook his head. "You know I'm not a patient man. To be honest, I can't wait for him to grow up so that I can at least get a good night's sleep. It's so hard to focus on putting on the play the Gods demand when I am sleepless and elbow-deep in excrement."

Rufio looked across the table at Sextus whose face had changed to something approaching disappointment as he looked at Felix.

"May I say something?" Sextus asked.

"Of course! You're among friends." Felix reached over and

pat Sextus' arm, but the other man's kind eyes remained fixed on Felix.

"For a long while now…since we were married really… Martia and I have been trying to have children. We love children, her especially, as I'm sure you can see… But the Gods have not seen fit to bless us with a child and that is, to both of us, deeply saddening. Only the love we have for each other has kept us together, strong… But there will, I suspect, always be a gap in our lives where the hope for a child was, a great 'what if' that will haunt us."

"I'm sorry to hear it, Sextus. Truly," Felix looked down at the table.

"You miss my point, Felix. Martia and I have only recently accepted the fact, and there is a sort of peace in that. Perhaps we will be so blessed in the next life, if the Pythagoreans are to be believed. At any rate, I urge you to be grateful, my friend."

"Grateful?" Felix repeated.

Sextus nodded. "Yes. Be grateful, in your words, in your heart, in your prayers… Let the Gods know it! For though you may be elbow deep in excrement, and your nights sleepless, time marches on. Nothing lasts, except for love. If you think your son is difficult now, wait until he is fifteen or so. Trust me, I have many nephews and nieces. There will be a point when your dark hair turns grey overnight for all the worry and frustration you will experience."

Felix unconsciously ran his hand through his hair. "You're not selling this life to me, Sextus, especially as you and your wife will have dark hair the length of your days," he chuckled, but Sextus did not laugh.

"Do you not think we would trade our dark hair, or our peaceful nights, in a second for the gifts which the Gods have laid in your laps?"

Felix's face darkened, and he filled his cup again. "You are wrong about love being the only thing that lasts forever, Sextus.

Take Terentius' work, for instance. It lives and breathes long after his death, and it shall continue to live on. That is immortality."

"Perhaps. But Terentius is long dead. I wonder what he is thinking in the Afterlife? What would he have done differently with the time the Gods allotted him?"

"I wish he would have written more," Rufio muttered.

Sextus looked quickly at Rufio, but then turned back to Felix. "I do not wish to be harsh with you, my friend, only to lend you a different perspective. Terentius' work may be immortal in a way, but you are not. And your children will grow up so very quickly. When the boatman comes for you, are you going to think on all the productions you put on across the Middle Sea, or about the legacy of love, or otherwise, which you have left to your child?"

Felix did not answer, but drank deeply of his wine.

"You speak true, Sextus," Rufio said, raising his cup to the other man.

"I speak from my heart to you both, whom I consider my dearest friends. I have had a lot of painful moments of reflection to think on this the last few years."

They were silent then, Sextus thinking of Martia and longing suddenly to be by her side.

Felix warred with himself, emptying and refilling his wine cup a couple more times, his mind struggling with the words Sextus had so daringly thrown at him. His jaw was set, and his eyes dark, but he did not speak. He would not speak.

Rufio, for all the dirt and dismay of raising a child in the world, knew in his heart that he was indeed grateful for his life. *Gods, I wish you to know it!* He had had excrement flung at him, borne many an aching head for the ring of wailing in his ears, and even set aside his purpose in reading and writing for long seasons of his life. But it was all worth it to him, for he was reminded of his blessings whenever he thought of Clara and Felicia. *My parents did not understand me,* he thought, *but I swear that I will endeavour to nurture and encourage my daughter in every way.*

"Well," Felix clapped his hands. "Considering the conversation we have just had, I would say that Apollo was right to have chosen this play of Terentius' for us to perform. Don't you think so?"

Sextus sighed and nodded half-heartedly. "Yes, Felix Modestus. Apollo knows all."

"He does. And tomorrow, we shall begin upon a grand adventure with our first rehearsal."

"Well," Sextus said, rising from his couch a little unsteadily. "I am for my bed and my wife. She cannot sleep well without me, nor I without her."

"But the night is young, and the wine is excellent!" Felix smiled, and winked at Rufio.

Sextus shook his head. "I am tired. But I am looking forward to the rehearsals." He looked at each of them. "Good night to you both."

"Good night, Sextus Annius," Rufio smiled.

Felix did not look at Sextus as he left, but shook his head. When the latter was gone, Felix turned to Rufio. "You believe what he said? Terentius is not immortal? Pff! A sacrilege!"

"He was right, Felix."

"What does he know? He doesn't even have children. He has no idea what it's like to be a father!"

"He knows what it's like to know he never will be. That seems worse."

"Come on, my friend. Now we're alone, let's drink into the early hours!" Felix shifted on his couch to lean toward Rufio.

But Rufio shook his head. "No. I'm tired too. I need sleep."

Just then there was a raucous singing in the distant atrium that echoed throughout the domus as the rest of the company returned from their escapades in the city.

"Fine then, the others will join me. You go to sleep, old man," Felix shoved Rufio mockingly.

It was at that moment that the children began crying, awoken by the newly-arrived drunkards who stumbled to their respective cubicula around the peristylium.

"Gods, not again!" Felix roared as he clenched his jaw and shook his head. "I'm not going. I'm not giving in!"

"Well, I'm going. Clara needs a good night sleep after all the feeding," Rufio said. "I'll see you in the morning."

"Fine," Felix said. "You go. I'll drink."

Rufio walked around the tables and made his way out. "Peli!" he hissed, and the dog slid off the couch to follow, pausing a moment to stare at Felix.

"You'll stay with me, won't you, Peli?"

Peli looked up with his mismatched eyes at the inebriated man, and then promptly squatted to squeeze out a turd beside Felix's couch before running after Rufio.

Felix tried to ignore the sudden stench and thrust his jaw out to finish the last of his wine. "What's a little more shit!" He stood from his couch, his ears filled with Thespis' wailing, and Electra's calls for help. "Atticus!" Felix shouted.

"Yes, Felix Modestus!' Atticus appeared at the far end of the triclinium.

"We are finished. There is a mess here you may wish to clean up." Felix pointed at the floor.

Atticus' shoulders slumped. "Yes, Felix Modestus. Good night to you."

Felix stumbled out of the triclinium and made his way around the peristylium to the staircase and to the upper level. For a brief moment, he noticed that his child was the only one crying now, and once he reached the top of the stairs, he looked down into the garden. There, beside the tinkling fountain, Rufio stood in the moonlight cradling his daughter as he told her a silly story about a donkey.

Felix noted that Felicia was mesmerized by her father's voice, that her big eyes gazed up at him with awe, and that a tiny smile tickled the sides of her mouth.

Rufio smiled too, though his eyes were tired, and his hair dishevelled. He smiled as if his life depended on it.

Felix felt a pang of jealously as Electra stepped into the corridor bouncing their wailing son in her arms.

"Get over here and help!" Electra hissed, her eyes wild in the semi-darkness.

"I'm coming!" Felix hissed back, before looking at Rufio one more time. "Good for you, my friend," he whispered, before following Electra into their cubiculum and shutting the door behind him.

VIII

HEAVE, OH!

After a warm, restless night, it was rosy-fingered Dawn who first roused Felix and Electra where they lay exhausted on their broad bed on the east side of the domus' upper story. The orange and pink light of early dawn crept in like a beautiful thief at the window to tickle their eyelids and slowly rouse them. In the plane tree outside, a pair of mourning doves cooed softly, heralds for that fine morning in late spring when the odyssey of bringing their production to life would begin.

It was always an exciting time for Felix, but this time he suspected that it would be one of his greatest challenges. His eyes opened slowly to stare at the wooden beams of the ceiling above and the rays of light angling their way through the window onto the sheets where one of Electra's long, olive legs jutted out from beneath. His eyes followed the outline of her body upward until her long, dark hair led up to her face.

Her eyes were open, still and sad, like dark pools at the heart of a wood.

"I'm sorry for last night," he whispered to her, not wanting to wake the baby on the other side of the room. "I drank too much wine, and…"

"What?" she asked softly.

"And Sextus upset me with what he said."

"What did he say?"

Felix shook his head slightly. "He held too big a mirror up to my face."

Electra gave him a tired, quizzical look.

He smiled a little sadly. "It doesn't matter."

"You love to look in the mirror," she said as she turned onto her back and stretched.

"I love you more."

Electra looked to see if he was playing with her, but his face was serious. She smiled and reached out to pull him on top of her. "Come," she said, glancing across the room at the still quiet cot. "Let's start this day properly…for good luck."

This time, they were undisturbed.

IT TOOK SOME TIME FOR THE ENTIRE COMPANY TO ROUSE themselves that lovely morning, even as the entire domus staff was already hard at work within the corridors and courtyard, and in the surrounding groves. The tinkle of bells about the necks of goats could be heard up the hill, accompanied by the peasant calls of their herder. Still, it took Felix, freshly bathed and feeling fully enthused for the day, to wake each of them by pounding a fist upon their individual doors and calling to each of them.

Groans and the sound of sick emerged from within a few of them, but eventually The Etrurian Players were awake. Some headed for the baths at the very back of the domus, while others pulled on wrinkled tunicae and stumbled to the triclinium where a light ientaculum of fruit, bread, cheese, and honey had been laid out. For those who were experiencing an inordinate amount of unease due to the volume of wine they had consumed, a separate table with cooked cabbage and sprouts in broth had been set out.

Clara, who had slept extremely well that night, entered the

triclinium to find Felix, Martia, and Sextus sitting and eating together while the rest of the company ate their cabbage in uncomfortable silence at the other end of the tables. She sat herself across from Sextus and Martia.

"Is Rufio, not ready?" Felix asked.

"He's coming," Clara said. "He's just dressing Felicia. And Electra?"

"She too is coming. She wanted to feed Thespis one more time before we get started."

"Did you do anything to help her this morning?" Clara raised an eyebrow at her old friend.

"I'll have you know that Electra visited the baths first while I watched over our son, so yes."

Sextus smiled to himself.

"And here she is," Martia said when Electra came in at the doorway wearing a red stola accented with gold. Her dark hair was braided and tied back to reveal her smiling face.

At the other end of the table, Fausto elbowed Beatrice whose eyes widened at the sight. "She hasn't looked this good in a while," he hissed into her ear.

Felix stood from his couch to take Thespis. "I'll hold him while you eat, my love."

"I'll only have a little water and fruit," Electra answered, smiling at everyone before she sat down. "I'm quite replete."

It was Beatrice's turn to elbow Fausto.

"Everyone, finish eating!" Felix said. "We have a big day ahead of us!"

There was a general murmur of conversation as everyone finished their food.

"I forgot my script!" Fausto suddenly burst out as the others began to move toward the odeon. "Sorry, I'll be right back, Dominus!"

"It's fine, Fausto. There is time enough," Felix replied, "Run and get it."

Fausto sprang from his couch and made for the domus' interior.

"Fausto, can you check on Rufio while you're there?" Clara asked.

"Yes, lady!" he called back over his shoulder.

Fausto emerged from his cubiculum grasping his copy of Terentius' play. He paused to listen. He could hear Rufio's voice as he spoke to his daughter on the upper floor, and so bound up the stairs to find him. *The cabbage and sprouts worked!* he thought, marvelling at how much better he felt. He knocked and entered the room. "Rufio?"

"It must be all that disgusting fish your mother ate!" Rufio said as Fausto came in.

"What's that you say?" Fausto said as he quickly covered his nose.

Rufio turned to look over his shoulder, one hand still on Felicia's wriggling tummy. "Oh! Sorry Fausto. I was speak to Felicia."

Fausto could see that Rufio was sweating. He glanced down to see a mass of soiled bracae upon the floor. "Is she all right? Do you want me to get Clara?" There was actual concern in the younger man's voice as he approached cautiously from behind Rufio's right shoulder.

"No need. I'm quite used to this." He paused a moment, one hand to his mouth. "Gwrra!" he heaved.

"What did you say?" Fausto asked from behind his hand.

"Nothing. Just…could you hand me a clean baby bracae from the table over there?"

Fausto turned to look and walked over. "These?"

Rufio huffed and turned, his eyes off of Felicia. "No. Those are mine, Fausto! The other ones, the smaller ones." He gestured wildly, not noticing Felicia had suddenly grown still, her baby hands balled into fists, and her lips pursed in concentration.

When Rufio turned back to Felicia, he spied her baby buttocks flexing again. "Oh, no you don't!" Rufio squealed and sidestepped.

Unfortunately for Fausto it was at that precise moment that he came up with the clean bracae, only to receive the full force of the baby's delivery upon his clean tunica and face. He stood stunned and confused for a brief moment but then as the feeling of wet heat hit, and the smell filled his nostrils, he screamed.

"Oh, I'm sorry, Fausto! You have to be quick! It happens to me all the time!" Rufio turned to look down at Felicia who fired another shot that thumped him in the sternum. "Not ag… again! Felicia…" Rufio whined. He turned to look at Fausto who stood absolutely still, his clothes and face spattered. "Don't cry, Fausto. It cleans easily."

"They're not tears, Rufio…" he growled back, his hands shaking.

"Sorry about that. You might want to hit the baths before rehearsal. Tell the others I'll be a bit longer."

Fausto turned slowly, the looser excrement falling to the floor from off his clothing, and then walked slowly from the room without another word.

Rufio watched him go and turned back to his daughter. "Are you quite finished?"

Felicia giggled and kicked her legs.

"That's quite enough fish for Mama, isn't it?" He reached for the new bracae and began wiping. "The others will be wait… Gwrra!"

A LITTLE WHILE LATER, RUFIO FINALLY APPEARED IN THE outdoor space where the others were gathered in the odeon of the domus, listening to Felix. He chewed a piece of bread in one hand, and held his daughter in the other.

"There's my little imp!" Clara said, going over to them. "What took you so long?"

"Do I smell?" Rufio asked her, his voice low.

Clara sniffed and recoiled but a little. "She got you again?"

He nodded and handed Felicia to her.

"And Fausto? I sent him to get you."

Rufio shook his head. "He didn't make it."

"Oh, no."

"Yes."

"Rufio, Clara! You joining us?" Felix asked from the stage, waving at Felicia with his hammy fist.

"Yes…yes. Sorry I took so long." Rufio greeted the others and sat at the end of one of the rows, as far from others as possible.

"Where is Fausto?" Felix asked. "He has one of the biggest roles to play."

"He's getting cleaned up," Rufio replied, his eyebrows raised.

Electra put her hand to her mouth and laughed.

"Well, we need to get started," Felix began. "I was just saying that the set pieces for this production are much simpler than before. Castor and Pollux have been working on the driftwood olive tree which will have real branches-"

"It sounds lovely, by the way!" Clara said, turning to look at the two carpenters who smiled back.

"And next will be a simple fountain of Attic design," Felix finished.

"What would 'Attic design' look like?" Pollux asked. "You still haven't told us."

"Just…you know…as they are about the city! Perhaps more of a well head." Felix said.

"Like a tap?" Pollux asked.

"I haven't seen any about the city," Castor added.

"Never mind! We'll talk about it later." Felix's impatience was already rising to the top of his mood.

"There's the one in the peristylium!" Beatrice said. "How about that one?"

"Great idea, Beatrice," Felix said. "Castor, Pollux, you can copy that one."

The two brothers looked doubtfully at each other, but said nothing more. "That's not really a tap," Castor murmured to his brother.

Felix continued. "We'll also need to get a nice ring for the character of Antiphila. One that will stand out in the glint of the firelight in the theatre."

"Something with diamonds and rubies perhaps?" Electra offered, a cheeky smile upon her lips.

"Something you could wear yourself afterward, you mean?" Felix winked back at her.

Electra shrugged.

Sextus Annius Sabinus raised his hand then.

"Please, Sextus," Felix said. "There is no need to raise your hand as though you're at the Academia. Do you have an idea?"

"I have a contact. An associate in the city who is one of the top jewellers in all of Athenae. He would certainly loan us a piece for the production, or at least sell it to us for a fair price."

"That sounds promising," Martia said beside him.

"It should be something recognizable," Clara suggested. "Perhaps a ring with a large face and an image of some sort in jewelled relief?"

Felix nodded, liking the ideas. "Sextus, would you be able to procure such a piece for the production?"

"Of course. Leave it to me, Felix." Sextus smiled, thrilled to be a part of things.

Clara reached over and took Martia's hand. "Our hands are roughly the same size, so you can measure it by Martia's."

The two women smiled and then all heads turned back to Felix.

"That's sorted, then," he said. "Quickly, for costumes… Apart from the character of Bacchis," here he looked to Electra, "the costumes will be quite simple and elegant. Single colours for each. The men shall have tunicae and cingula, and the women long peploi with the cingula hidden beneath the folds, as is traditional here." He looked to Beatrice. "No criss-crossing of ribbons, Beatrice. Remember, this is Attica, not Rome."

"Yes, Dominus," she said, thoroughly annoyed when Domela turned to look at her and touched the side of her nose.

Beatrice stuck her tongue out immediately.

It was then that Fausto stumbled into the odeon, his hair still wet, his clothes different than what they had been.

"And here comes our Syrus!" Felix declared. "Are you finished with your wardrobe change, Fausto, that we may begin our rehearsal?"

Fausto said nothing, but nodded and held up his scroll before sitting down beside Beatrice.

"What happened to you?" the girl asked.

He shook his head. "Don't ask." He eyed Felicia whose little face peered at him with large eyes from over her mother's shoulder. "She's a killer, that one," Fausto whispered to Beatrice who clearly looked confused.

"Fausto!" Felix boomed.

"Yes, Dominus?" he looked up.

"May we finally begin?"

"Yes."

"Good." Felix stood and mounted the small stage to walk slowly about the wooden planks. "*Heautontimorumenos*… The Self-Tormentor…" Felix paused and looked up to the blue sky above them. He had made his offerings in the lararium of the domus that very morning. *Please accept my offerings…* "May the spirit of Terentius be pleased with our production, and may Apollo smile upon it…"

Everyone in the odeon, including Atticus and some of the servants at the back, were silent as Felix poised himself to begin.

"Lest it should be a-"

A loud ripple cut the words off in mid air as young Thespis, so mesmerized by the sight of his father on high, let loose a flatulent bark where he sat in his mother's arms.

"Oh, dear!" Sextus said unwittingly beside them, his hand over his nose as the smell wafted among the seats.

Electra hung her head for a moment and, saying nothing, rose to go and change the baby.

"Shall I wait?" Felix called after her.

"No," she replied as she left the courtyard. "It's only the prologus!"

"Only?" Felix muttered. "It sets the scene, does it not? It pleads for the audience's understanding."

"Yes," Pollux began. "I was wondering about that. Why does Terentius seem to beg to the audience?"

"I don't know, Pollux!" Felix barked.

Rufio stood to look at Pollux. "I think it was because at the time, Terentius was receiving much criticism from the public. He wanted them to give the play a chance."

Sextus began nodding. "I have heard this as well."

"But Terentius' work is much respected now. We don't need to beg." Pollux did not seem to want to let it go. "It's not really a funny start, is it?"

"The prologus is not meant to be funny." Felix rubbed his face which was growing redder by the moment.

"It doesn't make sense."

"Maybe we should just change the play?" Felix was clearly angry now. "Who cares about transporting the audience to a golden age, a time long before our current one? Who cares about rural idylls?" Felix stepped to the edge of the stage. "Oh, I know! Why don't we set it in the mountains of Germania among the barbarians? Yes!" He spread his arms wide as if he had struck upon something. "We can have heads on spikes, warriors gnashing their teeth, and women who drink the blood of babes to honour their dark gods! How does that sound to all of you?" Felix looked at all of them.

"That doesn't sound funny at all," Pollux said, finding it hard to look at Felix.

"No. It doesn't!" Felix roared.

"Felix, please continue with the prologus," Clara said, standing up to block his view of the others for a moment. "They will understand once you perform it."

He nodded and closed his eyes. "Yes. Good idea." Eyes open again, he took a deep breath and began. "Lest it should be a matter of surprise to any one of you, why the Poet has assigned to an old man a part that belongs to the young, that I will first-"

In that very moment, as Felix was about to find his rhythm upon the road of that opening speech, his words stumbled upon seeing the goat, Nicodemus, charge toward the stage bleating in terror as Peli followed, his white teeth chomping at the latter's spindly legs.

"Aaah!" Martia cried as they sped past her.

"Peli stop!" Clara yelled as Rufio got quickly to his feet to stand between the dog and the goat.

Peli ceased his pursuit and looked from his master to his mistress.

Meanwhile, behind Rufio, Nicodemus had stopped before the stage and wheeled to peer at the canine from beneath Rufio's spread legs.

"GODS!" Felix roared. "Will everyone shut up!"

"Ah…Rufio?" Julius was pointing behind him.

"Peli go!" Rufio commanded, then turned only to see the

goat scrape the ground with his fore hoof and charge, horns down.

"Futuo!" Rufio squealed as he leapt vertically to avoid the horns aimed at Peli.

The goat rammed Peli who squealed and skidded to a halt, his teeth out.

Felicia began to cry then, and Clara handed her to Martia, so that she could go to check on Rufio.

But Rufio, now angered as if one of his farmyard animals had eaten part of the crop, turned on the goat. "No one rams my dog!"

"He's lost it," Beatrice whispered to Fausto who was already standing on his seat as if watching a burgeoning brawl in a tavern.

Rufio launched himself after Nicodemus and together he and Peli chased the beast from the odeon courtyard.

"I'm sorry," Clara mouthed to Felix who stood dejected and quite forgotten upon the stage, the scroll hanging at his side.

"I'll take Felicia for a walk if you like," Martia said to Clara.

"Thank you." Clara nodded and smiled at her before turning to sit.

Once the courtyard was quiet, all remaining eyes turned to Felix.

He stared back at them all, felt his heart racing, the angry blood pumping furiously in his neck and head. He took a deep breath before speaking. "We'll skip the prologus. I know it well. Act One, Scene One... Pollux, Julius... You're up!"

"Now?" Pollux asked, even as Julius, ever the professional, rose to his feet.

"NOW!" Felix shouted.

Pollux was on his feet and running to the stage as Felix

slumped down between Clara and Sextus, both of whom knew that it was not the time for comforting words.

Upon the stage, Pollux's Menedemus began to labour at his self-inflicted digging in the fields, sweating and grunting.

"Less grunting," Felix directed. "It's a field, not a brothel."

Pollux continued as Felix turned to look at Damon who stood at the back.

The mute nodded to his dominus and set his flute to his lips to bring the sound of country birdsong to life.

From the side of the stage emerged Julius whose aged Chremes, walking along, noticed his old neighbour, Menedemus, tormenting himself.

There was a pause, allowing a few moments for the one to contemplate the other, and then…

"Although this acquaintanceship between us is of very recent date, from the time in fact of your purchasing an estate here in the neighbourhood, yet either your good qualities, or our being neighbours (which I take to be a sort of friendship), induces me to inform you, frankly and familiarly, that you appear to me to labour beyond your years, and beyond what your affairs require."

"Excellent," Sextus whispered to himself, awed by the skill with which Julius wielded his voice.

Felix nodded and smiled, grateful for the veteran actor.

Chremes - for that is who Julius was now - continued as he approached Menedemus.

"For, in the name of Gods and men, what would you have? What can be your aim? You are, as I conjecture, sixty years of age, or more. No man in these parts has a better or a more valuable estate, no one more servants; and yet you discharge their duties just as diligently as if there were none at all." Chremes cast his eyes over his neighbour's lands before turning to the aged labourer. "However, early in the morning I go out, and however late in the evening I return home, I see you either digging, or plowing, or doing something, in fact, in the fields. You take respite not an instant, and are quite regardless of yourself. I am very sure that this is not done for your amusement. But really, I am vexed how little work is done here. If you were to empty the time you spend in labouring yourself, in keeping your servants at work, you would profit much more."

Menedemus at last ceased his digging and managed to stand up straight, his hand to his lower back.

"Good, good…" Felix muttered.

"Have you so much leisure, Chremes, from your own affairs, that you can attend to those of others which don't concern you?"

"I am a man, and nothing that concerns a man do I deem a matter of indifference to me…"

Clara leaned close to Felix, a smile on her face, her eyes locked onto Julius and Pollux. "We're off." She nudged him.

Felix smiled at last. "Yes, we are."

In the past, whenever The Etrurian Players would set out on the adventure of an entirely new production, it would be with great confidence, with an air of optimism and excitement which anyone undertaking anything would be supremely jealous of.

That was not the case this time as Felix Modestus struggled to wring the best out of his players who were, apart from Julius, forgetting their lines, stumbling over each other, or simply losing the play's plot no matter how many times they read Terentius' script.

Felix persisted, however, lashing them verbally as though he were a Persian satrap whipping his terrified front lines.

At first, it was Fausto who bore the brunt of Felix's frustration, for the younger man could not, it seemed, find humour in the slave Syrus' actions or words.

Over three days, they had barely run through the first and second acts in anything approaching a fulsome way, even though Martia had taken it upon herself to care for the children as much as she could on her own so that the company could rehearse in relative peace. Clara and Electra, of course, stepped in to relieve her and feed the children from time to time, but it was a great consolation that Martia had a knack for calming the children.

Sextus, of course, worried that his wife was becoming too attached to other people's children, but he could not bring himself to stop her, to erase the smile that seemed to constantly brighten her features in that increasingly tense domus. And tense it was, so much so that he took any opportunity to go into the city to meet with other magistrates and discuss trade and policies affecting both Rome and Athenae.

On the third painful day of rehearsals, Felix's nerves received a bit of a respite as Rufio and Julius brought out Clitipho and his father, Chremes, for the third scene of the first act.

Clitipho entered from his father's domus onto the street, speaking to his friend Clinia within.

"There is nothing, Clinia, for you to fear as yet: they have not been long by any means: and I am sure that she will be with you presently along with the messenger. Do at once dismiss these causeless apprehensions which are tormenting you."

"Rufio," Felix interrupted. "Good. But use your arms more. We need more physicality."

Rufio nodded but did not respond, waiting for Julius' Chremes to speak.

"Who is my son talking to?" Chremes said from the side of the stage, spying Clitipho emerging from his domus.

"Here comes my father, whom I wished to see; I'll accost him. Father, you have met me opportunely."

"What is the matter?"

"Do you know this neighbour of ours, Menedemus?"

"Very well."

"Do you know that he had a son?"

"I have heard that he has; in Asia."

"He is not in Asia, father; he is at our house."

Chremes' eyes widened as he looked around. "What is it you say?"

"Upon his arrival, after he had just landed from the ship, I immediately brought him to dine with us; for from our very childhood upward I have always been on intimate terms with him."

"You announce to me a great pleasure. How much I wish that Menedemus had accepted my invitation to make one of us; that at my house I might have been the first to surprise him, when not expecting it, with this delight!"

As the other players lolled on the seats of the small odeon, Rufio and Julius attempted to bring the conversation between father and son to life. But, though they had no trouble recalling their lines, the great hurdle was in inserting humour.

They spoke of the imminent arrival of Bacchis, the courtesan whom Chremes was led to believe was Clinia's mistress, but was in fact his own son's who spoke to him in that moment. The conversation focussed on Clinia, the newly-arrived friend from Asia, the son of Menedemus.

"What does Clinia say?" Chremes asked, stepping up close to his son.

Clitipho looked around. "What does he say? That he is wretched."

"Wretched?" Chremes threw his hands in the air and rubbed his shaking head. "Whom could we less suppose so? What is there wanting for him to enjoy every thing that among men, in fact, are esteemed as blessings? Parents, a country in prosperity, friends, family, relations, riches?"

"Damon, accent each of those as Julius says them!" Felix said over his shoulder, and the flute piped up.

Julius nodded and repeated. "Parents, a country in prosperity, friends, family, relations, riches?"

"Good!" Felix said.

Chremes carried on. "And yet, all these are just according to the disposition of him who possesses them. To him who knows how to use them, they are blessings; to him who does not use them rightly, they are evils."

There was a pause as Julius waited for Rufio to speak his line, but the latter was lost in the words he had been listening to.

"Rufio?" Clara hissed from the front row.

"Oh, uhm…yes. Sorry." He turned to Felix and then back to Julius. "It's just… I was thinking of the words of Chremes' character. Terentius' is spot on in his observations, isn't he?"

Felix sighed. "Yes, he's very thought-provoking, Rufio. Can we save the philosophical discussion for later, and just stick to the script? I don't want to lose this flow."

Rufio shook his head, his eye catching sight of his satchel, for he had been making his own notes while the others rehearsed, his mind bursting with ideas brought on by Terentius' play. "Sorry, yes…" He turned back to Julius who nodded encouragingly back at him. "Aye, but he always was a morose old man; and now I dread nothing more, father, than that in his displeasure, he'll be doing something to him more than is justifiable."

"If you don't insert some humour into this, Rufio, I'll do something more to you!" Felix suddenly roared.

"I told you it wasn't a funny play," Fausto said most unhelpfully from where he lay sprawled on his seat.

Felix wheeled, as if ready to flay the young player, but Rufio interrupted.

"Felix, this scene is not meant to be hilarious," Rufio

corrected, quite confident in his appraisal of the text he knew so well. "It's smart-funny, remember? It's the anticipation of-"

"I DON'T CARE!"

There was a sudden, deep, and uncomfortable silence then as no one dared speak and, far back in the peristyle garden of the domus, Thespis began to wail.

"We'll never get through this if you don't control yourself!" Electra growled at her husband before leaving the odeon to go to her son who was now giving poor Martia an earful.

Clara then took it upon herself to address the company. "Take a few minutes, everyone!" She then turned to Felix, her hand on his slumped shoulders. "Felix…"

"I'm sorry," he said. "I'm sorry I brought you and Rufio all this way for nothing."

She knelt down in front of him then to get him to look at her. "We've only just begun. You can't expect perfection so quickly, especially not with this play."

"Clara's right, Felix," Rufio said as he and Julius came down off of the stage. "There's a reason so few companies perform this play."

"All the more reason for us to undertake it!" Julius added. "And I know of only one director to manage it: The Felix Modestus!" The old man winked at Felix who smiled sadly up at him. "Give it some time. Be patient."

"I know you're right," Felix replied.

Sextus approached then, for he had returned in time to see the rehearsal of the latest scene. "With you, Clara, Rufio, Julius and Electra, things cannot but go well, Felix. The others will find the way, led by the veterans, and Rufio's knowledge of the play."

"Thank you, Sextus!" Rufio smiled.

Sextus continued. "You've been at it for three solid days, however, with little progress."

"Please don't remind me!" Felix balled his fists. "Apollo

demands discipline and restraint in the pursuit of artistic perfection. We're not even close!"

Sextus walked to stand in front of Felix with the others. "But Dionysus is the patron of the theatre in Athenae, and he encourages freedom and ecstatic pleasure, does he not?"

"Giving my lot that kind of direction could be perilous for us all," Felix joked.

Sextus smiled. "Yes, I can see that. But I can also see that the company is tired, and a thoughtful play is more draining than a mime. Do you think everyone could use a break? Perhaps tomorrow, give them the day off so that they can go into the city. This is a beautiful domus, but never leaving it can feel like a prison."

"It would do us some good." Felix stood suddenly and clapped his hands. "Yes. Thank you, Sextus. A bit of fun might enliven everyone and bring the humour to the surface. Julius, go tell the others."

"With respect, Felix," Julius replied. "As the father of our company, I think it would mean more coming from you."

Felix smiled, and then went to tell the rest of the company.

"I've never seen him so distressed about a production," Julius said to Sextus, Rufio, and Clara when Felix was gone.

"It's Athenae," Sextus offered. "Theatre is a serious business here."

Rufio and Clara clasped hands and followed the other two men into the domus, Rufio gathering his satchel as he passed.

AFTER A STRANGELY QUIET, RESTFUL NIGHT, THE NEW DAY THAT followed saw everyone rested and ready to head into Athenae to enjoy all that the city had to offer. Some of the company took ientaculum in the triclinium, enjoying the morning feast that Atticus had laid out for them, but most were so eager to get to the city that they went straight to the outer courtyard.

Three litters were waiting with their bearers sitting beneath the olive trees that flanked them.

"Where are they?" Fausto asked Castor and Pollux as he approached the central fountain where they were sitting in the morning sunshine. He pulled a chunk of the bread he had grabbed and looked around. "I can't wait to go back into the city. What a place!"

"Yeah, we know why you want to go back so badly," Castor teased, elbowing his brother.

On the other side of the fountain's rim, where Damon lay on his back looking up at the sky, the sound of grunting emerged and they all laughed.

"Even Damon knows why you love it here!" Beatrice chided Fausto who shrugged. "Are you wearing perfume?"

"Careful you don't attract a Greek oil merchant instead, Fausto!" Pollux teased. "Your pretty face will get you into trouble."

"But where are the others?" Fausto paced about the fountain.

"They're coming," Julius said as he and Domela entered the courtyard one after the other. Julius wore his finest tunica for the occasion, a long grey one with threaded acanthus borders in red and green, and Domela wore a green stola tied with silver-coloured ribbon such that it accented her squat, curvaceous figure. Her hair was loose about her shoulders which were covered by a crimson shawl.

Beatrice eyed the older woman for a moment. "Where do you think you're going all dressed up like that?"

Domela walked up to her and smiled most disingenuously. "Thank you for noticing, Beatrice." She leaned forward to whisper. "Julius loves me in this." Then she spoke louder as she pretended to look the girl up and down. "If we go to the temple, I would prefer to look respectable to the goddess. It's better than looking like a kitchen maid, no?" She moved off to join Julius in waiting beneath one of the adjacent olive trees.

Beatrice fumed in silence, looking down at her grey tunica and the single brass bangle that hung lonesomely about her thin wrist. "Cunnus," she hissed.

"Ignore her," Fausto said beside her. "She needs all that extra stuff. You don't."

Beatrice smiled thinly and pushed him.

"Finally!" Castor burst out as Felix, Electra, Rufio, and Clara entered the courtyard with the children, followed by Sextus and Martia who looked as well turned out as any emperor and empress.

"Good morning, Dominus!" Fausto saluted playfully.

Felix grunted.

"Are we taking litters into the city?" Beatrice asked Electra as she passed.

Electra smiled as she smoothed her indigo stola and flung back her dark curls. "We are, but as there are only three litters, the rest of you will have to walk."

Beatrice looked down at her leather sandals, shrugged, and smiled. "I'm fine with that. It's a beautiful day!" She was secretly pleased to see Domela sigh as she looked down at her own sandals which were fastened tightly about her thick feet. She looked at Rufio then. "I recognize that tunica!"

Rufio smiled as he spun playfully to show her the deep blue tunica with golden meander borders which she had made him for the production in Rome. "It's still my favourite!" Rufio said, making Beatrice clap joyfully. He adjusted the satchel which, of course, he brought with him, and climbed into the litter assigned to him and Clara.

"Are we going already?" Castor asked.

"You keep it up, Castor, and you can stay and work on the set designs!" Felix said, his voice most annoyed.

"Take your time, Dominus. It's early."

"I thought so," Felix replied.

"What's wrong with Felix this morning?" Clara asked Electra as she hoisted Felicia higher on her hip.

Electra leaned in as if to let the children clasp hands. "He was so stressed that he couldn't pleasure me last night, even though Thespis was sleeping soundly."

Clara coughed.

"You asked."

"I suppose that would upset him, knowing Felix." Clara answered.

"Quite," Electra said. "I had to take it upon myself, which annoyed him even more." Without another word, she climbed into her litter and reclined across from Felix with Thespis nestled beside her, dressed in a miniature tunica of white and gold to match his father's.

Clara handed Felicia to Rufio, and then climbed up into the litter, careful not to rip her crimson stola as she did so. Once in, she took Felicia from Rufio and the child began to gaze at the necklace of golden seashells about her mother's neck.

"Felix," Sextus called out. "We shall travel with you to the Olympieion, but then Martia and I will carry on. I have some meetings in the agora, and Martia is going to pick the ring for the production."

"Most generous of you, Sextus," Felix replied before he climbed into the litter beside his wife.

"Open the gates!" one of the house servants called out and the great iron double gates creaked open.

"Master Rufio! Master Rufio!"

"Stop!" Rufio said to the litter-bearers who had just lifted the litter. He stuck his head out to see Atticus running toward him, eyeing Peli suspiciously where he stood beside the litter. "What is it, Atticus?"

"I see that you are bringing your dog with you into the

city."

"Yes, is that not allowed?"

"Oh, it is. It's just that if he misbehaves, as I know he is wont to do, then there could be trouble."

"What kind of trouble?" Clara asked as the rest of the company filed past their litter and moved out onto the road to go down the hill.

"If he harms anyone, or desecrates a temple, then…well… I have seen them hang dogs before. That is all." Atticus looked most uncomfortable sharing this information.

Rufio did not seem worried. "Would you prefer I leave him here with you and Nicodemus?"

Atticus thought about it for a moment, about the chaos that had ensued since their arrival, and shook his head. "I'm sure it will be fine, so long as you keep him close to you at all times."

"Very well. We'll see you later today."

"Enjoy!" Atticus called back, relieved to have the domus empty for a spell.

Rufio leaned over the edge of the litter to speak to Peli as the bearers lifted them again. "You hear that? They hang naughty dogs in Athenae!"

Peli stood still as the litter set off through the gates, looking from his master to the interior of the domus, once, twice, three times, before barking once and charging out of the gates after the others.

It was a beautiful morning to travel down the wooded slope between the hills of Ardittos and Agras. Sunlight stretched from over the peaks of Hymettos to warm their backs as the litters made their way through the wood of pine, oak, and wild olive. Mourning doves cooed softly in the branches within the wood, their lovely chorus occasionally halted by the loud cawing of a crow hunting for carrion deeper in the trees.

The calm was broken by the company farther down the path as they burst into a song about a taverna maid at Ostia who hungered for sailors until she found her true love.

Clara laughed. "That's a new one. Not sure how Sextus and Martia will feel about that."

Rufio smiled as he gazed out into the woods. "I think they're much more liberal in their thinking than we suspected."

"True enough," Clara said, hoisting Felicia onto her lap as the litter swayed back and forth. "I do feel for her. You can see how much she loves children."

"I know." He reached out to touch his daughter's hair with his right hand, his left holding onto his satchel so that it would not tumble out of the litter.

"Why did you bring that? You think you'll get work done today?"

He shrugged. "You never know when the Muse will whisper to me."

Clara smiled at her husband and settled back while Felicia's small hands toyed gently with her face.

Rufio continued looking into the wood. *I wonder if the goddess does roam about those woods?*

Just as he thought he spied movement deep in among the trees, the wood began to thin and the high walls of the Panathenaic stadium appeared as if dropped there by the Gods. On their other side, down a wide path, there appeared a great marble plinth with a ship upon it.

"That's not something one sees everyday, is it?" Rufio pointed at the land-locked trireme which sat strangely at odds with its surroundings.

"I heard Castor and Pollux asking Atticus about that," Clara said. "That is the ship that is used to carry the goddess' sacred peplos to the Acropolis."

Rufio looked surprised. "But why do they keep it here?"

"I don't know, but it is beautiful, isn't it? There is so much mystery to this city."

The litters turned left to follow the path across the front of the stadium, and then crossed the river where the bridge arched over the Ilissos toward the Porta Hadriana. Other pedestrians and riders stopped to watch the group as they passed, wondering at the strange Latin song that cracked the morning peace.

"A little more grace now!" Felix barked at them from within his litter as they approached the gate.

"Kalimera, Praetor!" one of the guards greeted Sextus as his litter passed.

"Good morning to you, Arcas!" Sextus replied. "We have business in the city today."

The guard, whom Sextus had become acquainted with since arriving in the city, was friendly at his post, but imposing enough in his bull's hide cuirass and high, crested helmet to command the respect of his men and the pedestrians with whom he dealt. His Latin was excellent, for he dealt mainly with the population of Novae Athenae, but he still inserted a little Greek when he could. He uncrossed his thick arms and approached the praetor's litter, greeting Martia as he did so.

"Are these players with you, Praetor?"

"They are indeed, Arcas. They are The Etrurian Players!"

"Don't believe I've heard of them before," the guard said, his men behind him looking over the company who were silent now. "I've certainly seen some of them," Arcas added, looking at Castor, Pollux, Damon, Fausto, and Beatrice. "They like their drink." How could he forget seeing the troupe stumbling out of the city, drunk and singing to the sky?

"Erm," Sextus cleared his throat. "Yes, well...artistic inspiration takes many forms. I assure you they are hard at work for the Panathenaea."

"Praise, Athena," Arcas said, his hand on his armoured chest. "And the mutt following you, Praetor?" He pointed at Peli who was hiding beneath Rufio and Clara's litter. "Is it bothering you? Shall I have one of my men dispatch it for you? Gods know we have enough strays running about the city."

"Oh, no, no, no, Arcas. That dog is ours and he is in fact an integral member of the company!"

"He is?"

"Everyone loves a bit with a dog," Sextus added.

"In Rome, maybe. Here, I'm not so sure." Arcas shrugged. "Enjoy your day, Praetor."

"You as well."

"My lady," the guard bowed to Martia and waved them through.

Rufio then leaned out and looked down at Peli as their litter carried on. "You'd had better not piss on Sextus ever again. He just saved your furry neck!"

Peli eyed Rufio momentarily and then lashed him sloppily with his tongue before Rufio could pull back.

Felix nodded his thanks to the man, and the rest of the group passed beneath the arch of the gatehouse into the city. The sound of the Ilissos faded away as they entered the city into the square where the equestrian statue of Emperor Hadrianus towered over them. Sextus and Martia's litter pulled up alongside Felix and Electra's.

"We will carry on toward the agora," Sextus said. "Perhaps we will see you there later?"

"We'll see you soon," Felix said, distracted by the milling crowd staring at them, tempted to announce their arrival. He held back however, and turned to Sextus again. "Thank you for getting a ring for the production."

Sextus waved it off as if it were the least he could do, notwithstanding that most of the production was already paid out of his coffers.

"Remember, something that is recognizable and which will catch the firelight in the odeon."

Sextus nodded and his and Martia's litter carried on straight down the street toward the Acropolis.

"Maybe I should go with him to make sure he gets the right thing?" Felix said to Electra.

"I'm sure Sextus and Martia will pick something suitable. You stay with me. Besides, we need to go to the Olympieion."

Felix nodded and in that moment he spied his players who were afoot trying to sneak off toward the agora. "Just where do you think you're going?"

"To have some fun, Dominus!" Fausto said aloud, eyeing some passing girls even as he spoke.

"Not yet you don't!" Felix answered. "First, we're going to pay our respects to Zeus and Apollo, and then you may break away."

The group looked a little dejected, apart from Julius, but they fell into line and followed Felix's litter as it turned left down the street that led to the great temple of Olympian Zeus, the rooftop of which could already be seen above the neighbourhood.

In their own litter, Rufio made to speak to Clara who, he noticed, had fallen asleep among the pillows with Felicia nestled safely beside her. He smiled and watched them as the servants heaved the litter onto their shoulders once more and made their way down the street.

A FEW MINUTES LATER, THE ETRURIAN PLAYERS ARRIVED outside the walled precinct of the great temple of Zeus. The litters came to a stop beneath some olive and oak trees, the branches of which were rustled by a hot breeze that spun the dust about their feet.

While Castor and Pollux looked down the road toward the

arch of Emperor Hadrianus which led to the theatre district and the pleasures beyond, the others were busy looking up at the soaring columns and rooftop of the temple. Fausto elbowed them and pointed, and then all eyes were upon the temple.

There was an immediate sense of being small and insignificant that did not sit well with most of the players, as used as they were to being lauded, but that was perhaps the point, at least in Rufio's mind, as he thought about it. Felix's great successes had gone to his head, and hubris was never a good thing. *There is always something bigger than oneself,* Rufio thought as he clutched his satchel and turned back to the litter to wake Clara.

"Clara, we're here," Rufio whispered and nudged her gently. He reached in to take Felicia and then Clara slid down out of the litter to join the others.

Her eyes widened. "It always amazes me to stand so close to it."

"It's…big," Rufio muttered as they walked to join the others before the propylon.

"Who's this then?" Fausto said as they approached the entrance to the precinct where four statues of the same person looked down upon them.

"That's Emperor Hadrianus, Fausto!" Julius said, wondering why the younger man did not recognize him after seeing statues of him all about the empire.

"Well… I can see that!" Fausto recovered. "Why so many statues of him?"

"Because, Fausto," Julius continued, "after six hundred years of trying to build this temple, Emperor Hadrianus was the only one to actually complete it. He was a great patron of Athenae!" Julius bowed to the statue as he touched one of the bases, and then went through first.

Felix made his way to the front while Electra, holding

Thespis, fell in beside Clara and Rufio. "The Etrurian Players are here to pay homage to Zeus and Apollo!" Felix announced.

A few stray pedestrians looked at him, but there were no cheers, no thunderous applause.

Felix lowered his thick arms and grunted.

"Mind your hubris!" Electra hissed at him, her red lips pursed.

Directly in front of the propylon there was a bronze tripod that appeared to be sitting upon the hunched shoulders of defeated Persians, and beside that, a high column topped by a statue of the famed Athenian orator, Isocrates. But it was the temple itself that inspired awe, even among the most distracted of visitors. The vast rooftop, with winged acroteria upon the wide pediments, was supported by a veritable forest of one hundred and four polished marble columns that were seventeen meters high, and two meters wide.

"You could get lost in there," Beatrice said as they all stopped to look up.

"It is a wonder," Julius said beside her, his fatherly hand on her shoulder.

Domela came to stand on Julius' other side and pointed. "Look at all the statues of Emperor Hadrianus around the temple. There are so many!"

Beatrice looked askance at her. "Of course there are! He finished it, didn't he?"

Every few meters around the temple, bronze statues of Hadrianus stood as offerings of gratitude to the Roman phil-hellene emperor who had at last completed the temple as well as so much more for the city of Athena. The statues all led to a great colossus of the emperor at the west end of the temple. It glinted in the sunlight, the calm, bearded visage looking down on them as if picking out the Romans among so many Greeks, ordering them to behave whilst in Athenae.

"You're not going to visit the temple without an offering,

are you?" a woman suddenly shouted.

Rufio turned to see rows of offering sellers lined up along the inside wall of the temple precinct.

"She's right," Clara said to Rufio. "Let's get something."

They made their way with Electra to the woman's stall, ignoring the other vendors who were shouting to them.

"What do you have that is fitting for Zeus?" Clara asked the woman who was dressed in a pale blue linen tunica, her arms bare and covered in bronze bangles that jingled and mesmerized Felicia.

"Ooo, I have everything!" the woman said. "Laurel and olive wreathes woven with glass beads, oils, pottery by the finest artisans in Athenae…"

Rufio leaned over to look at the hastily-painted items and raised an eyebrow.

"I have bronze figurines, clubs of Herakles, the mighty son of Zeus, and miniature golden circlets."

"I think we just need a wreath," Rufio said.

The woman bent over and suddenly there was a loud clucking. When she stood, a flurry of white feathers erupted into the air. "I even have chickens!"

"There isn't much meat on that one!" Rufio marvelled. "It's half dead! You can't offer that!"

"Greek chickens are leaner than the Roman ones you're probably used to!" the woman bit back before depositing the bird back into its wicker cage beneath her table.

"I think we'll just take an olive wreath," Clara said. "The one with the blue beads."

"Ah, an excellent choice, lady!" the woman beamed. "That'll be one obol."

"Ah…" Rufio fished in his leather scrip, holding his satchel out of the way.

"That's about two and a half Roman asses," Clara calculated.

"That's Felix at a party," Rufio muttered.

Clara smacked his arm playfully. "We should also get a wreath for Apollo," Clara held up her hand and leaned into Rufio. "I think we could all use the help."

"Right." Rufio looked over the wares. "We'll also take that laurel corona with the yellow glass leaves."

"Another choice to please the Gods!" the woman said.

"How much?" Rufio asked, his coins in his hand now.

"Call it five asses even."

Rufio dropped the bonze coins into the woman's hand. "My thanks." He then picked up the coronae and turned to look for the others.

"Goodbye, omorfoula," the woman said as she waved to Felicia who reached out for the shiny baubles on the table.

"I hear Thespis starting to cry," Clara said as she turned to see Electra and Felix coming their way from one of the other vendors along the precinct wall. "Over here!"

Electra arrived first, bouncing Thespis to calm him. "He woke suddenly."

Then, as if by magic, he was quiet. His eyes locked onto Felicia's, and the storm abated as rapidly as it had arrived.

"These two are going to be trouble," Felix said as he joined them, his arms filled with a basket of offerings from votive pieces in clay and bronze, to flowers and wreathes, and even a miniature, jewelled corona for the King of the Gods.

"Is that all you have?" Felix said, looking at Rufio's offerings.

Rufio shrugged. "Yes. One for Zeus, and one for Apollo Delphinios' altar on the other side of the wall."

Felix nodded. "Of course. I bought enough for everyone to give something. I know they're saving their coin for the tabernae and brothels afterward." Felix looked around. "Where are they? This temple is so sprawling, I can't see the people for the columns!"

"There they are," Electra pointed, "gathered before the steps of the pronaos. They've travelled the world, and yet they always look like bumpkins when things become serious."

"Hey, there's only one true bumpkin here!" Rufio puffed out his chest and cheeks playfully, making the children giggle.

Electra leaned over and smelled him. "At least the smell of the farm has quit you!"

Rufio turned to her, but she smiled, a rare and hypnotizing occurrence.

"We're wasting time!" Felix said. "Let's go." He marched off toward his players. "The Gods wait for no man!"

Rufio, Clara, and Electra followed Felix who was already with the others, handing out offerings.

"Wait! Where's Peli?" Rufio said suddenly, turning about to look. "He's gone!"

"He'll be fine," Clara said. "He's probably just exploring. He'll find us. He always does."

Rufio shook his head in frustration before continuing on. "Should have left him at the villa," he muttered.

When The Etrurian Players were all gathered in front of the Olympieion, they stood as if struck dumb for a moment, staring up at the structure.

"It's rather large, isn't it?" Fausto commented.

"That's what Calypso said to me the other night!" Pollux laughed.

"Who's Calypso?" Domela could not help asking.

It was Castor's turn to laugh. "She's Pollux's favourite lupa at the House of the Nymphs!"

"Oh," Domela grunted, annoyed she had blundered into that, especially as Beatrice was laughing into her hand.

"Are we going in, or not?" Electra asked, stepping forward to go up the wide, white stairs.

Everyone followed, Rufio last as he craned his neck to look up at the blue and gold ceiling at the top of the soaring

Corinthian columns. He felt as though he were stepping into a forest of titanic birch trees, their white trunks rising up to the heavens. The sound was strange in that forest, coming and going, bouncing off of the great bronze doors that seemed more fitting for the halls of Olympus than of anything in the mortal realm. Rufio gulped and stepped through the doors to catch up with Clara and Felicia.

There were many people in the temple, but one would not have thought so for they were dwarfed by the stature of everything within it - bronze tripods, altars, fountains, and the columns leading along the sides of the massive cella, drawing all eyes to the chryselephantine statue of Olympian Zeus.

The King of the Gods was seated upon a great marble throne with a sceptre in one hand and the Goddess Nike in the other. He looked down on the mortals around him, stern and expectant. At his feet was a broad marble altar groaning with offerings which the priests were continually moving and removing to make room for more.

The troupe of players approached, each placing their chosen offerings upon the altar before stepping back and to the side, the scented smoke of incense swirling about them, clouding their eyes just enough to make them wonder whether they had strayed into a dream for a brief moment.

"Father Zeus..." Felix said as he, Electra, and Thespis stepped to the front of the great altar. "Grant us victory in the performance ahead. We honour you and offer you these gifts in thanks." Felix placed the miniature corona on the altar, Electra a bronze votive of Nike, and then they both laid a large glass eye on Thespis' behalf.

"Father Zeus," Electra whispered. "Please bless and protect our son, now and always."

They were silent for a few moments before they stepped aside. Then Rufio, Clara, and Felicia approached.

Felicia stared up in silent astonishment at the King of the

Gods whilst Rufio and Clara jointly held out the olive wreath.

"Father Zeus, Protector of Travellers…" Clara said. "Thank you for bringing us safely to Athenae. We honour you."

Rufio bowed his head, his arm touching Clara's, his eyes closed. "May our actions lead us to our victories, Oh, Jupiter… I mean Zeus!"

Clara looked at him quickly.

"Father Zeus," Rufio corrected.

"Do not worry, Roman," a nearby priest said as he emerged from a cloud of smoke to the right. "In this temple, Zeus and Jupiter are one, the merging of two worlds as Hadrianus, who watches over this great temple, intended."

Rufio looked at the priest. "Thank…thank you." Rufio heard a great flapping and looked up to the ceiling above the statue where an eagle was perched upon a beam. "Is that…" he began, clearly astonished, but the priest interrupted him.

"Zeus welcomes your offering. Now, please move along to allow others to pay their respects."

Rufio turned around to see a long line of people snaking down the cella and through the doors to the light beyond. "Oh, right. Sorry." Rufio followed Clara and Felicia, and together they went to join the others who were making their way back out of the temple.

Once they were all gathered outside in the sunlight, Felix turned to address them.

"Before you all disperse to your various distractions, there is one more thing to do." He looked at his players. "It was Apollo who sent us here. It is Apollo to whom we should offer our sincere thanks."

They all nodded, some turning their eyes to the sun in the sky above, others in the direction of the stairs to the left of the temple, those that led down to the river and the shrines beside it.

"Follow me," Felix said, leading the way.

Damon struck up a gentle tune upon his flute then, and The Etrurian Players made their solemn procession into the shaded quiet around the temple of Apollo Delphinios. They all grew silent, apart from the music, as they descended the stairs and emerged onto the area before the temple. The law courts of the Panhellenion were closed, it seemed, and farther down the riverbank, the temples of Chronos and Rhea stood like shadows among the plane, pine, and olive trees.

The Etrurian Players stood before the temple of the god who had sent them there and, without a word, they set about fashioning their own wreaths of olive to offer to Apollo.

Felix looked on, proud that they did not need the instruction. *Apollo, please accept all of our offerings.*

Rufio, holding onto the laurel wreath they had purchased, looked at Clara. "Let's go in before the others."

Clara nodded and, hoisting Felicia more comfortably in her arms, followed Rufio through the bronze doors into the temple.

After the sheer magnitude of the temple of Zeus, the temple of Apollo seemed minute, though its thick Doric columns were wide and sturdy. Inside, the scent of woodsmoke and incense was strong as they walked down the cella toward the main altar, flanked by bronze tripods in which flames flickered.

Rufio and Clara stood before Apollo, his eyes seeming to gaze down upon them, his fingers hovering above the strings of his lyre as if ready to pluck the notes that they heard only in dreams. Together, they raised the wreath, each holding a side, and laid it upon the altar, the fire from the nearest tripod catching the yellow glass among the leaves.

"Apollo, we honour you…" Clara began.

"Guide us and inspire us in this wonderful play," Rufio added. "Help us to make the Athenians feel its true meaning."

Apollo's marble eyes gazed down upon them, through

them, and in that moment, the temple serpent slithered around the altar, passing before their feet, to go to the other side.

Clara froze for a moment, but Rufio held her hand. "He has heard us."

Just then, the others came in from the pronaos and the bronze doors, the murmur now hushed as they followed Felix through the cella to the altar.

Rufio and Clara stepped back to allow them through, Clara standing beside Electra so that the children could quiet each other.

One by one, the members of the company placed their olive wreaths upon the altar, their prayers and hopes their own. Then Felix stepped forward to place the small bronze votive statue of Apollo upon the altar.

"Oh Apollo, Lord of Light, and Art, and Music... Master of the Muses... The Etrurian Players are here to honour you, and to thank you for bringing us to this great city of Athenae..."

Domela jumped slightly when she spied the serpent make its way from behind the altar to the far side of the temple, but other than that, all was quiet but for the flickering flames.

"Oh, Apollo!" Felix raised his muscled arms. "Look favourably upon our humble production of *Heautontimorumenos*. May we do your faith in our skills the utmost justice. Humbly, we ask for your blessing. Please accept our offerings."

Felix lowered his arms and stepped back. For a brief moment, he felt uncomfortable beneath Apollo's gaze. He bowed his head.

It was at that opportune and silent moment of reflection that Felix's son decided to make his own flatulent offering, and it echoed about the temple harsher than any musical note Damon could have summoned upon his flute.

Felix's eyes widened in horror and he raised his head. "I... I'm..."

The players looked at each other, unsure what it meant, and then the scent of Thespis' soiled bracae embraced them all.

"Gwrra!" Fausto heaved.

"Apollo, we thank you!" Felix said hastily before turning and leading them all out of the temple.

Electra's face was ashen at the experience, but she secretly hoped that Apollo would understand.

Gasping in the fresh air outside, the players were grateful for the light and air about Apollo's temple.

"Can we finally go, Dominus?" Castor asked from where he leaned against an olive tree, inhaling deeply of the warm air.

"We need to change Thespis," Electra told her husband. "Just let them go."

Felix nodded. "Very well. Off you go, the lot of you. Enjoy, for tomorrow our rehearsals recommence in earnest!"

"Yes, Dominus!" several of them clapped before making their way to the stairs that led away from the river and back up to the Olympieion. They were all gone within seconds, Julius and Domela bringing up the rear of the eager procession to the agora.

"I'll help you," Clara said to Electra, and the two of them went to a quiet spot along the riverbank to clean and change the wriggling infant in Electra's arms.

"I pray to the Gods," Electra said as they walked, "that Thespis is someday as prolific in his art as he is in his excretions." She smiled at her son. "You're going to give your father an ill humour!" The two women laughed as they walked.

Felix however, stood staring back at the temple, silent in another, more apologetic, prayer to Apollo.

Rufio stood there with his satchel, looking from the river, to Felix, and to the temple. He decided to give his friend a quiet moment, and so began to walk around the edge of the law court to look down the river. The quiet in that place soothed his generally anxious mind, and he knew that if they had more time, he would just settle himself beneath a tree and write until his eyes closed and he was enveloped in sleep. "Like him," Rufio said to himself as he spied the same rough-looking man he had seen before sitting beneath an oak tree scribbling furiously upon a long scroll. "Hey, oh!" Rufio called out and waved to the fellow. "What are you working on?" he said as he approached the younger man.

The man continued his work, his hand not pausing as he wrote.

"I asked what are you working on?" Rufio said again as he got closer, but then something stopped him in his trajectory toward the stranger. "Do I know you?"

The man finally stopped and looked directly into Rufio's eyes. "Free me! Make them *see* me!"

"What did you say?" Rufio asked, his heart racing inexplicably as he remembered some thread from a long-ago dream. "Who are you? You from Rome? You sound like it."

The man went back to writing, ignoring Rufio's questioning.

"Must be from Lugdunum," he muttered.

"Who are you talking to?" Felix asked as he appeared at Rufio's shoulder.

"Him." Rufio pointed to the man who was now walking away. "Where are you going?"

"Ah… Rufio?" Felix gripped his friend's shoulder. "There's no one there."

"Of course there is!" Rufio protested. "Look at him walking away. A most unfriendly person!" He shouted at him.

Felix shook his head. "I think we need a drink." Felix began to pull Rufio away. "Ah, I see him!" he suddenly shouted.

Rufio wheeled around quickly. "Finally!"

"There!" Felix said. "Peli! Come on, boy! Good dog!"

Farther down the river, from between the temples of Chronos and Rhea, a blur of black and white came charging toward Rufio and Felix.

"Where have you been?" Rufio shouted at his four-legged bit of mischief.

As Peli ran, he slowed to sniff at something.

"Look, see!" Rufio pulled at Felix's tunica as Peli paused beside the departing man who pat his furry head before carrying on his way.

"All I see is Peli pissing…again!" Felix said.

"The man was petting him."

"All right, my friend. Time to go. I think you've had too much sun already." Felix pulled Rufio away as Peli joined them.

"But we're in the shade here!" Rufio protested.

"Come. The women are waiting for us." Felix pointed to where Electra and Clara stood with the children by the stairs leading up. "Athenae awaits!" Felix said as he and Peli walked to join them.

Rufio turned one last time to look the other way. Nobody was there. "Am I going crazy?" He shook his head and, holding his satchel to his body, went to join the others.

THEY FOUND THE LITTER-BEARERS DOZING IN THE MID-morning light, all of them leaning against the two litters which they had parked along the outer precinct wall of the Olympieion.

Felix sighed when he saw them. "Arise! *The* Felix Modestus has returned!" His voice echoed in the street, turning the heads of several pedestrians within earshot as the litter-bearers jumped to. "Onward!"

"Felix," Electra said to him. "Clara and I will ride in our litter. We need to feed the children again. You and Rufio can go in his."

"Fine. Yes. Very well." Felix steered Rufio to the other litter. "If I ate as much as my son, you would have to roll me to the agora!"

Rufio looked across at Clara. She smiled and nodded to him that she was in agreement with the plan and climbed up into the slightly larger litter before closing the curtains.

"Where to, Dominus?" the head litter-bearer asked Felix as he climbed into the litter to face Rufio.

"The agora. But go by way of the sanctuary of Dionysus."

"Yes, Dominus!" the man replied before giving his men a count to lift. "Ena, deo, tria!" The litter-bearers all lifted and grunted at once and, a moment later, they were swaying down the cobbled street toward the great arched gateway that had been erected for Emperor Hadrianus' visit to Athenae.

"The emperor is everywhere in this beautiful city," Felix commented as he flung the curtains wide so that they could see everything. The crowds were thickening, going toward the theatre district and the agora, so it was possible to view things at a reasonable pace. Felix also enjoyed that the Athenians were watching him as they passed, of course. "Even the upper story of the arch looks like the scaena frons of a theatre."

Rufio leaned out to look up and saw what Felix was referring to. Three doorways rested atop a great arch through which traffic passed into the older part of Athenae. There was an inscription which Rufio tried to make out as they passed. "'This is the city of Hadrianus, and not of Theseus'".

"Well, it's not wrong. Most of the city beyond the gate, including the great Olympieion, was completed by Hadrianus." Felix leaned out to look up at the gate from the other side. "'This is Athenae, the ancient city of Theseus'. Well, at least our Roman forbears gave credit where credit was due."

"I should hope so," Rufio said before a blur of black and white darted past his side of the litter. "Peli, no!" he shouted, but he was too late to stop Peli from darting in and out of the thick crowd and frightening a woman carrying a basket of field greens upon her shoulder.

A loud cry went up as a flurry of soaring stalks went down into the dirt at the people's feet.

The woman scrambled to pick up her produce before they were all trampled.

"I'm so sorry!" Rufio said, and as their litter passed her, he dropped a couple dupondii in among her produce.

She looked up at Rufio with stormy blue eyes. "Futuere, Roman ass!"

"I said I was sorry!" Rufio protested, wishing he had not dropped his coins. He turned back to Felix. "I'll bet she doesn't know a lick of Latin, but for that!"

Felix laughed, and reached out to grip Rufio's leg with a huge smile on his face. "It's good to be together again!"

Rufio smiled back and laughed. "I miss it, even though you sent the gaudiest wagon in Athenae to pick us up!"

"I knew you would enjoy that!"

Rufio shook his head, then leaned out again to see Peli trotting alongside the litter, nearly tripping up the bearers. "Did you see how blue that woman's eyes were?"

"Yes," Felix said gravely. "We'd better get you a mati in the agora before you shit yourself and fall over." He then made to spit three times at Rufio.

"I see that Electra has rubbed off on you!" Rufio laughed, wiping his face.

"Hmm." Felix frowned and looked out at the crowds as they passed.

"What?"

"Nothing."

"I know that look. What's wrong?" Rufio stared at Felix, the litter swaying back and forth as it picked up a bit of speed, and then slowed again.

"Electra is not happy with me today."

"Why?"

"I've been so distracted…supremely stressed, actually!" Felix shook his head.

"So? It's normal, isn't it? You're running a theatre company, and you are in the birthplace of theatre, at the behest of Apollo himself, to perform a play you're not sure will be well-received."

"Thank you for putting it thus, Rufio."

"It's normal that you have a lot on your mind is all I'm trying to say."

"I know that. But what is *not* normal is…" Felix shook his head. "Never mind. It will be fine."

"What?" Rufio pressed.

Felix looked around as if to make sure no one was listening, then leaned closer to Rufio and whispered. "I've been so stressed and distracted…I…I couldn't pleasure Electra last night."

"Ha!" Rufio could not help but chuckle, however briefly. "You?"

"Venus denied me my usual skills, which are not inconsiderable, I'll have you know!"

Rufio held up his hand. "Yes, all right. I'm sure. But Felix, you need to go easy on yourself. There is a lot going on. It's normal to be distracted."

"For you maybe."

Rufio smiled. "Actually, things in that particular department are rather good!"

Felix observed his friend for a moment, and though his first inclination was jealousy and bitterness, he quickly overcame it. "Well, at least one of us is victorious for Venus."

"I'm sure it was an isolated incident," Rufio reassured him. "Who knows? After a day out and a bit of relaxation, you'll be as excited as a satyr in a grove of nymphs!"

One of the litter-bearers chuckled at that.

"Laugh again and I'll have you flogged!" Felix barked.

"Yes, Dominus!" the man replied quickly.

Felix leaned out to his left and pointed. "Look, Rufio! The great theatre of Dionysus. Slow down here!" he shouted to the litter-bearers.

To the right of the litter, surrounded by a low wall, was the sanctuary of Dionysos Elefthereus, a place of peace in the middle of what was otherwise a crowded throughway. A wide altar to the god sat in the middle of an area of green grass and wildflowers, and on the left side of the sanctuary were two temples to Dionysus, the walls of which were filled with musical instruments, theatrical masks, and other offerings from the performers who had either hoped for victory, or achieved it. More offerings lay at the feet of the great chryselephantine statue of Dionysus in the larger temple.

"Incredible," Rufio said below his breath as he looked upon the high scaena frons and the heights of the cavia which seemed to climb up the rocky hillside of the Acropolis. The seating clung like ivy to the rock up to the columned monument of Thrasyllos, the long ago choregos who had been an Athenian citizen who financed and prepared dramatic productions not paid for by the state. "I feel dizzy just looking up at it." Rufio looked to the right of the theatre of Dionysus to see a large, square, covered structure almost built into the side of the theatre. "And that?" He pointed.

"That is the odeon built by Pericles. Well…originally built by Pericles. The dictator, Sulla, destroyed that one, and so it was rebuilt by King Ariobarzanes of Cappadocia."

"No wonder people aren't welcoming to Romans here." Rufio shook his head.

"That is where the musical contests for the Panathenaea take place."

"We should come and see some performances while we're here," Rufio said as the litter moved along.

Felix was quiet.

"What's wrong? Aren't you amazed by all of this? I suppose you've been here many times before. Unlike me."

"It's not that. When I look at these wondrous monuments to art and creativity here, in this place, I feel…I feel like an imposter."

"Ha! You? Come on, Felix. You can't be serious? You're the most sought after company around the Middle Sea. Kings and emperors want you to perform."

"Ah, but here, in Athenae, in the place where our craft began, they see through all of that. The favour of kings and emperors comes and goes, but the performances live on forever…the good ones anyway. How can I live up to that?"

Rufio did not quite know what to say. He understood in a way, for when he began to set his stylus to a sheet of papyrus, it was all he could do not to think of the great poets and playwrights he had read all the days of his life.

"In that theatre, for instance…" Felix pointed to the theatre of Dionysus which they had just passed. "Do you know who performed there during the Panathenaea and the Dionysia?" Rufio nodded, but Felix continued anyway. "Sophocles, Aristophanes, Euripides, Menander, and others won laurel crowns here! How can I not worry when we are in this place?"

"I understand that, Felix, but you are the one who brings those works to life, and whom people love for it."

"I know, but I still can't help but think about it."

"Where has your trust in the Gods gone, Felix? Apollo himself has blessed you, and entrusted you to do this!"

Felix did not respond, for the thought only roused more of the anxiety which he hated himself for. He breathed to calm himself.

They were silent for a moment as the litter-bearers picked up speed and passed the long stoa of Eumenes, the King of Pergamon. The stoa, which provided shelter for theatre-goers and pedestrians, stretched from the theatre of Dionysus and the monument of Nikias all the way along the Asklepieion and toward the odeon of Herodes Atticus.

"There is so much here," Rufio said as he watched some people conversing in the shade of the stoa while others were writing or just enjoying the midday sunlight as it beat down.

"And there it is," Felix nudged Rufio and pointed again.

"What?"

"The odeon where we will make or break our reputation as the greatest theatre company in the empire. Slow down!" he told the litter-bearers who were sweating quite profusely now.

Beyond a small grove that was a sanctuary of the Nymph stood the newest odeon of Athenae, built by Hadrianus' friend, Herodes Atticus. It rose up in four stories of stone arches to a pediment from which the tiled rooftop fanned out to completely cover the cavea of the odeon. Statues stood looking out from the arched niches above, and below a few musicians wandered in and out of the higher archways of the metaskenion.

"Can we go inside?" Rufio asked. "It must be magnificent!"

"Another day," Felix said, not wanting to see the seating for five thousand spectators, nor bear the harsh silence of the interior.

"I do wonder," Rufio said, "why we are performing a play in the odeon. Isn't it for musical performances?"

"I guess they're dumping the Roman company in the Roman building."

Rufio shrugged. "Then I suppose we'll have to give them the best Roman performance they'll have ever seen, won't we?"

Felix eyed him and could not help but smile. "You're unusually optimistic these days. What's happened to you?"

"I don't know. I'm just happy, I suppose." Rufio did not realize it but he clasped his satchel tightly to his body when he said that.

Felix noticed, but did not say anything, for he was still too distracted by the looming walls and archways of the odeon they were passing. "We have to make this work," he muttered as he took it all in.

"We will," Rufio said.

"First, we need to put some life into this production! On to the agora now. Faster!" Felix barked as he spied the litter with Electra and Clara pulling away.

The bearers grunted and pressed on between the Pnyx and the Hill of Ares toward the agora of Athenae.

"They certainly are taking their time!" Electra said to Clara as she slid out of the litter where she had the bearers park it beside the fountain at the southwestern entrance to the agora. She took Thespis down and held the curtain aside for Clara to disembark with Felicia. "I'm so thirsty. I feel like I've been in the desert for a week!"

Clara laughed and nodded. "It's no wonder, Electra. Your son drinks without end. Come, let's get some water at the fountain while we wait for our men."

"We will walk from here," Electra said to the litter-bearers.

The men nodded and went to sit in the shade to wait for the other litter.

The small fountain house lay just off of the road, in the shadow of the Hill of Ares, the place where the Athenian court passed judgement and where the God of War himself was once tried by the other gods of Olympus. The sound of trickling water echoed playfully off of the walls and ceiling of the open-sided fountain where the two women sat on the edge, taking turns cupping their hands to drink while the other held the children.

"What is taking them so long?" Electra said as Thespis

began to whine. She took a little water and rubbed his face gently, tickling him until he giggled.

"I'm guessing they went slowly so that Felix could tell Rufio about the theatres. We didn't really have a good view of them when we arrived."

"I'm sure everyone could see you in that wagon Felix sent!" Electra laughed. "*The* Felix Modestus can be such a child!"

"It's the key to staying youthful and keeping up with you, my dear!" Felix's voice came down the street as the other litter appeared in front of them.

"It's about time!" Electra said as she and Clara stood to meet them.

The litter was set down beside the other one and out slid Felix and Rufio, the former heading straight for the fountain to take a few great gulps of the fresh water before turning to kiss his wife.

"Oh, now you're interested, are you?"

Felix looked sheepish for a moment, but said nothing.

"Everything all right?" Rufio asked Clara as he came up to her, adjusting the strap of his satchel.

"We're just fine." She touched Felicia's nose and smiled.

Felix turned to the litter-bearers. "Take the litters around to the Porta Hadriana. We'll see you there later for the journey back."

"Yes, Felix Modestus!" the head litter-bearer said.

Felix turned to Electra, Clara, and Rufio. "Shall we walk?"

"Lead the way." Rufio fell into step beside Clara and Felicia and, together, they followed Felix, Electra, and Thespis who was looking over his mother's shoulder at Felicia.

COMPARED TO THE FORUM ROMANUM, THE ANCIENT AGORA OF Athenae was much more sedate, though no less crowded. As the beating heart of Athenae, there was much in the way of activity with citizens, officials, priests, and philosophers mingling to talk, or coming and going from the various stoas, temples, shrines, the bouleuterion, and the great odeon and gymnasium of Agrippa.

Rufio craned his neck as they walked, taking it all in.

"What do you think, Rufio?" Electra asked over her shoulder as she walked proudly beside Felix.

"I think I don't see many women about," he replied, spying the looks from some pedestrians.

"Never mind that. What about the place?" Electra persisted. "Much of this was here when Rome was but a mud hut village."

"Well," Rufio protested. "I'm not so sure about that!"

"I am!" she replied, her head high.

"She's very proud of her heritage," Clara whispered to Rufio who simply nodded.

"It's quite beautiful, Electra," Rufio said aloud. "You are right."

"Of course I am!"

"Why is that man stark naked?" Clara suddenly said.

As they came along the thick columns of the temple of Ares in the centre of the agora, they saw a bearded man with short, unkept hair standing in the shade of the odeon of Agrippa, beneath the great statues of Triton. He was indeed naked, and not very clean. He stood beside his tunica, which had been thrown down upon the ground beside him, and he was exercising, stretching, and puffing out his chest to try and match the monstrous sculptures above him.

"Oi, take it inside the gymnasium!" Felix yelled.

"Shhh! Felix!" Electra hissed, averting her eyes from the man. "That's Melampus, the seer. Just ignore him. Don't draw attention to us." Electra walked more quickly, and the others tried to keep up.

But it was too late. The naked seer stopped his calisthenics and stepped into the sunlight beyond the shadows. "YOU!" he shouted, pointing directly at Rufio. "YOU! Bag man!"

Rufio felt his heart begin to race. *Please no curses. Please no curses.*

Melampus began to follow them, his eyes wild but never leaving Rufio's back. "YOU, WAIT!"

"I don't want any tips or fortunes told, thank you!" Rufio said. He could not help but notice that the Athenians passing by them paid no heed to the completely naked - and, frankly, quite dirty - man in their midst. Rufio put up his hands as if to fend off the seer's musty smell.

The seer continued in his pursuit, and so Rufio fell back to put himself between the man and Clara and Felicia. "Have you seen him yet?" Melampus finally said, ceasing his pursuit.

Rufio stopped dead and turned. "What did you say? Seen who?"

Melampus touched the side of his big nose, his bushy eyebrows rising and falling a couple of times, and then promptly turned and went away.

Rufio stood there for a moment, rooted to the spot as the dust of the agora swirled around him.

"Rufio, come on!" Felix shouted from up ahead where they were heading for a wide stoa along the Panathenaic Way.

Rufio ran after the others, wanting to put as much space between himself and the seer. "Where did you say we can get those evil eye mati things?" he asked.

THE TWO-STOREY STOA BUILT BY ATTALUS, RULER OF Pergamon, was a long, covered colonnade with over forty rooms on the ground floor. From these, merchants sold their wares to the people of Athenae, and there was everything from clothing, food and spices, to ceramics and votive offerings.

As soon as Electra, Felix, Clara, and Rufio came into view,

the merchants came to life, appearing at their doorways with special offers that were, apparently, available that day only, just for them.

Electra ignored the many pleas for her business as she passed slowly, whilst Clara offered her polite 'thanks, but no thanks'.

"What a beautiful baby!" one merchant called out. "I have some tunicae that will help him match the beauty of his mother!"

"Lady of Rome!" another called to Clara. "The finest gold ornaments for you and your lovely daughter! Wrought from the best mines in all of Graecia!"

"They are persistent, aren't they?" Rufio said once he caught up to Felix.

"They are, but it's still not so bad as Ephesus. I've cracked many a skull of a merchant who dared to lay hands on Electra. Saved the poor bastards, really."

"Saved? By cracking their skulls?" Rufio looked up at Felix.

"Yes. If I had let Electra have at them, they would have been dead! Then where would the company be without our leading archimima?"

"Of course," Rufio shook his head.

Just then, Electra turned and went into a shop.

Clara followed her and waved Rufio and Felix over.

The shop, aptly-named 'Eyes on You', was run by a merchant from Corinthos who seemed to know Electra immediately.

"The great Electra is in my shop again! At last!" The man was tall and thin, with an artisan's hands, long fingers stained with paint and clay. He reached out to take Electra's free hand and kissed it before turning to Felix. "And *The* Felix Modestus! It is an honour. I had heard you were coming to Athenae for the games."

"Biton," Electra smiled. "It is good to see you again."

"And you, lady!" The man turned his attention to Thespis. "And you are a mother now! Wonderful! Ftousou!" he spat.

"These are our friends, Biton," Felix said. "They come all the way from Etruria to perform with us."

"Ahh, well…" The merchant turned and bowed to Clara who held Felicia close, out of range of more spitting, and to Rufio who had just joined them. "You have a beautiful daughter, lady."

"Thank you," Clara replied.

Biton turned back to Electra. "I am guessing that you require some matia for these beautiful children?"

"Yes, indeed," Electra answered. "They garner a lot of attention, and so we require the Gods' protection at all times."

"You've come to the right place! I have the greatest selection in all of Athenae!" Biton stood aside to show the interior of his shop.

Rufio felt dizzy as he looked around, for everywhere his gaze went, it was met with the deep, penetrating stare of eyes, dark blue, pale blue, turquoise, and other shades of blue he had never even seen before.

"Perhaps something small, for the children? An anklet, or a necklace?" Biton showed Electra and Clara to a table with jewelry laid out upon it and they began to browse. He then turned to Felix and Rufio. "Ah, Felix Modestus. As ever, the jealous eyes of the world rebound from your magnificent person. I don't suppose you require a new mati?"

Felix smiled. "No. I still have the one you sold me last time. But thank you, Biton."

The man turned to Rufio then, and gasped. "Your friend, however!" He shielded his eyes as though he were Icarus on his way to the sun, pained and blinded. "He has the mati upon him, and badly too!"

"I do?" Rufio said, panic in his voice. "It's that damned naked seer out there!"

Biton shook his head, still shielding his eyes. "No. Melampus is of no harm. You…you have been gathering your mati for some time, it seems. Have you argued with many people on your journey here?"

"Ye…yes," Rufio answered as Biton began to lower his hands.

"Have you been sick of late?"

"Yes. Quite."

"Have you looked at someone with blue eyes as well?"

"Yes!" Now Rufio was worried.

"There is something more. You also have an otherworldly mati upon you. Yes, yes… Quite discomfiting."

Rufio put his hand to his chest as he felt his heart racing. "Gods! I knew it! I should have stayed home! I feel faint!"

"Well, it's no wonder!" Biton said. "With all that you've been through. And now, you are to perform?"

"Maybe I shouldn't?" Rufio wondered.

Felix's eyes shot wide and he looked at Biton directly, shaking his head violently as Rufio bent over to catch his breath.

Biton nodded and turned back to Rufio. "That is not the answer. Glory awaits you upon the stage, to be sure. But you must be protected!"

"Anything!" Rufio declared. "What do you have?"

Biton led Rufio to where several matia hung from a wooden rod. "You require a medallion, and a strong one at that." His hands hovered over several of varying sizes. A few were entirely of glass, others with eyes set in bronze or silver. At last, Biton's hand rested upon one with a large, brilliant blue lapis eye set in the middle of a gold medallion with granulation around the edges. "This is the one that will offer you the most protection!"

Rufio looked at the medallion, instinctively clinching his leather purse beneath his satchel. "That looks expensive."

"It is, but the Gods prefer gold. It is purer than other metals. It draws their immortal eyes to you more easily, and so offers you more protection." Biton took down the medallion and hung it around Rufio's neck so that it rested upon his chest.

"It's the size of an apple!" Rufio protested.

"Yes, but a golden one!" Biton offered. "As though from the bough of the Hesperidean tree itself!"

"It's a bit gaudy for me," Rufio said.

Biton shrugged, and made sure to rub his eyes, so blinded was he by the mati clinging to the man before him.

Rufio looked from the medallion upon his chest to Felix. "What do you think?"

Felix smiled but nodded. "It will offer you protection, that's for certain!"

Biton nodded. "As always, The Felix Modestus knows all."

"Clara?" Rufio turned to her and spread his arms wide.

Clara's eyes locked onto the medallion, but she forced herself not to laugh. "Well…it's…ah… If you like it, then you should get it, Rufio."

Rufio still was not sure.

To help him along, Biton held up a polished, bronze mirror for him.

Suddenly, Rufio felt something beside his leg and looked down to see Peli standing there looking up at him. The dog barked, surprising Biton who had not seen him.

Biton screamed and the mirror he held whipped back into his eye.

The women turned to look as Biton held his face, and Peli continued to bark.

Rufio stood looking from his dog to the merchant and back. "I'm so sorry. He does that," he said to Biton. "Peli, where have you been?" He crouched down to hold his dog back from Biton.

Peli began to lick at the medallion. "You like it? Shall I get it?"

Peli barked again.

Biton noted this and stood straight again. A bruise was already forming beneath his left eye. "The Gods do speak through animals sometimes, do they not?"

"They do," Rufio said. "Not sure about this one, though." He cast an embarrassed look at Peli. "I'm sorry about your eye."

"It is of no consequence. An eye for an eye."

"We'll take it, Biton," Clara said, coming up to them. "And this anklet for our daughter."

Biton looked at the golden chain with a single eye upon it which Clara held out. "An excellent choice."

"How much?" Rufio asked, reticent but not so much as to now refuse in the face of an injured man.

"Three aurea for the medallion and a denarius for the anklet. A special offer for special friends."

Rufio grumbled beneath his breath but fished in his purse for the right amount, before dropping the coins into Biton's hand.

Electra then paid for the simple mati set in silver upon a rope necklace which she had picked for Thespis. "Thank you, Biton," she said as the merchant hung the mati around Thespis' neck.

"Thank *you*, lady. Thank you, all!" he said, rubbing his eye and wincing as they went out of the store. "May the Gods protect you!"

When they were out walking along the colonnade again, Rufio looked down at Peli. "Your timing could be better."

Peli barked and it reverberated in the stoa.

"So what do you all think?" Rufio said, sticking his chest out with the golden medallion resting upon it. "Does it suit me?"

Clara smiled, and Felix shrugged, but Electra spoke up. "Not really, but it will protect you. Gods know, you need it, Rufio Pagano!"

Felix laughed and followed her and his flailing son.

"Come, my love," Clara said, smoothing his hair and tucking the medallion beneath the hem of his tunica. "You are as handsome as ever."

Rufio could not help but smile. He kissed her, and then touched Felicia's soft cheek. "This thing is so big, it will protect us all, I'm sure."

"I'm sure. Come, let's catch up with Felix and Electra."

They roamed the rest of the shops, enjoying the shade offered by the stoa and the hot breeze that whirled about the rows of columns.

Rufio and Clara were reluctant to buy anything else, but Electra did pick out a new bangle for herself, as well as a deep blue tunica with a silver meander pattern for Thespis.

When they reached the south end of the stoa, Felix turned to them. "I'm famished! Shall we eat? There's a wonderful taberna just off of the Roman agora."

"Roman agora?" Rufio asked, clearly confused. "I thought this was the agora?"

"It is," Electra said. "This is the better one, but there is also a Roman one."

"Really?" Rufio began to get excited.

"Come," Felix said. "I'll bet that's where the others have got to."

They stepped onto the cobbled street at the end of the stoa and turned left. This time, Peli remained with them.

They had only walked a few steps when Rufio turned to look at a building to their right. "A library!" he said excitedly. "Can we go in?"

"Oh, Rufio. I'm too hungry. I need to sit," Clara said. "Besides, they won't allow children and dogs in there."

Rufio looked back at the building. He had a strong urge to go in. "Fine then. I'll meet you all at the taberna. Is the agora straight down this street?"

"Sort of. Just ask someone," Felix said. "We'll be at the Taberna Thesias."

"Taberna Thesias," Rufio repeated. "All right. I'll be along shortly."

The others went ahead, with Clara looking back over her shoulder briefly as she walked.

Rufio looked down at Peli who had remained behind with him. "Go," he said. "Stay with Clara and Felicia."

Peli barked and ran off down the street.

Rufio turned to look at the entrance to the library. It was not an enormous building, but it was clean and well-kept, at least on the outside. In this home of learning, Democracy, and theatre, he wondered what wonders he would find within, behind those red-painted exterior walls and shaded colonnades.

Above the library's main entrance, the inscription read: *To Athena Poliades and to the emperor Caesar Divi Nervae Filius Nerva Traianus Optimus Augustus Germanicus as well as to the city of Athens, the priest of the philosophical Muses, T. Flavius Pandainos, son of the successor Flavius Menander, dedicated at his own expense the outer galleries, the peristyle, the library with the books and all the ornaments contained therein, as well as to his children Flavius Menander and Flavia Secundilla.*

"All right then." Rufio laughed to himself at how his countrymen could be so verbose. He walked beneath the inscribed lintel into the dark interior.

It took his eyes a moment to adjust after the bright light of the agora, but once they did, he gasped.

The walls of the library were stock full of pigeon hole shelves filled to capacity with scrolls and tablets that rose up to the cedar-beamed ceiling. Each section was labelled with small, marble plaques that were inscribed with the subject, and then smaller pieces of papyrus on which the names of authors were written in beautiful script.

Rufio adjusted his satchel and began to walk slowly among the stacks in the direction of a small inner courtyard from which most of the light originated. The only flames in that place were from small lamps that hung from the marble columns across from the myriad books.

Another inscription upon a marble slab read: *No book shall be taken out, since we have sworn it. It will be open from the first hour until the sixth.*

"Damn," Rufio muttered, realizing the library would be closing at the sixth hour of daylight, which was imminent. He felt his stomach rumble.

"Thelete boethia?" a man said from the courtyard.

Startled, Rufio turned to see a slightly older man in a crisp, floor-length, white tunica coming toward him. He had keen eyes, a neatly trimmed beard shaded with white, and dark wavy hair. He carried a few scrolls carefully in his arms, as though they were as precious as tiny birds in spring.

"Oh, I…ah…I just wanted to look."

"Ah! You are Roman!" the man said.

"Well… Etrurian, to be specific, but yes." Rufio felt at ease immediately, for the man smiled broadly. "I am in Athenae for the Panathenaea, with my family and friends and…"

The man looked at Rufio's satchel and smiled. "You are a fellow bibliophile, I see."

Rufio stopped his babbling and nodded. "Yes. I was passing by and just had to come in." He looked around. "It is a beautiful library, you have."

"Thank you," the man inclined his head. "I am Phemius, the librarian of Pandainos' family library."

"I saw the name on the lintel. It's a most impressive collection." Rufio looked around again, unable to stop gazing.

Phemius smiled. Of course, he understood. It was a paradise to him as well. "And your name?"

"My name is Rufio." Rufio looked around again. "Do you have many plays in your collection?"

"Hmm." Phemius set the scrolls he had been holding on a nearby table and rubbed his beard. "I'm afraid this collection is comprised mainly of philosophical treatises from across the empire. We also have a large collection related to the Cult of the Muses…the rituals, monuments across the empire and such. There is, however, a large collection of plays and theatrical treatises at the larger library, the one built by Hadrianus."

"A larger one?" Rufio was amazed and his reaction made Phemius smile.

"This is your first time in Athenae."

"Yes, it is."

"Hadrianus' library is a great deal larger than this one though, to be honest, I prefer the intimacy of this place. It is easier to hear the voices of the authors."

"You hear them?" Rufio asked, suddenly hopeful.

"Well, in a manner of speaking, yes. Certainly." Phemius looked around at the stacks. "Each scroll, every author, has a voice, a temperament, a purpose. They are as close to being immortal as mortals can get."

Rufio nodded. He liked the librarian.

"Unfortunately, I am about to close for the day," Phemius said. "We are quite strict about the hours and, in Athenae, the sixth hour is well-protected for the prandium, and for sleep."

"Or reading?" Rufio ventured.

Phemius nodded. "Or reading." He began to show Rufio to the exit. "Are you a playwright yourself?"

"Well…yes, in fact. I am…or at least I'm trying to be. What gave it away?"

"Well, Rufio, you are in the library asking about plays. You have a well-worn satchel with the edge of a scroll jutting out, and your fingers are stained with ink." He laughed kindly. "It was a safe assumption."

"Quite."

"Is one of your plays entered in the competition?" Phemius looked doubtful. "That would surprise me, since you are Roman and it is only open to Greeks."

"No, actually. Well, I am in the midst of writing my first play…or…trying to do so, at least. I am here with The Etrurian Players."

"You're a performer?" Now Phemius was surprised.

"Yes, but, well, not a very good one."

"I have heard of your troupe. Quite the success in Rome, I remember hearing."

"I suppose it was." Rufio could still, occasionally, hear the cheering of the crowd in the theatre of Pompey.

Phemius cleared his throat. "Are you ready for the Athenian crowd? They can be quite snobbish when it comes to the theatre."

"So I've heard," Rufio answered. "I think the question is, perhaps, are they ready for The Etrurian Players?"

"I suppose we'll find out!" Phemius laughed again. "Well, may Apollo and the Muses smile upon your performance, Rufio from Etruria."

Rufio turned to exit, but then turned back to Phemius. "Would it be all right if I come back to look at the collection?"

"Of course! In fact, I can show you the collection of plays and theatrical treatises at the large library if you like, on another day, of course. I can leave my assistant in charge here."

"Thank you. I would enjoy that." Apart from Clara, it was not often that he met someone with the same interest in books.

"Out of curiosity, is there anything you are specifically interested in?"

"I like most playwrights, but at the moment, Terentius is occupying my thoughts." Rufio pursed his lips, not wanting to say more.

"Terentius is one of my favourites!" Phemius said. "Most underrated, if you ask me. So much insight for such a young man!"

"That is what I keep telling everyone, thank you!" Rufio threw his arms up. *Finally, someone understands!*

"It is truly a shame what happened to him," Phemius said, his voice saddened.

"Why? What happened?"

"Didn't you know?" Phemius asked, but Rufio shook his head. "Terentius died in Athenae. When he was just twenty-five, he came to Athenae to write and find inspiration and… well…he died here. Quite alone and without friends, as the story goes."

Rufio looked down at the veins of the marble floor where the sunlight from outside reached in. He looked up. "That is very sad indeed."

"Yes," Phemius said. "So much thoughtful comedy from his hands, and yet such a tragic end for one so young."

"Well, I've kept you long enough," Rufio said. "I'll return when I have the opportunity, if you are agreeable to it."

The librarian's smile returned. "Certainly, but remember, before the sixth hour of day."

"Thank you," Rufio said as he turned and stepped through the doorway into the midday sunlight. He heard the door close and lock behind him before he turned right to walk down the narrow, cobbled street toward the Roman agora. He felt as though a heavy weight were laid upon him then, a great sadness at what he had just learned. "Dead at twenty-five? Here?"

It was unthinkable…and worrisome.

IX

THE ROME ANTICS

L ost in thought after what the librarian had just said to him, Rufio wandered down the street outside the library toward the next agora, the forum built by Caesar and Augustus for the people of Athenae. He came to a high archway that consisted of four wide, doric columns that supported a broad pediment topped by an equestrian statue. Upon the lintel, there was an inscription. Rufio craned his neck to read it aloud to himself.

"'The People of Athens, from the donations made by the god Gaius Julius Caesar and his son the Emperor Caesar Augustus to Athena Archegetis, when Eukles of Marathon was general of the hoplites, who succeeded his father Herod in the responsibility and as an envoy, in the year when Nikias son of Sarapion of Athmonon was archon.'"

"Look, friends," someone said in perfect Latin from the midst of a passing group of men. They all wore richly coloured chitons and flashed with gaudy, golden bracelets. "A Roman who can read! What will they think of next?"

At first Rufio did not realize they were referring to him, but when he looked at the man who had spoken - a handsome man with smooth skin, a neat beard, and dark wavy hair - he was staring directly at him from the middle of his gang of peacocks.

Rufio smiled at the man with pursed lips and, emboldened by the great mati now hanging about his neck, made the sign of goat horns in their direction. "Cunne!" he shouted after them.

They laughed, and carried on through the archway into the forum.

Suddenly, Rufio felt homesick. As he stood there with the crowds flowing past him, all he could think of was Etruria, their home, their vines, their orchards and fields, and the surrounding green of the hills. He thought of Errol, and felt a pang as he remembered Stella roaming their land with her strange, would-be husband. The world of people and vast swathes of marble felt foreign to him, no matter how many books the libraries had.

He sighed and walked on through the gateway and propylon until he came into the sunshine on the other side where a brilliant field of white stretched out before him. The forum built by Caesar and Augustus consisted of a large open court completely paved in marble, such that legions could have held drills upon it, and its reflection could have twinkled on the high windows of Olympus. It was completely surrounded by deep, shaded colonnades, the rooftops of which were supported by grey Hymettos marble columns crowned with brilliant, white ionic capitals. Because of the roof and the heat, the air smelled of cedar in the sunshine. He could also discern mixed spices, perfumes, incense, and grilled food, all of which was sold by the merchants who had set up their shops and stalls the entire length of the colonnade. There were clothing and perfume sellers, wine merchants, produce stands with colourful mounds of spring vegetables, bakers, and butchers whose rhythmic chop chopping of meat provided a cacophonic chorus for the market.

A donkey brayed on the far side of the forum, and the sound reverberated across the court, reminding Rufio of Stella.

He shook his head and plodded across the courtyard as if setting out upon a great expedition.

"How am I going to find them in this?" he said to himself.

Already feeling the heat and sunlight acutely, he headed for the south colonnade to walk in the shade, only to be immediately harangued by the sellers there.

"You look like you could use some new clothes! Come here! I have just the thing! How about a handsome Greek chiton?"

"No, thank you," Rufio said as he passed the merchant.

"You look like a scribe! Come here! I have the *best* papyrus quality in all of Athenae, right here!"

Rufio paused briefly, but then continued walking, even as the papyrus merchant stood in the middle of the aisle continuing to call after him. Suddenly thirsty, he stopped at a fountain where clear fresh water poured out of a niche in the wall on his right. He reached out with his cupped hands to first drink and then splash his face.

He wrinkled his nose abruptly at a smell he had grown to despise, but before he could run from it, a round and smiling face caught his eye.

"Hello! Come here. Yes, you!" The man nodded and waved to Rufio from where he stood in the middle of the aisle with a small wine jug and a cup.

"You selling wine?" Rufio asked, drying his hands on his tunica and walking over to the man.

"It is some of the best wine you will ever taste, my friend. From my island of Chios. Here, let me pour you a sample… No charge at all." The man was squat but fit, and a bit older than Rufio. He had thin, snowy white hair which danced atop his head and contrasted with his darkly-tanned skin. He poured the clear, golden wine out of the pitcher into the cup and handed it to Rufio.

Rufio smelled the wine, swirled around in the clay cup, and sipped. His eyes widened as it played about the inside of his mouth. "This is excellent!" he gasped. "So fresh and light!"

"Didn't I tell you?" the man's eyes twinkled as he smiled and pat Rufio on the back. "My name is Policarpos. I live in Athenae with my wife, but we are from Chios. My brother sends me the wine."

"I make wine as well," Rufio said, "in Etruria, that is."

"I could tell that you were not Greek. It is wonderful to meet you…"

"Rufio. Rufio Pagano."

"Are you here on business?"

"My troupe is here to perform in the Panathenaea. Well, at the end of the Panathenaea, that is."

"Blessings upon Athena!" Policarpos exclaimed. "What is the name of your company?"

"The Etrurian Players."

"I look forward to the performance eagerly. My wife, Ploumi, she longs to go to the theatre!"

The man's equally squat wife smiled at Rufio as she approached, her hands clasped tightly in front of her apron in an attempt to halt the tremors that appeared to plague her.

Rufio looked down at the cup again. "May I buy some of your wine? I would love for my wife to taste it!"

Policarpos shook his head. "Oh, I don't sell wine. My brother only sends it to me to share with friends and with customers because it goes so well with my wares."

"What are you selling then?" Rufio asked, a little disappointed.

"Fish!" the man returned.

"Oh? Really?" Rufio was even more disappointed, but before he could extricate himself, Policarpos was pulling him toward his stall.

"You see? I have a wide variety of fruits from Poseidon's realm. I have tuna, mullet, rays, sea bass, grouper, swordfish, sturgeon, and eels which I keep fresh. See here?" He reached into a basin full of writhing water and pulled out a wriggling black eel.

Rufio recoiled.

"I suppose eel isn't for everyone," Policarpos said, putting the leviathan back. He then proceeded to present the catches of the day which were laid out in colourful rows upon a marble basin, and then dipped his hand into a basket of oysters which clinked as they fell about.

The smell of the fish hit Rufio and he felt his gorge rise. *Gods, get me out of this!* He looked at the eyes of the fish and noted their various expressions. The mullet were accusing, the bass bored, and the rays merely shocked. The piled, silvery sprats rioted in the thousands, their smell accosting Rufio's nostrils. "I'm afraid that I don't really enjoy fish that much." Rufio tried to say it kindly, for the man was genuinely friendly and kind.

"Oh, well…that's because you haven't had the right fish!" Policarpos said. "I can help you there. Let me give you two of these red mullet for you and your wife. They were just caught this morning. Take them home with you. They are already gutted. Grill them with olive oil and squeeze some lemon over them. A pinch of salt and you will experience the best fish ever!"

Is there such a thing? But Rufio could not bring himself to say it aloud as Policarpos was already wrapping the fish in broad fig leaves and tying them with hemp string.

"There! A gift to welcome you to Athenae, Rufio Pagano!"

Rufio smiled and accepted the stinking package graciously.

"Come back and tell me how much you enjoyed them, yes?"

"I will. Thank you, Policarpos. Now, I must go and find my friends."

"Of course! May the Gods guide your day, Rufio!" Policarpos turned to tend to a customer who had just approached with a large basket, ready to buy much of his stock.

It was then that the smell of grilled meat rescued Rufio's nose. He continued walking along the colonnade, his stomach churning unbearably even as he held out the fishy package. At last, he came to a smoky stall where a man and woman grilled various meats upon sticks which hung upon two grooved marble arms over a bed of glowing charcoal.

"You look hungry, friend! Would you like some fresh meat?" the man said as his wife stood by ready to serve.

Rufio stopped. "Yes!" he answered immediately. *It could be hours before I find the others,* he thought. "What meat is it?"

"All sorts!" the man said proudly. "We have cockerel, lamb, offal, octopus, and…oh, I forget what this one is…" He turned to his wife and she shook her head ever so slightly.

Rufio spotted this and recoiled a bit, wondering if it might be dog or some such meat that was easily to hand. "I'll have a stick of the lamb please."

"One lamb, coming up!" the man said. "Would you like bread?"

"Yes," Rufio replied.

The man promptly placed the stick in a piece of flat bread over which he drizzled a little oil and sprinkled some sea salt from a bowl. "That will be two asses."

"Two asses for a stick of meat?" Rufio could not believe it.

"Things are pricier in the forum," the man replied. "We have to pay for the space."

The woman piped up then too. "You also asked for bread, salt, and oil."

"I did not ask for the salt and oil." Rufio considered not taking it, but then he spied their slightly tattered clothing and reminded himself that he had once had no more than a few asses to his name. "Very well. Here. If I don't get sick, I'll be back."

The man lit up. "We'll be waiting!" He handed Rufio the wrapped meat. "There will be a very special price for you next time you visit!"

Rufio smiled. "I'm sure. Thank you." He carried on down the colonnade, eating as he went and marvelling at the flavour of the meat. *It is good!* He was glad of it, and so was his stomach. He reached the end of the colonnade where he noticed a grain merchant measuring out amounts of barley in variously-sized bowls carved into the marble. Then, he turned right and made his way through what appeared to be another propylon that led up some stairs to a court dominated by an octagonal tower with a weather vane on top.

Never having seen anything quite like it, Rufio stopped to look up at the images of the winds on each side, Boreas, Kakis, Apeliotes, Eurus, Notus, Livas, Zephyrus, and Skiron. Each side had a sundial upon it and in observing these, Rufio noted how very late it was. "Ach!"

"What is wrong friend?"

Rufio turned to see two neatly attired men sitting beneath a nearby olive tree in the shade of the small tower, drinking wine and conversing easily as they observed the people around them.

"We are addressing you, man. Do you require assistance?" The man who had just spoken had a black, curly beard that ran upward into his identical hair, the line of which was almost in the middle of his head, leaving his great creased forehead visible. "He looks quite distraught, does he not, Philemon?" he said to his friend.

"He does. The man needs a drink!" the second fellow cried as he stood and waved Rufio over. He had a broad, practiced smile with perfect, white teeth that seemed to bite at the air as he spoke. Laughter lines ringed his eyes and mouth, but they only seemed to make him more handsome in a way. "We won't bite you! Come!"

Rufio approached them slowly, shocked by how difficult he was finding it to remove himself from the forum. "I was just surprised by the time."

"People often have that reaction when they pass the horologion. They are enjoying themselves so much in the forum here that they forget the time!" The happy one, the one named Philemon, slapped his thigh. "That is why we like to sit here and observe, is it not Zonas?"

The bearded man with the big forehead nodded slowly. "Yes. It is amazing to me how people worry so about things they cannot control, but then are lax in the things they can control, such as being on time."

Rufio sighed. *Oh no. Philosophers…* "Speaking of which, I am on my way to meet some friends and-"

"And you are late," Zonas said, shaking his head.

"Unfortunately, yes, so I really must be-"

"Why all this rushing about…"

"Rufio. Rufio Pagano."

"Rufio Pagano!" Philemon smiled. "A wonderful name! "I am Philemon, and my stoic friend here is Zonas."

"Pleased to meet you, but I really must-"

"Have a drink!" Philemon interrupted again, already pouring what looked like water into a small cup. He handed it to Rufio.

"Thank you," Rufio said. "I am quite thirsty." He downed the clear liquid and immediately felt as though his throat was on fire. "Aaah!" he coughed.

"Ah, I see!" Philemon said. "You are not acquainted with skinos of the islands!"

Rufio wiped his mouth and caught his breath. "No…it's good. I was just expecting water."

"A new experience then!" Philemon smiled his toothy smile.

It was Zonas' turn to speak. "You chose to drink the cup

without asking what it was. Now you must live with that decision."

Rufio looked sideways at the big-headed philosopher. "I suppose I will. I don't regret it, however, for now that I know…" He held the cup out to Philemon who grinned as he refilled it. "…I can now enjoy it." He downed the liquid again, forcing himself not to cough.

Philemon nodded. "Yes, my friend! We'll make an Epicurean of you yet!"

"When you are nursing your sore head later," Zonas said, "then you will have a new lesson to take away with you back to…" They both looked up at Rufio who still stood before them.

"Etruria."

"Excellent!" Philemon said. "Our Etrurian brother! Will you sit with us for a spell to enjoy the sunshine and passing populace?"

Rufio looked at Zonas' face, for the man seemed to be testing his every word and decision, analyzing him. "I really must go and meet my friends," Rufio said, casting another look at one of the sun dials upon the horologion.

Zonas nodded his approval.

"Very well," Philemon said. "But be sure to enjoy yourself in the goddess' fair city, Rufio!"

"I will," Rufio began to go, but then turned back to them. "Can you tell me where the Taberna Thesias is?"

"It lies along the Peripatos, just up the hill, below the Erechtheion. Go out here, just past the latrine," Zonas pointed to a large square building directly behind Rufio, on the other side of the tower. "Go out that exit, turn right before the library, and then go to the right again until you are facing the Acropolis. The Taberna Thesias has a lovely view of the forum, the great library, and the Pantheon."

"The library?" Rufio looked pleased.

"The taberna is also beside the House of the Nymphs," Philemon added with a wink.

"All…right…" Rufio answered a little suspiciously. "Thank you both."

"Farewell, Etrurian!" Philemon called out. "Come see us again!"

"But only if you want to!" Zonas added.

Rufio walked quickly past the public latrine and out into the street, eager for a seat as he was feeling a little light-headed.

THE TABERNA THESIAS WAS ONE OF THE MORE POPULAR establishments near the agora and Roman forum. It was easily accessible along the Peripatos, the road which curved around the base of the north side of the Acropolis and which intersected with the Panathenaic Way, the great processional thoroughfare running from the Dipylon Gate of the city to the propylaea of the Acropolis.

With a splendid view of the library and forum from the lower slopes of the Acropolis, the Taberna Thesias had a broad, paved terrace where scattered olive trees provided shade at the front of the stone-built structure with a tiled rooftop. The smells of fresh bread and grilled meats wafted downhill from the taberna's two outdoor kitchens which flanked the building. The current proprietor, a burly man by the name of Boreas, was actually a retired legionary from Britannia who had wanted, when his time in the legions was completed, to live out his days in a place where he could actually see and feel the sun on a regular basis. Athenae was that place.

A few meters along the Peripatos from the Taberna Thesias was the House of the Nymphs, the popular lupanarium which visitors claimed was one of the cleanest in the city. This establishment was in the form of a two-story stoa with colonnades on both levels, but instead of rooms or niches for merchants, there were ornate bedrooms where the lupae who worked there plied their wares - and their patrons! - in ways that were both exotic and exciting. The lena of the House of the Nymphs was a tall, lean, and busty woman who went by the name of Circe. She was married to Boreas, said proprietor of the Taberna Thesias and, together, their businesses formed a much-visited duo of sophisticated entertainment. The women who worked for Circe were well-taken care of, and protected, for if ever there was trouble, Boreas and his small army of cooks would appear in no time, meat cleavers in hand, to remove any patrons who attempted to bring violence into the orbit of the pleasures on offer. The workers from both establishments formed an extended familia that commanded respect and a lot of coin.

The day was a fine one indeed, with the sun shining down on Felix, Electra, Clara and the two children where they all sat at a large table beneath the shady boughs of an olive tree at the front of the taberna's terrace.

Peli, who had remained with them, sat with his ears perked up, his mismatched eyes keen as he stared out from the edge of the terrace, down the rocky slope to the streets below. He whined a little, and Clara reached out to pet his head.

"Go find him then. Go now," Clara said.

Peli waited for an affirming look and then darted off.

"Rufio certainly is taking a long time," Felix said as he leaned back to feel the dappled sun on his face.

"He probably got lost in the library," Clara said with a smile. "I've never known someone who loved being around books so much."

"Not much in the way of libraries in Etruria though, is there?" Electra said as she carefully adjusted her hold on Thespis who dozed fitfully in her arms.

"No," Clara replied. "But thanks to all the scrolls Felix gifted Rufio in Rome, he now has his own library."

"Etruria suits you both, I think," Felix smiled. "You are enjoying life there?"

"The Gods have blessed us," Clara said, moving aside a wild lock of Felicia's blonde hair as she too dozed in her lap. "We couldn't be happier. It is clean and peaceful. Rufio and I have never been so happy in all of our lives." She made a sign against ill-omen before continuing. "And the latifundium is thriving - you've tasted the wine."

"If the quality of the wine is a measure of the quality of your life in Etruria, then I am supremely jealous," Felix said.

"I thought you loved Ephesus?"

Felix looked at Electra who pursed her full lips and took a sip from her cup. "The politics of Ephesus do wear on one so."

"You mean all of the wives you dallied with previously are having a difficult time letting go of the fact that you are a family man now," Electra added.

"Erm. That is part of it," Felix sighed but reached out to stroke his wife's cheek. "I don't care about them. But for some reason, Ephesus no longer feels like home. Everything we do is lauded, but it…it all lacks sincerity."

"You have too many sycophants." Now Electra smiled, though she spoke the truth.

"Maybe," Felix answered. "Perhaps we need a new challenge?"

"Well," Clara said. "I think Athenae may be that challenge, no?"

"The Gods work in mysterious ways." Felix agreed, but he grew silent.

Electra leaned in to speak to Clara. "You see? He is worried all the time lately."

"I can hear you," Felix said, rubbing his jaw.

"Good. Which reminds me… In the agora I bought you a tincture to help you with your libido."

"What are you talking about, woman?" Felix looked

embarrassed, for even as Electra said it, Boreas arrived with a platter of grilled fish for all of them. "Erm..." Felix turned a shade of deep purple.

"Here you go, Felix Modestus," the proprietor said. "Fresh this morning!"

"Thank you, Boreas," Felix replied slapping the veteran on his thick shoulder.

Boreas leaned down to whisper. "You know, if you need some help, my wife's girls are especially talented. They've helped many an older man such as us rise from the dead, so to speak." The big man winked. "Circe has told me that Amazonia is blessed by Venus herself and-"

"Yes, thank you, Boreas. That is most unhelpful. Why don't you-"

Before he could say more, Clara interjected. "Boreas... were you given that name because you are from the North and Britannia?"

Boreas turned to Clara, leaving Felix to his thoughts. "No, lady. My mother always said that I had a lot of wind as a child." He laughed heartily at that and smacked Felix's back just as he was ripping open a fresh crust of bread. "Enjoy your food!" He turned to leave, but then came back. "And if you are looking for the other members of your company, they are at Circe's!" He pointed down the Peripatos to the lupanarium where Fausto leaned upon the upper balustrade, naked on top, with his hair dishevelled.

"Dominus!" Fausto shouted and waved, but even as he did so, two long, slender arms reached out like tentacles to pull him back inside as laughter emanated from within.

Felix continued to stare in that direction. "Hmm."

"Don't even think about it!" Electra smacked his shoulder.

"Oh relax! I have much more pressing things upon my mind!" Felix stared at his plate as he peeled the meat off of one of the grilled fish.

Clara was saddened to see her old friend in such a state. Not that she worried over his lack of excitation with Electra - she really did not need to know that! - but rather his seeming panic and lack of focus. Felix seemed adrift and despairing, and it saddened her deeply to see it. "Felix?"

"What?" he snapped, but then caught himself and looked at Clara.

"Do you not enjoy performing any longer? Maybe it's time for something else? Or time to retire?"

Shock registered on Felix's face.

Electra nodded. "I've asked him the same thing, and he shouted at me." There was a hint of sadness in her voice as she turned to her husband. "There is no shame in it. You've amassed a considerable fortune over the years. Perhaps it is time?"

Felix's eyes were wide and alert now. "Have you both lost your minds? Stop acting? Stop performing? I am *The* Felix Modestus! I do not quit. I rise to meet every challenge the Gods send my way!" He beat his chest.

"Really?" Electra arched her plucked eyebrows.

"Don't even!" Felix growled. "It was one time!"

"I'm sorry, Felix," Clara said quickly. "I didn't mean to suggest that you don't want to perform. Just that perhaps a change is needed."

"No, no. I'm sorry," Felix said, clearly exasperated with himself. "The truth is that I *am* getting tired of travelling the Middle Sea. I love performing, but going everywhere in the world to do it is getting exhausting." He pounded his leg hard with his fist. "By the Gods, I've covered more miles that Odysseus himself!"

"Perhaps you're ready for a quiet life at last?" Clara smiled, and Electra scoffed playfully.

"Please... My dear, you do know me, no? I certainly know

myself, and I am not suited to a *quiet life*. I'm definitely no farmer."

"What about a permanent base?" Clara asked. "Perhaps Athenae, or even Rome?"

Felix shook his head. "I can't see it. Too many competing companies in Rome, and in Athenae…well…I'm still not sure of the reception we'll receive."

"I think you should stop worrying about that," Electra added, "and focus on making this production the best you can make it, my love." Her voice was tender suddenly, and this brought Felix back. She gripped his hand.

It was obvious to Clara that Felix and Electra shared each other's worries. "Electra's right," Clara said. "And we'll all help."

Felix nodded. "I agree. Thank you, both." He smiled then, setting aside his worries for the moment. "Let's enjoy the day, this food, and this excellent wine."

The three of them ate in comfortable silence for a few minutes, careful not to wake the children just yet so that they had time to finish.

But Felix was feeling talkative again, and so dove into another subject he had been wondering about. "Speaking of farmers, Clara, you have absolutely transformed our Rufio. I barely recognize him beneath all that joy and confidence!"

Clara smiled. "We've transformed each other or, rather, we've helped each other to find our true selves, I think."

"It's amazing what even a little support can do," Electra mused.

"Come now," Felix said to his wife, "this is not one of your hen circles where you complain about your husbands."

"This hen bites, remember?" Electra shot back, half playful, half not.

"I remember, and I respect her," Felix soothed. "Besides, you are not a hen, but a goddess among us, my love."

"Much better," Electra held her head high, and they both laughed.

Felix is learning… Clara thought.

Felix turned back to Clara. "Rufio *is* changed, but I can't help but think he is hiding something. He's always carrying that satchel around with him, but I never see him delve into it."

Clara smiled to herself. "I'll leave it to him to reveal what it is he's doing, for I know but a little."

"Well, at least he can't hide a mistress in that dirty bag," Electra laughed.

"Rufio is loyal to a fault," Felix added.

"There is no faulting loyalty to one's wife," Electra made sure to say.

"Of course, of course. But I do wonder what is going on in his mind." Felix rubbed his beard in thought.

Clara adjusted her seating position as Felicia began to jostle in her sleep. "There is no mistress in his satchel, that I can assure you. He does carry around some scrolls for reading, and some blank ones for writing, along with styli and ink."

"Do you know what he's writing?" Electra asked.

"No. Not exactly. But whatever it is, it does weigh heavily on him. That I do know."

Felix was curious, sitting straighter in his chair. "I'll have to ask him what-"

Before Felix could finish, a loud, high-pitched voice that could have belonged to a soprano shepherd in the hills, raked over the entire terrace.

"The Felix Modestus! By Bacchus, we are in the same place again!"

Without turning, Felix's face darkened and his eyes closed as he breathed calmly and deeply. "Tell me it isn't *him*. Have the Gods completely abandoned me now?"

"Who is it?" Clara asked as she peeked over Felix's thick shoulder to see a seemingly jovial man of medium build and wavy brown hair striding over from the centre of a group of laughing men and what appeared to be a monkey.

"It is Cassius Cantor," Electra hissed. "He is the leader of The Rome Antics. They're a pantomime company out of Rome. Felix hates him."

Clara looked at Felix who was rallying himself for the interaction, and before she could say anything, Felix was standing to meet the man.

"I thought that was you!" the newcomer howled.

Cassius Cantor saw himself as the 'Emperor of Comedy' from Rome, and put it about, wherever he plied the Middle Sea, that he had been crowned thus by Emperor Septimius Severus himself. It was doubtful that that was true, but no one had ever challenged him on it, apart from Felix, and so he carried on with the self-proclaimed title. His voice notwithstanding, he was a somewhat handsome man who enjoyed female company most of the time, at least when he was not drinking and carousing with his company of nine so-called 'actors'.

The Rome Antics' success, Felix was certain, had come about because after the Ludi Apollinares in Rome, when The Etrurian Players' fame reached unimaginable heights, Cassius Cantor and his company, who had only performed in the dark squares of the Suburra before that, had put out the word that the great Felix Modestus had taught him everything he knew. This fictional attachment to Felix and his victorious company helped to make a name for Cassius and The Rome Antics.

"What do you want, Cassius?" Felix growled as he looked down on the approaching man.

"To say hello. That is all. A most civilized greeting from one great actor to another." Cassius Cantor's smile was impossibly wide, his green eyes sparkling in the afternoon sunlight. "How are you, old friend? I had no idea you were in Athenae! I see you are surrounded, as ever, by beautiful women." He winked at Electra and stared and smiled at Clara, that is until he noted the child in her lap.

"We're not friends, Cassius. And don't pretend that you didn't know we would be in Athenae. You've shown up wherever we've gone the last several months. You're like a barnacle upon the hull of our company trireme."

"A barnacle!" Cassius smiled. "That's rather unfair. Especially as The Rome Antics have been performing twice as much as The Etrurian Players have. Remember, we're everywhere, doing everything!"

"You really do need a new slogan, worm." If Electra could wield daggers with a look, she just thrust several at Cassius.

"Ah, the beautiful Electra!" He bowed to her. "I assure you, this 'worm' is effective enough. Have you given any more thought to our offer to be our own archimima when Felix tires of his greatness?"

"You can only dream of the greatness I've achieved," Felix said, stepping between his wife and child and Cassius Cantor.

"If that is what I desired, of course I could. But I prefer to make things up as I go. *A play a day!* I usually say! That way, people never tire of our performances."

Felix laughed. "You don't write plays, and you certainly don't perform them. You're more like buffoons performing skits like monkeys at a Suburran dinner party."

"People *love* a bit with a monkey!" Cassius protested, then turned to the one of his mates who held said monkey. The man pinched it, and it screeched on cue before slapping him across the face. "See? Momo is so cute!"

"Monkeys are disgusting," Felix countered. "Theatre should elevate people. What you do is an abomination to the craft and to performance."

"That is merely your opinion, my friend. Even the lowest of society need to feel the ache of a good belly laugh."

"Stop using my name for your own ends." Felix was in

deadly earnest, and Electra thought she saw him glance at a knife upon the table, one which she deftly slid beneath a platter.

"If I do so, it's because I look up to you," Cassius said. "Besides, I see that you have grown very busy…" He nodded toward the child in Electra's arms. "Children are a blessing, so I've heard, but they do sap creativity and lustful drive so."

"What would you know about it?" Clara said, her chin high as a breeze tousled her hair.

"Nothing, admittedly, but if all mothers were as lovely as you, I would have an army of children. I don't believe I caught your name."

"I didn't offer it," Clara replied.

"There is yet some mystery left then," Cassius turned back to Felix. "There's no need to be so angry, my friend. You are a family man now, and that is respectable enough. You had a good run."

Felix's fists grabbed hold of Cassius' hem.

Thespis began to cry, and Clara stood with Felicia, ready to back away with her child.

"Felix, there's no need for violence," Cassius said, continuing to smile calmly up at him.

"How about I do the world a favour and wipe the smile off of your smug face!" Felix shouted.

In that moment, the rest of The Rome Antics all stood up from their long table to come to the rescue of their dominus.

"What's going on out there?" Boreas' deep voice bellowed from the smokey interior of the taberna.

Peli found Rufio without issue after Clara sent him on his mission. The canine even managed to steal a piece of meat from off a butcher's table as he ran past, chomping on it in a most frenzied way as he careened down the street in the direction his senses told him. When he finally found his master, Rufio was standing beneath a high statue of the goddess Athena, staring up the sloping street in the direction Peli was coming from.

Behind Peli, an angry man was running, waving his skinning knife.

"Cacare," Rufio muttered. "Peli!" he shouted, slapping his leg. "Come here, boy!"

The dog arrived, panting and licking his chops, tail wagging furiously as he found Rufio.

"Did you piss on that man waving the knife?" Rufio asked.

Peli spun round and hid behind Rufio's legs, a deep growl in his throat.

"Is that your mutt?" the heavy-set man demanded as he too came panting up to Rufio, stopping a few feet away.

"Yes, I'm afraid he is. What seems to be the problem?" Rufio looked at the man's leg for any signs of urine. "I'm sorry, he does do that."

"What? Steal?" The man was enraged. "That's the second time he's done it!"

"Steal?" Rufio looked down at Peli. "Better you had pissed on him."

"What did you say?" the man asked, his face as red as a Peloponnesian pomegranate. "I don't know what things are like where you're from, Roman-"

"Etrurian, actually," Rufio corrected.

"You're all the same. Ignorant and ill-mannered!"

"That's not fair."

"But here," the man continued, "if an animal disturbs the peace like that, or steals, we kill it."

"There's no need for that, my good man." Rufio was trying desperately to stay calm, to keep the man calm so that he didn't raise any alarms. "I apologize for this irreverent cur. I know he is *bad*," Rufio shot a look at Peli, "but he is mine, and I won't have anyone harming him. He is too good an actor."

"A what?" Now the man was clearly confused. "You're mad."

"Please, just tell me what he's stolen and I will pay you for it."

"He stole a piece of tenderloin from right off my table. Twice!"

"Was it beef or pork?" Rufio asked.

"What does it matter? They're both expensive."

"Now, now… I raise livestock on my own farm. I know what's what. Beef or pork?"

"Fine then. It was beef."

Rufio raised and eyebrow.

"All right! It was one beef and one pork."

"How much?" Rufio started fishing into the pouch which had been hidden by his satchel, careful not to jingle the coins and alert the man to the possibilities of payment.

"Four asses for the beef, and two for the pork."

"Fine then." Rufio dipped his hand into the pouch. "Here's three dupondii." He held them out and the man grabbed them with a meat-wet hand, his knife down by his side now.

"If he does it again-"

"If he does it again, I'll skin him myself, all right?"

Peli whined at that, but Rufio looked down quickly and shook his head reassuringly.

Without another word, the butcher was going back the way he had run. When he was gone, Rufio knelt to grab Peli by the scruff of the neck.

"What am I going to do with you? Pissing on servants, shitting in the villa, brawling with goats, and now stealing expensive cuts of meat?" Rufio shook his head. "Hopefully, that's all the mischief for a while. Now, take me to Clara and Felicia!"

Peli began to walk up the street toward the shadow of the Acropolis.

Rufio sighed when he saw it was the same way that the butcher had gone, and set off at a quick walk after his meat-loving companion.

RUFIO HEARD THE SHOUTING WHEN HE WAS STILL RUNNING UP the street that led to the Peripatos. When he arrived at the intersection, he spotted Peli darting to a broad terrace with olive trees.

Felix's voice was loud and angry, and several other voices were added to the auditory rumble.

Rufio ran up, his satchel swaying awkwardly from his shoulder as he climbed the stone steps and found Clara holding Felicia who was crying with Thespis who had just been handed to her by Electra. Peli stood before Clara and the children, growling and barking and there, in the middle of a small crowd of tatty Romans and cooks with cleavers, stood Felix holding another man up by the hem of his tunica and shouting into his face.

"Hey, ho! What's going on here?" Rufio shouted, pushing his way to Felix's side. "Care to let me in on it?"

"NO!" Felix roared.

"Stand back, fellows!" the man in Felix's fists said to his compatriots.

"How about 'yes', Felix?" Rufio urged before whispering. "This is not the best marketing plan you've had for the company. You really want the Athenians to see you like *this*?"

"I don't believe we've been introduced," Felix's adversary said from his perch, extending a hand to Rufio.

Rufio looked at him. *He's strangely calm for a man about to have his face pushed in!* "Felix, how about you put this rascal down and have a drink with me?"

"You're late," Felix said.

"Ah, Rufio! *The* Rufio!" the man said, looking back to his fellows. "From Rome! Remember?" His compatriots nodded, slightly confused, but remembering the name, the performance. "I am Cassius Cantor, leader of The Rome Antics, the greatest pantomime company in the empire!"

"So?" Rufio bit back, not liking this man's familiarity. "You're a buffoon then?"

"A very successful one!" Cassius smiled, and in the interaction he felt his feet touch the ground again. "I was just complimenting Felix on his illustrious career and-"

"You were just leaving," Felix said evenly.

Cassius smoothed the sleeves of his ruffled tunica and shook his head. "Leave? But we just got here, and my company is thirsty after performing in the streets of Athenae all morning! Isn't that right?" he asked his men.

"YEAH!" they shouted.

Cassius turned to Felix and Rufio. "Why don't we push our tables together and talk about the theatre and plans for the future?"

"Just leave off, Cassius!" Electra shouted from Felix's shoulder.

"Only if you come with me, lady!" Cassius dared.

Felix pushed him hard and he flew backward in a most dramatic, pantomimic fashion into all of his company, knocking most of them down.

"THAT'S ENOUGH!" Boreas's voice ripped through the crowd as he approached, flanked by his cooks who were now ready to follow orders as though he were a centurion upon the battlefield. "Felix Modestus, I must ask you to leave immediately. This is bad for business!"

"What?" Felix asked, clearly incredulous.

Boreas leaned in and whispered as his cooks ushered The Rome Antics back to their tables. "I don't like the little shit any more than you do, Felix Modestus, but you got physical first - I saw it - and they are regulars who spend a lot of coin on food and women."

"*We* will be spending inordinate amounts of money here as well, Boreas. And you're asking us to leave?"

"Just for today," Boreas said. "You see the other customers looking most uncomfortable?"

Felix could see several other tables where Athenians sat, shaking their heads at the scene, even as they considered leaving.

"To show my good faith," Boreas whispered, "the wine and food are on the house. No charge."

Felix looked at the man and nodded. "Very well. We'll leave." He turned around. "Electra, gather our things. We're leaving. But we're paying for the meal," he said back to Boreas. He then removed the leather pouch that hung from his cingulum and, without looking, opened it and tipped the contents onto the table - six denarii!

"That is far too much!" Boreas said, unbelieving of what he just witnessed.

"Put the balance toward cleaning up the mess you'll have after those panto-fools have finished gobbling."

Cassius Cantor heard that and immediately stood, bowed with a flourish, and sat down again to the applause of his fellows.

Without another word, Felix turned to leave with Clara holding both children, and Electra carrying their purchases.

Rufio was left standing there, still clearly confused. He looked at Boreas who was scooping up the silver coins, and then spied Peli beneath the table, eating the food that had been spilled in the scuffle. "Peli, come!" he said.

Peli looked up, lifted his leg, and watered the table.

"Go on!" Boreas shouted at the dog who shot after Rufio's departing form.

When Rufio caught up with the others down the Peripatos, he stopped Felix. "Who was that? What was all that about?" He looked at Clara and Electra's clearly upset faces.

"That...that...whoreson!" Felix shouted.

"Who's calling?" a young lad asked from where he was sweeping outside the House of the Nymphs beside them.

Felix ignored the lad and looked up to the second story. "Fausto!"

"Yes, Dominus!" Fausto emerged once more into the sunlight, his face red and smiling. "Shhh!" he said behind him. "Just a second!" He turned back to Felix. "Yes?"

Felix sighed. "When you, Castor, Pollux, and Damon are finished carousing with Circe's women, make your way straight back to the villa. We have rehearsing to do!"

"What about Beatrice?" Fausto asked. "She's here too!"

"All of you!" Felix shouted.

"Right then," Fausto saluted before two sets of arms pulled him backward and a couple of siren voices laughed over him.

Rufio chuckled, but when he turned back to Clara and Electra, he could see they were not amused. He quickly took some of the packages from Electra who then took Thespis from Clara.

"You took too long," Clara said to him.

"I'm sorry. I got waylaid. You all right?"

She sighed. "We're fine. Just...that man was most annoying, and on purpose!"

"The bastard has always been like that!" Felix said. "Every time I see him, anywhere in the empire! He's like a leech, sucking the blood from our success!"

"A pantomime group?" Rufio said, adjusting his grip on the fish he still carried among all the other parcels. "You can't be serious?"

"The Rome Antics have, for some insane reasoning of Chaos' making, been very successful." There was bitterness in

Felix's voice, and the look upon Electra's face said that this had been going on for some time, that they were both exhausted from fretting over it.

"Well, you just have to ignore him. Pantomime is far different from the productions you put on, Felix," Rufio tried to say. "And Cassius - that's his name, right? - his voice is so grating. No wonder he's in pantomime! He doesn't have to speak any lines that way!"

Felix laughed. "That makes a lot of sense, Rufio."

"Of course it does! That's probably the last time you'll have to deal with him. Just let's forget about it and focus on making this the best production yet!"

"Listen to Rufio, Felix. He's right!" Electra added. "You just have to ignore that lotium-drinking cunnus!"

It was Clara's turn to laugh, for she had rarely heard Electra speak the language of the taberna.

The mood was lightening as they walked along the Peripatos toward the eastern side of the Acropolis.

Clara sniffed at the air then, scenting something unpleasant, until her senses rested on Rufio. "Tell me that isn't you."

Rufio looked at her. "Ha! No. It isn't me. It's this!" he held up the wrapped fish which he still carried. "I was given some fish in the forum."

"You hate fish," she said.

"I know!" he laughed, still carrying it.

Clara smiled to herself. Rufio could always make her smile.

Up ahead, they passed a beggar sitting by the roadside. The man was old, wearing only a homespun tunica that was torn in several places to reveal his emaciated body beneath. "Spare an ass," the old man said. "For a bit of food?" He held out a shaking hand.

"Go ask a man named Cassius at the Taberna Thesias back there. He's got loads and loves to be charitable!" Felix said.

The old man looked back and made to get up, but before

he did, Rufio stopped him.

"Here," Rufio said. "I'm told these are fresh and very good." He handed the beggar the packet of fresh fish and carried on walking after the others.

The old man eagerly unwrapped the packet to find the two fish staring back at him. "What am I supposed to do with these!" he shouted at their backs.

Rufio turned to look back and just as he did so, one of the fish hit him square in the chest! "You ungrateful - *gwrra!*" he heaved. "I hate fish!"

"So do I!" the beggar yelled back before heading in the direction of the taberna.

They walked as briskly as they could toward the Porta Hadriana of the city where the litter-bearers were supposed to be waiting for them. The children were getting raucous once more, and they were in need of feeding. Felix, Electra, Clara, and Rufio felt exhaustion weighing on them and longed for the calm interiors of the litters.

They emerged from beneath a high arch onto the broad avenue that led to the square before the gate and the neighbourhood of Novae Athenae. It was not as crowded as it had been earlier in the day as many were still resting after the cena with most businesses still closed. A steady flow of people were making their way into the great bathhouse on their right, however.

"I could certainly use a bath," Rufio muttered to himself as he still smelled the clinging scent of the fish. The thought of his proximity to the naked seer, Melampus, earlier also did not give him any hygienic confidence. "Pwau!" He sniffed. "Peli could too!"

Peli wagged his tail as he trotted along between them.

"Back at the villa, Rufio," Clara said. "I'm so tired, I need to get home."

"There they are!" Felix said as he pointed to the litters where they were waiting around the base of the equestrian monument of Emperor Hadrianus in the middle of the square.

"I suppose Sextus and Martia are still somewhere in the city?" Electra wondered.

"It's fine," Felix said as they arrived at the litters. "We'll see them back at the villa."

They could tell that Felix was driven now, though whether it was from his interaction with Cassius Cantor, or from the fact that they had missed an entire day of rehearsal, none could tell. He held Thespis who was, by now, bawling his eyes out and calling Felicia to join him. Their voices echoed around the square.

"Time to go!" Rufio said, parting the curtains so that Clara could climb in with their daughter.

The litter-bearers, who were scattered about the monument, dozing in the midday sun, got to their feet, rubbing their eyes as their leader urged them on. "Where to, Dominus?" he asked Felix.

"Back to the villa," Felix said as he climbed in after Electra and shut the curtains.

Once Clara was settled, with Felicia safely nestled on her chest, Rufio climbed in with the parcels, his big mati necklace falling out of his tunica as he did so.

"I'm going to have to get used to that hanging around your neck," Clara said as the curtain closed.

Rufio sniffed again as he sat. "That can't be me!" He looked around to see Peli's face peeking beneath the curtain, begging to be allowed into the litter. "Not a chance! No! You smell like a cyclops' anus! Down!"

Peli dropped to the ground, his tail no longer wagging as he waited for the litters to set off.

"Forward!" the head litter-bearer called out and the two

litters set off toward the gate.

Felix was quiet as Electra fed Thespis. The sway of the litter as it picked up speed on the other side of the Ilissos River lulled him. His thoughts were dark and whirring, of the play that still eluded him, the city where they were supposed to perform it, and now the presence of The Rome Antics. He found the latter the most disturbing of all, and so he sat in sullen silence as they went.

Clara sighed as Felicia ate, and would have fallen asleep were it not for the frustration she felt.

Rufio, who clung to the parcels so that they did not tumble out, watched her with curiosity. Her usual joy and optimism were dimmed. "What is it?" he asked.

"It's nothing."

"You sure? Doesn't look like nothing. It's that fish smell, isn't it? I'm sorry, I couldn't help-"

"No, love. It's not the fish. I don't even smell that anymore."

"That's a relief," Rufio relaxed. "What is it then?"

"That man…Cassius Cantor…the leader of The Rome Antics…"

"What a silly name for a troupe!" Rufio laughed, but then his face darkened when he saw that Clara really was upset. "Did he do something to you?" He balled his fists which still clutched the string around the parcels.

"No. It was something he said."

"What?"

"It really bothered me."

"What did he say?" Rufio could feel his anger rising and imagined himself going back and knocking the smug look off the man's face.

"He said that children only sap creativity and lustful drive." She looked sad then, but Rufio smiled and reached across with one hand to stroke her leg. "Do you think that's true?"

"Oh, my love. Would you let such an idiot convince you of something like that when we know better?" He winked at Clara and her smile returned.

"No."

"As far as lust, I think we're doing all right in that area. We make offerings to Venus regularly, and she rewards us, does she not?" *Felix might not be so lucky,* he thought, but did not say it aloud.

"Oh, yes. The goddess is very generous with us." Clara had a suddenly sly look in her eye that Rufio found exciting.

He cleared his throat and blushed a little before he continued. "As for children sapping one's creativity…well…I would be a very pathetic man indeed if I let my child or family be the scapegoat for my own failings."

"Tell that to Felix."

The litter slowed as it began the ascent up the road and, as Clara finished feeding Felicia, she and the child dozed off almost immediately.

Rufio looked at his family and smiled to himself, felt warmed by the great gratitude he felt in being with them. However, after a few moments, he could not help but think of what Phemius, the librarian, had told him about Terentius. *To die here in Athenae, alone, with so much more to write?* It was a deeply saddening thought for Rufio. He thought of the brevity of the life he was living, and as he watched his child sleeping in his wife's arms, still working her tiny mouth in a subtle sucking motion as she slept, so beautiful and calm, he became acutely conscious of the fact that he was now a father. He thought sadly of his own father too, and of what kind of father he wanted himself to be for his daughter.

"I won't be like him. Never," Rufio said to himself.

He looked out from behind the curtains and in that moment, he spotted the glint of the white marble temple hidden back among the trees on the Hill of Ardittos. After a second, it was gone again, but something drew him to that monument of the Goddess Artemis, hidden in among the trees in that lonely place.

"Oh, Terentius… I'm sorry for you…" Rufio could not help but feel for the fallen playwright. He thought of the play their company was struggling to come to grips with, and was suddenly filled with a determination to make a success of it. He felt a chill, however, at the flashing image of a man upon a beach that, in that moment, accosted his mind. "We have to make this work."

Free me! a voice shouted at the back of his mind. *Free me!*

"AAAH!" Rufio shouted and fell out the side of the litter onto the rocky surface of the road. He shook his head, trying to wrest the image that had flashed so vividly in his mind.

"Rufio?" Clara called from within the litter which had stopped a few paces away.

"I'm fine!" he called out, gripping the medallion about his neck as he lay prostrate. He suddenly felt something in his ear and shook violently when he realized it was Peli who had rushed up to lift his leg over him. "Bad dog!" Rufio shouted as Peli bolted in the direction of the villa just up the road. Rufio wiped the side of his head with his shoulder. "Go ahead," he told the litter-bearers who were obviously struggling not to laugh. "I'll walk the rest of the way!" he called to Clara.

"All right!" her muted voice said from within.

Rufio gathered the parcels he had dropped and plodded on after the litters. He tried not to look into the woods to his right.

A few hours later, after everyone had bathed and rested, Rufio found Martia sitting in the peristylium garden with the two children. She sang calmly to them, and they listened intently, each occupying one of her knees.

"Good evening, Rufio," she said as he approached.

"You really have a way with them, you know?" Rufio said, sitting on the couch opposite.

"They are wonderful," Martia beamed. "Juno has indeed blessed you."

Rufio felt deeply for her, for he could see that she loved children dearly. The fact that she could not conceive seemed so unfair. "Thank you for helping us with them."

"It is my absolute pleasure, believe me. I know so many ladies in Rome who refuse to care for their children themselves, and I never understood it. I admire Clara and Electra for doing so themselves."

"It is not always easy," he said.

"No. But is that not the way with things that are worth doing?" She smiled at him.

Rufio nodded. "That is true."

"They are all waiting for you in the odeon."

"You'll be all right alone with them?" Rufio reached out to stroke Felicia's head.

"I will."

Rufio smiled and went into the triclinium at the other side of the garden. There, he filled a cup with wine from a silver pitcher that had been set out on one of the tables. He then made his way into the odeon where tripods had been lit around the periphery to give enough light.

"There he is!" Felix said from where he stood upon the stage. "No longer stinking of fish and urine?"

The entire company, including Clara, turned to look back at Rufio.

He made a show of sniffing himself. "I'm as sweetly-scented as a field in spring!"

"Then let's get started!" Felix said, his chest out, his arms wide. "Pollux. Julius. You're up! Act one, scene one!"

X

DISAPPOINTMENT RISING

I*t's better. Definitely…much better. But still not very funny,* Felix Modestus thought as he lay in bed beside Electra, his arms behind his head, his chest rising and falling as he tried to calm his racing mind. He had slept very little each night, and he was exhausted. But he was also relieved that The Etrurian Players had finally run through the play a few times, that they were starting to find their rhythm. However, they were still attempting to grasp the tenor of Terentius' humour. *Such a complicated piece!* Felix's breathing grew more rapid such that he could see his heart beating upward beneath his muscled chest. *Oh, Apollo! Why could you not have commanded me to perform a tragedy?* He sighed, a bit too loudly.

"You know… Thespis is still sleeping soundly," Electra whispered from beneath the mound of her tousled hair beside him. "I can tell by his breathing."

"Then you best not speak too loudly," Felix answered, patting her naked thigh with his hand and stroking it.

"I do believe that Venus commands us in this moment, husband." Electra turned over and stretched, her long naked body fully revealed.

Felix looked at her and smiled. "My mind is too busy, love. Thoughts of the play, of the business…of…"

"Of The Rome Antics?" She shook her head and climbed

on top of him, massaging his chest with her long fingers and moving her hips in a most tantalizing fashion. "Let me help you, *The* Felix Modestus… Husband…"

Felix tried to focus upon her, so beautiful, so full of morning eroticism, but his lack of interest in that opportune moment only served to make him angry with himself. "I feel like Tantalus, submerged in water, unable to bite at the fruit hanging above my head, or drink of the water surrounding me.

"Things have been going well, Felix," she whispered as she leaned over to kiss him, her dark hair falling about his face like the aulaeum before a performance. "I want you, my love…"

Felix fumbled with her body, not like the experienced lover she knew so well, but rather like a nervous youth on his first journey into Venus' realm.

After a few embarrassing moments, Electra stopped in her passionate attempts and looked down at his body. "What's wrong?"

"I told you."

"A busy mind never stopped you before."

"Well, this time, it has. I'll make it up to you later." Felix's hands fell from her hips to his sides. "I'm sorry."

Electra pursed her lips, and she glanced at the marble dressing table where her bronze mirror, makeup and several phials lay. The morning sun, was only just coming in at the window, rays off of the Charioteer's spinning wheels, and the sound of birdsong resonated in the pine forest outside. "Wait a moment." Electra jumped off of the bed and walked across the room to her dressing table where she searched for a moment before finding what she wanted. She returned with a small phial of blue glass with a cork stopper, and climbed back into bed. "Here." She handed him the phial. "Drink this."

"What's this?" Felix asked. "Where did you get it?"

"It will help. Trust me. I bought it in the agora the other day."

"Yes, but *what* is it?" Felix held up the small blue glass in the ray of sunlight to see a seemingly viscous liquid inside. "Are you trying to poison me?"

"No. I'm trying to excite you, but it's obviously not working. This," she tapped the phial, "will help."

"You want me to drink some aphrodisiac you bought in the agora?"

"I want you to make love to me. Now." Electra's dark, glassy eyes stared intently at Felix, expectantly, but when he looked back, she knew that he would have none of it.

"I don't need this!"

She looked down again. "You obviously do!"

"How dare you, woman?"

"Oh come now," she hissed. "All men need a little help once in a while. It is nothing to be ashamed of."

Felix's eyes widened so much that he suddenly resembled one of the theatrical masks in their prop stores. It made her laugh, and with that one act, his rage exploded. "How dare you!" he yelled.

"How dare I?" she yelled back, only just noticing that Thespis was starting to wince, his usual preliminary act before crying. "How dare you not satisfy me!"

Felix sprang from the bed, strode across the room, threw open the door and went to the balustrade overlooking the garden below. Grasping the phial, he threw it down onto the pathway along the flowerbeds where it broke. He returned to the room and slammed the thick door. "Don't you ever speak to me like that again, woman, or I'll get my pleasure from the lupae down at the House of the Nymphs!"

Electra turned to him as she rocked Thespis in her arms. "They would laugh you out of the brothel, *old man*!"

"What did you call me?"

. . .

On the other side of the upper floor, Rufio looked from the large table where he was writing by lamplight, taking note of some of the things which had come to mind in his sleep. He made a worried face at Clara who was feeding Felicia in the bed. "That doesn't sound good."

"No. It doesn't," Clara answered. "I suspect Electra gave him the phial she bought in the agora the other day."

"Phial?"

"An aphrodisiac to…help him."

Rufio shook his head. "That was not a good idea. No wonder he's shouting."

They heard the door slam again as Felix stormed out of the room across the courtyard and stomped downstairs to go to the baths at the back of the villa.

"I imagine Atticus is rushing to light the hypocausts right now," Rufio said.

"Poor man," Clara added. "He didn't know what he was in for with all of us."

Rufio set his stylus down, closed his tablet, and went over to the bed. He smiled and kissed Clara. "I'm glad I'm not so beset as Felix is."

"As am I…" she winked and kissed him again. "You'd better go and try talking to him. Else we'll not have a good day of rehearsal."

"And we need it!" Rufio said, pulling a tunica over his head and sliding his feet into his sandals.

Peli jumped up from beside the desk where he had been laying and ran to the door, his tail wagging as he turned to look at his dominus.

"I'm coming," Rufio said to the dog before turning back to his wife. "Wish me luck."

"Good luck," Clara said.

Rufio opened the door and Peli went out first, running

down the stairs to sniff around and to urinate among the shrubbery.

At the bottom of the stairs, Rufio stopped to listen. He could hear the groans of the entire company in the cubicula of the lower level where they had been awoken in a most violent fashion. Above, Thespis' cries were now consistently loud. The day had definitely begun. A loud licking caught Rufio's ear.

"Peli, what are you doing?" he asked his four-legged companion who was keenly nosing at something by the flowerbeds. Seeing that the dog paid him no heed, Rufio carried on through the peristylium toward the triclinium and the baths beyond to find Felix.

THOUGH FELIX AND ELECTRA SAID LITTLE TO EACH OTHER, THE villa was calmer after everyone had eaten and taken it in turns to visit the baths. By mid-morning, some of the company had gathered in the odeon to go over their lines. Meanwhile, Castor and Damon were in the villa's workshop beginning the design work on the Attic fountain Felix had demanded, the only other set piece apart from the driftwood olive tree which was already nearing completion.

When Rufio re-entered the odeon, having finally had his ientaculum, he was dismayed to find Felix as sullen and tight-lipped as he had been earlier. Rufio had tried to get Felix to talk when they were in the baths but it had been to no avail. They had soaked in silence, Felix not speaking, and Rufio not asking.

"Felix Modestus!" Sextus Annius Sabinus came into the odeon courtyard with a broad smile upon his lips, holding a small leather purse in his hand as he strode toward him. "I have good news for you."

"Yes, Sextus. Please, some good news!" Felix answered, meeting the praetor in the middle of the small orchestra.

"I have the ring at last!" Sextus said, holding up the pouch in triumph. "And it is more beautiful than I could have imagined!"

Felix sighed out loud, and Rufio came to join him, as did Clara and Electra, who had just entered from the triclinium. Domela arrived with Julius, and Pollux jumped down off of the stage where he had been rehearsing quietly.

"I couldn't believe it when the craftsman showed me. His previous description did not do it justice!" Sextus was excited and fumbled with the straps on the leather pouch, but eventually he succeeded and reached in to take out the ring.

"Ooooo!" came the collective gasp as the sunlight hit upon the ring.

The jewelled ring that was to be the vehicle for the revelation of Antiphila as the true daughter of Chremes and Sostrata consisted of a large oval amethyst in the middle of which was the goddess Vesta, seated with a bowl in her lap. The goddess' sacred flame within the bowl was made up of a ruby that drew the eye immediately to the centre of the ring. Around the edges of the oval face were a dozen tiny diamonds that glinted at every which angle.

"It's perfect, Sextus!" Felix said, smiling at last as he took the ring in his hand and held it up to see how the light hit it. "The odeon where we are performing is covered, but with enough torches around the stage the light should still catch it." He turned it over to see the golden band with granulation around the edge of the oval, and looked up at Sextus. "This must have cost a talent!"

Sextus shrugged. "Not so much as that, but enough. I don't mind, Felix. It's all for the cause!"

"Even Apollo will shield his eyes from its brilliance!" Fausto added, craning his neck to see over the others.

Electra promptly spat at him. "No sacrilege!"

"Stop spitting at me!" Fausto retorted.

"Clara." Felix turned to her. "You are the one who will be wearing it in the performance. Here…try it on."

Clara held out her right hand and Felix tested it to see which finger it would fit until he landed on the middle digit.

"You have to be careful that it doesn't fall off," Sextus added. "We don't want any of the jewels to dislodge."

"It's quite snug," Clara said, turning her hand over and showing it to Rufio who was at her shoulder now.

"Quite pretty!" Rufio said. "Well done, Sextus."

"Martia helped get the price down," Sextus said. "She was eager to have it when the play is finished."

Felix looked at Electra whose face was suddenly very still. He knew she had wanted the ring when it was all over. It was their tradition. "Sextus, thank you for procuring this. It's absolutely perfect!"

Everyone nodded in agreement.

"So, are we rehearsing or not?" Pollux clapped loudly and bounded back up onto the stage.

"Yes, Menedemus!" Julius replied as the aged Chremes.

"That's the spirit!" Felix yelled.

"I shall leave you to it," Sextus said quickly. "I'll go and help Martia with the children in the peristylium." He went out quickly, not wanting Felix to miss out on the sudden enthusiasm.

"Right!" Felix clapped loudly. "Now that we have the ring, let's start with scene one of the fourth act. Domela and Beatrice…on the pulpitum! Fausto and Julius, to your hiding place at stage left." Felix went up onto the stage to give Domela the newly-acquired ring. "Do not drop this."

She gulped. "Yes, Dominus. I will. I mean, I won't!"

"I know you won't." Felix smiled. "Ready?"

She nodded nervously, took a breath, and held the ring up as she and Beatrice took up positions at what was the house of Chremes, her house.

With the rest of the cast seated now, Felix called it. "Begin!"

Sostrata entered the scene from her domus with her nurse, Canthara, in tow.

"Unless my fancy deceives me, surely this is the ring which I suspect it to be, the same with which my daughter was exposed."

"More awe in your voice, Domela!" Felix directed. "Make your eyes pop so that the audience can see your shock!"

Domela shot her eyes wide as she held the ring up to observe it with Beatrice as the nurse beside her.

At the left side of the stage, Chremes observed to Syrus, "Syrus, what is the meaning of these expressions?" Even as he said so, the older man clambered onto his servant's back the better to see.

Everyone laughed at that unexpected turn as Sostrata continued.

"Nurse, how is it? Does it not seem to you the same?"

Canthara crossed her arms and stuck her nose in the air. "As for me, I said it was the same the very instant that you showed it me."

"Beatrice…" Felix warned. "The nurse is not haughty."

Beatrice tried again, this time holding Domela's hands as they both looked upon the ring. "As for me, I said it was the same the very instant that you showed it me!"

"Good," Felix whispered.

"But have you now examined it thoroughly, my dear nurse?" Sostrata asked again.

"Thoroughly." Canthara's eyes widened as she brought the blinding jewels close to her eyes for inspection and sighed.

"Then go indoors at once, and if she has now done bathing, bring me word. I'll wait here in the meantime for my husband."

At that moment, to stage left, it was Syrus' turn to climb onto the back of his master, the better to hear and see.

"Excellent!" Felix howled.

"She wants you, see what it is she wants," Syrus said to Chremes who was beginning to sweat from the servant perched upon his back. "She is in a serious mood, I don't know why; it is not without a cause. I fear what it may be!"

Chremes shrugged his servant off of his back so that Syrus fell with a thud upon the pulpitum. More laughter came from the audience. "What may it be? In faith, she'll now surely be announcing some important trifle, with a great parade." He wiped his brow as he shook his head in dismay.

"Ha! My husband!" Sostrata suddenly said, wheeling on Chremes who then shoved Syrus back out of sight so that Fausto rolled away.

"Ha! My wife!" Chremes said, walking toward her as if nothing had happened.

"I was looking for you."

"Tell me what you want."

Sostrata placed her hands upon her husband's shoulders as she spoke.

"Julius," Felix said. "Move away a little instead of closer. Recoil slightly at her touch. Remember, you're afraid of what she is going to declare."

Julius nodded and waited for Domela to continue.

"In the first place, this I beg of you, not to believe that I have ventured to do anything contrary to your commands." Sostrata pursued her retreating husband, step for step.

"Good idea, Domela!" Felix said.

Sostrata explained the history of what had happened after she had given birth to a baby girl, so many years before, and how she had given the child to an elderly woman of Corinth to be exposed because she herself could not do it.

Chremes in turn, allowing for compassion and maternal

affection, worried immediately that the elderly woman might have profited by their child, selling or enslaving her. He backed away as Sostrata persisted in touching and pleading with him all about the stage.

"My dear Chremes, I have done wrong, I own. I am convinced. Now this I get of you; inasmuch as you are more advanced in years than I, be so much more the ready to forgive so that your justice may be some protection for my weakness."

At this, Chremes' face softened and he stopped his retreat.

Everyone watching leaned forward, rapt by the unfolding scene of revelation.

"As we women are all foolishly and wretchedly superstitious, when I delivered the child to her to be exposed, I drew a ring from off my finger, and ordered her to expose it, together with the child; that if she should die, she might not be without some portion of our possessions."

Now Chremes took her gently by the shoulders. "That was right; thereby you proved the saving of yourself and her."

Now Sostrata raised her hand to show her husband the ring. "This is that ring."

Chremes' eyes widened as hers had at the outset of the scene, a perfect mimic, "Whence did you get it?"

"From the young woman whom Bacchis brought here with her."

"Ha!" Syrus said to himself from the far left.

"What does she say?" Chremes asked.

"She gave it to me to keep for her, while she went to bathe. At first I paid no attention to it, but after I looked at it, I at once recognized it, and came running to you."

As the two of them discussed finding out how the girl had come to have the ring, wanting confirmation one way or another, Syrus fretted to the side, his hair drenched from sweat, that is from the water with which Fausto had decided to wet his head.

"I'm undone!" Syrus said. "I see more hopes from this incident than I desire. If it is so, she certainly must be ours." He listened to further converse, of the elderly woman's name, one Philtere, and how they knew not if she was still living. "Tis the very same. It's a wonder if she isn't found, and I lost!"

More laughter from the audience then before Chremes spoke. "Sostrata, follow me this way indoors." He led her to their home.

"How much beyond my hopes has this matter turned out!" she said, her relief palpable. "How dreadfully afraid I was, Chremes, that you would now be of feelings as unrelenting as formerly you were on exposing the child."

Chremes paused in the doorway and held her hands. "Many a time a man can not be such as he would be, if circumstances do not admit of it. Time has now brought it about, that I should be glad of a daughter; formerly I wished for nothing less."

With the end of the scene there was a thoughtful silence and then applause.

"Brilliant!" Felix shouted. "By Apollo, you three have got us off on the right foot today! Well done!"

"Thank you, Dominus!" Fausto said, pushing back his sodden hair.

"Just the right amount of humour, but also perfectly tender at the end!" Felix was all smiles.

Rufio was silent as the others went toward the stage, those final words of Chremes' having struck a chord with him. *I am glad of a daughter!* he thought, most fervently.

"What do you think?" Felix said to Rufio as he walked past Clara and Electra, who were deep in discussion.

Rufio stood. "I think it's a tough act to follow."

"Fausto can handle it. Scene two is all Syrus!" Felix laughed.

"I'm sure he can," Rufio said as he stood. "I'll be back. I

just need to do something. Carry on without me for now." He turned and left suddenly.

"Where are you going?" Felix said after him, but Rufio was already gone. "You'll miss mine and Fausto's plotting scene!"

Electra appeared at his shoulder then. "Perhaps we should go back to the very beginning of the third scene of the third act?"

Felix turned to her. "What for? Now? You don't even have lines in that scene."

Electra smiled but her eyes were hard as she looked into her husband's. "No. But you wanted to open it with Chremes happening upon Clitipho and Bacchis, no? What was Chremes' line to his son? 'Did I not see you just now putting your hand into this courtesan's bosom?'" Electra sighed. "Perhaps directing that will make you more interested in me?" she whispered in Felix's ear, her long, elegant fingers gripping him subtly before she left the odeon.

"Woman!" Felix roared at her back. "Electra?"

There was no response.

Felix turned to Clara who pretended not to have heard, but suddenly laughed, her face red beneath the strands of her blonde hair. "Oh really?" Felix said, completely exasperated. "You know that Clitipho is played by your husband!"

Clara walked up to Felix and gently tapped the side of his bearded cheek. "She's your wife."

"Your sympathy is overwhelming," Felix said to her as she left. Felix raised his hands and slapped his sides. "When did I say we were taking a break?" He turned to see Fausto, Castor, Pollux, Damon, and Beatrice looking at him and trying not to laugh. "Don't any of you dare, or you'll regret it."

Damon trilled a note on his flute that sounded like a swallow circling the courtyard.

"Take a break!" Felix roared before storming off.

• • •

Clara entered the garden and went up to Sextus and Martia who were sitting humming a tune to Thespis. The child was reaching out to touch the leaves of an oleander which tickled him and made him giggle. "Does Rufio have Felicia?" Clara asked them.

Martia smiled and nodded toward the far side of the garden where Rufio was walking around the peristylium with Felicia in his arms.

"He told us about the scene you just finished," Sextus said.

"Ah." *Now I see,* Clara thought.

"Felix told us that was the scene you'd be working on," Sextus added. "It was a kindness."

"Even in a comedy..." Martia added, "...talk of exposing children is unbearable to me."

Clara reached out to lay her hand upon the other woman's shoulder. No words were required. She then went to join Rufio and Felicia in circling the peristylium. "You all right?"

"I'm fine," Rufio said. "I just wanted to hold her."

Clara leaned in as they all walked together. "Too much 'smart funny'?"

"I suppose," Rufio replied with a sigh. "I was wondering..."

"What?"

"Did I tell you what the librarian, Phemius, said?"

"No. What did he say?" Clara tickled Felicia's chin and the child giggled, a sound like spring water falling into a pool.

"He said that Terentius died alone here, in Athenae."

"I didn't know that. How sad."

Rufio nodded. "He was young too. Not more than twenty-five. But that scene...the themes of parenthood..."

"What is it, my love?" Clara stopped him walking and faced him.

"I don't know..." Rufio's face screwed up in thought and he kissed his daughter's head. "I feel his pain, like he may have experienced the same lack of love when he was young, the same as Clinia and Clitipho do at times."

"That's the whole point, isn't it?"

"Yes, but…" Rufio was frustrated at his inability to find the right words. *How will I ever write my own play if I can't formulate a thought!* "I just wondered if Terentius didn't feel *exposed* himself in a way…to the world's harshness…to the cold loneliness of life."

"Perhaps…" Clara kissed his cheek. "Thankfully, you are not alone, Rufio."

He smiled and kissed her back. "Yes. The Gods have smiled on us." He bounced Felicia a little and her hand walloped him on the nose.

"Oh, Felicia!" Clara said as she took her from Rufio who was rubbing his nose. "Don't hit your pater." She laughed as she said it, for the comical look on Rufio's face. "Maybe she's practicing for the pantomime?"

"Don't even say it!" Rufio said immediately, kissing the chubby little fist. "She's just practicing fighting off the boys."

"Hmm. That's it."

The rest of the rehearsal that day was taken up with the remainder of the fourth act. This time, Atticus too watched from the back of the courtyard, silently admiring the masterpiece unfolding before his eyes. He could not believe that The Etrurian Players were his dominus' guests beneath the roof he managed.

When Felix Modestus stepped onto the pulpitum to begin the third scene, the company fell silent.

Felix's Clinia, whose love for Antiphila, the long-lost daughter of Chremes and Sostrata, had been unwavering, came walking onto the scene speaking to himself.

"Nothing can possibly henceforth befall me of such consequence as to cause me uneasiness. So extreme is this joy that has surprised me. Now and then I shall give myself up entirely to my father, to be more frugal than even he could wish."

"You need to play it funnier," Electra said from the front row.

"Shhh. This is the 'smart' part," Felix bit back, nodding to Fausto to say his lines next.

Fausto snuck onto the other side of the stage, pretending to hide from Clinia, the son of his dominus' neighbour, Menedemus. "I wasn't mistaken; she has been discovered, so far as I understand from these words of his." He stepped forward so that Clinia could see him. "I am rejoiced that this matter has turned out for you so much to your wish."

"O, my dear Syrus, have you heard of it, pray?"

Rufio leaned in to whisper subtly to Clara. "Is it just me or is Felix terrible right now?"

"I never thought to see it!" she whispered back. "It's as if he's just reading through it."

Syrus continued. "How shouldn't I, when I was present all the while?"

"Did you ever hear of anything falling out so fortunately for anyone?"

Syrus turned to the audience in a most annoyed way. "Never."

Finally, some laughter.

"And, so may the Gods prosper me, I do not now rejoice so much on my own account as hers, whom I know to be deserving of any honour."

"I believe it. But now, Clinia, come, attend to me in my turn. For your friend's business as well - it must be seen to - that it is placed in a state of security, lest the old gentleman should now come to know anything about his mistress."

"O, Jupiter!" Clinia raised his arms to the sky, no smile to match his emotions.

"Is he going to do it like that?" Castor whispered to Pollux who simply shook his head.

"Do be quiet," Syrus said.

"My Antiphila will be mine."

"Do you *still* interrupt me thus?" Syrus asked.

But Clinia did not speak. Suddenly, Felix's arms dropped to his sides and he looked at the company seated before him. "I can't do this."

There was a sudden, collective gasp from everyone, for they had never heard *The* Felix Modestus say anything of the sort. Nor had they ever witnessed such a hideous performance from him. They were silent as Felix stepped down off the pulpitum, leaving Fausto alone.

"I need a drink and a walk," Felix said as he went directly out of the courtyard.

"Felix, come back here!" Electra was on her feet. "You need to lead the rehearsal!"

"YOU DO IT!"

Everyone stood and milled about in the small orchestra, trying to ascertain what was going on.

"I've never seen the dominus give up like that!" Beatrice said to Pollux.

"We're going to be a laughing stock," Fausto said.

"And not the good kind of laughter," Castor added, shaking his head.

"Stop it! All of you!" Julius suddenly shouted at them from the heights of the pulpitum which he had stepped onto.

They looked up at him as though he were Caesar standing upon the Rostrum in the Forum Romanum.

"Our leader has a lot on his mind," Julius said. "Can you not see that? Do you not see what a titanic task Apollo has set for us, for *Felix*? This is perhaps the most difficult play we have ever attempted to put on. Tragedy is easy compared to this... this..."

"Smart funny play?" Domela finished.

"Yes!" Julius pointed at her, excited, his face red with intensity. "This 'smart funny play'. It is not easy, as we know, but we are getting there. We need to improve ourselves and inspire our dominus who has always inspired us!"

Rufio nodded and smiled up at Julius.

Beatrice, however, was scowling as she looked from Domela to Julius.

The latter spotted this. "And yes, Beatrice, everyone… Domela and I have been laying with each other for some time. Accustom yourselves to that notion. I've bled for this company upon every stage around the Middle Sea, so I deserve it!"

Domela smiled up at her Caesar and blew him a kiss.

"Now!" Julius continued. "While Felix is collecting himself, I'm taking charge!"

The company clapped.

"Act three, scene three!"

"Are you sure you want to do that one?" Rufio asked Julius.

"Yes. You've avoided it long enough, and we know how Felix wants to start it. Electra, Rufio…get up here!"

"I've never seen Julius so authoritative," Fausto said to Beatrice.

"It's that woman!" Beatrice hissed, looking at Domela.

Domela heard her and turned to face her with a smile. "Yes. It is. All he needed was to make offerings to Venus." She winked.

Beatrice made a gagging motion and went to sit with Damon on the other side of the cavia where he was spinning some notes on the flute to set the scene.

"Good luck," Clara whispered to Rufio as he followed Electra onto the stage

"Stand off to the side," Julius directed. "As though you are in hiding." He pointed. "I'll stand here so that Chremes can spy what you are up to."

"Is this really necessary?" Rufio pleaded, catching Clara's eye while she covered her mouth to silence her amusement.

"Yes!" Julius commanded.

"Gods, all right!" Rufio retorted, turning to face Electra's dark stare. He gulped.

"Right," Julius said from Chremes' vantage point on the other side of the stage. "Clitipho, put your hand into her bosom and kiss her neck."

"This is going to be good!" Castor said to Pollux.

"He was a good actor, that Rufio!" Pollux added.

Rufio gulped as Clitipho's hand hovered over Bacchis' full bosom. His eyes widened as it landed, but so did Electra's. He pretended to nuzzle her neck, and at the same time heard her hiss in his ear.

"If you get erect I will castrate you myself!"

Chremes stormed onto the scene, just in time. "Pray, what does this mean? What behaviour is this, Clitipho? Is this acting as becomes you?"

Bacchis disappeared and Clitipho turned to face his father, Chremes.

Rufio looked down briefly to make sure all was well. *Phew!* "What have I done?"

"Did I not see you just now putting your hand into this courtesan's bosom?"

"Yes, you did!" Pollux hooted from the cavia.

Now Syrus came onto the pulpitum from the side. "It's all up with us - I'm utterly undone!"

"What, I?" Clitipho answered. Rufio shrugged his shoulders and spread his arms wide, the palpable guilt he felt making it all the more comedic.

Chremes rushed toward him pointing at his eyes. "With these self-same eyes, I saw *it* - don't deny it. Besides, you wrong him unworthily in not keeping your hands off." Here Chremes motioned as if feeling an imaginary woman's body.

The laughter was louder at that, and the air lightened in the courtyard.

"…for indeed it is a gross affront to entertain a person, your friend, at your house, and to take liberties with his mistress."

Rufio was so red at that point that Clara felt sorry for him as she watched, but the others laughed all the more at Clitipho's humiliation, even as Chremes smacked him across the face.

"Yesterday, for instance, at wine, how rude you were-"

"'Tis the truth," Syrus said from his hiding place.

"How annoying you were!" Chremes barked. "So much so, that for my part, as the Gods may prosper me, I dreaded what in the end might be the consequence. I understand lovers. They resent highly things that you would not imagine."

"But he has full confidence in me, father, that I would not do anything of that kind."

"Be it so. Still, at least you ought to go somewhere for a little time away from their presence." Chremes circled his son then. "Passion prompts to many a thing. Your presence acts as a restraint upon doing them. I form a judgment from myself…"

The act carried inexorably onward to its end with Chremes continuing to chide Clitipho, and Syrus coming forward to whisper to Clitipho that he should not touch the courtesan who was - as part of the scheme - supposed to be the lover of Clinia. All the while Syrus took Chremes' side openly, the conniving servant.

When all of Syrus' plotting was finished and they reached the end of the third act, The Etrurian Players clapped loudly in the small odeon, including Electra, Clara, and Atticus at the back of the courtyard.

Julius and Fausto made a show of bowing, whilst Rufio came to sit down beside Clara, making sure to put her between him and Electra. He felt Castor and Pollux patting his back and shaking him.

"Well done!" Castor said.

"You survived!" Pollux added.

Electra turned to them. "He did, but you might not!"

The two of them shut their mouths quickly.

After a few minutes, Julius mounted the stage again to address the company. "Let's keep this momentum...for Felix!"

They all cheered.

"Act five, scene one! Pollux, join me. Menedemus and Chremes are up!"

FELIX SAT ALONE BENEATH AN OLIVE TREE, ACROSS FROM THE fountain in the first courtyard where the litters were parked. He gripped a clay wine jug, tipping it continuously to his mouth. His hands shook, he sweat, and his heart raced, though whether it was from panic, or disgust with himself, he could not say.

"Oh, Apollo...why am I undergoing this trial?" he said to the sun as it bent westward.

In that moment, Felix realized that it was panic, sharp, and shooting, a humiliating panic that beset his mind and body. He had never...ever...performed upon any stage in so terrible, unconvincing, or stunted a manner as he had that very day, and it shook him to his core. He drained the pitcher, wanting only for the oblivion Rufio's vintage could offer him, but its effects were as water, his mind so bent on tormenting him. He cast the pitcher against the side of the fountain where it shattered.

He looked around quickly, ensuring that no one was near - the servants had all fled when he stormed into the courtyard - but it was not because of the broken jug. Rather, it was because of the flow of tears which he could not dam up. As he sat there beneath that shivering olive tree, Felix Modestus wept uncontrollably, his fists balled, his veins bursting with what felt like desperate Promethean fire, furious and strong. He was impossibly chained.

Felix had only ever wanted to give joy to the world, for he had had little of it as a child, apart from when he was with Clara and Rufio. But now he dreaded, more than anything, not being able to do even that, to carry out the purpose which the Gods had given him so long ago in that Etrurian wood.

"I will not die in the place where my art was born." Felix wiped his eyes, stood up, and calmed his breathing as he tilted his head skyward. "I'm not giving up," he encouraged himself, turning to walk back into the villa.

Before he got a few steps, a sudden, pained howling filled the courtyard, and he wondered for a moment whether he was going mad, whether the sound emanated from deep within his own body!

The howling grew louder and Peli's head appeared from the other side of the fountain where he had, apparently, been lying in the shade against the cold marble.

"What's wrong with you?" Felix asked as Peli moved slowly and awkwardly, as if something were amiss with his back legs, spread out as they were. "What is-"

Before Felix could finish, a loud bleating pierced the air, and both he and Peli turned to see the resident goat, Nicodemus, staring down his horns at Peli, a fore hoof scraping at the ground.

"Well this should be interesting," Felix muttered, unable to take his eyes away from the encounter.

The goat charged to pin Peli against the fountain, but Peli dodged, crying out painfully for some unseen reason. Nicodemus crashed into the fountain, dazing himself, and at the moment Peli took the opportunity to sink his teeth into his enemy's rump before running out of the gates of the villa compound, his behind still moving most strangely.

Nicodemus shook his head, looked up at Felix with his strange goaty eyes, and then went to collapse beneath a tree on the other side of the courtyard.

"That *was* funny," Felix muttered as he went back into the villa, wondering if they could train the goat to do that on stage.

Just inside the atrium, Felix met Rufio who came up to him, panting.

"There you are!" Rufio said.

"Here I am," Felix replied.

"Are you all right? We were worried about you."

"I wasn't, no." Felix wiped his sweaty forehead. "But now I am." He sighed and was silent for a moment. "I heard you all laughing and clapping."

"Julius took over for you, to give you some time. It went well."

"That's something, at least." Felix was not sure if he was happy about that. "I suppose every legatus needs a good tribunus."

Rufio put his hand on Felix's shoulder. "Every legatus needs a break from time to time for all the pressure they're under."

Felix stared at his friend and a somewhat sad smile emerged. "Thank you."

After a moment, Rufio asked, "Have you seen Peli? I heard him howling strangely. I've never heard him do that."

"Yes," Felix replied, looking back into the courtyard. "He went out."

"Gods! What is so complicated about this that you don't understand it, Fausto?"

After ientaculum the next day, and before the start of the day's rehearsals, Felix undertook to help Fausto understand once and for all the plots that Syrus was undertaking to acquire money to pay the courtesan, Bacchis, for her help in the deception of Clitipho's father, Chremes.

It was not an easy task.

"How can I be convincing if I don't understand the plot?" Fausto said as they ate in the triclinium that morning.

"Maybe if you spent less time at the House of the Nymphs, and more time reading the script, you would understand?" Electra said.

Fausto had turned on her. "Thank you, *Great Mother*, for the advice." His momentary rebellion ended the second Electra's gaze fastened on him. Fausto looked away. "Anyway…I need the release. It helps my creativity."

"Haha!" Rufio could not help his outburst. *Must make a note of that*, he thought.

"Fausto," Felix continued from his perch on the stage, his muscular legs swinging off the edge. "Time to think with the apparatus in your skull, not in your bracae."

"Too much thinking stunts a man," Fausto said.

Felix looked at Rufio and Clara who shrugged.

"Listen. I'll go over it one more time. Focus on me now, or I'll pay Circe not to allow her lupae to engage with you!"

Fausto leaned forward, squinting, his ear cocked to hear every word. "I'm ready."

"Syrus…that's you, Fausto,…he arranges for Clinia's - his dominus' friend, Clitipho - his long ago girlfriend, Antiphila, to come with Clitipho's mistress - the courtesan, Bacchis - to Clitipho's father's domus. You with me so far?"

"Yes, I think so," Fausto replied, rubbing his head as if to promote more circulation to understand.

Felix continued. "Antiphila is posing as Bacchis' servant so that she and Clinia may be reunited. At the same time, Clitipho and Bacchis may spend time together, but in secret, because Chremes is led to believe that the courtesan is the mistress of his neighbour's son, Clinia. As a result, the unknowing Chremes tells his neighbour, Menedemus, Clinia's self-tormenting father, not to welcome him home because he has brought a spendthrift mistress with him. "

Fausto shut his eyes and nodded unconvincingly.

"You're losing him, Felix!" Pollux shouted from the back of the courtyard.

Felix spoke more slowly. "In order to get the money to pay off Bacchis, Syrus tells Chremes that Antiphila was pawned to Bacchis by the old woman who is now deceased. Syrus tells Chremes that Bacchis wants to sell the girl. He advises Chremes to tell his neighbour, Menedemus, to buy Antiphila from Bacchis as it is a very good deal when, really, it would mean Clinia and Antiphila could be together, and Bacchis paid off at the same time. Chremes doesn't believe Menedemus will go for it, but says he will try. Do you understand so far, Fausto?"

"I think so."

Felix looked up at the company and they were all listening intently then. *Good to have a review, I guess,* he thought to himself. "When Sostrata, Chremes' wife, sees Antiphila's ring she realizes that the girl is their daughter whom Chremes had ordered exposed as a child. Syrus realizes that his plot may be ruined by this discovery and that he may not be able to pay Bacchis off as a result. Clinia, however, is overjoyed because now that it is apparent that Antiphila is of acceptable stock, his father, Menedemus, will allow him to marry Antiphila. But Syrus, tells him that he may tell his father, but that he should not tell Chremes because then, Clitipho will be in trouble when it is discovered that Bacchis is actually *his* mistress!"

Fausto sighed and shook his head.

"Listen carefully now, Fausto…" Felix leaned forward, speaking more slowly. "Bacchis, who is impatient for her payment, threatens to expose Syrus' lies. Syrus then tells

Bacchis to go to Menedemus' domus where she will get paid. But then Syrus tricks Chremes by telling him that Clinia has told his father, Menedemus, that Bacchis is actually Clitipho's mistress and that he himself wishes to marry Antiphila."

"That's true though, right?" Fausto looked up.

"Yes!" Felix said. "But Chremes does not know it is the truth. He thinks they are tricking Menedemus, but it is himself who is actually being tricked! Syrus says to Chremes that he should actually go along with the 'ruse' and offer to give Clinia, his son's good friend, dowry money as well as giving Clitipho money to give to Bacchis to pay her off on behalf of Clinia." Felix thought for a moment, worrying that he was getting confused himself at such a late hour in the plot, but he grasped the strand of the story again and held on tight. "Menedemus is finally reunited with his son, Clinia, but he then encounters Chremes who tells him that his son is deceiving him with a false declaration that he wishes to marry Antiphila, Chremes' newly-found daughter."

"But that is true," Fausto said. "Clinia does wish to marry Antiphila!"

"Yes," Felix answered, "But Chremes believes it is a lie because of what Syrus has told him. Menedemus is convinced by Chremes that his son is lying to him and agrees to go along with Chremes' plot to catch him in the lie."

"In Clitipho's lie?" Now Beatrice was asking.

"In what he believes is Clitipho's lie, but which is actually Chremes'." Felix stood up as they headed into the final act. "Menedemus tells his son that his marriage to Antiphila will go ahead. Clinia is thrilled, but Chremes is confused that Clinia does not ask for money for a dowry for the wedding. Chremes then realizes that Syrus has played him, that *he* is the subject of Syrus' plot and not Menedemus. He worries that Bacchis and her entourage will ruin him financially."

Domela piped up then. "I thought Bacchis was now at Menedemus' domus?"

"But she is still staying at the domus of Chremes," Felix corrected. "Menedemus then gives Chremes the same advice which he gave to him at the beginning of the play: that he should make his son obey him. Chremes asks Menedemus to help him save his son from Bacchis by pretending that he is disowning him and giving all of his estate to Antiphila as a dowry for her marriage to Clinia. Clitipho then has to choose between his mistress, Bacchis, and his inheritance. Syrus is then plotting when he tells Clitipho to ask his mother, Sostrata if he is really her son. Sostrata is upset by this question and quarrels with Chremes, her husband. She convinces Chremes to give Clitipho back his inheritance on the condition that he give up Bacchis and marry a respectable girl."

"What happens then?" Fausto asked. "It does end abruptly as I recall."

The others nodded behind Fausto.

Felix crossed his arms. "Clinia and Antiphila are permitted to marry. Bacchis is paid off with part of the dowry after Clitipho is forced to give her up and marry someone else - who, we don't know. In the final lines, Clitipho persuades his father, Chremes, to forgive Syrus for the tricks he has played on him."

"That's it?" Fausto asked, seeking confirmation.

"Yes, Fausto. That's it."

Fausto nodded. "I think I understand."

Felix stared at him for a moment, considering slapping some sense into him, for he could tell Fausto's mind was already hearing the siren call of the lupanar in the city. He clapped his hands loudly. "Right. Let's start from the beginning! And I want everyone listening intently!" Felix climbed onto the pulpitum and looked out over his players. He suddenly felt nervous. He felt the rising panic, a most foreign and uncomfortable feeling. The company's eyes looked up at him expectantly. He took a breath and ploughed on with his prologus...

"Lest it should be a matter of surprise to any one of you, why this poet has assigned to an old man a part that belongs to the young, that I will first explain to you..." Felix paused, struggling to control his breathing which was, usually, perfect. "And then, the reason for my coming I will disclose. An entire play from an entire Greek one, the *Heautontimo-rumenos*..."

"TERRIBLE! ABSOLUTELY TERRIBLE!" FELIX RAGED ABOUT THEIR vast cubiculum later that night. "I don't know what's wrong with me!"

"I have an idea!" Electra bit back, as she tried to calm Thespis by walking him about the room, contrary to the direction Felix went.

Felix turned angrily toward her and grabbed his crotch in response.

"You're such a child!" she shrieked, making Thespis cry more. Finally, close to tears, Electra relented and sat down upon the bed to feed Thespis yet again.

No sooner had the child's wailing abated than there was a loud howling ranging through the woods beyond the villa walls.

"By the Gods, this hillside is haunted," Electra looked worriedly toward the window. "It must be Artemis' hounds following her as she visits her temple in the wood."

Felix stopped at the window and listened. "It's probably just some excited dogs... Sounds familiar, actually." He shook his head. "You're not hearing me though!"

"What? What, oh great one?" Electra wiped her brow where her dark hair stuck to her forehead. "What am I not hearing?"

"I'm stuck! Can't you see that? Have you ever seen me act so poorly?"

Electra knew she had not, but she was wary of indulging his dark mood so much that he could not regain his talent, and other things. She took a breath, suddenly exhausted, and pressed on. "Felix…my husband…do you think that no other creators, whatever their art, are ever without self-doubt? The ponos of creating something is never ending."

"Another one of your Greek words, woman?"

"You know this word. You live it everyday. Perhaps not so acutely as now, but you do. Tell me what it means."

Felix felt as though he was being schooled, but his mind was spinning too quickly to fight her. "It means 'toil'."

"Yes. Toil…hardship…struggle. You know that it is at the very heart of what we do."

"Do I?" Felix looked at her.

"Well, perhaps in the past creating has come far too easily for you. Perhaps this play is Apollo's way of taming your hubris and making you work harder for what you want?"

"I don't know *what* I want anymore."

His words shocked and frightened Electra, for he had always been a man of utmost certainty and unshakeable confidence. *Are we glimpsing the end?* she wondered, suddenly very afraid. She knew she needed to motivate him and there was only one way to do so, or so it seemed to her. Electra looked down at her son's beautiful face and dark hair where he suckled at her breast, and whispered to him. "Brace yourself, my son. I'm about to prod a titan." Electra's features hardened, and she stood up, still holding her son to her chest. "Listen to me now, Felix Modestus."

Felix, who had gone back to pacing in front of the window, stopped to look at her. "Please. No more. Ponos…yes, I understand your philosophy. Every time we are in Graecia you decide to indulge in such talk." He waved her off.

But Electra steeled herself for what she knew would light a fire beneath him. "It's time you stopped indulging in your parade of self-pity, Felix."

"What did you say?"

"You heard me! Where is *The* Felix Modestus? What have you done with him?"

Felix looked around, quite confused by the sudden turn of her voice. "I'm right here, woman!"

"No. You're not. All I see is a self-indulgent, self-entitled *actor* who doesn't want to work hard enough!"

"Take that back, woman!"

"I've never seen you like this. It's as though you are a… a…"

"A what?" he demanded.

"An amateur!" *That should do it.*

"AAAH!" Felix screeched as if he had been stabbed, his hand even going to his chest which rose and fell with fury. "How dare you?" he growled. "I'm a professional!"

"Do you think that Cassius Cantor frets as much as you are before The Rome Antics perform?".

"How can you even mention that ingrate to me?" Felix shook his head. "I never thought I would hear such cruelty from you." Felix spread his arms wide. "You don't love me. That much has become evident!"

"I do love you…with all my being! But you are acting like a baby!" Electra turned her back on him and switched Thespis to her other breast. "You won't even try to act anymore, and you won't even make love to me."

"For all I knew, you wanted to poison me with your tincture!"

The howling outside became louder, but Felix ignored it this time, the pounding of blood in his ears deafening him to all else.

"I don't want to see you until you get yourself together,"

Electra declared. "Tomorrow, I command you to go into the city and do whatever it is you need to do to get unstuck! Even if that means having ten lupae thrash you into consciousness!"

Felix was taken aback by that. He crossed his arms. "Really. *That* is what you suggest?"

"It's what I command!" Electra returned, though somewhat regretfully.

"Fine!" Felix said as he gathered his tunica, cingulum, sandals, and a pouch heavy with coin.

"Where are you going at this hour?" she asked as he stormed toward the door.

"To spend the rest of the night in the baths in preparation for a day of debauchery…as you *command!*" He slammed their cubiculum door.

"Please, Venus and Apollo…" she said in a low, desperate voice. "Let him be healed that he may come back to us…back to me."

Electra looked down then and saw that Thespis was fast asleep, though his little mouth still moved. She extricated him from her breast and laid him down on the soft bed beside her, to watch him sleep calmly as she worried about what Felix would do.

XI

RIOTOUS ROMANS

When the sun was up the following morning, its rays already stretching far into every room on the east side of the villa, everyone was still asleep in their cubicula, having been unable to do so well into the night due to Felix and Electra's stormy interaction.

The birdsong in the forest without the villa walls had swelled to a fever pitch among the pines, and the distant sound of a herd of goats could be heard somewhere up toward Hymettos where a shepherd called to them in a series of whoops and clicks.

Still, no one woke, that is, until Felix emerged from the bathhouse.

"Men! Players! Awake! Awake!" his voice echoed throughout the villa, startling the few servants who had taken the opportunity to doze whilst the guests remained asleep. "Arise, men of The Etrurian Players!"

"What is happening?" Rufio asked Clara from beneath his pillow.

"What is he doing now?" Clara returned, rubbing her eyes and turning toward Rufio.

They said nothing more, hoping that was the end of Felix's call, but then he bellowed even more loudly from beside the fountain in the peristylium garden directly below.

"Where are my players? Come! Rise! Today we are going into the city for a day of great debauchery and inspiration! Electra commands it!" Felix tore at a crust of bread and then drank from a wine cup which he had taken from the triclinium. He sat down on one of the couches about the garden fountain and muttered to himself. "We'll show her what fun there is to be had."

"What is he talking about?" Rufio moaned as he turned onto his back and stared up at the ceiling, blinking himself awake.

"It sounds as though you are being summoned," Clara said as she rose from the bed to go and get Felicia who was now awake and looking in her mother's direction. "I'm coming, darling." She picked up her daughter and returned to the bed to feed her. "Ooo! Cacare!" Clara said suddenly, her nose wrinkled. "Felicia's certainly keeping her own schedule!"

Rufio sat up. "It's we who are not." He shook he head. "Here, give her to me. I'll change her. You go to Electra and see what all this is about."

Clara slid a fresh tunica over her body and went barefoot out of the room, trying to avoid being seen by Felix.

He did see her, however. "Clara!"

"Felix," she replied, leaning over the railing to look down at him. "What is going on? You've woken the entire household with your shouting!"

"Yes. I have! Wake your husband and tell him it is a day for the men!"

"Fine then. But first, I'll speak with your wife."

"Don't bother!" Felix crossed his arms as Clara proceeded to his and Electra's cubiculum.

"Electra?" Clara whispered. "Can I come in?"

"Yes!" Electra answered.

Clara opened the door to find Electra sitting on the bed in the sunlight with Thespis sleeping beside her. Her eyes were dark with lack of sleep, and the faint outline of salty streams lay upon her cheeks.

Clara went directly to sit on the bed beside her. "What is happening?"

"We argued last night."

"I know that. We all do!"

Electra shook her head. "I'm sorry, but the man is impossible!"

"Why is he shouting and rallying the men to go into the city? Rufio is quite confused."

"Yes, he would be. He is happy with you, whereas Felix is supremely unhappy. He is being a child and needs to get unstuck. I've had it!" Electra wiped her cheeks and looked Clara in the eyes. "I told him to go the city and do whatever it takes to get unstuck…drinking, whoring, whatever it takes!"

"You said that?"

"Yes. I was desperate. He can't act…he won't touch me…" She shook her head wildly. "He's a mess!"

"So a visit to the lupanar is the cure?"

"Do you have a better idea?"

Clara thought about it. Of course she had plenty of other ideas, but she also knew that the ship of Felix and Electra's unique relationship always righted itself after the storm. "So, I should tell Rufio to go with him?"

"If you don't mind. I would feel better if Rufio where there to talk sense to him."

Clara smiled. *Oh, he'll love that!* "All right. I'll let him know." Clara bent down to hug Electra. "How about while the men are doing whatever it is they need to do, I take you shopping. We can bring Martia along and have a relaxing day just for us."

"I would like that." Electra smiled sadly and gripped Clara's hand. "Once Felix and the others are gone, we can get ready."

"I'll tell Rufio." Clara went out the door and made her way around the gallery back to their cubiculum. She looked down at Felix who was looking up at her.

"Wake your husband, Clara!"

"I am, but you need to calm down, Felix," Clara said, turning away from the door to stare at him. "Isn't this excessive?"

"No. It isn't!" he replied.

"Fine then." Clara turned and went into the cubiculum.

"Come on, men! Time for drink and for women…and I'm paying!" Felix bellowed as he shook his full purse.

Castor and Pollux opened the door of their cubiculum and stuck their heads out. "You're paying, Dominus?"

"Yes!"

"We'll be ready in a moment!" The brothers shut their door and began to get dressed.

"Felix?" Julius emerged from his room, his wispy hair floating about the top of his head. "What about rehearsals? We've had a breakthrough."

Felix shook his head. "You have. I haven't. I need a day without theatre, without drama."

"Well you certainly had a night of drama!" Beatrice emerged from her cubiculum.

"Beatrice, you can come as well if you want," Felix smiled.

"I thought it was just for the *men?*"

"I know you can drink with the best of us. You're welcome to join us!"

Beatrice looked at Julius, and then back to Felix. "No thank you, Dominus. I'll stay here and continue to work on the costumes."

"Suit yourself," Felix answered. "Julius?"

The older man shook his head. "I'm too old for what you have in mind, I think. I'll remain behind to help Beatrice and work on the fine details of the props with Domela."

Felix's mouth grew small as he looked back at Julius, but he nodded. "I understand." He stood as Julius went back into his cubiculum, and shouted once more. "Fausto, Damon! You coming?"

Damon emerged from his cubiculum with his flute in hand, a happy tune pipping up as he approached.

"Good man! You shall have first pick of the lupae!"

Damon twirled a quick note and sat down on one of the couches.

After a few moments, Fausto, Castor, and Pollux all emerged to join Felix and Damon in the courtyard.

"Rufiooo!" they chanted. "Rufiooo!"

"Do I have to go?" Rufio asked Clara as he dressed himself, having already performed his ablutions. "I really don't feel up to it."

"I know," Clara said. "But Felix needs you. You've seen how he is."

"Yes, I know." Rufio secured his money pouch on his cingulum and went to pick up his satchel.

"I don't think you should bring your work with you," Clara said. "You won't have time for that. You also wouldn't want to lose it."

"But I may be able to find Phemius so he can show me the large library."

"This is not that kind of outing, my love."

"So, you want me to go whoring too? Honestly, Clara, I'm too tired for that. Besides, the only woman I want in this world is you. None other."

Clara kissed him. "I know. If I didn't, do you really think I'd be encouraging you to go?"

"I'll try and talk some sense into Felix and calm him down. He's been under a lot of pressure."

"He has. Though much of it is of his own making." Clara picked up Felicia and nuzzled her nose. "I told Electra that I would take her and Martia shopping later. She needs some fun too, I think. So, we may see you down there anyway."

"Maybe," Rufio said before kissing her again. "I'll try and get Felix to sit for a quiet drink in the shade so that we can talk. I think he just needs some quiet time without pressure." He opened the door. "See you later?"

"Enjoy!" Clara said, waving Felicia's hand at Rufio.

"Doubtful, but I'll try." Rufio winked and closed the door.

"There he is! Rufiooo!" The sound of the group slammed into Rufio as he emerged from his cubiculum.

"Look!" Pollux said. "He's even left his work behind!"

"All right, all right!" Rufio said. "Are Sextus and Julius joining us?"

"They declined my invitation," Felix said. "It's just us six." Felix grabbed an apple from the tray of food that Atticus had had set in the garden for them.

The others all took food as well, cleaning the tray like a swarm of Egyptian locusts, and then followed Felix out of the garden.

Once silence settled on the villa again, Martia turned to Sextus where they sat upright in their bed, both wide awake.

"Do you think we should cancel the performance?" Martia asked her husband. She had seen how worried he was, though he gave no indication of that to anyone else. "If this goes awry, it could harm your reputation here in Athenae."

"I know. I've thought about it, my love. Yes. But what sort of friend would I be to Felix if I abandoned him or sabotaged his production at the first sign of trouble? One commanded by Apollo no less! They are our business partners, but they are also our dearest friends now, aren't they?"

Martia smiled and leaned against him. "Yes. They are. They never judge us, or take advantage of us."

"I agree. They have become our familia, no matter how raucous and mad they can be. Felix...all of them... have changed our lives, and I wouldn't have it any other way. No matter how uncomfortable or embarrassing it might be at times."

"Nor would I have it any other way." Martia sighed, and climbed on top of her husband. "I'm so proud of you, Sextus!" She pressed her lips to his.

THE SIX MEN WALKED INTO THE CITY AT FELIX'S COMMAND. "No litters for real men of action!" he had told them as they made their way downhill through the wood toward the Panathenaic stadium. "Today, we lay hold of life!"

Oh, that sounds convincing! Rufio rolled his eyes as he nearly ran to keep up with the miniature mob.

Fausto, Castor, and Pollux talked excitedly about their preferred lupae and how tremendous it was that they were to see them again, and Damon, who ambled alongside them, his flute clutched in his hand, hooted at every wish the other three expressed.

"Calypso is the best by far!" Fausto bragged. "She's younger, and more agile. She could be a tumbler really! Felix! Why don't we hire her for the company?"

"I'm sure she prefers to keep her tumbling to the cubiculum, Fausto!" Felix laughed.

"You've got it all wrong, Fausto," Castor added. "Medusa is the best lupa there. She entangles you first, and then gets to work."

"Does she turn you to stone?" Rufio asked, shaking his head.

"Yes!" Castor said proudly. "Well, only a part of me!"

Damon howled and made an obscene gesture as he spun away.

"They're both fine, to be sure," Pollux conceded, "but Amazonia is the best woman by far. She's tall, and strong, and goes to battle in the bed!"

Felix laughed out loud at that as they turned onto the road in front of the stadium. "And I'll have them all at once!" he declared. "You three can find other lupae today!"

They booed him as he laughed in return, their noise drawing looks as they crossed the bridge over the Ilissos River and approached the Porta Hadriana.

A great howling exploded from the forested banks of the river to their left, followed by a baying of hounds.

"Peli?" Rufio ran to the side of the road, his hand against the wall of the small temple there. "Peli!" he called again, whistling loudly.

"Rufio, let's go!" Felix called from where they had stopped in the middle of the road.

"I thought I heard Peli," Rufio said, turning slowly away from his view of the trees. "He was out all night."

"So what? Let him live a little!" Felix pulled Rufio to his side. "As you should too!"

Rufio shook his head. "I think I'd rather visit the library today."

"Nonsense!" Felix gave him a dark look before turning to the trooper in charge of the gate. "Salve, Arcas!"

"Salve!" the soldier returned, walking out from his men to greet them. "You are early today, Felix..." He tried to recall the rest of the name of the man before him to whom the praetor had shown such respect.

"Modestus," Felix finished.

"*The* Felix Modestus!" Fausto added with what he thought was well-time hilarity.

"Are you men already drunk?" Arcas asked more seriously.

"Not yet," Felix answered. "But I'm sure they will be. But don't fret! I'll keep them in line. We've been hard at work on our production for the Panathenaea and need a respite."

"Praise Athena," Arcas said in a low voice. "Very well. Just try not to disturb the peace. This isn't Rome, you know."

"We are all quite aware of that," Felix said.

"Move along!" Arcas waved them through and Felix led the way. "Wait!" he added quickly, pointing at Rufio.

"Ye…yes?" Rufio answered.

"You're the one with the black and white mutt with the mismatched eyes, right?"

"Yes! Have you seen him?"

"Yes. He's been causing trouble. Barking and howling strangely for close to a day now. We've had several complaints."

"Did you see him?" Rufio was worried now, and ignored the others who were waving to him from the other side of the gateway.

"He ran into the trees along the river. Didn't look right if you ask me. He was running rather strangely. Is he rabid?" Arcas asked. "I know the Praetor Sabinus said he's a part of your company, but if he continues like this we'll have to hunt him and put him down. You understand?"

"Yes, I do. But please, don't kill him. He really is a good dog. And he is not rabid, I assure you. If you see him just tie him up and I'll get him on my way back out later today."

"Can't make any guarantees. Best if you get to him first."

"I understand."

"Rufiooo!" the others called from within the gates. "Rufiooo!"

"Go on!" Arcas said as Rufio ran after the others. "Romans…" he muttered to himself.

.   .   .

ATHENAE WAS AS BEAUTIFUL AS EVER THAT DAY. THERE WAS NOT a cloud to mar the perfectly blue sky, and the columns, arches, and monuments of the city shone so brilliantly it was as if they had been newly scrubbed. The people who roamed the streets seemed to take pride in their great city and in themselves. Togate Roman men walked alongside sophisticated Greeks in long chitons, seemingly deep in conversation, while groups of women in brilliant-coloured stolae and himatia talked in whispers out of the sun, smiling at the latest gossip that passed among them, some of it about the very men who strolled past them. There was always someone to talk about in Athenae, for the least bit of errant behaviour garnered a great deal of attention in that somewhat more subdued city of the empire.

"What in Hades is that?" Pollux suddenly said as the group strode down the crowded avenue that led directly to the Acropolis from the Porta Hadriana. All of them stopped, stepped aside, and watched. Like most of the Athenians around them, their attention focussed on a passing Egyptian merchant.

The man was bedecked in long cotton robes the colour of papyrus sheets, but eminently more supple. His dark hair and beard were oiled, and he wore kohl about his dark eyes which gave no indication that he was aware of people's staring. Around his neck, wrists, and ankles were necklaces and bangles of purest gold with orbs of polished lapis lazuli which drew the eye of many a passing lady. He had three servants with him: a bookkeeper or secretary who took notes when he said something, a heavily muscled bodyguard who did stare back at the crowd, and then a slave who stood several feet behind him, holding a long, arched parasol over his head.

"Can someone please explain this to me?" Pollux was quite perplexed, but so were many others around him. It was not the merchant's bold gaudiness that he remarked upon, nor the size of the staring bodyguard that bothered him. It was the slave in the rear. "Do you not see what I'm seeing?" he asked his fellows and other citizens around him.

Everyone nodded and then, out of their shocked stupor, began to point and talk so that a murmur rose along the street.

"That slave is covered in flies!" Pollux added.

"We see that, Pollux," Felix said, stepping forward into the street.

"May I ask why?"

"He's a honey slave," Felix stated. "I saw a couple the last time we were in Alexandria."

"Do I want to know what that means?" Rufio now asked, feeling terrible for the young man.

"Well, the flies can get quite bad on hot days, especially in Aegyptus," Felix explained. "So, some of the rich will cover one of their slaves in honey and have them follow them wherever they go. As a result, the flies do not bother the owner, but land on the slave covered in honey."

"That's disgusting!" Pollux shouted, his sentiments echoed by a few in the surrounding crowd.

"Oh, I don't know," Felix returned. "I actually thought about trying one out in Ephesus. The flies are bad there too."

"It's barbaric!" Pollux added. "I mean…look at him, you can barely see him for all the flies!"

"Can we go to the lupanar already?" Fausto asked, stepping between his friends and the view of the honey slave.

"I feel like I need to visit the baths," Rufio muttered, catching one last glimpse of the Egyptian.

"Let's go!" Pollux said, leading the way. "I can't be around this any more."

"Why's your brother so upset by that?" Rufio asked Castor. "I mean, yes, it's disgusting, but I'm sure there are worse things."

Castor leaned in close to Rufio. "He had a similar experience when he fell in a latrine drain trying to retrieve an intaglio ring he had dropped in there. He was so covered in shit that the flies harangued him all the way to the baths. I'd never seen so many flies! Well…until now, that is."

"Ah." Rufio fell back to walk beside Felix. "Please don't get a honey slave."

"I decided against it. A waste of good honey."

"Of course…" Rufio said uncertainly. Felix was in a strange mood.

They followed the others whose pace had picked up as they approached the east slope of the Acropolis to join the Peripatos at the grove on the eastern side. They followed the road for a bit, and the sounds of laughter reached their ears as they drew even with the sanctuary of Aphrodite and Eros.

"The House of the Nymphs calls us!" Fausto howled as two lupae came out onto the upper story to wave at him, their pert breasts smiling at their returning young Adonis.

Rufio stopped Felix in the middle of the road. "You're not really serious about the lupanar, are you?"

"Of course not!" Felix crossed his arms. "I just wanted to make Electra think I was."

"What?"

"You think if I tumbled with a few lupae it would improve my daily situation? Honestly, Rufio. You have met my wife, haven't you?"

"Well, yes, but…"

Felix looked up at the lupae leaning on the balustrade of the House of the Nymphs. "As tempting as it is… No. I have other things on my mind."

"Felix! You coming?" Castor asked as the others went in.

"You lads have fun!" Felix yelled back before unhinging the purse from his cingulum and throwing it to Castor. "Enjoy!"

"Thank you, *The* Felix Modestuuuus!" he sang before running inside.

Felix turned to Rufio. "Let's go."

"Where?"

"The agora. I may not have decided to sample the delights between the lupae's legs, but I still want to drink my face off!"

"You don't want to go to the Taberna Thesias? It's right here."

Felix shook his head. "Why? So I can hear the others all rubbing along at my expense? No. We'll find quieter place." Felix began walking down the path toward the agora. "Oh, and you'll have to pay. I gave all of my coin to Castor just now."

As they walked, Rufio hefted the small pouch he carried, wondering if he had brought enough. Felix seemed thirsty.

THE AGORA ON THE NORTH SIDE OF THE ACROPOLIS WAS extremely busy by mid-morning with the meat, wine, and olive oil sellers out in force. There were stands with fresh vegetables laid out in colourful terraces upon wooden stands that drew the eye. Offering sellers stood beside their tables replete with votive statues and phials as well as a few chickens and doves in wooden cages. The latter were intended for those making offerings at the Pantheon which loomed over the eastern wall of the agora.

Rufio and Felix entered at the eastern propylon and went along to the north colonnade where a small, nondescript taberna had a few tables and chairs in the shade of the arcade.

"Who's that waving at you?" Felix asked, pointing to the other side of the great court.

Rufio strained his eyes to see, then sighed. "It's the fishmonger I met the other day. He gave me the free fish."

"Looks like he might give you some more," Felix laughed. "He seems quite thrilled you're back."

"Let's just sit down. I've barely eaten anything today, you wanted to leave so quickly."

The two of them sat at a table with two chairs at the edge of the courtyard, beside one of the thick grey columns, with a view of the agora and the looming Acropolis beyond it.

"It really is a beautiful city, Athenae," Felix said as he leaned back and waved to the server, a young man in a plain brown tunica and sandals.

"Then why don't you seem happy to be here?" Rufio asked as Felix gazed up at the Parthenon and the colossal statue of Athena beside it.

Felix turned to the approaching server. "We want a large pitcher of wine…Nemean…the blood of Hercules…and keep it coming."

"Shall I mix it with water?" the lad asked.

"No. No water."

The server looked shocked.

"You sure about that?" Rufio asked. "People will raise their eyebrows seeing *The* Felix Modestus drink unwatered wine in public."

"I don't care. Let them talk. And stop calling me *The* Felix Modestus."

"I thought you wanted me to?"

"I did. Now, I don't." Felix turned back to the awaiting server. "Bring bread, cheese, sausage, and oysters if you have them fresh."

"We do, sir."

"Good. That will be good for a start," Felix replied, turning back to the court. "Bring the wine first."

"Yes, sir." The lad turned to leave.

"And the bread!" Rufio piped up as he was leaving. He turned back to Felix. "So, you going to tell me why you aren't happy to be here? I mean, this city is amazing. So much better than Rome!"

Felix turned to Rufio. "You think so?"

"Why not? It's less crowded, and safer, and it doesn't stink so much. Well, not where we're staying anyway."

"If you were living in the alleyways of Piraeus you wouldn't be saying that. Few people live the way we are at the Atticus villa."

"Surely, you've accumulated enough profits over the last few years to live in such a way."

Felix shook his head. "Yes. To a degree. But almost everything we make, I put back into the company. Doing what we do costs much more than you think. Why do you think we need Sextus so much?"

"But Sextus is our friend," Rufio said, taking the wine the server had just poured and smelling it. "Surely, he is happy to continue to support The Etrurian Players."

"He is. Of course," Felix answered. "And after you and Clara, he is my closest friend."

"So? What's the worry then? You have a successful business partnership that doesn't seem to infringe on your friendship. Seems ideal."

"Finances and coin are finite, even for someone like Sextus. Besides, I don't know how long our business will remain *successful*." Felix downed his wine and refilled it immediately. "I mean, you've seen how I've been acting lately. If I've fallen so low, then it's only a matter of time before Apollo strikes me down and rips my gift away completely." Felix rubbed his face roughly. "If he hasn't already done so."

Rufio watched the people coming and going all over the agora. He wondered at the array of circumstances laid out before them as if upon a vast stage. Each of them had their struggles, their triumphs, their joys, and their tragedies. That was life beneath the Gods gaze! "Beautiful and terrible all at once."

"What did you say?" Felix refilled Rufio's cup as the server arrived to set down a platter of sizzling sausage, cheese, a crusty loaf of bread, and the oysters. He also set down a plate of grilled sardines.

"We didn't order these," Rufio said, looking up at him.

"They're from Policarpos, the fishmonger on the other side of the agora," the lad replied, pointing and waving.

The fishmonger and his wife, Ploumi, waved back in Rufio's direction.

Felix laughed. "Seems you've made some friends." He waved back at them on Rufio's behalf.

"I didn't have the heart to tell them I hate fish."

"I'll eat it for you," Felix said, taking one of the sardines and popping it in his mouth and chewing. "These are excellent!" Felix stood and clapped in the fishmongers' direction and the couple bowed and smiled broadly.

"Gwrra!" Rufio had his hand to his mouth.

A few other guests at tables behind them looked in his direction, a little panic in their eyes.

"He's fine," Felix said to them. "He's been learning Dacian. Can't get his tongue around the sounds."

The other guests nodded and went back to their food.

"Surely you can try not to heave every time a fish is nearby."

Rufio nodded and stared straight ahead. After a moment, he cut some of the sausage and pressed it into a hunk of the bread. He sighed before biting. "This is good."

"Why did you say 'beautiful and terrible' before?" Felix asked, returning to his earlier question. "What is beautiful and terrible?"

"Life is, isn't it?" Rufio finished chewing. "I was looking at all the people walking around here. Everyone is dealing with something, aren't they? They all have beauty in their lives - in some form, anyway - but they also have tragedy. That's mortal life, isn't it? A series of highs and lows. That's what Terentius wrote about…life!" Rufio shuddered at the sudden flash of his dream in his head then, but rallied himself to make his point to Felix.

"I'm starting to wonder about Terentius," Felix muttered. "Did he really know life? He died so young, *and* alone, if what that librarian told you is true."

"I don't know. I think even someone as young as that can be a great observer of life around him. But I'm sure that even in his short number of years, Terentius had a series of victories and losses. I mean, even with his writing alone."

"What would you call *Heautontimorumenos?* A loss?"

Rufio shook his head. "I would say it's his greatest victory."

It was Felix's turn to shake his head as he poured more wine. "I suppose one man's victory is another's failure."

"Felix," Rufio said, turning toward his friend, trying not to note the blank faces of the sardines staring up at him from their pool of oil and salt. "You are mortal too, just like all of these people before us." Rufio gestured to the passing crowds. "You have enjoyed more victories than most of them, but now the Gods are testing you. You may feel you are at a low point, but low points end and can turn into highs."

"I don't want to be just one of the crowd, Rufio. I never have. You know this."

"I know." Rufio knew it was true. Felix had always been the strongest, the loudest, the most skilled at what he did.

"What if Apollo has commanded me to perform this play to finish me off? What will I do with my life after that happens?"

"I think Apollo has commanded you to perform this play to make you stronger, to help you decide exactly what you want to do with the beautiful and terrible life you've been given!" Rufio smiled, quite proud of himself.

"You really love this play, don't you?"

"It's a work of genius, but at the same time it portrays feelings that most people can connect with and relate to."

"Well, I'm glad you see it. Because lately, I see it as a pain in my ass." Felix suddenly looked deflated, his wine cup pausing at his lips. He shook his head. "I never thought to see myself unable to act, or…or to make love to my woman," he whispered. "You know she bought a tincture to make me erect? Me!" He downed the rest of his wine and refilled his cup. "It's humiliating. I threw it into the peristylium when she handed it to me."

"I've heard this can happen when the mind is weighed by worries. You've put a lot of pressure on yourself lately." Rufio pat his shoulder. "That, coupled with crying babies, mountains of shit, and sleepless nights will lay any man low. It's only temporary."

"I don't want to talk about my inability to achieve an erection. I refuse to accept that!"

"Well, there's always the lupanar," Rufio ventured. "Electra did give you permission."

"Are you kidding?" Felix laughed. "That was a test, Rufio! If I took her up on that, she'd turn me to stone like a Gorgon."

"I know. Just checking." Rufio winked. "There's hope for you yet."

They continued to eat and drink with the taberna server eventually bringing another jug of wine, more sausage, and bread. Felix continued to slurp the oysters, and Rufio continued to try and hold down his food at the sound. The sun was high now and lit the vast marble courtyard so that it was almost blinding.

"This would be a good space for a performance," Rufio noted after a while.

Just then, as if on cue, a cart rolled into the agora from beneath the gate of Athena Archegetis to their right.

"I don't believe this," Felix muttered.

"What?" Rufio looked around.

"It's those panto fools," Felix growled as his eyes focussed on the donkey-cart and the ten men around it, one of whom had a monkey on his shoulder.

"Is that that group from the Taberna Thesias the other day?"

"Yes. Cassius Cantor and The Rome Antics." Felix spat in their direction.

"Clara told me about him." Rufio pulled at a crust of bread and watched. "Looks like they're setting up for a performance."

"Setting up for their idiocy, more like." Felix crossed his arms. "Let's see what new ways they've devised to make us Romans look bad to these Greeks."

"Maybe he'll surprise you?" Rufio ventured. "Looks like they have a lot of props." Rufio pointed to the cart which had a large tarp over it.

Two of the men began to fold it back, and once they had, it became apparent that it was full of only one item.

"Is that…"

"Yes," Felix answered, his lips pursed. "A cart filled with cocks."

Felix, Rufio, and most others passing by stopped to watch Cassius Cantor and his men unload a series of giant, stuffed, leather phalluses with painted red knobs. They placed them in a large circle to create a sort of arena, and then the monkey jumped down off of the one man's shoulder to grab what looked like two wooden, painted roosters from the back of the cart and place them in the middle of the circle.

"I don't know what to say," Rufio said.

"I hate monkeys," Felix growled.

"Domini et dominae!" Cassius Cantor suddenly hopped atop the driving bench of his company's wagon to address the entire agora. "We are The Rome Antics, and we are about to perform a comedy of such raucous joy that you will go through the rest of your day smiling and laughing and feeling good about the world!"

"That's quite a bold statement!" someone shouted at him from the butchers' stalls in the south colonnade.

"Yes, it is!" Cassius Cantor replied with a bow from atop his cart, just as his donkey brayed.

People were already laughing.

"If you are interested in drama, laughter, and a bit with a monkey, then gather round and be amused!"

To Felix's dismay, a good number of people began to assemble in a great circle about The Rome Antics.

Cassius Cantor smiled and spread his arms wide. "We now present to you, good people of Athenae… The Cock Fight!" He immediately leaped down off of the wagon and joined his troupe of men around the circle of phalluses, whilst one of them played a wild flute, accompanied by the monkey, Momo, on the tambourine.

Felix shook his head. "Here we go."

Rufio craned his neck to watch as The Rome Antics began to hoot, holler, and guffaw as their roosters had at each other in the fighting pit.

"This is ridiculous," Felix said, pouring himself more wine. "Look at those fools! That's not theatre, it's buffoonery!"

"People do seem to like it," Rufio ventured, though he could not see the skill in the performance.

The Rome Antics were a group of gruff and clumsy fools, made dumb by the Gods, gathered around the two wooden fighting cocks in the middle, pointing, grunting, making rude gestures, and cheering to the sound of a wild flute and the jerky chiming of the monkey upon the tambourine.

"Is this it?" Felix heckled, but his voice went unheard as the audience in the middle of the agora cheered as one of the roosters fell over, surrounded by blood which one of the actors shot from a wine skin at his side.

"I suppose there's a reason no one remembers the names of pantomime writers," Rufio said, though he stood to get a better look as the crowd thickened.

"I can't watch anymore," Felix added. "I've lost my appetite. Here," he turned to Rufio. "Hand me your purse. I'll go pay so we can get out of here."

Without looking, Rufio handed Felix his coin purse.

Felix saw how Rufio was watching and stormed off to pay.

"Something's happening!" Rufio said as the owner of the dead rooster pushed his opponent.

There was a sudden pause in the action, but then every man there picked up one of the giant, stuffed phalluses and began swinging them like clubs.

"There's a fight!" Rufio yelled back to Felix as he returned to the table.

"Of course there is. Why do you think he's called it *The Cock Fight?*"

The circle spread wide and the audience backed up with it, as if they were drawn into a lewd dance, with knobby phalluses swinging this way and that as The Rome Antics shouted, and grunted, and sweat, laying into each other full force, knocking each other over onto the ground. Some men beat opponents' faces with the phalluses, and others duelled as if they were swinging gladii. Yet another rammed one into the behind of his foe.

The crowd, however, seemed most to enjoy the monkey, Momo, who had flung himself upon one of the prostrate men and was beating his fallen phallus with his tambourine, the man grunting in pain with each movement of the simian's percussion.

When all but one of the cocks remained standing - this, of course, being a victorious Cassius Cantor - the rough audience of men and street urchins burst into wild applause, cheering through gap-toothed smiles.

Felix looked around the fringes of the agora where well-dressed Athenians and Romans looked on in disgust, shaking their heads and muttering about the obscene pantomime they had just witnessed. "Some people still have taste," he said to Rufio.

Rufio looked from the one group of onlookers to the other and saw that there were more who seemed disgusted than entertained. Those beneath the colonnades of the agora who were laughing were pointing at and mocking The Rome Antics, and not a few made crass remarks about the idiocy of Romans.

These last comments Felix heard loud and clear, and it made him angry, not at those who had spoken the words, but at Cassius Cantor. "He's humiliating all of us, that panto fool!"

"I don't think so," Rufio answered, trying not to smile. "Just himself."

Just then, after the company took a round of bows for their audience, Cassius Cantor stepped up onto the wagon again to address the agora. "We do hope that you enjoyed our unruly production! If you did, please consider feeding the monkey with a coin or two!" He pointed to Momo who was prancing around the attendees with a small bucket in his hands.

Cassius Cantor continued with his announcement. "The Rome Antics will be performing here, in this spot, two more times today, so be sure to come back for more laughter and monkey mayhem!"

People applauded and the crowd began to disperse as they all went back to their business around the agora.

Cassius spotted Felix and Rufio where they stood and, the small bucket in hand, he ran over to them as his company loaded the phalluses back into the wagon. "I'm so glad you came to watch the show, Felix Modestus! What did you think?" He looked from Felix to Rufio expectantly. "I wrote it just last night!" He seemed genuinely proud of the fact. "We were sowing and stuffing cocks all night!"

"I'll bet," Rufio laughed.

Cassius turned to him. "You… You're the husband of that pretty one that was with Felix and Electra." He looked at Rufio's hands. "You, at least, can appreciate how quickly this came together."

"Me? Why?" Rufio stepped forward, still agitated at the man's mention of Clara.

Cassius pointed at his fingers. "You're a fellow playwright, no?"

"Well…how did you know that I-"

"Your fingers are stained with ink. And you're in the company of *The* Felix Modestus! You must be a writer!" Now he turned to Felix. "Tell me, my friend. Truly… What did you think? Quite good, eh?"

Felix stared down at Cassius Cantor, his thick arms crossed, his breathing steady. "I think that you are a disgrace, Cassius. You and your *company*."

"Surely not!" Cassius laughed and held up the bucket. "Look how full this is! They loved it!"

"You humiliated yourself for a rabble's pleasure, and embarrassed all of us. Did you see the people beyond your ring of cocks who were mocking you, who were disgusted by you? They were laughing at you, Cassius!"

But Cassius Cantor simply smiled and shook his head. "What do I care if a few Greek snobs think we're crass and lowbrow? We made many others laugh, Felix. Who cares if they were laughing *at* us. We brightened their tired day, and they went away smiling after dropping some of their hard-won coin into our humble bucket. I'd say that's a theatrical victory, wouldn't you?" Just then, Momo came to stand beside Cassius' leg, leaning upon it as if it were a column in the street.

Felix shook his head. "No, Cassius. It's not theatrical at all. It was shit."

"Well, I'm sorry you feel that way." Cassius shrugged. "I have to go now, my friend." He wiped his sweaty brow. "I've got enough in my bucket to treat my men to lupae and lunch!" He turned and left, but Momo remained there for a moment, staring up at Felix and Rufio, his little fangs bared in a hideous smile.

"I'm going to kick that thing," Felix growled, and the monkey turned and scurried after Cassius, his tail straight up in the air. "I can't watch these idiots any more. Let's walk." Felix turned and made his way toward the gate of Athena Archegetis to their right.

Rufio followed, smiling to himself at the ludicrous scene that had just played out before him. He did remember a time when Felix laughed out loud in the streets of Rome when companies such as Cassius' had performed on the steps of temples, but that easy side of Felix's had, it seemed, disappeared. "Wait for me!" Rufio grabbed a last bit of sausage and went after him.

THE SUN LIT EVERY CORNER OF THE ANCIENT AGORA AT THE western end of the Acropolis. A warm breeze blew in from the sea and managed to reach the city, tickling the branches of the pine, olive, and plane trees. The cicadas had begun their daily concert, now that the heat had arrived, their shiny, winged bodies flickering in the sunlight as they dashed from one tree to another, like arrows from tiny bows shooting every which way.

Felix and Rufio walked in uncomfortable silence, though, despite the beauty of the day.

Rufio knew that Felix needed to talk, to unburden himself further, but he could also see that he was not ready. *I'll follow his lead,* he thought as they crossed the Panathenaic Way and walked between the odeon and the temple of Ares. Rufio cast his eyes about warily to see if the naked seer, Melampus, was lurking about. He wasn't. However, a loud pack of dogs came careening down the hill where the temple of Hephaestus over-looked the ancient agora.

People hissed at the passing hounds and tossed small stones at them to stopper their gruff cacophony, but the dogs pressed on as unworried as a group of cataphracts in battle. At the back of the pack, nipping and snarling at the other dogs' legs was a familiar blur.

"Peli! You get back here this instant!" Rufio shouted, taking a few quick and futile steps. "Peli!" he shouted again, even as the pack ran down the street between the stoa of Attalus and the library of Pandainos.

"Just leave him," Felix said, pulling Rufio along as if with some sudden purpose. "At least he's made some friends!" He laughed.

Rufio did not. "I just don't want him executed. You heard what that guard, Arcas, said about the strays in the city."

"Don't worry. If Peli survived in Rome, he can survive anywhere."

"Just like us, I suppose," Rufio forced a smile and slapped Felix on the back.

Felix stopped abruptly and turned to Rufio where they stood in front of the shrine to the Eponymous Heroes. "You're exactly right!"

"About what?" Rufio wiped his sweaty brow, squinting in the high sunlight.

"About us surviving Rome. Do you remember that perfor-mance?" Felix's eyes sparkled.

"How could I forget? I think of it almost every day," Rufio admitted.

"So do I!" Felix began to walk again, past the shrine on their left, and the tholos on their right, taking the road past the Areopagus toward the south slope of the Acropolis. "These Greeks are a wonderful people, but we Romans are tough!"

"Except we're Etrurian, remember?"

"Even better! We've got the best of both!" Felix punched a fist into his other hand. "We put on a magnificent production in Rome and came out victorious, even though we faced financial ruin and enslavement, Suburran thugs, a traitor in our midst, and not least, the Roman mob!"

Rufio sighed. "Maybe we can *not* do all that again?"

"You miss my point… If we survived all of that, we can certainly make a show of it here in Athenae!"

"Hmm. Yes. I see your reasoning, to be sure, Felix. However, we have a different play this time, a much more difficult one. Perhaps all that conflict in Rome - the threat of death! - played more of a role than you give credit?"

"That's what we need! Some conflict! Rufio, you're brilliant!"

"Well, I don't know about that…" Rufio rubbed his fingernails on his tunica, but then grew serious. "Isn't a lack of humour, mountains of dirty baby bracae, and a limp-"

Felix shot him a look.

"I mean…well…you know what I mean! Isn't all that conflict enough?"

"Those are frustrations, not conflict! We need a battle!"

Rufio shook his head. "I don't know about you, but my thoughts and my writing, and a farm hand who loves my donkey are battle enough for me. Let alone getting up in front of an audience again!"

Felix nodded, as if he had not heard him that time. "A battle. Yes. I gave birth to my son, and felt like a god…"

"I'm pretty sure Electra took care of that part," Rufio said, his finger in the air.

"…I've never felt like that," Felix continued, "except at the end of our performance in Rome. It's time to reconnect with that feeling."

"This is progress. Good. Now, how do you propose to go about it?"

"Battle plans, start here!" Felix stopped and pointed to the great odeon of Herodes Atticus. "Come. Let's go inside!"

"Now? Don't we need permission, or at least to have Sextus talk to someone for us?"

"Fortuna favours the bold, Rufio!"

"Now you're quoting Virgilius?"

"Yes!" Felix strode beneath the great arches into the dark of the portico of the odeon, and into the back of the stagehouse.

A caretaker at a wide table looked up at them, his face lit by a burning lamp in the dark. "Can I help you?" the man asked, a little sleepily. It was nearing the sixth hour after all.

"I am Felix Modestus, leader of The Etrurian Players, and we are set to perform here during the Panathenaea this year."

The man rubbed his eyes and opened a large wax tablet, searching the notes on it with the point of his bronze stylus as he squinted down at the writing. "Hmm. You are not performing during the Panathenaea. You're Romans and-"

"Actually, we're Etrurian," Rufio corrected.

The man looked up, annoyed. "Same thing." He scrolled to the bottom of his list and nodded. "Yes, I see here that you are performing *after* the great festival." He looked back up at them. "That's good. You could have a full house. No competing performances after the festival is finished."

"Excellent!" Felix said, his clap echoing in the large space.

The man shook his head. "Or not. Might be that everyone goes home before you perform. Only Apollo and Athena know."

Felix smiled. "Yes, they do."

Rufio stepped forward. "We are actually guests of the

Atticus family, staying at the villa at the eastern edge of the city. You know the one, yes?"

"Ye…yes. I do." Now the man was paying attention.

"A beautiful place!" Rufio added.

"I've never been inside," the man said.

"Well, at any rate…" Rufio continued. "We're in the middle of rehearsals and, well, we need to take a look at the layout of the odeon here to make sure our set pieces will be appropriate. Can we go inside to take a look?"

"I suppose that would be fine." The man set down his stylus and closed his tablet. "I just lit all the torches so that one of the local magistrates could give some mad Egyptian a personal tour of the place. Bastard had a poor slave covered in honey and flies following him everywhere!"

"Some people," Felix stifled a laugh, shaking his head. "Sounds terrible."

"It was. I just finished cleaning up all the honey he dribbled on stage and in the cavia!"

"We won't spill any honey, we promise," Rufio reassured the man.

"Good. I'll put the torches out when you're done looking around. But don't take too long. It's almost the sixth hour, and I need to rest."

Rufio looked at him. "Yes. I can see how very busy things are."

"We won't be long," Felix said, leading Rufio up the stairs to the area behind the scaena frons. It was quiet there, muffled.

"Is this bigger than Pompey's theatre in Rome?" Rufio asked.

"No. Unless it feels that way because of the roof."

Rufio inhaled and could smell the scent of the cedar beams far above. He looked to where Felix stood in the middle doorway leading onto the stage. Felix paused in the dim light, and for a moment, Rufio thought he did look like some sort of god, or even a hero like Orpheus, coming out of the Underworld's gateway. *Except he's trying to lead himself out of the darkness.*

Felix stepped out of the arch onto the boards of the pulpitum, his breathing deep and calm as he spread his arms wide to take it in, to embrace it all.

Rufio walked through the arch to Felix's left, his heart racing as he looked across the small orchestra to the steep seating of the cavia. It was much smaller than the theatre of Pompey in Rome, but somehow the intimacy of it made it more intimidating. *We'll be able to see everyone's faces!* he thought before turning to look back and up at the massive, four-storey scaena frons. Each level had nine niches that gave access to viewing galleries above. Statues stood in elegant poses between each of them, as if there were a constant audience of gods, goddesses, and literary and theatrical heroes all of whom would sit there and pass judgement on every performance.

"The acoustics are impressive," Felix said in a low voice that carried around the odeon. "I can even hear my breathing."

Rufio looked around, up at the cavia where the torches lit the area to the topmost row. "Incredible."

Felix walked to the front of the pulpitum and stared at his imaginary audience. "Rufio," he said.

"What?" Rufio answered as he turned on the spot to observe the beauty of the odeon.

"Would you mind if I tried my prologus again?"

Rufio smiled. "Of course not. Battle plans, right?"

Felix nodded. "Exactly."

Rufio descended the short stairs to cross the half-circle orchestra, and sat himself on the first row of seating as Felix prepared himself with a few more deep breaths.

Felix paused for a few moments and then his eyes opened, and a smile spanned his bearded face.

"Lest it should be a matter of surprise to any one of you,

why the poet has assigned to an old man a part that belongs to the young, that I will first explain to you, and then, the reason for my coming I will disclose." Felix's voice was confident and inviting. He then began to move back and forth slowly, as if to address the audience on all sides of the cavia. "An entire play from an entire Greek one, the *Heautontimorumenos*, I am today about to represent, which from a two-fold plot has been made but one!"

Rufio smiled, for Felix's voice was back, his pronunciation of the Greek name of the play like a song made to be spoken in that very odeon. At the back, he spotted the caretaker peering around the corner, silent as a mouse, an eager glint in his eye.

"I have shown," Felix continued, "that it is new, and what it is. Next I would mention who it was that wrote it, and whose in Greek it is, if I did not think that the greater part of you are aware…"

Felix found himself in the world he loved most, playing the role he was meant to play in that moment. He was the medium between the dead and the living, the translator of words, and of melody, and of feeling. He continued with his prologus, relishing every word of it.

Rufio was proud then, and relieved, for Felix Modestus was climbing back into the world from out of the gaping maw of the Underworld into which he had thrown himself. He hoped that he would remain. Rufio felt a chill on the back of his neck then, a cold prickle of the hair and skin, and for a moment he thought it was Felix's performance. Then, he froze in his seat, and turned his head slowly to his left to see a young man, scroll in hand spilling to the ground. He watched the performer upon the pulpitum most intently, mouthing every word that was spoken as if he knew it by rote.

Rufio was about to ask the man who he was, but the moment he made to open his mouth, he froze, for he recognized him from different places all at once. *The beach...near Apollo's temple on the Ilissos...my dream!* Rufio's heart raced, so loudly that he thought he could hear it reverberating in the odeon. *Terentius?*

The young man turned then and put his finger to his thinly-bearded mouth for silence.

Rufio's eyes widened and he tried to focus on Felix's words, even as he grasped his panicked chest.

"Do you make proof, what, in each character, my ability can effect." Felix approached the middle of the pulpitum again, taking a couple steps backward as he neared the end of he prologus. "If I have never greedily set a high price upon my skill, and have come to the conclusion that this is my greatest gain, as far as possible to be subservient to your convenience, establish in me a precedent, that the young may be anxious rather to please you than themselves..."

Felix closed his eyes again, but this time his smile remained.

Rufio looked to his left again to see the apparition nodding and open his mouth as if to speak.

"FELIX!" a shout came.

Rufio looked to his left again, but the young man was gone. "What?"

"No good?" Felix asked.

"What?" Rufio answered, quite confused. "No, it was...you were..."

"What?"

"Perfect." Rufio stood, but then the shout came again.

"FELIX! RUFIO!"

"Is that?" Rufio asked.

"Fausto?" Felix turned to see Fausto burst into the odeon from the doorway at stage left.

"There you are!" Fausto said, heaving and out of breath. "I heard your voice from out in the street!"

"What is it, Fausto?" Felix asked, gripping him by the shoulders. "Are you out of coin?"

"No…no! A fight!"

"You?" Felix looked to see if anyone was pursuing him.

Fausto shook his head. "Not me. All of us!"

"With whom?" Rufio asked as he jumped up onto the pulpitum to join them.

"The Rome Antics, those bastards! They came to the House of the Nymphs. The monkey stole our coin and they threw me out of Calypso's cubiculum, and-"

"All right, Fausto!" Felix shook him. "Calm down! Where are the lads now?"

"I told you! Fighting! They're fighting all of The Rome Antics! I came to find you. We need help!"

"Where is the fight?" Rufio asked.

"In the new agora!" Fausto pulled away. "We need to help them!"

Felix nodded and flexed his shoulders. "Oh, we'll help them all right!" He looked quickly to Rufio and smiled, his eyes wide. "To battle!"

Cacare! Rufio thought as he ran after Felix and Fausto.

Just before leaving, however, Felix stopped in front of the caretaker. "What's your name, friend?"

"Cosmo. What of it?"

"What did you think? Good?"

"It was all right," the man replied.

Felix spied the remnants of tears in his eyes, smiled, and ran for the sunlight outside. "TO BATTLE!"

THE HUBBUB FROM THE NEW AGORA COULD BE HEARD ABOVE the din of the rushing crowd, the whirring cicadas, and the shouts of the city officials who burst from their offices in the bouleuterion to see what chaos was shaking the calm of Athenae.

Some people panicked when shouts of battle echoed around the ancient agora, thinking that barbarians were at the city gates. They either ran in the opposite direction to gather their belongings and families at home before the assault, or they ran in the direction of the raucous clamour that seemed to explode out of the new agora.

Felix, Fausto and Rufio sprinted past the tholos at the entrance to the agora, down the length of the middle stoa, and leapt across the broad Panathenaic Way. Felix grabbed hold of an olive tree as he jumped, using it to propel himself out of the way of a passing wagon and accidentally ripped a bough from it as he passed. They carried on past the library of Pandainos, and bolted down the street toward the new agora.

"Woohoo!" screamed the naked seer, Melampus, from his spot beside the odeon of Agrippa. "You go to a great fray!"

"Rufio Pagano!" the librarian, Phemius, then called as they passed. "Would you like to tour the library now?"

Rufio looked back over his shoulder as he ran. "Another day, perhaps?" Then he collided with a bean seller's stall, sending the crop skittering all over the cobbled street.

"Watch it, Roman!" the man yelled.

Rufio rolled away, narrowly missing a pile of donkey excrement, found his feet, and carried on after Felix and Fausto.

"What was that about?" Phemius said as he arrived beside the bean seller.

"Now I have to pick all these up!" the man made a sign against evil at the backs of the fleeing Romans.

Phemius pat the man on the shoulder and carried on down the street in the direction of the noise.

. . .

When Felix and Fausto exploded into the new agora from the gate of Athena Archegetis, the scene laid out before them was one of pure chaos.

Rufio arrived panting and leaning on his knees as Felix scanned the vast, paved courtyard, fashioning an olive crown from the bough of olive he still held. "What do we do?" Rufio asked.

"We get stuck in!" Felix immediately ripped his tunica off over his head, tore away his bracae, and set the olive crown firmly upon his head. "To battle!"

Rufio watched for a second as Felix charged in, followed immediately by Fausto.

The surrounding colonnades were packed with shocked and excited onlookers which made the space more like a palaestra than an agora. In the middle of the courtyard, beside The Rome Antics' wagon, Castor, Pollux, and Damon stood in their bracae alone, surrounded by Cassius Cantor and the other nine Rome Antics. Castor had a bloody nose, and Damon gripped his ribs, howling as he did so. At the front, Pollux faced off against three others, landing a blow here, and taking another blow there. Around the circle of sweating, fighting men, a pack of dogs ran, and barked and snarled like some canine cavalry nipping at the rear of the enemy's lines.

"The Felix Modestus is HERE!!!!" Felix shouted as he grabbed the nearest of Cassius' men and hurled him into the side of the wagon.

"Felix!" Castor shouted, turning to Damon, "Felix is here!"

Felix immediately went to the wagon, grabbed what appeared to be a great club, and pulled it from the wagon to face Cassius Cantor and the others. When he swung, it was with one of the massive, stuffed leather phalluses.

"Please, Felix Modestus!" Cassius Cantor pleaded before his muscled nemesis. "Not my knobs!"

But Felix was deaf to his pleading and promptly swung

with all his might, striking Cassius Cantor so hard across the cheek that he sent him back several feet. Felix swung, again and again, as though he were an angry farmer cutting the winter wheat in a storm.

"Ho, ho!" called out the Athenian actor, Cadmus, from the south colonnade, leaning in to pull his fellow thespian, Aegisthus, and the playwright, Telephus, forward. "This is going to be good!"

Fausto then leaped atop the wagon and threw phalluses to each of The Etrurian Players who formed up around their leader. He threw a last one to Rufio and was promptly knocked off of the wagon by Numa who had the monkey, Momo, on his shoulder. Fausto fell to the ground and rolled away, swinging at one of the stray dogs that took a nip at him.

Numa hurled phalluses to The Rome Antics from his perch and then promptly jumped down to face off against Rufio.

"Peli!" Rufio shouted, distracted by the racing form of his dog. Then, he felt himself thrown backward as Numa's phallus hit him across the face with a loud smack. Rufio scrambled to his feet, and swung back, missing Numa, but striking the monkey from off his shoulder, sending it hurtling through the air.

The simian landed with a screech and was immediately swiped up in Peli's jaws as he ran by.

"Ohhh! The monkey!" someone shouted from the crowd.

"What is wrong with that dog?" asked another, looking at the strange prance of Peli's back legs.

Rufio swung again at Numa, knocking him back into the wagon so that he fell unconscious to the ground. His eyes searched for Peli again, and he stopped suddenly, for as Peli ran with the monkey in his maw, he also dealt with what appeared to be an overly engorged phallus of his own, which bounced painfully upon the ground.

Momo clutched onto the dog, his mouth agape with little fangs, even as he beat Peli's red prick with his tiny tambourine!

"Hey, that's my dog!" Rufio shouted, about to run after Peli, but stopping when Fausto shouted.

"Rufio, help!" Fausto was taking a beating from Piso and Lycus, the shorter of Cassius' crew.

Rufio immediately ran to aid Fausto, grabbing a rope from off the wagon as he passed, and collided with Piso. He swung hard at him with the red-painted knob, and then pounced to hog-tie him.

"Did you see that?" one of the butchers exclaimed. "Impressive!"

But most eyes were on the other side of the courtyard where the naked and crowned warrior took on five men by himself.

"Is that *The* Felix Modestus?" someone asked.

Another answered. "No, no. That's Hercules, returned to Athenae!"

A loud cheer went up at that, and Felix felt more exhilarated than he had in an age. So much so that he roared with his phallic club held high above his head, his chest heaving. He paused then and turned, fully aware of the crowd's eyes upon him, the enemy actors encircling him, slavering like hyenas before the lion. And then, he spoke clearly for all the world to hear, the words of famed Euripides…

"I took on a cloak of youthful flesh, of all the toils I then endured what need to tell? What did I not destroy, whether lions, or triple-bodied Typhons, or giants or the battle against the hosts of four-legged Centaurs? Or how when I had killed the Hydra, that monster with a ring of heads with power to grow again, I passed through a herd of countless other toils besides and came to the dead to fetch to the light, at the bidding of Eurystheus, the three-headed hound!"

The crowd roared and cheered, and even The Rome Antics lowered their phalluses.

"That was beautiful, Felix Modestus!" Cassius Cantor said, but even as the words left his bloody lips, Felix swung hard and knocked him backward.

The Athenian actor, Cadmus, turned then with a smile to Aegisthus, and together they called out a bit of Euripides' chorus. "He's a foreigner! And a foreigner who ruled our citizens most brutally at that!" They laughed, bowing to their fellow citizens who applauded their well-timed words.

The Rome Antics all leapt upon Felix again, howling and swinging with phallus and fist, and The Etrurian Players waded into the fray to their dominus' aid so that the courtyard was even more chaotic than it had been.

From the steps of the east propylon, the philosophers Philemon and Zonas looked on, the one with a smile upon his lips, the other a mask of severity.

"Look how he lets the life inside rush out upon the world!" Philemon marvelled as he watched Felix.

Zonas shook his head. "The heart is great which shows moderation in the midst of prosperity."

Philemon looked at him. "Seneca? Really?"

Zonas shrugged and they looked on.

"Where are the guards?" asked someone as the brawl spilled into the market stalls beneath the north colonnade. Women screamed, and people ran in every direction to avoid the rioters only to run into the racing dogs.

"Peli!" Rufio shouted, having seen Momo suddenly skitter across the courtyard to leap upon Damon's back.

Damon howled as the creature pulled his hair.

"Damon, hold still!" Castor shouted, preparing to clobber the miniature attacker, only to be pulled back by two more Rome Antics.

"Leave my monkey alone!" Numa shouted, ready to beat Castor.

"Leave my brother alone!" Pollux roared, picking up Numa by the groin and shoulder and hurling him into Cassius Cantor who had just been laid low by Felix.

"Everywhere! Doing everything!" someone shouted from the crowd, mocking The Rome Antics' tagline.

Finally, a contubernium of the urban guard marched into the agora, the optio shouting at the top of this lungs so that it echoed over everything. "STOP NOW!"

The slither of gladii could be heard, and others screamed.

"Peli!" Rufio shouted as he ran by them, chasing his dog.

"What in Hades is going on here?" the optio muttered, seeing giant stuffed phalluses littering the court, among tipped tables, and broken wares.

Peli stopped running in the midst of the large group of dogs which had stopped to eat thrown food near the wagon in the middle of the agora, and Rufio rushed to grab him.

"Peli, what is wrong with you? I've been worried-" His words died in his throat as he saw what Peli was up to or, rather, into.

A terrible sound rent the air, a pained, horrific howling, as Peli rocked back and forth on the back of a bitch in the pack. The other dogs bit at him, even as he tried desperately to satiate himself.

The guards were by now rounding up the brawlers, and the hubbub was dying down beneath the angry shouts of the upset traders.

"Peli!" Rufio shouted and ran in, kicking at the other strays, trying to grab hold of his dog's back legs and extricate him from his task.

Laughter erupted around the court then, even as the guards lined up Felix, Castor, Pollux, Fausto, Cassius and his men.

"Hey you!" one of the guards shouted at Rufio.

It was at that most inopportune moment that Clara, Electra, Martia, and Sextus came down the steps of the eastern propylon.

"What's happening here, Zonas?" Sextus asked the philosopher he knew.

"I'm most sorry, Praetor," Zonas replied. "Seems your friends have had a bit of a scuffle."

"What?" Clara and Electra said in unison, breaking from the crowd in time to see Felix naked, and the rest of the company battered, bloody, and under arrest.

"Rufio?" Clara shouted.

Rufio looked up from where he was pulling at Peli who was stuck into his canine companion.

Castor and Pollux looked at Rufio, from where the guards had them at sword point, and started to laugh. "Didn't we see that scene on a vase in the potters' street?"

Someone in the crowd heard that, and the laughter spread, people all pointing to the man and two dogs putting on a show in the middle of the courtyard as the irate wife looked on in humiliation.

Clara shook her head and turned away. "I don't believe this!" she said to Electra.

Felix finally saw where Electra stood and met her eyes. There was a faint flicker of a smile on her lips. "My Hercules," she whispered.

Martia blushed, and Clara turned to Electra.

"Really?" Clara said.

"Arrest these riotous Romans!" an aged Athenian nearby shouted.

Sextus turned to speak to the man, but then someone else shouted.

"Banishment!"

"Not for Hercules!" added a young Athenian woman.

"Death!" a few others demanded.

"Oh dear…" Sextus sighed, and turned to his wife, Clara, and Electra. "Our cena will have to wait. All of you go back to the villa. I'll see what I can do."

Peli finally finished, and the bitch ran off leaving Rufio holding Peli's back legs whilst he stared in Clara's direction, his face as red as an overripe pomegranate.

Clara shook her head and turned away, even as Rufio was forced into line with the other rioters.

"To the cells with them!" the optio shouted, and the crowd applauded the departing Romans for a most entertaining afternoon.

Felix broke away from his guard's grasp at the gate of Athena Archegetis, bowed, picked up his clothing which he had dropped there, and walked away with a great smile upon his face, the sunlight glistening on his sweaty form.

XII

HERCULES UNCHAINED

The people of Athenae felt a great relief that evening as the yellow and purple light of early summer dusk blanketed the city with calm. No enemy had been at the gates that day, no invasion of their beloved polis underway. The Gods knew that the people of Athenae had suffered terribly in the past, but they had always overcome it, prevailed against terrible odds.

However, that did not stop a small band of disgruntled merchants from lodging their complaints at the offices of the agora, wanting recompense for the damage to their wares and the loss of stock that occurred in the riot started by the Romans.

In the triclinia of domi around the city, there was great talk that evening of the rioters in the new agora. Some relayed the story as a brawl among visiting merchants, while others said it had begun as a protest against the notoriously bad theatre troupe known as The Rome Antics who had been seen lately about the agora and in the streets. Some said their monkey had been lifting purses since the day they arrived in Athenae. Still other gossips claimed they heard that the fight broke out in the lupanar called the House of the Nymphs, that it had begun when a lupa chose one man over another.

A very few suggested that it had been a fight between rival

theatre companies, but most dismissed this out of hand as something too mundane to have instigated such a great battle. Most citizens preferred to focus their attention on the vision of Hercules coming to the aid of the smaller band of combatants with his nephew, Iolaus, and Cerberus in tow. Whether they had been there or not, this was the talk of the city, and it was this sighting of the respected hero alone that stayed the sentence of death that a minority of citizens called for.

Whatever people's view or thoughts on the origins of the riot, all were left wondering what happened to the phallus-wielding fighters and their Hercules. That is, until it was put out that they had been jailed.

It was getting dark at the southwestern edge of the ancient agora, but that did not stop people gathering by torchlight in an area between the Areopagus, the Pnyx, and the Hill of the Nymphs, just inside the Melitides Gate of the city. They were in fact gathered around the desmoterion, the state prison of Athenae, for inside were all of the combatants of that day's riot including, some whispered, Hercules himself. People of all classes, including some daring women, had gathered there to try and catch another glimpse of the hero. Others offered prayers, and burned offerings upon the altars of the agora, while most simply gathered to gossip and hear the retelling of those exciting moments by some who had actually been there that day.

Extra guards had been brought in and posted about the walls of the long, rectangular building in an attempt to prevent the crowd of onlookers from barging into the prison to free the rioters. The members of the Boule, the citizens council of Athenae, and some magistrates from Rome were meeting into the night to decide what to do.

Inside the prison, beyond the gate and the guard tower that overlooked it all, the seven cells were filled to capacity, the jailers pacing the small lane between the two cell blocks, worrying over the crowd beyond the walls whose constant murmur continued to make them nervous.

The four cells toward the end of the prison, beside the walled court, had already been filled with a gang of cut-purses, three sheep thieves, and a smuggler from Piraeus earlier in the day. The remainder of the cells, including the large one with a bath, were now filled with the rioters.

The jailers could hear the men inside talking, or throwing the occasional insult across the way at their supposed foes, but they said nothing. If Hercules was indeed among them, they did not want to anger him for fear that he would take vengeance upon them afterward. Instead, they brought him a plate of bread and cheese, and clean water to drink, enough for him and his nephew Iolaus.

"THIS BREAD ISN'T THAT BAD," FELIX SAID AS HE RIPPED A hunk from the loaf that the silent jailer had given him. "Fausto, pass it around." Felix handed the platter to him and it went around the cell to Rufio, Castor, Pollux, and Damon who all sat on the cracked dirt floor with their backs to the wall, as far as possible away from the bucket that served as the privy. On the floor, beside Rufio, Peli lay sleeping deeply, panting as he did so, utterly exhausted by his escapades.

Rufio watched his dog and pat his head gently, avoiding the overly-used area of his genitals which finally seemed to be deflating.

"Is he all right now?" Fausto asked, nodding toward Peli.

Rufio shrugged. "I just don't know what happened. He's never been like that. At least, not for so long!"

"Long is right!" Castor joked. "I thought he turned into a horse!"

Pollux laughed at that, but Rufio did not see the humour in it.

"That monkey certainly gave him a good beating," Fausto added. "Hideous thing!"

There was a sudden screeching on the other side of the prison as Momo hurled himself around The Rome Antics' cell. Rufio got up and went to the barred door. "Shut that thing up!"

"You shut up!" the man named Numa shouted back.

"You there!" the jailer slammed his stick against Numa' fingers which had been gripping the bars. "Iolaus has spoken! Shut that monkey up!"

"That's not Iolaus! Nor is that Hercules!" Numa bit back, only to have his fingers bear the brunt of the jailer's frustration again.

Rufio looked confusedly at the jailer and turned back to his compatriots in the cell. "I don't know what is happening." He looked at Felix who was still wearing his olive crown, smiling broadly as he ate some of the cheese. "What are you so happy about?"

Felix looked up at him. "I feel amazing! Don't you?" He set the platter down and raised his arms above his head to stretch and sigh. "What an exhilarating day!"

"I think you got clubbed on the head," Rufio replied.

"I was the one who did the clubbing, my friend." Felix turned to Castor and Pollux. "Did you see the state of those bastards when it was all done?"

"We got them good, Dominus!" Pollux said. "Every one of them was bloodied."

"I'm just glad I found you!" Fausto said, his mood lightening more now.

"How exactly did it all start?" Rufio asked as he settled himself back down beside Peli. He stroked the dog's muzzle and lifted his hand in disgust at the stickiness he found there.

"Oh, don't worry, Rufio," Castor added. "It's just honey. I saw Peli licking that Egyptian honey slave's leg at one point."

Rufio sighed and shook his head, wiping his hand on the dirt floor. "Anyway, how did all this start?"

"What does it matter?" Felix said. "It was thrilling, and we won the day, and the crowd!"

"You can't be serious!" Rufio shouted back at him. "We're sitting here, awaiting a death sentence, and you still see the day as a success?"

Felix nodded. "They won't execute us."

"Well, they aren't letting us go either, are they?" Rufio said, turning back to Fausto. "So?"

Fausto shrugged. "Like I said, we were at the House of the Nymphs, having a wonderful time-"

Damon howled with delight at that.

Fausto continued. "That stupid monkey stole the coin Felix had given us, like I said, and then The Rome Antics stormed into the cubicula where we were having a wonderful time with each of our lupae. They threw our clothes down onto the street and pulled us from our ladies' arms, saying we couldn't pay!" Fausto shook his head. "Calypso, Medusa, and Amazonia tried to protest, but by then it was too late."

"Too late for what?" Rufio asked.

"To stop the fight," Pollux added. "They set on us as soon as we were outside. It was two of them to one of us, plus that bastard monkey who was running around waving the purse in our faces."

Fausto continued. "When Circe called for her husband and he and his cooks came with their cleavers, we all ran down the hill toward the agora."

"I told Fausto to go and find you both while we held them off," Castor added. "Luckily for us, he did."

"None of this is lucky, Castor," Rufio said. *I just want to be back with Clara and Felicia.* "We're now sitting in jail just a few steps from where the Gods tried Ares on the Areopagus. Now, we're awaiting trial as common brawlers to these Athenians. Definitely not gods!"

"Calm down, Rufio," Felix said, still smiling. "We are gods in our own right!"

"Yes!" Pollux clapped his hands. "You said it, Dominus!"

"Greater men than us have died within these walls," Rufio said, his voice dark.

"Like who?" Fausto asked.

"Socrates for one!"

"Socrates?" Fausto shrugged. "Never heard of him. How do you know?"

Rufio pointed to a spot on the wall where a bunch of writing had been etched by previous prisoners.

Fausto turned to look at it and tried to make out the Greek words. "'Ο…Σωκράτης…ήταν…εδώ.' What does that mean?"

Rufio did not answer.

"Somehow, I don't think the great philosopher would have carved into the stone that he was here." Felix laughed.

"But he was, wasn't he?" Rufio said. "Maybe they'll make us drink hemlock too and put us out of our misery!"

"You're overreacting." Felix stared at Rufio. "And you're wrecking my good mood."

"Good!"

"What's hemlock?" Fausto asked. "Does it taste good?"

"Tastes like Cassius Cantor's arse!" Pollux laughed.

"Then I don't want any," Fausto replied.

Rufio stood again and went to the door to try and catch a glimpse of the night sky and get a breath of fresh air. He could hear the murmur of people outside the prison, as well as the splash of water in The Rome Antics' cell. "They have a bath?" He turned to the others behind him, but they were already back to talking about their lupae's favourite tricks, while Felix rested against the wall, smiling and eminently proud of himself. "Clara will never speak to me again after this. I'm a terrible father and husband. I've let them down."

"Clara will be fine," Felix said, suddenly at his side. "As will Electra."

"You sure about that?"

Felix smiled. "Oh, yes." Felix remembered his wife's parting smile as he was marched from the agora. "Now step aside, Rufio. I need to ask the jailer something." Felix whistled out through the bars and one of the jailers walked up, avoiding looking at his eyes.

"Ye…yes?" the man said.

"I need fresh air. And I want to speak with the prisoner named Cassius Cantor. The leader of that lot!" Felix pointed across the way.

"I…uh…"

"The Gods demand it, man. Hurry!" Felix said, adjusting his olive crown.

"Yes, yes. Of course! But only yourself…Herc…um…sir."

"That is acceptable," Felix replied.

The jailer unbarred the door and let Felix out into the crisp night air.

Felix turned back to the cell. "I won't be long," he told Rufio, and winked. "Send him to the courtyard."

"Yes." The jailer then went to The Rome Antics' cell. "Cassius Cantor?"

"It is I!" Cassius replied, appearing at the bars.

"Your presence is requested in the courtyard."

"I am at your disposal, good man," Cassius replied with a smile. He turned back to his fellows. "Try to stay quiet, lads." Cassius exited the cell and the jailer promptly closed and barred the door once again. "Lead on."

"He's waiting in the courtyard," the jailer pointed down the short alleyway to where Felix was waiting, his back to them as he looked up at the silver slice of the moon.

Cassius Cantor walked slowly toward Felix whose bulky form, even then, looked like that of a god's. "It's not fair, you know?"

"What's not fair, Cassius?" Felix replied without turning.

"To have such skill, and good looks to match it." Cassius looked back to see if the jailer was watching them. He was. "You've even got our jailer and the people of Athenae believing that you're Hercules incarnate. Is there anything you cannot do, Felix Modestus?"

Felix turned to face Cassius. Even in the dim light, he noted the black eye and cut lip he had given him.

Cassius winced as he laughed and worked his jaw. "You certainly hit like Hercules!"

"You deserved it."

Cassius shrugged. "Perhaps. But with this face now, at least I won't need to wear a mask to perform."

"Why did you and your men have to steal my lads things? If you hadn't, none of us would be here."

"In truth, Felix, it was the monkey who started it. The lads just got overzealous. I had promised them a good time at the lupanar and…well…when they saw The Etrurian Players already engaged with their favourite she-wolves, seems they couldn't help themselves. They've quite fallen for Circe's ladies! Besides, it was all just a bit of fun. We Romans need to stick together."

Felix shook his head. "I'll be surprised if Boreas and Circe let any of our men near the place again after today."

"Oh, I don't know. You'd be surprised how the stink of a scandal can actually smell sweetly to some."

"It's all a joke to you, is it?" Felix took a step closer to Cassius, but the man did not budge.

"Life is a constant joke, my friend. The ultimate comedy!" Cassius spread his hands wide.

"You're the joke, Cassius." Felix turned on him. "You know,

Rufio thinks they are going to execute us. If Socrates didn't make it out of here, why should we? Most Romans don't have a proud history here in Graecia."

"Clearly you haven't heard what they're saying outside these walls," Cassius muttered.

"What?"

"Nothing." Cassius shook his head. "They won't execute actors, Felix. You know that. They appreciate us too much!"

"You sure about that?"

"They especially won't execute the greatest actor around the Middle Sea."

"Please, Cassius. You think your buffoonery makes you the greatest actor from Hispania to Judaea?" Felix's voice was disdainful, so much so that he felt a very slight pang of guilt.

"Not, me!" Cassius laughed. "I'm talking about you, Felix Modestus!"

Now Felix was at a loss for words.

Cassius smiled and sat down upon a stone bench along a nearby wall. "You know, I've admired you ever since I saw that performance in Rome at the Ludi Apollinaris." He shook his head in wonder. "You...your entire company really...inspired me that day. I can't see you all perform enough."

"Is that why you follow us everywhere we go?" Felix walked over and sat beside him.

Cassius grew serious. "I worried that if I stopped seeing you perform, then I would cease to be inspired." His smile returned then and he grinned sheepishly at Felix. "And the publicity for The Rome Antics when we're with you isn't so bad either."

Felix sighed.

Cassius continued in earnest. "I know we have different styles, but they serve no less a purpose."

"And what's that?"

"To entertain. To make people think, or to help them

escape their worries and ills for a short period of time. We both accomplish that…just in different ways." Cassius leaned on his knees and groaned for the pain. "I don't mind at all living in your shadow, Felix Modestus. I like the shade!"

Felix crossed his arms and leaned against the wall, his eyes trailing up to the stars set by the Gods in the sky above. For the first time ever, he felt no animosity toward Cassius Cantor, not for the flattery he heaped upon him, but for the simple truths he was not embarrassed to utter. "You know, Cassius, I-"

"You there!" A different jailer and two other men suddenly appeared at the entrance to the walled courtyard.

Felix looked up, confused by the interruption. "Yes, what is it?"

"You're both free to go. You and your men."

"All of us?" Cassius asked.

"Yes. All of you!"

"But how?" Cassius stood and walked over to him.

"The misunderstanding has been cleared up. The Boule does not see the merit in keeping you all here, let alone executing actors."

Cassius looked at Felix and grinned.

"Are you going to leave or do you want to remain in the desmoterion indefinitely?"

Cassius piped up. "While I do admire your fine facilities, good man, I believe I shall leave. Thank you for your hospitality!" Cassius bowed and went to join his men who had gathered before the gate.

Felix stood tall then and walked from the courtyard, past the jailer and his men who backed away as he did so, and stopped at the open cell door where Rufio and the others were waiting. "We're free to go."

"Thank Apollo!" Fausto said as he, Damon, Castor and Pollux all went to the door.

Felix looked at Rufio who was trying to wake Peli. "You going to carry him?"

"I think I may have to," Rufio replied as he wedged his arms beneath Peli's exhausted body. "Pah! He stinks!"

"You can both bathe back at the villa. Come. Let's get out of here." He stepped aside so that Rufio and Peli could go out first. Alone in the cell, Felix looked around one last time, his eyes resting on the Greek writing that said 'Socrates was here'. "Life is a comedy." He shook his head and left the cell to join the others.

Castor approached him. "There's a massive crowd outside, Felix. What do we do?"

"We'll go straight to the villa. No stopping. And no more fighting with The Rome Antics." He looked at his company. "You hear me? There's a truce now."

They all nodded and went out the door, following Cassius and his men.

Outside the desmoterion, a large half-circle of guards with torches kept the crowd back, but not so far that Felix, Cassius and all their men could not see all of the curious, intent eyes focussed upon them, searching for the hero.

Felix waited at the doorway for a moment, just out of sight, and saw Sextus standing with a couple of members of the Boule in front of four litters. He saw Sextus staring at him and the scowl upon his face was one that Felix would never have thought possible. He took a deep breath, adjusted the olive crown which he still wore, and walked slowly out the door.

A hush fell over the crowd as everyone stared, frozen in place in the presence of their Hercules.

Felix did not meet anyone's eyes, for what demigod would? He walked directly toward Sextus who was speaking to Cassius most intently.

"No more!" Sextus said angrily. "Or I won't be able to stay the sentence next time!"

"Thank you, Praetor," Cassius said. "We are grateful to you." He stepped aside, winked at Felix, and joined his men.

"You got The Rome Antics out too?" Pollux asked Sextus.

Sextus turned on him. "Of course I did! They're Romans too!" He shook his head, clearly flustered by hours of deliberation with the stern-faced members of the Boule who waited nearby to ensure the rioters all behaved themselves when they emerged from the desmoterion.

"Thank you, Sextus," Felix said to him.

Sextus shook his head. "Just get in the litters so we can get out of here. We'll talk about this later."

The Etrurian Players climbed into the litters with Castor and Pollux in one, Damon and Fausto in a second, Rufio and Peli in a third, and Felix to join Sextus in the fourth.

From within the litter, Damon began to play a solemn but building tune upon his flute which had escaped the battle unbroken.

It was then that Felix, standing before the litter, turned to look at the crowd, his eyes bright in the firelight of the torches held by the guards. "People of Athenae..." he began, waiting for the shushing about the crowd to abate. He looked at Cassius Cantor who stood nearby with his men, not daring to leave yet. "The Gods have blessed The Etrurian Players...*and* The Rome Antics! To witness them both perform is to experience the divine!"

People sighed and gawked, and one woman in the front of the crowd even fainted as Felix disappeared into the litter.

"Thank you, Hercules!" someone shouted, and the entire crowd joined in.

Cassius Cantor watched the litters pull away into the darkness and smiled. "Brilliant. Absolutely brilliant."

. . .

Eventually, the small crowd of citizens who had been following the four litters through the streets of Athenae fell away to return to their homes in the city to tell their families that they had seen Hercules, and even caught of glimpse of his nephew, Iolaus, who had carried Cerberus. It was whispered that the supposed hound of Hades was much smaller than expected and bore only one head, but most chose to leave out that detail when relaying their sighting. They had seen Hercules after all! And they had received his recommendations for a divine theatrical experience on top of it!

The litters were completely quiet by the time they left the city and crossed the Ilissos at the Porta Hadriana, their dark silhouettes swaying as the hired litter-bearers carried them through the darkness, following and followed by men with torches to light the way.

Finally, after a seeming eternity of silence, Sextus spoke to Felix. He was calmer now, having forced himself to be calm, for the deliberations - the humiliating pleading - with the Boule had been intense and draining. "What were you thinking, Felix?"

Felix looked up at Sextus, the crown still resting upon his brow, and stared right back at his business partner and friend. He smiled, but Sextus did not return the smile. "I was defending my men. They were attacked."

"This was no common taberna brawl, Felix. You destroyed the agora. You're fortunate no one was killed."

"It was just a bit of fun, Sextus. Nothing to worry about. Besides, it turned out to be good publicity."

"Publicity? You are joking, right? I arrived at the agora with your wives and my own to find you stark naked swinging giant cocks around and bloodying fellow Romans in front of half the city. Publicity?" Sextus shouted, and his voice was swallowed by the darkness of the forest on either side of the road. "I never would have thought you so irresponsible…so stupid!"

"Please, my friend. Don't overreact."

Sextus crossed his arms and shook his head in dismay. "Overreact? You just don't understand, do you? Not only was I, a Roman dignitary in Athenae, humiliated in front of the Athenian council… If that wasn't bad enough, you and your entire company were almost executed this day. Literally! I could be riding back to the villa now to tell your wives and children, little though they be, that their husbands and fathers were to be executed for public lewdness and rioting. They even wanted to hang the dog!"

"Ha. Good luck with that."

Sextus ignored Felix's attempt at humour. "I just don't know where we go from here, Felix. It may be that this partnership is not working out. You yourself have not been feeling inspired anymore. You told me yourself. Perhaps we should just cancel the performance and leave while we are all still breathing?"

"Don't say that, Sextus!" Felix reached out to grip his hand. "I'm myself again, I promise. Today had a healing effect that I cannot explain, but I *am* better now. Truly!"

"You were supposed to just visit the lupanar and get it out of your system. Gods know why Electra ever agreed to such a thing, but she did. And you couldn't even do that!"

"I was never going to do that." Felix sighed. "Lately, I've just been…I don't know…frustrated, I suppose."

"With what? What has you so agitated that you would risk everything? Assist me in understanding, Felix, because, Gods help me, I cannot."

"I suppose that I have been frustrated by this new role as a parent. When Thespis was born upon the sea, brought into the world with my own hands, I felt like anything was possible. I felt power, greatness, and a love that goes beyond anything I ever thought possible. But then, as the reality of this new burden set in…that I was now in charge of a tiny life which I must protect at all costs, but which takes up almost all of mine and Electra's time…"

"What?" Sextus' voice was curt, almost angry.

"I suppose I have been experiencing some regret at the loss of certain freedoms I've enjoyed for a very long time. Perhaps the brawl was part of that? I don't know."

"The loss of certain freedoms?" Sextus repeated. "Do you hear yourself? What I wouldn't give to be in your position! *The* Felix Modestus…poor fellow…he has had to sacrifice his own selfish whims in order to be father to a beautiful child!"

"There's no need to mock me."

"I'm not. I'm trying to give you a different perspective. Do you know what Martia and I would give to be in your position? You know our situation. I've already told you. How dare you whine about being a father! Martia cannot have children…she never will. But I know how fortunate I am in her, in our love. I cannot have a child with her, but I know with absolute certainty that I do not want to have a child with anyone else. Even my family have urged me to take another wife, a fertile one, but I've refused. It's not meant to be in the Gods' eyes that Martia and I are blessed with children, and I accept that because I am blessed in other ways. We all have our sacrifices to make, Felix, and I'm happy to make mine. As you should be to make yours, for all the ways in which the Gods have blessed you!" Sextus turned away, unable to look upon Felix in that moment.

Felix did not know what to say. He had never felt such shame, even more so than when he had not been able to perform upon the stage in previous days. The club with which Sextus had just battered him was greater than any Hercules had ever wielded, and he knew that he had needed that beating. Felix remembered the day Thespis had been born, the maelstrom of feelings, the utter confidence that it was all part of the Gods' plan for him. He remembered the love he felt for his wife, the perfect conviction of it, how he had felt that that was as close as he would ever come to divinity.

He knew he had rolled his weighty hubris to the top of a very high mountain, so much so that it had been inevitable that the Gods would force him back down again. Rather than see the changes in his life for the blessings they were, he had seen his new role as something lesser than what he had been, and that had been, perhaps, his greatest failing. Felix rubbed his face and closed his eyes, trying to escape into the darkness behind his lids. He breathed deeply, in and out as he realized the truth of what Sextus had said, knew how blessed he truly was. When he opened his eyes again, Sextus was looking at him.

"You're right, Sextus. I've been ungrateful for my blessings, but also insensitive to you and Martia. I'm truly sorry, my friend. All that you've said is true. I have been more selfish than I have any right to. I've let all of you down." Felix put his hand up as Sextus was about to interject. "It's true. Only the truest of friends would say to me what I needed to hear. If you no longer wish to be partners in this venture, to be the patron of The Etrurian Players, I completely understand. The last thing I wanted to do was to humiliate you, Sextus. That was never my intent."

"I know," Sextus sighed. "Felix, do you think I could so easily dismiss a partnership…no, a friendship!… such as this?" He smiled. "Another one of mine and Martia's blessings has been to become acquainted with you and yours. Every adventure has its mountains and valleys, no?"

"True enough." *He is truly a great man!* Felix thought. "I'm glad that you don't wish to desert us."

"I can handle a few hundred old Greek men!" Sextus waved a theatrical hand.

Felix's eyes widened. "A few hundred?"

"Yes. The entire Athenian Boule turned out to debate your sentencing"

"Really? Gods…I…I just don't know what to say to that."

"Don't say anything," Sextus smiled uncomfortably as he remembered the collective dismay of the Athenian council. "Just make sure you show them how great you really are when you stand before them in the odeon."

"Oh, we will. Don't you worry, Sextus."

"Good. I'm glad to hear it."

"And don't worry about us getting into trouble again for, by Apollo, I swear we won't let you down."

Soon after, the litters arrived at the villa and were ushered through the maintenance entrance at the back and into the courtyard behind the utility shed, stables, and servants' quarters. It was late and the villa was quiet but for Atticus, who was there to meet the litters, and the bath servants whom he had ordered to stoke the fires of the hypocausts so that the waters were warm enough.

"Is everything all right, Praetor?" Atticus asked Sextus who descended the litter first. He wrung his hands as he stood there. "I was worried for our guests."

Sextus looked back at the drowsy players falling out of the litters. "As well you should have been, Atticus. The Boule nearly executed them."

"Executed?" Atticus gripped his chest in panic as he counted the players who tumbled out and walked toward the bathhouse. "But none were."

"All is well," Sextus rubbed his face as the exhaustion began to set in. "It may well have been the most important speech of my career…talk of the strong bonds between Rome and Athenae, the glory of artistic and theatrical tradition, and the fallibility of even the greatest of men."

"And that swayed the council?" Atticus asked.

"Not until I mentioned Apollo's command to Felix Modestus on Delos. A few of the council members had heard what happened there, and so the Boule did not want to anger the god by executing the company he had sent to Athenae."

"Thank Athena…and Apollo!" Atticus gasped. After a moment of silence, as Sextus watched to ensure Felix and the others had gone to the baths, Atticus spoke again. "Lady Martia asked me to tell you that she has retired but that you should wake her when you arrive. She was quite worried."

"Thank you, Atticus. Good night."

"Good night, Praetor." Atticus watched Sextus go back into the villa and then turned to see Rufio kneeling beside the prostrate form of his dog outside the bathhouse doors. "Is everything all right, Rufio Pagano?"

"Oh, Atticus. I am alive, and so are the rest, but this day…" Rufio shook his head. "Not what I had envisioned."

"Nor any of us. Are you not bathing with the others?" Atticus did not say so, but he could smell both Rufio and his dog quite profoundly.

"Yes, I will. But first, I wonder if you might have one of the servants bring a bucket of warm water and some rags. I need to wash this one after his…his…orgy."

"I'm sorry… His what?" Atticus leaned forward.

"His ordeal. Forgive me. I am very tired."

"I understand. I shall fetch the water myself from the tepidarium. I'll be back in a moment." Atticus took a bronze basin which hung from an iron hook on the workshop wall nearby, and went into the baths.

"It's all right, boy. I'll get you cleaned up," Rufio whispered to Peli who lay on his side, still panting, his tongue lolling out the side of his mouth.

"Here you go," Atticus said as he returned and set the water basin down. "And here are the rags." He took three from off of his shoulder and set them on a bench nearby. He then filled a shallow bowl with water from a nearby tap that was fed from one of the mountain springs, and set it down beside Peli. "In case he wants to drink."

"Thank you, Atticus," Rufio said. "I can handle it from here. Please get some sleep. It's the middle of the night."

"It is almost morning," Atticus replied, looking at the sky. "But yes, I think I shall sleep a little before starting on ientaculum for all of you."

"I think the day ahead will be a quiet one, Atticus. Do not hurry on our account."

Atticus nodded and smiled sadly as he looked down at the poor dog which Rufio began to scrub with a wet rag. "Good night then."

"Good night, Atticus." When he was gone, Rufio turned his attention back to Peli. "What happened to you? You gave me such a scare."

Peli's mismatched eyes turned from his sprawled position to look up at his master.

"I'm just glad you're safe. But you can't do that again. You hear me? No!"

At the half-scolding sound of Rufio's voice, Peli sat up and licked his hands.

"You can be so naughty, and yet it's so hard to stay angry at you." Rufio continued to scrub at Peli with the wet rag, switching to a fresh one as the first became blackened. "Stand up."

Peli rose up slowly onto all fours and bowed his head to lap at the water which Atticus had placed there for him.

Rufio continued scrubbing. "I'm glad to see you're not excited anymore. Remember, you're a dog, not a Satyr," he said as he cleaned Peli's belly and behind. "Gwrra!" He shook his head and paused to collect himself.

After Rufio had thoroughly filthied all three rags and turned the basin of water to a dark stygian hue, he stood stiffly and looked down at Peli who was now wagging his tail and looking up at him. "I'm going to get cleaned up now. You go to Clara," he commanded. "Quietly. Shhh," he said, putting his fingers to his mouth.

Peli did not bark, but remained quiet, having been trained to that when Felicia had been born.

"Go now." Rufio shooed him and Peli walked stealthily into the villa to go back to where he knew his mistress and infant charge were sleeping.

Rufio sniffed at himself. "Now, it's my turn," he said as he went into the bathhouse.

By the time Rufio entered the tepidarium, the others had all finished and gone straight to their cubicula to sleep off the day's adventure. It was quiet but for the dripping of water and, as he soaked, Rufio wondered if he should not just sleep there. But he was so exhausted that he feared he would drown and not know it, so he went about his business with oil and strigil, scraping the dirt from his body, and then finishing off with a cold plunge in the frigidarium. Atticus had set out towels for all of them and one set remained for Rufio, along with a phial of rosemarinus oil which he rubbed into his skin.

When he emerged from the bathhouse, into the small odeon of the villa, he walked quietly through the triclinium, around the peristylium, and up the stairs to the second storey. He found Peli sleeping outside Clara's cubiculum door, and as he was about to enter, he paused to look out over the garden, thinking he heard a lark saluting the morning. "What?" Rufio strained to hear, but then stopped when he realized the joyous sounds were not coming from the sky or the trees outside the villa, but from Felix and Electra's cubiculum.

Rufio smiled to himself. "Everything's back to normal at least." He then turned and went to his own cubiculum door. He bent down to pat Peli, who opened his eyes to ensure it was his master, and then went inside.

In the dim light cast by a single oil lamp upon the broad desk, Rufio could see Clara sleeping soundly with Felicia beside her, nestled safely in among the pillows. He did not have the heart to wake her, and so he went to the larger of the couches that were in the room and collapsed.

EVER SINCE CLARA HAD SEEN RUFIO AT, QUITE LITERALLY, THE tail end of the riot in the agora, she had been fuming against her better judgement. She had been happy for him to spend time with Felix, and to help their friend if he could. She had also been looking forward to meeting them later in the day for a cena in the sunlit afternoon around the Acropolis. She had worn Rufio's favourite stola and even had Beatrice do her hair especially so as to take her husband's breath away when he saw her.

Time together with friends, and a bit of romance had been the plan in Clara's mind. Instead, however, she had found Rufio in the midst of a brawl, engaged in a strange threesome with Peli and a yelping four-legged third party.

Clara's first reaction at the time had been to grab a broom and slap some sense into both her dog and her husband. But when she saw the guard march Rufio and the others off at sword point, the fear she had felt then overwhelmed any sense of humiliation and anger.

The time in which she had waited with Electra and Martia, cradling Felicia like a talisman, whilst Sextus remained in the city pleading for the men's lives, had been the longest hours of her life. She had uttered prayers to Apollo who had sent them there, and to Athena in whose city they were guests, hoping that they would intercede on behalf of her errant husband.

When Sextus finally sent word that he had brought all of them home safely, a great wash of gratitude had flowed from Clara's eyes. She had collapsed upon the bed beside Felicia with prayers of thanks to the Gods, even as she had fallen asleep, exhausted from a day of worry.

It was near the fourth hour of daylight when Felicia woke Clara, hungry and in need of a change. Clara sat up in the bed to feed her and spied Rufio sleeping upon the couch, bathed in a pool of sunlight. She smiled and thanked the Gods beneath her breath once again that they had brought him home safely. There was no anger or frustration to be felt, no sign of embarrassment or dismay. There was only a relief as sharp as any scythe wielded on their latifundium. That relief cut through all else.

When Clara finished feeding and changing Felicia, trying to be as quiet as possible, she saw Rufio begin to shift upon the couch. She went over to him, sat on a stool beside, and leaned down to kiss his forehead with tear-soaked lips while Felicia's tiny hand struck out and smacked her father's neck.

"Ah!" Rufio's eyes shot wide for a second, but when he spotted his two favourite people in the world, he relaxed and smiled back, though a little nervously. "It's good to see you."

Clara wiped her eyes. "It's so good to see you."

Laying there, his body aching and tired, Rufio reached out and put his hand in hers. "I'm sorry."

"You're safe. That's all I care about."

Rufio sat up and leaned in to hug his wife and daughter, grateful for their touch, their smell, the sound of their voices.

"Did they treat you very badly in there?"

Rufio shook his head. "No. They wouldn't dare mistreat Hercules."

"What do you mean?"

"You wouldn't believe me if I told you." Rufio stood when he heard the scratching at the door and went across the cubiculum to let Peli in. "There's my little Cerberus!" he laughed as Peli pounced on him, tail wagging.

Peli then rushed to Clara and Felicia, his tail wagging so wildly that it threw him off course a couple of times.

"And you!" Clara said, handing Felicia to Rufio before kneeling to greet the canine. "We were worried about you, you naughty boy!"

"Naughty is right!" Rufio said, holding his daughter close. "This city is going to be overrun by an army of black and white mongrels." He shook his head. "I tried to clean him last night, but he still smells."

Clara sniffed Peli and recoiled immediately. "Wha! Who stinks?" she asked, making Peli whine and wag his tail all the more. "Who stinks?"

A great honk emanated from Felicia's bracae, making Rufio jump before he laughed. "We have a winner!"

Clara made to get up and take her, but Rufio held up a hand.

"I'll do it, my love," he said. "I missed it."

Thank you, Gods, for keeping him safe, Clara thought.

THE CENA DOUBLED AS IENTACULUM THAT DAY, FOR IT WAS already nearing the sixth hour of day when everyone met in the triclinium to eat and recount in full the tale of the great battle between The Etrurian Players and The Rome Antics the previous day.

Julius, Domela, and Beatrice listened in astonishment to all of it, while Clara, Electra, Sextus, and Martia relived the mortifying moments leading up to their arrival on the chaotic scene that had sent all of Athenae into a tumultuous tizzy.

"I must say, Felix," Sextus said as he smiled and wiped his brow, "life alongside all of you is anything but dull!"

The entire room burst out laughing.

"You even have the city believing Hercules has returned!"

Felix inclined his head, and Electra reached over to stroke his muscled arm.

Clara and Rufio exchanged smiles, for Felix and Electra had been the last to arrive in the triclinium, their faces still as flushed as rose petals, arms interlocked, their smiles spread across their exhausted faces.

In the early hours of the morning, Electra had asked Martia to take Thespis, and she had done so willingly, for the child seemed to now fall into a deep state of quiet whenever he was with her, keen to observe her bright eyes and gentle smile. Martia had also been happy to help Electra, now that Felix was back, for though she had put on a brave face for the duration of his incarceration, she could tell that beneath it all there had been unbearable worry. The perpetrators had, after all, been Romans misbehaving in Athenae, and Greeks did not easily forget the past.

Felix suddenly held up his cup. "I would like to thank Sextus for saving our skins this past night." He looked directly at Sextus then. "I am sorry for the frustration we have caused you, my friend. It will not happen again, for there is peace between us and The Rome Antics now."

"Really?" Julius asked.

"Truly," Felix answered. "Cassius Cantor and I have reached an understanding." Felix laughed. "He's actually not that terrible!"

Julius shook his head in disbelief. "I guess prison really does change a man!"

"Not prison, Julius. Battle. And Cassius and I have fought ours. Now it is done, and the time has come to focus on the performance to come!"

"Now that's what I like to hear!" Sextus said, raising his cup back to Felix. "To the play!"

"To the play!" everyone repeated.

"And I want to assure everyone that I am my old self again," Felix said. "No more amateur theatrics from me! Rufio and I went to the odeon and I performed my prologus."

"Really?" Clara turned to him.

"That's where Fausto found us," Rufio whispered.

"I'm back," Felix declared, "and better than ever!"

"I'll agree with that," Electra said, a smile on her lips.

Felix kissed her hand.

"Are we rehearsing today, Dominus?" Beatrice asked.

"Today, we rest. You may do what you wish. For myself, there is something I need to do without further delay."

"May I make one request?" Sextus asked.

"Of course, my friend!" Felix replied.

"Can everyone just stay out of the city for a couple of days?"

The laughter rang throughout the villa.

An hour later, as the sun was beginning to tilt westward, Felix, Electra, Rufio, Clara and the children were making their way slowly through the pine-clad pathways of the woods beyond the villa's walls. Peli ranged occasionally ahead of them, but for the most part he remained at Rufio's heels, his urge to venture far afield dampened for the time being.

The air was hot and sweetly scented with pine and wild thyme, and the cicadas whirred away as they flit from tree to tree. The forested slopes felt like a world apart from all they had seen thus far, from Athenae, from the villa. Their senses were heightened as they walked.

Electra and Clara held the children close, stopping occasionally to let their little hands explore the texture of a tree's bark, or the cool surface of a rock.

Felix and Rufio flanked the women and children, the one with a bow and quiver of arrows at the ready in case a boar came charging out of the thicket, the other carrying a hemp sack with offerings for the goddess whose temple they sought.

"Where did Atticus say the temple was?" Rufio asked as he adjusted the sack over his shoulder.

"He said we were to follow the deer path downhill from the villa until we near the top of the Panathenaic stadium-"

"Downhill is right!" Clara added as she picked her way over a fallen tree, careful not to catch the hem of her stola upon it. "I would have dressed differently had I known we were going this far through the wood."

"Felix had a strong need to make an offering to Artemis," Electra said, smiling at her husband. "I think it's a good idea."

"It is," Rufio acknowledged, "but I like to know where I'm going. I don't want to wander into the necropolis on Ardittos hill by mistake."

"It's day, Rufio," Felix added. "The dead are not concerned with you beneath Helios' light." Felix stopped. "There! I see the stadium!" He pointed to a high retaining wall set into the hillside, the white blocks out of place among the dark tree trunks, rising out of the dirt and pine needle covered forest floor. They stopped to orient themselves and Felix pointed to the hill rising up just the other side of the stadium. "We have to go up there."

"Can we rest here a little?" Rufio asked.

"No. Let's keep going," Felix insisted, plodding on ahead, followed by Electra and Thespis, then Clara and Felicia.

Rufio hoisted the sack again and brought up the rear with Peli beside him, the dog's senses more alert now as he nosed the air and peered into the shadows.

The path rose steeply now, and though there were visible

pathways on the forest floor, they did not seem well-trodden by any man. Just past the stadium, the hill of Ardittos rose up on their right, its dense crown of pine and cypress overlooking the stadium on one side, and the Ilissos river on the other.

"Is that it, Felix?" Clara asked as she spotted a small temple at the top of the hill, hidden in among the trees.

"No. Atticus said that one is the temple of Athena-Tyche. The temple of Artemis Agrotera is on the other side of the hill."

"Up and down, up and down," Rufio complained, wiping his brow.

"Would you prefer to be in prison?" Electra said, looking at Rufio over her shoulder.

"No. No, thank you," he replied. "Though the food was excellent, the view was dismal."

Electra laughed and it sounded delightful in that wood.

They carried on until the path peaked and then began to descend once more, but then the pathway spread out in five different directions.

There was a sudden rustling in the the brush then, and rapid hoofbeats on the forest floor.

Felix pulled back his bow quickly, his arrow pointed in the direction of the sound.

"No! Don't!" Electra said. "It's a deer! Artemis' animal."

The deer froze and stared at them for a moment.

"Peli, stay," Rufio urged, and surprisingly he did.

The deer then bolted down the second path from their right.

"The goddess is leading us," Electra said, pointing in the direction the deer had gone. "We follow."

They followed in silence, picking their way downhill through the forest until their view at last opened up onto a broad terrace surrounded by a low retaining wall.

"It's beautiful!" Clara said as they approached the sanctuary of Artemis Agrotera. "I never would have thought this to be here."

"I glimpsed it from the road far below," Rufio said, "but everyone was saying how difficult it is to find."

"If the goddess had not shown us the way, we probably would not have found it," Electra said as she followed Felix.

The sanctuary consisted of a cleared rectangular area surrounded by a low marble wall. In the middle was a small temple with four ionic columns at the front, and four at the back, each of their capitals still faintly gilded. Around the circumference of the temple was a faded blue and white frieze depicting ancient battles, and episodes from the goddess' life. In the pediment of the temple was a simple crescent moon, one of the symbols of Artemis.

The temple doors were open, though it was dark inside, and before the temple was a broad altar of white marble where hunters had left bloodied arrowheads and a couple of skinning knives. The far retaining wall looked out from over the Ilissos and the temples along its riverbank, to the titanic form of the Olympieion, the great temple of Zeus, and then to the distant Acropolis crowned with the temple of Athena Parthenos.

Electra stood at the wall with Clara and Rufio. She wiped a tear from her eye.

"Is everything all right?" Clara asked her, reaching out to touch her shoulder.

"Yes," she answered. "I just don't know why, but the sight of this city from this spot…it's…it's just so beautiful. I have missed it."

While Clara put one arm about Electra, her other holding Felicia, Rufio looked back to see Felix standing before the temple, staring into the darkness of the cella.

"Perhaps we should make our offerings," Rufio suggested, watching Peli to make sure he did not leave the confines of the sanctuary.

"Yes, let's," Electra agreed.

They went to stand before the altar and Rufio set the sack upon the ground to reach in and take out the items they had brought. To Electra he handed the small clay pot of Hymettos honey, and to Clara he gave the bundle of crescent-shaped cakes which Atticus had provided that morning. For himself, Rufio pulled out a piece of papyrus on which he had written out the lines he remembered of the goddess' hymn.

With Thespis in her arms, Electra placed the honey upon the altar, and prayed silently to the goddess whom she had always admired for her strength.

Clara, with Felicia trying to reach for the cakes, placed the beautifully-wrapped bundle upon the altar and said her own prayers to the goddess, expressing her hopes for care and protection for the child who squirmed in her arms.

It was then Rufio's turn. He unrolled the papyrus and, looking up at the temple, uttered the words written thereon. "I sing of Artemis, whose shafts are of gold, who cheers on the hounds, the pure maiden, shooter of stags, who delights in archery, own sister to Apollo with the golden sword…"

Rufio paused, having found his breath, steady now, Peli somehow at his side suddenly, knowing. Electra and Clara listened intently to his words as he continued.

"Over the shadowy hills and windy peaks she draws her golden bow, rejoicing in the chase, and sends out grievous shafts. The tops of the high mountains tremble and the tangled wood echoes awesomely with the outcry of beasts, earthquakes and the sea also where fishes shoal."

A wind picked up then, hot and swirling in the sanctuary, and Electra and Clara held the children to their chests, close, to avoid the dust as Rufio pressed on through squinting eyes.

"But the goddess with a bold heart turns every way destroying the race of wild beasts, and when she is satisfied and has cheered her heart, this huntress who delights in arrows slackens her supple bow and goes to the great house of her dear brother Phoebus Apollo, to the rich land of Delphi, there to order the lovely dance of the Muses and Graces. There she hangs up her curved bow and her arrows, and heads and leads the dances, gracefully arrayed, while all they utter their heavenly voice, singing how neat-ankled Leto bore children supreme among the immortals both in thought and in deed."

When Rufio finished, the wind seemed to fade away with a sigh. As the dust settled, they saw Felix's form standing before the temple entrance, and before any of them could utter a word to him, he strode into the darkened sanctum alone.

THE FAINT GLOW OF A SINGLE CLAY LAMP BURNED UPON THE altar in the temple of Artemis Agrotera which was as dark and deep as the forest on a moonlit night. It smelled of cedar and juniper, but with a hint of blood and iron. Behind the altar was a statue of Artemis who ran alongside her stag and hound, her golden bow at the ready. All sound was muted within the goddess' sanctum, and Felix could hear the beating of his quickening heart as he approached the altar.

The walls of the temple were adorned with an odd mixture of faded flowers and ribbons, and a variety of shields, daggers, swords, bows, and hundreds of Persian bronze arrowheads which were remnant offerings to the goddess after the great battle of Marathon when the temple had been built.

Coiled in the corner behind the altar, the guardian of the temple slept in darkness, continuing to digest the myriad vermin who came in from the forest.

When Felix arrived before the altar, his face lit by the lone flame, he looked up at the goddess' image, his arms spread wide, and closed his eyes.

"Divine Artemis, Goddess of the Hunt... Protector of Children... Sister of Art-Loving Apollo... I honour you."

Felix paused, having forgot all that he wanted to say to the goddess, things he had wanted to request ever since the strong urge to visit her temple had come upon him. He breathed deeply, tempering the frustration he began to feel with himself. "Oh, Artemis...You who do battle and hunt, while also leading the dances of Muses and Graces...I ask for your help. I have escaped imprisonment and death at the hands of the Athenians, but to what end? I wish more than anything to give to your Far-Shooting brother a production worthy of his faith in me and my company. I wish to honour him. Yet I also wish to do right by...to protect...my wife and my son. I would be both the greatest player, and father and husband of the age, but I know that few mortals are granted so much."

Felix opened his eyes and leaned on the edge of the altar to look up at the goddess.

"Oh Artemis, I am torn between my art and my family. I have journeyed far...laboured hard... Will you guide me along with your divine brother? Help me to fulfill a destiny not of humiliation and defeat, but rather of victory and renown."

He looked at the goddess' divine aspect again, the silence seeming to deepen as though she were expecting something. And so, Felix took the pugio he had tucked into his cingulum and held it with both hands so that it glinted in the firelight. A thought came to him then, and without further delay, he cut the side of his hand just enough to draw blood. Red droplets fell onto the altar where he placed the blade.

"I offer you this blade and my blood, Divine Goddess. Please accept my sincere offerings and guide me to victory, whatever that may look like in the eyes of yourself and your art-loving brother."

Felix felt slightly faint then, and fell to his knees, his thick hands gripping the edge of the altar as his ears began to ring.

Honour Apollo in Athena's great city. Your victory is at hand.

Felix looked up quickly, his vision blurring as he peered beyond the flame to the goddess' visage.

From artful victory to life's triumph you shall go, but not without the passing of creativity's torch… Your offering is accepted…

The voice faded away in Felix's mind and on the wind that now came in at the temple door.

"Felix?" came Electra's voice from the light outside. "Is everything all right?"

The spinning in Felix's head stopped and he rose to his feet to bow before the goddess. "Thank you," he whispered before turning to go out.

WHEN FELIX EXITED THE TEMPLE, HE FOUND ELECTRA standing directly before the entrance, holding Thespis in her arms and staring at him with a worried look upon her face.

"Is all well?" she asked. "Did the goddess accept your offerings?"

Felix nodded, though he did not smile. "She did." *That voice… It echoes in my head still.* He then kissed his wife and took his son into his arms. "All will be well, Thespis. You will see. Someday…you will see." He turned back to Electra. "I know you miss this city," he said as they both turned to look over the wall and river to Athenae and the Acropolis. "If all goes well, we can move here if that is what you want?"

"Thank you," Electra said. "But let's see how things unfold. Besides…so long as I am with you, my husband, I am home." She kissed Felix back then, more lingering this time, even as Thespis began to wriggle and cry.

Felix laughed and tickled his squirming son. "Someday, you too will find your love, little one. For now, you must eat and grow strong and skilled."

Thespis let out a great wet wind then, smiling in a most relieved way up at his father.

"Yes, my boy. And shit and break wind. You can do that too! Just not in public when you are older, for it is uncouth!"

Electra howled with laughter and reached out to take Thespis. "I'll change him."

"No, my dear. I can do it. You go and sit with Clara for a few minutes. I see that Rufio is already engaged in changing soiled bracae, and so I shall join him."

"All right then," Electra smiled and went to rest with Clara where she sat upon the sanctuary wall, Peli dozing at her feet as she looked out at the city.

Felix walked over to Rufio who was in the midst of changing Felicia.

"If I had a sestertius for each pair of bracae I changed, I would be able to stop farming!" Rufio said as he finished tidying up is daughter. "She is prolific!"

"But would you want to either stop farming, or stop changing bracae?" Felix asked.

"Truly, no."

"Then you are going about the Gods' business."

Rufio held up his hand which had some excrement on it. "Is this the Gods' business then?"

Felix laughed as he began changing Thespis. "No, Rufio. That is your daughter's."

Rufio was rubbing his hand on the dirt to clean it when Felicia sounded another horn. "Oh, no! You see?"

Felix looked aside at his friend and laughed, but it was then that Thespis sounded his own loud note and took a shot at his father's chest.

"Gwrra!" Rufio heaved. "Gwrra!"

Felix was silent.

"Now that's funny!" Clara joked with Electra as they watched their husbands struggle, their laughter echoing about the sanctuary as though two nymphs had come out of the wood to dance and sing about the goddess' temple.

"Gods, I need some wine!" Felix said.

"And a bath," Rufio added. "Gwrra!"

After the children and the men had been cleaned up, they began to make their way back to the villa. They had remained at the sanctuary longer than expected, and now the sun's chariot was racing with wheels of orange fire to the distant horizon.

Felix walked with his bow and thick quiver of arrows slung over his shoulder, while Electra and Clara carried the children more carefully over the darkening forest floor.

Rufio, who had offered to carry all of the satchels and left-over food, followed behind them with Peli back at his heels, unwilling to be away from his dominus.

The woods were getting dark quickly, and looked unfamiliar in the late light of day. They walked up and down, and then up again, following faint pathways.

As the others turned down a pathway to their left, however, Rufio stopped suddenly. "Hey!" he shouted into the woods to his right as he strained to see. "Hey, you!"

Felix stopped and looked back. "What's he doing?" he said to Electra and Clara.

"Rufio?" Clara called back to Rufio who stood shouting into the wood with Peli alert beside him, ears pricked high.

Without another word, Rufio charged off in the other direction. "Hey, stop!"

Felix turned and went after him. "That's the way to the necropolis!" Felix called, but Rufio and Peli were already gone.

"It's him!" Rufio said to Peli as he charged through the underbrush. "Wait!" he called to the man he had seen along the river and in the theatre. "Why are you following us? Stop! I just want to talk!"

The man Rufio saw continued to walk, dragging his long, unfurled papyrus scroll on the forest floor as a reluctant bride drags her flame-coloured train to her new home.

"Are you all right? Stop now!" Rufio shouted.

The man stopped most suddenly and immediately turned to face Rufio and Peli who was now beginning to bark and whine. Beyond the man's shoulder, Rufio could see the moss-covered tops of monuments and broken grave stelae.

"FREE ME!" the man shouted with tears in his eyes, even as he was swept backward through the air into the mass of ancient monuments.

Rufio stared, dumbfounded. He did not notice the great boar that suddenly charged out of the forest, its head levelled at him.

"Rufio!" Clara's scream echoed somewhere in the fading light behind him.

Conscious now of the beast bearing down on him, Rufio dropped the satchels, took Peli up in his arms and turned to run. "BOAR!" he shouted, as he ran with Peli wiggling and barking into his ear, snarling over Rufio's shoulder at the animal pursuing them.

The animal was too fast, however. Rufio could hear its grunting breath closer and closer to him. As he turned to see those angry red eyes bent on goring him, three swift arrow shafts plunged into the animal's right side sending it straight into the trunk of a wide oak tree with a thunderous crunch.

Rufio dropped to his knees, utterly breathless, not ten feet from the dead beast.

"Rufio!" Clara shouted, Felicia now crying in her arms as she ran toward her husband.

"I'm fine!" Rufio called out, looking up, expecting to see

Artemis somewhere in the wood. Instead, he saw Felix atop a fallen tree, his bow strained against a fourth arrow.

"Is it dead?" Felix called, jumping from the top of the tree.

"Oh, it's dead all right!" Rufio called back.

Peli now approached the dead boar, barking furiously at it and spinning around several times in hysterics.

Felix arrived, followed by Clara and Electra.

"By Artemis," Electra said. "It's enormous!"

"That would have killed you, Rufio!" Clara chided. "Why did you run off like that?"

"I thought I saw someone I knew," Rufio answered.

"Here?" Clara replied.

"I don't know!" Rufio said loudly, still panting from the pursuit.

Felix leaned on his bow, smiling now as he looked down at the boar.

"What are you happy about?" Rufio asked. "That thing almost killed me!"

"Looks like we're feasting tonight!" Felix said.

A smile spanned Rufio's face. "Forget the fish! We're having Etrurian wine and boar!"

The two of them cheered and jumped about while the women shook their heads and tried to calm the children.

Peli, who was clearly confused by the myriad emotions displayed by the group, decided to take a bite at the boar, then turned and lifted his leg upon it.

An hour later, in the outer courtyard of the villa, The Etrurian Players were gathering in preparation to go out and search for their dominus and the others. They had been gone for far too long and with darkness falling, Atticus had warned Sextus that something might have happened.

The praetor had rallied the group, along with servants from

the villa, and was preparing to send them out in search parties of three, armed with torches, spears, and bows.

"This is exciting!" Fausto said. "I've never hunted before!"

"We're not hunting, you idiot!" Castor chided him. "Felix, Electra and the others should have been back a long time ago. We're searching for them!"

"I know," Fausto said. "But if I see a rabbit or something, I'll take a shot."

"You couldn't hit a horse if you tried!" Pollux said.

"I like horses!" Beatrice protested.

"All right, all right!" Julius said at the front of the group. "We need to find Felix and the others fast! Each group is armed and has a torch. Atticus' men will lead each group down a different forest path. Don't shoot any which way, or else you might hit one of us. Got it?"

Beatrice gulped. "Yes."

"We'll find them, dear," Domela said to her. "Don't worry."

Beatrice nodded.

"Let's go!" Julius said, leading the way like Caesar. Behind him, the groups were gathered and stepped forward as the bar was lifted and the gates groaned open. They went but two steps before they stopped dead.

Before the gates was a great muscled form with a massive boar slung across his shoulders.

"It's him! It's Hercules!" one of Atticus' servants shouted.

"No it isn't!" Julius said. "It's Felix!"

"Sorry we're late!" Felix bellowed as he pushed his way into the courtyard. "We decided to do some hunting!"

A cheer went up around the courtyard as Felix hefted the boar and dropped its dead weight onto the ground beside the fountain. "Who's hungry?"

ACT IV

SUMMER HEAT AND HISTRIONICS

XIII

WRITING AND THE SHADE

"If my love affairs had been prosperous for me, I am sure she would have been here by this; but I'm afraid that the damsel has been led astray here in my absence."

Clinia, Menedemus' estranged on, stood pacing in the street outside of his father's domus, the worry clearly etched upon his face, visible in his every movement as he waited for, and fretted over, the imminent arrival of his beloved Antiphila.

"Many things combine to strengthen this opinion in my mind; opportunity, the place, her age, a worthless mother under whose control she is, with whom nothing but gain is precious."

Onto the scene then came Clinia's good friend, Clitipho.

"Clinia!"

"Alas, wretched me!"

"Do pray, take care that no one coming out of your father's house sees you here by accident." Clitipho looked around quickly, worried that Clinia's return home should no longer be cloaked from his tormented father's eyes as they wished it to remain for the moment.

"I will do so, but really my mind presages I know not what misfortune," Clinia said.

"Do you persist in making your mind upon that, before you

know what is the fact?" Clitipho chided. "She'll be here presently."

"When will that presently be?" Clinia sat upon the edge of the fountain in the square, his head in his hands.

"Don't you consider that it is a great way from here? Besides, you know the ways of women, while they are bestirring themselves, and while they are making preparations, a whole year passes by."

Clinia looked up, his face fraught with emotion. "O Clitipho, I'm afraid."

His friend placed his hand upon his shoulder in sincere reassurance. "Take courage. Look, here comes Dromo, together with Syrus." He pointed at their two servants coming along the road. "They are close at hand…"

Loud applause and cheers rang out from the cavia of the small odeon of the villa as the rest of The Etrurian Players applauded Felix and Rufio. It was with great relief that the company had been watching Felix rehearse that morning, never missing a beat, or word, or wry expression of his features.

Rufio stood to the side and applauded too, for it seemed that Felix Modestus had returned from his artistic exile, a fact which Rufio joked was partially due to feasting on mountain boar and Etrurian wine.

Felix smiled at his company and breathed deeply for a moment, not because he was nervous, no. That imposter had left with his tail between his legs. This great breathing was one of a return to the pulpitum. It was out of gratitude to the goddess who had, evidently, heard his prayer. He winked at Electra who held Thespis in her arms. Felix then put up his hands to quieten everyone.

"That's better!" he clapped Rufio on the back, grateful for his friend's honest delivery, though he knew Rufio preferred to be sat with a stylus and sheet of papyrus to performing. "Something is missing though… Damon!"

"Yaaaw!" Damon replied from the middle of the cavia.

"Let's try accenting our scenes with sounds of the outdoors. Something to tickle the minds and imaginations of the audience, just enough to draw them further into the illusion of our scene, but not so much as to distract from the dialogue or action."

Damon nodded, stood, and set his flute to his mouth. At first the sound was of a buzzing of cicadas which quickly grew muted and then turned to the sweet song of larks, and then the calming refrain of mourning doves.

The sounds were so mesmerizing that even Felicia and Thespis turned in their mothers' arms the better to see where the sounds were coming from.

"Those children are going to grow up thinking birds have two legs, two arms, and a big forehead!" Castor joked.

"Three legs from what the lupa said!" Pollux added, causing Damon to place his flute in a different place and point it in his direction.

"All right, all right," Felix hopped off the pulpitum into the orchestra. "That was perfect, Damon! Do you think you can sustain that on and off throughout the performance since we are not including any songs or choral arrangements?"

Damon nodded with a grunt.

Felix smiled when he saw Sextus grinning at the back of the cavia where he sat with Martia and Atticus watching the rehearsal.

"Let's keep our momentum!" he said to the group. "Fausto, Castor… Act two, scene three. Syrus and Dromo arrive onto the scene with Clinia and Clitipho apart from them."

Fausto and Castor jumped up from their seats and took to the stage like hungry lads at a banquet.

Felix and Rufio stood aside to listen as Clinia and Clitipho's servants came walking onto the scene…

"Do you say so?" Syrus asked.

"'Tis as I told you, but in the meantime, while we've been carrying on our discourse, these women have been left behind."

"Don't you hear, Clinia?" Clitipho whispered from the right. "Your mistress is at hand."

Clinia smiled with a world of relief. "Why yes, I do hear now at last, and I see and revive, Clitipho!"

IT HAD BEEN DAYS SINCE THE RIOT, AND FOR ALL THAT TIME, The Etrurian Players had remained at the villa focussed on rehearsing and perfecting their performances, finalizing costumes, and making adjustments to props.

Only Sextus had ventured into the city for business, and when he returned it was often with news of public curiosity about Hercules and the theatre companies he had lauded when released from prison.

"I assure you," Sextus told everyone, "that The Rome Antics have taken full advantage of your recommendation, Felix, or, rather, of Hercules'. They're drawing massive crowds near the odeon and the stoa of Eumenes. I've never seen a street performance draw so many Athenians!"

Felix smiled to himself. *I knew Cassius would take advantage of that,* he thought. "If Cassius Cantor is good at anything, it's sniffing out a promotional opportunity!" Felix laughed and turned back to Sextus. "Any other word?"

"While The Rome Antics are there and dominate the scene for now - much to the dismay of some local actors and play- wrights - it is The Etrurian Players who are talked about by citizens in the tabernae and the agora. You may not be able to return to the new agora to do your shopping anytime soon, but when you eventually do make an appearance in the heart of the city, the timing must be perfect."

"Worry not Sextus," Felix said, his hand on his shoulder. "We're not going to the agora anytime soon."

"What?" Fausto said, most distraught. "But I told Calypso I'd be back soon!"

"Don't worry, Fausto!" Pollux ribbed him. "I'm sure she'll find someone else's coin to take."

Julius walked up to Fausto. "Don't make the mistake of falling in love with a lupa, my boy. Therein only lies heartbreak."

"And a painful burning sensation between the legs," Castor added with a chuckle.

"How would you know?" Fausto shouted at him.

Castor put up his hands. "My medicus told me."

"You're both disgusting!" Beatrice piped up from the broad trestle table she had set up in the courtyard to work on the costumes. That stopped the burgeoning argument, for ever since they had returned from prison, she had been upset for all the worry they had caused her, and she had not been silent about it.

"Well, perhaps we should get back to work," Julius said.

"Quite right," Domela added.

"Quite right," Beatrice mimicked as she sewed away, her head bobbing as her gaze went from Domela to Julius.

Though the others did not say anything, most of them noticed the newfound energy with which Julius undertook his roles. True, he had always been one of the best players among them - across the entire Middle Sea! - but there was no denying the fact that his not-so-secretive relationship with Domela had given him an added, youthful edge. His performances at rehearsal were inspiring everyone else to greatness, as were his constant words of encouragement to each of them on the side.

"Felix?" Julius said.

"Yes?"

"Might I suggest that we undertake the fourth scene of the second act next? Electra and Clara haven't had many opportunities to rehearse."

Felix looked at Electra and Clara and they both nodded their agreement. "Good idea! This can be the final scene we do before the sun reaches its zenith. It's starting to get hot!" Felix wiped the sweat from his brow and went onto the pulpitum to wait.

Clara handed Felicia to Rufio who sat beneath one of several awnings that Atticus had set up, and Electra handed Thespis to Martia who, as usual, took him into her arms most willingly and where he fell asleep almost instantly.

"Right," Felix began. "Bacchis and Antiphila appear down the road from the homes of Menedemus and Chremes. Clinia and Syrus stand apart from them, listening from behind the fountain..."

Electra and Clara stepped onto the pulpitum, the latter's arm laced through the other's as they walked slowly about the stage.

Felix and Fausto stumbled over each other as they moved around the bucket that stood in for the fountain, always out of sight of the two women.

"Upon my word, my dear, Antiphila," Bacchis began, "I commend you, and think you fortunate in having made it your study that your manners should be comfortable to those good looks of yours, and so may the Gods bless me, I do not at all wonder if every man is in love with you." The courtesan, with full lips that somehow managed to pout and smile at once, looked Antiphila up and down and pat her hand. "For your discourse has been a proof to me what kind of disposition you possess. And when now I reflect in my mind upon your way of life, and that of all of you, in fact, who keep the public at a distance from yourselves, it is not surprising both that you are of *that* disposition, and that we are not; for it is your interest to be virtuous; those with whom we are acquainted will not allow us to be so. For *our* lovers, allured merely by our beauty, court us for that. When that has faded, they transfer their affections elsewhere; and unless we have made provision in the meantime for the future, we live in destitution."

The two women rounded the fountain for a third time and then sat facing the orchestra as Bacchis continued.

"Now with you, when you have once resolved to pass your life with one man whose manners are especially kindred to your own, those persons become attached to you. By this kindly feeling, you are truly devoted to each other, and no calamity can ever possibly interrupt your love."

Felix watched Electra speak Bacchis' words from Clinia's hiding spot on the other side of the fountain. For a brief moment, she caught his eye, and his smile, touching the spot above her heart upon the utterance of the word 'love'. *All is well,* Felix thought.

Rufio waited for Clara to utter her next lines, for though she had few in the play, when she spoke, she captivated her audience.

Antiphila then replied to Bacchis. "I know nothing about other women; I'm sure that I have, indeed, always used every endeavour to derive my own happiness from his happiness."

Clinia's head appeared above the edge of the fountain, as he was unable to help his enthusiasm. "Ah! 'Tis for that reason, my Antiphila, that you alone have now caused me to return to my native country. For while I was absent from you, all other hardships which I encountered were light to me, save the being deprived of you."

Antiphila suddenly cocked her head, having heard the voice, and in that moment a flute mimicking the sound of Clinia's voice piped up in the street, and she went back to her converse with Bacchis.

"I believe it," Syrus whispered to Clinia with whom he was crouched in the dirt, listening.

"Syrus, I can scarce endure it! Wretch that I am, that I should not be allowed to possess one of such a disposition at my own discretion!"

"Nay," Syrus said, hissing at Clinia who was now moving around the base of the fountain as the women began to stand and carry on. "So far as I understand your father, he will for a long time yet be giving you a hard task."

Bacchis suddenly looked past Antiphila to see Clinia staring up at them most intently. "Why, who is that young man that's looking at us?"

Antiphila turned with Bacchis and squealed, falling back into the courtesan whose bosom caught her. "Ah! Do support me, I entreat you!"

"Prithee, what is the matter with you?" Bacchis asked.

"I shall die, alas! I shall die!" Antiphila swooned, still supported by Bacchis.

"Why are you thus surprised, Antiphila?"

"Is it Clinia I see, or not?" the younger girl replied as the young man stood up from the ground, brushing himself off, aided by Syrus in the same task whom he then shooed away.

"Whom do you see?" Bacchis asked.

Before she could answer, Antiphila launched herself from Bacchis' supportive bosom directly at Clinia who also leapt toward her. They met in a loving embrace.

"Blessings on you, my life!" Clinia said, holding her out to look upon her.

"Oh my long-wished for Clinia, blessings on you!"

At that precise moment, Syrus threw flower petals into the air above their heads, and then pretended not to have done so as they looked around.

"How fare you, my love?" Clinia asked her, grasping her hands.

"I'm overjoyed that you have returned safe."

"And do I embrace you, Antiphila, so passionately longed for by my soul!" Clinia said, kissing her hands.

Syrus stepped forward quickly. "Go indoors, for the old gentleman has been waiting for us some time."

"Stop!" Rufio suddenly called out. Felix, Clara, Electra, and Fausto all stopped and looked at him. "End of scene!"

Felix turned toward him. "Yes, we know, Rufio. But let us finish the action."

Clinia and Antiphila pulled apart and they went all together into the house of Chremes where the women would be staying.

When the scene was done, Felix turned to the audience. "Damon, excellent thought to cover Clinia's speech with your flute. That was funny!"

Damon stood and bowed, saluting with his flute.

"And Electra, my love, it was funny the way Bacchis caught Antiphila. Just funny and titillating enough for the more conservative Athenian audience."

"Better to tantalize slightly than hit them over the head with a giant phallus, wouldn't you say?" Electra stared at him, unable to hide her smile after a moment.

"Quite, my love," Felix replied before turning to Julius. "Anything else you spot?"

Julius stood up. "Yes, it was somewhat difficult to see and hear you and Fausto behind the fountain. Perhaps Electra and Clara can have their conversation to one side of the fountain instead of in front of it. That way, you and Fausto can be upon the ground on the other side, more visible to the audience.

"Yes!" Felix clapped. "I was worried about that as we were playing it out." Felix then turned to Rufio. "Any other input?"

"How about less kissing?" Rufio replied as he stood, bouncing Felicia to calm her.

"Oh, Rufio!" Clara chided as she hopped down off the

pulpitum, strode toward him, and planted a long kiss upon his lips.

Rufio smiled as her lips lingered upon his, and when he felt her take Felicia from him, he made to swoon and fall backward over his seat to flip over and land face down in the grass.

Damon fluted a descending scale and everyone laughed and applauded.

THE ETRURIAN PLAYERS REHEARSED FOR DAYS ON END WITH A discipline that surprised Sextus, Martia, Atticus and the servants. Before long, the month of Julius was upon them, the days long, and bright, and the temperatures soaring to sweaty heights.

It was not long before the realization dawned on the company that the Great Panathenaea was but a few weeks away, at the end of Augustus, or rather the middle of the Attic month of Hekatombaion as some of the more conservative Athenians still referred to it.

This meant that they needed to focus more than ever, though that became difficult during the hottest days of the year as the great bowl of Athenae came to a boil beneath the summer sun.

During one midday break, as they sat in the shade of the olive trees in the peristylium sipping cooled Samian wine and eating fresh figs, Felix talked with the others about some ideas he had come up with to make the action upon the stage more interesting.

"There is a lot of talking about people in the play. What if those characters who are being discussed by others are standing off to the side miming the action?"

"*Mime* the action? I don't know about that," Rufio said. "It could get quite confusing for all of us on stage. We don't want to distract from the words being spoken."

"While you're at it, just put giant knobs in their hands so they can wave them at the speakers to make sure the audience knows who's speaking," Pollux added.

"No more knobs," Fausto agreed, his hand touching the side of his head.

"True. Quite right!" Felix caught himself. "Not sure what I was thinking there." Felix leaned back on his couch.

"I think you need to stay true to Terentius' vision, Felix." Clara sat up beside Rufio. "It's all about the words, the meaning and feeling of them."

"You seem to forget, husband," Electra said, reaching out to touch his shoulder from her couch beside him, "in a Greek play, there are few distractions."

"And this is Athenae," Julius added. "We're not in Rome."

"Yes, yes, I'm well aware." Felix scratched his beard. "The success of The Rome Antics tells another story, however."

"Let them do their thing, and we'll do ours," Castor said.

Felix smiled at the confidence his players were displaying. He had only been musing about adding things, no doubt due to the heat that played with his mind, but it was good to see them asserting themselves when it came to their strengths. "We'll keep things as they are. Let Cassius' lot bandy about with their stuffed bollocks."

"Knobs," Fausto corrected.

"Whatever!" Felix clapped back.

"I can see their next show now," Pollux said. "The Cunnus Kerfuffle."

Everyone burst out laughing.

Felix looked at them all, one eyebrow raised. *And yet,* he thought. *Here we all are, talking about them!* Now he could not help but laugh.

The cicadas' song bloomed then to a deafening height as the Gods hammered them with midday heat.

"That's it," Felix said. "No point baking here any longer.

The shade does not help at one point. I'm going to try and sleep before Thespis wakes."

"Not without me, you're not," Electra rose from her couch, smoothed her stola and clasped Felix's hand.

"I was hoping you'd say that," Felix whispered to her before they left the others there in the courtyard.

"I'm tired too," Domela added from the couch at the back where she and Julius had been listening to the banter.

"Quite right," Julius stood with her to follow.

"Talk about a cunnus kerfuffle," Fausto whispered to Castor.

Julius turned and walked up to Fausto. He leaned down, grinned, and spoke. "She's lovely to me. And at least I don't have to pay her."

"Haha!" Castor howled at the same time that Damon trilled a few mocking notes on the flute.

Julius lightly tapped Fausto's reddening cheek with his palm, and then went after Domela.

"We've got to get back into town," Fausto said to Castor, Pollux, and Damon.

"I don't want to know!" Clara said, shaking her head. She looked at Rufio. "Felicia is going to be up any moment. I'll get her before she starts crying."

Rufio set his cup down, picked up the satchel which had been sitting on the ground beside him, and followed her to leave the others to their longing for lupae. He caught up with Clara at the stairs. "I was thinking of going into the city."

"You were?" She turned on the stairs to look down at him.

"Well, not into the city proper, but to the shrines and temple of Apollo along the Ilissos. It's quiet and cool there, and…well…I could use a change of scenery. Couldn't you?"

Clara nodded. "We can doze in the litter on the way."

"We can bring Peli too. He's been so good lately."

"Exhausted and *good* are different, but yes, I see your point. We'll have to put a lead on him though."

"I'll go ask Atticus for a litter, a rope, a blanket, and maybe some food to nibble."

Clara was going to say they did not need all of that, but then Rufio looked so happy at the prospect that she just smiled. "It sounds lovely."

WITHIN THE HOUR, RUFIO, CLARA, FELICIA, AND PELI WERE on their way down the road behind the opaque white curtains of the litter as it swayed gently in the hot breeze. Rufio dozed while Clara fed Felicia, and Peli, who was tied to a long rope which was, in turn, tied to Rufio's ankle, ran alongside the litter.

The litter-bearers eyed the dog warily as they carried their load, sweating and grunting in the summer sun.

But Peli seemed not to care about their stomping and shuffling feet, prancing along, tail wagging as though he was happy to be out in the world once again.

Atticus had supplied them with a picnic, and even added some food for the litter-bearers whom he had told could sleep in the shade while they waited, away from their guests of course.

The streets seemed deserted as they went, with any sane citizen retreating indoors at that hour of the day. It leant an eerie feeling to Athenae, but also painted it with an ancient purity that soothed Clara as she lay there, stroking her daughter's sweaty brow as she fed.

The litter turned off of the road, just before the Porta Hadriana, and the bearers headed into the wood along the treed shoreline of the Ilissos. In the shade, it grew darker within the confines of the litter.

Clara turned her head to look at Rufio who had begun to

snore a little. She covered her mouth so as not to laugh out loud at the sight of him gripping his satchel to his chest, a rope around one ankle, and their picnic nestled between his feet.

Before long, a dappled light penetrated the litter's hangings as it was set down beneath the trees near the temple of Apollo Delphinios.

"We're here, lady," the head litter-bearer said, aware from the snoring that Rufio was not awake.

"Thank you," Clara replied. She sat up and nudged Rufio. "My love. Time to wake. We're at the shrines."

Rufio's eyes opened slowly and he turned to her and smiled. "I slept so deeply," he said softly.

"No. Stay!" one of the litter-bearers suddenly said.

Peli started barking loudly.

"Well the peace was nice while it lasted," Rufio said to Clara, smiling and stretching. A second later, the rope grew taut and he was whisked out into the sunshine from beneath the white curtains. "Aaah!" Rufio shouted as he was dragged along the ground.

One of the litter-bearers grabbed his hand as he passed, in an effort to lend him some aid, but as Peli continued to pull at the other end, Rufio lifted off the ground as though he were upon an invisible rack!

"Peli, NO!" Clara shouted. The dog obeyed immediately, much to her surprise, and pranced back toward Rufio who had dropped back to the ground, Peli's leg thinking about lifting beside him.

"Don't you dare!" Rufio growled at Peli.

"Are you all right, sir?" the litter-bearer asked, helping Rufio to his feet.

"I'm fine. I've had worse." Rufio brushed himself off and pointed to the litter. "Atticus has sent food for all of you to enjoy in the shade while we're down here. My wife has it for you."

"Thank you," the man bowed and accepted the bundle of food from Clara. "Do let us know if you need anything. We'll just be on the other side of the temple." He looked around cautiously.

"Are you all right?" Clara asked the man.

"Oh yes, lady. Fine. It's just…"

"Just what?"

"They say this riverbank is haunted. So ancient it is. That is why the law court is closed most of the time. They only use it for overflow trials."

Clara looked around at the calm sunny spot in which they stood. "I don't think there are any lemures here at the moment."

"That may be, but I wouldn't want to come down here at night."

"We will keep that in mind. Thank you," Clara said before turning back to see Rufio gathering up his satchel, and the papyri and styli that had fallen out onto the crisp grass. "We will call you if we feel uneasy."

The man gulped and made a sign against ill omen on his forehead.

Clara turned back to Rufio. "Do you want to untie him for now? Just in case?"

"Oh no!" Rufio shook his head, looking at Peli. "I'll untie myself, but not him. Come, you! There's a nice shady tree here by the river waiting for you." Rufio led Peli to the shoreline and a plane tree that stood there. He untied the rope from his ankle, which had a red ring around it, and tied it about the trunk. "There. It's long enough for you to go a few paces, but not too far." He knelt down. "I'm keeping my eye on you."

Peli whined and licked Rufio's face before he could pull back.

"If you're good, I might let you run about a little. But not now. Not after that display."

Peli lay down, defeated.

"Good." Rufio went back to help Clara with the blanket and food which they set up near Peli in the shade along the river.

It was peaceful among the temples of Apollo, Chronos, and Rhea, and the sanctuary of Zeus Panhellenios. No one seemed to be around, and the old law courts adjacent to the temples were firmly shut for the day. It was difficult to believe that they were just outside the city walls.

Rufio settled himself against the bowl of a willow tree whose branches reached down into the water. The lithe and leafy limbs caressed the river, swaying with the light current as it bubbled over rocks and tufts of grass and dirt. The sound was soothing and that, coupled with the melody of birdsong made Rufio feel calmer than he had in a while.

"The litter-bearer seems to think this place is haunted," Clara said to Rufio as she stood Felicia up, holding her hands as she wobbled upon her tiny legs.

Rufio smiled as he watched, mesmerized by his daughter's skill. "She'll be walking in no time!"

"Yes, she will… Io, my girl!" Clara beamed.

Rufio looked upon his wife and daughter, the sight of both of them making him feel that all was right with the world. "Well, it certainly doesn't seem haunted by malicious spirits here," he said. "The tomb on the hill above our farm at home…now *that* is haunted!"

Clara sat Felicia on the ground between her legs and fed her a piece of fresh fig, so sweet it made Felicia's eyes bulge in delight.

"I think she likes it!" Rufio laughed. "Maybe not too much, else we'll be changing bracae all night long!"

"I wouldn't have it any other way." Clara stroked her daughter's hair and looked at Rufio as he took out his small writing desk, a sheet of papyrus, his stylus and ink. She wanted to ask what he was writing, but thought better of it, wanting him to take advantage of inspiration while it struck. It was, after all, a rare calm they were experiencing. Instead, Clara turned Felicia around to face her and began to show her blades of grass, a pine cone hot from the sun, and a pebble that was smoothed by the flowing waters of the Ilissos.

Peli, bored on the other side of the tree, crawled upon his belly until he was pressed against Clara's side, his furry face looking up at Felicia who reached out to touch one of his pointed ears.

"Gentle, love. Peli doesn't like his ears pulled."

But Peli let the child do as she wished, and then licked her hand, making Felicia giggle at the feeling.

"I don't know where that mouth has been," Rufio muttered without looking up, a thin smile on his face.

"He's clean enough for now," Clara said as she pet Peli's head and neck. "He smells like sun-baked soil and pine for the moment."

"There is no end to the blessings of this day," Rufio finished writing something before letting the papyrus curl back up. He then reached into his satchel and pulled out a small wreath of rosemarinus. "I'm going into the temple for a moment."

"Be careful not to step on the snake," Clara said.

Rufio nodded. "Right. I'd forgotten about him." He walked toward the temple of Apollo which was not far off. He could hear the litter-bearers laughing and talking in the shade of a wild olive tree on the other side of the temple. He looked at the small altar outside the temple and saw that the Etrurian olive wreath he had previously left was upon the ground. He walked over to it, picked it up, shook the dirt from it and set it upon the altar again. "For you, Lord Apollo." Rufio then mounted the steps to the temple entrance and walked between the thick Doric columns to go in.

Inside the temple, the bowls of the bronze tripods burned with low flames into which incense had been dropped, scenting the air and pleasing the god. At the far end, in the cella, Apollo stood with his lyre, gazing down the aisle at those who came to pay homage to him.

Rufio stood just inside the threshold, waiting until his eyes adjusted, searching for any sign of the temple priest, or even the temple serpent Clara had reminded him of. Neither were present. *No doubt they're both sleeping someplace like everyone else in Athenae,* Rufio thought as he walked.

The temple seemed different from the last time he was there with Felix and the entire company. His senses were piqued by everything around him, and the hair on the back of his neck prickled such that he turned around to make sure no one was there. Assured that he was indeed alone, Rufio approached the altar before Apollo and there saw the range of their previous offerings, including the laurel wreath with the yellow glass leaves which he and Clara had offered. He found that comforting somehow.

"Lord Apollo," Rufio began. "Humbly, I come before you to ask for your protection, your blessing in our endeavour, and…and for your guidance and inspiration. Shine your light upon me so that I may put into words the story I feel in every part of my soul. I have only ideas and images at the moment, but I know that they are meant to…to form a whole and coherent tale that will please you. For now, please accept my offerings…" Rufio held up the corona of rosemarinus and then unrolled and read the snippet of the hymn which he had just written out from memory.

"I will remember and not be unmindful of Apollo who shoots afar. As he goes through the house of Zeus, the gods tremble before him and all spring up from their seats when he draws near, as he bends his bright bow. But Leto alone stays by the side of Zeus who delights in thunder; and then she unstrings his bow, and closes his quiver and takes his archery from his strong shoulders in her hands and hangs them on a golden peg against a pillar of his father's house. Then she leads him to a seat and makes him sit: and the Father gives him nectar in a golden cup welcoming his son, while the other gods make him sit down there, and queenly Leto rejoices because she bare a mighty son and an archer. Rejoice, blessed Leto, for you bare glorious children, the lord Apollo and Artemis who delights in arrows; her in Ortygia, and him in rocky Delos, as you rested against the great mass of the Cynthian hill hard by a palm tree by the streams of Inopus..."

Rufio rolled the papyrus back up and placed it upon the altar. "As we are in Athenae, I thought it best to use your father's ancient name..." Rufio breathed deeply, nearly coughing from the smoke of the cedar incense wafting around the main altar. "My mother...she did not bear a great archer, such as yours did. I am but a farmer and scriptor...but... Lord...I do what I do with utmost sincerity. Guide me in the time to come...my words...my actions...for myself...and for the family with which I have been blessed."

There was movement at the right corner of the altar then and Rufio took a step back as the head of the temple serpent peeked over the altar's surface.

Rufio froze and watched, unable to dislodge his feet from where they were planted on the cracked marble floor of that ancient temple.

The serpent, a thick, gleaming apparition of crystalline black and green, with eyes the colour of yellow heliodor, slid across the top of the altar, weaving slowly amongst the offerings to Apollo that where piled there. Though as thick as Rufio's arm, the serpent did not disturb the offerings set out for his master, but safeguarded them for the Far-Shooter.

Rufio gulped as the serpent paused in the middle of the altar, its forked tongue jutting out rapidly to touch the wreath and the papyrus which Rufio had set there. "Please accept my offerings, Lord Apollo."

The serpent seemed to stare at Rufio, the latter clasping his hands as if locked in an uncomfortable silence with someone.

"Lord, please watch over and protect my wife and child, and shine your divine light on my endeavours. I…I will…if all goes well…I will build a temple in your honour when we return to Etruria."

The serpent's head rose up and, for a moment, Rufio worried that it might strike, but then it slid calmly down the front of the altar, between Rufio's feet, brushing him gently, and disappeared into the darkness beyond the glow of the tripods.

Rufio backed away a few paces and then turned and went out into the daylight, breathing deeply of the fresh air as he leaned upon one of the columns.

There were moments he could remember in his life, turning points of import. He somehow knew that this was one of those moments. He felt it. But he could not see with absolute certainty what it all meant. He only knew that Apollo had heard him, and would help him, so long as he helped himself. "There is a Muse for all seasons…" Rufio said, a sudden urge to write that down. He looked to where Clara and Felicia were with Peli.

Clara waved Felicia's hand in Rufio's direction, their faces the most beautiful thing Rufio had ever seen.

He smiled back and walked forward, missing the temple steps, only to fall headlong into the dirt before the temple. He rolled quickly and came to his feet in one smooth motion, brushing the dirt from his tunica and looking around as if he had been tripped.

Clara laughed and blew him a kiss.

Rufio skipped across the grass and dirt toward his family, his daughter giggling at how silly her father looked and, the more she giggled, the sillier he got. When he finally arrived, a little breathless, he bent over to kiss them both before sitting in the shade against the willow tree.

"Did Apollo accept your offerings?" Clara asked.

Rufio was already balancing his writing desk upon his knees, his stylus poised above the papyrus. "I believe he did," he replied without looking up. "I just want to write something down before I forget…and…there." He looked up and smiled.

"That's all? You're not writing anymore?"

"I'm formulating," Rufio shrugged.

"Formulating? Really?"

"Yes." Rufio grinned.

"All right then." Clara picked up Felicia. "Pater's formulating! Yes he is!" Clara suddenly sniffed. "Woo! So are you by the smell of it!"

Suddenly, Peli's nose was in there to confirm the deduction.

"Peli, back!" Clara said. "Rufio, can you take her?"

Rufio stood up and took Felicia while Clara fished around in one of the satchels for clean bracae.

"I'll change her," Rufio said, taking the bracae from Clara and setting about the business of cleaning his daughter.

Clara leaned back against the tree behind her and took a moment to look around. It was indeed very peaceful, strangely so all of a sudden. "I think it's so hot even the birds are sleeping now."

"It is a different world here," Rufio said as he cleaned one hand on the grass. "Gwrra!"

"Oh, Rufio. Really?" Clara laughed.

"Must be this Greek food."

"Hmm." Clara reached to take a piece of bread and cheese that they had brought. "So can you tell me what you've been working on? I see you scribbling away all the time, but it doesn't look like poetry or prose."

"I've been formulating."

"Yes, you said that. Formulating what?"

"A play, of course…"

"Of course." Clara smiled.

"But I don't know how to describe it. I have so many ideas that come to me at once, like flickers of sunlight on the sea. It's difficult to remember, so I write them down for now."

"So, a play…"

"Yes."

"About what?"

He waved at a fly that buzzed about Felicia as he sat her up, all clean now, and leaned against the tree with her in his lap. He held his stylus in his hand and she fastened onto it, most curiously. "I want it to reflect life in a most sincere way."

"Sincerity is always good."

"Yes. I was toying with…well…"

"What?" Clara leaned forward, intrigued by the perplexing look upon his face.

"Well…I was thinking of a story that reflects my own life in some ways."

"Really?"

"It's just a thought. I mean, who would have thought that poor Rufio Pagano would find himself so blessed, here with you." He smiled. "And with you!" He looked down at Felicia's big eyes, then back at Clara. "Obviously not my life verbatim, just snippets…chance happenings."

"And this will be 'smart funny'? Like Terentius?"

"What else?" Rufio smiled. "He's my favourite."

"I think you should write it, whatever *it* is. I'm so proud of you."

"Thank you." Rufio raised his one hand which he had on the stylus to make a flourishing motion. "But don't say anything to anyone, all right?"

"I won't. But, Rufio be-"

"I mean, if people knew, then that would be too much pressure. Felix would want to produce it and-"

Clara nodded distractedly now as she watched Felicia's stylus-wielding hand rise and fall in concert with her father's as though they were conducting a chorus.

"Who knows, maybe by the time I'm finished writing it this little one will be old enough to play a part and-"

"Rufio!" Clara said, but too late.

Felicia's little hand plunged downward clutching the stylus and buried the bronze point of it in Rufio's thigh.

"Ooww!" Rufio howled, only to be joined by Peli in the same sound.

"I tried to warn you," Clara said as she took Felicia from Rufio so that he could extricate the stylus from his muscle.

He pulled up the hem of his tunica to see where it was bleeding. "Gods, she's strong!"

"I tried to tell you."

"It's fine. Just a scratch, but I'd better rinse if off." Rufio stood and walked to the riverbank to hoist his tunica and splash water on his thigh.

Peli strained at his rope to join him, and choked himself with the effort as he whined.

"Maybe you should take him for a walk?" Clara said. "You did promise him. And he's been good."

Rufio turned to look back at her. "I can do that."

Clara was already untying the rope from Peli's neck when Rufio stood up.

"I'll keep him on the lead though, because if I don't he'll… run away." Rufio watched as Peli shot off down the river toward the temple of Cronos and Rea. He sighed and hobbled after Peli. "Peli! Come back here!"

"Sorry!" Clara called out as she watched Rufio amble away. She then looked down at Felicia. "Hungry, my girl?"

. . .

Rufio tried to run after Peli, but the canine was much faster, and the throbbing in Rufio's leg was getting worse. "Come back here! Peli!" he shouted, following the sound of barking.

When Rufio found Peli, he was standing directly in front of a man who was leaning against the bole of a pine tree, beside which was an aged statue of Apollo. "Peli! Leave that man alone!" Rufio called, hurrying toward them before the man lashed out at his dog.

But the man seemed unbothered by the dog barking in his face, or indeed by the pine resin that seemed to be dripping down the trunk and onto his rather ragged brown tunica. To Rufio's surprise, the man was wholly engrossed in scribbling away on a lengthy piece of papyrus. When he got closer, and recognition dawned on him, he stopped. His sweat turned from hot to cold in a matter of moments, and there was no other sound in the area apart from the hot summer wind tickling the branches of the pine the man sat against.

"Salve," Rufio said to the man as he approached more slowly. "I'm sorry about my dog."

"What dog?" the man said without looking up from his work. Then, he barked sharply at Peli who whined and raced to Rufio's side.

"I remember you," Rufio dared to speak. "Are you him?" Rufio gulped. "You are…Terentius?"

"Is that a question, or was it meant as a statement of your certainty?" he said without looking up.

"Honestly…I don't know what I'm certain of, apart from the love of my wife and daughter."

"I wouldn't know about that."

"Please tell me. Are you him? Are you Terentius?"

The younger man looked directly at Rufio then. "I *was* Terentius." There was an edge of anger and frustration in his voice, but also a thread of deep sadness, of regret.

"Why did you not stop the other day at the temple of Artemis? That was you, was it not?"

The man went back to writing. "I cannot stop whenever I choose. At the close of the day, I must go back to the place."

Rufio gulped. "What place? What were you up to?"

"To be suspicious is not a fault. To be suspicious all the time without coming to a conclusion is the defect."

"Did you just quote your own words at me?" Rufio asked, but received no response. "What are you writing now?"

"Everything."

"Everything?" *I've finally cracked,* he told himself. *I'm speaking with a shade!*

"Everything I did not get the chance to write."

"But you're writing it now."

He shook his head. "I write, yes. I see it. But if I turn it to you?" The shade turned the papyrus toward Rufio and the moment he set eyes upon it, the script disappeared. "My words are for myself, and for the Gods."

"What happened to you?" Rufio asked, suddenly very sorry for him.

"Life happened to me."

"Why did you come to Athenae in the first place?"

"I came here for inspiration, to walk in the footsteps of the great playwrights who came before."

"And?"

"And they shunned me. And I became ill."

"Were you alone?"

"Surrounded by people, and utterly alone but for my thoughts and words."

Rufio tapped at the right side of his head as a ringing was increasing in volume in his ear.

"You said you would free me." The shade stated it matter-of-factly, suddenly. Then, he uttered a title he loved with all his being as if he were singing a melody made for the Gods. "*Heautontimorumenos*... It is my torch in the darkness."

Rufio began to back away, his discomfort now far outweighing his curiosity.

"You said you would free me," the shade repeated.

"I don't know what you mean," Rufio replied, stopping his retreat and tapping his head again. "Free you from where? You roam about at will. If you want to leave Athenae, you can come back to Italy with me on my ship."

The shade shook his head. "No. Free me from here. From this." He motioned to the world about them. "I am stranded. I have no will anymore."

"I don't understand. How am I to free you if you are-"

"Shhhh!" the shade put his finger to his lips as he had done in the odeon. The resin from the tree dripped heavily now onto the shade's shoulders.

It sent a cold chill down Rufio's spine, even in that summer heat.

"The play Apollo demanded. It has been the one wish the Gods have granted me. You and your players must make the Athenians see what true Roman drama is when you perform. Make them see me for what I am."

"And what is that?" Rufio asked.

"What you want to be... Worthy of remembrance..."

The ringing reached such a pitch that Rufio shut his eyes and fell to his knees. The last thing he heard was Peli howling.

"RUFIO!" CLARA'S VOICE CAME INTO HIS CONSCIOUSNESS. "Rufio!"

Her voice came in and out like waves, as though he were underwater. As his hearing rose above the surface, Clara's voice was joined by the sound of singing birds and the percussion of a thousand cicadas. The trees above him seemed to bend and sway as he opened his eyes, but then he felt something strange on his head. He tried to rise from his awkward angle upon the ground but he could not.

"Rufio, stop! Your head is stuck to the tree!" Clara sat Felicia on the ground beside Peli who stood guard over her, and set about trying to extricate Rufio's head from the resinous trunk of the tree he had fallen against. "What were you doing? Did you faint?" She observed the back of his head where it was stuck. "Oh, dear..."

"Lady Pagana! Do you require assistance?"

Clara looked to see the litter-bearers coming toward them. "Yes. Yes, please!" She turned back to Rufio whose eyes were open now, though he still looked confused.

"What in Hades is happening?" Rufio muttered.

"You're stuck against the tree. Just give us a moment..." She stood and picked up Clara. "He fainted against the tree and now his head is stuck."

One of the litter-bearers chuckled, but the leader smacked him upside the head.

"Was he attacked?" the leader asked, pointing at Rufio's thigh which appeared to have a small stab wound surrounded by dried blood. "I would put some of that pine resin on it."

"Yes, yes. We can do that!" Clara said, bouncing Felicia who was becoming agitated. "Can you just get him off the tree and into the litter so we can go back to the villa?"

"This is the most violent picnic I've ever seen!" one of the other litter-bearers said as the four of them leaned over Rufio who was starting to wriggle like an animal in a trap.

"Hold still, dominus," the leader said as he drew a small knife from his belt.

"Wait! Oh...not the hair!" Rufio protested, but they held his flailing hands.

The leader leaned down, pressing the blade against the tree and slowly sawed between it and Rufio's head. He did not cut far enough though, for when Rufio was pulled up, some of his hair remained stuck to the tree.

"OW!" Rufio cried, his hand feeling at the back of his head.

"No, don't touch!" the leader said, but it was too late.

Rufio's hand stuck to the back of his head, and when he pulled it off, a bit more hair came with it. "Gods, it's hot!" he said, sweating profusely, his face red with heat and frustration.

"Let's help the dominus back to the litter," the leader said to two of the others, before turning to the third. "You help the domina with their belongings."

"Wait!" the man said. "We forgot…" He leaned down to put his finger in the sap, and then spread some on Rufio's thigh wound. "There."

Rufio stared wildly at the man. "Thank you!"

The man nodded and followed Clara back to the picnic spot.

"I'm coming, Rufio!" Clara called to him as he was carried away most awkwardly by the three servants, one holding him by the shoulders, the other two by a leg each.

When they got to the litter, they set him down and rolled him in through the litter's open curtains. "We'll get you back to the villa soon, dominus."

Rufio nodded, but did not speak. He was focussed on stopping the vertiginous effects plaguing his head at the moment.

A minute later, Clara arrived with Felicia, Peli, and the fourth litter-bearer carrying the food and Rufio' satchel.

"Did you get everything?" Rufio asked.

"Yes, we did. Don't worry yourself, my love." Clara looked worried, her eyes searching his. "Let's just get you home." She adjusted the items at their feet and invited Peli to jump up amongst them, which he did immediately. After she closed the curtains, Clara called out to the litter-bearers. "We're ready."

The litter immediately rose up, settled upon the bearers'

shoulders, and began to move off. Rufio pulled aside the curtain to catch one more glimpse of the temple of Apollo before it disappeared from his sight. "I feel nauseous."

"Was it your old head injury? Did you get dizzy?" Clara made to stroke his head but stopped when she felt the stickiness of the resin there. "Just lean back and rest. We'll get you cooled off when we get home."

"I really don't know what happened. I was running after Peli…yes you!" He wagged his finger at the canine curled up at their feet. "Then, Peli went up to Terentius and started barking at him and-"

"I'm sorry… Did you say Terentius?" Clara and Felicia seemed to look at him.

"Yes. Alright? Yes. I saw Terentius."

"A different Terentius then."

"No. *The* Terentius. Or, rather, his shade. I've seen him before. I just never said anything."

"Is this the same man you said you saw after the temple of Artemis?"

"Yes!"

Outside, the litter-bearers each made a sign against ill omen, for they could not help but hear what their passengers were saying. As they did so, one of them tripped and the litter tilted suddenly.

"Careful out there!" Rufio shouted, his head pounding.

"Apologies, dominus!" the leader said as they climbed up out of the forested riverbank and onto the road by the Porta Hadriana.

"Rufio, I'm going to ask Atticus to call a medicus when we get back. That old head injury seems to be acting up. I wonder if the heat isn't making it worse."

"I'm perfectly fine!" Rufio said.

Clara observed his supremely red face and unsteady eyes. "Yes, my love. But I'm going to ask anyway."

Rufio shook his head. "I'm not mad, Clara. I've been seeing Terentius."

"Dreaming of him, you mean."

"Well, yes. But I've also *seen* him several times. He's stuck."

"I'd say so. He's dead!" Clara ran her hand over her face. *He's really hit his head hard this time.*

"He's a bit odd…troubled even…"

"I should say. If you've talked with him, what did you discuss?"

"Well, he doesn't say much. He's writing most of the time. It's rather hard to get his attention."

"What was he writing?" Clara asked, almost regretting having done so.

"Everything."

"Everything?"

"That's what he said. But what he keeps saying to me is that I…we…need to free him. He's trapped here, you see?"

"No. I don't."

"Well, I'm guessing that if what Phemius, the librarian, said is true, he died here in Athenae when he was quite young and alone. In fact, he said he was lonely."

"Terentius said he was lonely?"

"Yes. He said he was surrounded by people, but lonely when he was here."

"Over two hundred years ago."

"Yes, it's been a while. I can see his frustration."

"How do you free him then?"

"He said that to be free, we need to make the performance of *Heautontimorumenos* such a success that the Athenians finally see what true Roman drama is, see him as worthy of their remembrance."

"He sounds like a picky shade."

"I'm in deadly earnest." Rufio crossed his arms and leaned back upon the pillow to stare at the curtained roof of the litter.

"If Peli could talk, he would confirm it all. He's the one who found him."

Clara looked at Peli, his mismatched eyes staring back at her. She sighed and held Felicia close to her chest.

"Oh! And by the way," Rufio said. "We're building a temple to Apollo on our land when we get back to Etruria."

By the time the litter pulled into the courtyard of the villa, the sun was making its way down in the west. They had all fallen asleep in the litter which the bearers had put down gently beside the central fountain.

"There they are!" Felix's voice echoed about the courtyard as he, Sextus, Martia, Atticus, and Electra holding Thespis came out. "How was the picnic?" he asked as he swung the curtains aside to see their groggy faces.

"Don't ask," Rufio said.

"It was delightful," Clara added quickly, "until Rufio hit his head against a tree."

"What?" Felix asked. "How did that happen?"

"I said don't ask," Rufio repeated. "I need a bath. Atticus, are they ready?"

"Yes, Rufio Pagano," Atticus said, approaching most cautiously to help Rufio out of the litter.

"Good." Rufio stood and up with him came the pillow which had adhered to his head.

Felix put his hand to his mouth to stifle his laughter. "You've got something on your head, my friend."

"Leave it!" Rufio barked without looking at any of them. "I'll get it off in the bath." Rufio marched away, aided by Sextus who leant him an arm to steady him on his feet.

Clara came around with Felicia from the other side.

"Are you all right?" Electra asked her, reaching out to touch her cheek.

"I'm fine. We did have a lovely time, but…I think his old head injury is causing him some delusions." She turned to Atticus. "Would you mind sending for a medicus to have a look at him?"

"Right away, lady," Atticus said, turning quickly to go into the domus.

Clara turned back to Felix, Electra, and Martia. "He says he's been seeing Terentius and speaking with him."

Atticus stopped in his tracks and turned back to them.

"Terentius?" Felix asked. "*The* Terentius? *Our* Terentius?"

"He insists on it, yes." Clara wiped the sweat from her brow. "I'm just worried about him. Atticus?" Clara looked at him. "Please do fetch a medicus."

"Sorry, lady. Yes. Right away!" Atticus went into the domus. *Perhaps I should tell them,* he thought. *No. Not now.*

"Come," Martia said, "let me hold Felicia for you. You look absolutely distraught!"

"Thank you," Clara said, handing Felicia gently into Martia's care so that she would not awake. "I think this heat is playing with me as well."

Felix watched as Electra, Clara, Martia, and the children went inside. When they were gone, he sat on the edge of the fountain beside the litter and looked up at the purpling sky. "Terentius? Apollo, what are you trying to tell us?"

He then spotted Rufio's satchel still in the litter, beside Peli who was still curled up among the pillows. He reached out to take the satchel and Peli growled a little. "Oh, relax you."

The growling stopped and Felix took the satchel out and opened it. He pulled out a scroll with some scribbles on it. "Hmm… Good title!" He looked from the papyrus to the domus, and smiled before putting it back. "Oh, Far-Shooting Apollo…you see all, don't you?"

XIV

THE PANATHENAEA

The summer weeks flew by as swiftly as any swallow diving in the evening air, and soon it was time for the Panathenaea in honour of the goddess Athena. The preparations for the greatest festival of the Attic calendar were completed with every deme of the city making a contribution. Foremost among the completed tasks was the weaving and embroidering of the goddess' ceremonial peplos which would be carried from the slopes of the hill of Agras upon the ceremonial trireme.

The entire city, ports, and surrounding countryside were more abuzz than all the apiaries on the slopes of Hymettos combined, as people came from all over to watch and take part in the religious ceremonies, athletic competitions, cultural and theatrical events, and all else that accompanied the eight-day festival.

It was the day of the great Panathenaic procession, and all who were taking part in that ancient rite had gathered before dawn in the area between the massive Dipylon Gate and the Sacred Gate at the northwest of the city, the covered walkways and towers overlooking where the river Eridanos flowed into the city, and where the road led to Eleusis. It was a gathering of organized chaos in which Athenians and Hellenes from other parts of Graecia and the empire came together. There were priests and priestesses, young men and women, warriors, victors in the Crown Games, including the Olympiad, winners from the previous festival's competitions, and famed Athenian actors and playwrights. More than anything, there were horses, hundreds of them, all neighing, whinnying, pissing and shitting in the area outside the Sacred Gate near the Pompeion, the warehouse where the marshalling of the procession took place, and where the city officials and Roman dignitaries gathered.

Shouts went up everywhere as the parade marshalls and the troops lending them assistance tried to ensure that all participants knew their roles and place in the procession.

"What do you think is the hold-up?" Sextus asked his friend, Publius Leander Antoninus, a Roman magistrate in Athenae with whom he had grown quite close over the years. "People are going to start fainting soon from the heat."

"Don't worry, my friend," Publius said. "This is quite normal. The Athenians put on a good show of being unorganized, but then it always goes off beautifully. As well as any triumph in Rome!"

Public Leander Antoninus was Sextus' senior, but not as conservative in his views as others. He had three daughters and was married to an artist from Delphi. They lived on the slopes of Hymettos, not very far from where the villa of Herodes Atticus was located.

Both men were dressed in their formal toga praetexta with broad purple stripes on the hems, indicating their official status. They sat in the shade of the Pompeion's peristylium, outside one of the many rooms where the higher-ranking participants and priests dressed for the occasion.

"The ship is on its way, Magistrate," one of the soldiers reported to Publius, saluting before turning and leaving.

"That's a relief," Publius said to Sextus. "That's the trickiest part of the procession, really."

"I saw it on my way here, just off the road on the hill of

Agras. Magnificent!"

"It really is incredible how they manage to get a full-sized ship all the way here from Novae Athenae. But, as it carries the goddess' sacred peplos, I suppose every effort is put into it. They are pushing it on its mechanism all the way here, through the streets, and will turn onto the Panathenaic Way for the procession."

"I can't wait." Sextus beamed. It was an ancient tradition he had long read about and wanted to see. Yes, it had probably evolved since it was first held over seven hundred years before, but it looked like it would still be impressive. "I've been meaning to thank you again for arranging for The Etrurian Players to take part in the procession. It's quite an honour for them."

"Think nothing of it, Sextus." Publius waved it off shyly. "This is the birthplace of the dramatic arts, and what better place for the greatest theatre company in the empire to be? I'm just sorry that they had to be placed at the end of the procession. The priests are quite strict about non-Athenians not participating. This small victory of ours is indicative of the changes afoot, I think. For better or worse, I suppose."

"I know. But I am happy to help my friends," Sextus said with a smile.

"And the other company?" Publius asked. "The Rome Antics?"

Sextus' smile faded a little. "It is a sort of peace offering between them. Rather than exclude them, I thought it best to let them take part. I have spoken with Cassius Cantor, their leader, and he promises that they will not embarrass Rome."

"I'm not sure they could embarrass Rome anymore after what happened in the agora!" To Sextus' relief, Publius laughed.

"I know. But it is a small price to pay to allow Felix Modestus to focus on the task at hand. In just a little over a week, we'll find out if Athenae is ready to accept Roman drama."

"The very thought of it fills me with dread, Sextus. I won't lie. But the Gods sometimes do the unexpected. Maybe this will be one of those times?"

"I hope so."

"Is the production ready? Are they ready?"

"Yes. They are. I've been watching their rehearsals and, I tell you, Publius, I've never seen anything so magnificent."

"I can't wait to see it! Where are The Etrurian Players anyhow?" Publius asked. "I should like to meet them and congratulate them on their success. I mean, even Hercules has endorsed them to the people of Athenae!"

"Yes, well… That's Felix for you!" Sextus shook his head. "I think they are at the fountain inside the Dipylon Gate. Some of them are a little worse for wear after the Pannychis last night."

Outside the Pompeion, sitting on the edge of the covered fountain inside the titanic Dipylon Gate of the Kerameikos, The Etrurian Players awaited word from the marshals that they were to line up for the procession. They mingled like ants upon the roadway, minute in the shadow of the high walls and roofed towers of Athenae's most fortified gate which stood between the city and the necropolis beyond where the monuments of many famed Athenians gleamed in the sun.

Felix had thought to have the company dress in the costumes they were to wear in the play, and Clara to bear the jewelled ring with Vesta upon her finger to catch the sunlight as well as the crowd's attention. But he decided against all of that, and made them all wear white peploi and tunicae or, in Fausto's case, a chiton.

"Shouldn't we have worn our costumes, Felix?" Pollux

asked, his voice gravelly from the previous night's drinking. "I saw The Rome Antics in theirs."

Felix shook his head. "All the more reason not to. This procession is not about us. It is about honouring the goddess Athena. If we want to win over the people of the city, we need to appear pious."

"Some of the Athenians weren't so pious last night," Castor said, his voice echoing the abuse of the previous night.

"Why did you all have to drink so much?" Electra said as she paced with Thespis in her arms. She stopped and stared at Castor, Pollux, Fausto, Damon, and Beatrice who had all snuck up onto the Acropolis the night before for the sacred vigil of the Pannychis in which the paean for Athena was sung, the sacred dances performed, and prayers and offerings made throughout the night to the goddess, mostly by the youth of the city, overseen by the priests and priestesses of Athena.

"They had wine, Electra. We drank it." Pollux dipped his head back into the fountain to try and soothe his aching head.

"You certainly did!" Electra snapped. "And you Fausto, why are you wearing a chiton that is too small for you?"

"It's new. I like it!" Fausto snapped back, pulling the hem down as hard as he could. He had bought it the day before at the lupa Calypso's insistence.

"You look ridiculous!" Electra added.

"Why are you so grouchy?" Castor asked.

"This is my city. I don't need any more embarrassment!"

"You keep screeching, and you will be embarrassed," Fausto said.

"Careful, Fausto," Felix stepped forward. "And she's right. That thing is so short, I can see your testicles. Are you putting on a puppet show?"

Damon laughed and howled at that, and then promptly bent over to vomit in a corner behind him.

Fausto bent over to look at himself, and quickly pulled his

hem down some more, only for it to rise back up. "Oh well. I hear that the Pyrrhic dances are done naked anyway. When in Athenae…"

"He's going to humiliate me!" Electra turned to Felix.

"Don't worry. It will be fine. Why are you so wound up? We're lucky to even be taking part in the procession."

"I'm the only Greek in our troupe. This procession is one of the greatest, most sacred events to be undertaken!"

"Which is why we should enjoy it, Electra. At least while it lasts." Felix put his arm around her and kissed both her and Thespis. "I know you're disappointed we can't go all the way up to the Parthenon as most of us are not Greek, but we will go after and make our offerings to the goddess. Don't worry."

Electra nodded and sat down in the shade of the fountain with Thespis, cupping her hand and drinking a little.

Julius and Domela stood apart from the others, marvelling at the costumes of some of the participants as they waited for the sacred ship to arrive. There were hoplites calling on the great military traditions of ancient Athenae, the warriors dressed in cuirasses polished to a brilliant shine to match the helmets tilted back upon their heads. Their round hoplon shields gleamed with the sigils of the ancient families, and their dori, the long spears they carried, rose up like a forest, their leaf-shaped blades glinting like birch leaves in fall.

"Look at the lovely dancers!" Domela said, pointing to the large gathering of maidens, dressed in pure white peploi, their long hair tumbling like waterfalls in a wood about their shoulders, their heads graced with floral coronae. They smiled, and laughed, and danced about as they waited beside the stalk-still phalanxes of the hoplites. "I used to be that lovely, you know," Domela said with not a little regret.

Julius took her arm, no longer afraid to openly show his affection for her in front of the company. "You still are."

Domela blushed and leaned upon his shoulder.

Beatrice, who was watching them, smiled a little and looked to Fausto beside her where he was groaning and leaning upon a column. Catching a glimpse of his unfortunately hiked-up chiton, she shook her head and went back to observing the other participants in the parade.

There was an array of priests and priestesses, the hieropoioi and athlothetai, all holding the implements of their offices, along with bows of sacred olive, oak, and bay. Accompanying them were young girls, the kenephoroi, similarly dressed with garlands in their hair, four of the tallest of them carrying an ornate peplos for the goddess, and others leading several white cows and sheep. All of the animals had gilded horns and were bedecked with fragrant garlands. The girls talked amongst themselves while occasionally soothing their tethered charges who would be offered to the goddess.

There were also actors with their great theatrical masks tucked beneath their arms, musicians who warmed up upon their lyres, tambourines, sistra, and drums. There were bakers and metics in purple robes with their baskets and carts of breads, honeycombs, and cakes for the goddess, Attic oil merchants with amphorae of oil for the goddess, and wine-bearers who stood near the priests with their enormous and ornate orange and black ware amphorae depicting scenes of the goddess' life. These would be used to pour the sacred libations.

A great cheer rose up and the earth shook as the horsemen of the Panathenaea arrived through the Sacred Gate. These hipparchoi were chosen from among the best and most beautiful horses and riders of each deme of Athenae and the surrounding areas. They rode bareback upon their mounts, some of the riders dressed in chitons, and others completely naked, seemingly at one with the horses beneath them, commanding them perfectly. They milled about the entire gathering, by far the largest complement in the procession.

Then came the dignitaries and offerings from Athenae's ancient colonies, even as far away as Massilia in Gaul or the colonies around the Black Sea.

"It is strange to see the ancient power of Athenae displayed so prominently," Electra said to Felix. "It fills me with pride, but it also makes me sad for some reason."

"It is quite a spectacle," Felix said as he watched The Rome Antics arrive through the Dipylon Gate, colourfully dressed in their pantomime garb. They did not stop to speak with them, but Cassius Cantor waved and smiled as they waded into the awaiting crowd.

"What an abomination having them in the procession," Electra growled.

"They'll behave…I hope," Felix said. "Sextus said they will be behind us in the procession at least, but before the excrement gatherers following behind."

Castor heard him. "Yes, with the shit where they belong!"

Felix turned toward them. "I don't want any trouble. Got it?"

"Yes, dominus."

"We want to win over the city, not have them turn on us again." Felix rubbed his face. "It's going to be a long day."

"You feeling all right?" Clara asked Rufio who stood beside her rocking Felicia who had just settled down. "We can bow out if you want."

"No need. I'm fine. I'm just glad I don't have to organize this thing." Rufio tickled Felicia's chin and pointed to a pure black stallion nearby.

Clara relaxed, and laced her arm through his, her head upon his shoulder. She had been worried about him since his ravings at the shrines along the Ilissos, but was relieved that he had not been injured. She looked at Rufio and reached up to touch the back of his head gently.

"Is it fully-grown back?" he asked, touching the patch on

his head where he had been stuck to the pine tree.

"Just about. But please don't do that again. The medicus said that because of your previous injury, you need to be extra cautious when it comes to your head. Lucky that tree was so resinous. The sap cushioned your fall."

"I'd rather not think about it," Rufio replied, grateful that he had not concussed himself and fallen into fevered dreams where Terentius would no doubt have continued to harangue him. *Though, he seems to be doing it anyway!* Rufio thought. He cast a quick eye over the massive gathering before him, worried that Terentius' shade might have infiltrated the procession.

Rufio seemed to be spotting the shade whenever he went outside the villa walls. That very morning, he had been up early, nervous about the procession, and found himself in the olive grove, outside the south wall. He had seen the shade, sitting against a tree, scribbling away as usual. It asked him why he was not also writing and Rufio, completely annoyed with the shadowy vision, turned and went back inside muttering to himself. It was then that Atticus happened upon him in the courtyard.

"Rufio Pagano… Have you seen him again?"

Rufio jumped, Atticus' face lit grotesquely by one of the burning braziers.

"My apologies. I did not mean to scare you." Atticus stepped back, hands out.

"See who?" Rufio asked.

"I heard lady Clara and Felix Modestus speaking…saying that you believe you saw Terentius."

"Yes, yes. I know. I hit my head. I'm mad! Isn't that what everyone is saying behind my back? You know, I really ha-"

"I believe you, Rufio Pagano."

"Wait…what?" Rufio looked around to see if anyone was near, but they were all inside getting ready to make their way in the dark to the city. "You believe me?"

Atticus nodded. "I have seen him too. The shade, that is."

"How do you know it's Terentius? There must be many shades with a necropolis so near."

"He's dressed like a Roman. Dirty, dishevelled, deeply sad…carrying a long scroll on which he is always scribbling?"

"Yes." Rufio gulped.

"I have seen him. As have some of the shepherds. The residents of this villa, my dominus' family, have talked about it over the generations, or so I've been told. They do love theatre, after all. They've even made offerings to Terentius' shade."

"I didn't think to do that," Rufio muttered.

"It seems to me, you are."

"How so?"

"By putting on the play."

Rufio felt sad in that moment. "Phemius, at the library, told me what happened to Terentius here in Athenae."

"A true tragedy," Atticus said. "And a great loss for drama so early on."

"Has the shade spoken to you or anyone else?"

Atticus shook his head. "No. You are the first to have had any interaction with him. The Gods are trying to say something, I suppose. But some members of the familia have seen the shade. My dominus actually found it quite disconcerting at times. That is why he does not remain in residence here for long. It is too unnerving. I continue to make offerings to appease him…but perhaps…"

"Perhaps what?" Rufio had asked.

"Perhaps the success of the *Heautontimorumenos* is the healing that he needs?"

The rest of the company then came into the courtyard to depart for the city.

The conversation continued to replay itself in Rufio's mind as they stood in the Kerameikos waiting for the procession to start.

As they watched the crowd grow thicker and thicker, Rufio pulled Clara closer to him. "I love you," he whispered.

The morning sunlight was starting to peek over the city walls, and spread across the crowds. Clara's eyes lit up and Rufio could not help but smile.

"The ship is here!" someone shouted, and everyone turned eastward to see the sacred trireme, a symbol of Athenae's strength, seemingly floating along the ground as though on water.

The Etrurian Players and everyone else pressed forward to catch a glimpse of the ship as it floated toward them.

"Well that's something we don't often see!" Domela said, her soprano voice high over the rest of the company's exclamations.

"It's a theatrical trick," Julius explained. "They have a mechanism that helps the ship move along as though it is on water. Quite brilliant, really."

"Look, Felicia!" Clara said to her daughter as she pointed.

Rufio stood beside them and watched, rubbing his eyes to ensure he was not seeing things. He was not.

The crowds lining the streets of Athenae parted before the sacred trireme as though they were waves cut through by the ship's bronze-beaked prow.

"What a magnificent display!" Felix said as he stood beside his wife, holding his son.

The trireme had a long sleek hull that had been newly cleaned and polished, and the great frowning eyes on either side of the prow, freshly painted in blue, white, and black, stared down on the people. The short oars that jutted out from three levels all had colourful ribbons attached to them, and the deck was lined with sailors, and hoplites with their gleaming bronze helmets down over their faces. Music flowed all around the ship, like gulls at sea.

Damon leapt up on the edge of the fountain the better to see and hear, his flute clutched in his right hand.

The most wondrous thing upon the ship, however, was the sacred peplos of the goddess Athena, which hung upon the yardarm of the ship and served as the sail. It billowed in the hot breeze, proudly displaying the embroidered scenes, or aristeia, from Athena's battles and feats in the Wars of the Giants and other confrontations.

"I've never seen anything like it!" Beatrice said.

Electra turned to her. "The embroiders are chosen by the Boule from among the most skilled artisans in each deme."

"Those images seem to be alive!" the younger woman said.

Electra smiled and turned her attention back to the trireme which began to slow as it came into the midst of the assembled participants in the procession.

The trireme turned then to point in the direction of the Panathenaic Way, the processional route from the Kerameikos of Athenae, through the ancient agora, and on to the propylaea of the Acropolis.

The voices of the marshalls could be heard giving orders somewhere far off in the crowd, and so it was back to waiting.

"Well, if it isn't *The* Felix Modestus," a haughty voice said as four men approached from the direction of the Pompeion on the other side of the road. "Or should I call you, Hercules?" The man and his friends laughed.

Felix handed Thespis to Electra and turned to face the four newcomers. He had known the hateful timbre of the actor Cadmus' voice immediately for he had had run-ins with him, and his friends Aegisthus, and Zotikos in the past. They were all actors born out of Athenae's theatrical traditions, and saw themselves as the very pinnacle of the performing arts across the Middle Sea, even though they rarely left the city.

"I see they are letting you join the procession," Aegisthus said beside Cadmus.

"Who are these jokers?" Castor said to Pollux who shrugged his shoulders.

The three actors looked identical, each with a carefully-trimmed beard and short, wavy hair, meticulously placed. The fourth man, a playwright by the name of Telephus, stood slightly apart from his friends, his long hair and smile setting him distinctly apart from them.

"I hear you are performing Terentius?" Telephus said to Felix.

"Word gets around," Felix replied. "Telephus, what are you still doing with these arrogant pricks?"

The playwright made no reply, but smiled and turned his head away to laugh.

"I think it a disgrace that Romans should be included in our sacred festival," Zotikos said, staring down his long nose at The Etrurian Players. "It's not right."

"What's not right is that hideous face of yours!" Electra spat at his feet.

"Electra…" Zotikos smiled thinly. "Always a pleasure."

"We are looking forward to your performance at the end of the festival, Felix Modestus," Aegisthus said, his light blue eyes unnervingly bright in the morning sunlight. "I wonder if they will banish you from Athenae afterward."

"They haven't yet," Felix replied. "Besides, if they haven't ejected you for your less-than-stellar Oedipus, I think we're pretty safe."

Aegisthus stepped forward to get in Felix's face, but not before Rufio pushed him.

"Don't even think about it, landica!"

"Ah, the lovely language of the Latins," Cadmus said, putting an arm out to stop Aegisthus from furthering the confrontation. "You must be the Iolaus to Felix's false Hercules."

Suddenly a group of men crowded in behind Cadmus, Aegisthus, Zotikos, and Telephus.

"Is there a problem we can help you with, Felix Modestus?" Cassius Cantor said, surrounded by his troupe who were all staring at the Athenian actors and playwright.

"Yes! Of course!" Cadmus exclaimed, turning to face them. "The pantomime pricks have arrived! Tell me, Cassius, how many beggars have you tricked into giving you money while here?"

Cassius Cantor smiled easily at the man, blowing sideways to get a strand of his bangs out of his face. "Just your wives."

It was Cadmus' turn to lunge but not before a loud voice called out.

"What's the meaning of this?" Sextus Annius Sabinus said as he waded into their midst, followed by Publius Leander Antoninus. "This is a sacred occasion!"

"Your little Romans shouldn't be here, Praetor!" Cadmus hissed. "They're a disgrace to the goddess!"

"You would do well to get over yourself, Cadmus," Publius said. "It's time to get to your positions for the procession."

"Gladly, Magistrate." Cadmus took a last look at Felix and left, followed by Aegisthus, Zotikos, and Telephus who turned and mouthed an apology to Felix.

"I can't abide that man!" Publius said to Sextus.

"We are of like mind, Magistrate," Felix said.

"Everyone," Sextus said to the group, "this is my friend Publius Leander Antoninus, one of the Roman magistrates here in Athenae. He and his wife Delphina have invited us to dine with them a few days from now."

"Thank you for the invitation, Magistrate," Clara said.

The man smiled and put up his hands. "Please, call me Publius. I only want snobs and fools like Cadmus and his friends to call me 'magistrate'." He smiled warmly and was about to speak when music began to fill the air.

First the gentle thrumming of a drum began, followed by a long, solemn note on a cornu from atop the Dipylon Gate. As the procession marshalls gave some final orders, the sound of flutes rose up into the air, followed by tambourines, and sistra, and a chorus of girls' voices singing the hymn to Athena…

"I begin to sing of Pallas Athena, the glorious goddess, bright-eyed, inventive, unbending of heart, pure virgin, saviour of cities, courageous, Tritogeneia. From his awful head, wise Zeus himself bare her arrayed in warlike arms of flashing gold, and awe seized all the gods as they gazed…"

It was then, in perfect concert, like an army arrayed for battle, that the procession marshalls made their final command and the entire procession lurched into motion as the sound of music filled the sunlit world about them.

"All right!" Sextus said to The Etrurian Players and The Rome Antics. "Do not disgrace Rome this day. Understood?"

"We understand, Praetor," Cassius Cantor said, winking at Felix.

Sextus and Publius went to join their group from Novae Athenae who were permitted to walk in the procession with the deme representatives, just ahead of The Etrurian Players.

Felix looked at Cassius, unable to hold back a smile.

"We've got your back, Felix Modestus!" Cassius said before turning and going back to where his troupe waited for him on the other side of the road with the dung scoopers.

The music rose to a glorious height all around them, but it was unlike any music they had heard before, so soft and sacred, as if Orpheus himself were among the musicians, accompanying the girls who continued with their hymn to Athena…

"But Athena sprang quickly from the immortal head and stood before Zeus who holds the aegis, shaking a sharp spear; great Olympus began to reel horribly at the might of the bright-eyed goddess, and earth round about cried fearfully, and the sea was moved and tossed with dark waves, while foam burst forth suddenly, the bright son of Hyperion stopped his swift-footed horses a long while, until the maiden Pallas Athena had stripped the heavenly armour from her immortal shoulders. And wise Zeus was glad... And so hail to you, daughter of Zeus!"

The colossal peplos of Athena that was upon the ship billowed and snapped as the wind filled it.

At the front of the Panathenaic procession went the four lithe girls carrying the ornamented peplos of the goddess. All eyes watched them as they passed to the front, paused, and then began their walk along the Panathenaic Way.

Next came the the priestesses of Athena all in white, singing to the goddess as they were followed by the Athenian women bearing gifts for their godly patron.

Behind them, young girls and some of the Attic herdsmen and shepherds urged on their force of flower-bedecked cows and sheep who would be sacrificed at various altars along the way. The herdsmen made their calls to move the animals forward, and the girls, each holding an animal by a lead, whispered softly to them to calm them, to tell them they were an honour to Athena.

Behind them came the metics, the non-Greek residents of Athenae, dressed all in purple robes and carrying sweet cakes and honeycombs from the the surrounding countryside. These were followed by the musicians whose music weaved through the entire procession before and behind, many of them playing the drums, sistra, and tambourine, but others playing the sacred notes from the aulos and cythara. They were joined by the famed actors of Athenae, Aegisthus, Cadmus, and Zotikos who carried large theatrical masks from their greatest performances, and the playwright Telephus who carried a scroll on which he had written a poem to the goddess.

"The music is so beautiful," Clara whispered, almost as if she were in a daze.

"It is," Rufio agreed, holding Felicia who was also silent, her ears picking up the melody. Rufio turned to look at Felix who smiled at him. He could tell Felix wished they had a more prominent position in the procession, but even he knew that this parade was not at all about The Etrurian Players. There would be no coin tossing or riling of the crowd this time.

Felix put his arm around Electra who held their son close as she wiped a single tear from her cheek. "You all right?"

Electra nodded. "I did not realize now much I missed this place."

"This is taking forever!" Fausto whined, only to be smacked by Castor.

"Shh. Just listen will you?" Pollux said.

It was then the turn of the sacred trireme to move and, as if Boreas himself began blowing from his distant northern cave, the ship moved forward as if of its own accord. The ribbons upon the oars fluttered in the wind, and the hoplites and sailors upon the deck stared ahead to their sacred destination: the Acropolis.

In the wake of the ship came the older men of Athenae, those who carried the wisdom of the past, who guarded and shared it. They moved slower than others, but there was no cause to rush, for they had undergone a lifetime of toil and were an honoured part of the Panathenaea. They held in their gnarled hands bows of sacred olive, the life-giving tree that Athena herself had given to the city in the distant past.

A great clip-clopping echoed about the plaza of the Kerameikos then as the drivers of nine four-horse chariots fell into a steady trot behind the old men. In the cab with each driver stood a fully-armed warrior with spear and hoplon, whispering prayers of their own to the goddess as they rolled slowly forward, flowers from the crowd raining down on them as they passed, guarding the women who came behind them. These were the skilled craftswomen of Athenae who had woven the colossal peplos upon the sacred trireme. They walked to cheers of thanks from the crowd massed at the fringes of the procession, all grateful for the labours they had undertaken for an entire year.

A horn then sounded, and the infantry joined the procession behind the craftswomen. They marched in perfect unison, small phalanxes of armed hoplites from each of the ancient demes of Athenae, their footfalls shaking the ground, but not so much as what came next.

The horsemen of the Panathenaea rode forward, their horses prancing, charging, and rising up upon their hind legs with wild manes fluttering in the wind. They whinnied and neighed proudly as if their lord, horse-taming Poseidon were among them, blasting upon his great conch horn that they do him proud. Some rode bareback, some wore breeches, and others chitons, and some had donned flowing chlamydes, the mantles worn by young men. Some others rode fully naked, their muscled torsos as much to honour the goddess as their skill in riding.

Rufio, who had been admiring the horses intently, turned back to see the dung-scoopers at the ready behind The Rome Antics, for the cavalry had been standing still for some time. He noted, however, that even they seemed to be taking pride in their task, for they were to keep the goddess' city clean.

"There's Aristides of Athenae!" Pollux said, pointing to someone two groups ahead. "You see his head above the others, wearing the olive crown?"

"Who's he?" Beatrice asked, standing on tiptoes to be able to see.

"He won in the boxing at the last Olympic Games." Pollux turned to Castor. "I wonder if he'll compete in the Panathenaic Games?"

They continued to watch as the crowd of athletes marched forward, some wearing chitons, some naked to display their hard-won scars and physiques, but all of them wearing their coronae of victory which they had won at each of the crown games of Isthmia, Nemea, Delphi, and of course, Olympia.

"I think they're all going to compete here!" Pollux said excitedly.

The athletes were followed by the deme representatives from Colonus, Melite, Ceiriadae, Coele, Cydathenaeum, Scambonidae, and lastly an honorary delegation from Novae Athenae, or Adrianopolis.

Standing in the last group, Sextus turned to wave to Felix and the others before he began his slow walk with the other delegates along the Panathenaic Way to the ancient agora.

"Romans!" one of the marshalls hollered at them. "You're next! The Etrurian Players first, and then The Rome Antics! Now!"

"Come, friends!" Felix bellowed. "Walk with dignity, though we be at the tail end!" Felix walked forward with Electra and Thespis beside him. Behind them came Rufio, Clara, and Felicia, then Julius and Domela, Castor and Pollux, Fausto and Beatrice, and lastly Damon who played a sound of Hesperidean birds upon his flute that seemed to capture those among the onlookers who had not already moved on to follow the procession.

The Etrurian Players walked slowly behind the deme representatives, picking their way carefully over the piles of horse, cow, and sheep manure which the animals had deposited as they waited.

"I think the dung collectors will be staying here," Rufio said to Clara as he shook his sandalled foot free of equine excrement. He looked behind to see Cassius Cantor and The Rome Antics coming up between piles of dung, jumping, singing, and tumbling nimbly through the mess. They were followed by the dung collectors who shovelled with great skill and speed, dumping each load into the back of one of three carts that followed them. "That's a lot of good dung," Rufio muttered. "I hope they use it for the crops in the surrounding fields."

Clara smiled to herself, but focussed on the walk ahead as they left the Kerameikos and moved into the ancient agora between the temple of Ares and the altar of the twelve gods.

The agora was packed to capacity with onlookers pressing in upon the Panathenaic Way on both sides, cheering, throwing flowers, and singing along with the hymns to Athena that were repeated by the chorus of girls at the front of the procession.

"What a sight!" Felix said as the sacred trireme's mast and the colossal peplos moved through the agora, toward the Eleusinium and then the cursed Pelasgicon on the Acropolis' north side.

The cheers of the crowd were deafening in the confines of the agora, and the air seemed to be scented with a million fragrant flowers that were floating through the air to land upon the crowns of the participants, and on the steps and alcoves of the temples, stoas and other buildings of the agora.

The crowd, however, having enjoyed the display of the Panathenaic horsemen, followed by the parade of crown games victors, grew quiet once their respective demes passed. They stared at the strange addendum to the procession, those two Roman theatre troupes that had caused so much distress in the new agora a short distance away.

But then a child at the front of the crowd spied Felix, and began to shout. "It's Hercules! It's Hercules!"

Others in the crowd craned their necks to see, and soon many were pointing.

"What do we do?" Rufio asked behind Felix.

"I have an idea. Just smile and wave, and I'll say something."

"What are you going to say?" Electra asked, quite nervous now.

"Don't worry. I've got this…" Felix cleared his throat and

then stepped forward, his arms spread wide, his voice deep and strong. "For the honour of rich sacrifice is always offered to you, nor is the last day of the month forgotten, nor the songs of young men, or the choral chants. On a windy hill loud shouts of gladness resound to the beat of maiden dance-steps the whole night long."

A great applause rose up at Felix's recitation from Euripides' play, *Heracleidae*, that spoke to the very event in which they were participating.

Electra sighed, and touched Felix's shoulder. "Well done, my husband."

"We have to do something, don't we?" Felix said before beginning the recitation anew for those at the other end of the agora.

They came even with the library of Pandainos and there, Rufio spotted Phemius standing with others of the library staff watching the procession. He waved to the librarian who spotted him and waved back, only to be quickly distracted by The Rome Antics behind them as they carried Cassius Cantor upon their shoulders while hooting and hollering something about Minerva.

Electra shook her head. "Don't they know the goddess' proper name?"

"Don't mind them. We're much more sophisticated." Felix glanced back to see his players walking calmly in procession, except for Fausto who was tugging at his short chiton as the lupae from the House of the Nymphs called out to him from the street between the stoa of Attalus and the library of Pandainos. "Well, most of us are," Felix muttered.

As the front of the procession slowed, things grew quiet as they stopped to make sacrifices, the first of which were dedicated to Athena Hygieia. Another group of priestesses broke off and moved up to the Areopagus where more preliminary sacrifices were made. Prayers echoed over the procession, and the smell of blood and burning wood and flesh wafted in and about the gathered crowds.

The Etrurian Players watched from behind as the front of the procession snaked its way up the great staircase at the bottom of the propylaea, the monumental entrance leading onto the Acropolis. It was here that only true Athenians were permitted to continue, and while some broke off from the procession to make offerings to the goddess at the threshold of her sanctuary, most continued up the steep stairs, including the young girls carrying the peplos of Athena, the priestesses, and women with gifts. The Athenian girls and herdsmen who led animals helped their flocks to navigate the marble stairs, some of the animals growing nervous as they approached the end, but fulfilling their purpose nonetheless. Athenians then accepted the gifts of cakes and honeycombs from the Metics among them, and carried them beneath the high pediments of the propylaea, followed by the musicians whose melody echoed in the small forest of columns as they passed beneath the great entrance.

To those below, waiting at the bottom of the staircase and among the trees at the high walls of the back of the odeon of Herodes Atticus, it was as if they were seeing the Athenians among them ascend to Olympus. They disappeared into a world beyond their reach where music and song was played for the goddess, and the smoke from offerings and incense began to surround the top like clouds about a high mountain eyrie.

As the priests set about sacrificing a single, pure white cow at the temple of Athena Nike, which rested upon a small promontory overlooking the staircase, the sacred trireme pulled up slowly at the bottom of the stairs. To the sound of the sacred hymns, the sailors upon the ship lowered the colossal peplos of the goddess from the yardarm and it was, in turn, handed over to the craftswomen who had woven it as they arrived behind the four-horse chariots. These sacred labourers carried it slowly up the stairs, the soldiers upon the ship forming an honour guard about them as they went into the propylaea.

The chariots and horsemen of the Panathenaea ordered their ranks on the lower slope before the stairs as the rest of the procession arrived and made their way in, including the crown games victors, and the Athenian representatives for each deme of the city.

When The Etrurian Players arrived, they stood at the bottom of the stairs to look up at the shining entrance of the propylaea.

"This is where our path ends," Felix said to his company.

"I wish we could go up," Clara said. "It looks so beautiful."

"It looks crowded," Rufio commented.

Electra was quiet as she stared up the great staircase watching the last of the Athenians go in. She kissed and bounced Thespis who was starting to wriggle in her arms.

"You can go in with Thespis if you want to," Felix said to her.

She shook her head. "I want to go in as a family," she said. "We'll come back later during the festival."

Felix kissed her and turned to see Sextus coming up to him.

"How did it go?" Sextus asked. "I heard people calling out for Hercules."

"Can I help it if they recognize me?" Felix smiled.

"Well, there wasn't a riot, so I suppose all is well."

As the others talked, some of them looking at the horsemen behind them, or up at the sacred trireme, Rufio wandered off to the right to look up at the high walls of the odeon. He thought of Terentius, of what, according to the shade - and to Atticus, apparently - was riding on the success of their performance. He could not shake the image of that lonely Roman sitting against a tree along the Ilissos. He did not want to mention it to Felix or the others, for that would have increased the pressure on them tenfold, or at the least made them think he was mad from the thump upon his head. He touched the wall of the odeon, remembering the shade sitting next to him as Felix had rehearsed his prologus. "Apollo, please guide us in our endeavour…"

"Rufio?" Clara called to him as she and Felicia approached. "Sextus says that he reserved tables at the Taberna Thesias for all of us. We're leaving now."

"Hmm." Rufio turned to her, but his eyes gazed off to somewhere else, some place where his thoughts still lingered.

"Are you all right, my love?" She reached up to place her hand upon his cheek.

Drawn back into the present by her touch, he looked at her and smiled. "I'm fine. Just thinking of the performance. It's just nine days until will take to the stage."

"I know there have been a lot of distractions this time, but we *are* ready. You do see that?"

"But will we be ready on the day? Performances are mercurial. We can be perfect in rehearsal, but then beneath the gaze of the crowd, it can all fall apart. It's much safer to be the one with a stylus in one's hand."

"Is it? I should think creating the words from nothing but what the Gods give you is more dangerous. Actors interpret what is already created, but setting the words down for the first time? That is a true act of creation."

Rufio smiled at her. "I suppose it's just my nerves. They affect me overmuch."

"And I know how you overreact before, and are amazed at your success afterward, whatever the endeavour may be."

"You know me well."

"I love you well," Clara countered with a kiss. "Now, let's join the others. I'm famished, and Felicia is going to have to eat soon."

They walked to join the rest of The Etrurian Players and

all together they processed from the propylaea stairs around the Peripatos to the Taberna Thesias.

The Taberna Thesias was brimming with clientele, so it was fortunate that Sextus had arranged to have tables set aside for them on the terrace out front. It was a beautiful and hot day, and the breeze coming from the sea to the west roused the sunlit grapevines that provided shade for the entire terrace.

Boreas' servers went back and forth in a steady stream from the outdoor kitchens with sizzling platters of lamb and goat meat, and whole shock-eyed fish that stared up from beds of wild dill, celery, and bay. Girls travelled among the tables with pitchers of water and wine, and young boys carried loaves of freshly-baked bread in woven baskets to accompany it all. There were platters of wild greens drizzled with oil, salads, figs, and for those who were willing to pay, a lemon or two for the table.

When the praetor arrived with his wife and The Etrurian Players a great cheer went up as they walked past the line of people waiting to get in, and sat down at the row of tables which Sextus had reserved for them at the far end of the terrace.

"What's all that about?" Beatrice asked Fausto.

Fausto smiled and pulled her along with him. "Wouldn't you take notice if Hercules joined you for lunch?"

"They still believe that?" Beatrice asked, shaking her head and worrying that the immortal hero might seek to punish Felix for his audacity.

"Just go with it," Castor said behind them.

Felix sat with his back to the crowded taberna and the rest settled themselves around the table. Immediately a serving girl brought pitchers of water and wine and proceeded to fill all of the clay cups that had been set.

"Boreas says that the meat and fish will take some time, Praetor," the girl said. "We are much busier than he expected. He apologizes."

"No need," Sextus replied with a smile. "If you can bring the salads, some bread and cheese first, we can start with those. Our company is quite hungry."

"Right away, Praetor." The girl left, dodging the other servers as she went back into the taberna.

"What are they doing here?" Pollux growled as he saw Cassius Cantor and The Rome Antics eating, a few tables away.

"Ahem…" Sextus looked down the table at Pollux. "Cassius Cantor and his company are here at my invitation, in honour of the day…and as a guarantee of their good behaviour."

"They'll make you a pauper, Praetor!" Castor added. "If you think we eat a lot, they are as locusts!"

Sextus laughed. "I'm sure my finances can handle it. Besides, I'm only paying for their meat, nothing more."

Castor shook his head in amazement.

A few moments later, all of their cups filled, Sextus looked across at Felix. "Will you do the honours? The words of Euripides once more?"

Felix nodded and stood with his cup aloft to the Acropolis looming over them, where the ceremonies for Athenians were coming to a conclusion. The entire taberna grew quiet as all the patrons and servers paused to stare at the broad back of the Hercules in their midst. "Oh, Athena…" Felix began. "For the honour of rich sacrifice is always offered to you, nor is the last day of the month forgotten, nor the songs of young men, or the choral chants. On a windy hill loud shouts of gladness resound to the beat of maiden dance-steps the whole night long." His words lingering on the breezy, heated air, Felix then tipped a little of his wine onto the ground. Everyone followed suit. He then drained the entire cup and sat again to the applause of most people there, the loudest of all being Cassius Cantor. Felix smiled to himself.

"You're enjoying this, aren't you?" Electra said as she leaned to kiss his cheek.

"Celebrity is fleeting, my beautiful wife. Of course I'm enjoying it." Felix turned to the rest of the players who had full cups once again. "To celebrity and The Etrurian Players!"

They all cheered at that.

"Rufio," Clara said as she fed Felicia a bit of fresh fig. "Are you still lost in thought? You're staring off again."

"I'm sorry. No. Not really. I was just looking at the great library down the hill. We only have a little over a week until the performance and I still haven't been to see it."

"Why don't you go now?" Clara asked, casting an eye about the tables. "Seems like it may be some time before the food arrives."

Rufio looked around. He was hungry, but he had to admit to himself he did not feel like the usual banter. "You know, I think I will. Do you mind?"

Clara smiled. "Of course not. I'm quite happy to rest here and talk with Electra and Martia. You go."

"I'll try not to be too long. Save me some meat if you can." Rufio stood and stepped back from the table.

"Where are you going?" Felix asked him.

"To the great library. I've been meaning to have a look before we leave."

"The food is coming, Rufio!" Fausto said.

"I'll be back soon. Start without me." Rufio then bent down to kiss Clara and weaved his way through the tables and down the path toward the new agora and the library on the other side of it. As he went, a group of lupae from the House of the Nymphs passed him in a perfumed cloud of brash colours. Rufio felt a couple of hands grab at him, amidst giggles, and quickly checked for his purse which, thankfully, still hung at his belt. He looked back at them and one with wild hair, the one named Medusa, winked at him as she followed the others into the taberna.

THE GREAT LIBRARY COMPLEX BUILT BY EMPEROR HADRIANUS stood directly beside the new agora's enclosure, its monumental west-facing entrance just down the street from the arch of Athena Archegetis. The thoroughfare was tightly-packed with citizens who had been to the Panathenaic procession and were now in search of food and drink. Many were gathered in small groups talking excitedly about the day, their favourite part of the ceremonies, and the sighting of Hercules among the participants.

Rufio shook his head and tried desperately not to laugh as he heard this last, attempting to forge a path for himself through the throng to the great library's only entrance. After passing the forum, he came to the library complex. To his right, a row of seven soaring green Corinthian columns topped by statues of the gods towered over him, with seven more of the same on the other side. In the middle was the propylon leading into the library which, it struck him, was more like a temple. It had four massive pink columns of Phrygian marble supporting a pediment over which three statues of winged Nike looked down on the mortals below.

Rufio stopped to look up and admire the work, but the crowd pressed in around him, including several shifty-looking characters who seemed more at home in the bowels of the Suburra of Rome than in front of that great place of learning in Athenae. His hand securely around his money purse, Rufio mounted the central staircase and left the noisome environs of the city street for the dark quiet of the library.

It was a world apart, for beyond the tall doors and dark

interior of the library's propylon, a new realm opened up before Rufio.

Unlike the library of Pandainos, which had been small and intimate, the great library built by Hadrianus was monumental and vast. Once inside, a great rectangular peristylium with a hundred pink and blue-veined marble columns spread out to either side. These supported an ornately-carved and painted cedar roof that provided a much-needed respite from the hot Athenian sun.

Rufio was immediately struck by the quiet around him. A serene, mosaic pool that seemed to capture the sunlight sat in the middle of the sprawling garden. All around it were statues, flowerbeds, and trees beneath which had been set marble benches with ornately-carved legs where people could sit, read, think, and discuss. As Rufio stepped to the edge of the garden, he could see niches and small lecture halls on the north and south sides of the peristylium, but inevitably, his eye was drawn to the large structure at the eastern end of the complex, the bibliostasion. This was a large hall divided into several rooms with gilded ceilings and alabaster accents. Statues of Athenae's great philosophers and playwrights stood sentry beside Rome's emperors among frescoes that brought the walls to life.

All of this beauty was, however, secondary to the innumerable precious books that were kept in the niches of the high, cedar armaria that lined each room, nearly from floor to ceiling.

Rufio decided to walk around the peristylium to the bibliostasion when, after a few steps, someone came out of one of the lecture halls.

"Rufio Pagano?"

Rufio turned to see Phemius with another younger man, both of them carrying scrolls, bronze ink pots, and styli. "Salve, Phemius."

"What are you doing here? I thought you would be celebrating with your compatriots. You made a good showing in the procession."

"Yes, you saw that?" Rufio looked sheepish. "We brought up the rear quite well."

"It's an honour to take part in the Panathenaea, no matter your position," said the man with Phemius.

"All right, Laius," Phemius turned to the other. "There's no need to correct our guest. Here…" He handed his scrolls to the younger man. "Go and set these out in the hall for this evening's debate."

Laius, carefully balancing his load in his arms, went off down the colonnade and into one of the lecture rooms.

Phemius turned to Rufio. "We're hosting a debate of the merits of Rome's presence in Athenae since the time of the Republic."

"Merits? You sure that won't cause a riot?" Rufio stopped himself, his face a deep shade of red.

But Phemius smiled. "Not the sort of riot you are acquainted with," he chuckled. "By the way, I am glad they did not hang all of you. It would have been a loss to the world of theatre."

"I'm glad they didn't hang us too," Rufio said.

"Why don't you come to the lecture this evening? You could add your voice to the debate."

"I'm not one for debating, I'm afraid. Besides, I think they might tear me limb from limb at the first mention of Sulla."

"It is true that Sulla was unbelievably cruel to Athenae and her people, but Caesar, Marcus Antonius, Augustus and others did much for the city. And of course, Emperor Hadrianus did more than any other Roman for Athenae. You're standing in one of his greatest gifts to the city at this very moment."

Rufio looked around. "It is magnificent…"

"Would you like a tour?" Phemius asked.

"If you have the time, yes. The company is at the Taberna

Thesias now, but I thought I would come and look while they wait for the food to arrive."

"Let me show you around," Phemius said, leading the way along the peristylium.

As they walked, Rufio took it all in as if it were an oasis in the desert. Not that he had ever seen the desert. Etruria in high summer was as hot and dry a world as he had ever seen. He admired every detail of the place as they walked, the colour of the marble as the sun illuminated the surfaces, the way the sunlight reflecting off of the vast pool cast sparkling orbs on the walls and private corners where the silence was a deep comfort to thought.

"I could write for hours here," Rufio said as they reached the eastern end of the peristylium.

"Yes. It is a wonder," Phemius replied. "It's normally busier than this, but because everyone is celebrating the start of the Panathenaea, it's more quiet than usual." Phemius stopped at the tall cedar doors of the first hall of the bibliostasion, pushed them open and led Rufio inside. "Here we are..."

Rufio gasped as he entered the hall, for he had never seen so many scrolls in all his life.

Across a floor that was adorned with polished marble in hues of white, orange, blue, and grey, pink columns with white corinthian capitals supported two levels of books that were kept safe and dry in a multitude of cedar armaria.

Phemius stood in the middle of the hall's marble floor and smiled at Rufio's reaction. "Impressed?"

"'Impressed' is not the word," Rufio replied as he turned around slowly. "I never thought to see such a collection as this."

"This is the first room of the bibliostasion. There are two more."

Rufio looked at him. "Two more like this?"

Phemius laughed. "One more like this on the other side. The central room is larger."

"Larger? What works are in here?"

"This room contains treatises on nature, and the histories of the Gods, as well as military accounts. The similarly-sized hall on the other side is dedicated to political discourses, philosophy, histories and so forth."

"And the central hall?" Rufio asked.

"Let me show you." Phemius led Rufio though a side door that led from the first hall to the second, central hall and the two of them were swallowed up by the vast space as though two mortals had stumbled into the halls of Olympus itself. Phemius walked to the middle of the hall and bowed respectfully to the statue of Emperor Hadrianus which stood in the tall, central niche looking down at them.

Rufio followed suit awkwardly, and then cast his eyes about the library. "I can't get over this. It's almost too much to comprehend."

"I understand you. I have worked here for most of my life," Phemius said, "and I have yet to truly understand the amount of knowledge that inhabits these armaria."

Rufio spied the scrolls, some of them hundreds of years old, that stared out from the shadows of the cedar cabinets. It was as if each book had its own numina that called out to him, urging him to read its scroll, whispering of the secrets held within. "What does this room contain?"

"Ah, this room contains works on architecture, including the great structures of Athenae's Periclean age, artistic sketches, all of the known treatises on arithmetic and the study of the universe, and works on the religious rites and traditions of all known peoples across the empire." Phemius turned to Rufio. "It is also where we store copies of every known work of literature, poetry, and drama."

Rufio turned to him quickly. "You have some plays here?"

Phemius chuckled, but not mockingly. Rather he was joyful at the response he could give. "My friend, we have copies of all plays ever written here."

"Where?" Rufio asked.

"Up there." Phemius pointed to the second storey of the bibliostasion, just above the statue of Hadrianus. "Come, I'll show you." Phemius led Rufio to a small doorway which led to a narrow, marble stairwell that led up. They exited a second door and found themselves on the small walkway behind the columns fronting the armaria of the upper floor.

Rufio paused and gripped the column beside him to steady himself as he peered over the edge. "Has anyone ever fallen from up here?"

"Not yet," Phemius replied. He reached out to take hold of Rufio's sleeve and pulled him back against the wall. "This way." He made his way to the right, along the walkway until they reached the niches above the emperor. "Here we are." He then opened the high double doors of the two nearest armaria to reveal an array of scrolls, both large and small, the shelves labelled with the names of myriad playwrights and authors.

"By Apollo and the Muses…" Rufio said as he craned his neck to read the names. "Aeschylus… Agathon… Aristias… Aristophanes… Sophocles… Euripides… Menander… Rhinthon… You have them all! Even some I've never heard of! Chionidis?"

"Ah, yes. A comic poet from before the Persian wars." Phemius smiled. He always enjoyed the awe and respect true acolytes of the theatrical arts displayed when they set eyes upon the collection. "And look here in the next cabinet."

Rufio stepped to the cabinet closest to Emperor Hadrianus and spied all of the Roman names. "Gods, you have all of Andronicus' works! Accius… Ennius… All of Plautus and Naevius' works… Seneca, of course." Rufio looked shocked. "You have the tragedies of Pacuvius?"

"We do indeed. And those were not easy to come by. Emperor Hadrianus and Herodes Atticus were great lovers of the theatre and both spared no expense in trying to obtain copies of every known literary and dramatic work. Even Plato tried his hand at playwriting." Phemius pointed to the other cabinet.

"I don't see Terentius," Rufio said, his voice betraying his disappointment.

"Ah… Terentius is here." Phemius pointed to a sparsely populated shelf at the bottom. "Our collection would not be complete without his work."

Rufio knelt down to touch, but looked up at Phemius before doing so. "May I?"

"Yes, but carefully. They are quite old. My predecessor believed that those may even have been left in Athenae by Terentius himself."

Rufio took out one particularly old scroll. "Andria," he said.

"Yes, *The Girl from Andros*. Some say his first work. And there are *Hecyra, Eunuchus, Phormio, Adelphi* and, of course *Heautontimorumenos*, my personal favourite."

"Yes. Of course. If only he had lived longer, this shelf would be full."

"There may only be a few works, but what works they are!"

Rufio nodded and saw something small and dull in the faint light. He reached in to pull out a worn bronze stylus. "What's this?"

"Ah, is that still there?" Phemius held out his hand for Rufio to give it to him. "This shouldn't be there. The bronze might corrode and degrade the papyrus beside it. I thought I had removed it, but someone keeps putting it back."

"Why is it there in the first place?" Rufio asked.

"I'm not quite sure. It's always been here. One of the staff heard before that it was found with one of the older scrolls of Terentius'."

Rufio felt a chill then. "Do you think it was his?"

"It certainly looks old enough," Phemius said.

"May I hold it again?" Rufio asked.

Phemius handed the stylus back. "It is amazing how so mundane an object can represent so much."

Rufio looked down at the stylus and picked it up. He was surprised by how warm it felt to the touch, almost hot. It made his heart race to hold it. "It's as if one were holding the armour of Achilles, or Hercules' club."

"You do have a dramatic mind, Rufio Pagano. It is obvious that the stylus is your weapon of choice."

Rufio handed the object back to him and stood up, leaning against the cabinet as the void over the edge swayed in his vision.

"Perhaps one day soon, we shall have a copy of your play on these shelves? I know you are taken up with rehearsals for the production, but how is your own work coming along?"

"Oh, ach…" Rufio stood back as Phemius closed the armaria, hiding the precious scrolls from his view once more. "I don't know, really. Sometimes I wonder if I am experiencing delusions of greatness."

"Is that not the way with most playwrights? Seems to me the delusion is an essential ingredient at the outset."

"Do you think?"

"I know." Phemius smiled.

"You're mocking me."

"Not in the least. I'm most sincere." They began to make their way back around the walkway to the hidden stairwell. "Writing a play is a skill that comes with practice, no? It is your ponos, your toil. You must not give up."

"Sometimes I feel like doing just that, but then…then I am urged to carry on by way of some thought in the early hours of morning."

"That is the time when the Gods speak to us. I would not

ignore it." When they arrived at the lower level, once more looking up at Emperor Hadrianus' draped image, Phemius turned to Rufio. "You know, I believe that it is all well and good to read the great plays of the past, for they do enlighten us and give us much-needed perspectives and an appreciation of the world around us." He pointed up at the armaria where they had just been standing. "Such a collection is meant to be studied, to be performed whenever possible. But, it seems to me that if one wishes to truly connect with people, one needs to give them a human experience through one's own eyes, a new perspective of the world that is unique to you."

"Just as Terentius does."

"Exactly," Phemius replied. "Aristophanes said it in *Birds* that by words the mind is winged."

"So he did." Rufio smiled.

"Don't give up, Rufio Pagano. Who knows? It may be that some day, your words will help people to fly."

RUFIO HAD SPENT MUCH LONGER AT THE GREAT LIBRARY THAN he intended and so, after bidding his host a hurried farewell and thanking him for the tour, he plunged back into the sweaty streets to make his way back to the Taberna Thesias.

As he walked, he could not help but think on the treasures he had set his eyes upon in the library, and how Terentius, a truly wonderful playwright, occupied so little shelf space. It saddened Rufio to think how the shade of Rome's greatest playwright - in his opinion, at least - now wandered alone in the liminal spaces of Athenae, unable to go beyond its borders. Rufio could also not help but wonder what that meant for his own hopes and dreams.

When Rufio returned, it was to find the taberna nearly empty and the servants clearing the tables, except for the few that were still occupied by Felix, Electra, Clara, Sextus, Martia, and the children. "You ate already?" Rufio said as he arrived, his eyes scanning the empty platters upon the table.

"You were gone for over an hour, Rufio!" Felix said.

"What took you so long?" Clara asked as he sat down beside her.

"Phemius gave me a tour of the great library."

"Magnificent, isn't it?" Sextus said as he poured Rufio some of the wine which they had been enjoying in the afternoon sunlight.

"Truly," Rufio said as he took a big gulp from his cup. "I went to the second story to see the armaria that contain the theatrical collections." He shook his head. "They have copies of everything ever written. Even Pacuvius!"

"Really?" Felix leaned forward.

Rufio nodded and then jumped as Peli's head suddenly appeared in his lap. "What are you doing here?" He looked at Clara. "What's he doing here?" he asked her as he rubbed the hound's head.

"Seems he got away from Atticus," Clara laughed. "He arrived just as the food did."

Rufio looked at Peli and ruffled his jowls. He then looked at the table and saw that all that was left were a few grilled fish and the crumbs of a loaf of bread. "All you left me is fish?"

Everyone smiled.

Rufio began to turn red and he felt his hunger more acutely at that moment than he had all day. "The Greeks are too crazy for fish! Fish…fish…FISH!" He reached out reluctantly, too hungry not to try, and took up one of the grilled sardines.

"Go on, Rufio," Felix said. "You might like it!"

"Doubtful." Rufio tilted his head back and lowered the sardine but before he could take a hesitant bite, he lost his grip on the tail and it plunged into his throat. "Gwrra!" He turned and immediately coughed it up onto the ground.

Peli sniffed it quickly, then looked back at him.

"Ahh!" Rufio coughed and downed his wine. "I need something else. I just can't!"

It was then that Clara pulled away the napkin covering a last clay plate in the middle of which lay a succulent skewer of lamb meat covered in oil and herbs. "Don't worry, my love. I saved you some meat." She kissed his cheek and set the plate in font of him.

"The Gods love you!" Rufio said to her, the relief washing over him.

"You know, Rufio, the sardines will keep your hair from going grey," Electra said from down the table where she cradled Thespis.

"Thanks, but I'd rather have a head of snowy white hair and a plate of steaming meat than attempt to eat one more fish!"

Felix chuckled. "Didn't that nice fishmonger give you some fresh fish? Surely you enjoyed that?"

"I did not."

"Rufio…" Clara sighed. "It was a very kind present!"

"Present? It would have been diarrhea!"

"Oh dear," Martia covered her face.

"Rufio, please!" Clara said, her face reddening.

"What?" As Rufio's head was turned, Peli chose that exact moment to snatch up the skewer of lamb and bolt.

"No! Bad dog!" Rufio shouted as he knocked back his chair and ran after him. "Give that back!" It's mine!" he yelled as he chased Peli down the Peripatos.

"Should we tell him we've ordered another platter?" Sextus said, unable to contain his laughter.

"No. We can just bring it back to the domus with us," Clara said, shaking her head. "He'll chase Peli all the way back anyhow."

XV

THE MEAT OF IT

Felix Modestus had originally thought he would try and keep his players away from the myriad distractions of Athenae and the activities and events of the Great Panathenaea. After all, they had a play to put on! However, as he lay abed that night, sweaty from his and Electra's late night exertions, Thespis sleeping soundly in his crib on the other side of the vast cubiculum, he thought back on how rough a start the company had got off to, and how far they had come since.

Heautontimorumenos was not an easy task, but they had persevered and become intimately acquainted with Terentius' intended plot, finding just the right amount of humour and pathos that would give them a chance of winning over the Athenian crowd. The Etrurian Players had rehearsed, endured Felix's own crisis, been in a riot for which they had been jailed and nearly executed, and still they were rehearsing their parts like the professionals they were.

"I think they can enjoy some of the festival," Felix whispered to himself in the dark.

"What?" Electra said groggily from beneath the sheet beside him, her hand reaching out to stroke his chest.

"Nothing, love. Sleep." Felix kissed her tousled hair and stared out the window at the silver moonlight.

· · ·

THE NEXT MORNING, AFTER A SHORT REHEARSAL OF THE second act, the company was pleasantly surprised when Felix announced that they were done for the day and that they could go and enjoy the first full day of the Panathenaea which included the musical and rhapsodic contests.

"Are you sure, Dominus?" Beatrice asked. "There's still much to prepare for, no?"

"Yes," Fausto agreed. "The performance is just nine days away!"

"And we're ready," Felix replied.

"Are you certain, Felix?" Julius stepped toward the pulpitum of the small odeon.

Felix turned to Castor and Pollux. "Are the set pieces finished? The olive tree and the fountain?"

The brothers looked at each other, and then back at Felix. "Yes, Dominus."

"We'll just have to cut the fresh olive branches the morning of the performance to insert into the trunk."

"Good." Felix turned to Beatrice and Domela. "And the costumes are all fitted and ready?"

"Yes," they said at the exact same time.

Beatrice frowned, but it disappeared quickly enough. "Yes, Dominus. This time was much easier as the costumes are not as elaborate for this production."

"And you all know your lines perfectly well," Felix added. "We can have short rehearsals each morning and evening, but the days can be spent enjoying the festival. If anyone is worried about one of their scenes, we can work on it together. And of course, we'll do a full run-through the day before."

"Thank you, Dominus!" Fausto shouted and everyone else clapped.

"Just remember to keep a low profile this week. No brawling in the agora or the lupanar. And for Apollo's sake, stay away from The Rome Antics."

"Don't worry, Felix!" Castor said.

Felix eyed them. "All right. Off with you!" he said and the company dispersed.

Rufio came and sat beside Felix on the edge of the pulpitum. "Shall we go and see the musical contests? I suppose I should while I'm here. I don't know when we'll be back."

"I'm not going to anything," Felix said.

"Why not? Some of the greatest performers and athletes in the world are here for this!"

"I need to focus, and I don't want to see anyone else perform."

"Why not?" Rufio asked.

Felix shook his head. "I… I don't know. This is a difficult play and…and I don't need anything to affect my confidence."

"Is it even possible for your confidence to be shaken, Felix?" Clara said as she approached.

"You'd be surprised, my dear."

"We can stay with you," Rufio said. "You know. Go over some of the scenes together."

Felix shook his head. "No. You go ahead. I just need to rest my mind and soak in the baths." He smiled. "Besides, if you were ever to hear a reading of Homer, the Panathenaic rhapsodic contest is it."

"If you're certain," Clara said.

"I am. Electra is staying too, so if you want you can leave Felicia with us and go just the two of you."

Rufio looked at Clara and she looked back at him hopefully.

"Why not?" Rufio said.

"Just tie Peli up," Felix added. "I don't want him pissing in my bath."

When Rufio and Clara were gone, Felix sat alone upon the pulpitum looking up at the pure blue sky above. He breathed deeply, in and out, and smiled to himself. "Apollo… Thank you for this labour…"

THE CITY WAS ABSOLUTELY BUZZING WITH ACTIVITY FROM THE first hour of daylight, for people had come from all over the city and farther afield in Attica to attend the Great Panathenaea. Though many came for the athletic and equestrian contests on the second, third, and fourth days, the musical and rhapsodic contests of the first day were extremely popular.

When the day's opening sacrifices were completed on the Acropolis and at the altars and shrines of the agora, the crowds then found their way to the sanctuary of Dionysus at the end of the Street of the Tripods where offerings were made to the god who presided over, among other things, festivity and theatre. The sanctuary, with its temples, altars and statues, lay just to the south of the great theatre of Dionysus beside which was the titanic odeon originally built by Pericles where the day's contests were to be held.

By the time Rufio, Clara and the others stepped through the propylon leading into the sanctuary, the sacrifices were coming to an end and people were beginning to file into the entrances without any semblance of a line.

"I don't think we'll all be able to sit together," Clara said to Julius who followed her and Rufio along with Domela.

"No," Julius replied. "This is a popular event. We'll sit where we can." He and Domela were then swallowed up by the crowd as they followed Castor, Pollux, Damon, Fausto and Beatrice who had rushed ahead.

"Is there even seating in this venue?" Rufio asked Clara.

"Yes, but not that much. Come," she said, pulling on his hand. "Let's push our way in."

Suddenly, Rufio was not so keen on attending the festival. It was packed, mostly with Athenian men, many of whom appeared to be artists and musicians themselves. Rich and poor attended, though the latter were somewhat less numerous in number as their labours did not necessarily allow for a day without work, let alone eight.

It was a shock to go from the bright, morning light into the dark, torch-lit interior of the odeon. As Rufio and Clara entered, they had the feeling of stepping into a thick forest, for all around them were close to a hundred stone columns that supported a high cedar and tile roof designed to resemble a tent. There was seating on four sides and in the centre was a small, square orchestra with a single stool for the performers. Nearby, a statue of Dionysus presided, the god's lifelike eyes seemingly excited to hear what artistic offerings the mortals before him would bring.

"Over there!" Rufio pointed to a bench at the top of one block of seats where they could both sit. He pulled Clara along, stepping carefully up the side, ignoring the tutting of those already seated, and settled themselves on the uppermost row. "Just in time," he said to Clara. "Look how full it is!"

"It's standing room only now," Clara looked down at the spaces between the seating blocks where people crammed themselves in among the stone columns, straining to see if any performers had yet stepped onto the orchestra. "I see the others." Clara pointed to the other side of the odeon and waved.

Beatrice and Fausto waved back, and Damon twirled a few notes upon his flute which silenced the crowd suddenly as they thought the performance was beginning. When people realized it was not a performance, the buzz of discussion erupted once more.

"I feel like I should be back at the villa working," Rufio muttered, feeling quite warm in the crowded space.

"You can't be writing all the time, my love." Clara turned

to him and placed her hand upon his cheek. "You need to take in art in order to create it."

"I suppose. But how will listening to a reading of Homer help?"

"The words have a power all of their own, as does music. And it's not just Homer. We may also hear bits of Pindar and Hesiod. It's very exciting! You'll see. This is something we'll not ever see in Rome." Clara was beaming with excitement.

Rufio could not help but smile at her. "I wonder if Terentius sat here during this very festival?" He pictured the shade fleetingly, and looked around quickly to make sure it was not there staring at him.

Just then, Clara leaned upon his shoulder and grasped his hand. "I'm glad we came."

"Me too," he said, relaxing into his seat as a tall man in a long, white, pleated chiton stepped into the orchestra.

The murmur of the audience faded to nothing as all eyes turned to him.

"All hail Dionysus who presides over this place, and all hail our divine goddess and patron, Athena, whose festival this is!" The man spoke perfectly, his pace just so, his voice projecting to every corner of the odeon so that everyone there could hear. "On this first day of the Great Panathenaea, we assemble to hear the very best musical and rhapsodic performers of our time." He looked around to let that sink in, meeting the eyes of people on all sides as he turned slowly. "We shall begin with the musical contests, the youth competitors preceding the adults, and then the same for the rhapsodes. If anyone disrupts the competition in any way, they will be removed from the event and banned for the remainder of the Panathenaea. We are here to honour our patron goddess with the very best in human achievement." The speaker stopped, looked at the judges in the first row of one of the seating blocks, and then raised his hands to the roof, as if he were praying to the Gods. "Let the contest begin, and may Victory crown the worthy!"

The audience applauded and struck up conversation for a few brief moments before a lone, blond, curly-haired boy of no more than fifteen walked into the orchestra holding an aulos, a double-reeded flute. To Rufio's surprise, the lad seemed eminently calm, even under all of that scrutiny. He set the two reeds to his mouth, wetting them first, took a deep breath and, after a moment, blew a long, melancholic note. That note turned to two, more urgent notes that were reminiscent of two young horses playing in a Thessalian field, charging this way and that, enjoying a freedom from another age.

Clara and Rufio leaned forward in their seats, drawn in by the music as they, and everyone else there present, recalled youthful memories of carefree play, the long-forgotten idylls of childhood.

The youth's song then changed, slowed, was pulled inexorably into a different melody, the one flute by the other, as though days of childhood revelry had been stopped by some tragedy with a long shadow, the death of a favoured pet, perhaps, or of a kindly grandmother. As the melody came to its end, the audience was left with a lingering sense of hope that drew them out of their sadness just enough to make smiling possible once again. And just like that, the boy lowered his aulos and bowed to great applause.

Many in the audience wiped away tears, clapping, and praising whilst the judges made notes on the large wax tablets each of them held in their laps.

"And that's the first one!" Clara said to Rufio, her eyes watery.

Rufio could only shake his head. "I bet his parents are proud."

The man in front of them turned in his seat, his eyes likewise pooling. "That is young Demophon. He is an orphan."

"How sad," Clara said.

The man agreed and turned back to face the orchestra as they waited for the next competitor.

For the next hour, youths ranging from twelve to twenty stepped into the orchestra, each of them seemingly better than the last but for one poor boy whose nerves got the better of him, causing him to shudder on one note. Though it was a fleeting mistake, and the rest of the performance was flawless, it was so jarring that much of the audience flinched as though they had been cut by a blade.

It had been heartbreaking to see the boy run out of the orchestra, tears streaming down his red face.

A murmur arose as the last of the youth competitors finished and the judges made their notes.

Clara turned to Rufio. "What do you think so far?"

Rufio shook his head. "I don't know how the judges will decide. It's an impossible task. They were all magnificent! And they have to give the prize to one person?"

"No. In the Panathenaea, prizes are given to the winners, but also to those who achieve second place."

"Still… Not an easy task." Rufio pointed across to the other side of the odeon where Beatrice appeared to be comforting Damon whose face was buried in the palms of his hands. "Looks like Damon was quite moved."

Clara watched. She often wondered what was going on in Damon's head. It was not easy to speak with him, but she greatly admired his skill with the flute and had often wondered where the feeling with which he played came from. "I think all of these performers are touched by the Gods in some way," Clara added.

"No doubt," Rufio agreed. "Do they receive an olive or laurel corona if they win?"

"Oh, much more than that!" the man in front of them turned again.

Rufio and Clara looked at him. "Yes?"

"Indeed!" the man said. "The winners and runners-up in the youth category receive amphorae crafted by the finest workshops in Attica, filled with the best Attic olive oil."

"One amphora for such skill?" Rufio asked, a little disappointed.

"No, no, no…" the man replied. "Six amphorae for the runner-up, and sixty for the winner."

"Sixty!" Rufio exclaimed a little too loudly, causing others to turn and look at him.

"Yes!" the man said. "And it is more for the adult competitors. In addition to the same number of amphorae, they also receive close to a talent in silver."

"A talent?" Rufio looked from the man to Clara. "Surely the oil is enough of a prize?"

"It is a tradition that goes back hundreds of years," the man said proudly. "Athenae honours those whose labours honour the goddess Athena in her home."

"All the emperor gave us was a corona," Rufio muttered to Clara.

The man perked up. "Are you musicians?"

"No. We are actors," Rufio said.

"Actors?" The man looked doubtfully at Clara and back to Rufio.

"We are part of The Etrurian Players. You may have heard of us?" Rufio clarified.

"Can't say that I have," the man replied, beginning to look bored.

"Well, we'll be performing in the odeon built by Atticus the day after the festival. You should come and see us."

"Perhaps," the man replied, already turning. "We should stop talking now. The adult competition is about to begin."

Clara smiled to herself when she saw Rufio's face.

So rude! he mouthed to her.

"You are a wonderful writer and actor, my love," Clara said, "but Felix is the better promoter."

Rufio shrugged and turned to listen to the announcer who had returned to the orchestra.

"And now Athenians and xenoi, we come to the adult category in the instrumental and cytharody competition. Here are gathered the greatest musical performers you will ever bear witness to. They have toiled at their art for most of their lives, honing and perfecting their skills to honour the goddess. Some are competing for the first time, while others are returning champions of the Panathenaea!"

The audience applauded at that, and that applause increased tenfold as the first competitor walked out.

"And now, a former champion in the Panathenaea… Antiocheis!" the announcer said before leaving, for this first competitor needed no introduction.

A tall, thin man with a thin, dark beard strode across the floor, inclining his head somewhat humbly to the audience. He carried a kithara which seemed most ancient, the wooden soundbox dark and polished with age. After a few moments of soaking up the adoration, he seated himself on the stool so that he faced the row of judges.

"I wonder if he'll be any good?" Rufio whispered to Clara, only to bear the brunt of a wicked glare from their nosy neighbour.

Clara set her hand upon Rufio's and together they watched and listened.

The silence filled the odeon immediately from the rafters to the floor, all attention on the musician who, it seemed to Rufio, appeared to have retreated into a trance. His eyes were closed, and he held his kithara upon his lap, balancing it with care and skill.

A single chord, strummed across all seven strings, roused the audience as though it were a splash of cold mountain spring water in summer. Another followed, leading into a scale that tickled all of the notes that were most pleasing to the Gods. Antiocheis' fingers created sounds upon that instrument that seemed to be new to the world, but which told a story that many could relate to, of love found, and lived, and ultimately lost.

Clara wiped her eyes and held Rufio close as she listened, for the heart-wrenching melodies made her feel as though she and Rufio were following Orpheus into the depths of Hades as he searched for his Eurydice. She and Rufio were hidden safely among the black rock of that dread realm, watching as Apollo's son played for his life and his love, leading her out of darkness to the world above. But then, only at the final moment, he turned too soon and she was pulled back into the darkness to end the song on another darker and deftly-played chord.

The audience was left sobbing, only applauding when Antiocheis stood and bowed.

"How is anyone going to follow that?" Rufio asked. "I mean, we've heard a few lyre players in our time, but this…"

"The kithara is no hobbyist's instrument," Clara said. "Only a very few can master it."

"And they're probably all here!" Rufio added. "Although, I don't know that anyone is going to be able to compete with that."

It was not long before Rufio realized he was wrong in thinking so, for as the competition progressed, each musician played with a skill that tickled the audience's senses and wrung their emotions such that even one of the judges in the front row fainted at the beauty of a particular song played upon the kithara by a young competitor of no more than twenty-five years. While servants roused the fallen judge, the young man continued playing, mastering his shock and continuing to the end.

One musician after another performed, each as good or

better than the last. Some played the kithara, and others the aulos. Some were accompanied by canary-voiced boys, and others by strong baritones whose songs spoke of summer fields, and homes, or of journeys to faraway places where only the Gods trod. Everyone there felt like they had been through a labyrinth of emotion and human experience that would light their waking hours and nighttime dreams for weeks to come. It was such that by the end of the performances, the audience talked of little else than the epic task laid bare before the judges.

"Is that it then?" Rufio asked Clara, leaning to one side slightly. "I believe my ass has fallen asleep."

"Shhh! Tut, tut!" the man in front of them hissed. "The rhapsodes are about to begin!"

"Oh, calm yourself, grandfather," Rufio bit back, having had quite enough of him. "Don't think I haven't seen you ogling the young men up there!"

"I'm admiring the beauty of their skill and craft," the man protested.

"I'm sure," Rufio scoffed, and the man turned forward to be silent.

"Do you want to leave?" Clara asked Rufio.

"We're here now. We might as well listen to the rhapsodes. I wonder if any actors will be performing?"

Just then, the Athenian actor, Aegisthus walked into the odeon to a roar of approval.

"Does that answer your question?" Clara asked.

Rufio peered down to the orchestra. "That's that snooty one! Aegisthus, is it? He wasn't very nice to Felix."

"I suppose we'll see if his performance is any better than his manners," Clara said as she leaned forward to listen.

Aegisthus stood in the middle of the orchestra as though he were bathing in sunlight, his eyes closed beneath his dark, normally angry brows. He had one hand upon his heart, the other at his side and as he took a breath to begin, the first syllable that everyone heard was that of a bird.

Aegisthus caught himself and looked to the rafters in search of the arrogant sparrow. When not another sound was audible, he breathed again only to have the bird rob him of his first words.

The entire audience, including the judges, looked to the rafters a second time.

Aegisthus walked in a slow circle a couple of times, collecting himself for a third try.

Then Rufio spotted Damon bending over while, beside him, Beatrice and Fausto were red-faced as they seemingly tried not to howl with laughter.

"Watch Damon," Rufio whispered to Clara, and just then, as Aegisthus puffed out his chest to begin his rhapsode, Damon set his flute to his mouth and bent down covertly.

Just as the famed Athenian actor was about to speak, the bird twittered mockingly in one corner of the odeon, and then in another, flitting here and there such that Aegisthus gasped in frustration and stormed out of the orchestra.

Many audience members laughed at that, unable to contain themselves.

"The Gods must not want him to perform," one bejewelled lady said nearby.

"Or Damon of Rome," Rufio laughed into Clara's ear, causing her to stopper her own laughter.

Once Clara had collected herself, she caught Damon, Beatrice, and Fausto's attention and shook he head, her lips pursed tightly.

Damon put up his hands in surrender, having enjoyed the moment.

A minute later, after the judges were certain the bird had left the odeon, the dark, imposing figure of Zotikos walked into the orchestra to begin that part of the competition in earnest.

"I recognize him too," Rufio said. "He's not a nice fellow, but I do hear he's talented."

"Let's see," Clara said.

Zotikos of Athenae stood confidently in the middle of the orchestra, his stare grabbing hold of the audience, meeting theirs head-on and unflinching. He took one step forward, and then…

"All day long her sails were full as she held her course over the sea, but when the sun went down and darkness was over all the earth, we got into the deep waters of the river Okeanos, where lie the demos and city of the Cimmerians who live enshrouded in mist and darkness which the rays of the sun never pierce neither at his rising, nor as he goes down again out of the heavens, but the poor wretches live in one long melancholy night. When we got there we beached the ship, took the sheep out of her, and went along by the waters of Okeanos till we came to the place of which Circe had told us…"

The audience was immediately enthralled, spellbound by Zotikos' voice, as though Circe herself had empowered him. But they were also filled with dread, for all knew the words of Odysseus as he described his descent into the house of Hades.

Futuo! Rufio thought. *Shades.*

"Here Perimedes and Eurylokhos held the victims, while I drew my sword and dug the trench a cubit each way. I made a drink-offering to all the dead, first with honey and milk, then with wine, and thirdly with water, and I sprinkled white barley meal over the whole, praying earnestly to the poor feckless ghosts, and promising them that when I got back to Ithaca I would sacrifice a barren heifer for them, the best I had, and would load the pyre with good things. I also particularly promised that Teiresias should have a black sheep to himself, the best in all my flocks. When I had prayed sufficiently to the dead, I cut the throats of the two sheep and let the blood run into the trench, whereon the ghosts came trooping up from Erebus - brides, young bachelors, old men worn out with toil, maids who had been crossed in love, and brave men who had been killed in battle, with their armour still smirched with blood; they came from every quarter and flitted round the trench with a strange kind of screaming sound that made me turn pale with fear. When I saw them coming I told the men to be quick and flay the carcasses of the two dead sheep and make burnt offerings of them, and at the same time to repeat prayers to Hades and to Persephone; but I sat where I was with my sword drawn and would not let the poor feckless ghosts come near the blood till Teiresias should have answered my questions…"

Rufio and Clara gripped each other's hands as Zotikos wove his spell, for they could see the shades, smell the blood and burning flesh of offerings as much as anyone there. The young and the old there present shook in secret beneath their stolae, tunicae and chitons.

Zotikos spoke of the ghost of Elpenor, and the shade's description of his death on Circe's island, and how he would bring the God's anger down upon Odysseus should he not give him rites.

Rufio had a thought that he should perhaps offer something to his own demanding shade, but he then remembered that Terentius had made his own demands which, especially now, seemed more urgent than ever.

Zotikos continued… "Thus, then, did we sit and hold sad talk with one another, I on the one side of the trench with my sword held over the blood, and the ghost of my comrade saying all this to me from the other side. Then came the ghost of my dead mother Antikleia, daughter to Autolykos. I had left her alive when I set out for Troy and was moved to tears when I saw her, but even so, for all my sorrow I would not let her come near the blood till I had asked my questions of Teiresias.

"Then came also the ghost of Theban Teiresias, with his golden scepter in his hand. He knew me and said, 'Odysseus, noble son of Laertes, why, poor man, have you left the light of day and come down to visit the dead in this sad place? Stand back from the trench and withdraw your sword that I may drink of the blood and answer your questions truly.'

"So I drew back, and sheathed my sword, whereon when he had drank of the blood he began with his prophecy. 'You want to know,' said he, 'about your return home, but heaven will make this hard for you."

Zotikos stopped his monologue and bowed his head.

Only then did the audience applaud and the judges scratch their marks into the fragrant bees wax of their tablets.

"Not bad," Rufio said to Clara.

"I would have chosen a different passage, but yes," she said, "his skill is undeniable. Not as good as Felix, but still…"

"Who's this now?" Rufio asked as another of the Athenian actors came on. "I recognize him as well. He was with Zotikos."

"And now," the announcer began as the crowd quieted a little more. "Another of our great Athenians…Cadmus!"

Into the orchestra strode Cadmus, knowingly handsome with his carefully-placed hair and trimmed beard. He had a pouty stare that he aimed strategically about the odeon before settling himself in the centre and spreading his arms wide.

"Men come and go as leaves year by year upon the trees. Those of autumn the wind sheds upon the ground, but when the season of spring returns the forest buds forth with fresh vines."

"It's from the Iliad," Clara whispered to Rufio who nodded and leaned forward. "The words of Glaukos."

Rufio looked at her and smiled, proud that she was so quick to remember.

"It is so with the generations of humankind, the new spring

up as the old are passing away. If, then, you would learn my descent, it is one that is well known to many. There is a city in the heart of Argos, pasture land of horses, called Ephyra, where Sisyphus lived, who was the craftiest of all humankind. He was the son of Iolaus, and had a son named Glaukos, who was father to Bellerophon, whom heaven endowed with the most surpassing comeliness and beauty. But Proetus devised his ruin, and being stronger than he, drove him from the district of the Argives, over which Zeus had made him ruler. For Antaea, wife of Proetus, lusted after him, and would have had him lie with her in secret; but Bellerophon was an honorable man and would not, so she told lies about him to Proetus. 'Proetus,' said she, 'kill Bellerophon or die, for he would have had converse with me against my will.' The king was angered, but shrank from killing Bellerophon, so he sent him to Lycia bearing baneful signs, written inside a folded tablet and containing much ill against the bearer. He bade Bellerophon show these written signs to his father-in-law, to the end that he might thus perish; Bellerophon therefore went to Lycia, and the gods conveyed him safely."

No one spoke as Cadmus relayed the tale, his solid, arrogant voice barring any comment of whisper in the audience, the manner in which he spoke casting every mind there back in time to that age of heroes.

"When he reached the river Xanthos, which is in Lycia, the king received him with all goodwill, feasted him nine days, and killed nine heifers in his honour, but when rosy-fingered morning appeared upon the tenth day, he questioned him and desired to see the written signs from his son-in-law Proetus. When he had received the wicked written signs, he first commanded Bellerophon to kill that savage monster, the Chimaera, who was not a human being, but a goddess, for she had the head of a lion and the tail of a serpent, while her body was that of a goat, and she breathed forth flames of fire; but

Bellerophon slew her, for he was guided by signs from heaven. He next fought the far-famed Solymoi, and this, he said, was the hardest of all his battles.

"Thirdly, he killed the Amazons, women who were the peers of men, and as he was returning thence, the king devised yet another plan for his destruction; he picked the bravest warriors in all Lycia, and placed them in ambuscade, but not a man ever came back, for Bellerophon killed every one of them. Then the king knew that he must be the valiant offspring of a god, so he kept him in Lycia, gave him his daughter in marriage, and made him of equal honour in the kingdom with himself; and the Lycians gave him a piece of land, the best in all the country, fair with vineyards and tilled fields, to have and to hold.

"The king's daughter bore Bellerophon three children, Isandros, Hippolokhos, and Laodameia. Zeus, the lord of counsel, lay with Laodameia, and she bore him noble Sarpedon; but when Bellerophon came to be hated by all the gods, he wandered all desolate and dismayed upon the Alean plain, gnawing at his own heart, and shunning the path of man. Ares, insatiate of battle, killed his son Isandros while he was fighting the Solymi; his daughter was killed by Artemis of the golden reins, for she was angered with her; but Hippolokhos was father to myself, and when he sent me to Troy he urged me again and again to fight ever among the foremost and outdo my peers, so as not to shame the blood of my fathers who were the noblest in Ephyra and in all Lycia. This, then, is the descent I claim."

Cadmus ended with an immediate bow and, so sudden was it that it took the audience a moment to catch on and match it with their applause.

"What did you think?" Clara asked Rufio.

"I mean, it's a great story but…I don't know… Are points taken away for arrogance?"

Clara chuckled.

"And is it just me or the dark lighting in here, but did I see him try and sneak in a scratch of his bottom when he turned?"

Clara covered her mouth to keep her laughter from boiling over.

Rufio smiled to himself. He always did love it when he could make her laugh.

It was then that a very young man walked into the orchestra, his eyes darting all around him.

The murmur of the crowd continued faintly as people asked their neighbours who this newcomer was.

He was no more than twenty-two years of age, young among all the veterans of the competition, with a plain, knee-length chiton that might have been homespun by his mother or young wife.

"And now, a first-time competitor in the sacred Panathenaea," the announcer said. "Alexandros of Thebes!"

There was some muted applause, which Clara and Rufio added to with some pity for the young man whom nobody seemed to know.

"I can't bear to watch," Rufio said, covering his eyes for a moment, feeling for the young man and the imminent humiliation.

But the young man rallied himself and transformed before their very eyes. He was taller now, his chest out, his eyes staring to some far off place as he mouthed a silent prayer to the Gods.

Then, he spoke…

"I beseech you, splendour-loving city, most beautiful on earth, home of Persephone; you who inhabit the hill of well-built dwellings above the banks of sheep-pasturing Acragas: be propitious, and with the goodwill of gods and men, mistress, receive this victory garland from Pytho in honour of renowned Midas, and receive the victor himself, champion of Hellas in that art which once Pallas Athena discovered when she wove into music the dire dirge of the reckless Gorgons which Perseus heard pouring in slow anguish from beneath the horrible serpent hair of the maidens, when he did away with the third sister and brought death to sea-girt Seriphos and its people."

The young Theban paused to let his words wash over the audience, as refreshing as the foam on Seriphos' pebbled shore.

Rufio leaned in to Clara. "What is this reading?"

Clara answered without looking at him. "It's Pindar's Pythian Twelve. What a start!" she whispered.

Alexandros of Thebes walked a small circle, his head down, but then he looked up again, as though to address the Gods sitting on the terraces of Olympus.

"Yes…he brought darkness on the monstrous race of Phorcus, and he repaid Polydectes with a deadly wedding-present for the long slavery of his mother and her forced bridal bed; he stripped off the head of beautiful Medusa, Perseus, the son of Danae, who they say was conceived in a spontaneous shower of gold. But when the virgin goddess had released that beloved man from those labours, she created the many-voiced song of flutes so that she could imitate with musical instruments the shrill cry that reached her ears from the fast-moving jaws of Euryale."

Rufio was quiet as he listened, awed by so much skill in one still so young, and of course somewhat jealous of the words of the ancient poet that still managed to capture the attention of an audience in such a way.

"The goddess discovered it; but she discovered it for mortal men to have, and called it the many-headed strain, the glorious strain that entices the people to gather at contests, often sounding through thin plates of brass and through reeds, which grow beside the city of lovely choruses, the city of the Graces, in the sacred precinct of the nymph of Cephisus, reeds that are the faithful witnesses of the dancers."

Alexandros stopped suddenly to look at the faces of the audience, his eyes finally resting on the bench of judges.

"If there is any prosperity among men, it does not appear without hardship. A god will indeed grant it in full today… What is fated cannot be escaped. But that time will come, striking unexpectedly, and give one thing beyond all expectation, and withhold another."

The hall was silent and his final words lingered in the air. People felt a flutter of excitement in their chests, for it had been a very long time since an artist of Thebes had so beautifully performed the words of that city's favoured son.

The applause that broke free of the restrained crowd was deafening and as young Alexandros bowed to each side of the odeon, his hand upon his heart, Rufio could see the glimmer of tears upon the cheeks of many there, caught in the firelight like rubies upon their faces.

As the judges were making their notations, Alexandros of Thebes left the stage calmly, though all was chaos and praise about him.

Over the next hour, several other competitors came and went, some singing, accompanied by musicians upon the flute or aulos, others doing their very best to perform their monologues in such a way that they had a chance against the newcomer from Thebes. It was whispered among the spectators that one particularly good performer, a man named Theophile of Chios, was even descended from Homer himself.

"The goddess must be pleased," Clara said. "They're all so good!"

"They are," Rufio answered as he rubbed his bottom and shifted from one cheek to the next to try and wake it. "I don't envy the judges."

Then the crowd hushed as Aegisthus dared the orchestra once more, his face calm, the red depth of his complexion shallower than before as he scanned the rafters for his hateful avian adversary.

Clara looked across at Damon and wagged a finger at him.

He nodded back and put his hands up.

Before anyone could interrupt or annoy him, Aegisthus ploughed on with his monologue.

"Think of your father, O Achilles like unto the gods, who is such even as I am, on the sad threshold of old age."

Aegisthus paused after that first shot, allowing the audience's minds to catch up to him and discern the words of King Priam to the Greek hero, Achilles, as he begged for the body of his slain son, Hector.

"It may be that those who dwell near him harass him, and there is none to keep war and ruin from him. Yet when he hears of you being still alive, he is glad, and his days are full of hope that he shall see his dear son come home to him from Troy…"

There was pain in Aegisthus' voice, a pain and feeling that one would not have expected from his haughty demeanour in the streets of Athenae. He became the pained person of Priam in that moment.

"'But I, wretched man that I am, had the bravest in all Troy for my sons, and there is not one of them left. I had fifty sons when the Achaeans came here; nineteen of them were from a single womb, and the others were borne to me by the women of my household. The greater part of them has fierce Ares laid low, and Hektor, him who was alone left, him who was the guardian of the city and ourselves, him have you lately slain… Therefore, I am now come to the ships of the Achaeans to ransom his body from you. Fear, O Achilles, the wrath of heaven; think on your own father and have compassion upon me, who am the more pitiable, for I have steeled myself as no man yet has ever steeled himself before me, and have raised to my lips the hand of him who slew my son.'"

Aegisthus sighed painfully as he re-enacted Priam's kiss upon the hand of Achilles. Then, he continued…

"Thus spoke Priam, and the heart of Achilles yearned as he bethought him of his father. He took the old man's hand and moved him gently away. The two wept bitterly - Priam, as he lay at Achilles' feet, weeping for Hektor, and Achilles now for his father and now for Patroklos, till the house was filled with their lamentation. But when Achilles was now sated with grief and had unburdened the bitterness of his sorrow, he left his seat and raised the old man by the hand, in pity for his white hair and beard; then he said, 'Unhappy man, you have indeed been greatly daring; how could you venture to come alone to the ships of the Achaeans, and enter the presence of him who has slain so many of your brave sons? You must have iron courage: sit now upon this seat, and for all our grief we will hide our sorrows in our hearts, for weeping will not avail us. The immortals know no care, yet the lot they spin for man is full of sorrow; on the floor of Zeus' palace there stand two urns, the one filled with evil gifts, and the other with good ones. He for whom Zeus the lord of thunder mixes the gifts he sends, will meet now with good and now with evil fortune; but he to whom Zeus sends none but evil gifts will be pointed at by the finger of scorn, the hand of famine will pursue him to the ends of the world, and he will go up and down the face of the earth, respected neither by gods nor men. Even so did it befall Peleus; the gods endowed him with all good things from his birth upwards, for he reigned over the Myrmidons excelling all men in prosperity and wealth, and mortal though he was they gave him a goddess for his bride. But even on him too did heaven send misfortune, for there is no race of royal children born to him in his house, save one son who is doomed to die all untimely; nor may I take care of him now that he is growing old, for I must stay here at Troy to be the bane of you and your children. And you too, O Priam, I have heard that you were aforetime happy. They say that in wealth and plenitude of offspring you surpassed all that is in Lesbos, the realm of Makar to the northward, Phrygia that is more inland, and those that dwell upon the great Hellespont; but from the day when the dwellers in heaven sent this evil upon you, war and slaughter have been about your city continually.'"

Aegisthus breathed slowly, his eyes meeting the audience.

"'Bear up against it, and let there be some intervals in your sorrow. Mourn as you may for your brave son, you will take nothing by it. You cannot raise him from the dead, ere you do so yet another sorrow shall befall you.'"

Aegisthus raised his shaking hands up, as though it were he who spoke to godlike Achilles in that tent beneath the walls of doomed Troy.

"And Priam answered, 'O king, bid me not be seated, while Hektor is still lying uncared for in your tents, but accept the great ransom which I have brought you, and give him to me at once that I may look upon him. May you prosper with the ransom and reach your own land in safety, seeing that you have suffered me to live and to look upon the light of the sun.'

"Achilles looked at him sternly and said, 'Vex me, sir, no longer; I am of myself minded to give up the body of Hektor.'"

Aegisthus closed his eyes and bowed his head, even as the audience applauded and wept and raised their voices to the rafters in praise of his valiant return.

"Not bad," Rufio said to Clara as they stood and waited for the rows before them to file out.

"Quite a display, yes," she agreed, however reluctantly. Clara looked upon her husband and noted the great sadness in his eyes at that moment. "You all right?"

Rufio nodded, but unconvincingly.

"Tell me," Clara said, lacing her arm through his as they

walked out into the orange evening light. "Don't brood. It's not good for your digestion." She smiled. "Tell me, Rufio."

"It's just… Seeing all those amazing performers… I know I will never be as good as them. I suppose now I really do understand why Felix did not want to come. We're performing in a week's time! How are we to follow any of that?" Rufio pointed to the great odeon and shook his head. "The expectations of these Greeks are far beyond what I'm capable of."

Clara smiled sadly at him. She could see him chiding himself behind his eyes. "Rufio…my love… That is because they know *what* to expect of their competitors. I would say we are at an advantage for our performance, for they have no expectations of us. If they do, they are quite low indeed. They don't expect great theatre from Romans, even though Felix and the others are well-known. Their arrogance blinds them, and together, our company is more than capable of ripping away the veil that hides the world from them."

Where they stood, in the shade of an olive tree along the wall of the sanctuary of Dionysus, Rufio leaned in to kiss Clara, his hands gently holding her face. "I love you."

"And I love you," she replied. "And I believe in you."

"And I you."

The crowd was dissipating now as people sought out their homes or one of the various tabernae about the Acropolis.

Rufio and Clara walked along the path until they were back on the Street of the Tripods. "That last performance…" Rufio said.

"Priam and Achilles? The one Aegisthus performed?"

"Yes. As much as I hate to admit it, he was very good." Rufio wiped at his eyes.

"What is it?" Clara asked, though she suspected what he would say.

"Can we go back to our daughter now? I feel as though we have been away from her for too long."

Clara smiled and nodded. "That is the beauty of our life, Rufio. We *can* go back to her."

"There they are!" Fausto suddenly burst from the crowd of pedestrians followed by Castor, Pollux, Beatrice, and Damon. "Do you both want to go to the taberna with us?"

"Where are Julius and Domela?" Clara asked.

"They're walking back to the villa," Beatrice added as she caught up.

"We're going to go back as well," Rufio said to them. "You go ahead."

"Suit yourselves!" Fausto said without waiting for another word. He practically skipped away with Beatrice, followed by Castor, Pollux, and Damon who unleashed his skills upon the flute, turning people's heads as he went, making them wonder where those birds were perched.

"Home, then?" Clara said.

"Home," he agreed, eager to hold Felicia, and even to see Peli who had by then, no doubt, bitten half of the domus servants and littered his way through the villa.

As they made the long walk through Athenae, over the Ilissos, and up the hill of Ardittos to the villa, birds and cicadas singing in the hot, pine-scented air, Rufio could not help but feel the sting of self-doubt hampering his every step. He thought of the young performer from Pindar's Thebes, and of the actor from Chios who claimed descent from Homer himself. Their skill had been incredible, and on a par with Felix, but it was the words they had spoken that really struck Rufio.

How can I hope to compose such words and images to move people's hearts so? he wondered as his sandalled feet crunched upon the path. *I don't have any pedigree such as those performers. I'm an Etrurian farmer, born of a father who had never even read a single scroll!*

"Rufio?" Clara suddenly said, holding him close as they walked.

"Yes?"

"I love you."

And with those simple, heartfelt words, Rufio felt his worries melt away, and he thanked the Gods for his good fortune.

That night, Rufio dreamed of King Priam begging the Greek hero, Achilles, for the body of his son, Hector. The scene, the dream, was as real as anything Rufio had lived through.

As he lay sweating in bed beside Clara on that hot, Athenian summer night he found himself in the tent of Achilles watching as the old king fell to his knees and kissed the hands of the man who had murdered his son and desecrated his body. From the shadows, Rufio could see the amphorae of wine and oil, the chests of gold booty, and weapons and armour piled high, taken from slain enemies. He could smell the sweat and incense, hear the flicker of flames from bronze tripods and lamps hanging from the tent's beams.

Rufio watched as Achilles stood beside the rack holding his god-forged armour, that cursed armour that would be the cause of so much pain and envy. He spied the change in the great warrior's face and eyes, his entire body, as King Priam's words, his love for his son, penetrated Achilles' heart.

Rufio Pagano wanted to weep at the sight.

"Fathers and their children…"

Rufio turned suddenly to see Terentius sitting beside him. "What are you doing here? This is my dream!"

"No. It's mine. What are _you_ doing here? Shouldn't you be rehearsing?" the shade chided.

Rufio shook his head, his eyes screwed tightly in confusion. "Shades don't dream."

"Of course they do!" Terentius said. "Consciousness is not

earthly."

"Don't bring philosophy into this," Rufio poked his chest and retreated quickly when he realized Terentius was made flesh in his dream. "I just want to take in this scene."

Terentius nodded and looked back to Priam and Achilles. "I have visited this tent many a time," the shade admitted. "Fathers and their children…"

"Yes, you said that."

Terentius turned his eyes to Rufio, a little too close for comfort.

I guess shades don't believe in personal space, Rufio thought.

"You above all others should understand the meaning of this, the thread of life which it represents."

"Oh, come now!" Rufio hissed, hoping Achilles would not see him and cut him down.

"Fathers and their children… It is the heart of the matter, the great part of life which I endeavoured to portray in the play!"

"But I heard that you grew up a slave?"

"Slavery is a state of mind." Terentius stated.

"Tell that to Syrus," Rufio said.

"Syrus does as he pleases," Terentius added. "He is but a character meant to test and direct the real action and focus of the play: the relationship between the fathers and sons."

"I have a daughter," Rufio insisted, wishing that the shade would leave the tent so that he could have a good look at the armour of Achilles before he woke up.

"It is the same for both," Terentius said. "Fathers and their children…"

"But I thought you didn't know your father?"

The shade looked to Priam, the noble king risking the last thing he had in the world, his life, to get back the body of his beloved son. "I had a father, though I never knew him."

Now Rufio felt badly.

"But how could you write so…so accurately about the relationship between the fathers and their sons if you never knew your own?"

Terentius stood from the pile of carpets upon which he sat and looked down at Rufio. "I am human, and I think nothing human is alien to me."

"That's it? You're human?" *And he's quoting himself again!*

"That is everything in the telling of a tale. Even one such as this." He pointed to where Achilles led Priam out of the tent, leaving the two of them bickering in the shadows. "You would do well to remember that when you set your stylus to papyrus."

Rufio stood to face him. "You're not human any longer. You're dead."

The shade smiled. "Am I dead if you and your company continue to fret over my words? Fathers and their children… I may be trapped in Athenae, but I am not dead."

Rufio began to edge away, feeling a longing for his wife and child, but Terentius reached out to grab hold of him with icy, ink-stained hands.

"The time is nearly upon us. Make the Athenians feel my words! Free me! Fathers and their children!"

"You said that!" Rufio shouted at him, pulled away, turned and ran. His only thought was to get away from the handsy shade at that moment, and so vigorous was his escape that he ran headlong into the armour of Achilles, falling to the ground with a great bronze clatter!

"Futuo!" Rufio shouted from the floor of the cubiculum where he had fallen off of the bed. He stared up from his low position and noted the wooden beams of the ceiling which were lit with bright morning light.

There was a loud panting that came in at the door, and

then approached at a rapid pace just before Peli appeared above, lashing Rufio with his tongue.

"All right, all right! I'm fine, you!"

Peli plopped himself down beside Rufio, the latter simply staring up at the ceiling while he enjoyed the cool relief of the floor beneath him. The sound of cicadas came in at the open window, and out the cubiculum door, he could hear voices echoing throughout the villa.

"I suppose everyone else is awake?" Rufio asked his canine companion.

Peli nudged him with his snout and licked his face again.

"All right, all right! I'm getting up!" Rufio pushed himself to his knees and then up to sit on the edge of the bed as he rubbed his face. Incense burned in a small dish upon the desk by the window, the smoke of eastern sandalwood blowing into the room to revive his senses. He stood with a groan, went over to the wide bronze bowl filled with fresh water, and splashed his face.

After slipping on his indigo tunica and fastening his cingulum and caligae, Rufio stood looking down at the broad table where his scrolls of notes were spread around a blank piece of papyrus. He picked up one of his bronze styli and held it for a moment over the page. His hand shook a little, but he calmed it as Terentius' words came back to him. *Fathers and their children…* Rufio remembered. He looked down at Peli who was still waiting for him. "Did Clara send you to fetch me?"

Peli whined and placed his paw upon Rufio's leg.

"We'd better go then. I need to say something to the company."

FELIX MODESTUS HAD NOT HAD A GOOD NIGHT, WHICH WAS surprising considering that he had stayed away from the musical and rhapsodic contests of the previous day so as to keep his mind calm and focussed. Though he had done his best to adhere to the Herculean persona he had recently adopted, the feeling of uneasiness he had previously thought to have conquered now returned.

That morning, everyone - well, everyone but Rufio - had arisen early, keen to rehearse before setting off to watch the second day of the games which included the athletic contests for boys and youth taking place in the stadium just down the hill. Everyone seemed at ease in their roles, their lines learned, their timing near-perfect.

As Felix held Thespis on his lap, watching Electra and Clara rehearse their parts in the fourth scene of the second act without flaw, he realized with a deep sadness that the usual excitement he felt at the approach of a performance was distinctly lacking.

And it worried him.

Felix felt his son's soft, dark hair and smiled when those big brown eyes looked up at him. However, it confused him all the more. He realized he cared more for the child than for what was happening upon the stage, though he could hear Antiphila's words.

"I know nothing about other women: I'm sure that I have, indeed, always used every endeavour to derive my own happiness from his happiness."

There was silence then as Clara's voice faded out.

"Erm, Felix?" Electra was staring down at him from the stage. "While I do love that you are interested in our son, you have a big part in this act, do you not? Clinia and Syrus cannot spy upon Bacchis and Antiphila without Clinia upon the stage."

Felix looked up and saw the entire company staring at him. "Oh, ah, yes… I just wanted to check on him." He turned to Domela. "Can you hold Thespis for me?"

Domela rushed over and took the child into her arms.

Felix climbed onto the stage to join Fausto where he spied upon Electra and Clara. He cleared his throat, and set off…

"Ah! Tis for that reason, my Antiphila, that you alone have now caused me to return to my native country; for while I was absent from you, all other hardships which I encountered were light to me, save the being deprived of you."

"I believe it," Syrus said to himself.

WHEN RUFIO ARRIVED ON THE SCENE, IT WAS TO SEE CLINIA and Antiphila embracing upon the pulpitum of the odeon.

"I'm overjoyed that you have returned safe." Antiphila was saying.

"And do I embrace you, Antiphila, so passionately longed for by my soul!" Clinia said before kissing her.

Syrus looked around, and then his eyes met Rufio's. "Go in-doors, for the old gentleman has been waiting for us some time."

When the act finished, everyone turned to follow Fausto's gaze to where Rufio stood at the back of the courtyard.

"Don't look at me!" Rufio said.

Upon seeing her father, Felicia reached out her arms to Rufio from where she had been sitting comfortably in Martia's lap while Clara rehearsed.

"Good morning!" Rufio said as he accepted his daughter from Martia and hoisted her in his arms. "I'm sorry I slept so long."

"You were exhausted. I thought I shouldn't wake you," Clara said as she came down off the pulpitum to greet him.

Castor leaned in to whisper to his brother. "*Exhausted.*" He winked.

"From the long contest yesterday, *cunnus!*" Rufio bit back over his shoulder with a chuckle.

The brothers smiled and went back to discussing what they

would see that day.

"I'm sorry I missed rehearsal," Rufio said to Felix as he approached.

"It's fine. We're just going through the motions."

Julius looked quizzically at Electra when they heard that, but said nothing.

"Well, I was speaking with Terentius last night and-"

"Sorry, what?" Fausto interrupted. "Rufio, did you say you were speaking *with* Terentius?"

Rufio turned quickly to see everyone staring strangely at him. "No. Apologies. What I meant to say was that I was thinking about Terentius…about the play…and it occurred to me that the true meaning of the play might help us all."

"And what is that, Rufio?" Felix asked. There was a hint of annoyance in his voice.

Rufio just smiled at him. "I've been thinking a lot about it, and this play is about being human, not heroic, or godlike, but rather, just human. Terentius wrote about fathers and their children - sons in this case."

"I thought Terentius was born a slave?" Julius said.

"He was, but that doesn't mean he didn't long for parents, or at least a father. If anything, he would have observed fathers and their children all around him quite keenly."

"So what are you saying?" Felix asked as he sat on the edge of the pulpitum.

"That this play is about fathers and sons. It is trying to say that living life through one's children is bad. That fathers must learn from their mistakes, just as Menedemus does, and how Chremes should take his own advice. It's about being an ally to those you love."

"That's it!" Sextus burst out from the back of the court-yard. "Rufio, you've hit upon it!"

"I have?"

"Yes! Terentius may have been alone in the world, but the

line spoken by Chremes…" Sextus turned to Julius who spoke the words.

"I am human, and I think nothing human is alien to me."

Rufio's eyes widened and he looked about for the shade in some corner of the courtyard.

"That's it!" Sextus was on his feet, his enthusiasm spreading through the company. "The play is not just about fathers being allies to their sons, but of humans being humane, and understanding of each other!"

Rufio thought for a moment before speaking. "It's as if Terentius is craving kindness and understanding."

"Is?" Fausto asked, clearly confused by Rufio's words. "You're acting very strange, Rufio."

"I'm sorry," Rufio quickly recovered. "I'm still groggy from wine and sleep. What I mean is that it is clear that Terentius *was* craving the kindness and understanding he thought humans should give to each other, the kindness and under-standing which he clearly did not always receive himself."

"How sad," Martia said as she leaned against Sextus.

"It makes sense," Electra said. "That explains why the prologus is so pleading. I thought him weak at first, to open like that, but now it seems that he was just setting the tone for the play."

Felix looked at everyone as they discussed, and much to his great sadness, he felt like an outsider listening in on the conver-sation when really he should have been the instigator of it.

"It all makes even greater sense now. Thank you, Rufio!" Pollux said. "I feel the bright light of celebritas upon me now!"

"That's just the sun burning your face," Castor quipped, shaking his head.

"Speaking of burning faces… Felix, can we go to the stadium now?" Fausto asked. "The athletic competitions have surely begun already."

"Yes, fine. Go ahead, Felix said, "We're done rehearsing for the day."

Electra turned to him. "Already? We've only gone through one act today!"

"It's fine," Felix replied, avoiding the questioning look from Sextus at the other end of the courtyard.

Fausto clapped and went out with Beatrice, Castor, Pollux, and Damon who had all been waiting to go.

"You're certain you don't want to do any more today, Felix?" Julius asked.

"I'm sure," Felix replied, already leaving the courtyard.

The others simply stared at each other in confusion.

Electra shook her head as she accepted Thespis from Domela. "I just don't know what's got into him."

THE FIFTH DAY OF THE PANATHENAIC GAMES ARRIVED, AND with it the highly-contested tribal competition in which each deme of Athenae put forward twenty-four of the most beautiful citizens to take part in the Pyrrhic dances. These groups of beautiful citizens numbered the same as a comic chorus and wore nothing but a helmet and carried a shield, all to honour the Goddess Athena and commemorate her victory over the Giants. As the populace were acquainted with many of the competitors, that particular day of the games was especially popular with the locals, the presence of outsiders being somewhat frowned upon. And so, after a few mornings of what were excellent rehearsals, The Etrurian Players remained at the villa rehearsing for almost the entirety of the day.

"I'd dance naked with a helmet and shield!" Fausto said when Felix finally called an end to the rehearsals around the sixth hour.

"I'm sure you would!" Castor said.

"What do you think, Beatrice? Should I try to sneak in and give it a whirl?"

Beatrice looked suddenly at Fausto. "Why are you asking me? I don't want to see you dancing about like some crazed satyr!"

Damon then jumped up on one of the benches of the odeon to offer a few notes.

"I don't want to see you do it either, Damon!" Beatrice shouted.

"You know, Fausto," Electra said. "If you were to try and sneak in and dance in the Pyrrhic competitions, and if you got caught, which you would, they would cut off your manhood."

Fausto stopped dancing immediately, a look of extreme discomfort on his sweaty face. "Really?"

"Absolutely," Electra said, her gaze dark and gorgon-like.

Fausto gulped.

As she fed Felicia, Clara leaned in to whisper to Electra. "Would they really do that?"

"No. I don't think so," Electra replied, making Clara laugh.

Fausto looked even more uncomfortable.

"I, for one, am just fine with staying here and resting today," Pollux said as he laid back and stared up at the sky. "I'm exhausted after watching three days of athletic competition and horse races."

"Did you not enjoy it?" Rufio asked as he rolled up his copy of the play.

"I did, but one can only watch so much of men running, jumping, and beating each other to a pulp."

"Careful, brother," Castor said. "You're sounding as old as your Menedemus!"

"Yeah, Pollux! You have to admit that that wrestling bout the day before yesterday was something else!"

"It was indeed," Pollux said, sitting up and starting to laugh.

"Why, what happened?" Julius asked, sipping from the cup of wine he was sharing with Domela.

"Well," Pollux began, "we were watching the athletic competitions for the men in the stadium down the hill. There had been many bouts - too many if you ask me - and it was past the sixth hour of the day. The competitors are supposed to remain on site the entire time as the competition moves quickly."

"Oh, get on with it!" his brother chided.

"There was a bout between an Athenian and an Ionian Greek. It started off well, each of them throwing and pinning the other with great skill, but then the Ionian started walking funny."

"Was he injured?" Rufio asked.

"No. He just didn't look right. Anyway," Pollux continued. "They wrestled for about a minute until the Athenian picked up the Ionian and slammed him hard onto the dirt of the skamma."

"So, the Athenian won?" Julius asked. "Sounds like an exciting bout."

Pollux had a doubtful look on his face. "Well, yes, and no. There was a bit of chaos at the end of the bout, even some screaming."

"Why, what happened?" Julius asked, not having heard the story.

Everyone was turned to Pollux, listening and wondering why Fausto, Castor and Damon were trying not to laugh.

"Are you going to tell us?" Electra said impatiently.

"Yes," he replied. "It seems that there was a reason for the Ionian's strange movements. He had been holding something in the whole of the day, so when the Athenian slammed him onto the ground, he shit himself more than an ox with diarrhea!"

"What?" Clara cried.

Pollux nodded. "It went everywhere, including in the Athenian's face, and upon the referee's chiton!"

"Gwrra!"

"It's not that bad, Rufio!"

"It's not your lovely story, Pollux… Gwrra! It's…" Rufio covered his nose. "I think Thespis needs a change of bracae!" He looked over the bench to the grassy ground where Electra had laid him to stretch out.

"Finally!" Electra said, bending to pick up her son.

"You see, Pollux?" Felix said from where he had been sitting in silence upon the edge of the stage. "If you want to see someone shit themselves, you just have to hang around here. We have hourly shows!"

"Mundus stercoris!" Rufio laughed, but stopped when he noted the dark look on Felix's face.

"I'll change him," Felix said, sliding off the stage to take Thespis from Electra.

"Gwrra!"

Felix shook his head as he walked past Rufio. "How a farmer who shovels shit all day can't handle a baby's droppings, I'll never understand!"

"It's not my baby!" Rufio called after him. "Boy, he's grumpy."

Electra was silent.

"Hopefully he'll feel better after the convivium tonight," Clara said, placing her hand on Electra's arm.

"He'd better be," Electra said.

"When did Sextus say we were to go to Public Leander's villa?" Julius asked.

"For sunset," Clara answered. "Apparently the villa is just up the hill a short distance."

"That's convenient! We won't have far to stumble home!" Castor said.

"If you're planning on embarrassing Sextus and Martia, you can stay here!" Electra stood. "I'm going to bathe and get ready. Clara, Beatrice, Domela? You coming?"

All the ladies stood and followed Electra.

Clara, who was finished feeding Felicia, handed the child to Rufio. "Here. Can you watch her?"

"Of course. Take your time," Rufio said.

Just then, Felicia's bracae erupted.

"You can change her as well!" Clara called over her shoulder.

Rufio nodded with pursed lips. "Come on you," he said to his smiling daughter, holding her to his chest. Just then, Felicia's dangling legs kicked and walloped Rufio in the plums. "Oooo! Have you grown taller?" he grimaced as he left the odeon courtyard.

"I'm never having children," Fausto said as he covered his nose.

"It was funny when that wrestler shit himself though," Pollux mused.

Julius shook his head and began gathering the stray scrolls.

THE REST OF THE AFTERNOON WAS SPENT RESTING, BATHING, and preparing for the convivium being held for The Etrurian Players at the villa of the magistrate, Publius Leander Antoninus and his wife, Delphina.

Sextus and Martia were very much looking forward to the evening, for though Publius was a Roman official, he also had a great appreciation of art, especially as his wife, Delphina was a skilled painter from the slopes of Parnassus. Sextus did worry, however, whether some members of the company might get a little too raucous for their hosts, and so he asked Felix to ensure that they behave, at least to some extent.

Felix smiled and reassured him. "Don't worry, Sextus. I'll let them know that if they get out of line, I'll beat them." He winked.

"But they're free now, Felix. You can't just beat them.

They're your friends!" Sextus was immediately sorry he had said anything.

"Then I shall beat them freely!"

Sextus' eyes bulged from his face, but as Felix started to laugh, he relaxed. "I thought you were serious!"

"I know I've been of a mood lately, but do you really think I would so such a thing? Don't worry, my friend. They'll behave. Athenae has tamed them somewhat."

Sextus looked doubtful.

"All right, maybe not. But it will be fine." *It better be,* Felix thought.

AS DUSK BEGAN TO COVER THE SLOPES OF HYMETTOS AND THE cicadas slowed in their plaintive song, the litters set out from the villa with Castor, Pollux, Damon, and Beatrice following on foot behind them.

Peli barked wildly from his tied position beneath an olive tree when they left. He did stop, eventually, much to Rufio's relief, though the latter did not know that it was because Nicodemus had arrived and was circling the canine with his blank eyes.

"I feel badly leaving him behind," Rufio said to Clara as their litter swayed its way up the road.

"He'll be fine. He has Nicodemus to keep him occupied now. They seem to be getting along." Clara looked up from feeding Felicia and smiled.

"Getting along? I think either one would be happy to see the other on a souvlaki stick in the agora!"

"Oh, Rufio. Gods forbid it!" Clara shook her head, and when Felicia had finished, she handed her to Rufio while she adjusted her stola. "She should be fine for quite a while now."

Rufio looked down at his dozy daughter. "She'll sleep through the evening."

"Perhaps. You know, I'm quite excited about this evening. We've met Publius, and he seemed quite nice, but from what Martia said of Delphina, she is absolutely lovely. And a skilled painter!"

"Really? Well, I would prefer it if she were a skilled cook, but we'll have to wait and see."

"I'm guessing they have servants."

"Speaking of servants…I wonder how Errol is handling things."

"I'm sure he's fine," Clara reassured him. "And don't start worrying about Stella."

"I'm not," he insisted. "All right, I am! But I think I want to get rid of that farmhand who's after her. I swear, if we get back and there are little donkey-men clip-clopping about the yard, he's in for it!"

"I don't think that's how it works."

"Anyway," Rufio shook his head as if to rid himself of the thoughts. He felt Clara's grip on his leg and looked up at her. "You look beautiful by the way."

"I thought you would like me to wear this indigo stola to match your tunica. Can we have fun tonight, and leave the worries of the production behind?"

"Sounds good to me. You know, I think this will be my last performance."

"It's not that bad. I think you're quite good in the role of Clitipho."

"I don't meant that. I'm actually fine with the role and have loved this play since I read it when I was a youth. Not that I fully understood it when I was young, but now…"

"Now it means something more?" Clara touched their daughter's foot where it jutted out from the hem of her tiny white stola.

"Yes."

"But a last performance? Isn't that a bit extreme? It's a nice change of pace, I find, though if Felix asks us to travel to Babylon for the next performance, I think we'll have to say 'no'."

"And who knows what they eat there!" Rufio felt his stomach rumble. "I just don't think that my purpose is to be an actor. I can do it, but is it what the Gods intend for me?"

"I think you know what the Gods intend," Clara said. "We're quite fortunate."

"Yes," Rufio agreed, his mind too muddled to properly portray his thoughts. "I just hope that they have some decent meat."

THE ETRURIAN PLAYERS' PROCESSION ARRIVED AT THE VILLA OF Publius Leander Antoninus shortly thereafter. The litters passed beneath a torch-flanked arch where they were greeted by smiling servants whose heads were crowned with ivy. They were led up a long path toward the villa which was situated on a slight rise in the land within a walled enclosure. The main domus was surrounded with fragrant jasmine and pink and white oleander that rustled in the evening breeze.

The villa itself was a rectangular, two-storey stone structure that surrounded a large courtyard which contained orange, lemon, and pomegranate trees that provided some shade during the hot days, and dancing shadows at night.

Rufio noted quickly, as he peered out of the litter's curtains, that outside the walls of the villa itself, there was a farm with Attic olive trees, whose branches were groaning with unripened fruit, as well as a heard of sheep and goats. The whinny of horses reached his ears, and a strong bitter tang intruded on his nose. "I think I smell an olive press."

"Seems that way," Clara agreed. "It's not working now, but the smell will get stronger when the season arrives."

"It's no latifundium, but this is a nice family farm," he

observed as the litters came to a stop on the circular path of the courtyard before the domus.

When all the litters were lowered, the curtains were thrown aside and everyone disembarked. Those who had been on foot arrived just after that, Damon playing a pastoral ditty on his flute just as the evening's hosts emerged from the large main door of the villa.

"Welcome, friends!" Publius Leander said as he and his wife approached to greet their guests.

Publius Leander Antoninus and his wife Delphina were not the sort of people one would have expected of a Roman magistrate's family. Rather than the formal toga praetexta that he had been wearing at the Panathenaea, Publius Leander now wore a crimson tunica with a simple meander border embroidered with golden thread and belted with a brown leather cingulum. His wife, Delphina, looked like a majestic sea nymph, her skin darkened from being in the sun. She wore a light, gap-sleeved tunica of a shade of blue that lay somewhere between the sea and summer sky, her simple silver bangles jingling as she reached out to take Martia's hands.

"How lovely it is to see you all," Delphina said with a great smile. "Welcome to our home." She turned to motion to two of her daughters who lingered in the background, their eyes casting looks over the company of players coming up to join them. "These are our two younger daughters, Hadrea and Lavena."

Fausto, Castor and Pollux immediately stepped forward but were barred from going farther by Felix's muscled arm.

Hadrea was of about twenty years of age with a dark, olive complexion and black hair, the same as her mother's, and Lavena, the younger by about two years, had long blonde hair that tumbled down in curls about her shoulders. The two young nymphs smiled at the company behind Felix.

"It's lovely to meet you all," Electra said as she stepped forward.

"Oh, my dear. I've long been an admirer of your skill upon the stage," Delphina said to her. "And is this your son?" She looked to the child in Electra's arms.

"This is Thespis," Electra said with a proud smile.

"Of course he is!" Delphina marvelled at the child. "So handsome, like his father."

Felix bowed his head. "Felix Modestus, at your service, lady."

"You may also know him as 'Hercules'," Fausto piped up, shooting a quick wink at the daughters who giggled in return.

"My husband told me something about your Athenian adventures, Felix Modestus, but I would like to hear more from you about it over the cena."

Sextus stepped forward then. "And these are Rufio Pagano and Clara Probita, with their daughter Felicia."

"A pleasure, lady," Rufio said, before turning to Publius Leander. "Thank you for the invitation, Magistrate."

"Please," Publius said, "here we are simply Publius and Delphina. We don't stand on any ceremony. Anyway, Sextus outranks me!" Publius laughed.

"And I am just Sextus, a great fan of the theatre and proud sponsor of The Etrurian Players!" Sextus waved his arm to present the rest of the company. "May I present the greatest theatre company in the empire… At the front, you see Fausto, Castor and Pollux. The one with the flute is Damon…he works magic upon the pipe. Then you have Beatrice, a magnificent costume maker and actress in her own right. And at the back, Domela, the newest member of the company, and of course, Julius, our veteran."

"It is a great pleasure to meet all of you!" Delphina smiled warmly.

"Please, come inside!" Publius said, motioning to the

entrance. "There is wine and plenty of food. Kaleos and the cooks have prepared a feast for us!"

"I do hope you enjoy fish!" Delphina said as she led the way inside, her daughters lingering to meet the company.

"Oh, no," Rufio muttered to Clara as they followed their hosts into the domus.

"You'll be fine," she said to him, unable to hold back her smile. "I think we're going to have a lovely evening…"

THE INTERIOR OF THE VILLA WAS A WORLD UNTO ITSELF, FOR every wall was decorated with intricate frescos that exploded with life and colour. There were scenes of bull-leapers soaring over thrashing horns, and underwater scenes with dolphins frolicking in the watery plains of Neptune's realm. As the party trouped down the corridor to the triclinium at the back of the villa, they passed depictions of everyday life such as olive picking in groves, and shepherds tending their flocks on the steep Hymettan mountainsides looming over them among wildflowers and their attendant bees. There were horses in long-grassed fields of spring where poppies exploded in rich fluttering reds, and small boats with fishermen bringing up their catch from the wine-dark deep, the nets painted so skillfully that they seemed to flutter before one's eyes.

Clara stopped before the fishing scene. "Delphina, when Sextus and Martia mentioned that you're a skilled painter, I had no idea how much they were playing it down. Did you paint all of these?"

Delphina stopped beside her. "That's very kind of you, dear. Yes, I did paint them."

"These could decorate the imperial palace on the Palatine Hill, Delphina!" Felix said behind them.

"Oh, now," Delphina blushed. "Surely you exaggerate,

Felix Modestus!" she laughed. "It is but something I do for the sheer pleasure of it, and to fascinate our daughters."

"When they were younger, at any rate," Publius Leander said as he joined them, the procession to the triclinium having been waylaid by the art. "Now, our daughters are distracted by other things," he said with a tired smile and pointed down the corridor to where Hadrea and Lavena were talking excitedly with Fausto, Castor, Pollux, and Damon about the riot they had heard their father speak of. "I worry for them."

"Have no fear, Publius Leander," Felix said. "I'll tell my players that your daughters are off limits, and that they shouldn't even speak to them."

"Oh, please don't," Publius said. "I meant that I was worried for your players, Felix Modestus!" he laughed. "For were Socrates and Plato still among us, they would have much admired our girls. They are too brilliant for their own good, I sometimes think, for conversation with them is like combat in the arena. It can turn the brain so that it is battered and bruised, leaving one exhausted and longing only for music and drink!"

"Oh, Publius!" Delphina nudged him. She turned to the others. "Pay him no mind!"

"Well, it sounds as though we have come home then!" It was Felix's turn to laugh. "For music and drink are our favourite fare!"

"Let us hope that we have provided for more than that!" Delphina said as she continued leading the way.

A servant wearing an ivy crown and a plain white chiton opened a set of double doors which led into a brightly lit triclinium with a long row of tables already set with courses of bread, cheeses, and salads. These were surrounded by couches covered in plush cushions all of varying shades of blue that shimmered in the light cast by hanging bronze lamps about the room.

But it was the walls once more that took centre stage, for they were covered in a deep forest setting that enveloped the diners who could peer into its green depths to catch a glimpse of a forest nymph, or a prancing satyr. Upon a lonely rock beside a spring, there sat Apollo, thoughtful as he plucked at the strings of his cythara.

Damon immediately wove a spell with his flute that brought the forest to life as everyone filed into the triclinium.

"Sextus, you and Martia take the lectus medius," Publius said, pointing to the couch for high status guests.

Sextus led Martia to the middle couch on the end, while Publius showed Felix and Electra, along with Thespis, to the lectus summus, and Rufio, Clara and Felicia to the next one down and so on for the rest of the company.

Hadrea and Lavena sat at the very far end, as far from their parents as possible, with Beatrice pressed between them, flanked by Castor and Pollux on the one side, and Fausto and Damon on the other.

When everyone was seated, Publius and Delphina settled on the lectus imus reserved for the hosts, beside the couch which was occupied by Julius and Domela.

Publius then clapped and servants emerged from various doors holding craters of watered red and white wine which they offered about the table. "In honour of our guests, we have opened our stocks of Falernian and Chian wine. We hope you enjoy!"

"Publius Leander, that is too much!" Sextus said. "Such vintages!"

"Nonsense, my friend. How often do we play host to the greatest theatre company in the empire?"

"You favour us, Publius Leander," Felix said. "I just hope that your fellow Athenians feel the same way about us in a few days time."

"It is true that our Athenian audience is…well…how

should I say it? They have very high standards, and are perhaps more discerning than most when it comes to the theatre. But I feel confident that you will emerge from the great odeon victorious."

It was meant as a great compliment, but for some reason, Felix grew silent at that. "From your mouth to Apollo's divine ears, Publius Leander," he muttered.

Martia looked around their silent end of the tables and spoke up. "Sextus and I have had the privilege of watching The Etrurian Players bring Terentius' play to life and I must say that I am moved no end by how they have managed it with such skill. Athenae is in for a real treat!"

"Here, here!" Sextus said.

"Our family shall be there in force," Delphina said, raising her cup. "To Apollo and Dionysus!" she tipped a bit of wine onto the floor and the party followed suit before taking a first sip.

"And to The Etrurian Players!" Publius added, raising his cup a second time and drinking. "Now, I urge you all to eat, for there are many courses to accompany our evening of happy converse!"

Without waiting for the servants to serve, The Etrurian Players reached for the food.

"My Gods," Delphina smiled. "Have you not been feeding your people, Felix Modestus?"

"I apologize, lady."

"On the contrary," Delphina said. "Nothing makes a Greek mother happier than to see her food eaten so eagerly!" she laughed.

"'Eager' is an understatement," Felix replied. "When we were in Alexandria, they caused quite a stir as they ate their way through the marketplace, for the authorities feared a plague of locusts had descended upon the city!"

"Ooo!" Domela hooted at that from down the tables. "Dominus, you are cheeky!"

Everyone laughed and tucked in.

The first course consisted of bowls of glistening olives, hard-boiled eggs, platters of raw vegetables, salads of fresh greens, and of course, fish and shellfish.

"You see!" Rufio hissed into Clara's ear as a particularly prickly prawn stared at him with beady black eyes from a bed of greens. "Fish. Not a jot of meat anywhere."

"Shh!" Clara nudged him as she fed Felicia a piece of egg. "This is the gustatio. Just hang on."

"Your daughter is extremely well-behaved, Clara Probita," Delphina said to her, smiling at the wide-eyed girl. "So beautiful!"

"Thank you, Delphina. Yes, we are blessed, indeed."

"Like yourself and Electra, I would have my daughters with me almost always. I fed and cared for them myself, though many of our acquaintances insisted I should get a nursemaid to do all of that." Delphina grew a little quiet. "I would not have missed a moment."

"How did you cope when Publius was away on official business?" Sextus asked.

Delphina smiled and looked over her shoulder to a silent older woman who stood by. "Kaleos has always been a great help."

"I thought you didn't have any help?" Electra said as she struggled to keep Thespis from grabbing at the food on her plate.

"Well, we all need a little. But Kaleos is a friend, not a servant. She has been like a second mother to our girls."

Publius turned to the woman. "Kaleos, are you sure you won't sit with us?"

"I've already eaten, Publius, don't fret. I'm just happy to see this domus so full of life." Kaleos smiled, the creases of her sun-tanned skin stretching as she did so, like an aged comic theatre mask. "We haven't had this many people here since Adara and poor Alene were here with Emrys and that Egyptian man."

"His name is Ashur," Publius added, "and he is a good man."

"I know he is," Kaleos replied, "but that didn't help poor Alene, did it?"

"Please, Kaleos. Can we not?" Delphina said, her face suddenly quite sad.

The other end of the table burst out laughing at something at that moment, creating an uncomfortable contrast.

Julius and Domela looked that way, not wanting to intrude on the more serious conversation to their left.

"Who are Adara and Alene?" Electra asked.

"Oh, ehm…" Publius began to squirm a little as he looked to Delphina, but she put her hand upon his and smiled.

"It's fine, dear. I am proud of our daughter."

"You have four daughters?" Clara asked.

"Three," Delphina said proudly. "You've met Hadrea and Lavena already." She nodded to the other end of the tables where the two girls were laughing along with Beatrice and the others. "We have a third daughter, our eldest… Adara."

"What a beautiful name," Clara added. "Is she…is Adara…"

"Oh, she is married," Publius put in quickly, "to a Roman tribune, actually. Someone very close to Emperor Severus."

"We all met the emperor after our last performance in Rome," Felix commented as he dropped a clean fish bone onto his plate. "But I'm happy to count myself among the ranks of players rather than of the legions. It's a much safer life!"

Rufio looked from Felix's fish remnants back to Publius. "You seem somewhat reticent about your daughter's match." *How will I ever be able to hand my daughter over to someone else?* he thought, though he knew it was silly to begin to worry about such a thing so soon.

"Oh, well, Tribune Metellus Anguis is a good and honourable man. It's just that he…well…danger seems to follow him wherever he goes, and so too then our daughter, Adara." Publius stared at his plate for a moment. "At least that wretched Plautianus is no longer terrorizing the empire."

"Isn't he the Praetorian prefect?" Clara asked.

"I heard about this!" Rufio said. "He was cut down in the imperial palace and thrown to the street below."

"Sounds like something out of Euripides!" Felix added.

"It was real enough," Publius said, glancing quickly to his wife. "Our son-in-law was there and had to leave Rome for Etruria after."

"That is where Adara is now," Delphina added, "along with our grandchildren."

"You have grandchildren?" Martia asked, not having heard of them before.

"Yes, two. Phoebus and Calliope." Delphina composed herself. "Though, we haven't yet met them. We hope to get to Etruria and see our daughter and her children by the time Saturnalia comes around."

"Where in Etruria do they live?" Rufio asked, happy to talk about home. "Do you go often?"

"No," Publius answered.

"The Metelli have a villa rustica on a latifundium somewhere mid-way between the via Cassia to the east and the via Aemilia Scauri to the west."

Rufio and Clara looked at each other and then back to Publius and Delphina.

"Surely you are joking?" Rufio said.

"Why would we joke about such a thing?" Publius asked.

"It seems as though your son-in-law is our very own neighbour!"

"Really?" Publius was shocked.

Rufio nodded. "Truly. Senator Quintus Metellus…he owns the villa, the one on the other side of the hill from us."

"Erm," Sextus cleared his throat. "Senator Metellus is no longer among the living."

"Really?" Rufio said. "I suppose that explains it. I haven't heard of him harassing my workers for several months now. Not since last year," he said to Clara who nodded. Rufio looked back to Publius. "Can't say that I'm sad the senator is gone. He gave my own father no end of trouble. But I do remember sometimes seeing the tribune when he was young, as well as his older sister…Alene… Oh."

Publius and Delphina looked sad at that moment.

"Is this the Alene you mentioned earlier?" Clara asked "The one you said visited you here?"

"Yes," Delphina said. "She was…murdered…in Numidia. She saved our grandchildren from an attack."

"How awful. I'm so sorry," Rufio said. "She was a lovely girl."

Clara elbowed him.

"She was," Delphina replied.

"At any rate," Publius spoke more loudly now, attempting to insert some jollity into his voice. "We shall go to Etruria at the end of the year."

"Please do pay us a visit when you do," Clara added.

Publius nodded, but then looked down the table. "Does everyone have enough wine?"

"Hail, Publius Leander Antoninus!" Castor shouted with a raised cup.

Publius nodded and forced a smile before waving to the servants waiting near the doors that led to the kitchens. "Time for the prima mensa!" he announced to more cheers from the players.

Electra could see that Delphina was saddened then, that

her thoughts lingered on her eldest daughter. "Lady, I am sorry that we have made you sad."

Clara looked up too. "We really did not mean to. Rufio especially enjoys talk of home. Of Etruria that is."

"Not at all," Delphina said, her smile returning. "It is part of raising children, as you shall both find out. We give everything to them willingly…we nurture them…pray for them… raise them, and then they leave for lives of their own."

Rufio and Clara reached out to touch Felicia, and Electra stroked her son's hair as he masticated most comically upon a piece of cooked carrot.

"We also wipe their bottoms without end!" Felix chuckled. "Some stages of their lives I am happy for them to end. Let the curtain fall upon dirty bracae and sleepless nights!"

"Here's to that!" Castor called out.

Delphina smiled sadly. "Don't wish the time away, Felix Modestus, for it passes in the blink of an eye. While they are young and at home, you can keep them safe."

Before more could be said, the servants filed in with platters of cooked tuna with wine sauce, rock eel in a mulberry sauce, and prawns steaming with an attic honey glaze.

Rufio sighed. "I'll never eat again," he muttered, but just as he looked up most reluctantly at the table, his eyes were met with a platter of steaming goat's meat, and chicken stuffed with attic olives and vegetables. "This looks magnificent! I could almost weep!"

As Rufio reached for the chicken, the servants brought platters of boiled greens, artichokes, and beans as well as more bread. Everyone's wine cups were refilled and a general clamour rose for the beauty of the feast.

"This is delicious!" Rufio exclaimed.

"So glad it's to your liking, Rufio Pagano," Publius smiled.

Felix could not help but chuckle at his friend who seemed eminently relieved at the sight of meat.

"The artichokes are wonderful as well," Clara added.

"They are a rarity here for us," Delphina added. "We can grow many, but the moles usually get at them before we can harvest."

"Oh, I have a remedy for that!" Rufio said, looking up as he dropped a chicken bone onto his plate. "Cats."

"Cats?" Publius asked.

"Cats," Rufio repeated. "They are a wonder for protecting artichokes from moles. One or two cats and your crop will be safe!"

Publius smiled. "Well then. I suppose we shall get some cats!"

Delphina smiled at Rufio. "I don't suppose you eat much fish on your latifundium in Etruria, do you?"

Rufio shook his head. "No, lady. Mostly chicken and boar for me."

"Well in that case, do try as much of the fish as possible while you are here," their hostess replied, motioning to the servant behind Rufio to serve him. "Try the eel. It is especially tasty!"

Before Rufio could reply, a ladle of glistening eel was dropped onto his plate, the sauce dousing his chicken.

"Thank…thank you…" he said. "Gwrra!"

"What did you say?" Publius asked.

"Oh," Rufio caught himself. "Rare! What a rarity!"

Publius smiled, and nodded his agreement. "Yes, we are quite lucky with the fare available to us here in Athenae."

Rufio smiled and reached for the goat meat.

THE EVENING WORE ON AND THE CONVERSATION GREW LOUDER and moved on to happier topics, other than death and fish even though, to Rufio, the two were not mutually exclusive. They spoke of the ongoing games, and elaborated on their favourite contests, the athletic competition being one of the favourites among the men.

Pollux, of course, made sure to recount the wrestling bout they had attended which ended in a mess for the competitors, and a bit of discomfort for the spectators, especially those who had been cheering from the front row. "Honestly, I've never seen anything quite like it!" Pollux said, downing the remnants of the expensive Chian vintage he had been enjoying.

"Yes, well…" Publius adjusted his position upon his couch. "I'm sure the Panathenaea will not witness such a thing ever again."

"Let's hope not," Sextus added. "I think that tomorrow's torch race should prove a cleaner affair."

"But no less dangerous," Publius said. "At the last Panathenaea, two of the runners in the torch relay got too close to each other and the one lit the other on fire as they ran!"

"Surely you're joking!" Pollux cried from the other end of the triclinium. "How is that possible?"

"The man still had oil on his body after visiting the baths that very morning. When his opponent's torch crashed into him, he went up like that!" Publius snapped his fingers.

Rufio smiled at Clara, for they had both noticed that their host was also enjoying the wine he had so generously offered them.

"Did the man die?" Sextus asked. "Surely that would have been a bad omen for the games!"

Publius shook his head. "The man ran directly for a horse trough filled with water at the end of the stadium and dove in. He suffered minor burns."

"Incredible!" Pollux shook his head in disbelief. "I should have liked to see that."

"The great sacrifice takes place tomorrow as well, does it not?" Felix asked.

"It does," Delphina answered while her husband refilled

everyone's cups. "It is the day of the hecatomb upon the great altar of Athena on the Acropolis."

"Are non-Greeks permitted to attend?" Clara asked. "I would like to show Rufio the goddess' great temple."

"One should not come to Athenae without honouring Athena, that is certain," Delphina said. "If you can stomach the smell of smoke, and blood, it is not to be missed. Afterward, they distribute meat to the people."

"Meat?" Rufio perked up.

Delphina smiled, noting the remnants of eel still swimming in his plate. "Oh, yes. More meat than one could ever imagine."

Rufio turned to Clara. "I think we should go to that."

"Yes, you would," she replied, kissing his cheek.

"After the hecatomb, there only remain the boat races at the port, and then the awards and feasting on the final day." Publius sat himself back down beside his wife. "Will you all attend the rest of the events?" he asked the table.

"I do not know, Publius Leander," Felix answered. "We are supposed to perform after the festival."

"Of course!" Delphina was now very excited. "Sextus has told us all about the production, and of course we have heard talk of your triumphs all about the Middle Sea."

"But not in Athenae," Felix muttered.

Publius nodded. "Our Athenian audience can be quite haughty when it comes to theatre."

Delphina smiled and shook her head in respectful disagreement as she caught Felix's eye. "I think that my countrymen may surprise you, Felix Modestus. Yes, they can be pretentious about their theatre, but they also have a great appreciation of theatrical performance coupled with thoughtful plot."

Everyone paused to listen to Delphina now, for though quiet and unassuming, her kind demeanour had a commanding presence.

"I have not seen your company perform before, but from what I have heard of you from our friends, Sextus and Martia, and from how seriously you take your craft, I have no worries that the people of Athenae have the potential to laud you. The question is, are you up to presenting your laudable selves to this city?"

"Self-doubt has been my enemy of late," Felix said to Delphina.

The Etrurian Players looked at each other in complete astonishment at the admission that had just slipped from Felix's mouth.

But Delphina nodded her understanding and smiled at him. "It is part of the process of great artists such as yourself, no?"

"Speaking of great artists, you've seen my wife's frescoes adorning the walls of our domus, yes?"

"Please, husband," Delphina protested.

"No, wait," he said. "I could see many of you admiring them as we walked to the triclinium."

"We were indeed!" Clara smiled.

Publius continued. "My wife will not sing her own praises, so I do it for her. At any rate, when Delphina began every one of those frescoes, she was riddled with doubt, certain that what was in her mind could not possibly grace the walls as she envisioned it."

"How can it even be possible?" Delphina added as though she were in mid process.

"But when she finished each of those paintings, she quite surprised herself. There were times when she did not even recall painting particular sections!"

Martia reached out to hold Delphina's hand. "The Muses were with you, and speaking through you then."

Delphina nodded. "For those who are meant to create, whose purpose it is to bring beauty to the world, however much or little, the Muses are their constant companion, through all the seasons of one's life."

The gathering was silent, each person thinking on how that applied to him or herself. It was a responsibility, and perhaps a burden. But mostly, it was a blessing.

In that moment, however, Felix Modestus felt it as a great, crushing weight. He reached out to Electra to take his son into his arms. Thespis was a comfort to him, and when he was holding him, he felt stronger, better and more capable.

Delphina smiled at that, and as the others at the far end of the table began to engage in more conversation, Felix looked up at his hostess.

"I would do right by this little one. Leave him a legacy which he can be proud of when he thinks on me."

"You already have, husband," Electra said, her hand about his shoulders in a surprisingly tender act.

"You just need to do right by yourself, Felix Modestus," Delphina said. "Apollo and his Muses have given you a gift, and a purpose. It is for you and your allies about this table to see it through."

Felix nodded silently as he looked into his son's eyes.

"We all worry for our children, Felix," Publius said. "The Gods know *we* continue to do so."

"It is that worry that consumes us now," Electra said, "not theatre, art, or performance."

"You are new parents, and caring for one's child can be a healthy obsession," Publius added. "But the Gods reward sincerity of action and thought in a wonderful way, do they not?"

"Publius," Delphina laid her hand upon her husband's arm, for she could see the raw emotion suddenly coming into his voice, his eyes, his shaking hand which she steadied for him.

"I look upon our daughters here, and think on our daughter in Etruria who has been through so very much and, I suspect, will go through much more…and I am filled with dread."

"You will upset our guests," Delphina said softly.

But Publius shook his head. "I have a point, my dear. When I find myself overwrought with worry, I think on a story related to Socrates."

"I think we shared a cell with him!" Fausto said, having overheard the name.

Publius continued. "The story goes that when Socrates' father, a sculptor named Sophroniscus, found that he did not know what to do with his son's evident brilliance and thoughtfulness, while balancing the life of art he was already engaged in, he went to the Oracle of Delphi for advice."

"What did the Oracle say?" Felix asked, remembering acutely then the day Thespis was born.

"The Oracle said 'let the boy do whatever comes into his mind and do not constrain or divert his motivations, but let them be.'"

"I have not heard that story," Sextus said, most interested. He gripped Martia's hand and kissed it, knowing how the conversation was affecting her.

"When I worry about balancing my purpose in this life with the welfare of my daughters, I think of the Oracle's advice to Sophroniscus. It is both comforting and freeing, but not easy by any means. I need to constantly remind myself."

"What Publius is trying to say," Delphina said softly, "is that your art and parenthood are not mutually exclusive. The one nurtures the other. The Gods have given you a gift and purpose, Felix Modestus. Trust that they will do so for your son." She turned to Clara and Rufio. "And for your daughter." She smiled, but the smile did fade ever so slightly. "It is the only thing to help you through the years and trials to come."

There was a deep, thoughtful silence at their end of the triclinium.

"Kaleos," Delphina turned to the older woman. "Please tell the servants it is time for the secunda mensa."

"Yes, Delphina," Kaleos said before leaving the triclinium.

"I need some air," Felix said, and stood to hand Thespis back to Electra before going out of the open doors at the back of the triclinium that led to the olive grove beyond.

"I fear that we have upset him," Publius said.

"*Heautontimorumenos* weighs heavily upon him," Sextus replied, watching Felix's form fade into the darkness without. "Will he be all right?" he asked Electra.

The latter looked about the table, worried that the rest of the company had overheard. "He will. He always is," she replied. *Apollo, give him strength,* she prayed.

"Do you have a cubiculum I might use to feed Felicia?" Clara asked Delphina.

"Yes, of course, my dear. I'll show you to Adara's cubiculum. There are a couple of couches where you can do so in comfort."

"I'll join you," Electra said as she too stood from the couch and followed with Thespis.

The servants filed into the triclinium then to clear the table and, much to Rufio's relief, take away the platters of fish heads and bones. More lamps were lit, and Kaleos burned chunks of incense in bronze bowls at either end of the triclinium so that the scented smoke wafted about to clear away the smell of fish.

The table was then set for the third course with platters of honeyed pastries, nuts, figs, apricots, grapes, and strawberries. These were accompanied by goat's cheese which had been made by Kaleos' husband who continually guarded the food stores up the mountainside.

As the warm comfort of the evening and the wine settled upon everyone, it seemed as though a soft blue-gold light, enriched by the couch cushions and drapery, infused the gathering.

Julius and Domela whispered in quiet converse upon their couch, while the rest enjoyed the company of Publius and Delphina's younger daughters.

How strange a twist that their older daughter should have married my neighbour's son in Etruria, Rufio thought to himself as he gnawed happily upon a piece of lamb which he had grabbed from a platter on its way back to the kitchen. He had usually stayed away from his neighbours because of the senator, that horrid paterfamilias who made Rufio's father look as though he had kindness and patience to spare. *Now that he's crossed the dark river, perhaps I'll pay the family a visit?*

Then again, Rufio wondered if that would be a bad idea. The insinuation from their hosts that their eldest daughter was in constant danger around the tribune was unnerving. *Such a shame,* he thought, for he liked his hosts. He also understood their worry for their daughter, how deep and early that worry could take root. *If I wasn't being harassed by that needy shade, it would be all I would think about!*

As Sextus, Martia, Delphina and Publius fell into easy conversation, Rufio stared out of the open doors to the darkness beyond to try and spot Felix. When he could not find him, he stood stiffly, and a little drunkenly. "I'm going to check on Felix," he said to Sextus who smiled and nodded, for he too had been worried about their friend.

As the others about the tables stood and stretched and conversed while more wine was served, Rufio made his way outside into the sweet air of the Attic night.

"THERE YOU ARE," RUFIO SAID AS HE APPROACHED FELIX'S hunched form where he sat upon a stone bench tucked away in the olive grove.

The moon was enormous overhead, and its light made the trees' leaves appear to be wrought of fine silver where they shivered in the warm breeze upon the mountain. There were hints of jasmine on the breeze too, and a tang of pine.

"You having a good time?" Rufio asked when Felix did not answer.

"Hmm," came the muted reply. "The Gods feel closer here, do they not?"

Rufio sat straight and looked up at the moon. "I suppose."

"I feel their gaze more acutely. Apollo is watching me, judging me."

"Apollo favours you, Felix. He always has done. You know that."

"Perhaps before…but now he is testing me. That is why he sent us here. Not for victory, but to tempt defeat."

"Don't say that," Rufio knew how much the entire company relied upon Felix, his strength and certainty, and what it would mean if those qualities were lacking. It was an enormous amount of pressure, to be certain, but Felix had always been a capable leader.

"Did you know that upon the temple of Apollo at Delphi, there are over one hundred and forty inscribed maxims?"

Rufio looked at Felix, quite confused by this sudden turn. "I have heard about the Delphic Maxims, but did not know there were so many. Why?"

"Of all of the maxims, 'Know thyself' is the one I remember."

"Well, of course. Everyone recalls that one."

Felix stared down at his hands and sighed in the moonlit darkness. "It is the most prescient for me."

"Why? What's got into you, my friend?"

"I no longer *know* myself, Rufio. I don't know who I am. The purpose the Gods had given me when we were young… that purpose which was so vivid, so real… I feel it slipping away from me, and I'm helpless to stop it."

Rufio was at a loss for words now. He was no stranger to

self-doubt, that was certain, but what Felix was describing went far beyond nervousness about the coming performance. His psyche was in turmoil, and what good was an Etrurian farmer when it came to that? *I have to try…*

"Felix," Rufio said as he turned on the bench and reached up to set his hand upon his bulky shoulder. *Is that a tear?* Now Rufio was panicking. "It seems to me that the Gods are always testing us, especially those whom they love."

"You think so," Felix scoffed.

"Yes. I've read something of these Greeks' belief in 'ponos', their hardships and toils. They believe it is important because it gives one purpose and makes one stronger."

"You've been spending too much time in the library."

"Actually, I would have liked to spend more time there. You should have seen all the scrolls. I mean…you gifted me a wondrous collection of works, but this! This was something on another-"

Felix stared at him.

"Sorry. I… What I'm trying to say is that Apollo may be testing you because he loves you and believes in you so much. Trials are not supposed to be easy."

Felix sighed. "Rufio, I can see you're trying to help. Really. But this is not about finding humour in something that is lacking it, or a fear of not impressing the Athenian snobs… I actually don't care about that anymore."

"I'm sorry. I know. I heard you," Rufio stood and looked down at Felix. "It's about feeling that your purpose in life is slipping away. I suppose like a legionary whose sword is wet with blood, losing a grip upon it in the midst of battle. He's losing his lifeline." *Oh, that's good! I should use that!*

"You're not making any sense. That Chian wine has got to your head."

Rufio crossed his arms. "Maybe…it was delicious." He stepped forward and put his hands on Felix's shoulders as he faced him. "All I'm saying is that maybe your purpose in this life…what the Gods intend for you…is not slipping away, but rather…just changing."

Felix looked up at that.

"Like the seasons." Rufio stood back, winked, and made his way back to the triclinium. "Think about it," he said over his shoulder as he went toward the warm glow of light inside.

Felix felt his heart racing within his chest then, his mind a maelstrom of doubt and fear, uncertainty and guilt. His familia was depending upon him, more than ever now, and he was letting them down. "I'm in a labyrinth with no string…" he whispered as he stood to lean upon the nearest olive tree, his hand clasped tightly about one of the limbs.

It was then that Felix heard the soft notes of Damon's flute flowing out of the triclinium doors like the smoke of the incense that had been lit. He had not heard Damon play that melody before. It was filled with longing and gratitude at once, and painted a picture of warm summer nights one would still remember in the dark days of winter.

Felix walked slowly toward the villa's light and could see their hosts and all the members of his company listening in silent admiration to Damon's music as he played for them at the far end of the triclinium with his eyes closed.

The face of every person there betrayed different emotions, though the same melody played about their ears. There was joy and calm, restitution and longing, anxiety and fear, hope and exhilaration.

Their hosts thought of their daughter far away, and of the grandchildren they had not yet met.

Sextus and Martia thought of the children they would never have, and the gratitude they felt for each other.

Julius and Domela wondered that they had found happiness so late in their lives, and Castor smiled that after so long, he and his brother were still the best of friends.

Fausto looked upon Beatrice with new eyes, and she met his look with a joyous smile.

Hadrea and Lavena saw the adventures to come, and Kaleos marvelled that not that long ago, those girls were squealing babes in arms like the children who visited them that evening.

Rufio and Clara remembered the pain of years of longing and separation from each other, and then together they thought of their daughter, their home, and how risk and change could bring about the greatest of joys.

Electra, cradling Thespis to her chest as he slept, stared at Felix, and prayed to the Gods to give her the strength she needed to be able to help him in whatever way was needed. As the music danced in her ears, she thought that she could never love another the way that she loved him.

And as Felix met his wife's eye, he felt how undeserving he was of her and their child, and how disappointed Thespis would be when he someday learned how his father, *The* Felix Modestus, panicked like a frightened child before the theatre mob of Athenae.

Even Hercules had his share of tragedy, and Felix could feel his coming fast upon him.

THE INEBRIATED ENTOURAGE RETURNED TO THE VILLA LONG into the night as dew already settled upon the forest ferns and leaves of bitter laurel. They were met by Atticus and a few groggy servants who had kept torches and braziers burning in the courtyard and throughout the domus.

"Did you have a good evening, Praetor?" Atticus asked Sextus.

"A lovely evening, thank you, Atticus," Sextus whispered so as not to wake the children who slept soundly in their mothers' arms.

One by one, The Etrurian Players filed past Atticus, some stumbling in at the gate and others alighting from the curtained confines of the litters. They all smiled at him as they passed, but Rufio stopped.

"Where is Peli? Please tell me he did not wreak havoc upon you." Rufio rubbed his face roughly, trying to rid his mind of the cobwebs that were already forming.

"I am happy to report that Peli was indeed well-behaved. He and Nicodemus did have one encounter, but this time the hound outdid the goat."

"Oh, he bit him?" Rufio could imagine the goat's spindly, bleeding leg in Peli's gnashing teeth.

"No. Peli urinated upon Nicodemus as he slept." Atticus stifled a laugh.

"Oh. All right then." Rufio nodded. "I'm sorry. Peli has a habit of doing that."

"My leg knows it well, Rufio Pagano."

"Good night then."

"Good night."

Rufio followed Clara who was already heading upstairs behind Electra, and there they found Peli waiting for them outside the cubiculum door.

"Do you need help?" Martia asked Electra at the top of the stairs.

"I'll be fine. Felix should be along soon."

"I'm afraid the evening has got the better of our dramatic general," Sextus said from where he looked down into the peristyle garden.

Electra sighed and walked around to her cubiculum.

When Rufio and Clara turned to their own door, Peli stood up, his tale wagging vigorously.

"Did you wait up for us, Peli?" Clara whispered, as she cradled Felicia.

"Good boy," Rufio said, bending to pat the canine. "Come,

time for sleep. Who knows what tomorrow will bring?"

Clara smiled at him, for the optimism in Rufio's voice lightened her heart immensely.

STILL IN THE COURTYARD, ATTICUS WAITED FOR THE LAST OF the guests to disembark from the litters. With some concern, he began to walk toward the last one. There had been a time, some years past, when one particularly old guest had passed away in one of the litters, and that moment came back to him in most unwanted fashion. He was about to reach out with a shaking had to pull aside the curtains when two muscled legs slid out. "Ah!" Atticus squealed. "Felix Modestus? Is that you?"

"If it is not me, then some imposter has stolen my legs and abused my body with heady wine and thoughts." Felix stood as he held one of the litter's posts. "Yes, Atticus. It is I."

"The lady Electra and young Thespis are already abed."

"The child sleeps," Felix said dully. "That is good. I shall sleep in the garden tonight."

"Are you certain? The cubiculum is much more comfortable, and there are no scorpions."

"Perhaps a small bite will rouse my carcass," Felix said, confusing Atticus further.

"Very well Felix Modestus. I shall bring you a blanket."

"No need. Good night, Atticus." Felix walked slowly through the atrium, into the peristylium, and plopped himself down on one of the couches about the fountain. His breath was deep and laboured as he stared up at the huntress moon before his eyes shut and his tortured dreams began.

WHEN FELIX OPENED HIS EYES THE NEXT DAY, THE SUN WAS already high in the sky, his face hot and sweaty. He could hear Thespis wailing on the upper floor of the villa, and Electra's voice desperately trying to soothe their son with the song that was a constant in her arsenal of lullabies.

From one of the cubicula - Fausto and Damon's, he thought - Felix could hear the sound of vomiting, and at the far end of the peristylium, Peli was barking as he faced off against a bleating Nicodemus.

"Gods, is this a villa or a barn yard?" Felix shouted.

"If it bothers you so much, come and help!" Electra shouted from on high.

"Good morning, Felix!" Clara said as she rushed past him from the triclinium and up the stairs to Electra's aid.

"Stop it, you two! Shoo! Naughty goat!" Rufio said as he emerged from the triclinium with Felicia in his arms, dispersing the duelling quadrupeds who darted off into the courtyard at the front of the villa. "Peli's going to miss that goat when we're gone," Rufio laughed. "I found him covered in goat droppings this morning outside our door!" He sat down on the couch opposite Felix, bouncing Felicia on his knee. "Uncle Felix is looking rough."

"Don't shout, Rufio," Felix groaned as he sat up.

"I'm not. Did you sleep well?"

"No." Felix went to the fountain, cupped his hands, and splashed his face. "I drank too much. I'm not usually affected by so little wine."

"Little?" Rufio laughed. "It was a fine vintage, and you drank nearly an entire amphora on your own!"

Felix looked up from where he leaned on the fountain's edge. "No! Really?"

"In truth, I don't know. I drank my share as well." Rufio stood and walked to Felix's side.

Felicia reached out and slapped his shoulder.

"Good morning, little one," Felix muttered. "Please tell my son to stop singing. He's not as good as he thinks."

"I think he's actually got better," Rufio joked.

"Not when my head aches as it does." Felix stretched. "I think I'll go straight into the baths."

"Atticus had the hypocausts stoked first thing."

"I only need the frigidarium," Felix replied.

"Well, when you're finished and you've eaten, Sextus wanted to speak with you. He's gone into the city for something, but will be back soon."

"Did he say what it's about?"

Rufio shook his head. "No. Probably something about accounts, I imagine." Rufio suddenly cocked his ear. "Ah. There it is. Your son has stopped singing."

"Thank the Gods," Felix muttered as he went in search of the baths.

A COUPLE OF HOURS LATER, FELIX KNOCKED ON THE TABLINUM door, Atticus having informed him that Sextus had returned.

"Yes, come in!" Sextus said, standing to greet Felix as he entered, newly bathed and grasping a cup of water. "Did Bacchus get the better of you, my friend?"

"It seems so," Felix replied rather sedately. "I'm afraid our rehearsals will occur later today."

"Are you not going into the city for the sacrifices today?"

"What sacrifices?"

"The hecatomb is offered to Athena up on the Acropolis. There will be a great feast afterward. Everyone is going down for it soon!"

"I thought you were just down there?" Felix asked.

"Oh, I just nipped down quickly to ask something of one of the other magistrates."

"What for? What was the urgency?"

"Well, that is what I wanted to speak with you about." Sextus suddenly looked quite awkward and motioned for Felix to sit in one of the two chairs by a window with him.

"You worry me, Sextus. Are we in some kind of financial distress?"

"Oh, no. Not at all. It's just that…well…"

"Come, man. Out with it."

"I have noticed your distress, Felix."

"My distress?" Felix's faced darkened. "What do you mean?"

"I don't want you to take this the wrong way, by any means. I consider you my closest friend, but I'm worried for you."

"What cause have you to worry?"

"Felix, come on now… I see how much anguish you've been feeling throughout the preparations for this entire production. It doesn't seem like…"

"What?" Felix's voice was unusually aggressive.

"Felix," Sextus' voice was calm. "Your heart isn't in this one, is it? Be honest with yourself."

"Why would you say that, Sextus? I'm always ready for a challenge. And this one was given to me by Apollo himself!"

Sextus sighed. "Everyone is worried about you, and your doubts are having an effect upon them, the way a general without confidence affects his troops before a battle. They're worried."

"They haven't said as much to me. I think you're imagining things. Maybe it's you who is worried?"

Sextus nodded. "I am worried! There is a lot riding on this performance. The Etrurian Players have been the most lauded company about the Middle Sea for the last couple of years. But fame is fleeting, is it not?"

"Not for us," Felix said. "Not for me!" he insisted.

"All I'm saying is that maybe this one time, it's a mistake. Maybe we should cancel the performance?"

"Cancel? You mean quit!"

"I mean postpone. I've spoken with my friend in the city, and he says that the people would not notice too much if the performance did not go ahead. The Panathenaea will have finished, and everyone will be exhausted from the games. We could arrange to perform the production back in Rome where it will be appreciated. We could return to the theatre of Pompey where you enjoyed such a magnificent victory!"

Felix was shaking his head. "You're backing out on us, Sextus!" Felix's voice was hurt, accusatory in a way that Sextus had never heard before.

"I'm worried. Is it not better to cancel the performance than to present the Athenians with a mediocre production? If it is not well received, it could end it all! The Etrurian Players would not be welcomed anywhere. There would be no funding, and no faith in your abilities. The damage of one bad performance in Athenae could bring down the entire company."

Felix jumped to his feet, knocking his chair over and against the wall. "I can't believe you. I thought you were my friend! I thought you believed in us!"

"I do, Felix, please! I also know that you are human, and that at times the best strategy is to back down and try again."

"Tell me Sextus, now that I see that you know everything… What should I tell my son when, one day, he asks his father why, when at the peak of his career, he quit before performing at the Great Panathenaea? What should I say to him then? How could I live with myself?"

"You can tell him that you did it to save The Etrurian Players."

Felix pointed at him. "No! You know why? Because there won't be such a company to save! The Gods will turn their backs on us if we don't see it through!" Felix went to the door and opened it. "Don't you dare cancel!" he shouted, and then slammed it shut.

Sextus stood and righted the chair which Felix had knocked over. He then sat at the table with his head in his hands. "By Apollo…it was good while it lasted."

XVI

AFTER THE STORM

The sixth day the Panathenaea arrived. The summer heat had reached fevered heights, and the city sweltered more than anyone living could remember. As citizens and slaves walked thought the streets, they shielded their eyes from the swirling dust which seemed to have gathered everywhere except along the banks of the low-flowing Ilissos where many escaped to dip their heads for relief.

With the torch races having finished in the stadium, the sweaty crowds that had packed it began to flow toward the high rock of the Acropolis where Athena's temple sat above her sacred city. Even though temperatures were scorching, Athena's fires would burn hot and bright as the flames were readied to receive the sacrificial hecatomb in the goddess' honour.

If one were visiting Athenae for the very first time, one would think that no goddess in all of the great Pantheon was more loved and honoured than Athena. Approaching the Acropolis, one might have been forgiven for thinking that as they made the hot, arduous climb to the great western propylaea, they were actually mounting the steps of Olympus itself. Every altar burned with scented offerings, and every low wall or barrier was hung with summer flowers and strands of ivy and of olive, the latter representing the gift of the goddess to the people of her city.

In the agora below, crowds lingered in whatever bits of shade they could find, against the walls of the stoas and other public buildings, and beneath the clusters of olive trees where the cicadas clamoured with a deafening roar. People crowded around fountains for a quick drink of water before choosing their moment to join the slow-moving crowd that pressed its way together at the first propylon to be spit out in a more orderly fashion up the winding path to the great propylaea.

The titanic serpentine crowd flowed up, their heads craned to see the small but glorious beauty of the temple of Athena Nike hanging above them, where the first heifer had been offered, prior to the hecatomb. Opposite Nike's temple, upon its massive pillar, the four-horse chariot, rededicated by Marcus Agrippa and Augustus, seemed to roll, its horses champing in the burning light.

The people of Athenae, and the xenoi who visited, passed into the maw of the great propylaea. Their exhausted and excited voices echoed about the soaring doric and ionic columns as they enjoyed a moment of shade before stepping out into the light to find themselves beneath the gaze of the bronze colossus of Athena, her speartip and helmet glinting in Helios' fiery light. To the goddess' left rose the great temple of Athena Parthenos, her victory over Poseidon for the patronage of the city displayed in brilliant colours upon the western pediment. The peaks of the temple soared, topped by the wings of the acroterion which, to some, appeared to be Zeus' own eagle come down from Olympus.

Clouds of smoke began to gather about the sanctuary of Artemis Brauronia to the right, and about the beautiful forms of the Caryatids of the Erechtheion to the left as they looked out over the sea of mortal heads swarming the temple, the people carrying their own meagre offerings for the goddess.

It was then that the smell of salt and sweat changed to the tang of smoke, blood, iron, animal faeces and urine. The sound of talk, and of singing, of flute and of tambourine shifted, and all ears were filled now with the lowing of a hundred cattle being led to the great altar of Athena on the north side of the temple, their fleeting cries piercing the suffocating air as the priests slit their throats and offered them up to the goddess.

Blood ran in torrents over the edges of the altar, pooling about the priests' feet, slicking the steps and engulfing the awaiting herd within the confines of the retaining wall. At the eastern end of the Acropolis, beyond the altar, the butchers were hard at work, cutting the sacred carcasses, reserving the bones and fat for the goddess' fires, and portioning the cuts of meat equally for each deme of the city and its citizenry.

Men, women and children arrived in droves, taking the path between the sacrifices and the Parthenon to the eastern end of the temple where, one slow step at a time, they entered the goddess' home through the great double doors.

People gazed up in wonder at the brilliant colours of the Parthenon's frieze as they approached, their eyes filled with bursts of blues, deep reds, and golden yellows depicting the very Panathenaic festival in which they were participating. The latticed walls of cedar filled the spaces between the columns to either side of the great doors of the pronaos, forcing an orderly entrance into Athena's earthly home. Once the people were inside, it was as though their voices were taken from them, or else offered willingly, for the silence within was deep and respectful as they stepped beneath the gaze of the titanic chryselephantine statue of Athena.

The goddess looked down, her face calm, confident, and full of care for her people. The ivory of her form shone with oil, and the gold of her triple-crested war helmet, robes, and the great shield depicting the Amazonomachy, the war between the

Greeks and the Amazons, reflected the firelight onto the pool of water at her feet, thus sending shimmering echoes of gold in all directions. Along with Athena's attendant serpent, sphinxes, gryphons, gorgons and winged horses, the Goddess Nike hovered in Athena's right hand, high above the rest of the gods who were all depicted in gold upon the marble plinth at Athena's feet.

Among the ancient weapons, armour, and shields that usually adorned the temple walls and columns, thick garlands of fragrant flowers were hung between the two levels of columns, accented by colourful drapes that fluttered and wafted the smoke that burned from the two giant tripods flanking the goddess' pool. The great cedar roof shimmered in the smoke and firelight of the massive, hanging bronze lamps in the form of soaring goddesses.

The people approached the smaller altars lining the walls of the cella in orderly rows, so much so that food, oil, flowers, perfumes, votive statues, birds and other offerings were soon heaped upon all of them. Their prayers and offerings made to the goddess, they then pressed through the crowd to the centre of the cella to look up at Athena, their prayers continuing in each of their minds. They admired the sacred peplos that had been woven for her which depicted the great battle between the Gods and Giants.

People smiled and bowed to their great patron goddess, some wept and continued to pray, and others found inspiration and a will to go on through whatever toils they endured, for who could not but be joyful when Athena herself was your patron and ally?

It was then that one group struck up the sacred Hymn to Athena, and soon a chorus of voices rose to the painted rafters, a melody to tingle the spine of Zeus himself to whose daughter the song was offered.

"Oh, Athena, guardian of the city," the people sang,

"Dread is she, with Ares she loves deeds of war, the sack of cities and the shouting, and battle. It is she who saves the people as they go out to war and come back. Hail, Goddess, and give us good fortune with happiness!"

Different groups took up the hymn, some men, others women, such that layers of baritone and soprano mingled to create a heavenly chorus to please the goddess' ear.

"THE ACOUSTICS IN HERE ARE AMAZING!" RUFIO SAID TO Clara as they stood in the middle of the cella's press, gazing up at the goddess.

"So what do you think?" Clara asked him as she leaned against his shoulder, holding Felicia close to her chest.

"I think it's a true wonder," he replied.

Just then, a shower of flower petals rained down upon them from the people crowding the railings of the upper level as they tossed joyous handfuls at the goddess' feet.

On Clara's other side, Electra held Thespis up, showing the goddess to her son, praying for his safety through life, wherever it may lead him.

"I remember coming here as a child," Electra said to Felix who protected her and their son with his bulk. "The goddess was just as strong and beautiful then as she is now, as she has been for hundreds of years." She looked at her husband and kissed him. "Apollo and Athena watch over us all, Felix. You don't need to worry."

Felix looked at the joy in her smile, the brilliance of the fire in her dark eyes. "Where are the others?" Felix asked.

Electra's smile faded slightly, and she shrugged. "I do not know."

"There they are!" Clara said, pointing to the upper storey where, to Athena's left, the rest of The Etrurian Players were singing and tossing handfuls of pink and white flowers over the crowd's heads.

The press of people was getting tighter, hotter, and sweatier. Rufio used the hem of his tunica to wipe the sweat from his forehead. "I need air," he said to Clara.

"Me too. The goddess has heard our prayers and received our offerings. Electra?" Clara said. "Shall we go back outside?" She noticed that Electra looked sad, her eyes watery pools as she gazed up at the goddess. "If you want to stay longer, Rufio can take Thespis for you. We can wait for you outside the temple."

Electra looked at her, and shook her head. "I'm ready." She glanced at Felix and noted that he seemed more concerned with the crowd pressing around them than her, or indeed the goddess to whom they had been praying. "Athena has received our prayers and offerings. We can go."

Rufio turned to indicate to the others on high that they were leaving.

Julius waved and nodded, and their heads disappeared.

AT THE EASTERN EDGE OF THE ACROPOLIS, BETWEEN THE shrine of Zeus Polieus, Protector of the City, and the tholos dedicated to Emperor Augustus, bakers at long tables handed out bread and honeyed cakes to the people as they filed out of the Parthenon, wading through the smoke and blood-scented air.

As he waited in line, Rufio looked up at the statue of Augustus beneath the roof supported by nine ionic columns and thought that the Roman looked quite out of place standing so haughtily in the shadow of the eastern pediment of the Parthenon which displayed the birth of the goddess Athena. "He doesn't look at all out of place, does he?" Rufio pointed with his thumb over his shoulder as he stood in line for the honey cakes.

Felix looked and nodded. "He certainly left his mark on the city."

"As will we," Rufio smiled and winked, but Felix did not respond.

They reached the bakers' tables and accepted the small loaves of bread and honey cakes, and then moved along to the eastern edge of the Acropolis to eat them away from the jostling crowd.

"The air is a little fresher over here," Rufio said as he fed Felicia a piece of bread while Clara held her. "What a view!" He and Clara turned to look across the tiled rooftops of the city and the district of Novae Athenae toward Hadrianus' triumphal arch, dwarfed as it was beside the titanic mass of the temple of Zeus, the Olympieion. From there, their eyes gazed toward the great horseshoe of the Panathenaic stadium.

"Look!" Clara pointed. "You can see the temple of Artemis Agrotera where we were."

"Strange," Rufio said. "It's so difficult to find when you're close, but then from here it's as plain as the frown upon Felix's face!" Rufio cast him a look.

"I'm not frowning," Felix returned, tearing into his small loaf of bread.

Electra shook her head. "You are." She turned back to Rufio and Clara. "The goddess sees all from her lofty home. On a clear day, you can see the temple of Aphaia on the island of Aegina, and the temple of Poseidon at Sounion where it overlooks the sea.

"Really?" Rufio turned to gaze out to the southeast, shielding his eyes and waving futilely at the smoke. "I don't see it."

"I think Athena's eyes are more keen than yours, Rufio!" Electra laughed.

"He reads too much in dim light at home," Clara said, both women staring at him.

"Or maybe it's all the smoke wafting over here from the great altar?" Rufio bit into one of the honey cakes. "Hmm! These are delicious!"

Clara smiled and took a bite of her own before giving Felicia a taste. The child's eyes widened perceptibly at the first gnawing bite and Clara laughed. "I think she likes it!"

"There they are," Felix grumbled. "Finally!"

Electra, Clara and Rufio looked to where the rest of The Etrurian Players were walking over to them, each with bread and cakes in hand.

"The bread they give at the circus in Ephesus is nowhere near as good as this!" Pollux said.

"If you're done stuffing your faces, maybe we can go!" Felix said suddenly.

Electra wheeled on him as the others went by, taking the path along the northern edge of the Acropolis, past the walled sanctuary of Pandion and toward the Erechtheion. "What is wrong with you? This is a sacred day…a sacred festival!"

People around them were staring as Electra raised her voice and Thespis began to cry.

"Ftousou!" She quickly spat on her son to protect him against the stares. "Felix, I don't know what's wrong with you, but you need to fix it. I've been trying to help you. I've been patient. But…" She shook her head wildly, some of her dark strands falling loose to blow in the increasing wind and choking smoke. "We're all relying on you, and our friends have come a great distance to be here for you and see that Apollo's will is done!"

"You don't understand," he growled and walked away, leaving her to follow alone with their son wailing in her arms.

As Rufio and Clara walked behind the great altar of Athena toward the northern edge of the Acropolis, the sound of lowing became deafening, the thudding of the priests' blades cutting into the victims' throats unnervingly audible on the other side of the low walls surrounding the sacrificial precinct.

"I think I'm going to be sick," Beatrice said to Fausto as they walked.

Fausto held her and looked back at Rufio and Clara. "We're going to go ahead. We'll see you back at the villa!"

"Go, go!" Rufio answered "We'll follow!"

Fausto, Beatrice, Castor, Pollux, Damon, Julius and Domela all walked ahead and made their way down the stairs that led into the city from the courtyard of the Arrephorion, the house of the young weaver women of the sacred peplos, at the northwest corner.

"I don't blame Beatrice," Clara said as she and Rufio came to a stop in the shade of the northern side of the Erechtheion, by the door to the Pandroseion. "The smell is rather strong now. I don't know how they'll get it clean again!"

"I'm surprised these Greeks didn't sacrifice a hundred fish!" Rufio said.

"I don't know that Athena would like fruit from Poseidon's sea," Clara said. Speaking of which, do you know what that is?" She pointed through the open arch of the Pandroseion to a singular, full, healthy olive tree.

"It's an olive tree," Rufio replied, his farmer's eyes immediately taking in the strength of the limbs, and the fullness of the fruit weighing down the branches.

"It's *the* olive tree," Clara said.

"What do you mean, *the* olive tree?"

"You saw the western pediment of the Parthenon as we came up, yes?"

"Of course. It's hard to miss."

Clara smiled. "Well, this is *the* olive tree which Athena gave to the city and which won her the contest for its patronage."

"Really?" Rufio's eyes widened as he approached the tree within its small courtyard. "It doesn't look that old."

Clara shrugged. "I suppose the tree is as ageless as the goddess."

Rufio paused and reached out to touch the tree with his eyes closed for a few heartbeats. When he opened his eyes, he knelt down and placed one of the honey cakes at its base.

"What are you doing?" Clara asked, smiling to herself.

"Making an offering to Athena for help with our own olive trees. If our trees could last even half as long as this one, then our latifundium will thrive for generations."

"It's a good idea, my love," Clara said, happy in her heart that Rufio regularly envisioned a bright and beautiful future for all of them.

Just then, Clara spotted Felix's bulky form storming past the the archway. "Felix, we're in here!" she said, but he did not stop.

Electra then appeared at the doorway and stopped when she saw them.

"What's wrong with Felix?" Clara went over to her, followed by Rufio.

Thankfully, Thespis calmed down when Felicia reached out with her honeyed fingers to grasp his hands.

Electra sighed. "Everything is wrong with Felix." She looked at Rufio. "Can't you talk some more sense into him?"

"Me?"

"Yes, you!"

"I've tried!" Rufio tried not to crumple beneath Electra's dark stare.

"Maybe Felix is just distracted," Clara offered, her hand on Electra's shoulder. "There is a lot going on with the Panathenaea, pressure from Sextus, The Rome Antics-"

"Riots…going to prison…" Rufio added.

Clara kicked him and turned back to Electra. "He'll be fine. You'll see. You know Felix. He'll come through."

Electra looked doubtful. "Perhaps he would have done before." She looked beyond the tree and the wall to the rooftop of the Parthenon. "He is changed...different."

They were silent, not knowing what else to say.

The wind picked up even more then, swirling the dust around the tree in the small courtyard of the Pandroseion. Dark clouds began to cut across that summer sky most suddenly, as if gathered by Zeus above Athenae, like black sheep herded into a tight pen.

"We should go!" Electra said suddenly, beginning to walk.

Rufio and Clara followed her out of the Pandroseion and along the path to the stairs down into the city from the Arrephorion.

"What's happening?" Rufio called out to Electra.

"A storm is coming!" she called over her shoulder.

"I haven't seen a cloud in weeks, and *now* there's a storm?" Rufio asked Clara.

They rushed down off of the Acropolis and went with Electra to the agora where they had arranged for the litter-bearers to await them.

Felix was already there, laying inside the litter.

Electra got inside and sat beside him without speaking.

"Let's go! Quickly!" Felix barked at the servants and the litters were hoisted, the curtains billowing like the sails of a ship at sea.

The children cried all of the way back to the villa, though the sound was not as deafening as the wind that whirled about them.

"Do you think my honey cake offended the goddess?" Rufio wondered out loud.

Clara shook her head but did not speak, for she was too

busy humming to Felicia to try and calm her as the day grew dark.

The storm was getting worse.

THE LITTERS MANAGED TO RETURN SAFELY TO THE VILLA, though it had been no mean feat for the litter-bearers who had trudged uphill against the water that was rushing down the paths of Hymettos. As soon as they were within the front courtyard and the gates closed securely behind them, the servants immediately set planks of wood before the gates in an effort to deflect the water and mud that was rushing down the mountain slopes with increasing velocity.

Sextus and Martia met them in the atrium where the impluvium was now overflowing with water.

"Thank the Gods you're all right!" Sextus shouted, for the sound of the rain upon the tiled rooftop was deafening.

"We were so worried," Martia helped Electra with Thespis.

"Have the others returned?" Felix asked them. "They said they were coming back ahead of us."

"Yes. They arrived at a run, just before you did," Sextus confirmed. "Everyone has gone to their cubicula to wait out the storm…though…I can't imagine it will end anytime soon."

Then, a clap of thunder cracked the sky overhead.

Thespis and Felicia wailed and the three women rushed inside to take refuge in their respective rooms.

There was also a loud barking and as Rufio turned, Peli came lunging through the air to land in his arms, wet and shaking and nuzzling into his dominus' chest.

"It's all right, boy! I've got you. We're back now."

Atticus followed with the end of the gnawed rope that he had used to tie Peli up. "He got away from me, Rufio Pagano. I am sorry!"

"It's all right. I'll take him. It's good you tied him up. He would have run into the city to get us!" Rufio began to go toward the stairs with Peli, but turned back to Felix. "You coming?"

Felix looked up at the opening above the atrium and felt the rain lashing his face as another crack of lightening raked the sky. He spread his arms wide as if to tempt the Gods.

"Felix!" Rufio shouted. "You should get inside!"

"I'm having the servants bring food and wine to each of your cubicula, Felix Modestus!" Atticus said. "Please, get to safety!"

They could barely hear each other, but Atticus tried again.

"I'll have mine in the peristylium," Felix said.

"There is no place that is dry in the garden, not even beneath the roofline!" Atticus tried, but Felix waved his hand.

"No matter. I find it refreshing!" Felix said before marching past Atticus, Sextus, and Rufio who clutched his wet dog to his chest.

The wind howled like an angry Fury and the three men scattered to their respective rooms and duties while, behind them, the two litters were toppled and slammed against the courtyard wall, the sound of their wood splintering almost as loud as the thunder.

When they were gone, Felix walked slowly through to the other side of the peristylium, his entire person sodden and squelching with each step. He settled himself on a bench at the far end of the garden, between the triclinium doors and beneath the awning of the roof.

A tile fell from the sky to shatter in the middle of the garden beside the fountain, but it did not startle him. No. Felix Modestus was as calm as he could be then, though everyone else in the villa was shouting and taking cover.

One of the servants came rushing up with a tray that had bread and cheese upon it, as well as a clay cup for wine. Another arrived with a pitcher that was filled with wine. They set them down on the bench beside Felix and bowed before rushing off.

Felix, his face and beard dripping, looked down at the tray where the bread was already as soaked as a sponge newly-plucked from the sea, and the cheese appeared to be back in its brine. He reached for the pitcher, tilted it back, and took a long draught. *Yes,* he thought, pleased. *Rufio's Etrurian vintage.*

As he let that nectar of memory roll around in his mouth, offsetting the taste of rain that he had had up until that point, Felix had a faint memory of spring storms in Etruria when he was young. They could come on as quickly there, the Gods getting just as angry. He could remember the thunder rolling over the hills, and the painful crack of lightning that lit the forest slopes of those steep-sided valleys. He could even remember the tears of some farmers whose crops of vines and olives had been destroyed when their protective nymphs had abandoned their plots. It never paid to neglect offerings to those protectresses.

That made Felix think. He had lost his way, he knew, though stubbornly he was loathe to admit it to anyone. *They don't understand anyway.* But he had to wonder as he sat there drinking, unfeeling of the wet anymore, if *he* had neglected those nearest to him, as well as the Gods who watched over him. He knew he was prone to hubris, but he did not relish the sting of guilt that he felt when he thought of Electra and of Thespis, nor even of his company and friends who had come at his request from so far away.

The theatre, his company, and his reputation had always been his entire life. But now, he could feel his attention and his priorities drawn in another direction.

He wondered, with some trepidation, if Rufio wasn't right after all.

Maybe my purpose is not slipping away… It's just changing.

He shook his head and drank deeply of the wine, wishing

for oblivion. "I don't like change, unless I choose it!" he shouted.

The wind picked up even more then, the shrubs in the garden pulling at their roots, the fountain overflowing as the water was blown sideways out of it.

Felix howled then, feeling wild, a part of him challenging the Gods to strike him and see where it led to.

The courtyard filled with white light as thunder clapped again and lightning burst overhead.

Felix shielded his eyes from the intense brightness and when he opened them he could see a dishevelled man in a rough homespun tunica standing in front of the fountain. He looked sternly at Felix, his arms crossed, shaking his head in supreme disappointment.

Felix jut his chin out at the man. "Est mundus stercoris!" he shouted before taking another long drink.

The man marched directly toward Felix, and before the latter could stand to meet him, he slapped Felix hard across the face sending him sideways onto the bench, the sodden bread and cheese a pillow for his head, and the rest of the wine flowing away with the rain.

THE STORM RAGED ALL THROUGH THE NIGHT, AND WHEN THE people of Athenae awoke the next day there was a brightness to the world, an intensity of colour and light that they had not seen in a while. Every building, every column, and every statue shone above the muddied streets where the whisking sounds of brooms could be heard as the clean-up began.

People spoke in hurried whispers about the omens they had witnessed or been told of by others who had seen them, or heard about them. Tongues wagged without end on every corner and at every fountain.

People talked of giant serpents emerging from the rivers

Ilissos and Eridanos to swallow dogs and cats whole, of winged horses and harpies clashing in the night sky webbed with lightning, and of the Gods holding back a new invasion of Giants who sought to lay siege to Attica. Some even whispered that the colossus of Athena had stepped down from her plinth before the Parthenon, brandishing her spear and shield and walking the perimeter of the Acropolis to defend it against all comers.

The stories spread like summer fires. But there was little time for all of that, especially for those who were in attendance for the games. On that seventh day of the Panathenaea, the flow of people went in the direction of Piraeus where the boat races were to take place.

The priests emerged from their homes to make offerings to Athena on the Acropolis, and it was confirmed that the goddess had accepted the hecatomb that had been offered the previous day. Her statues shone and her temple was unharmed by the storm. In addition to those propitious signs, the rivers of blood, ash, and bone that had flowed from the great altar upon the Acropolis had been completely swept away.

Athena was pleased.

Her hymns were sung and new garlands hung to replace those that had been destroyed by the wind and rain so that Athenae was reborn in the wake of the storm.

Up the slopes of Hymettos, detritus littered every forest pathway and the track that led to the city. Within the villa, Atticus had his servants up early, cleaning away debris that had blown in from the surrounding forest and groves, gathering broken bits of roof tile and pottery, and shovelling away the thick mud that had managed to flow beneath the gates into the main courtyard, despite the small blockade that had been placed outside. The domus steward decided to leave the peristylium garden until last, for Felix Modestus yet slept upon his plate of food at the back, and the surrounding cubicula of the other guests remained silent.

"Make sure the odeon is fully swept and tidy for The Etrurian Players," Atticus told his staff. "They have but two days until the performance." He picked up one of the stray scrolls of *Heautontimorumenos*, wiping away some of the mud and letting the water run off of it. "Such a wonderful play…" he muttered as he went over to where an iron peg jut from the wall beside the small pulpitum, and hung the scroll from it to dry in the morning sun.

Upon his marble bench-bed in the peristylium, Felix Modestus lay still and sleeping upon his meal of the previous evening. His mind was aware that the storm had ceased, that his beard was pressed with goat's cheese, and that wet bread filled his ear. But he did not care. He lay there upon the bench, not wanting to rise to face the day nor his wife whose wrath, he felt certain, would be unbearable.

He heard it then, the soft beautiful string of notes plucked upon a cythara. They slowed his heart and cleared his mind. *What's this? No one in the company can play like this!* he thought.

Felix felt the morning sun intense upon his face then, which was strange, for he had thought he was hidden beneath the roofline. However, the sun was hot and burning, bright and blinding. It made him squint hard, though he tried to open his eyes to see.

The music continued, and a deep, resonant breathing accompanied it, a sound of sunfire. It rose to a beautiful crescendo and then fell farther and farther, until it was out of hearing.

You have toils to undertake before your trial…Felix Modestus.

"Who's there?" Felix asked, shielding his eyes to try and

look through the intense sunlight. He wondered if it was the man who had slapped him across the face, but in his heart he knew it was not. "Your playing…it…it was-"

Felix stopped himself, for when he opened his eyes, he saw him for a brief second, he who was the reason for his being in Athenae. The sun's light shone as if deliberately turned to him, highlighting his curling sky-blue cloak, his star-whirling eyes, and the great cythara cradled in his strong arms. "Lord Apollo?" Felix said, his voice hoarse, but a croak in the vast auditory library of the world. "I…I…"

Felix fell to his knees before the god, but the light faded away as swiftly and as softly as the music that had roused him. He was alone in the courtyard again.

When he opened his eyes once more, it was to see Peli sitting beside him, staring with those unnerving eyes.

The dog's nose rose up as he detected something, and a moment later, Peli was licking the cheese from Felix's face.

"Get off me!" Felix roared, only to have Peli turn, lift his leg, and piss in Felix's general direction. "You spiteful cur!" Felix roared, his voice now reaching every corner of the villa. "Come back here! I'll cook you for breakfast!"

Felix rubbed his face and eyes as he made directly for the baths.

"What's all the shouting about?" Clara said as she turned over to face Rufio across the sleeping form of their daughter who lay peaceful and protected between them.

"I'm guessing Peli has helped Felix to start his day," Rufio chuckled, though why Felix was already up and about, he could not guess. The house had been quiet until then as far as he could tell as he lay there in bed observing the mess in their cubiculum.

At some point during the storm, when the thunder and

lightning were at their brightest and most deafening, the shutters had flown open and blown all of Rufio's scrolls, wax tablets, and styli off of the table and all over the floor. At the time, he had not concerned himself with cleaning things up, but with shielding Clara and Felicia from the flying debris.

Rufio kissed Clara, then his daughter's forehead before he groaned and swung his legs over the edge of the bed. He rubbed his face and pulled a couple of stray olive leaves from his hair, letting them fall to the ground with the rest of the detritus.

He went over to the bronze tripod with a bowl upon it, picked out more leaves that floated upon the surface of the water, and splashed his face. He then went to the window and opened the shutters fully before leaning upon the sill and looking out.

The forest and groves were bright and green, and the earth was rich and wet outside the villa walls. It would be dry by the fourth hour.

"So bright and colourful," Rufio muttered. "Reminds me of home."

Clara opened her eyes and looked across the room at him with a smile. "Everything reminds you of home."

He turned in the light at the window to look at her and Felicia. "You are my home."

"I don't want to get up yet," she said, leaning on one elbow and stroking her daughter's wild, downy hair.

Felicia's tiny lips moved in a pout, as if she were rehearsing for her breakfast.

It made Clara smile more. *Athena…thank you for protecting us this night.*

Rufio turned away from the window and began the task of picking up the bits and pieces of his work from about the room.

Clara began to laugh, and Rufio turned to her with an armful of scrolls.

"What's funny?"

"You are, my love. You're wearing papyrus scrolls and nothing else!" she giggled like a girl at the site of him.

"I'll dress then, shall I?"

She nodded. "I'm guessing Atticus will be here any moment to check that we're all right."

Rufio set the scrolls back upon the table and began to dress while Clara set Felicia to her breast and began to sing.

On the other side of the upper level, Sextus and Martia, who had just made love in the full brilliance of Helios' morning light which flooded their cubiculum, sat against the pillows of their bed holding each other closely, tenderly.

Sextus smiled, and wondered with some amazement that he was not feeling the sting of the great stress that had been at the back of his mind. It seemed that this production which he was funding with a fortune of coin, as well as his reputation, was doomed to fail. But even with those thoughts haranguing him, he felt supremely happy, and thanked the Gods for his good fortune. He stroked his wife's hair and kissed the top of her head as her face rested upon his chest. "I love you, Martia," he said.

"I know, Sextus," she replied. "I love you too. So very much." But there was sadness in her voice.

He knew it was not him, but that her thoughts were drifting back to the one thing they both desired more than any fortune or the good will of their society: a child of their own. Of course, he knew it was futile to hope for as much, for every medicus they had seen, every priest they had consulted, had told them the same thing, that the Gods did not intend for them to have a child of their own, but that they should help others. Martia's charitable work fulfilled but a small part of that need which she felt, he knew. He also knew that, for both of them, it had been a mixed blessing being around their friends' beautiful babies, helping to care for them, to entertain and interact with them.

What would happen when everyone went their separate ways yet again and he and Martia returned to their vast, empty domus in Rome?

"Let's not get up now, Sextus," she said as she held him all the more tightly. "I don't want to face the world just yet."

"Whatever you wish, my love."

For a while longer they lay there listening to the sound of birdsong and cicadas in the light and trees outside.

ELECTRA LAY BY HERSELF IN A POOL OF SUNLIGHT THAT flooded the cubiculum in which she and Thespis had spent a night of terror, him wailing, and her shielding him as she prayed to the Gods for protection from the storm. She remembered the summer storms of her youth, but that which she had experienced the previous night was unlike any other, angrier and more intense. She had wished throughout the night that Felix would burst through the doors to come to her side, but he never did.

She never imagined that she would see her husband, who was always so strong and certain, become so engulfed in self-doubt and, though he would never admit it to her, filled with fear. It altered her perception of him in a way that made her deeply sad and uncertain about the future. He had been like a god on Delos when Thespis was born, and a hero - albeit a selfish one - as he had fought The Rome Antics in the agora of Athenae.

Now, however, Felix Modestus was changed. He was more

of a man now instead of a god or hero, with all of the weaknesses and flaws that entailed.

Apollo and Athena…give him the strength to see his labours through to victory, she prayed.

Thespis finished suckling then, having done so the entire time she was lost in thought. He whined a little as his mother raised him and pat his back to encourage a great belch.

"Good boy," Electra said to her son with a small smile, though she did wonder at how her life had changed from long lazy mornings of love-making to suckling her child alone in her bed, the sheets smelling of sour milk rather than of heady eastern perfume.

Thespis' body tensed for a brief moment, and this gave Electra a flutter of worry, that is, until a great stench rose up from his bracae.

"And then there's that," she muttered. "At least you're reliable and on cue, my son."

Electra set him in the middle of the bed where he could kick wildly as he tried to escape the mess that clung to him, and went to gather the water, cloths, and new clothes for her son. Her own morning ablutions would have to wait.

A minute later, as Electra was changing Thespis whilst humming one of his favourite tunes - a bawdy marching song about Cleopatra, that made him giggle for some reason lost on her - Felix walked in, newly washed and glistening with oil.

"I see you're singing him the song I always sing for him," Felix's deep voice approached from the side.

Electra was glad to hear the guilt in his voice. "Cacare for cacare," she replied without looking at him.

Felix grunted and walked over to where his clothes hung and picked a plain crimson tunica from among the vast array of coloured and embroidered clothes he had brought. He slid it over his head, pushed back his wet hair, and sat to tie up a new pair of sandals.

"We're fine by the way," Electra said. "No need to worry."

Felix looked around the room at the scattered debris that fanned out from the window where the wind had rushed in. Scrolls sat in small puddles of water upon the terracotta flooring, and jewelry glinted in the morning light where it lay as if scattered by reckless thieves.

"I'm sorry, Electra. Are you all right? Is Thespis? He seems fine, shitting as usual."

"Yes, Felix. We're fine. It would have been nice to have you here while the wind howled and the shutters were nearly ripped off of their hinges. But we're fine."

The sound of the rest of the company rose up from the courtyard below.

"Sounds like the others are up." He sat on the bed beside her, Thespis' changing at an end. "It *was* a rough night."

"Oh, it was rough was it? I suppose drinking and passing out on a bench in the garden was quite a challenge!"

"Electra, come now. I just needed some time alone. I wasn't very good company."

"You haven't been good company for a while now."

"I have a lot on my mind. You know this." Impatience began to enter into his voice.

But Electra was not having it. "Don't you dare! We all have a lot on our minds. Everyone has a lot on their minds. While you were lolling in your stupor and self-pity downstairs, not thinking about us, *you* were on *my* mind." She shook her head as she riffled through her wardrobe for some clean clothes, settling on a blue gap-sleeved tunica with tiny golden Herculean knots at the shoulders. "I can't believe I worried for you, even while I was shielding our child's head from flying debris!"

Felix looked down at Thespis and touched his cheek with a thick finger. He was relieved he was unhurt.

"I wasn't just passed out, Electra. I was actually attacked!"

"By whom?" she demanded.

"Some mad man in a threadbare tunica walked in and punched me hard across the face. That's why I passed out."

"Is there no end to your dishonesty, Felix?" She walked up to him. "Where are the marks upon your face if you were struck so hard?"

His hand strayed to his cheek and he wondered about that, did not feel any hurt or bruising. "I don't know, but there was a man, and he was quite angry with me for some reason."

"Tell him to get in line." Electra marched toward the door and opened it.

"Where are you going?" Felix asked.

"It's my turn to bathe and feel whole again." She slammed the door but hollered from the other side. "You're on, Felix Modestus!"

Felix listened to Electra march her way downstairs, throwing some biting comment or other at the rest of the company as they greeted her in passing. He then picked up his son. "Time for your father's ientaculum then," he said. "Come, I'm starving."

As Felix walked to the doorway, holding his son to his chest, Thespis grunted and pushed out another eruption.

Felix stopped suddenly, the smell arresting his senses in a most unpleasant way. He held out his son to see the source of the odour dripping down his dangling legs. "We need to stop giving you figs."

WHEN FELIX FINALLY ARRIVED DOWNSTAIRS WITH THESPIS, IT was to find the entire company gathered around the tables in the triclinium.

"Dominus!" Fausto called to him. "You slept in the courtyard?"

"If you're not careful, Fausto, you will from now on," Felix growled. He looked around the table at the dour and thoughtful faces, and then sat himself on the empty couch between those of Sextus and Martia, and Rufio, Clara and Felicia. "Was anyone hurt last night?" he asked.

"No," Rufio said, his eyes going down the length of the tables where the conversation was suddenly muffled.

"Is Electra-"

"She's still in the baths," Clara said, staring at him. "She's not happy with you."

Felix shook his head. "She doesn't believe me that someone attacked me last night in the courtyard."

"What?" Sextus sat up. "Are you injured, Felix? Who was it?"

"Some mad man in a rough, brown homespun tunica. He just appeared out of nowhere and punched me across the face."

Rufio nearly choked on his honeyed bread. He looked at Felix's unblemished face.

"I've never seen him before, but he must live hereabouts. He had wild, long hair and an unkept beard."

"Oh!" Domela said out loud. "He must have smelled quite terrible!"

Felix thought about it for a moment. "Actually, I couldn't smell him."

"A shepherd maybe?" Castor ventured. "A sheep shepherd smelling of shit!"

"Sounds more like the title of a new play rather than an assailant," Pollux chuckled.

"He didn't smell!" Felix insisted. "But he was there."

"Well," Sextus said, "I'll speak with Atticus about putting more servants on watch. It may be that it was just some vagrant seeking shelter from the storm."

"I would have thought he might be seeking food, instead of a fight," Beatrice added.

Felix noticed Peli staring at him from behind Rufio and Clara's couch. "You stay away from me."

Rufio turned to look at his dog, and then back to Felix. He smiled. "Was it Peli who woke you up this morning?" he asked.

Felix did not answer at first. He thought better of speaking about who exactly woke him up. That was for him alone. "He started the day by pissing on me."

"Oh!" Domela squealed.

"Maybe Electra sent him to rouse you?" Fausto laughed.

Felix stared at him without speaking, and the younger man went back to his plate of food. Eventually, he addressed them all again. "So, is anyone up for rehearsing this play today? We're supposed to go on in two days."

The Etrurian Players looked at each other rather guiltily.

"What?" Felix asked.

Julius looked from Rufio and Clara to Sextus.

Felix noted that Rufio and Clara looked slightly upset about something while the others looked rather sheepish. "What is going on here? What were you talking about before I arrived?"

Sextus cleared his throat. "Felix, my friend. We were just discussing whether we should go through with the performance."

"You were? Without me?"

"The omens were bad last night," Beatrice said.

"The goddess was not happy with all of her offerings," Fausto added.

"I even heard one of the servants telling Atticus that he heard from the servant of a neighbouring domus that the odeon built by our host's family was struck by lightning last night." Pollux shook his head and crossed his arms. "Maybe the Gods have changed their minds about it? I mean, I'm eager to play Menedemus, but not if the Gods are against it now."

"Felix..." Sextus began, placing a hand on his shoulder.

"The omens were bad last night from the sound of it. It's not too late to cancel."

Felix looked at his son's big brown eyes and stroked his soft hair as he sat in the crook of his arm. He did not want to admit defeat. Giving up was something that he had never done before. But, if he was honest, there was a part of him that felt the temptation of great relief at the thought of cancelling the whole thing.

"Felix," Clara said. "Rufio and I are not in agreement with cancelling, especially so late. If you do cancel, you will never be able to perform in Athenae again, let alone visit."

Felix looked his two friends in the eyes. "Rufio, what do you think?"

Rufio looked about the table at the others and shook his head. "I think we've all been too distracted by the games and other goings on to focus on our work."

"We know our lines to perfection," Pollux said.

"That's not enough for this play, Pollux," Rufio replied. "We need to have immersed ourselves in it." He spotted Atticus come in at the doorway to the triclinium as if to report something, but he waited for Rufio to finish speaking. "When we performed in Rome, we were focussed upon our task."

"Apart from the odd brawl," Castor said.

"And near-fatal head injury," Fausto added.

"Yes, yes," Rufio said. "Apart from those. We were excited about the prospect, though we were deathly afraid of performing."

"*You* were deathly afraid," Felix corrected.

"Fine. I was," Rufio conceded. "But you are professionals. Would Apollo make such a demand of you, Felix, and then simply change his mind? I think the Gods operate with more sincerity than that, don't you?"

Felix stayed focussed on his son.

"But the omens, Rufio!" Fausto said. "Surely last night is a sign!"

"Erm," Atticus stepped forward then. "If I may… I have just had word from the city that there is no damage to the odeon. I receive reports on my dominus's properties whenever there is weather. I have also been told that the priests have determined that the goddess has accepted her offerings of yesterday, for the entire city is cleansed and brilliant. The storm washed all dirt and blood away, leaving Athena's polis shining in Helios' light."

Rufio turned back to everyone. "You see? The omens were *not* bad. They are good. Isn't it true that the Gods try us? They challenge us by tempting us to give up."

Felix stared across the table at Rufio. "Who are you, and what have you done with my friend?"

Rufio sat straight. "I'm Rufio Pagano. And *you*, you are *The* Felix Modestus!"

Clara smiled and winked at her daughter who sat in Rufio's arms, her big blue eyes looking up at her father.

"Well then," Sextus sighed. "If The Etrurian Players are determined, then so am I!" He clasped Martia's hand. "Is the performance proceeding then, as Apollo commanded?"

"I suppose it is," Felix said. "If we fail, let us at least do it with our heads held high."

Rufio noted the faint lack of determination in his friend's voice, but said nothing.

Felix continued. "Atticus, is the odeon cleared of debris?"

"Yes, Felix Modestus," Atticus nodded. "It is clear, and ready."

"Then finish eating, everyone. Dress rehearsal in one hour."

"All will be well, Felix. You'll see." Clara said as she and Rufio smiled across the table at him.

He did not smile back.

ACT V

THE JUDGMENT OF APOLLO

XVII

A DOG'S BREAKFAST

It was the final day of the Panathenaea. The people of Athenae rose across the city with a great feeling of anticipation for the last day of the games when all of the prizes would be awarded to the victors, and a great public feast would be held. There would also be celebrations in the various demes of the city to laud their local heroes if they were so fortunate.

In the wake of the great storm, fresh garlands had been hung upon every public building, altar, and temple to the Gods. New offerings were made to Athena, Patron of the City, and the rest of the Olympian pantheon. The Gods would feast alongside the people of Athenae that day as the Panathenaea came to its climactic end in honour of the Goddess.

On the slopes of Hymettos, at the villa of Atticus, The Etrurian Players had remained ensconced since the storm, rehearsing, going over all of the set pieces and costumes, and ensuring that things would be packed correctly for the journey to the odeon of Atticus in the heart of Athenae. They were focussed now, that is, all of them except for Felix.

The dress rehearsal had gone exceptionally well with Sextus, Martia, Atticus and the rest of the servants permitted to watch. There was a degree of laughter, but no howling. There were poignant moments, but no great sadness. It was a balanced play and performance, according to Sextus.

Felix, however, was not so certain. On that final day of the Panathenaea, the day before their scheduled performance, Felix lay in bed wondering if his doubts sprang from the fact that it was he who was not fully focussed upon the task at hand. He lay awake in bed, leaning upon one elbow, looking at his dozing son and wife. It made him smile to look upon them, especially now that he and Electra had made up.

It had been no mean feat to get back into his wife's good graces the previous day, but through sheer perseverance and strong will, Felix had broken down the high, stubborn wall which Electra had mortared between them. Felix ensured that she did not need to change one pair of bracae on their son the entire day, nor endure his crying when it was time for him to sleep. Felix did it all, on top of directing the rehearsal. All Electra had to do was ensure Thespis was fed.

When night fell at last, and Thespis was asleep in his crib, Electra and Felix lay together on that hot Athenian summer night, pleasuring each other as Cassiopeia sparkled in the night sky out of their cubiculum window.

"You are all that I need," Felix whispered to himself as he watched Electra and Thespis doze in the early morning sunlight. "Even if we fail tomorrow, and I never set foot upon a pulpitum again." He sighed and stretched. "Rufio's right…my purpose has changed…"

"What are you saying?" Electra's voice was groggy, her cheeks red with summer heat and sleep.

Felix reached out to brush aside a strand of her dark hair. "You're so beautiful."

She smiled and slowly opened her eyes. "You can stop trying so hard. I've forgiven you, even if you are seeing madmen in your sleep."

Felix tried not to think about that and determined that if he saw that assaulting rascal again he would lay him flat with one punch.

Electra reached out to touch his cheek, careful not to disturb Thespis who had, at some point in the night, started to cry and been brought into their bed. "Were you just talking about Rufio?"

"It's nothing," Felix said with a smile of his own. "I'm just…surprised at how…what's the word…*wise*, he's become."

"I'm not sure 'wise' is the word I would use," Electra said. "But he certainly is more confident than the first time I met him."

"That too."

"He is still silly though," Electra tried not to laugh, "in a most endearing kind of way."

"He is." Felix turned onto his back and looked up at the ceiling. "He always balanced me out when we were young, brought me back down to earth. And Clara, likewise, encouraged him to dream."

"And what did you do for him?"

Felix thought for a moment, feeling a little guilty that the answer did not immediately come to him. "I suppose I challenged him."

Thespis began to whine a little and turned to nuzzle his mother.

"There, there, my son. I'm here," she said as she began to suckle him. "He's growing so quickly."

Felix still stared at the ceiling. "I suppose Rufio is now challenging *me*."

"What?" Electra asked, her attention on their son.

"Does that make me the fool now?" Felix felt a prickle of panic.

"A fool wouldn't carry his pregnant wife through the streets of Delos to deliver their son the way you did. Don't you forget that, Felix Modestus."

Felix shook his head and turned to her. "I won't."

"What are the plans for the day then?" Electra asked. "Is anyone going into the city for the prize-givings and public feast?"

Felix sat up, his mind beginning to mull over the long list of final preparations. "I told the company that they could go into the city if they choose to, just that they have to be back here and sober long before the following morning."

"Ha," Electra laughed. "Maybe you are the fool to encourage them to the lupanar before tomorrow's perfor- mance. Who is going into the city then?"

"No one."

"Really?" Electra was genuinely shocked and the look upon her face said as much. "I would have thought that-"

"Nope. Not one of them wants to go to the award-giving, the public feast, or any of the other many celebrations. They asked me to do one final dress rehearsal today, and that is all. They want a day of calm before the next storm."

"Please don't tempt things, Felix. I can't weather another storm."

Felix laughed.

THE DRESS REHEARSAL LATER THAT MORNING WENT EXTREMELY well and, when it was done, the company set about packing everything up in the wagons for the journey to the odeon of Atticus in the city the following day.

After a rest, and some time in the baths for those who desired it, The Etrurian Players began to head to the triclinium for the feast that Atticus had ordered prepared for them on the eve of their performance. As they milled about, chatting with wine cups in hand, talking of how quickly their time in Athenae had passed and how wonderful it had been, Sextus approached Felix who sat alone upon one of the couches staring into the red depths of his cup.

"Are you all right, my friend?" Sextus asked as he sat down next to him.

Felix looked up and nodded, his lips pursed tightly together beneath the edge of his trimmed beard. "I think so. This city does cast a spell, doesn't it?"

"I feel it every time I come here," Sextus confirmed. "People excel here, in art, in politics… It puts one's own life into perspective."

"That is true, but I don't mean that necessarily. I mean…I feel closer to the Gods in this place. Like we are constantly being watched…judged even."

Sextus watched Felix closely. *He is still not the exceedingly confident man I thought I knew so well.* "Delos changed you."

"Yes, I suppose it did, but I've been in a constant state of change, in new territory ever since then."

"I imagine being a parent will do that." Sextus' voice was a little melancholy, but he covered it up quickly.

"I feel like Odysseus adrift, but with no home to go back to." Felix was silent for a few seconds, then shook his head and put on a smile. "Ach! I'm babbling."

"You do have a home, Felix. They are right there." Sextus nodded in the direction of Electra who was standing with Clara and Martia, holding Thespis in her arms as she stroked his cheek and talked with her friends. "Your Penelope and Telemachus go with you on your journey. That is more than Odysseus could ever have wished for."

"You grow more philosophical all the time, Sextus." Felix smiled again.

"A necessity of survival, I suppose."

Felix turned to face him. "Do you think these Athenians will truly approve of the play?"

"Does it matter?"

"I tend to think it does, yes." Felix raised an eyebrow.

"What I mean is that Terentius' work touches on themes of kindness, of parenthood, and the relationships between fathers and sons… That will make people think, in some cases, of happy memories, but also of much that is unpleasant to them. They may or may not approve of the play depending on how it makes them feel. I think the more appropriate question is, do *you* approve of the play and what you are doing with it?"

Felix nodded in thought, and when he did not speak, Sextus rose to go and sit with Martia who had settled on her couch.

The rest of the company also settled on their couches as Atticus ordered the gustatio to be brought out. The tables were quickly filled with bowls of olives, platters of cool, crisp vegetables, boiled eggs, and shellfish doused in garum, the latter a special treat.

"Oh good, more fruit from the sea," Rufio sighed as he picked up a carrot and bit into it.

"Rufio, you don't know what you're missing!" Fausto said from across the table as he made a little lagostino dance upon his plate.

Cradling Thespis as she sat on the couch beside Felix, Electra noted that everyone was looking to Felix who was taken up with looking at his son. "Maybe you should say something to everyone?" she whispered.

Felix looked up at his company and his friends. They were his familia, and he their paterfamilias. They needed words of encouragement from him. Felix stood up from the couch, his wine cup raised.

"My friends… I think that we can agree that this production has posed a bigger challenge that any of us could have imagined."

"You can say that again!" Pollux called out.

Felix put up his hand, for he needed to get through what he wanted to say to them. "But we have risen to the challenge that Apollo set for us, have we not?"

"YES!" they all said with a cheer.

"It is a good Roman play, my friends-"

"On a Greek subject matter!" Rufio added quickly.

"Eat your vegetables, Rufio!" Felix said quickly, making everyone laugh. "As I was saying… A good Roman play…and if these Athenians don't like it, then it's a tragedy of their own making."

"Heerra! Heerra!" Damon howled.

"Has Damon begun to worship Hera while we've been here?" Domela asked Julius beside her. "I never can understand him."

"He was agreeing with Felix," Julius said. "'Here! Here!' was what he said."

Fausto and Beatrice chuckled to themselves as Damon winked at Domela.

Felix set his cup down and raised both hands for silence. "We may not have been permitted to compete in the Panathenaea, but by Apollo we will not let this sacred festival peter out. Our performance will be a great punch to the gut of these Athenians so that they will never forget The Etrurian Players!"

Everyone cheered again.

"I am proud of you all, my friends," Felix added, his voice so low that nobody heard. "It has been a privilege to perform with all of you."

At the far end of the tables, when it became obvious that Felix had nothing more to say, Castor and Pollux, Damon, Fausto and Beatrice all fell into loud conversation as they ate and drank, debating the merits of each of the characters they had brought to life over the past months leading up to the morrow's performance.

Julius and Domela talked quietly, for he was protecting his voice, and she admiring his discipline in doing so while the other, younger members of the company hooted and laughed and drank.

Felix sat back down, his final words unheard by the others, except for Rufio and Clara who looked at him questioningly.

"What was that?" Rufio mouthed.

Felix waved it off and shook his head. It had not been the most rousing speech he had ever given, but it was all he had in that moment. He took Thespis into his arms, freeing Electra for a bit.

As Electra leaned to her other side to speak with Martia, and Sextus talked across the table to Clara and Rufio about the coming harvest back in Etruria, Felix sat there holding his son.

"We'll see what happens, my son. Only the Gods know for sure."

The servants cleared the platters from the gustatio and set about bringing in the prima mensa which included plates of rock eel and whole, grilled sea bream laid out upon beds of wild greens.

Rufio frowned and muttered, "Look at them! Like Suburran lupae spread out upon dirty sheets!"

A great bream head stared directly at him.

"I just can't. I–"

Just then, everyone bust out laughing and pointing at him, even as Atticus came to replace the platter before Rufio with another, bearing a mound of steaming, roasted and spiced goat's meat.

"Thank the Gods!" Rufio sighed and everyone applauded. "Now we can eat!" He turned quickly. "Atticus?"

"Yes, Rufio Pagano?"

"A platter of cheese please!" Rufio said with a smile.

"NO!" everyone cried.

Rufio began to laugh. "Got you!" He turned to his daughter. "Here, Felicia," he whispered. "Try this meat."

"She's already tried the eel, Rufio," Clara said with a smile. "She loved it."

He looked at Felicia again. She gripped the piece of goat meat, frowned as she put it to her mouth, and tossed it to Peli who lay beneath their couch and quickly gobbled it up.

The meal wore on into the evening, but eventually everyone stopped themselves well-short of their usual levels of consumption and made for their beds. One by one they left, first Clara and Electra with the children and Martia to help, then Julius and Domela, and the others until only Felix, Rufio, and Sextus were left.

"You ready for tomorrow, Rufio?" Sextus asked as he stood up and stretched.

"I think we all are...aren't we, Felix?" Rufio looked to his friend who had been relatively quiet the entire meal. "Felix?"

Felix looked up. "Oh, ah, yes. Tomorrow...yes. It'll be fine."

"Maybe you should get some sleep?" Sextus said. "I've always found that if I'm anxious or brooding, a walk through Hypnos' realm helps to revive me."

"You two go ahead. I'm going to stay up a while longer. I want to check the wagons one more time to make sure everything is ready to go to the theatre."

"If you insist," Sextus said. "I'm for bed. I need my wits about me when I deal with the Athenian politicians tomorrow. Good night, my friends."

"Good night, Sextus," Rufio said before turning back to Felix. "You want me to stay with you?" Rufio yawned. "You seem to not be...yourself. Is everything all right?"

"I'll be fine. I just need some time alone. You go ahead and get some sleep. Big day tomorrow."

Rufio nodded. "Good night, Felix."

"Good night."

When Rufio was gone, the servants set to clearing and cleaning the tables, preparing them for ientaculum the following morning.

Felix got up and went to the brazier-lit courtyard behind the kitchens. He wanted to make sure that the wagons were secure, that the trunks of costumes, the tree trunk, the freshly-cut olive branches, the amphorae and other set pieces were all packed and covered. The ring, he knew, was in Sextus' safe-keeping. Felix looked up at the moon in the sky and leaned his head against the wagon.

"Apollo, please see us through tomorrow," he prayed. "Shine your light upon us and guide us to victory, Lord, oh Divine Muses…"

Felix Modestus filled his lungs with evening air, held it, and let it out in a long, controlled breath. A part of him felt like it was his first performance again, but another part of him was world-weary, tired, and uncertain of what the next stage of his journey was. He knew he would not sleep that night, that he needed to reconnect with that part of him which he felt slipping away. "I don't like change, Rufio," he said to himself.

After a few minutes, Felix returned to the triclinium where, by the light of a few lamps that remained lit upon the table, he could see that it had already been set with pitchers of fresh mountain spring water, figs, and honey cake. Felix smiled, knowing that Atticus wanted to ensure his dominus' artistic guests were well-fed and prepared for their performance.

The performance.

Felix stood there in the semi dark thinking of all of the meals they had shared in that triclinium over the past months, the joy, the frustration, the chaos, and elation. "Why can't it all be simple?" he said to himself. *Odysseus with no home to go back to…* He remembered what he had said to Sextus. The latter had been right, of course, that his 'home' went with him everywhere. That was a blessing. However, it was nice, Felix knew, to have a place to set one's head down to rest peacefully, a place to call one's own. "Even Odysseus built his own home, his bed, about an olive tree."

He stopped suddenly and smiled to himself. "That's what I need. I good night's sleep at home." He turned and went to a table along one of the frescoed walls and there found a stack of papyrus sheets, styli, ink pots, and red ribbons. He took one of each, settled on the end couch at the tables, cleared a space, and began to write.

Felix turned to find Peli sitting still, wondering what he was doing at the table if he was not eating at it. "You hungry, boy?" Felix said, reaching out to pat Peli's furry head. He felt a little damp there and looked at his hand to see a bit of blood. "Been butting heads again with Nicodemus?" Felix looked him over closely, but Peli didn't seem to be bothered. He reached onto the table, pulled back the cloth over one of the plates, and handed Peli a piece of honey cake. "Don't tell Atticus," he whispered as Peli gobbled it up, tail wagging furiously as Felix went back to writing.

"...where I feel most at home. There. That should do it."

"Oh, I'm sorry, Felix Modestus," Atticus suddenly appeared at the doorway to the kitchen. "I thought you had gone to bed."

"Not to worry, Atticus. I am. I just wanted to make sure everything was prepared for tomorrow." Felix stroked Peli's head where it appeared at his thigh.

"I'm sure it will be a magnificent performance," Atticus smiled.

"Yes...they always are..."

"If I may, Felix Modestus..."

"What is it, Atticus?"

"Being my dominus' house steward, I have met a great

many artistic guests who have come through here. I have noticed that they all have a degree of self-doubt, even a little fear."

"Fear?" Felix asked.

"But I do not think it is a fear such as terror." Atticus came farther into the triclinium to be nearer to Felix. "It is more of a healthy awe of the gift Apollo and the Muses have blessed them with." Atticus rubbed his beard. "I have often imagined that that awe is essential to artistic success."

"How so?" Felix sat up.

Atticus shrugged. "I suppose that creating, blessing an audience with such emotional and rich experiences through art is… well…the realm of the Gods, isn't it? Without that healthy fear…that awe…it is just hubris, no?"

Felix smiled. "You're quite right, Atticus." Felix rolled up the papyrus and tied it with the red ribbon. "How many philosophers have you had as guests here?"

It was Atticus' turn to smile. "Quite a few."

"Well, I suspect that you could challenge any of them on any day."

Atticus bowed. "Thank you, Felix Modestus, but I am simply happy to set the stage where the creating takes place. It has been an honour to witness you and your company." He turned to go away and leave Felix to himself.

"Will you be coming tomorrow?"

"No. Witnessing the performance here, in this intimate setting has been joy enough for me, Felix Modestus. I'll remain here to prepare your triumphal feast." Atticus walked back into the kitchens.

Alone now with Peli, Felix held the papyrus scroll in his hands and looked down at it. "This is for the best, I think. It's the only way."

Peli looked up at him, head tilted as he looked at the rolled papyrus in Felix's hand.

"This isn't cake, you." Felix stood and placed the letter in the middle of the first table, beside the honey cake. He straighten his tunica and cingulum, then poured some water into a cup and drank before putting the stylus and ink pot back on the side table. "You going back to guard your dominus' door?" he asked Peli.

Peli whimpered and looked back at the table.

"No?" Felix stroked Peli's head. "Then sleep well and be good, our little Cerberus." Felix stood tall, breathed deeply, and left the triclinium. "Good boy," he said over his shoulder as he left.

Peli watched Felix leave and, after a couple of seconds, the canine turned back to the table which he approached like the most cunning of burglars, set his forelegs upon the edge, and stretched his furry neck to retrieve another piece of honey cake which he ate on the spot. A second helping followed that. In the midst of his third morsel, his attentions were distracted by the papyrus scroll, for it reminded Peli of the sticks which Rufio threw for him, and which he would sit chewing upon in the warm sunlight of home. Those memories in mind, Peli snatched the papyrus from off the table and disappeared into the villa.

Felix walked quietly through the villa Atticus, careful not to wake anyone. He arrived at the main courtyard beyond the atrium, his feet crunching on the stones on his way to the gate. There, he found one of the servants sleeping to one side.

When the man heard Felix approach, he roused himself. "Oh! Forgive me, Felix Modestus! You surprised me."

"Please open the gate," Felix said.

"You are going out?" the young man asked. "What of the Nymphs, Satyrs and shades that roam the wood? You may not come back?"

"That is always a possibility, I suppose," Felix said. "I may even meet Calypso herself." He winked.

"Sir?"

"Just open the gate, lad."

"Yes, Felix Modestus." The young man lifted the oak beam that barred the gate, set it down, and swung one side of the doors open a little.

"You can bar it behind me," Felix said as he stepped out and onto the road.

"Ye…yes, Felix Modestus."

Felix heard the gates barred behind him. He stood in the middle of the road and looked up at the brilliance of that Attic night sky pocked with constellations. He could see Hercules there, wrestling the dragon, Ladon, in the garden of the Hesperides. Felix smiled to himself. "Fitting."

He sighed, looking back a last time at the villa walls, and then began to walk, disappearing into the darkness and down the road through the forest.

THE DAY OF THE PERFORMANCE ARRIVED WITH A CHORUS OF birdsong as the first rays of Helios' fiery chariot breached the peaks of Hymettos, a cue for the first of the cicadas who still serenaded the hot days of summer in Athenae.

There was an air of excitement in the villa, a nervousness waiting to be unleashed as, in the various cubicula of the villa, the members of The Etrurian Players were roused by their personal creative daemons who tickled and tantalized their minds and hearts with thoughts of the performance to come. Would they remember their lines? Would they be funny enough? Would the audience in the cavia smile and laugh, or frown and boo? The chaos of a performance was something that could not be anticipated, for it was all too fluid, too dependent on a great many variables. All each player could do was their utmost with the skills they possessed. The performance was not until evening, but for the company of Felix Modestus, the warmup began early on the day of a performance.

RUFIO LAY ABED STARING AT THE CEILING AS CLARA FED Felicia, smiling sidelong at her husband.

"You aren't going anywhere are you?" Clara said.

Rufio turned. "Not this time," he replied with a grin.

"You ready for this?"

"As ready as I can be." He shrugged as if it did not matter so much, but inside he thought of Terentius and his - the shade's that is - pleas for release. "I'll just do my best."

"Well, in my experience, your best is quite astounding, my love."

Rufio took Clara's hand and kissed it. "What about you?"

"I'm going to enjoy it. I don't have that many lines. I'm more worried about the children keeping quiet backstage, but Martia is going to help with that. She's so kind."

"She is. She and Sextus are wonderful people. They really would make wonderful parents were they so blessed."

"I know," Clara said sadly. "Some things are not meant to be, I suppose."

Just then, the sound of vocal exercises and singing rose up from the courtyard below. A flute was added to the mix, and the villa was filled with a lively morning chorus to match the birds upon the mountainside.

"I guess everyone is awake," Rufio said as he sat up and took a deep breath. He looked over his shoulder at Clara. "Shall we?"

Clara raised Felicia and smiled at her. "What do you say, my girl? Shall we get your pater to the theatre on time?"

Felicia smiled and belched.

"I take that as a 'yes'," Rufio laughed.

. . .

THE SOUND OF THE COMPANY WARMING UP WOKE ELECTRA. SHE and Thespis had slept ever-so-soundly, so when she heard the warm-up, she rose with an unpleasant jolt.

As if feeling his mother's sudden panic, young Thespis set to stretching his own vocal chords in such a way that even the furniture would be roused.

"Oh, Thespis, not now!" Electra said as she went to his crib. "I know, I know… You've slept so long, good boy, and now you're hungry. Just please stop screeching so."

Once Thespis was feeding, his frenzy was reduced to a quiet murmur of satisfaction as Electra settled herself upon the bed, leaning against the pillows. She began to run over her lines in her mind, how she envisioned her performance. She tried to connect with Bacchis, the demanding courtesan she was to bring to life. "Apollo, bless this day," Electra prayed.

But then she turned to look at the other side of the bed, and noted that Felix had not slept there.

"That man! Again he's drunk himself to the floor downstairs!" Electra rose awkwardly up from the bed, Thespis still stuck to her breast. She marched over to the cubiculum door and opened it. "Felix!" she shouted down into the courtyard. "Felix Modestus, come up here at once!" Leaving the door slightly ajar, she went back into the cubiculum muttering. "Always running off, leaving me alone in bed now. What ever happened to our pre-performance lovemaking? I'll have to reinstate that!" She covered Thespis' ears.

When Thespis finished eating, Electra set him in his crib and slid a tunica over her head.

Felix had still not arrived.

"Felix!" she shouted.

"Electra?" Martia appeared at the door, already dressed in a beautiful green stola. "Is everything all right?"

"No," Electra replied. "I've overslept, I'm not ready, and Thespis needs changing. *And* my husband did not come to bed last night!"

"That's strange. Sextus did say that he left Felix in the triclinium last night. Maybe he fell asleep there? You go and have a look, and I will change Thespis for you. All right?"

Electra sighed and hugged her. "Thank you. I'll be right back!"

"Go, my dear. I'm sure Felix is somewhere in the villa, up early and excited for the day!"

Electra went out, still barefoot, wearing only a loose, white tunica. "Felix!" she called as she walked down the stairs.

"Electra?" Clara said as she emerged from their cubiculum, followed by Rufio who carried Felicia. "What's wrong?"

"Felix didn't come to bed last night," Electra said as the rest of the company watched her.

The Etrurian Players had all risen early to eat and gather in the courtyard of the peristylium to go through some vocal exercises, enjoying the food and spring water which Atticus had set out in the triclinium, but which they preferred to enjoy in the open air.

Electra turned to face all of them. "Castor, Pollux? Have you seen Felix today?"

The two brothers shrugged.

More panicked now, she turned to Julius and Domela, Beatrice and Fausto. "Have any of you seen or heard him?"

They shook their heads, and Julius rose from his seat to go to her. "He's probably checking the wagons again, my dear. Don't fret. Please, eat something. You have your own exercises to go through before the performance."

"I know, but we need to find him first." She raised her head. "Felix!"

The rest of the company followed suit, Castor, Pollux,

Damon and Fausto running in different directions throughout the villa.

"Felix!" they called, their voices echoing every which way. "Felix Modestus!"

It was then that Atticus arrived, a little breathless. "Lady Electra," he puffed, his brow sweaty.

The others returned to the courtyard then as well.

"We can't find him!" Castor said.

"He's not here!" Fausto added.

"Where's Felix?" Sextus said from the top of the stairs as he and Martia came down with Thespis.

Clara turned to them. "We can't find him."

"What?" Sextus rubbed his face and turned to Atticus. "Did any of the servants see him?"

"That is what I came to tell you," Atticus said. "Last night, I found Felix Modestus sitting in the triclinium alone…well… not alone…he fed that naughty dog my honey cake!"

Rufio looked down at Peli who sat beside him.

Atticus continued. "He was writing a letter on papyrus."

"A letter to whom, Atticus?" Sextus asked.

"I don't know, Praetor. But I did hear him say something about 'where he most feels at home'. I didn't know what he meant by it. It's not my place to pry. However, I was just told by the young man who guarded the gate last night that…" Atticus paused, as if trying to rally his courage.

"Spit it out, man!" Sextus urged.

"What is it, Atticus?" Electra said evenly as she approached the trembling steward.

"He…the lad, said that Felix Modestus went out the gate in the middle of the night. He did not return."

"WHAT?" Electra grabbed the hem of Atticus' tunica. "Do not play with me, little man. I'm in no mood for it!"

Rufio raised an eyebrow to Clara who rushed forward to extricate Atticus from Electra's grasp.

Atticus mumbled now. "I...I thought he might have come back in through the servants' gate at the back, but he is nowhere to be found. Not in the baths, not by the wagons."

"He's abandoned me!" Electra raged and was about to tear at her cheeks like Medea in a rage, but Clara, now helped by Julius, held her fast.

"Hold on now!" Sextus said, stepping into the company's midst. "What might he have meant by where he feels 'most at home'?"

"The brothel?" Fausto ventured.

"That's where *you* feel at home, idiot," Beatrice said, slapping his shoulder.

"Tab...tab...taberna!" Damon added with a stutter.

"No, no. He much prefers the wine here! Great wine, Atticus!" Pollux said.

"Thank you, master Pollux," Atticus replied with a quick bow of the head.

"Does he have a rich mistress here in Athenae?" Beatrice asked, getting her a vicious glare from Electra. "I mean...you know...there was that one time in Tyre when-"

"I'm sure that's not helping, Beatrice," Clara said quickly, cutting her off before Electra rushed her.

Everyone started throwing out ideas, but the more guesses they ventured, the more flustered Electra became. The children began to cry, and Atticus looked near to being overwhelmed by panic.

In the chaos, Clara looked back at Rufio. "What are we going to do?" she asked him.

Rufio rubbed his face as if to wake himself. Then, with a determined look, he shouted. "All right! Here's what we're going to do!"

Everyone quieted down and turned toward him.

"I'm going to go and look for him. I'll find him, and make sure he is at the theatre on time!"

"How?" Sextus said.

"I just will." Rufio looked down at his canine companion. "Peli will help me. The rest of you get ready. Do everything you would do anyway were Felix here. Bring the wagons and everything to the theatre as soon as you can and begin the setup so that we're ready well before the performance."

"What if you don't find him?" Electra asked.

Rufio looked around the company's faces and came to rest on Sextus. "Then Sextus will step in for Felix."

There was silence.

Sextus gasped and shook his head. "I...I couldn't, Rufio. No. It's not fitting for a Roman praetor to be upon the stage. Investing, yes. Acting, no. It can't be done."

"It can if we put a beard and makeup on you!" Beatrice added quickly.

Rufio smiled. "Yes! You know the lines, don't you?"

"Well...yes...I do, but-"

"Perfect!" Rufio said. "While the others are getting ready to leave, you can go over the lines one more time to make sure."

Sextus looked as though he wanted to run for it, but then, upon seeing all of the faces of the actors he so admired looking at him, pleading with him for help, something came over him. A bright determination filled his eyes and he stood taller. He looked at Martia and she nodded.

"You can do it, my love," she said to him.

"Very well! I'll do it for all of you!" Sextus said before turning to Rufio. "But please do try and find Felix, will you?"

"I will!" Rufio said. "Fausto? Toss me one of those pieces of honey cake. I faint without ientaculum!"

Fausto lobbed the largest piece he could find and Rufio caught it and took a bite.

"I'll see you at the theatre!" Rufio said before turning to kiss Clara.

"Good luck," she whispered to him.

"With you and Felicia, I don't need luck." He turned to leave. "Let's go, Peli!" Rufio called and the two of them rushed from the courtyard leaving the rest of the company dumbfounded at the unimaginable turn of events, wondering how they would ever succeed in their labour without their Hercules.

XVIII

FINDING FELIX

The morning was indeed beautiful, the sun warm and bright, the air scented with pine and wild thyme, the sky a brilliant blue that made one want to lay down and gaze upon it. But all of this was tainted by panic as Rufio raced downhill from the villa, Peli cantering beside him the way he did in flowering fields back home.

This was not, however, a calm Etrurian morning in which they ambled along the loamy furrows of Rufio's fields. It was Athenae, on the day of their performance, and the reason for their being there that the star of their company had inexplicably gone missing.

"What is he thinking?" Rufio huffed aloud as he and Peli came to the bottom of the hill and turned left to run past the stadium which was strangely quiet now that the games were finished. "Surely you can sniff him out!" he told his four-legged search companion. "What's that snout for if you can't?"

Peli barked, tongue lolling as he enjoyed the run with his dominus.

Rufio shook his head and slowed as he came to the bridge near the Porta Hadriana. A little breathless, he passed the shrine on the left and stopped when the guard, Arcas, approached him.

The man eyed Peli who went and pissed at the side of the

road on the plinth of a statue of Emperor Hadrianus that stood there. "You know, if I were in a worse mood, I'd give you a fine for all the urine your dog has sprayed on Athenae. He's turning the monuments yellow!"

Rufio gulped a little at the armour-chested commander of the gate. "I do apologize, Arcas."

When Rufio spoke his name, the man calmed slightly. "It's good you're guests of the Atticus family. They paid for the monument. And a lot of other things in the city," he muttered.

Rufio shook his head. "There's no time for that now. I have a problem."

"Don't we all."

"No. I mean a big problem."

"Is someone murdered?"

"No."

"A ransom demand? Those mountain shepherds can never be trusted. They get these ideas and-"

"No. Nothing like that. But someone has gone missing!" Rufio spread his arms wide as if trying to scare off an Arcadian bear in the woods.

"Who?"

"*The* Felix Modestus!"

"Isn't he supposed to perform today?" Arcus rested casually upon his pilum as if discussing the weather.

"Yes, yes he is! But he's missing! Disappeared! Vanished as if some forest nymph abducted him in the night!"

Arcas smiled. "Well…there are worse things."

"I need to find him."

Arcas smiled. "Calm yourself."

"Why? Why should I calm myself when we're supposed to take the stage in a few hours?"

"You performing as well?" There was doubt in Arcas' voice.

"Yes! But no one will be performing anything unless I find Felix Modestus!"

"*The* Felix Modestus," Arcas confirmed.

"Yes! He's missing!" Rufio wanted to punch the man, but did not relish going back to prison.

"No, he's not."

"He's not what?"

"He's not missing."

"You've seen him?" Rufio's eyes popped wide, but he was distracted by Peli who was barking furiously from the verge off the road where the trees stretched out along the shore of the Ilissos river. "Peli, shut up!" Rufio turned back to Arcas.

The guard nodded toward Peli. "He pisses a lot and has a fornication problem, but-"

"Felix…please, just tell me where he is if you've seen him."

"I'm trying to, little man. I was talking about your dog. He's got the scent it seems. One of my men saw *The* Felix Modestus go that way in the middle of the night. My man said he warned him against it at that hour, but he was determined."

"That way?" Rufio pointed.

"Yes," Arcas confirmed, his helmet's crest shivering as he nodded.

"Thank you!" Rufio shot off after Peli and the two of them disappeared into the trees.

"Romans," Arcas muttered as he went back to his men.

Rufio raced after Peli, beneath the soaring branches of pine and plane trees, the ground speckled with sunlight at their feet as though they raced across a mosaic of gold and green.

"Vipere!" Rufio shouted as he jumped, narrowly missing an asp that was sunning itself. "Felix!" he shouted. "Where in Hades are you? We've got a show to put on!"

No answer came, but Rufio and Peli carried on running,

eyes searching along the riverbank, among the trees and inside the entrances of the temples of Chronos and Rhea.

But he was not there.

Rufio came to a stop at last outside of the temple of Apollo Delphinios. He leaned upon one of the altars outside, gasping as he tried to catch his breath. "Why can't a day here start normally?"

Peli meanwhile ranged about the temple and then mounted the steps, barking.

In front of the open doors of the temple, the resident snake lay stretched out, its head somewhere around the corner to the left.

"Leave that snake alone, Peli!" Rufio coughed. "He's big enough to eat you, and then where would we be?"

Peli persisted in trying to get through the doors, and pawed at the serpent's tail until it started to move on. He then disappeared into the temple.

Rufio followed.

It was dark inside but for the light cast by a three-headed bronze lamp with crows, the birds of Apollo, upon it.

"Peli!" Rufio hissed as he walked up the aisle of the cella toward the main altar.

Suddenly, Peli popped up on the other side of the altar, his paws upon the marble edge, his nose sniffing at a scrap of paper among the offerings laid out to Apollo Delphinios.

"What are you doing? Get down from there!"

"Your friend was here earlier."

"AAAH!" Rufio shouted and spun at the voice behind him, his hands grasping at the altar and, in doing so, knocking the still, white body of a dove from off the surface.

Peli promptly grabbed the avian offering and was about to leave when the newcomer stepped in front of him. "Smart dog."

Rufio still struggled in open-mouthed silence as Peli, frozen to the spot, looked up at the rough-looking man and dropped the offering at his feet.

"You?" Rufio stuttered. "But how? Why?"

"I do hope you write better than you speak."

Rufio screwed up his face and stood up from his panicked perch upon the altar's edge. "Terentius?"

The shade nodded. "Who else?"

"Well… I mean. You could have been any number of other people…those that are *living* in particular!"

"You going to put that back?" Terentius nodded at the dove upon the floor, frozen there like a still life painted upon a villa wall.

Without taking his eyes off of the shade, Rufio bent down to retrieve it and set it back upon the altar. "Forgive my dog, Lord Apollo, for he knows not what he does." Rufio looked at Peli who still stared at the shade and then retreated behind Rufio's legs.

"He knows what he is doing…" the shade smiled. "Like I said…smart dog."

"For stealing from Apollo? I don't think so." Rufio looked down at Peli. "No cena for you today!"

"Not the bird. The parchment."

Rufio was confused for a moment, but then remembered the scrap of papyrus which Peli had been sniffing at. He turned and picked it up from the altar. "'Forgive me for doubting.' Who wrote this?"

"Did you not hear me? Your friend was here earlier."

"Felix?" Rufio looked at the parchment. "No. He's left us? Is that it? He's asking Apollo for forgiveness? Oh, Gods! He's left us!"

Rufio's heart began to race.

"But you are performing my play today!" The shade was suddenly flustered, wide-eyed and sweating, a sight which Rufio wished he did not have to see. "You must find him!"

"Why do you think I'm here?" Rufio snapped back. "I mean…Felix has been acting strangely, but I never thought that he would…I mean…he's never quit anything in his entire life!"

"You didn't suspect? I thought you were smart."

"Easy, you!" Rufio pointed at the shade. "Just cause you're dead…"

"And you are human, and all that is human should concern you."

"Don't quote yourself," Rufio said. "It's desperate."

"The words are worth repeating." The shade, Terentius that is, shook his strangely life-like head of unkept hair. "How did you know to come looking for your friend?"

"The…ah…the house steward…Atticus, he said he overheard Felix say that he was going to where he *feels most at home*."

"And where is that?"

"He lives in Ephesus! How should I know?"

"Because he's your friend!"

"Don't shout!" Rufio chided him. "It's strange when you do it."

Terentius crossed his arms and stared unnervingly at the mortal man before him. "You're thinking too literally. Where, or with whom, does he feel most at home…comfortable… safe…free to be himself."

"Well, with his wife and child, but he left them to go to…" Rufio's thoughts trailed away, and he looked from Peli to Terentius, the shade's eyes wide. "The theatre."

The shade nodded. "I watched him come alive when he rehearsed my prologus."

"He's in the odeon!" Rufio said. He then turned quickly to face the altar and statue of Apollo behind it. "Lord Apollo… please smile upon our production this day. Let Felix be here, I pray!" Rufio then turned and ran out of the temple. "Peli, come!"

Peli shot after Rufio more to flee the shade than to follow his dominus.

"I'm coming too!" Terentius called after them, following with a strange speed.

Rufio and Peli shot up the stairs to the titanic platform where the Olympieion rose up to the sky upon its forest of Corinthian columns. They raced across the court surrounding the temple, making their way for the arch of Hadrianus.

The faithful were already lined up to make their offerings in the temple, and they watched as the strange Roman charged across the courtyard, a dog at his heels, as he looked back and shouted to no-one behind them.

"Come on then!" Rufio shouted.

The people in line watched as the man and dog raced, both of them looking behind at nothing.

"Romans!" said a grumpy older man in a long chiton.

"Too many of them in Athenae now," said another.

Rufio did not hear them for his breathing was rapid as he ran, his heart pounding furiously in his chest. Sweat poured from his forehead in that summer heat as he barrelled through the arch of Hadrianus in the direction of the Acropolis.

"You have to see the play through!" Terentius shouted after Rufio.

"Quiet!" Rufio snapped over his shoulder. "If we don't, you'll just have to stay put here in Athenae!"

The shade wailed as it ran, and Rufio felt a chill. "This is not happening!"

"Rufio Pagano!" someone shouted from the steps of the stoa of Eumenes to his right.

A group of men stood around holding prop phalluses over their shoulders like shovels or spades, joking and laughing.

Cassius Cantor stepped out from among them, his the

largest of the props, and waved it at Rufio to stop. "What are you running for?"

"I'm looking for Felix!" Rufio slid to a halt to catch his breath. "Have you seen him?"

Cassius Cantor looked back at the rest of The Rome Antics. "Seen him? You saying he's missing?"

"Yes!"

Peli started barking at the monkey, Momo, who retreated to the shoulders of Cassius' man, Numa.

"Peli, stop!" Rufio said, seeing Terentius come up to stand beside him. Rufio gulped.

"Who are these fools?" the shade said, but Rufio did not respond.

"Rufio?" Cassius said again. "What do you mean, Felix is missing? Today's the performance!"

"Yes, I know, Cassius!" Rufio wiped the sweat from his face. "We woke up this morning and he was gone!"

Cassius Cantor looked at his men, and then back at Rufio. "This isn't good. We'll split up. There are ten of us. We can help you search."

"I'm going to the odeon now," Rufio said.

"Good," Cassius replied. "I'll search the Pnyx. Numa, you and Piso search the new agora. Carmine and Cato the old agora. Lycus, you and Julio head for the Taberna Thesias and ask Boreas if he's seen Felix. Remus, you and Vito head for Circe's and check with all of the girls to see if he's popped in to see any of them."

Remus and Vito smiled, but Cassius snapped his fingers in their faces. "No quickies! This is an emergency!"

Rufio looked at Cassius, confused by this sudden willingness to help.

"What?" Cassius shrugged. "We need to stick together, Rufio Pagano. Nothing can stop the play!"

"Perhaps I misjudged this fool after all," Terentius whispered to Rufio who waved at his own ear as though a fly were buzzing in it.

Cassius clapped his hands. "Get to it!"

The Rome Antics and their phalluses scattered every which way, and Rufio, Peli, and the shade of the playwright continued along the stoa toward the odeon of Herodes Atticus.

RUFIO AND PELI BURST THROUGH THE GREAT ARCHES OF THE odeon stopping suddenly as their eyes adjusted to the dark and Rufio caught his breath again.

"Who are you?" the caretaker, Cosmo, shouted at them, his voice echoing to the ceiling of the stagehouse. He stood from his table, a small club in his hand.

"I'm…Rufio…Pagano. I'm with The Etrurian Players."

"You aren't on until later today."

"I know. I'm…I'm just looking for Felix Modestus."

"*The* Felix Modestus," Terentius whispered.

"*The* Felix Modestus," Rufio repeated, looking askance at the shrugging shade. "Have you seen him?"

Cosmo set his club down and crossed his arms. "Big, strong fellow?"

"Yes."

"Tidy beard, good hair?"

"Yes, I suppose."

"The one folks are calling 'Hercules'?"

"All right," Rufio said. "Yes. And I'm Iolaus."

The caretaker scoffed. "No you're not."

"I am!" Rufio protested, but then put up his hands. "Have you seen Felix…or Hercules?"

"Yes."

"Yes?"

"That's what I said. Yes." Cosmo tilted his head backward toward the darkness beyond the torches. "He's in the odeon. Slept most of the night on the boards of the pulpitum."

Rufio charged past the caretaker, grabbed a torch, and went into the odeon followed by Peli and the shade.

IT WAS DARK IN THE ODEON, THE HIGH ROOFTOP LIKE THE ABYSS of a night sky absent its stars. There was a scent of burning frankincense, and the gentle, flowing sound of a man breathing in deep sleep.

As Rufio stepped onto the boards of the stage from the left doorway of the scaena frons, the light of the torch spread out like a rising sun until it revealed the sleeping form.

Peli walked hesitantly to where Felix slept in the middle of the pulpitum, sniffed the familiar person, and turned to face Rufio. His back leg twitched a little.

"Peli, no!" Rufio chided as quietly as he could, showing the canine the surface of his hand, an indication of the things to come if he woke Felix in such a way.

Peli lowered his leg, looked once at Felix, and descended the stairs leading from the pulpitum to the orchestra. He ranged about the altar of Apollo and Dionysus where the burning remains of an offering smouldered.

"You should have let the dog wake him thus," the shade said to Rufio. "*That* would have been funny!"

"Shhh, you!" Rufio said to Terentius.

The shade shrugged and walked to the edge of the pulpitum to look out at the seating of the cavia all around. "It's beautiful…"

Rufio knelt down beside Felix, holding the torch out and away from his sleeping friend. "Felix?" he whispered, reaching out to touch his friend's shoulder. "Felix Modestus."

Felix's breathing changed slightly, but the smile with which he had been sleeping remained, shortening but a little out of confusion as his eyes opened to see Rufio standing above him.

"Futuo, Felix," Rufio said, a little angry to see him so calm, for a small part of him had hoped to find Felix in crisis. "You have the entire company in a panic!"

Felix rubbed his eyes, his full smile returned, and pushed himself up. "I haven't slept that well since we've been here." He stretched.

"I need to light the torches!" Cosmo muttered as he entered one of the second storey doorways that led to the cavia from the right wing of scaena frons. "Your people arriving soon, Hercules?" he called out with not a little sarcasm.

"Soon enough!" Felix called back to the old man. "Cerberus guarding the gates to our Underworld, he is."

"Never mind that, you shit!" Rufio was no longer whispering. "We all thought that you abandoned us! Sextus is even preparing to do your part!"

"Sextus?" Now Felix was on his feet. "He's not up to it!"

"Well, he was ready in order to save the company in your absence."

"But I didn't leave!" Felix protested. "I knew I needed some sleep if I were to perform to my usual, excellent standard. I checked the wagons one more time and came directly here. Well…here, after I made an offering to Apollo at the temple."

The odeon grew bright then as the torches were all lit by Cosmo about the top tier of the cavia, the marble seating coming alive in veined shades of white and grey.

Peli barked, and it echoed throughout the theatre.

"By Apollo, Felix," Rufio said. "How were we to know all of this? You have no idea of the panic you've caused. And Electra! Well, I'd cover my bollocks if I were you, cause she'll have them for ientaculum if you're not careful!"

"What are you talking about?" Now Felix's smile was gone. "I told you where I went."

"How in Hades did you do that?"

"I left you all a note!"

"What, the one in the temple? The one that says 'forgive me for doubting…'?" Rufio poked Felix in the chest. "How were we supposed to find that?"

Felix shook his head. "Not that note! The one I left on the table in the triclinium."

"There was no note in the triclinium!"

"Oh yes there was! I wrote it on a piece of papyrus and tied it with a red ribbon!"

Rufio dismissed that with a wave of his hand and crossed his arms. "What red ribbon? What note?"

Peli barked at the two arguing men from the orchestra just below the pulpitum and they both looked at him.

"*That* red ribbon," Felix muttered as he pointed to the steaming pile of cacare which Peli had just deposited, and from which trailed a soiled red ribbon.

"Hey, *Hercules!* You going to clean that up?" Cosmo shouted as he lit the last torch. "These aren't the stables of Augeas! It's an odeon, and you have a show to put on!"

Felix waved to him and turned to Rufio. "He's your dog. You're cleaning that up."

Rufio sighed.

"You should use that!" Terentius said as he turned his attention from the cavia to the two mortal men. "Very funny!"

Felix turned suddenly, seeing him for the first time, and recognized him. "YOU!" He suddenly charged Terentius, a great fist lashing out for his face, only to fly from off the edge of the pulpitum into the orchestra, narrowly missing Peli's deposit. "Come back here!"

"Felix, calm down!" Rufio said. "He's been helping us!"

"Helping? That's the mad man who attacked me in the villa the other night!"

Rufio turned to the shade. "Why would you do that?"

"He needed a good slap to snap out of his stupor."

From the left wing of the scaena frons, the caretaker looked on as the two men seemed to be having a three-way conversation, both of them speaking in turn to an empty space upon the stage. He shook his head and went back into the stagehouse. "Actors," he muttered.

"Who is this vagrant?" Felix demanded, looking over the dirty, torn homespun tunica.

Rufio sighed. "Felix Modestus…meet Terentius, or rather the numina that was him."

The shade bowed and wiggled his ink-stained fingers at Felix. "Free me, Felix Modestus," Terentius said, his eyes wild. "Free me by putting on the performance of your life!"

Felix's face was ashen, his eyes wide. "Oh…Athenae…" he whispered before fainting into the shit at the foot of the altar.

"A red ribbon," Terentius smiled.

Rufio looked at him. "Did you have to?"

At that moment, there was a loud voice coming from the stagehouse.

"Rufio Pagano! We can't find Felix!" Cassius Cantor burst onto the scene and stopped. "He's nowhere to be seen!"

"I've got him!" Rufio called out as Cassius skidded to a halt at the edge of the pulpitum. "You can call off the search."

"Ach!" Cassius put his hand over his mouth when he spotted Felix face down in shite. "Who dares to assault our Hercules in such a way?"

Rufio looked at the shade standing above him and shook his head. "It's a long story. Please Cassius. Get some water and rags so I can clean him up."

Cassius Cantor nodded. "I'll grab some skinos perfume too. He's going to need it!" He ran off through the middle door of the scaena frons.

Rufio helped Felix up. The latter groaned and made to put

his hand to his face, but Rufio stopped him. "Oh, I would wait if I were you, Felix."

"Oh, my head…" He sniffed then. "Gwrra!"

"Gwrra!" Rufio echoed.

They both looked up at the shade who looked down at them from the pulpitum, his countenance laughing and wild. "Do you start every performance like this?" Terentius asked.

Felix looked hopefully to Rufio. "Please tell me this is a very bad dream."

"All right. It is."

"Really?"

"No, Felix. And we're going on in a few hours."

Cassius Cantor returned a short time later with two buckets of water from a nearby fountain, clean rags, a bottle of skinos perfume as promised, as well as a loaf of bread and some dried meat for Felix to eat.

"You look hungry," he said as he set the items down on the pulpitum, wrinkling his nose as he caught a whiff of the air about Felix.

"Not a word of this to anyone, Cassius," Felix threatened.

Cassius put his hand over his mouth. "I promise. Not a peep."

Rufio came over to get the water and rags. "Cassius, can you keep an eye out for the rest of the company? They should be arriving soon with the wagons and they don't know that we've found Felix."

"Happy to help, Rufio Pagano!" Cassius turned to go, but before he disappeared again, he turned back to Felix. "I won't say a thing, but… I may ask your permission to use this in a new skit for The Rome Antics. I can see it now! A great battle…but with pillows that are…stuffed with faeces! I'll call it *The Pillow Fight!*"

"Get out!" Felix roared.

"*Cacare for a Cushion?*"

"Futuere, you panto-fool!" Felix shouted.

Cassius smiled. "I'll take that as a 'yes'!" he said as he ran off.

THEY MANAGED TO GET FELIX CLEANED UP AND SMELLING LIKE a Chian mastic farmer in no time, and a good thing too, for shortly thereafter a great chorus of concerned voices erupted from behind the scaena frons as The Etrurian Players arrived through the arches of the stagehouse with the wagons.

Felix heard them and looked around for the shade. "Is he still here?" he whispered to Rufio, his eyes darting like a cat in a room full of shadows.

"No. He disappeared when Cassius returned."

"Good. I mean… Rufio, I don't know what's going on, but your madness is rubbing off on me, I think."

"Don't worry about that. You've got more immediate concerns, don't you think?" Rufio nodded back over his shoulder.

"WHERE IS HE?" Electra's voice penetrated every corner of the vast odeon such that even the torches seemed to flicker.

"I think they're here," Rufio said to Felix as the two of them chewed on bread and meat where they sat on the edge of the pulpitum.

Felix sighed and pushed himself to his feet on the wooden boards behind him. "Here we go."

Electra emerged from the middle of the three arches that led onto the pulpitum and made directly for Felix. Her hair was already done, half-transformed into the courtesan, Bacchis, with dark, oiled herringbone braids that joined at the back to trickle down her long neck like the Caryatids upon the Acropolis. Silver thread ran through them, glinting in the firelight. Her makeup had not yet beed applied, for she was sweating in her rage on the journey into the city.

Behind her, the rest of the company arrived and spread out, all of them staring at Felix, Rufio, and Peli who sat upon the newly scrubbed bit of the orchestra.

"You!" Electra pointed at her husband, and the anger and worry in her dark eyes gave even him pause. "I've had enough of your antics. I thought you a man, not a coward!"

The company gasped, but said nothing, for they too had been beside themselves with worry.

Sextus stood beside Martia who was holding Thespis for Electra. The praetor looked supremely relieved that they had found Felix, but the tension in the theatre was as palpable as the fog about Rome on a late winter morning.

"Electra, let me explain before you fly off on a harpy tangent." He caught her hand just short of his cheek and held her wrist fast. "Will you listen, woman?"

"I'm done listening!" she turned away, but then back again, her face in his. "Do you know what you've done to me, to all of us? We thought that you had finally cracked. We thought that you had left us, abandoned us because you're too afraid of the Athenian crowd."

"Is that what you think?" Felix said slowly, crossing his arms.

"Am I wrong?"

"I'm here, aren't I?" Felix puffed out his chest and looked at all of the members of his company. "Did you all doubt me so easily?"

They were silent for a few seconds before Pollux dared to speak. "Well…you have been acting a bit strangely lately."

"We've been worried for you, Felix," Julius added. "You've not been yourself."

Felix paced, nodding. "It's true. I've not been myself. But that's not because I was contemplating abandoning all of you, or that I'm losing my wits." *I don't think I'll mention seeing shades, though!* "But I have changed, it's true. Change is inevitable in all of us. Since I've known each of you, I've seen change in all of you. I've realized that it is not a bad thing to evolve as people, the same way that our art evolves. We are risk-takers, are we not? We do what very few others dare to!"

The company stepped forward, their eyes wide, the beginning of smiles upon their lips.

"We open our hearts so that the world might feel. And this play…this play excels in that. We are the only company that can successfully help the audience feel what Terentius wanted to relate."

"That still doesn't excuse the fact that you left us without a word!" Electra said.

"Erm," Rufio stepped forward. "It turns out that he did tell us."

"What are you saying?" Electra looked down at Rufio from the pulpitum.

"Felix did not abandon us. He actually left us a note."

"What note?" Electra demanded.

"Well," Rufio continued, "there was a note. He left it on the table in the triclinium, but someone ate it before we found it." Rufio nodded to the dog at his side.

"The dog ate it?" Electra scoffed. "Do you think I'm stupid, Rufio Pagano?"

"No, Electra. I certainly do not. I think Peli naughty and hungry all at once."

"How can you be sure he ate it?" Clara asked, coming to stand beside Electra.

"Well… We found the red ribbon that Felix had tied about it and-"

"Where?" Electra asked.

"Let's just say that we should all be so fortunate in our digestive functions." Rufio pinched his nose.

"Ahh!" Castor and Pollux echoed.

Peli barked.

Electra looked from the dog to her husband. "Is this true?"

"Yes, love." Felix smiled.

"You weren't fleeing my bed?"

"I'm not a madman. I just needed to focus on this place." Felix turned around. "This magnificent place." When he turned back, Electra was standing right in front of him. She kissed him and he could feel her breathing begin to calm.

"Don't do it again," she said.

Martia approached with Thespis, and Felix turned to take him in his arms.

"Ba-ba!" Thespis said, most unexpectedly to Felix.

Felix's eyes popped. "What did he say?"

Electra sighed. "Yes. His first word is 'Baba'. He's been saying it all morning, as if he had joined the search for you."

"My little man!" Felix held Thespis up and smiled at him wildly, making the babe giggle so that the joyous sound echoed about the odeon.

"Felix?" Sextus stepped forward. "If I may…we have a performance to prepare for. Am I correct in assuming the play is going ahead?"

Felix Modestus looked over his company, and their eager, sweaty faces. "Yes!"

They all cheered at that.

"Athenians, brace yourselves!" Fausto shouted. "The Etrurian Players are here!"

Another cheer rose up to the cedar rafters.

"Let's unload the wagons and set our stage!" Felix declared, and everyone set to work. Before joining the others, he took Electra aside, one arm holding their son, the other drawing her near. "I want you to know that I will never leave you. I love you." He looked at his son whose big eyes went from one to the other of them. "I love you both more than I can say."

Electra seemed to transform from a harpy to Venus herself before his eyes as she leaned in to kiss him again. "What's that smell?"

"Skinos, apparently. Do you like it?"

"Yes, I do. But there's something unpleasant behind it."

Felix looked around. "Let's help the others."

THE COMPANY MADE THEIR PREPARATIONS WITH EFFICIENT haste over the next couple of hours. While they set up their props within the great odeon, in the street outside Cassius Cantor and The Rome Antics entertained and distracted the gathering crowds with a somewhat brazen pantomime entitled *The Syrian Woman*, in which a queen continuously beat and executed a group of Praetorian guardsmen. It did not go unnoticed that the woman and lead Praetorian were meant to resemble Empress Julia Domna and Gaius Fulvius Plautianus, the expired Prefect of the Praetorian Guard.

"My fellow players!" Cassius came into the stagehouse sweating and puffing beneath his gaudy imperial dress. "We have them distracted so as to buy you more time in your preparations!"

"Cassius, what are you doing?" Felix asked as he heaved a prop amphora from off one of the wagons.

"Just a little performance of *The Syrian Woman* which I wrote earlier this year. They love it! Can't stop laughing!"

"I'll bet," Rufio said to Clara.

"Carry on, my friends, and gird your loins!" Cassius said to the company. "For the Athenians have gathered a great host to watch you!" He then rushed out for another performance.

"At least their expectations are being lowered before they see us," Beatrice said.

"Yeah," Fausto replied as he carried some fresh olive

branches through the scaena frons. "All their lives they've been waiting for us."

"Sarcasm is bad luck before a show, Fausto!" Domela shouted.

"I've actually never heard that before," Beatrice retorted, hands upon her hips.

"All right everyone!" Felix said. "Back to work!"

On the pulpitum, before the central doorway, Fausto, Damon, Castor and Pollux were busy setting up the driftwood olive tree, the trunk of which rose up from the wooden planks of the pulpitum, smooth and gnarled and lovingly shaped by them to resemble an Attic tree. They then set about attaching the fresh olive boughs which they had cut the evening before, and began inserting them into the holes in the trunk. Soon, the tree rose up, its branches spread wide as if to embrace the audience with flickering silver and green leaves and unripened fruit.

From the orchestra, Sextus looked up from where he, Martia and Peli were entertaining the children. "It looks wonderful, my friends!" he said excitedly.

"Thank you, Praetor!" Pollux called back, taking pride in the work he had undertaken for Menedemus' farm.

Meanwhile Clara, Beatrice, Domela and Julius had been busy setting out ceramic amphorae and pots, baskets of fresh vegetables, and spades about the pulpitum. These props were spread out to either side of the doorways of Chremes and Menedemus, which were located on either side of the olive tree. There was even a prop apiary near the doorway of Chremes who, Julius imagined, would take pride in the provision of his own Attic honey.

Just to the side of the tree, Felix and Rufio were busy assembling the fountain which had been crafted from wood by Castor, Pollux, and Damon, and then painted to look like marble by Beatrice. It consisted of a semi-circular basin with a high, flat back from which jut a serpent's head, mouth agape, for the water spout. There was no water or pump this time, as they had done previously, but the effect was sufficient. The fountain was large enough such that the actors could sit upon the edge in the course of the play.

Without looking up, Felix whispered to Rufio. "Psst. He's not here is he?"

"Who?"

"You know who. That…the… Terentius!" he hissed.

Rufio turned and looked around the odeon, the orchestra, the wings, the seating of the cavia. "I don't see him."

"Unless the shade is just floating above us now. He could be perched upon my shoulders at this very moment and I wouldn't know it." Felix brushed his shoulders for good measure and made a sign against evil.

"Oh, stop worrying. You're not the one he's been harassing for weeks," Rufio said.

"Weeks?" Now Felix looked up.

"Yes. He wants it to go well, as much as we do. He *needs* it to go well."

"What do you mean, *needs* it to go well?" Felix grabbed Rufio's wrist.

"Just don't worry about it. Focus!" Rufio then pushed at the fountain. "It won't tip, will it?" Rufio asked.

"'Focus', he says… I've got a shade for a critic now, and I'm to focus?" Felix shook his head and sat upon the fountain himself. "No. It's solid. Sextus?" he called down to the orchestra. "Should we have it at an angle?" He stood back to look at it from the edge of the pulpitum.

"I would leave it facing the audience directly so that it can be viewed properly from the wings of the cavia." Sextus smiled. "It all looks magnificent!"

For a final, added bit of realism, Castor and Pollux carried in several buckets of soil which they spread out in front of the domus of Menedemus, the titular 'self-tormentor', to represent the land which he farmed so intensely. When they were finished, they made small furrows in the soil, and placed one of the spades upon the ground beside it.

When it was all done, the company stepped down into the orchestra about the altar there, and looked up at their fine work.

"And so Attica comes to life before our eyes." Sextus smiled at the sight.

"Damon?" Felix said. "A little atmosphere please?"

From where he stood behind the group, Damon set his flute to his lips and proceeded to sound out the wind on the slopes of Hymettos. The buzz of bees in the apiary followed, and then the birds of Attica fluttered all about them to the rafters of the odeon and about the seating of the cavia.

Everyone marvelled at how he had mastered his instrument and the sounds of the world in which they had been living the past months. Even the children giggled and looked about.

Felix turned to Damon. "Perfect."

Damon lowered his flute and smiled proudly.

"Where is Electra?" Rufio asked, only just the noticing that she was not standing among them.

"I'm here!" Electra said as she emerged from the house of Chremes at stage left.

Fausto gasped. "By Bacchus!"

"It's Bacchis," Electra corrected as she walked to the front of the pulpitum and did a twirl for Felix. "Good?"

"Very," Felix said. "Our archimima will dazzle the audience."

Electra's costume consisted of a brilliant red, floor-length peplos accented with golden waves which flowed around the hems and her body in a most enticing way. Golden earrings in the form of discs dangled from her ears, and rings and bangles of gold adorned her fingers and jingled upon her wrists.

"Gaudy enough for a courtesan?" Electra asked.

"Perfect," Felix said as he hopped up on the pulpitum and kissed her hand.

"Well, now that I'm ready, how about the rest of you?" Electra said.

"She's right!" Felix said. "Everyone, get your costumes on, and apply your makeup if you need it."

At that moment, Thespis began to cry and from where he was in Martia's arms, he strained his hands toward his mother.

Electra looked at her son, and then down at her peplos. She sighed. "Come, my son. I'd better feed you now so that you don't wail during the performance."

"Everyone, ready yourselves!" Felix bellowed, and they all rushed to the stagehouse to prepare.

An hour later, the children were fed, and the rest of the players had all donned their costumes, plain tunicae and peploi, for the performance.

Beatrice and Domela had only just finished going around the group, helping with hair and makeup before seeing to their own.

Vocal exercises began anew in the midst of the chaotic progress such that the odeon echoed with the sounds of pre-performance preparations. This added to the excitement that was building in the street outside where a large crowd of Athenians had gathered, waiting to enter the great odeon for the performance.

"I think all of Athenae has turned out for this!" Fausto called down from the second storey of the stagehouse where he looked out onto the street. "Cassius and his lot are finished! He's coming in!" Fausto rushed back down to the ground floor and joined the group as Cassius entered.

"How are you, my friends?" Cassius Cantor said, skidding

to a halt before The Etrurian Players. "You all look magnificent! A bit plain perhaps, excepting yourself, Electra," he winked, "but magnificent nonetheless!"

"What is it, Cassius?" Felix asked as he finished drinking a cup of water.

"They grow restless in the street," Cassius said. "Are you ready?"

"Just about. Cosmo is lighting new torches." Felix replied. "Stall them for a few more minutes."

"I'll do my best." Cassius made to run out, but turned back quickly with a great smile. "Good luck, my friends. May Apollo and the Muses bless you!"

The Etrurian Players were silent for a moment and all looked at each other. There was a collective deep breath as the moment came upon them at last. It was time.

Felix stepped forward. "To the altar, everyone. We must honour Apollo." He picked up a small tinderbox and a piece of frankincense from one of the wagons and went up the stairs that led to the scaena frons and through the central door onto the pulpitum.

The Etrurian Players processed down into the orchestra and spread out around the altar.

Felix, his back to the pulpitum, added a handful of wood shavings to the bowl of the altar, poured a little oil on it, and then lit it with the flint and a small knife. The flames caught immediately. "We've come a long way on this particular journey. And it is not yet done. We have one final stretch before we reach our Ithaca, my friends. We have endured many trials. We are survivors. And so, we thank Apollo for bringing us here to Athenae, for challenging us and inspiring us." Felix placed the frankincense in the flames, and after a few seconds it began to smoke. "Oh Apollo, please accept the offerings of your humble players and bless this performance. May it be well-received and worthy."

Everyone bowed their heads and mouthed their own silent prayers and wishes.

Felix looked up at the theatre then and, to his astonishment, he saw the shade of Terentius staring directly at him, clutching a long scroll and stylus, hopeful and wild-eyed at once, desperate in his own prayers on the other side of the veil that separated him from the living. But rather than balk, or let fear fasten upon him, Felix Modestus stared back at the shade and smiled. "Oh Apollo, please bless our Terentius and his insightful work. May we do it, and him, justice."

The shade then turned and, dragging his scroll behind him, walked to the uppermost tier of the cavia to sit upon the top, central step.

"To Terentius!" the group said all together.

Felix led the group back through the scaena frons into the stagehouse. "Cosmo!" he called to the caretaker.

"What is it?"

"Let them in!" Felix shouted.

"Bout time!" Cosmo replied. "The theatre's under siege!"

Felix turned to Sextus and Martia. "Do you want to take your seats in the cavia now?"

Sextus looked at Martia and then back to Felix. "We thought that we would help out back here during the performance, if that is all right with you."

"Are you sure?" Clara asked. "Don't you want to see it from the cavia?"

Martia smiled. "Sextus and I feel like part of the company now." She shrugged. "We would like to help. We can keep the children calm while you're performing."

"You're more than a part of the company," Electra said with a great smile. "You are family now."

Martia's lip quivered ever-so-slightly, and Sextus held her hand.

"Right then. Peli?" Rufio called out, a long rope in his hand. "Come here, boy."

Peli looked up at him, wary, his head down.

"We can't have you pissing on the Athenians during the performance." Rufio tied one end of the rope about Peli's neck and the other end to one of the wagons. Peli barked and whined. "Shh. Don't worry. I've got something for you." Rufio then reached into the wagon and pulled out a roasted leg of lamb. "Atticus sent this for you." Rufio set it upon the ground and Peli set to chewing it. Rufio turned to see everyone staring at him. "What? He's already pissed against the olive tree!"

"Get ready," Julius said. "The audience is arriving."

THE ODEON BUILT BY HERODES ATTICUS CAME TO LIFE AND crowds of Athenians filed in from either site of the pulpitum and scaena frons. They gathered in the orchestra and in the aisles, and clustered in the cavia. It was as if the entire structure had lungs, taking great breaths, the audience flowing like blood through its excited arteries.

The din of voices was so loud that most did not hear The Etrurian Players going through their final vocal exercises. The players sang up and down the scale, they stretched, and they breathed.

Fausto panicked, and Beatrice calmed him as per their usual pre-performance routine.

Castor and Pollux gave each other some brotherly encouragement, while Domela admired Julius' calm demeanour as he went though the play in his mind.

Now that the children were settled and sleeping in the back of one of the wagons with Martia caring for them, and Peli gnawing and watching at the wheel of that same wagon, Electra stood aside and, eyes closed, focussed her attention upon her transformation into the courtesan, Bacchis.

Felix watched her from where he stood with Sextus and Clara observing his players. "I never tire of seeing her do that," he said.

"It is a wonder," Sextus said. "It's as though she has become another person before our very eyes." Sextus then fished quickly about in the small purse that was hidden among the folds of his toga. "Before I forget…here, Felix." He handed Felix the ring. "Safe and sound."

"Thank you, Sextus." Felix looked at the jewel-encrusted ring with the image of Vesta upon it, and then turned to Clara who put her hand out. Felix slid the ring onto her finger. "There. Now your transformation is complete."

"Where is Rufio?" Sextus asked, looking about the chaotic hall of the stagehouse.

"He's trying to see who's in the audience," Clara said, pointing to where Rufio peeked out from the central doorway of the scaena frons, his person hidden by the tree.

RUFIO STOOD THERE, PEERING INTO THE ODEON, HIS EYES scanning the audience members, many of whom he recognized. In the front row of the cavia, he could see Athenian and Roman officials, including members of the Boule council. Publius Leander Antoninus and his wife Delphina were also there in the second row, along with their daughters Lavena and Hadrea, the latter two looking about at who was in attendance and whispering to each other. In the middle of the orchestra stood the Athenian playwright, Telephus, his arms crossed as he listened to the snobbish opining of the actors Zotikos, Aegisthus and Cadmus who critiqued the set pieces before them.

"Cunne," Rufio muttered, but then smiled when he saw the librarian, Phemius, sitting alongside the philosophers Zonas and Philemon. Unfortunately, he also saw the Athenian seer,

Melampus, and he hoped that he would remain silent and unprophetic during the performance. Fortunately, however, he was dressed for once.

Three rows up he also spotted the champions of the Panathenaic musical and rhapsodic contests, Antiocheis, Alexandros of Thebes, Theophile of Chios, and even the fifteen year old orphan, Demophon, who had taken everyone's breath away. One might have thought the latter would be terrified to be among so many, but he sat calmly, his head high, his eyes curious, graciously accepting the kind words his admirers offered him, including those of Athenae's champion boxer, Aristides, who sat beside Demophon like a protective, older brother.

About midway up the cavia, a group of gaudy and glittering women shone out from where the lupae of the House of the Nymphs were seated, including Amazonia, Medusa, and Calypso. Of course, Rufio was not acquainted with them, but Fausto, Castor and Pollux had spoken so much about them, he could not mistake them. Beside them was their domina, Circe, along with the burly Boreas who sat like an angry bull that has been dragged to the arena against his will. His stern demeanour changed, however, the moment Circe turned with a sly smile to whisper something in his ear. As if by magic, he relaxed and kissed her hand.

"She is a witch!" Rufio said to himself.

Opposite the lupae, he recognized Polycarpos, the fishmonger, and his wife, Ploumi. And near them Arcas, the guard from the Porta Hadriana, and some of the members of his contubernium.

Rufio then saw the entire company of The Rome Antics as they filed quickly into the odeon to spread out and find seats like scattered leaves about the cavia. "Oh, Gods…" Rufio said under his breath, his eyes searching for Cassius Cantor, but not seeing him.

He then spotted the shade staring directly at him from the top tier.

Terentius looked at Rufio with panic in his eyes, his ghostly visage turning to indicate the full, tittering and vocally-doubtful crowd.

"It's going to be fine," Rufio mouthed to the shade, no longer shocked that he was in communication with the long-dead Terentius, for his pity had long ago overtaken his fear.

"You all right?" Clara said, appearing at Rufio's shoulder.

"Oh!" Rufio jumped. "Ah, yes. I'm fine. Just looking over the audience. It's a full house."

"Of course it is. They're curious about what us Etrurians can do." Clara smiled and gave a shuddering breath.

Rufio turned to her. "Are you all right? You ready for this?"

"I am." She looked back at the wagon where Felicia slept with Thespis under Martia's watch. "I'm fine."

"I love you," Rufio said, pressing his lips to hers.

Clara kissed him back and then tidied his tunica for him. "We can do this."

"Yes, we can." He smiled and stroked a strand of her blonde hair. "Antiphila."

"Clitipho." Clara smiled back. "Are you ready for your Bacchis?" Clara looked to where Electra stood.

"I suppose I have to be, don't I?" he laughed.

"You remember your lines?"

"I do," he replied, surprisingly calm. "I know this play from beginning to end."

"I know you do."

"Better tell Felix the odeon is now full." Rufio held her fast, however. "Look who it is." He pointed to a lone figure making his way to the top left of the Cavia. "It's Atticus!"

"I thought he wasn't coming?"

"I guess he couldn't help himself." Rufio looked back. "It's time."

They took one last look at the audience and descended the stairs to join Felix and the others.

"FELIX MODESTUS, PLEASE LOOK AFTER MY MONKEY FOR ME!"

Rufio and Clara arrived to find Cassius Cantor holding a large, covered wooden cage, pleading with Felix.

"Cassius, I have a play to put on!" Felix grumbled. "I can't watch your monkey for you."

"And I can't bring him into the cavia for the performance!" Cassius retorted. "He doesn't sit still and well…"

"Well what?" Felix demanded.

"He…he gets excited with the theatre, all right! You don't want Momo pleasuring himself while you're on stage, do you? He's liable to hit someone!"

"What a disgusting creature!" Electra said. "Get out, Cassius!"

"But I helped you. Do you have any idea how much it took to hold that crowd back? Do you know how much we've been building you up these past weeks? Everywhere we've gone, we've talked about The Etrurian Players, about *The* Felix Modestus! We've even fought those who besmirched your integrity! No company has ever had such wondrous advertising!"

Felix was silent for a moment, aware of the growing quiet on the other side of the scaena frons. "Fine. You can put the cage under the other wagon, away from Peli. If that monkey so much as screeches I'm putting him out in the street. Got it?"

"Yes, Felix. Thank you." Cassius rushed to put the caged simian beneath one of the wagons and then returned. "The best of luck to all of you!" he said with a great smile. "I must get to my seat now."

And with that, the final member of the audience went into the cavia.

Felix Modestus stood in the midst of his gathered players then, looking each of them in the eye and smiling to lend them his strength and confidence which, he was relieved to feel, had returned. He knew that perhaps he should give a rousing speech to his troops, like Scipio before Zama, or Alexander before Gaugamela. They were facing great odds with this performance and not only was their reputation at stake, but also the memory of the father of their comedy. They were fighting for more than themselves, Felix knew.

"It is time, my friends. We are ready, and we *are* the best company in the empire. These Athenians may not know it yet, but they soon will. I have faith in every one of you and I have no doubt that we will win over the hearts and minds of these Athenians. Just as surely as Leonidas won over those of all Greeks after the battle of Thermopylae."

Rufio leaned close to Sextus. "Didn't Leonidas get killed in that battle?" he whispered.

"They all did," Sextus whispered back.

"Who's Leonidas?" Fausto asked.

Felix looked at the young player.

"The fishmonger who likes Rufio," Castor added with a laugh that spread throughout the group.

Felix smiled. "My friends. We are The Etrurian Players! We've been crowned by the emperor, and praised by kings and satraps."

They all cheered.

"Let's have some fun!" Felix clapped and looked at Damon. "Damon, let the birds of Attica take flight!"

XIX

THE ETRURIAN PLAYERS PRESENT…

The great odeon was silent but for the anticipatory breathing of the audience in the cavia and the flicker of the bright torches that fanned around the fringes. A cough here, and a sniff there were joined by the odd whisper to a neighbour about the scene laid out before them of a lone olive tree, a fountain, and the doorways of two homes. There was freshly-tilled soil, and an apiary. Rural implements leaned against walls and lay upon the ground. Amphorae of various shapes, crafted from the clay of Attica, were grouped beside the doorways, like old men sunning themselves. It was a strangely familiar setting that awaited the action upon the pulpitum of the theatre.

And then the birds began to sing as if on a dewy spring morning in the Attic countryside. They flit from one side of the odeon to the other, in the branches of the shivering tree, and over the heads of those watching. Bees added to the chorus. For those who had been lucky enough in their youth to escape to such a place from the city, remembrances of rural idylls put a distinct smile upon their faces as the play began…

Felix Modestus stood in the central doorway leading onto the scene, his form hidden by the olive tree as he controlled his breathing and prepared. *Apollo and Athena...I honour you...*

He stepped over the threshold and as he did so, the bird-song and the buzz of bees faded away. He walked slowly around the tree to stand at the edge of the pulpitum facing the audience directly.

A sea of faces rose up steeply before him, like a rock face he had to scale, but rather than feel the sting of intimidation, Felix claimed the space and the audience's attention. His shoulders back, his head high, he smiled at them and began his prologus.

"Lest it should be a matter of surprise to any one of you, why the poet has assigned to a more mature man a part that belongs to the young, that I will first explain to you; and then, the reason for my coming I will disclose."

Felix could see he had their attention. He had known the first line was of utmost importance for that.

"An entire play from an entire Greek one, the *Heautontimorumenos*, we are today about to represent, which from a two-fold plot has been made but one. I would mention who it was that wrote it, and whose in Greek it is, if I did not think that the greater part of you are aware. Now, for what reason I have learned this part, in a few words I will explain. The poet, our Terentius, who expired in this very polis, intended me to be a pleader, not the speaker of a prologus. Your decision he asks, and has appointed me the advocate. If this advocate can avail as much by his oral powers as he has excelled in inventing happily, who composed this speech which I am about to recite. For as to malevolent rumours spreading abroad that he has mixed together many Greek plays while writing a few Latin ones, he does not deny that this is the case, and that he does not repent of so doing."

Felix paused to let that sink in.

"He has the example of good poets, after which example

he thinks it is allowable for him to do what they have done. Then, as to a malevolent old poet saying that he has suddenly applied himself to dramatic pursuits, relying on the genius of his friends, and not his own natural abilities...on that, your judgment, your opinion, will prevail. Wherefore I do entreat you all, that the suggestions of our antagonists may not avail more than those of our favourers. Do you be favourable. Grant the means of prospering to those who afford you the means of being spectators of *new* plays, those, I mean, without faults, that he may not suppose this said on his behalf who lately made the public give way to a man as he ran along in the street."

At the top of the central aisle, the shade of Terentius sat, leaning forward, his ghostly lips mouthing the words as if trying to tempt them from Felix.

Felix did not shudder, but spoke on toward the end of the prologus.

"Attend with favourable feelings. Grant me the opportunity that we may be allowed to act a quiet play in silence, that the servant everlastingly running about, the angry old man, the gluttonous parasite, the impudent sharper, and the greedy procurer, may not have always to be performed by with the utmost expense of voice, and the greatest exertion. For our sake come to the conclusion that this request is fair, that some portion of our labour may be abridged. For nowadays, those who write new plays do not spare an aged man. If there is any piece requiring exertion, they come running to us. But if it is a light one, it is taken to another company."

Felix smiled at Cassius Cantor for a second, before finishing.

"In the present one the style is pure. Do you make proof, what, in each character, our ability can effect. If we have never greedily set a high price upon our skill, and have come to the conclusion that this is our greatest gain, as far as possible to be subservient to your convenience, establish in us a precedent, that the young may be anxious rather to please you than themselves…"

Without another word, Felix turned and disappeared behind the olive tree as the birds of Attica began to sing once more.

"You have their attention now," Felix said as he came through the doorway.

Pollux stood there breathing deeply and slowly, trying not to rub his beard which had been dyed grey for his part as the aged Menedemus.

"We have this, my friend," Julius said to him.

The others stood below the platform looking up at the pair of them as each went to the doorways of their respective homes.

Pollux adjusted his plain brown tunica and cingulum, and stepped out…

The audience watched as an old man emerged from the domus to their left. He moved stiffly, which made his age evident, but he nevertheless set himself to the work of a younger man. With a groan, he bent to pick up his spade, and set to working the dark earth of his farm. The birds sang about him, and the sun beat down. He wiped his brow, the motion drawing attention to the saddened look upon his face.

From the doorway of the other domus, another old man emerged, more relaxed and agreeable, as if he was enjoying the autumn years of his life with ease and free of guilt. He spotted his neighbour labouring away at that early hour and walked over to him.

"Although this acquaintanceship between us is of very recent date, from the time in fact of your purchasing an estate here in the neighbourhood, yet either your good qualities, or our being neighbours, which I take to be a sort of friendship, induces me to inform you, frankly and familiarly, that you appear to me to labour beyond your years, and beyond what your affairs require."

The other man glanced up but continued in his toils.

"For, in the name of gods and men, what would you have? What can be your aim? You are, as I conjecture, sixty years of age, or more. No man in these parts has a better or a more valuable estate, no one more servants. And yet you discharge their duties just as diligently as if there were none at all. However early in the morning I go out, and however late in the evening I return home, I see you either digging, or plowing, or doing something, in fact, in the fields. You take respite not an instant, and are quite regardless of yourself. I am very sure that this is not done for your amusement. But really I am vexed how little work is done here. If you were to employ the time you spend in labouring yourself, in keeping your servants at work, you would profit much more."

Menedemus stood up and leaned upon his spade as he gave his attention to his nosy neighbour. "Have you so much leisure, Chremes, from your own affairs, that you can attend to those of others, those which don't concern you?"

The neighbour set his hands firmly on his hips as he replied with confidence. "I am a man, and nothing that concerns a man do I deem a matter of indifference to me."

"Yes!" Philemon, the Epicurean in the audience burst out, quickly covering his mouth.

But Chremes was undeterred. "Suppose that I wish either to advise you in this matter, or to be informed myself... If what you do is right, that I may do the same. If it is not, then that I may dissuade you."

"It's requisite for me to do so. Do you as it is necessary for you to do."

"Is it requisite for any person to torment himself?"

"It is for me," Menedemus retorted.

Chremes approached and placed his hand upon his neighbour's shoulder. "If you have any affliction, I could wish it otherwise. But prithee, what sorrow is this of yours? How have you deserved so ill of yourself?"

Menedemus, to the audience's shock - they were expecting a comedy after all - began to weep.

"Do not weep," Chremes said, "but make me acquainted with it, whatever it is. Do not be reserved. Fear nothing. Trust me, I tell you. Either by consolation, or by counsel, or by any means, I will aid you."

"Do you wish to know this matter?"

"Yes, and for the reason I mentioned to you," Chremes confirmed, eying the spade as he did so.

"I will tell you."

"But still, in the meantime, lay down that spade. Don't fatigue yourself."

"By no means." Menedemus shook his head.

Chremes then proceeded to try and take the spade from Menedemus, the two old men engaging in a tug-of-war with the farming implement. In the end, Chremes came out victorious and his eyes widened as he hefted his trophy from the struggle. "Whew! Such a heavy one as this, pray!"

"Such are my deserts."

Chremes set the spade upon the ground and crossed his arms. "Now speak."

"I have an only son, a young man… Alas, why did I say 'I have'? Rather I should say 'I had' one, Chremes. Whether I have him now, or not, is uncertain."

"Why so?" Chremes led his distraught neighbour to the

fountain nearby so that they could sit upon its edge as Menedemus unfolded his tale of woe.

"You shall know…" Menedemus began. "There is a poor old woman here, a stranger from Corinth. Her daughter, a young woman, he fell in love with, insomuch that he almost regarded her as his wife. All this took place unknown to me. When I discovered the matter, I began to reprove him, not with gentleness, nor in the way suited to the love-sick mind of a youth, but with violence, and after the usual method of fathers. I was daily reproaching him… 'Look you, do you expect to be allowed any longer to act thus, myself, your father, being alive? To be keeping a mistress pretty much as though your wife? You are mistaken, Clinia, and you don't know me, if you fancy that. I am willing that you should be called my son, just as long as you do what becomes you! But if you do not do so, I shall find out how it becomes me to act toward you. This arises from nothing, in fact, but too much idleness. At your time of life, I did not devote my time to dalliance, but, in consequence of my poverty, departed hence for Asia, and there acquired in arms both riches and military glory.' At length the matter came to this: the youth, from hearing the same things so often, and with such severity, was overcome. He supposed that I, through age and affection, had more judgment and foresight for him than himself. He went off to Asia, Chremes, to serve under the king."

"What is it you say?" Chremes was evidently shocked at so drastic an action.

"He departed without my knowledge, and has been gone these three months."

"Both are to be blamed, although *I* still think this step shows an ingenuous and enterprising disposition." Chremes shook his white head.

"When I learned *this* from those who were in the secret, I returned home sad, and with feelings almost overwhelmed and distracted through grief. I sit down. My servants run to me. They take off my shoes, then some make all haste to spread the couches, and to prepare a meal. Each according to his ability did zealously what he could, in order to alleviate my sorrow. When I observed this, I began to reflect thus: 'What! Are so many persons anxious for my sake alone, to pleasure myself only? Are so many female servants to provide me with dress? Shall I alone keep up such an expensive establishment, while my only son, who ought equally, or even more so, to enjoy these things, inasmuch as his age is better suited for the enjoyment of them? Him, poor youth, have I driven away from home by my severity! Were I to do this, really I should deem myself deserving of any calamity. But so long as he leads this life of penury, banished from his country through my severity, I will revenge his wrongs upon myself, toiling, making money, saving, and laying up for him.'"

Menedemus sighed and continued. "At once I set about it. I left nothing in the house, neither movables nor clothing. Every thing I scraped together. Slaves, male and female, except those who could easily pay for their keep by working in the country, all of them I set up to auction and sold. I at once put up a bill to sell my house. I collected somewhere about fifteen talents, and purchased this farm where I fatigue myself. I have come to this conclusion, Chremes, that I do my son a less injury, while I am unhappy. It is not right for me to enjoy any pleasure here, until such time as he returns home safe to share it with me."

"I believe you to be of an affectionate disposition toward your children, and him to be an obedient son, if one were to manage him rightly or prudently. But neither did you understand him sufficiently well, nor he you - a thing that happens where persons don't live on terms of frankness together. You never showed him how highly you valued him, nor did he ever dare put that confidence in you which is due to a father. Had this been done, these troubles would never have befallen you."

"Such is the fact, I confess. The greatest fault is on my side."

"But still, Menedemus, I hope for the best, and I trust that he'll be here safe before long."

Behind the scaena frons, the company watched and listened to Pollux and Julius perform, their dialogue engaging most of their watchers, for who among them did not long for youth, or pity the old? How many of them had reproving fathers? Many there felt for the father who had realized his fault and now tormented himself.

"A good start!" Felix said as he turned to the others.

Just then, Pollux entered the domus of Menedemus, his face covered in sweat.

"Well done, brother!" Castor slapped him on the back and handed him a towel.

"The hard part is done, Pollux. Now you can relax and tell the tale," Felix said.

Pollux breathed and nodded with a great smile.

"Rufio? Get ready," Felix said pointing to Chremes' door.

Rufio nodded, turned to Clara behind him, and winked. "Here we go…"

Chremes sat alone now upon the fountain, thinking on the sad tale that his neighbour had relayed to him. "He has forced tears from me, and I do pity him." He stood with a groan from the fountain's edge. "I'll go in-doors immediately. But what means this noise at the door of my house? I wonder who's coming out! I'll step aside here."

At that moment Chremes' son, Clitipho, emerged from his domus, turning back to speak to someone within. "There is nothing, Clinia, for you to fear as yet. They have not been long by any means: and I am sure that she will be with you presently along with the messenger. Do at once dismiss these causeless apprehensions which are tormenting you."

Clitipho, who was a lean, thinly-bearded young man, shook his head as he turned away from the domus door, dipping a finger in one of the amphorae of wine and tasting it. He clapped his hands and rubbed them together as if in anticipation, then turned, unaware that his father, Chremes, was standing not far off.

"Who is my son talking to?" Chremes asked himself before stepping out.

Clitipho jumped when his father appeared suddenly, bumping his head on one of the low branches of the olive tree. "Here comes my father, whom I wished to see. I'll accost him. Father, you have met me opportunely!"

"What's the matter?"

"Do you know this neighbour of ours, Menedemus?"

"Very well," Chremes replied, for he had just been engaged in a very personal conversation with the man.

"Do you know he has a son?"

"I have heard that he has…in Asia."

"He is *not* in Asia, father. He is at our house!"

Chremes' eyes widened, and he cast a glance toward the Gods in heaven. "What is it you say?"

"Upon his arrival, after he had just landed from the ship, I immediately brought him to dine with us. For from our very childhood upward I have always been on intimate terms with him."

"You announce to me a great pleasure," Chremes said to his son, his hands set firmly upon the younger man's shoulders. "How much I wish that Menedemus had accepted my invitation. Even yet, there's time enough…"

But Clitipho shook his head, stepped around his father, and

turned back to him. "Take care what you do. There is no necessity, father, for doing so."

"For what reason?"

"Why, because he is as yet undetermined what to do with himself. He is but just arrived. He fears every thing - his father's displeasure, and how his mistress may be disposed toward him. He loves her to distraction! On her account, this trouble and going abroad took place."

"I know it."

Clitipho relayed how his friend, Clinia, had just sent his servant, Dromo, into the city to fetch said girl who owned his heart, and how he had ordered their own servant, Syrus, to go with him upon the task.

"What does Clinia say?" Chremes asked of his son.

"What does he say? That he is wretched."

"Wretched? Whom could we less suppose so? What is there wanting for him to enjoy everything that among men, in fact, are esteemed as blessings? Parents, a country in prosperity, friends, family, relations, riches? And yet, all these are just according to the disposition of him who possesses them. To him who knows how to use them, they are blessings. To him who does not use them rightly, they are evils."

"Aye," his son replied, "but he always was a morose old man, and now I dread nothing more, father, than that in his displeasure he'll be doing something to Clinia more than is justifiable."

Chremes nodded as if in satisfaction as he turned to the audience. "I'll restrain myself, for that the other one should be in fear of his father is of service to him."

A few members of the audience nodded their approval of the sentiment.

"What is it you are saying to yourself?" Clitipho demanded, stepping to his father's side.

Chremes turned back to him. "I'll tell you. However the case stood, Clinia ought still to have remained at home. Perhaps his father was a little stricter than he liked. He should have put up with it! For whom ought he to bear with, if he would not bear with his own father? Was it reasonable that he should live after his son's humour, or his son after his? And as to charging him with harshness, it is not the fact. For the severities of fathers are generally of one character, those I mean who are in some degree reasonable men. They do not wish their sons to be always wenching; they do not wish them to be always carousing; they give a limited allowance; and yet all this tends to virtuous conduct."

It was Clitipho's turn to look to the audience with a great eye roll that caused a titter among the younger members of those silent observers.

Chremes continued. "But when the mind, Clitipho, has once enslaved itself by vicious appetites, it must of necessity follow similar pursuits. This is a wise maxim, 'to take warning from others of what may be to your own advantage.'"

"I believe so," Clitipho said with a wink to the fire-lit faces before him as his father went into their domus.

Clara handed Julius a cup of water as soon as he came backstage. "Wonderful," she said to him as he drank.

"We've tickled their minds," Julius replied with a sweaty smile. "Now, it's for Rufio's monologue." He turned to Felix who approached them. "He's doing so very well," he whispered.

"He's a natural," Felix said.

"So are you, Felix," Clara said. "Is your Clinia ready to win them over?"

"Yes."

"Shh," Electra hissed from the other doorway. "He's about to launch into the second act!"

The rest of The Etrurian Players crowded around back-stage to listen to Rufio.

WHEN HIS FATHER WAS GONE, CLITIPHO SAT UPON THE GROUND and leaned against the trunk of the olive tree, twirling a singular leaf in this fingers.

"What partial judges are all fathers in regard to all of us young men, in thinking it reasonable for us to become old men all at once from boys, and not to participate in those things which youth is naturally inclined to." He stood then, and paced the edge of the pulpitum. "They regulate us by their own desires, such as they now are, not as they once were."

He stopped and rubbed his beard. "If ever I have a son, he certainly shall find in me an indulgent father. For the means both of knowing and of pardoning his faults shall be found by me. Not like my own father who, by means of another person, discloses to me his own sentiments. I'm plagued to death, when he drinks a little more than usual, what pranks of his own he does relate to me! Now he says, 'Take warning from others of what may be to your advantage.'"

Clitipho mimicked his old man, extricating a few chuckles in the audience, but also a few glares from older listeners.

"How shrewd! He certainly does not know how deaf I am at the moment when he's telling his stories. Just now, the words of my mistress make more impression upon me." He pressed his hands to his chest as though he squeezed a great set of bosoms, hips swaying. "'Give me this, and bring me that,' she cries. I have nothing to say to her in answer, and no one is there more wretched than myself."

Clitipho sat upon the edge of the fountain, cupping a hand and splashing his face with cool water.

"But this Clinia, although he, as well, has cares enough of his own, still has a mistress of virtuous and modest breeding, and a stranger to the arts of a courtesan. Mine is a craving, saucy, haughty, extravagant creature, full of lofty airs. Then all that I have to give her is fair words, for I make it a point not to tell her that I have nothing. This misfortune I met with not long since, nor does my father as yet know any thing of the matter."

Clitipho stood again and, shaking his head in dismay, turned and left the scene.

When Rufio came backstage, he bent over, gulping in great breaths of air as Damon's birds soared over the audience's heads, accompanied by the bees which Beatrice let loose from the apiary with her own instrument.

When Rufio had caught his breath, he looked up at the others. "A tough crowd. Might have heard a titter here, or seen a nod there, but they are stoney-faced."

"Don't worry, Rufio. I've been watching," Sextus said with reserved excitement. "They're engaged. I can see it!"

"No time to relax now, my friend," Felix said. "We're about to go on."

Rufio breathed and stood up. He drank from the cup Clara had, and kissed her. Her smile was all the encouragement he needed.

Felix stepped out of the domus of Chremes first, and the short second scene of the second act was underway…

Clinia at last stepped out of doors, tired of hiding from his estranged father. He breathed and looked about, a nervous excitement visible in his brawny form.

"It's Hercules!" someone shouted in the crowd before him, causing a wave of whispers which he did not register. When the noise died down, Clinia spoke.

"If my love-affairs had been prosperous for me, I am sure she would have been here by this. But I'm afraid that the damsel has been led astray here in my absence. Many things combine to strengthen this opinion in my mind - opportunity, the place, her age, a worthless mother, under whose control she is, with whom nothing but gain is precious."

Emotion was etched upon his bearded face, as if he were weighed down by a thousand worries with which far too many were familiar.

"Clinia!" came the shout of Clitipho who rushed from his domus.

"Alas! Wretched me!"

Clitipho pulled at Clinia's tunic, attempting to redirect him. "Do, pray, take care that no one coming out of your father's house sees you here by accident!"

But Clinia's worries were persistent. He worried that some misfortune had occurred, for it was taking overlong for his love to arrive with his servant.

Clitipho slapped him across the face as if rousing a drunken man. "You don't consider that it is a great way from here. Besides, you know the ways of women, while they are bestirring themselves, and while they are making preparations a whole year passes by!"

"Too true!" one husband shouted from the audience, only to be followed by another smacking sound.

"Oh, Clitipho… I'm afraid."

"Take courage. Look, here comes Dromo, together with Syrus. They are close at hand!"

The two friends went to stand aside by Chremes' domus door.

From the audience's left, the two servants, Syrus and Dromo, walked onto the scene at a lazy pace, the latter looking back, worried, the former simply relishing the freedom of the open countryside.

"Do you say so?" Syrus asked.

"Tis as I told you! But in the meantime, while we've been carrying on our discourse, these women have been left behind!"

Overhearing the distant conversation, Clitipho turned to his anxious friend. "Don't you hear, Clinia? Your mistress is close at hand."

"Why yes, I do hear now at last, and I see and revive, Clitipho."

"No wonder…" Dromo continued. "They are so encumbered. They are bringing a troop of female attendants with them!"

"I'm undone! Whence come these female attendants?" Clinia panicked, and while he did so, Syrus told Dromo to go back and meet the women who, it seemed, also brought jewels, and gold, and much clothing. Not items to be carried upon the road at so late an hour.

Alone then, Syrus bent at the fountain to catch a drink. "Good Gods! What a multitude there is! Our house will hardly hold them, I'm sure. How much they will eat! How much they will drink! What will there be more wretched than our old gentleman?" He caught sight of Clinia and Clitipho walking toward him. "But look. I see the persons I was wanting."

Before they reached Syrus, Clinia stopped and pulled at Clitipho's tunica. "Oh Jupiter! Why, where is fidelity gone? While I, distractedly wandering, have abandoned my country for your sake, you, in the mean time, Antiphila, have been enriching yourself, and have forsaken me in these troubles, you for whose sake I am in extreme disgrace, and have been disobedient to my father… On whose account I am now ashamed and grieved, that he who used to lecture me about the manners of these women, advised me in vain, and was not able to wean me away from her - which, however, I shall now do - whereas when it might have been advantageous to me to do so, I was unwilling. There is no being more wretched than I."

"He certainly has been misled by our words which we have been speaking here," Syrus said to himself as he wiped his mouth and strode toward the two men. "Clinia, you imagine your mistress quite different from what she really is. For both her mode of life is the same, and her disposition toward you is the same as it always was, so far as we could form a judgment from the circumstances themselves."

"How so? For nothing in the world could I rather wish for just now, than that I have suspected this without reason."

Clitipho rolled his eyes.

"This, in the first place, then - that you may not be ignorant of any thing that concerns her. The old woman, who was formerly said to be her mother, was not so. She is dead."

Clinia and Clitipho gripped each other.

"This I overheard by accident from her, as we came along, while she was telling the other one."

"Pray, who is the other one?" Clitipho asked.

Syrus put up his hand. "Stay. What I have begun I wish first to relate. Clitipho, I shall come to that afterward."

"Make haste, then."

Syrus made a show of pacing as he had seen his elder dominus do when lecturing his son. "First of all, then, when we came to the house, and Dromo knocked at the door... A certain old woman came out. When she opened the door, he directly rushed in. I followed. The old woman bolted the door, and returned to her wool. On this occasion might be known, Clinia, or else on none, in what pursuits she passed her life during your absence. When we thus came upon a female unexpectedly. For this circumstance then gave us an opportunity of judging of the course of her daily life, a thing which especially discovers what is the disposition of each individual. We found her industriously plying at the web, plainly clad in a mourning dress - on account of this old woman, I suppose, who was lately dead - without golden ornaments, dressed, besides, just like those who only dress for themselves, and patched up with no worthless woman's trumpery. Her hair was loose, long, and thrown back negligently about her temples."

"My dear Syrus, do not without cause throw me into ecstasies, I beseech you!"

Syrus shook his head. "When we told her that you had returned, and had requested her to come to you, the damsel instantly put away the web, and covered her face all over with tears, so that you might easily perceive that it really was caused by her affection for you."

Clinia rushed forward to hug the servant and lift him off of his feet. "So may the Deities bless me, I know not where I am for joy! I was so alarmed before."

Syrus then, at last, informed his own dominus, Clitipho, that the other woman he made mention of was none other than Clitipho's mistress, Bacchis.

"Ha! What! Bacchis? How now, you rascal! Whither are you bringing her?" It was Clitipho's turn to panic.

"Whither am I bringing her? To our house, to be sure." Syrus examined his dirty fingernails.

"What! To my father's?"

"No great and memorable action is done without some risk," the servant replied.

"Quite so," a voice in the audience said. This was the stoic, Zonas, whom people quickly shushed.

Syrus made a slight bow to the philosopher, but was pulled back by his dominus.

"Look now... Are you seeking to gain credit for yourself, at the hazard of my character, you rascal, where, if you only make the slightest slip, I am ruined? What would you be doing with her?"

Syrus proceeded to tell Clitipho that the two women were

together and that he could not have the one without the other. He had, however, a plan that would allow him to indulge his mistress with presents, and himself with her presence.

Both Clitipho and Clinia stood before Syrus, arms crossed, their faces twinned in simultaneous expressions of doubt.

"Well, well, disclose this project of yours. What is it?" Clitipho demanded.

Syrus smiled and pointed at Clinia. "We will pretend that your mistress is his."

"Very fine! Tell me, what is he to do with his own? Is she, too, to be called his, as if one was not a sufficient discredit?"

"No. She shall be taken to your mother." Syrus now pointed at Clitipho.

"Why there?"

While Fausto outlined his Syrus' plan to Rufio and Felix, whose Clitipho and Clinia tried to keep up with the wily servant's plotting mind, Electra and Clara prepared for Bacchis and Antiphila's entrance at the start of the fourth scene of the second act. They adjusted each other's stolae, Electra straightening Clara's simple one, and Clara accentuating Electra's courtesanal cleavage.

"After this act, I'll need to feed Thespis," Electra sighed. "My breasts ache."

"Mine as well," Clara said, "but for now, we are Antiphila and Bacchis. You are a courtesan, not a mother."

Electra nodded and raised her head to turn to Beatrice, Domela, and a wide-eyed Damon who had been watching keenly. "Are Bacchis' attendants ready?"

Beatrice held up her tambourine, Domela her ivy garland and wine pitcher, and Damon his flute as he adjusted the blonde wig upon his head.

"Good. Just as we rehearsed," Electra said, turning to go to the far right and the road which led to the domus of Menedemus.

"Here comes Rufio!" Clara said, waving to him from the far side as he entered Chremes' home.

The flute and tambourine immediately set off, announcing the imminent arrival of Bacchis' entourage, and some of the audience applauded the appearance of Electra, their Hellene archimima.

Rufio went directly to Pollux and Julius who sat upon stools, gathering themselves for the marathon to come.

"The audience is pretty quiet," Rufio said as he passed them on the way to see Felicia who was with Martia in the wagon.

Peli stood up and wagged his tail furiously at his dominus' approach.

"Shh, Peli," Rufio said, his finger pressed to his lips. "Good boy," he said as he pat him and glanced down at the still-tempting leg of lamb. "Good. You still have some meat." Rufio leaned onto the back of the wagon to see Martia. "Everything all right?"

Martia smiled and nodded, her voice almost a whisper. "They've been sleeping on and off. I think the sound of the performance soothes them."

"Let's just hope the audience doesn't fall asleep." Rufio looked around, suddenly worried that his attendant playwright shade would appear to chide him.

"It's going wonderfully!" Sextus whispered as he joined them.

"Do you really think so?"

"I've been watching the audience from back here the entire time. They are fully engaged, and trying to decipher Syrus' plot." Sextus wiped his brow. "We may actually pull this off."

There was a loud rustle within the cage beneath one of the other wagons then.

Sextus shook his head. "That cursed monkey! He's the only one causing a disturbance. I've half a mind to throw him out into the street."

"As long as the cage is covered, maybe he'll stay silent," Rufio hoped, glancing at the scaena. "I'm going to go watch Clara and Electra in action." Before going, he turned back to Martia. "Thank you, Martia."

"Go, go!" she replied with a wave. "We're fine here."

Rufio rushed toward the back of the scaena and peered out from the middle doorway behind the olive tree.

THE ARRIVAL OF BACCHIS AND HER ENTOURAGE ROUSED THE audience, many of whom cheered for her chaotic arrival in the sleepy country village. Her attendants sang and whistled, playing upon the flute and tambourine as though they performed for the empress herself, serving their mistress wine and fanning her as she walked with the simple, silent and beautiful girl beside her.

Behind the tree, Syrus and his dominus' friend, Clinia, watched them from their hiding place, eyes wide.

"Upon my word, my dear Antiphila," Bacchis said as she looked her companion up and down. "I commend you, and think you fortunate in having made it your study that your manners should be conformable to those good looks of yours. And so, may the Gods bless me, I do not at all wonder if every man is in love with you."

Antiphila shook her head demurely.

"For your discourse has been a proof to me what kind of disposition you possess. And when now I reflect in my mind upon your way of life, and that of all of you, in fact, who keep the public at a distance from yourselves, it is not surprising both that you are of that disposition, and that we are not." Bacchis looked back and laughed at her gaudy attendants. "For it is your interest to be virtuous. Those, with whom *we* are acquainted, will not allow us to be so. For our lovers, allured merely by our beauty, court us for that. When that has faded, they transfer their affections elsewhere."

"You'll always be beautiful, Bacchis!" one of the lupae in the audience shouted.

Bacchis continued. "And unless we have made provision in the meantime for the future, we live in destitution. Now with you, when you have once resolved to pass your life with one man whose manners are especially kindred to your own, those persons become attached to you. By this kindly feeling, you are truly devoted to each other, and no calamity can ever possibly interrupt your love."

"Quite astute for a courtesan," the epicurean Philemon said to his stoic friend in the cavia.

Antiphila stopped and turned to Bacchis. "I know nothing about other women. I'm sure that I have, indeed, always used every endeavour to derive my own happiness from his happiness."

Upon hearing this, Clinia clambered onto Syrus' back the better to hear that sweet voice. "Ah! 'tis for that reason, my Antiphila, that you alone have now caused me to return to my native country. For while I was absent from you, all other hardships which I encountered were light to me, save the being deprived of you."

"I...believe...it," Syrus grunted under Clinia's weight.

"Syrus, I can scarce endure it! Wretch that I am, that I should not be allowed to possess one of such a disposition at my own discretion!"

"Nay, so far as I understand your father, he will for a long time yet be giving you a hard task."

Bacchis then, overhearing the voices from behind the tree, turned toward them. "Why, who is that young man that's looking at us?"

Antiphila turned to look as well, and as the music and voices of Bacchis' attendants died down, she set her eyes upon the man she had thought of for so very long. "Ah! do support me, I entreat you!"

"What's the matter with you?" Bacchis said, looking from the young man to Antiphila and back again.

"I shall die, alas! I shall die!"

"Why are you thus surprised, Antiphila?" Bacchis motioned for wine from one of her attendants to be brought.

"Is it Clinia that I see, or not?"

"Who do you see?" the confused courtesan asked.

But at that moment, Clinia burst from behind the tree, leaving Syrus to collapse in the dirt, and ran to embrace his long lost Antiphila. "Blessings on you, my life!" He caught Antiphila up in his strong arms.

"Oh my long-wished for Clinia, blessings on you!" the girl said, accompanied by some muted sobs in the cavia before them.

"How fare you, my love?" Clinia begged of her as he held her aloft.

Smiling down at him, a teary glint in her eye, she said, "I'm overjoyed that you have returned safe."

"And do I embrace you, Antiphila, so passionately longed for by my soul?"

Their kiss lingered and, while Bacchis observed, she and her attendants growing bored by the moment, Syrus approached, dusting himself off.

"Go indoors," the servant said, pointing to the domus of Chremes, "for the old gentleman has been waiting for us for some time."

FELIX, CLARA, ELECTRA, DOMELA, BEATRICE, AND DAMON came in through Chremes' door at stage left, and Damon immediately set his lips upon his flute to play a joyous tune to accompany the lovers' reunion.

"There is no applause," Felix noted, his smile fading immediately. "Why is there no applause at the end of the act?"

"This is Athenae, husband," Electra said. "They're reserving judgement."

"Not Circe's girls!" Rufio said. "They love you, Bacchis!"

Electra turned on Rufio. "Do you think?"

Rufio gulped. "It's what I do best." He turned quickly to Clara and kissed her. "You were wonderful."

Clara laughed. "Yes. With all six of my lines!"

"Where is my son?" Electra said as she marched toward the wagons. "I'm going to rip my stola if I don't feed him!"

As Damon's music slowed, Julius stood poised at Chremes' door, and Pollux at that of Menedemus. Julius smiled and nodded before stepping out amid the morning birdsong that now flooded the countryside about Chremes' farm…

"It is now daybreak. Why do I delay to knock at my neighbour's door, that he may learn from me the first that his son has returned? Although I am aware that the youth would not prefer this. But when I see him tormenting himself so miserably about his absence, can I conceal a joy so unhoped for, especially when there can be no danger to him from the discovery? I will not do so, but as far as I can I will assist the old man. As I see my son aiding his friend, and acting as his confidant in his concerns, it is but right that we old men as well should assist each other."

Chremes observed the side of the olive tree that faced his own domus, checking the leaves and fruit upon it, when Menedemus, said 'old man', appeared from his doorway.

"Assuredly I was either born with a disposition peculiarly suited for misery, or else that saying which I hear commonly repeated, that 'time assuages human sorrow,' is false. For really my sorrow about my son increases daily." He sighed long and painfully, struggling to stopper the tears that threatened to unman him. "And the longer he is away from me, the more anxiously do I wish for him, and the more I miss him."

Many a father in the audience was moved by this, their pitying eyes upon this Menedemus. But they remained silent and continued to observe the action upon the pulpitum with great interest.

From where he sat a few rows up, Publius Leander Antoninus thought that such pain was not the preserve only of fathers of sons, but also of doting fathers of daughters. He wiped at his cheek most subtly so that none could see. But his wife, Delphina, attuned as ever to his stoic silence, gripped his hand beside him, for she felt herself that such pain was not only the realm of men, but of loving mothers as well.

Chremes spotted his neighbour who was, only just then, populating his thoughts. "But I see him coming out of his house. I'll go speak to him." He approached around the olive tree to meet the man. "Menedemus, good-morrow! I bring you news, which you would especially desire to be imparted."

"Pray, have you heard any thing about my son, Chremes?"

"He's alive, and well!"

"Why, where is he, I beg you?" Menedemus rushed to his neighbour, his face undergoing profound transformation in the transition from despair to relief.

"Here, at my house. At my home," Chremes replied, looking back at his doorway.

Menedemus began to weep upon the edge of the fountain and asked to see his son.

But Chremes denied him, much to the dismay of the audience whose heads turned this way and that looking for companions in their disagreement with the meddler's decision.

"He does not wish you yet to know of his return, and he

shuns your presence. He's afraid that on account of that fault, your former severity may even be increased."

"Did you not tell him how I was affected?" Menedemus demanded.

"No."

"For what reason, Chremes?"

Chremes, spoke in orbit of his neighbour, explaining all the while how Menedemus' son, Clinia, was ensconced within Chremes' domus with his former mistress, a certain Bacchis, who was perfectly trained to extravagance, not least for all her attendants laden with clothes and jewels of gold like an eastern satrap.

It was obvious to the audience then that the plot of the wily servant, Syrus, had taken. The men believed Bacchis to be the mistress of Clinia. Now that the viewers were in the know, they watched the old men expand upon their misunderstanding.

When Menedemus asked if his son's woman was at Chremes' domus, the latter spread his arms wide as if pleading with Olympus for aid. He complained of the great expense of a single dinner for her and her retinue, the quantity of wine, and her pickiness with regard to the vintages. His son would need a fortune to keep his mistress and his happiness.

But Menedemus was undeterred, determined to accept his son's return no matter whom he brought along with him.

"If it is your determination thus to act," Chremes advised, "I hold it to be of very great moment that he should not be aware that with a full knowledge you grant him this."

"What shall I do?"

"Any thing, rather than what you are thinking of... Supply him with money through some other person. Suffer yourself to be imposed upon by the artifices of his servant. Although I have smelt out this too, that they are about that, and are secretly planning it among them. Syrus is always whispering with that servant of yours. They impart their plans to the young men, and it were better for you to lose a talent this way, than a mina the other. The money is not the question now, but this - in what way we can supply it to the young man with the least danger. For if he once knows the state of your feelings - that you would sooner part with your life, and sooner with all your money, than allow your son to leave you. Whew! What an inlet will you be opening for his debauchery! Aye, and so much so, that henceforth to live can not be desirable to you. For we all become worse through indulgence. Whatever comes into his head, he'll be wishing for. Nor will he reflect whether that which he desires is right or wrong. You will not be able to endure your estate and him going to ruin. You will refuse to supply him. He will immediately have recourse to the means by which he finds that he has the greatest hold upon you, and threaten that he will immediately leave you."

"You seem to speak the truth, and just what is the fact."

"I'faith, I have not been sensible of sleep this night with my eyes, for thinking of how to restore your son to you."

Menedemus took his neighbour's hands in his. "I request that you will still act in a like manner, Chremes."

"I am ready to serve you," Chremes replied, and asked what he wanted him to do.

"As you have perceived that they are laying a plan to deceive me, that they may hasten to complete it. I long to give him whatever he wants. I am now longing to behold him."

"I'll lend my endeavours. This little business is in my way. Our neighbours, Simus and Crito are disputing here about boundaries. They have chosen me for arbitrator. I'll go and tell them that I can not possibly give them my attention today as I had stated I would. I'll be here immediately."

When Chremes left, Menedemus stood alone, his eyes gazing skyward. "Ye Gods, by our trust in you! That the nature of all men should be so constituted, that they can see and judge of other men's affairs better than their own! Is it because in our own concerns we are biased either with joy or grief in too great a degree? How much wiser now is he for me, than I have been for myself!"

Many an audience member's head shook in dismay at that, for they knew the truth of it, that Chremes had been set upon the wrong path by his own servant, Syrus. When Chremes returned from his neighbours, Menedemus was waiting for him.

"I have disengaged myself, that I might lend you my services at my leisure. Syrus must be found and instructed by me in this business. Someone, I know not who, is coming out of my house. Do you step hence home, that they may not perceive that we are conferring together."

Menedemus rushed off into his domus, leaving Chremes to meet the newcomer.

"GET READY, FAUSTO. SYRUS IS ABOUT TO GO ON!" FELIX SAID.

It had been a long act for Pollux and Julius, the latter of which remained upon the pulpitum, a dominus in waiting for his wily servant.

When Pollux arrived behind the scaena frons, Castor and Beatrice were there to hand him water and a towel.

"Well done, brother!" Castor slapped his back. "Come, sit so that Beatrice can fix your face."

Pollux sat down so that the ageing upon his visage could be ameliorated by Beatrice's skilled hands.

While the others watched from the wings, and Damon's music tickled the audience's ears, Fausto stood at the doorway of Chremes' home, ready to burst onto the scene like a runner from the starting line at the games.

"Wait for the music to die away, Fausto," Felix said. "And… go."

. . .

To a deep silence in the air, Syrus the servant appeared, pacing wildly, his mind as awhirl as his hair. "Run to and fro in every direction," he commanded himself. "Still, money, you must be found. A trap must be laid for the old man."

From behind the tree, Chremes spied his man, nodding in acknowledgment of his rightness. "Was I deceived in saying that they were planning this? That servant of Clinia's is somewhat dull. Therefore that province has been assigned to this one of ours."

Syrus looked up, eyes wide. "Who's that speaking?" he asked before turning and seeing his dominus. Quickly, he looked to the audience. "I'm undone! Did he hear it, I wonder?"

"Yes, he did, you shit!" one of The Rome Antics yelled, only to be shushed by Cassius Cantor.

"Syrus." Chremes emerged from behind the tree.

The panic in Syrus' eyes was writ large, but the servant found his way to a story like an acrobat across the circus field. He spoke of wine, and then praised their houseguest, Bacchis, the mistress of his neighbour's son, Clinia. "Not like courtesans of former days, but as times are now, very passable. Nor do I in the least wonder that Clinia dotes upon her. But he has a father - a certain covetous, miserable, and stingy person - this neighbour of ours." He pointed to Menedemus' domus. "Do you know him? Yet, as if he was not abounding in wealth, his son ran away through want. Are you aware that it is the fact, as I am saying?"

"How should I not be aware? A fellow that deserves the mill," Chremes said, arms crossed.

"Who?"

"That servant of the young gentleman, I mean," Chremes replied, referring to poor Dromo.

"Syrus! I was sadly afraid for you!" Syrus said to himself.

"To suffer it to come to this!" Chremes turned his back to his servant, his face a plot in the making.

"What was he to do?" Syrus replied, eyebrows arched slyly.

"Do you ask the question? He ought to have found some expedient, contrived some stratagem, by means of which there might have been something for the young man to give to his mistress, and thus have saved this crabbed old fellow in spite of himself."

"You are surely joking." Syrus turned to his dominus, only slightly less confused and surprised than the audience whose eyes were fastened upon them.

"This ought to have been done by Dromo, Syrus."

"How now? Pray, do you commend servants who deceive their masters?" There was a vain hope in Syrus' voice.

"Upon occasion…I certainly do commend them." Chremes looked sidelong at his man.

Syrus nodded. "Quite right."

"Inasmuch as it often is the remedy for great disturbances. Then would this man's only son have stayed at home."

Syrus stepped to the front of the pulpitum to whisper to the audience. "Whether he says this in jest or in earnest, I don't know. Only, in fact, that he gives me additional zest for longing still more to trick him."

"And what is he now waiting for, Syrus?" Chremes was prying now, fishing for minnows of intelligence. "Is it until his father drives him away from here a second time, when he can no longer support her expenses? Has he no plot on foot against the old gentleman?"

"He is a stupid fellow."

Chremes smiled. "Then you ought to assist him, for the sake of the young man."

Syrus shrugged most humbly then, for the benefit of his master. "For my part, I can do so easily, if you command me, for I know well in what fashion it is usually done."

"Do it then," Chremes commanded.

"But hark you! Just take care and remember this…in case any thing of this sort should perchance happen at a future time, such are human affairs! Your son might do the same." Syrus winked to the massed onlookers beyond the orchestra.

"The necessity will not arise, I trust," Chremes stated.

Syrus looked relieved. "I' faith, and I trust so too. Nor do I say so now, because I have suspected him in any way, but in case, none the more. You see what his age is." Syrus turned away. "And truly, Chremes, if an occasion does happen, I may be able to handle you right handsomely," he said to himself.

Supremely proud of how he had handled and misled his servant, Chremes turned to go into his domus. "As to that, we'll consider what is requisite when the occasion does happen. At present do you set about this matter."

When his dominus was gone, Syrus heaved a sigh of relief and wiped his brow, for the day had grown long and hot. "Never on any occasion did I hear my master talk more to the purpose, nor at any time could I believe that I was *authorized* to play the rogue with greater impunity. I wonder who it is coming out of our house?" He stood aside then as the scene came to a close and more music filled the air about him.

Felix Modestus stood at the central doorway of the scaena frons, looking up through the branches of the olive tree to where Terentius' shade sat at the top of the cavia, among those mortal viewers. "Gods…what is happening?" Felix asked himself beneath his breath.

"What do you mean? I think it's going well, all things considered." Rufio pat his friend's shoulder. "We're more than halfway."

"I mean him," Felix said, eying the ghostly form of Terentius who appeared to be craning his neck so that his worried face could see the reactions in people's faces, hear the quiet commentary of their opinions as they waited for the third scene of the third act to commence. "A part of me is more worried about pleasing that shade - if there really is a shade - than about entertaining these Athenians."

"I know," Rufio said. "I never would have taken him to be so broody. If it were Plautus, the hauntings would have been more riotous."

Felix turned to Rufio. "That's not funny." He rubbed his eyes. "I think we're going mad."

"Then I've grown comfortable in my madness, I suppose," Rufio smiled.

Just then, Clara joined the two of them. "By the Gods, you two! What are you jabbering about at this moment? Rufio, you're about to go on with Julius and Fausto!"

"Oh…ah…right! Yes. I'm off!" Rufio went to join the other two at the door of Chremes.

Clara turned to Felix. "You all right?"

"I'm glad you're both here for this. I wouldn't have it any other way."

Clara hugged Felix and placed her hand upon his bearded cheek. "Do not worry. We're all here for you."

Felix smiled and turned to Electra who was coming up the stairs to the back of the scaena. "Is our beautiful Bacchis ready to show herself on the upper storey?"

Electra paused and eyed her husband with a sultry look. "Do we dare pull their attention away from those three?" She nodded toward Julius, Rufio, and Fausto who were just going through the door and onto the scene.

THE AGED CHREMES CAME OUT FIRST, HIS FACE RED AND furious as he chided his son, Clitipho, who followed in tow. Behind the latter their servant, Syrus, tagged along, his head cocked to hear all that was said, for he feared his plotting to be soon revealed.

"Pray, what does this mean? What behavior is this, Clitipho? Is this acting as becomes you?" Chremes shouted, turning quick on his son before the tree as the audience leaned in to hear what was said.

"What have I done?" Clitipho replied, his eyes already straying to the upper story of the domus where Bacchis appeared, adjusting her stola and painting her lips. Clitipho coughed, choking on his excitement.

"Did I not see you just now putting your hand into this Courtesan's bosom?" Chremes pointed up without looking, even as Bacchis made another tempting adjustment.

"That's too much! This isn't a pantomime!" Terentius shouted from his perch at the top of the cavia, unheard by any but Felix and Rufio who stumbled a little at the sudden outburst.

Syrus turned to the audience, pulling at his hair. "It's all up with us. I'm utterly undone!"

"What, I?" Clitipho said to his father, feigning innocence.

"With these self-same eyes I saw it. Don't deny it. Besides, you wrong him unworthily in not keeping your hands off. For indeed it is a gross affront to entertain a person, your friend, at your house, and to take liberties with his mistress. Yesterday, for instance, at wine, how rude you were!"

"'Tis the truth," Syrus added.

"How annoying you were! So much so, that for my part, as the Gods may prosper me, I dreaded what in the end might be the consequence. I understand lovers. They resent highly things that you would not imagine."

"But he has full confidence in me, father, that I would not do any thing of that kind."

Chremes slapped his randy son, the younger man holding

his reddening face, eyes wide and alert, even as he glanced again up at the tantalizing form of Bacchis.

"Be it so," Chremes continued. "Still, at least, you ought to go somewhere for a little time away from their presence. Passion prompts to many a thing. Your presence acts as a restraint upon doing them. I form a judgment from myself. There's not one of my friends this day to whom I would venture, Clitipho, to disclose all my secrets. With one, his station forbids it. With another, I am ashamed of the action itself, lest I may appear a fool or devoid of shame; do you rest assured that he does the same. But it is our part to be sensible of this and, when and where it is requisite, to show due complaisance."

Syrus sidled up to Clitipho then. "What is it he is saying?"

"I'm utterly undone!" the younger man hissed back at his servant.

"Clitipho, these same injunctions I gave you. You have acted the part of a prudent and discreet person," Syrus added.

"Hold your tongue, I beg," Clitipho retorted.

"Very good," Syrus said as he backed away.

"Syrus, I am ashamed of him!" Chremes said, approaching the two whisperers.

"I believe it! And not without reason. Why, he vexes myself even."

Clitipho turned upon his servant with surprised annoyance. "Do you persist, then?"

But Syrus only shrugged. "I' faith, I'm saying the truth, as it appears to me."

Clitipho turned to his father. "May I not go near them?"

"How now? Is there but one way of going near them?" Chremes demanded, exasperated.

Syrus turned to the audience then. "Confusion! He'll be betraying himself before I've got the money." He turned to his elder dominus. "Chremes, will you give attention to me, who am but a silly person?"

Chremes and Syrus stepped aside to talk, as the latter informed his dominus that his son should go somewhere out of the way, a walk some distance off. Chremes agreed.

"May the Gods extirpate you, Syrus, for thrusting me away from here." Clitipho crossed his arms, his face pouty as he looked longingly up at the window where Bacchis appeared no longer.

"Then do you for the future keep those hands of yours within bounds," Syrus chided Clitipho who marched off down the road. Syrus turned back to his dominus. "Really now, what do you think? What do you imagine will become of him next, unless, so far as the Gods afford you the means, you watch him, correct and admonish him?"

"I'll take care of that," Chremes said, his eyes watching his errant son go off on his walk. He then looked about to ensure they were alone, and turned back to his servant. "What have you done, Syrus, about that matter which I was mentioning to you a short time since? Have you any plan that suits you, or not yet even?"

"You mean the design upon Menedemus? I have just hit upon one." It was Syrus' turn to look about before speaking in hushed tones with his dominus. "This Courtesan is a very bad woman."

"So she seems."

"Aye, if you did but know. O shocking! Just see what she is hatching. There was a certain old woman here from Corinth, and this Bacchis lent her a thousand silver drachmae."

"What then?" Chremes asked, interested now so much coin was mentioned.

"She is now dead." Syrus hung his head. "She left a daughter, a young girl. She has been left with this Bacchis as a pledge for that sum."

Syrus went on to explain that the girl in question, who was currently with Sostrata, Chremes' wife, is to be a surety against the money which Bacchis was trying to wheedle out of Clinia, Menedemus' son.

The audience leaned forward along with Chremes, attempting to ascertain the matter of what Syrus was saying, hiding things this way and that like a shyster playing at cups in the agora.

"What then do you intend doing?" Chremes asked, rubbing his forehead.

"What, I? I shall go to Menedemus. I'll tell him she is a captive from Caria, rich, and of noble family, and if he redeems her, there will be a considerable profit in this transaction."

Chremes shook his head. "I'll now answer you for Menedemus… 'I will not purchase her.'"

Syrus began asking the reason, but before his master could answer, they were interrupted by a great noise at their own domus door, and so hid themselves apart to see what was afoot.

"It's all right," Beatrice said to Domela. "You'll be fine."

"So much depends upon this scene!" Domela hissed. "I don't want to disappoint my Julius."

"*Your* Julius?" Beatrice stood still, her feathers clearly ruffled. "He was all of *ours* before he was *yours*."

"Ladies," Clara interrupted, "is this really the time?" She held up the ring. "Here, Domela. You'll need this. Remember to move it about so the audience can see it glint in the firelight."

"Oh, dear. You are cute, but I have done this before."

Now Clara's feathers were ruffled.

But Domela looked out of the door toward Julius. "But I do love him so," she said with a sigh.

Clara and Beatrice looked at each other.

"Do it for Julius then," Beatrice said. "I see that he loves you too." Domela turned to her. "It's obvious."

Clara stepped back then as the two other women prepared for their entrance.

"Shall we, domina Sostrata?" Beatrice asked.

"We shall, nurse!"

And Damon launched into a cacophonous arrangement from above that roused the audience to the noise which Chremes and Syrus had heard.

Sostrata, the wife of Chremes, came into the street from her domus, her nurse following. She held up a large, bejewelled ring which caused not a few audience members to gasp. When it glinted, the sparks of ruby and diamond light glittered about the odeon as though one were beside the sea at midday in summer.

"Unless my fancy deceives me," Sostrata said, "surely this is the ring which I suspect it to be, the same with which my daughter was exposed."

Behind the tree, Chremes climbed atop the back of his servant. "Syrus, what is the meaning of these expressions?"

"Nurse, how is it? Does it not seem to you the same?" Sostrata asked her own servant.

The nurse, Canthara, looked at it, her eyes betraying the great certainty, and not a little awe, which she felt. "As for me, I said it was the same the very instant that you showed it me."

"But have you now examined it thoroughly, my dear nurse?"

"Thoroughly."

"Then go in-doors at once, and if she has now done

bathing, bring me word. I'll wait here in the mean time for my husband."

It was Syrus' turn to climb upon his dominus' back, panic in his bulging eyes. "She wants you! See what it is she wants. She is in a serious mood, I don't know why. It is not without a cause… I fear what it may be!"

"What it may be? I' faith, she'll now surely be announcing some important trifle, with a great parade." Chremes shrugged off his servant and stepped out to meet his wife.

"Ha! My husband!" Sostrata said excitedly as she rushed toward him.

"Ha! My wife!"

Sostrata prefaced her great announcement by saying that she did not want her husband to think that she had ever set out to do anything against him.

Syrus rubbed his sweaty face. "This excuse portends I know not what offense." He climbed up into the tree the better to spy upon the couple.

Chremes assured his wife that he would believe her, and Sostrata pressed on with the incredible tale.

"Do you remember me being pregnant, and yourself declaring to me, most peremptorily, that if I should bring forth a girl, you would not have it brought up?" She paused. "There was here an elderly woman of Corinth, of no indifferent character. To her I gave it to be exposed." Sostrata clasped the ring to her breast, her face a confusing mixture of regret and excitement to her Chremes.

"O Jupiter! That there should be such extreme folly in a person's mind." Chremes stepped toward her, wanting for more of the story as his wife explained further. "This, indeed, I know for certain, even if you were to deny it, that in every thing you both speak and act ignorantly and foolishly. How many blunders you disclose in this single affair! For, in the first place, then, if you had been disposed to obey my orders, the child ought to have been dispatched. You ought not in words to have feigned her death, and in reality to have left hopes of her surviving. But that I pass over - compassion, maternal affection - I allow it. But how finely you did provide for the future! What was your meaning? Do reflect. It's clear, beyond a doubt, that your daughter was betrayed by you to this old woman, either that through you she might make a living by her, or that she might be sold in open market as a slave. I suppose you reasoned thus: 'anything is enough, if only her life is saved.' What are you to do with those who understand neither law, nor right and justice? Be it for better or for worse, be it for them or against them, they see nothing except just what they please."

Sostrata shook her head, tears in her eyes, glinting as brightly as the jewels in her hand. "My dear Chremes, I have done wrong, I own. I am convinced. Now this I beg of you… inasmuch as you are more advanced in years than I, be so much the more ready to forgive so that your justice may be some protection for my weakness."

Chremes looked upon his wife, and pat her shoulder. "I'll readily forgive you doing this, of course, but, Sostrata, my easy temper prompts you to do amiss. But, whatever this circumstance is, by reason of which this was begun upon, proceed to tell it."

Sostrata wiped her eyes, took a breath, and set upon the tale to better enlighten her husband. "As we women are all foolishly and wretchedly superstitious, when I delivered the child to her to be exposed, I drew a ring from off my finger, and ordered her to expose it, together with the child that if she should die, she might not be without some portion of our possessions."

Chremes nodded. "That was right. Thereby you proved the saving of yourself and her."

Sostrata then held out the ring before Chremes' eyes. "*This* is that ring."

Chremes took it and observed. "Whence did you get it?"

"From the young woman whom Bacchis brought here with her. She gave it me to keep for her while she went to bathe. At first I paid no attention to it, but after I looked at it, I at once recognized it and came running to you."

"What do you suspect now, or have you discovered, relative to her?" Chremes stood at the front of the pulpitum looking out at the crowd, his back to his wife as he thought on the circumstances just described to him.

"I don't know. Unless you inquire of herself whence she got it, if that can possibly be discovered." Sostrata stood again at his side.

From his perch, Syrus shook his head wildly, like a fretting sparrow returned to its nest to find it in disarray. "I'm undone! I see more hopes from this incident than I desire. If it is so, she certainly must be ours."

While Chremes and Sostrata discussed the woman to whom the baby had been given to expose, Syrus appeared to lay out more plans to his and his young dominus' benefit.

"How much beyond my hopes has this matter turned out!" Sostrata said as she and her husband went toward their domus to find the girl. "How dreadfully afraid I was, Chremes, that you would now be of feelings as unrelenting as formerly you were on exposing the child."

Chremes stopped at the threshold of their home, his face softening. "Many a time a man can not be such as he would be, if circumstances do not admit of it. Time has now so brought it about, that I should be glad of a daughter… Formerly I wished for nothing less."

Sostrata hugged her Chremes most fervently, and together they went indoors.

. . .

Whilst Fausto extricated Syrus from the tree upon the pulpitum, his antics receiving a few sniggers from the audience as he tumbled and toiled his way out of the clinging branches, Felix and the rest of the company greeted Julius and Domela with glassy eyes.

"Well done, both of you," Felix told them.

In the wagon with the children, whom Electra and Clara had just fed, Martia wiped her eyes as she held the children once more, safe and sound, with Peli sitting guard upon the ground below.

"What is it my dear?" Sextus said as he approached. "Are you uncomfortable in the wagon bed? I can take over if you like."

Martia shook her head. "No. It's not that. It's that scene, when they discover their long-lost daughter. To think the child would have been exposed when so many are not granted a single babe!"

Sextus reached over the side of the wagon to take his wife's hand. "It's not so anymore. Only in the most barbarian corners of the empire."

"I wish so much that-" Martia's voice caught and she stopped the wave of regret with a deep breath. "It is no matter. The Gods assign joys as they see fit."

"We have yet much joy between us, my love," Sextus said, his eyes full of love for his wife.

"I know," Martia smiled. *And I know he would never leave me,* she thought. *For that, I am grateful.*

Syrus at last fell from the tree, brushed himself off, and stepped toward the edge of the pulpitum to address his audience.

"Unless my fancy deceives me, retribution will not be very far off from me. So much by this incident are my forces now utterly driven into straits. Unless I contrive by some means that the old man may not come to know that this damsel is his son's mistress. For as to entertaining any hopes about the money, or supposing I could cajole him, it's useless. I shall be sufficiently triumphant if I'm allowed to escape with my sides covered." He rubbed his side nervously, imagining the lashing he was at risk of receiving should his plotting be discovered.

"I'm vexed that such a tempting morsel has been so suddenly snatched away from my jaws. What am I to do? Or what shall I devise? I must begin upon my plan over again. Nothing is so difficult, but that it may be found out by seeking. What now if I set about it after this fashion…" Syrus paced a little as he considered his options. "That's of no use. What if after this fashion I effect just about the same? But this I think will do. It can not. Yes! Excellent. Bravo! I've found out the best of all. I' faith, I do believe that after all I shall lay hold of this same runaway money!"

Feeling more optimistic, Syrus walked for a little until he spied Menedemus' son, Clinia, approaching and speaking to himself.

"Nothing can possibly henceforth befall me of such consequence as to cause me uneasiness. So extreme is this joy that has surprised me. Now then, I shall give myself up entirely to my father, to be more frugal than even he could wish!"

"I wasn't mistaken," Syrus said to himself. "She has been discovered, so far as I understand from these words of his." He then advanced on Clinia. "I am rejoiced that this matter has turned out for you so much to your wish!"

Clinia looked up and smiled, his bulky shoulders spread wide. "O my dear Syrus, have you heard of it, pray?"

"How shouldn't I, when I was present all the while?"

Clinia spied olive leaves in Syrus' hair and glanced up at the tree beside them. "Did you ever hear of anything falling out so fortunately for anyone?"

"Never."

"And, so may the Gods prosper me, I do not now rejoice so much on my own account as hers, whom I know to be deserving of any honour."

Syrus rolled his eyes and mimicked the more muscular fellow beside him. "I believe it. But now, Clinia, come, attend to me in my turn. For your friend's business as well…it must be seen to…that it is placed in a state of security, lest the old gentleman should now come to know any thing about his mistress."

"Oh, Jupiter!" Clinia roared joyfully.

"Do be quiet."

"My Antiphila will be mine!"

"Do you still interrupt me thus?"

As Clinia walked about, his mind drifting in an idyll of his own making, dreaming of the joys to come, Syrus fretted over his plan, trying most ardently to focus Clinia on the task of preserving Clitipho from being discovered by Chremes, and of still laying hold of the coin required.

"This must be seen to," Syrus explained. "That your friend's business as well is placed in a state of security. For if you now go away from us, and leave Bacchis here, our old man will immediately come to know that she is Clitipho's mistress. If you take her away with you, it will be concealed just as much as it has been hitherto concealed."

"But still, Syrus, nothing can make more against my marriage than this. For with what face am I to address my father about it? You understand what I mean?"

Syrus explained, much to Clinia's obvious surprise and relief, that he did not wish for him to lie to Menedemus. "I bid you do this: Tell him that you are in love with Antiphila, and want her for a wife, that this Bacchis is Clitipho's mistress."

"You require a thing that is fair and reasonable, and easy to be done. And I suppose, then, you would have me request my father to keep it a secret from your old man."

"On the contrary, to tell him directly the matter just as it is."

Clinia looked doubtful, as if the truth in all these plots were so far gone, it had returned like a surprise visitor. "What? Are you quite in your senses or sober? Why, you were for ruining him outright. For how could he be in a state of security? Tell me that."

"For my part, I yield the palm to this device. Here I do pride myself exultingly in having in myself such exquisite resources, and power of address so great, as to deceive them both by telling the truth, so that when your old man tells ours that she is his son's mistress, he'll still not believe him."

"But yet, by these means you again cut off all hopes of my marriage. For, as long as Chremes believes that she is my mistress, he'll not give me his daughter. Perhaps you care little what becomes of me, so long as you provide for him?"

Syrus shook his head in frustration. "What the plague, do you suppose I want this pretence to be kept up for an age? 'Tis but for a single day, only till I have secured the money. You be quiet. I ask no more."

Eventually, Clinia agreed to go along with the servant's plot to tell the truth, and to have Bacchis brought over to the domus of Menedemus.

Electra stood poised at the doorway of Chremes, ready for Bacchis' entrance. "Are you ready, Beatrice?"

"Phrygia is ready, yes," Beatrice replied, standing at her mistress' shoulder.

Electra heard Thespis whine a little from the wagon, but focussed her attention on the task ahead. *Martia is with him,* she reassured herself.

"Felix and Fausto are ready," Beatrice said as Damon's birds began to quieten in the tree above where the two men were hiding.

"Quickly, Beatrice!" Electra hissed, a little panicked. "My first line!"

"To a very fine purpose, upon my faith-"

Electra then sent Bacchis out beyond the scaena...

"To a very fine purpose," Bacchis declared to the audience, fully aware of the two men listening to her. "Upon my faith, have the promises of Syrus brought me hither, who agreed to lend me ten minae. If now he deceives me, oft as he may entreat me to come, he shall come in vain. Or else, when I've promised to come, and fixed the time, when he has carried word back for certain, and Clitipho is on the stretch of expectation, I'll disappoint him and not come. Syrus will make atonement to me with his back."

"She promises you very fairly," Clinia whispered to Syrus.

The latter rubbed his back at the promised lashes. "But do you think she is in jest? She'll do it, if I don't take care." They watched as Bacchis and her servant, Phrygia, came to a stop in the street.

"They're asleep... I'faith, I'll rouse them." Bacchis raised her voice so that all in the vicinity might hear. "My dear Phrygia, did you hear about the country-seat of Charinus, which that man was showing us just now?"

Phrygia looked confused, but tried to stay thoughtfully abreast with her mistress. "I heard of it."

"That it was the next to the farm here on the right-hand side," Bacchis said louder still.

"I remember."

The audience leaned in, wondering what the courtesan

could be up to, for she was now appearing as wily as the servant, Syrus!

"Run thither post-haste. The captain is keeping the feast of Bacchus at his house."

"What is she going to be at?" Syrus climbed upon Clinia the better to see and hear.

"Tell him I am here very much against my inclination, and am detained. Tell him that by some means or other I'll give them the slip and come to him." Bacchis smoothed the length of the brilliant stola along her hips and pinched her cheeks.

Phrygia smiled and bowed to her mistress before turning to go, when Syrus leaped from atop Clinia's back to stop her.

"Upon my faith, I'm ruined! Bacchis, stay, stay! Prithee, where are you sending her? Order her to stop." Syrus was upon his knees before the courtesan, pretending to kiss the hem of her stola when actually he was attempting a cheeky peek beneath it.

Bacchis ignored him and turned back to Phrygia. "Be off."

Phrygia turned again to go, but Syrus grabbed her tunica so that now, he held both women fast from his base position as he looked up.

"Why, the money's ready," Syrus blurted hurriedly.

"Why, then I'll stay," Bacchis said, motioning for Phrygia to stay.

"And it will be given you presently." Syrus got to his feet, but Bacchis reached out to press him back down like a hound too given to climbing upon one's lap.

"Just when you please, do I press you?" Bacchis demanded.

Syrus proceeded to tell her that in order for her to get the money, she needed to move herself and her entire entourage to the domus of Menedemus.

"What scheme are you upon, you rascal?" Bacchis demanded.

"What, I? Coining money to give you." Syrus turned and winked at the audience.

Bacchis relented and let herself be led to Menedemus' domus, while Clinia looked on with wide eyes from behind the tree, shaking his head.

When Dromo answered the door, Syrus urged him to take them in.

"Ask no questions," Syrus hissed. "Let them take what they brought here with them. Chremes will hope his expenses are lightened by their departure, for sure he little knows how much loss this trifling gain will bring him. You, Dromo, if you are wise, know nothing of what you do know."

Dromo curtsied to Syrus. "You shall own that I'm dumb."

Syrus nodded his agreement and turned to make way for Bacchis and Phrygia who entered Menedemus' home.

Clinia emerged from his hiding place, reluctantly following the perfumed retinue into his father's domus, but not without laying a smack upon Syrus' head as he passed.

As Felix, Electra and Beatrice came through the scaena, it was to the sound of restless babies.

Clara was busy walking around with Felicia while Martia, now out of the wagon, was walking around with Thespis.

Peli tugged at his rope, only calmed a little when Rufio tossed him another piece of meat.

Beneath the far wagon, within the cage, Momo let out a screech that was, thankfully, covered by the music Damon piped into the odeon at the changing of the scene.

"What is happening here?" Felix demanded. "Are we unravelling?" He turned to see if the audience heard any of the ruckus, but they seemed to be in discussion, many pointing at the servant Syrus, who lazed in the street before his dominus' home. "Oh no…" Felix spotted Terentius then, the shade moving up and down the aisles of the cavia listening at times to conversation, other times shouting at people who doubted the plot. "Rufio!" Felix called as low as he could. "Rufio, come here!"

Rufio rushed up to the back of the scaena to meet Felix. "What?"

"Look." Felix pointed to the far right. "You see him?"

"Where? Who are you talking about?" Rufio gulped. "Oh."

"He's going to ruin his own play."

"Nobody can see him."

"We can."

"And only us," Rufio said.

Felix shook his head. "If people start feeling nauseous or ill because the dead playwright is whispering in their ear, they will start to leave."

"What do you want me to do? Go out and lay hold of the shade? The only thing we can do is let him alone while we do our parts."

Felix turned quickly to the others in the hall behind him. "Will someone shut up that accursed monkey?"

"What do you want us to do?" Castor asked.

"I don't know, just give the cage a kick. Hand him some figs. Anything!"

There was a loud squeal and then silence.

"Felix," Rufio said. "Relax. We're in the final stretch."

"Really? We still have miles to go!" Felix turned to Julius, who stood to the left at Chremes' door, and nodded. "Go."

CHREMES EMERGED FROM HIS DOMUS INTO THE BRIGHT DAY, a look of great relief etched upon his wrinkle-worried face. "So may the Gods prosper me, I am now concerned for the fate of Menedemus, that so great a misfortune should have befallen him. To be maintaining that woman with such a retinue!

Although I am well aware he'll not be sensible of it for some days to come, his son was so greatly missed by him. But when he sees such a vast expense incurred by him every day at home, and no limit to it, he'll wish that this son would leave him a second time." He then turned to find his servant lazing in the street beside the fountain. When he spied Syrus, he marched straight over to him and gave him a kick. "Syrus... How go matters? You seem, then, to have effected something, I know not what, with the old gentleman."

Syrus got quickly to his feet, looking quite proud of himself. "As to what we were talking of a short time since? No sooner said than done."

Chremes smiled. "Upon my faith, I can not forbear patting your head for it." And he did so. "Come here, Syrus... I'll do you some good turn for this matter, and with pleasure."

Syrus rubbed his chin, his turn to smile, and proceeded to tell Chremes how Clinia had carried out his instructions. "Clinia has told Menedemus, that this Bacchis is your Clitipho's mistress, and that he has taken her thither with him in order that you might not come to know of it."

Chremes nodded. "Very good."

Syrus looked to the audience quickly, and then back to his dominus to present the hidden truth as a plot of lies to the unknowing man. "Why yes, pretty fair. But listen what a piece of policy still remains. He is then to say that he has seen your daughter...that her beauty charmed him as soon as he beheld her, and that he desires her for a wife."

Chremes' smile faded and he looked angrily at his servant. "What, her that has just been discovered?"

"The same. And, in fact, he'll request that she may be asked for."

"For what purpose, Syrus? For I don't altogether comprehend it."

Syrus shook his head. "O dear, you are so dull." He went

on to explain that if Clinia is engaged to Antiphila, then money will be given to him for the wedding.

But Chremes shook his head as if doing so would disperse the mist that clouded his thoughts. "But I neither give nor betroth my daughter to him."

"Just as you please. I don't mean that in reality you should give her to him, but that you should pretend it."

"Pretending is not in my way; do you mix up these plots of yours, so as not to mix me up in them. Do you think that I'll betroth my daughter to a person to whom I will not marry her?" Chremes sat upon the fountain, his old arms crossed, his head still shaking.

Syrus took it upon himself to sit beside his dominus. "It might have been cleverly managed… And I undertook this affair for the very reason, that a short time since, you so urgently requested it."

Chremes' head stopped shaking. "But still, I especially wish you to do your best for it to be brought about…but in some other way."

Syrus' eyes widened as he had yet to add another plot upon the plot. "It shall be done. Some other method must be thought of. But as to what I was telling you of - about the money which she owes to Bacchis - that must now be repaid her. And you will not, of course, now be having recourse to this method… 'What have I to do with it? Was it lent to me? Did I give any orders? Had she the power to pawn my daughter without my consent?' They quote that saying, Chremes, with good reason, 'Rigorous law is often rigorous injustice.'"

The older men in the audience nodded their assent for this and, as if annoyed by their urging, Chremes tutted them.

"I will not do so," he insisted.

"On the contrary, though others were at liberty, you are not at liberty… All think that you are in good and very easy circumstances."

Chremes sighed, for he cared what others thought, men concerning themselves with the affairs of men and all… "Nay rather, I'll at once carry it to her myself."

But Syrus quickly urged that his son, Clitipho, should be the one to take the money to Bacchis because Menedemus now believed that Bacchis was Clitipho's mistress, which was the truth, except in the eyes of Chremes who had been so mislead.

"I'll bring it," Chremes finally relented, and so went off to his domus to collect the small fortune.

WITH THE CLOSE OF THE FIFTH SCENE OF THE FOURTH ACT, THE audience began to murmur. Some were confused by Syrus' layers of plots, others doubtful that it could all be carried off without a hitch.

"My head is beginning to ache with all this thinking," Numa said to Cassius Cantor beside him.

"It's brilliant!" Cassius beamed. "They're carrying it off wonderfully!" The leader of The Rome Antics looked about the audience. "But I don't know if it is loud enough to engage the audience. They should have added more tumbling and folly."

"I'm worried about Momo," Numa said, staring at the scaena frons. "I heard him squeal at the start of the scene."

"Don't worry," Cassius said, "I'm sure they're taking good care of him."

"You know what he's like when he's in his cage for too long!"

Cassius looked quickly at his man. "It doesn't bear thinking about right now. Pray the Gods don't allow it to come to that."

Farther down at the front of the cavia, Zotikos, Telephus, Aegisthus and Cadmus were in discussion of the plot, the staging, the performances and every other aspect of the play. They spoke in hushed tones amongst themselves however, fully aware of how sound carried in the odeon.

A couple of rows up from them, Publius Leander Antoninus and Delphina observed the arrogant artists engaged in their small colloquium.

"Sadly typical of them," Publius said to his wife. "No one can ever be allowed to better them in anything."

Delphina smiled. "Oh, I don't know. There is yet time enough for Felix and his company to win them."

Publius looked doubtful, but was quickly distracted by the things the lupae from Circe's were saying several rows up about what they were going to do with the young man playing Syrus.

"Dear me," Delphina said, a smile upon her lips.

"He may get that lashing after all from the sound of it," Publius said, making his wife laugh out loud.

"It certainly is a convoluted plot," the philosopher, Philemon, said to his neighbour, Zonas, the stoic. "I wonder at the mind that created this as an entertainment."

Zonas smiled at his friend. "Great pleasures are worth a bit of work, aren't they?"

"I prefer my pleasures to come easily," Philemon replied, glancing up at the lupae in the audience.

"They may come easily, but they will not hold your attention for long. The more work you put in, the longer lasting the feelings that are wrung from you." Zonas looked at the pulpitum with a smile. "I'll remember this for some time, I suspect."

"I prefer not to work for it," Philemon said, unaware of the cross-armed shade standing directly in front of him. "I feel a tickle in my nose," the philosopher said.

"That's just the seer, Melampus," Zonas clarified. "He's sitting over there."

"Ah…yes. That's it." Philemon pulled a perfumed handkerchief from his sleeve and pressed it to his nose.

Above them, at the top left of the cavia, Atticus sat alone in silence, watching and waiting. He had seen the production come to fruition as if he had seen sculptors choosing a block of stone to work, and then witnessed their thoughtful chiselling for months. Now, he was at last seeing the sculpture revealed, and he worried for them.

"Apollo…" he said in a hushed breath as the music of Damon's flute and Beatrice's tambourine filled the air. "Please aid The Etrurian Players…" He then leaned forward to watch and listen as Rufio and Fausto stepped onto the pulpitum…

"THERE IS NOTHING SO EASY BUT THAT IT BECOMES DIFFICULT when you do it with reluctance," Clitipho said to himself as he took a frustrated stroll. "As this walk of mine, for instance, though not fatiguing, it has reduced me to weariness. And now I dread nothing more than that I should be packed off some-where hence once again, that I may not have access to Bacchis. May then all the Gods and Goddesses, as many as exist, confound you, Syrus, with these stratagems and plots of yours. You are always devising something of this kind, by means of which to torture me."

Syrus chased after him. "Will you not away with you to where you deserve? How nearly had your forwardness proved my ruin!" He made a breast-fondling motion in front of his young dominus and threw his hands up in the air.

"Upon my faith, I wish it had been so. Just what you deserve!" Clitipho pushed the servant but, emboldened, Syrus pushed back.

The audience gasped at his servile audacity.

"Deserve? How so? Really, I'm glad that I've heard this from you before you had the money which I was just going to give you."

"What then would you have me to say to you? You've made

a fool of me…brought my mistress hither, whom I'm not allowed to touch!"

Syrus wrung his hands in mockery but he smiled and explained that Bacchis was no longer at his father's but at the domus of Menedemus, and that his father would be giving him the money soon that he should be able to present it to Bacchis himself.

"Perhaps you are joking with me," Clitipho said, distrust in his features.

They saw Chremes coming then with a bag of coin.

Syrus turned to his young dominus. "Take care not to express surprise at any thing, for what reason it is done… Give way at the proper moment. Do what he orders, and say but little."

Clitipho nodded and turned to meet his father.

"Have you told him how it is?" Chremes demanded of Syrus.

"I've told him pretty well every thing."

Chremes turned to his son. "Take this money, and carry it."

"Go!" Syrus urged Clitipho. "Why do you stand still, you stone? Why don't you take it?"

"Very well, give it me," Clitipho said stiffly as he took the bag with a jingle.

Syrus then led Clitipho to the domus of Menedemus to present the money to Bacchis, whilst Chremes awaited their return in the street outside.

The old man seemed tired as he looked up at the leaves of the olive tree and observed the home which he had worked so hard to keep.

"My daughter, in fact, has now had ten minae from me, which I consider as paid for her board. Another ten will follow these for clothes, and then she will require two talents for her portion." He mumbled as he calculated the amounts in mid-air. "How many things, both just and unjust, are sanctioned by custom!" He shook his head in a most piteous way. "Now I'm obliged, neglecting my business, to look out for someone on whom to bestow my property, that has been acquired by my labour."

"JULIUS IS READY!" CLARA SAID TO FELIX AND POLLUX WHO awaited at the door of Menedemus' domus.

Rufio came to stand beside her along with Sextus. "This audience is so hard to read," he said to her.

"We're doing what we can," Clara said, "and I'm so proud of you."

Rufio gripped her hand. "Almost there." He looked about the odeon for Terentius and found him seated in the front row alongside the Athenian actors and the playwright, Telephus. "If only they knew," Rufio said to himself with a chuckle.

"Knew what?" Clara asked.

"Oh, ah…nothing." Rufio looked at Felix and Pollux. "Go now!" he whispered.

The two men put on their smiles and marched out to start the scene with Julius.

"MY SON," MENEDEMUS SAID WITH A GREAT SMILE. "I NOW think myself the happiest of all men, since I find that you have returned to a rational mode of life."

Clinia smiled, his shoulders relieved of the weight and worry he had carried for so long. All watching him could feel his relief and his joy as he cast a hopeful look to the sky above.

But Chremes stood aside, watching, listening. "How much he is mistaken!"

Menedemus noted Chremes waiting for him and strode over at once, leaving his joyous son to dream of the bright days to come. "Chremes, you are the very person I wanted. Preserve, so far as in you lies, my son, myself, and my family."

When Chremes asked what he wanted, Menedemus proudly outlined the wish of his son - and of himself! - to marry Antiphila, Chremes' newfound daughter.

"Have you already forgotten what passed between us, concerning a scheme, that by that method some money might be got out of you?" Chremes demanded.

"I remember," Menedemus replied with a smile.

"That self-same thing they are now about."

Menedemus shook his head. "What do you tell me, Chremes? Why surely, this courtesan, who is at my house, is Clitipho's mistress."

"So they say, and you believe it all! And they say that he is desirous of a wife, in order that, when I have betrothed her, you may give him money, with which to provide gold trinkets and clothing, and other things that are requisite."

Doubt began to poison Menedemus' previously joyous heart. "Alas! In vain then, unhappy man, have I been over-joyed. Still, however, I had rather anything than be deprived of him. What answer now shall I report from you, Chremes, so that he may not perceive that I have found it out, and take it to heart?" He looked back at Clinia who was oblivious to their conversation which undermined his joy at that very moment.

"Say then, that you have seen me, and have treated about the marriage."

"I'll say so. What then?"

"That I will do everything…that as a son-in-law he meets my approbation. If you like, tell him also that she has been promised him."

Menedemus spread his arms wide and smiled once more. "Well, that's what I wanted!" He watched Clinia go back into his domus. He turned back to Chremes.

"Assuredly, before very long," Chremes continued,

"according as I view this matter, you'll have enough of him. But, however that may be, if you are wise, you'll give to him cautiously, and a little at a time."

Menedemus nodded. "I'll do so."

The two men departed for their respective homes, and the street was quiet again but for a single bird cooing in the tree above.

FELIX CAME BACK THROUGH THE DOORWAY OF MENEDEMUS' home and breathed a great sigh. They were at last upon the fifth act. He had never before wanted to rush a performance, or been so eager for it to finish.

Felix leaned against the stone wall between the doorways as Pollux, Domela, and Julius awaited their entrance. He realized that he was not afraid of the audience, nor even of the bad reviews that were no doubt coming their way. The play was in his nature, and so the performing of it was a thing of ease.

As he stood there, watching his company, his friends, hurry about and prepare for their action with military precision, he realized that what he was afraid of was not having time with his wife and child. The world and many in it vied for his attention, but there were only really two people to whom he wanted to give it wholeheartedly, and a small handful of friends with whom he wanted to share his joy.

That made Felix smile.

"What are you smiling at?" Clara asked Felix as she and Rufio approached. She looked to where Felix was watching Electra walk calmly around with Thespis in her arms, a woman greater than any Bacchis in all her glory, smiling at the child she adored.

"Fortuna loves you, Felix," Clara reassured.

"I know," Felix said, "even though the Athenians don't."

Rufio looked out beyond the scaena. "Why do you say that?"

"Come now, my friends," Felix said. "They hate it. This is the most sedate performance we've ever given."

"Oh I don't know…" Clara searched for something encouraging to say, but Felix's smile confused her.

"It's all right," he said. "I'm fine with it. We've done what we came to do. It's time for the last stand, and I'm glad you're here for it."

The three of them turned to watch and listen as Pollux, Julius, and Domela walked out onto the pulpitum, the first through the door of Menedemus, the other two out of Chremes' domus.

"I AM QUITE AWARE THAT I AM NOT SO OVERWISE," Menedemus said to himself, "or so very quick-sighted. But this assistant, prompter, and director of mine, Chremes, outdoes me in that. Anyone of those epithets which are applied to a fool is suited to myself, such as dolt, post, ass, lump of lead… To him not one can apply. His stupidity surpasses them all."

At that moment, Chremes came onto the street with his wife, Sostrata, beside him.

"Hold now, do, wife, leave off dinning the Gods with thanksgivings that your daughter has been discovered. Unless you judge of them by your own disposition, and think that they understand nothing, unless the same thing has been told them a hundred times. But, in the meantime, why does my son linger there so long with Syrus?"

"What persons do you say are lingering?" Menedemus said just then, stepping in front of Chremes.

"Ha! Menedemus, you have come opportunely. Tell me, have you told Clinia what I said?" Chremes asked.

And Menedemus proceeded to explain that he had indeed

told him that Chremes will allow him to marry his daughter. Menedemus, with a proud air about him, explained that Clinia did not ask him for any money, but that there was true joy that he would be united with Antiphila.

Menedemus experienced no small amount of annoyance when Chremes laughed at this, certain that this was only part of the scheme hatched by Syrus and the rest of them to trick the two old men out of coin.

While the two men argued, Sostrata busied herself with prettying the front of their domus, checking the flowers and writing upon a wax tablet, seemingly planning the dinner which her husband had told her to leave off planning.

Meanwhile, as Menedemus explained again that neither Clinia, or anyone else, had asked him for money for golden jewels, clothes, and attendants that would be needed for the bride, Chremes grew more annoyed at his own confusion, his suspicions obviously whirling out of control. Menedemus explained that all Clinia asked was that the marriage be concluded that very day.

"You say what's surprising. What did my servant Syrus do? Didn't even he say any thing?" Chremes asked.

"Nothing at all."

Chremes grew red-faced and smacked the air in lieu of his servant's back.

"For my part," Menedemus added, "I wonder at that, when you know other things so well. But this same Syrus has moulded your son too, to such perfection, that there could not be even the slightest suspicion that Bacchis is Clinia's mistress!"

"What do you say?"

Menedemus smiled and lowered his voice as he explained that in an inner room of his domus, a bed was made up, and into this room went Clitipho, Chremes' son.

"I'm alarmed," Chremes said.

"Bacchis followed directly."

When Menedemus confirmed that Clitipho and Bacchis were alone in the room, and that Clinia was unbothered by any of it, Chremes looked deflated and sat upon the fountain's edge, splashing his face to prevent his fainting.

"Bacchis is my son's mistress. Menedemus…I'm undone."

Menedemus could not help but smile a little.

"Do you laugh at me? You have good reason. How angry I now am with myself! How many things gave proof, whereby, had I not been a stone, I might have been fully sensible of this? What was it I saw? Alas! wretch that I am! But assuredly they shall not escape my vengeance if I live…"

Menedemus grew serious then, and turned to his neighbour. "Can you not contain yourself? Have you no respect for yourself? Am I not a sufficient example to you?"

"For very anger, Menedemus, I am not myself."

"For you to talk in that manner! Is it not a shame for you to be giving advice to others, to show wisdom abroad and yet be able to do nothing for yourself?"

Chremes turned to Menedemus, his eyes seeking advice, for the old man appeared lost in his fury. "What shall I do?"

"That which you said I failed to do…" Menedemus stood and took a step forward, hand upon his bearded chin. "Make him sensible that you are his father. Make him venture to entrust every thing to you, to seek and to ask of you, so that he may look for no other resources and forsake you."

"Nay, I had much rather he would go any where in the world, than by his debaucheries here reduce his father to beggary! For if I go on supplying his extravagance, Menedemus, in that case my circumstances will undoubtedly be soon reduced to the level of your spade."

They both look at the tilled earth before Menedemus' domus, the spade still lying there at the ready.

"What evils you will bring upon yourself in this affair, if

you don't act with caution! You'll show yourself severe, and still pardon him at last, that too with an ill grace."

There were understanding nods, and satisfied smiles in the audience then, for in that moment, the self-tormentor had become the wise advisor.

Menedemus looked to Chremes after a few silent moments, and asked about the proposed match between Clinia and Chremes' daughter, Antiphila. For all that obsessed Chremes in that moment, Menedemus could not help but press for his son's happiness.

"On the contrary, both the son-in-law and the connection are to my taste," Chremes said, standing to shake his neighbour's hand.

When the conversation turned to a dowry for Antiphila, Chremes' aged face lit up, his skin stretched by his cunning smile.

"I did think that two talents were sufficient, according to my means," Chremes said. "But if you wish me to be saved, and my estate and my son, you must say to this effect, that I have settled all my property on her as her portion."

Many a young man in the odeon gasped at that, for they well-suspected the effect that would have upon the pleasure-loving Clitipho whom many of them identified with.

"What scheme are you upon?" Menedemus asked.

"Pretend that you wonder at this, and at the same time ask him the reason why I do so."

"Why, really, I can't conceive the reason for your doing so."

"Why do I do so? To check his feelings, which are now hurried away by luxury and wantonness, and to bring him down so as not to know which way to turn himself." Chremes was determined. Of that there was no doubt, for he was determined to have his way. He held Menedemus fast by the arms. "And now let your son prepare to fetch the bride. The other one shall be schooled in such language as befits children." He stopped, and looked quite thoughtful, his pale bushy brows arching. "But Syrus…"

"What of him?"Menedemus asked.

"What? If I live, I will have him so handsomely dressed, so well combed out, that he shall always remember me as long as he lives. To imagine that I'm to be a laughing-stock and a plaything for him! So may the Gods bless me, he would not have dared to do to a widow-woman the things which he has done to me."

The new plot thus hatched, both men went into their respective homes, the silence deep behind them at the sudden turn of events.

As Damon played a frantic tune, Beatrice's tambourine making an occasional crash, Pollux, Rufio, and Fausto prepared to go on.

It was that point in the play where the end was tantalizingly near, where the story would either win over the audience or all would come tumbling down about their sweaty heads.

Felix stood by with Electra, holding their son now as if to show him the world beyond the scaena, and Clara stood beside him too with Felicia serving as a guarantor of Thespis' silence. Martia and Sextus too joined them, as did Domela and Castor.

The entire company was pressed to the back of the scaena to watch.

Rufio turned from the doorway of Menedemus' domus, and winked at Clara before he led Pollux and Fausto out into the street.

"Prithee, is it really the fact, Menedemus, that my father can, in so short a space of time, have cast off all the natural affection of a parent for me? For what crime? What so great enormity have I, to my misfortune, committed? *Young men generally do the same.*"

Menedemus, trained to his role, put out his hands. "I am aware that this must be much more harsh and severe to you, on whom it falls, but yet I take it no less amiss than you. How it is so I know not, nor can I account for it, except that from my heart I wish you well."

Clitipho paced backward and forward, as if caught in a storm made only for himself, but when his father appeared, Menedemus left him to his father's wrath.

"Why are you blaming me, Clitipho?" Chremes demanded. "Whatever I have done in this matter, I had a view to you and your imprudence. When I saw that you were of a careless disposition, and held the pleasures of the moment of the first importance, and did not look forward to the future, I took measures that you might neither want nor be able to waste this which I have. When, through your own conduct, it was not allowed me to give it you, to whom I ought before all, I had recourse to those who were your nearest relations." He turned his back to his son, his demeanour stern and unyielding. "To them I have made over and entrusted everything. There you'll always find a refuge for your folly - food, clothing, and a roof under which to betake yourself."

"Ah me!" Clitipho shouted.

Chremes wheeled on his son. "It is better than that, you being my heir, Bacchis should possess this estate of mine." He pointed to his own doorway where, at that moment, Bacchis appeared to be measuring the doorway of that domus in preparation for the changes she envisioned.

Syrus rushed to the front of the pulpitum, seeking aid from the blank faces before him. "I'm ruined irrevocably! Of what mischief have I, wretch that I am, unthinkingly been the cause?"

"Naughty slave!" the lupa, Calypso, shouted.

"Would I were dead!" Clitipho cried, but his father came to his side, voice less harsh, but still firm as required.

"Prithee, first learn what it is to live. When you know that, if life displeases you, then try the other."

Clitipho gasped and turned quickly, as astonished at his father's cold-heartedness as the rest of the young men watching.

At that moment, Syrus stepped forward, getting lower to the ground the closer he got to his dominus. "Master, may I be allowed to…"

"Say on."

"But may I safely?" Syrus asked.

"Say on."

"What injustice or what madness is this, that that in which I have offended, should be to his detriment?"

"It's all over. Don't you mix yourself up in it," Chremes said, looking down upon his servant. "No one accuses you, Syrus, nor need you look out for an altar, or for an intercessor for yourself."

Syrus did just that, his head turning this way and that, seeking safety at some god's altar, but there were none to hand. He turned back to his dominus. "What is your design?"

"I am not at all angry either with you, Syrus, or with you, Clitipho. Nor is it fair that you should be so with me for what I am doing." With those final ominous words, Chremes marched into his home.

Syrus and Clitipho turned to each other, the two of them alone in the street. Together, they fretted over their uncertain futures, of starvation and homelessness.

But the exercise proved food for Syrus' wily thoughts as he sat himself against the trunk of the olive tree to meditate upon one final attempt.

While his servant closed his eyes, as focussed as a Pythagorean at sunrise, Clitipho grew increasingly impatient.

He strolled about the street and observed the silent onlookers who gazed at his worried face, a face fearful for survival. Clitipho looked upon his father's domus, and then his gaze focussed upon Menedemus' titanic spade. This last made him recoil. Finally, he could no longer hold his tongue, and turned back to Syrus. "What is it, then?"

Syrus opened his eyes slowly, and smiled. "It is this... I think that you are not their son."

"How's that, Syrus? Are you quite in your senses?"

"I'll tell you what's come into my mind. Be you the judge. While they had you alone, while they had no other source of joy more nearly to affect them, they indulged you, they lavished upon you. Now a daughter has been discovered, a pretence has been found in fact on which to turn you adrift."

Clitipho looked to the sky, shocked at this turn of fate. "It's very probable."

"Now consider another thing. All mothers are wont to be advocates for their sons when in fault, and to aid them against a father's severity. 'Tis not so here."

"You say true. What then shall I now do, Syrus?"

"Question them on this suspicion! Mention the matter without reserve. Either, if it is not true, you'll soon bring them both to compassion, or else you'll soon find out whose son you are."

Clitipho agreed with his servant's advice and went straight to the home that was yet still his home to make his case to his parents.

When he was gone, Syrus walked to the edge of the pulpitum.

"Most fortunately did this come into my mind. For the less hope the young man entertains, the greater the difficulty with which he'll bring his father to his own terms. I'm not sure even, that he may not take a wife, and then no thanks for Syrus. But what is this? The old man's coming out of doors! I'll be off.

What has so far happened, I am surprised at, that he didn't order me to be carried off from here. Now I'll away to Menedemus here. I'll secure him as my intercessor, for I can put no trust in our old man!"

Fausto came bursting through Menedemus' doorway and skidded to a halt upon the boards. The look of exhilaration upon his face made the others smile.

"Well done, Fausto!" Rufio said, thrusting a cup of water into his hand.

The younger man drank greedily and wiped his mouth. "I stood at the edge of the pulpitum and stared them straight in the eyes. What a thrill!"

"You've done that a thousand times before, Fausto," Beatrice said.

"Yes, but it's different here. This place! I feel like more than just mortal eyes are upon us."

Rufio and Felix turned to hear what Fausto was saying.

"I don't know… Maybe it's how close we are to the goddess' great temple? That must be it!" Fausto clapped and went to watch as Julius and Domela prepared to go on for the third scene of the fifth act.

"Don't say it," Felix whispered to Rufio. "Just don't."

Rufio nodded and went back to watching with the others.

Peli barked once as he strained at the rope which tied him to the wagon, curious about the covered cage some distance away.

"Peli, shhh!" Rufio hissed.

"Really, sir, if you don't take care, you'll be causing some mischief to your son!" Sostrata turned on her husband, a wagging finger in his face. "And indeed I do wonder at it, my husband, how anything so foolish could ever come into your head!"

"Oh, you persist in being the woman? Did I ever wish for any one thing in all my life, Sostrata, but that you were my contradicter on that occasion? And yet if I were now to ask you what it is that I have done amiss, or why you act thus, you would not know in what point you are now so obstinately opposing me in your folly."

"Alas! You are unreasonable to expect me to be silent in a matter of such importance."

The audience leaned in as the domestic squabble rose in volume, for many there sided with Sostrata that her husband had gone too far.

Still, others seemed to believe Chremes had acted wisely, for there was little else he could do to curtail his son's reckless behaviour.

"I don't expect it. Talk on then, I shall still do it not a bit the less."

"Don't you see how much evil you will be causing by that course? He suspects himself to be a foundling!" Sostrata paced desperately before her house. "Am I to admit that he is not my son who really is? Because my daughter has been found?"

"No," Chremes responded, "but for a reason why it should be much sooner believed. Because he is just like you in disposition, you will easily prove that he is your child, for he is exactly like you. Why, he has not a single vice left him but you have just the same. Then, besides, no woman could have been the mother of such a son but yourself. But he's coming out of doors, and how demure! When you understand the matter, you may form your own conclusions."

Clitipho came rushing into the street then, seeking his parents who, much to his relief, were standing there before him. He then threw himself at his mother's feet most pitifully. "If there ever was any time, mother, when I caused you pleasure, being called your son by your own desire, I beseech you to remember it, and now to take compassion on me in my distress. A thing I beg and request - do discover to me my parents!"

Sostrata looked to the Gods for strength before answering her son who now claimed he was not her son. "I conjure you, my son, not to entertain that notion in your mind, that you are another person's child."

Clitipho pulled back from her suddenly. "I am."

Sostrata cried out, and turned to her husband. "Wretch that I am! Was it this that you wanted, pray?" She grabbed her son's arm and pulled him closer. "So may you be the survivor of me and of him, you are my son and his! And henceforth, if you love me, take care that I never hear that speech from you again."

Chremes stepped forward to Clitipho. "But I say, if you fear me, take care how I find these propensities existing in you."

"What propensities?" the son asked of the father who now was not his father.

"If you wish to know, I'll tell you - being a trifler, an idler, a cheat, a glutton, a debauchee, a spendthrift! Believe me, and believe that you are our son." Chremes turned to the audience, proud of his own plotting.

"This is not the language of a parent," Clitipho insisted, turning away from them.

"If you had been born from my head, Clitipho, just as they say Minerva was from Jupiter's, none the more on that account would I suffer myself to be disgraced by your profligacy."

Sostrata winced as though a dagger had been thrust into her bosom. "May the Gods forbid it."

"I don't know as to the Gods," Chremes said."So far as I shall be enabled, I will carefully prevent it. You are seeking that which you possess - parents. That which you are in want of, you don't seek - in what way to pay obedience to a father, and to preserve what he acquired by his industry. That you by trickery should bring before my eyes! I am ashamed to mention the unseemly word in her presence." He pointed at Sostrata who was fanning herself beneath the olive tree. "But you were not in any degree ashamed to act thus."

Clitipho, desperate and downtrodden, walked aside to stand at the edge of the tilled field before Menedemus' domus. "Alas! How thoroughly displeased I now am with myself! How much ashamed! Nor do I know how to make a beginning to pacify him."

As Rufio, Julius, and Domela played out their domestic scene of scandal and displeasure beyond the scaena, Pollux prepared to make his entrance. He breathed deeply, slowly, preparing for the final scene.

"You can do it, brother."

Pollux turned to see Castor standing there, flanked by Felix, Fausto, Beatrice, Electra, and Clara.

"You have proven yourself in a lead, Pollux," Felix said. "No, go out there and save Clitipho from his father's haste."

Pollux smiled, stuck out his chest, and marched out into the street.

"Why really," Menedemus said to himself as he came outside. "Chremes is treating his son too harshly and too unkindly. I'm come out, therefore, to make peace between them. Most opportunely I see them both."

"Well, Menedemus, why don't you order my daughter to be sent for, and close with the offer of the portion that I mentioned?" Chremes winked at him, though his son and wife winced in the background.

"My husband, I entreat you not to do it!" Sostrata shouted, clutching Clitipho.

"Father, I entreat you to forgive me," the son added.

At that moment, Menedemus bent to pick up the spade that had been his labour for so long, and leaned upon it as he spoke in a low voice to Chremes. "Forgive him, Chremes. Do let them prevail upon you."

"Am I knowingly to make my property a present to Bacchis? I'll not do it!" He was resolute in his decision it seemed, and the more that became apparent, the more Clitipho sweat and squirmed, his mother clinging to him.

"If you desire me to live, father, do forgive me."

Sostrata, Menedemus, and Clitipho pleaded with Chremes to forgive, to forgo his plan of disowning, but he remained obdurate for several painfully-long heartbeats that had everyone leaning forward the better to hope and hear.

"On this condition, then, I'll do it. If he does that which I think it right he should do," Chremes declared, turning to face his son.

"Father, I'll do anything!" Clitipho fell to his knees, arms wide in supplication. "Command me."

"You must take a wife."

Clitipho's face shrivelled as his hopes were dashed. "Father." He had little to say, and though Menedemus offered a positive answer in his stead, Chremes would not hear from anyone but his son.

"Do you hesitate, Clitipho?" his mother demanded.

Chremes huffed, unsurprised. " Nay, just as he likes."

"He'll do it all," Menedemus offered, eyeing the prostrate son of his neighbour.

Taking a breath, Sostrata laced her arm through her husband's then and spoke to their son. "This course, while you are making a beginning, is disagreeable, and while you are unacquainted with it. When you have become acquainted with it, it will become easy."

That brought about a few knowing smiles among the populace of the audience.

Clitipho wrung his hands, his face a mixture of emotion that betrayed his mental toils in that moment. He could see no way out, no longer see the worth in pursuing the life of debauchery into which he had so willingly flung himself. With a great sigh of acceptance he turned to his parents who were his parents once again. "I'll do it, father."

"My son, upon my honour," Sostrata began, wasting no time at all. "I'll give you that charming girl, whom you may soon become attached to, the daughter of our neighbour Phanocrata."

"What? That red-haired girl, with cat's eyes, freckled face, and hooked nose? I can not, father!" he pleaded.

"How nice he is! You would fancy he had set his mind upon it," Chremes declared.

"I'll name another!" Sostrata obviously rifled through the list of young maids in her mind.

"Why no," Clitipho said. "Since I must marry, I myself have one that I should pretty nearly make choice of."

Chremes looked doubtful, and Sostrata enticed.

"The daughter of Archonides," Clitipho offered.

"I'm quite agreeable," Sostrata confirmed for her husband who nodded, satisfied that he had prevailed.

But Clitipho paused and stepped aside to watch as Bacchis and her entourage emerged from the domus of Menedemus to depart down the road and out of his life. He waved, unseen by any, especially by Bacchis who had no need of him any longer. But he was not bidding farewell to his mistress, but to his younger, indolent self. When Bacchis had disappeared, he turned back to his mother and father.

"Father, this now remains," Clitipho said, turning back and motioning for their servant to approach.

"What is it?" Chremes asked, trying not to smile.

"I want you to pardon Syrus for what he has done for my sake."

Syrus presented himself before his dominus, his head bowed.

Chremes looked at his neighbour, Menedemus, and saw that, with a smile, he was putting away his heavy spade, leaning it against the wall beside his door. Chremes then looked back at his son, his wife, and finally, his wily servant. "Be it so," he said.

All was silent as Chremes placed his hand upon Syrus' head and then brought him to his feet. He set his palm gently to his son's cheek, and kissed his wife's hand.

He then walked to the very edge of the pulpitum to look upon the vast audience rising up before him.

"Fare you well…and grant us your applause."

The silence was deafening.

XX

THE SILENCE AND THEN SOME

The audience stared back at Julius who stood at the forefront of the pulpitum with Pollux, Rufio, Fausto and Domela behind him. The audience made not a peep and so, his head held high, Julius turned to the others.

"Time to go," he mouthed, and the five of them immediately turned to disappear into the homes of Chremes and Menedemus.

"What's happening?" Felix demanded, his face filled with panic as they arrived behind the scaena frons.

The panic began to spread to the rest of The Etrurian Players as they stared from one to the other, all of them looking to Felix.

"Start packing up, quickly!" Castor said as he began to throw items into one of the wagons.

"They're going to tear us apart!" Fausto said, blinded by desperate tears that started to well. "This has never happened before."

"I'm sorry, lad," Julius said to him. "There is a first time for everything, good and bad. Domela." He turned to her. "Help me pack things up."

"I don't understand!" Felix roared, rushing to the scaena to peer out at the silent crowd.

Rufio was at his side in a moment. "They're just sitting there. And then there's… By Apollo, no!"

"Felix, help us!" Electra said, balancing Thespis on one arm and gathering items with the other.

"Maybe I can talk to them?" Sextus said to his wife who was standing with Clara and Felicia. "Oratory can be good for more than just politics and jurisprudence!"

The scene backstage became more chaotic, but Felix and Rufio could not tear themselves from the view, for in the middle of the orchestra, they could see the shade of Terentius staring up at the crammed cavia, his hands waving as he shouted at them, rubbing his wild hair in frustration.

"YOU STILL REFUSE TO SEE ME, ATHENIANS!" the shade shouted at them before weeping silently at the painful eternity he would have to spend behind the veil of Athenae's days and nights. "Apollo, Lord of Light and Creativity! Why?" Terentius pleaded. "Why, Lord?"

Rufio pulled at Felix's tunica. "We have to do something!"

"What can we do? If they didn't like it, they didn't like it!" Felix felt his heart racing. "We have to get out of here, now!"

Felix turned to see Clara rushing up to meet them.

"What are we going to do?" she asked, but then they heard it, like the trickle of water after a week in the desert.

Applause.

THE PLAY HAD ENDED, AND CASSIUS CANTOR AND NUMA SAT there watching as Julius and the others left the pulpitum in silence, more like to a funeral procession than a triumphal parade.

"Why is no one clapping?" Numa whispered.

"I…I'm not quite sure." Cassius Cantor looked around the odeon at the audience's faces, spying his other players spread about them, each of his men looking at him with confused looks.

Upon closer inspection, he could hear women and girls sniffling and wiping their eyes. Young men sat still, heads down, and older men with crossed arms reflected deeply on what they had seen.

Each person there was lost in thought, all of them thinking of their own familial relations, their loves, their life's mistakes, and their deeds well-done.

"Right," Cassius said with a determined look upon his face. "Time to break the spell." He stood up, followed by Numa and the rest of The Rome Antics about the odeon, and they all began to clap and hoot.

All around the odeon, people snapped out of their thoughtful trances and followed suit, and soon the sound of cheers and wild applause exploded in every corner of the cavia causing the torches to flicker in their brackets.

People were then on their feet, roaring their approval and calling out for The Etrurian Players to return to the pulpitum.

"Stop packing, my friends!" Felix said to his players. "They LOVE us!" Felix turned to Rufio. "Thank Apollo for Cassius and his men!" As the others joined him and Rufio, he turned back to the latter. "Don't tell anyone I said that."

Rufio smiled and put his finger to his mouth.

"Where is my son?" Felix turned to see Electra coming toward him. "I will show my son what a triumph looks like!" Felix took Thespis in his arms and clasped hands with Electra before leading the way out onto the pulpitum.

"Shall we, my dear?" Julius said to Domela as they followed.

The rest of the company went too, relieved and sweaty-faced as they stepped into the odeon to be engulfed by the uproarious approval of the Athenians.

"I was afraid for a moment," Clara said to Rufio.

"Me too. Can I hold her for this?" he asked.

She smiled and handed Felicia to him.

He looked at his daughter and saw the wide-eyed wonder as she pointed to the pulpitum beyond the scaena. "I think she likes it!"

"Oh, dear," Clara said, taking his hand and pulling him out to join the others. Before they went, she turned to Martia and Sextus. "You coming?"

"We shouldn't. We didn't perform," Sextus put up his hands.

"Nonsense!" Rufio said. "You're one of the producers, *and* you're both part of our familia!"

Martia and Sextus looked at each other, smiled, and followed Rufio and Clara out.

When he saw them leave, Peli began to bark, his voice swallowed by the applause. He pulled at his rope, straining and whining until finally, he set to chewing it, his mis-matched eyes straying every few seconds to the screeching, shifting cage beneath the other wagon.

THE ETRURIAN PLAYERS EMERGED FROM BEHIND THE SCAENA frons and the Athenians all rose to their feet, their hands waving and clapping like a thousand palm fronds at a parade.

Cassius Cantor roared and whistled and Felix Modestus smiled and waved back.

When the entire company was lined up, they bowed, and handfuls of flower petals were thrown at them to dot the orchestra floor.

Felix held Thespis up for all to see, and pulled his wife close to him, a true family man before the Athenians who valued such things.

"Why are people crying?" Pollux shouted beside Rufio. "Look at all the wet faces!"

"Yeah! It's supposed to be a comedy!" Fausto yelled back as he waved at the row of lupae blowing him kisses.

"It's the genius of Terentius' humour to get at the truth we all seek!" Rufio said.

And there, seen only by Rufio and Felix, Terentius stood in the middle of the orchestra, a rain of flower petals falling about his head. The shade wept as the Athenians lauded his story at last. He turned then to look up at the company that had come to his aid, his teary eyes meeting those of Felix and Rufio, and he too began to applaud the players.

Rufio and Felix felt a twin chill as the shade looked upon them and praised them.

Thank you, Terentius said, his pale, ink-stained hand upon his sleeping heart. *Thank you.*

And with that, he was gone.

Just as the applause began to abate slightly, a loud screeching could be heard, followed by a loud barking when, into the middle of the orchestra plunged a monkey pursued by a wild-eyed hound.

"Peli!" Rufio shouted.

"Momo!" Numa cried.

The two animals raced in circles about the feet of the Athenian actors Aegisthus, Cadmus, and Zotikos who had risen from their front row seats along with the playwright, Telephus, to be the first to congratulate Felix and his company.

"Peli, stop chasing that thing!" Rufio called out, handing Felicia to Clara and jumping off the pulpitum to try and grab his dog.

This only fired people's applause more and the sound reached to the rafters once again as Momo pounced onto

Rufio's back, using it as a jumping point to go up into the cavia. But when Peli attempted the same, Rufio spun and caught him in his arms.

"Oh no you don't!" Rufio said as he held his wiggling canine.

"Now that's a performance!" Cassius Cantor shouted with glee.

The crowd descended the aisle, many of them wanting to congratulate the players, to meet their summer's Herakles, or touch the arm of the famed archimima, Electra.

One by one, the people of Athenae placed olive crowns upon each of the players' heads, symbols of respect and of victory which, in the people's eyes, The Etrurian Players had earned by their toils.

Fausto was surrounded by admirers of his Syrus, and Julius and Pollux were praised for their portrayals of the old, wise, and foolish men.

"The play was anything but a torment!" Telephus said to them. "If you are amenable, I may have a play for you both at a later date," he whispered, casting a look at the Athenian actors who surrounded Felix. "I'm trying to break onto the Roman scene." He winked and went over to Rufio who still clutched Peli. "A bit with a dog… Hmm." Telephus looked thoughtful. "I think I'll try that."

"At your peril," Rufio laughed.

"When is your play coming out?" Telephus asked.

"My play?"

"Yes! You're the playwright in the group, no?" He pointed at Rufio's ink-stained fingers.

"Oh, I'm a farmer, that is all," Rufio said.

Telephus looked at him and leaned in. "Farmers are important and have a unique perspective of life, Rufio Pagano."

"I have very little time to write."

"There is always time to write." He clapped Rufio on the back and left to join the actors.

"What was that about?" Clara asked.

"Not sure."

They were surrounded by admirers, but a space formed about the Athenian actors and Felix.

Zotikos stepped forward to meet Felix.

Immediately, Castor, Pollux and Damon closed in beside him.

Aegisthus and Cadmus were there behind Zotikos and, when Rufio saw this, he set Peli down and went to join them.

Aegisthus stared at Felix for a moment, as if ready for an argument, but then the arrogant actor's features gave way to a slight smile. "I don't know how you did it, Felix Modestus, but this production was something else."

"You know, Zotikos, I can't tell if you're offering a compliment, or an insult," Felix said, taking a step forward.

But Zotikos shook his head. "I don't think I laughed out loud even one time during this *comedy*…"

People around them were listening now, and they could feel the growing tension.

Zotikos continued. "But I *felt* the entire piece. A perfect picture of human life. 'I am a man, and nothing that concerns a man do I deem a matter of indifference to me…' Wonderful. Amazing, and well done!" Zotikos extended his hand. "I congratulate you, and your company!"

Felix shook the actor's hand and smiled. "I'm glad that you enjoyed it."

Zotikos turned to the Athenians behind him and made a show of applauding The Etrurian Players. "A magnificent performance!"

The applause resumed, and Zotikos departed with Aegisthus and Cadmus in tow, unaware of the yellow stain which Peli had just placed upon the hem of his long chiton.

Telephus saw this and smiled at Felix as he followed. "Thank you."

"Well, that was unexpected," Julius said to Felix.

"It certainly was."

A sea of smiling faces passed before the company's eyes, and a chorus of compliments filled their ears as the audience members filed past them to offer their thanks and praise.

"You did it, my friend," Publius Leander said to Sextus as he and Delphina joined him and Martia. "A great success."

"It was wonderful," Delphina said, clasping Sextus' hands. "You should be proud."

"I am," Sextus said, wiping his forehead. "It was hard-won, I tell you."

"I see you have found your place with your adoptive family, Sextus. I am happy for you." Publius looked at the group who had graced his domus not long ago, but he said nothing more.

"Come, husband," Delphina said. "We should leave them to their celebrations."

Publius nodded. "Yes. Do be sure to see us before you return to Rome."

"I will," Sextus replied.

"He seems so sad," Martia said when they were gone.

"He worries for his daughter."

"Would that I could have such worries," Martia said.

Sextus gripped her hand. "Come. Let's join the others."

The crowd was still thick and as varied as though they were in the streets of the agora.

"I loved how subtle the play was, how true to life it seemed," the philosopher, Philemon, said as he stood with Zonas, Phemius, and Rufio.

"And yet, a reminder of what is important in life," Zonas added with a dash of stoicism.

Phemius set his hand upon Rufio's shoulder. "Truly, you did justice to Terentius' greatest work."

Rufio smiled to himself. "I hope so."

"You did," Phemius nodded. "I must be going now, Rufio Pagano, but if you have time, do stop by the library before you return to Etruria. We can talk of plays and of writing."

"I would like that." Rufio shook his hand, and those of the philosophers. "Thank you for coming."

"Making friends?" said a voice that approached Rufio from behind, making him jump.

"Bacchis- I mean, Electra!" Rufio said with a nervous laugh, trying not to look at her thrusting breast.

But Electra only laughed joyfully and gripped his hands. "Thank you, Rufio."

"For what?"

"For helping Felix. You are the very best of friends to him…and to me. Thank you."

Rufio relaxed and smiled. "Any time. We're family, after all."

"We are." She turned to go back to Felix.

"You were a wonder to watch perform, as ever, Electra."

"I know," she replied with a twinkle in her dark eyes. "So were you."

In the front row of the cavia, Rufio could see Fausto surrounded by the lupae of Circe's, with Castor and Pollux looking on jealously.

"You wish you were him?" Clara asked.

Rufio shook his head. "No. I'm perfectly happy where I am, thank you very much." He kissed her and Felicia. "I didn't think that-"

"It was well…well…well done, sir!" the seer, Melampus said suddenly, grabbing Rufio and Clara's hands in turn. "Very entertaining. You will go far, you," he said, poking a dirty finger into Rufio's chest. "Keep at it, yes. Keep at it!"

"Ah…I will… Thank you?" Rufio stuttered as the seer moved on.

"Why isn't that man wearing clothes?" Clara asked.

"He was…and now he isn't," Rufio said as Melampus' naked form marched out of the odeon into the night.

The Etrurian Players basked in the glory of their hard work for a while longer.

Felix and Damon spoke at length with the Panathenaic victors, Antiocheis, Alexandros of Thebes, Theophile of Chios, and Aristides of Athenae. They also wished the young Demophon the very best of luck in his burgeoning career.

"If you ever want a place in our company, let me know," Felix said to the fifteen-year-old.

The young man smiled and followed his fellow victors out.

There was some loud conversation in the cavia still where The Rome Antics all sat together, going over the performance they had just witnessed and how they could further their own catalogue by adapting such 'thinking plays' for their street performances.

Rufio was about to say something when the smell of fish reached him ahead of the fishmonger, Policarpos, and his wife, Ploumi.

"Rufio Pagano," Policarpos said quietly as he approached. "Ploumi and I just wanted to say that we enjoyed your performance immensely. We do not usually attend the theatre. The audience in Athenae is not normally as open to those who are not as knowledgeable when it comes to plays."

"We felt very welcome here!" Ploumi said to Rufio with a smile. "We felt we actually had something in common with these characters."

"It's all down to Terentius' words," Rufio said.

Policarpos shrugged. "I don't know who Terentius is, but I do know that you all told the story in a way that we could all be a part of it. In fact, it has urged us to action!"

"How so?" Rufio asked, trying not to gag at the fishy perfume they bore.

"Our own son… He left us when we insisted he too become a fisherman." Policarpos looked down in shame. "I told him to leave, and so he did." He looked up. "But now, after this play… I am going to contact him and tell him that he is welcome home no matter what he has chosen to do with his life."

"What does he do, your son?" Clara asked.

Ploumi smiled sadly. "He is a fullo."

"Oh!" Clara did not know what to say. "Why did he not want to be a fisherman?"

"He said that he didn't like the smell," Policarpos said with a shrug. "It's not for everyone."

"I suppose not," Rufio said, trying not to laugh, for a fullo did people's laundry by stomping in a vat of urine all day.

"But I know *you* like fish, Rufio Pagano!" Policarpos said excitedly. "That is why Ploumi and I have brought you some fresh herring!" He then retrieved a bundle of fig leaves from his satchel and presented it to Rufio like a trophy. "A gift from us to you."

Clara smiled to herself.

"Tha…thank you," Rufio managed. "And thank you for coming."

The couple nodded and set off with broad smiles.

"Good luck with your son!" Clara called after them before turning back to Rufio. "They seem nice."

"Gwrra!" Rufio shook his head. "Take it, please!"

"Is that herring I smell?" the caretaker, Cosmo, said from their left.

"Yes!" Rufio shouted. "Here, Cosmo! As payment for your aid!" Rufio lobbed the fig bundle to him.

"As long as they're fresh!" Cosmo called back.

When the last of their fans departed, The Etrurian Players looked up at The Rome Antics who were now coming down out of the cavia to meet them.

Cassius Cantor stepped forward with a great smile to meet Felix. "I really enjoyed that, Felix Modestus. Thank you!"

"It is I who should thank you, Cassius," Felix admitted. "Without your cue to these Athenians, we might have fled before we knew they enjoyed it."

"If there's one thing The Rome Antics know how to do, it's make noise!" Cassius and his entire company cheered at that. "I'm glad you stuck with it."

"Me too," Felix said.

"Perhaps we can team up some time?" Cassius ventured. "We could do a panto-drama! Yes! A new genre that makes people laugh *and* cry out loud!"

"And we could have a bit with a monkey!" Numa ventured excitedly.

The Etrurian Players shifted uncomfortably behind Felix who, for a few moments, said nothing. Then, he smiled and extended his hand to Cassius. "That sounds like an intriguing idea, Cassius. I'll give it some thought."

"Do, Felix. If we can pull it off, we'll have even Emperor Severus wetting his bracae!"

"That is an image!" Felix said.

"Farewell then!" Cassius said to the group at large. "We're off to Cilicia to entertain the pirates, but we'll see you back in Ephesus soon!"

"May Apollo guide you!" Felix replied graciously as The Rome Antics made their exit.

The odeon was suddenly very quiet as The Etrurian Players found themselves alone again, alone except for the sound of slow footsteps coming down the far right aisle of the odeon.

Atticus, who had been sitting at the top of the cavia silently, watching the flow of fans surround the company, at last made his approach.

The entire company turned to him.

"Atticus!" Felix said. "We're thrilled you came to watch! Tell us…what did you think?"

Atticus thought for a moment and then began to nod slowly, his eyes eventually rising to meet Felix's. "I think, Felix Modestus, that I have never seen anything quite like it. I have seen and met a great many artists as steward of my dominus' villa, played host to many who believed they were the very best at what they did. But," he paused again, "I can honestly say that you…all of you…are truly gifted. You have taken a difficult, beautifully-convoluted story, and made it a part of all of our lives. No production has ever made me feel the way I do at this moment."

"Thank you, Atticus," Felix said as he stepped forward to meet the man. "Coming from you, that is indeed high praise. I know that you see much."

Atticus shook his head. "I speak the truth."

"To Atticus!" Fausto shouted.

"To Atticus!" the company echoed.

"Now. I must get back to the villa to oversee the convivium." Atticus bowed and then left the odeon as quietly as he had entered it.

When they were at last truly alone, Felix climbed up onto the pulpitum, with Thespis still in his arms, to look down at his company gathered around the altar in the orchestra. "Before we go, I have something to say."

"Get on with it! We're hungry!" Pollux laughed.

"Don't worry, Pollux!" Felix answered. "There is food enough waiting for us all! But first, I just wanted to say that… to admit…" Felix felt his throat catch, and fought back the foreign urge to weep. He looked at his son's face and stroked his cheek with his index finger. "This production has been a struggle for us, for me especially, and I couldn't have come through it without all of you. Each of you has been a champion before and behind the scaena. Julius and Pollux, you won the day with your performances, and our Syrus was perfection!" Felix smiled at Fausto. "But each one of you is essential to our familia and the work we do." He saw Sextus and Martia and smiled at them. "I can't thank you enough." He turned to Rufio and Clara then. "For you to have come to our rescue again, from so great a distance…it is a true expression of friendship and love."

Clara gripped Rufio and Felicia closely, her eyes welling.

"I know," Felix continued, "that I have shown weakness of late. A thing I am not wont to do, normally. But I am not ashamed. I am a man. That is all. I'm a simple player, a friend, a husband…" He winked at Electra. "And a father." He kissed his son. "And I'm grateful for all of it, for the changes that have occurred…and the changes yet to come."

Rufio nodded, and looked up at his friend, happy to see Felix smile back at him.

"Here, here!" Julius called out, his arm around Domela whose smile spanned her rosy face.

"I'm a mortal man, and that's all right with me!" Felix declared.

"But you're our Hercules!" Pollux shouted.

"Not anymore!" Felix retorted. "But I am *The* Felix Modestus!"

The Etrurian Players cheered their leader, their brother, their friend.

"Now!" Felix declared. "Time to celebrate! Back to the villa!"

XXI

INK AND DIRT

The Etrurian Players celebrated most fervently that night at the villa of Atticus, basking in the wondrous afterglow of a job well-done. And the fact that the Athenian theatre-goers did not tear them limb from limb was an added gift that encouraged them to celebrate all the more.

Atticus had spared none of his dominus' coin when it came to putting on the post-performance convivium, as was the tradition of that art-loving domus when their guests' artistic toils came to successful conclusions. For Felix Modestus and his company, however, Atticus had delved deeper into his dominus' purse than was usual so that he might put on a more lavish feast.

Tripods and braziers lit every corner of the villa complex on the slopes of Hymettos. Music and song made by the relieved players of the empire's greatest company filled the air so that Apollo himself might hear the echo of it across the water on sacred Delos where he had first put into Felix's head and heart the great task to be done.

The triclinium tables were packed like a newly stocked market with platters of raw and cooked vegetables, boiled eggs, olives and figs, fresh breads and, now that the performance was over, an array of cheeses that were most welcome to do their worst on performers. There were of course platters of fish -

sardines, wrasse, sea bass, and scorpini - grilled over coals in the outdoor kitchen and doused with garum or oil from the estate. These were placed as far as possible from Rufio who, to the surprise of many, was eyeing the platter of shrimp, octopus, and tiny calamari.

"You sure about that?" Clara asked him when he said he was thinking about trying the calamari.

"It smells so good!" He nodded and went down the tables to pick one up. He observed the tiny fried emissary of Neptune's realm, the tentacles that looked like writhing hairs. "Just one bite," he said before popping the whole thing in his mouth.

All eyes were upon Rufio as he took the first, hesitant mastication. His face was calm at first, but then his chin wrinkled, and his eyes shut as his jaw appeared to recoil.

"He's losing it!" Castor yelled.

Try as he might to get it down, Rufio could not manage the mollusc. "Gwrra!"

The half-chewed calamari shot from his mouth to soar across the table and bounce off of Fausto's forehead to land on the floor at his side.

"Ahh!" Fausto shouted.

Beatrice broke into laughter beside Fausto and looked down as Peli came to investigate the fallen food, only to sniff at it and turn away.

"Apologies, Fausto!" Rufio said. "But the calamari doesn't seem to agree with me or Peli."

"Do you think so?" Fausto shouted playfully, throwing a piece of bread at Rufio who caught it with a relieved smile. Fausto turned to Beatrice who was still laughing. "You like to see me embarrassed, don't you? Ha ha!" He nudged her playfully.

Beatrice's smile faded a little as she stared at him.

"What?" Fausto asked.

"I like to see you."

"All right," he said. "I suppose as long as you have eyes to see, you shall see me."

But Beatrice merely pursed her lips. "Why did you not go with your lupae tonight? Didn't they offer you an evening of free pleasures for your Syrus?"

Fausto shrugged and looked at his platter of food. "I wasn't about to leave you to celebrate our victory alone, was I? Not with all these old folks!" A raw carrot suddenly smacked into the side of Fausto's head.

"Who are you calling old, little boy?" Julius called out, laughing.

"No one at all!" Fausto replied with a chuckle.

Beatrice smiled again as she took a sip of her wine. She saw Domela snuggle up to Julius and the subsequent smile that spanned the veteran actor's face.

"She's not so bad as all that, is she?" Fausto asked Beatrice as they watched the older couple.

"No. Not bad at all," Beatrice replied.

Atticus' people continued to bring out more food for the players, including legs of lamb and goat, boar's meat, boiled chicken with honey and peppercorns, and an array of songbirds wrapped in wild sage leaves.

Most importantly, perhaps, the wine flowed from beginning to end as servants ensured that no one was left with an empty cup unless they desired it. Atticus had ordered one of the amphorae of his dominus' vintage from his vineyards in Nemea to be opened, and it facilitated the joyous and raucous celebrations very well indeed.

Sextus raised his cup of rich red Nemean to Felix and smiled. "I toast you with the 'Blood of Hercules', as they call it. Congratulations, my friend. From what people were saying to me after the performance, it was a stunning success. I'm sorry I doubted you." Sextus' eyes were glossy, not because he had drunk more than was usual for him, but because he was glad of the company in which he found himself, company which made him, and Martia nestled beside him, feel more at home than any gathering back in Rome.

"There's no need to apologize, Sextus," Felix said as he raised his cup in return. "I'm sorry I gave you reason to doubt me."

Electra laid her hand upon Felix' chest and smiled. "My husband forgets that doubt is a part of the process."

"You never doubt yourself, though, do you Electra?" Rufio asked.

Electra turned and winked. "In public, no. In private…"

There was a hush down the tables as the company strained to hear Electra admit her mortality.

She looked at them all and held her chin up. "In private, that is only for the Gods, and my husband to know."

Felix kissed his wife's hand most tenderly at that. *Thank the Gods, we've survived another one!* But he did wonder at the thought, for he used to immediately begin planning the next show, his mind turning over the choice of play, the ins and outs of the production and what new things could be done to further crown his company's career. In that moment, however, Felix thought only of Thespis who was sleeping soundly in his and Electra's cubiculum on the second storey, checked on occasionally by Peli and, shockingly, Nicodemus, who had finally decided to tolerate his new canine companion.

"What about you, Rufio?" Martia asked from across the low table. "Do you experience doubt?"

They all turned to look at Rufio.

Clara smiled to herself, for she knew that he did in every aspect of his life.

Rufio sipped his wine and looked up thoughtfully. "I do. Yes. In farming, just as in theatre, I am riddled with it. But, I suppose that if one recruits reliable, skilled, and knowledgeable people…friends whom I can trust…then no amount of doubt can overcome us as a group."

"Running the latifundium is like running a theatre company, I suppose," Clara said, looking at her husband. "There are good times, and bad, things that we can control, and things that we cannot. As long as we remain sincere in our actions, give the Gods their dues, and continue to believe, all is well."

"Quite, my love," Rufio said to Clara as he gripped her hand.

"And with your writing?" Felix asked, his dark eyebrow arching high over his right eye. "Do you have doubts?"

Rufio was quiet for a moment as he imagined his scribbled notes, papyri covered in false starts, and his ink-stained fingers. "The doubt is dark and deep when it comes to putting a stylus to papyrus," Rufio said, "but I'm learning how to swim in it."

Felix nodded. "I think we all learned to swim this time around. The currents are constantly shifting now."

They were silent for a moment as the banter at the far end of the tables grew louder.

Felix stood up, cleared his throat to speak and, after a few moments, the gathering settled down. He looked upon his players, his friends, and smiled. "I am so proud of all of you. Apollo sent us what seemed to be an impossible task, but we rose to the challenge. I know it was different this time…"

There were nods of agreement about the tables, for they had all felt the sting of doubt, the fear of humiliation, at some point on their journey in Athenae.

"I know it was for me," Felix admitted. "But by helping each other, by toiling harder than we have before, we overcame the challenge of our trial."

"I'd say!" Pollux shouted. "We got the Athenians to enjoy Terentius' 'smart-funny' play!"

"I still don't understand the whole thing," Beatrice said,

shaking her head so that her hair fell out and about her shoulders.

Felix exchanged a quick look with Rufio, and then pressed on. "The Athenians may not have understood the entirety of the plot, Beatrice, but I believe they felt it…" Felix was silent, his eyes meeting those of his company.

Julius stood then, though the action was a little slow and swaying, and raised his cup. "To The Etrurian Players!"

"To The Etrurian Players!" everyone shouted.

Damon immediately set his flute to his lips and began to play a triumphant tune that got Castor and Pollux to their feet and dancing like the priests of Mars in Martius.

Felix ran to join them, as did Rufio and Fausto, followed by Julius and Sextus.

Everyone laughed and clapped as the men danced about the triclinium, feet shifting and stomping, arms swinging, smashing imaginary gladii upon imaginary shields. They had returned from battle victorious, and Beatrice and Domela added their voices to the song of welcome victory.

Meanwhile, Clara and Electra moved closer to Martia, for she seemed lost in thought, her eyes betraying the reticent smile upon her lips.

"What is it, my dear?" Electra said to her as she and Clara sat to either side.

Martia looked at both of them and grasped their hands. "I cannot say it aloud."

"What is wrong?" Clara asked, worried at the shaking she felt in their friend's hand.

Martia shook her head. "I'm just going to miss you. You are both…all of you are…well, you are the family Sextus and I have never had. I will miss you so much."

"You can come to us in Etruria any time, Martia," Clara said. "We would love to have you and Sextus stay."

"I would like that."

Electra sighed. "Ephesus is so far away, I know, but I will write to you all the time. Besides, I have a feeling we may be moving."

"Really?" Martia asked. "Leave Ephesus?"

Electra shrugged. "Why not? Besides, it is not what it used to be. And, being here, back in Graecia has been...well...healing."

"It has!" Martia said quickly. She looked at the two women and hugged them tightly.

Felix, Rufio, and Sextus fell out of the dancing line then to catch their breath as they watched the women together.

"When do you have to return to Rome?" Felix asked Sextus.

"The day after tomorrow, I'm afraid. I have to meet a couple of members of the Athenian Boule first, but then we take ship for Ostia."

"And you, my friend?" Felix asked Rufio.

"A few days. As soon as the Hippocampus makes berth in Piraeus, Captain Memnon will send word."

"And then back to Etruria for the harvest?" Sextus ventured.

"Yes. Back for the harvest." Rufio surprised himself that he had not thought of home as much of late, but now that they spoke about it, the long list of things to do began to flood his mind. "I suppose I'll have to swap ink-stained fingers for dirt-stained hands now."

Felix put his hand on his friend's shoulder. "There's no reason you can't bear both ink and dirt together, my friend. If anyone can do it, you can."

Rufio offered an awkward smile.

THE TWILIGHT OF THE COMPANY'S VICTORY LINGERED FOR YET A few more days as The Etrurian Players allowed themselves to indulge more readily in the pleasures of that ancient polis of colour and light. When Julius, Pollux, Castor, Fausto and Damon returned to the agorae of Athenae, it was to the cheers and congratulations of an admiring public, rather than the mocking jeers and plaintive shouting of a disgruntled populace.

"Seems like Terentius and our performance have saved us from the Athenians' anger," Pollux observed as he smiled back at a group of ladies.

"Apollo and the Muses must love you, my friend," Julius laughed as he walked arm-in-arm with Domela, enjoying the sun upon his uplifted face. "Your first performance in the agora was anything but stellar."

Damon trilled a few notes in reminiscence of that riotous occasion.

"Oh, I don't know," Beatrice added from where she walked with Fausto. "Though they won't admit it, even these Greeks enjoy a bit of panto."

Fausto laughed to himself. "I guess The Rome Antics weren't so bad after all."

"Let's just enjoy a day without mischief for once, shall we?" Julius said as he led Domela to a shaded taberna to seek some wine.

"You go ahead!" Castor called out. "We're going to say a final farewell to Circe's island!" He pushed Damon in the opposite direction toward the street that led up to the House of the Nymphs on the Peripatos.

Pollux turned. "Fausto, you coming? We should bid farewell to Calypso, Medusa and Amazonia!"

"No. You three go ahead," Fausto waved him off. "Beatrice and I are going to find some posca."

Pollux's face twisted up. "Doesn't sound like a fair trade, but all right. I'll bid them farewell from Syrus!" He turned and ran after his brother and Damon.

"Are you sure you don't want to join them?" Beatrice asked. "I don't mind."

Fausto stopped in the middle of the new agora's courtyard and stared at her. "I'm sure," he said as he took her hand and they began to walk. "Besides, by Venus, I've had this bad itch since my last visit there…"

Beatrice let go of his hand with a chuckle.

EARLIER THAT MORNING, AS THE SUN FILTERED THROUGH THE pine and olive wood surrounding the villa, Felix, Electra, Rufio, Clara and the children had gathered in the courtyard to bid farewell to Sextus and Martia whose ship awaited them at Piraeus to take them back to Ostia and Rome.

As the birds sang to the new day from the villa's tiled rooftop, it was difficult to hold back the tears for, in truth, they did not know when they would all be together again.

Martia found it especially difficult. She would miss the freedom that being with the players afforded her and Sextus, a simple freedom of being themselves. The society in which they dwelled in Rome, was simply not like that. "I will come and see you in Etruria, if you don't mind," Martia said to Clara as she hugged her and kissed Felicia's forehead.

Clara felt her heart tighten and hugged her back tightly. "Come anytime. Come for the harvest!"

"I would like that," Martia said as she turned back to Electra who held Thespis out to her for a final cuddle.

"He will miss you," Electra smiled.

"I will miss him," Martia rubbed her nose on Thespis' and the child laughed joyously.

"I will miss you too," Electra added, wiping a tear from her eye.

Martia turned and hugged her. "I'll imagine you in Alexandria, mesmerizing your admirers like Cleopatra, your little Caesarion in your arms."

"He'll probably be running by the time you get there!" Clara said with a laugh. "I can't believe how quickly these two imps have started to sit and crawl!"

They gathered around the children for a final display of their new skills about the fountain in the courtyard.

The three men standing nearby smiled at the sight.

"It will be difficult for Martia to be without her newfound sisters," Sextus said with a sad smile. "And for me without the inevitable excitement you all bring into our lives!" He laughed.

"And we will miss our brother-in-art, Sextus," Felix said, placing a muscular arm about him.

Sextus grinned. "You have the funds I gave you for the Alexandrian production?" Sextus grew serious again for a moment, for the previous day he and Felix had gone over the accounts line by line, planning for the next performance.

"Yes. The coin is secure. The Alexandrians won't know what hit them!" Felix clapped.

"What play are you going to be performing?" Rufio asked.

"Euripides' *Tragedy of Hercules*. I had a dream last night that I was wearing a lion skin and carrying a club." Felix puffed out his chest. "I feel that the hero was telling me something, sending me a sign."

"Yeah, a sign that you enjoyed clubbing people with a big knob," Rufio laughed.

Felix shook his head. "They do like to riot in Alexandria!"

"Gods, no," Sextus said, his hand on his face.

Felix winked at Rufio. "But we'll see if we can tame them. Make them weep with a tragedy!"

Rufio was quiet, for he too now felt the sting of imminent departure, though they yet had a couple of days left to them.

Sextus sighed then and went over to his wife. "My love…

I'm sorry, but we need to go. I'm not the only official on the ship."

Martia nodded from where she sat on the fountain's edge playing with the children. She stood and straightened her stola. "May the Gods guide you safely to your destinations."

"And you, my dear," Electra hugged her one last time before scooping up her son who was beginning to crawl but was blocked by Peli who sniffed his face.

"The wagon is ready for you, Praetor," Atticus said as he approached. "They will take you and lady Martia to Piraeus."

"Thank you for everything, Atticus," Sextus said. "Please tell your dominus how very appreciative we are of his hospitality and that we are happy to return the favour next time he is in Rome."

"I shall do so." Atticus bowed and backed away.

Sextus and Martia then climbed into the wagon and looked back at the group, including Peli who sat beside Clara whining as he looked up at them with his awkward eyes.

The villa gates opened and, heralded by birdsong, the wagon rolled out and down the road.

Electra wiped the tears from her eyes, her son looking up at her with a strange expression, and then gently pressing his cheek to hers. "Come," Electra said. "Time to introduce you to some new foods, young man."

"What about me?" Felix laughed.

"You can eat too, husband!" Electra called back.

Clara stood with Felicia and went to Rufio's side. "What are you thinking?"

"I don't know," he answered, stroking Peli's head. "I'm just not fond of goodbyes."

"It is a shame that our chosen familia is so spread out."

"It is." Rufio kissed her then, just as Felicia plunged her lips into theirs, mimicking the action. Rufio laughed. "But as long as I have you two near, anything is possible."

Together, they went back inside the villa.

When the wagon was father down the road, nearing the Panathenaic stadium, Sextus turned to his wife.

"I thought you would be inconsolable right now. I for one am deeply sad to leave them all behind."

"They are our chosen familia now, aren't they?" Martia said with a smile.

"Exactly! So why are you not weeping?"

"Because I'm too happy, my love."

"About leaving?"

"No, Sextus." Martia took his arm and drew him close. "About missing my menses."

"About missing your-" The words stopped in Sextus' throat and he looked into his wife's eyes to make sure she was not having him on. "You mean?"

Martia nodded, and then a tearful joy filled her eyes, adorning her lashes, her cheeks, and her smiling lips. "Yes."

"By the Gods! It's…it's… What a day!" Sextus beamed. "I love you so much."

"I love you too," Martia said, kissing him as their laden wagon rolled alongside the Ilissos.

It was no easy thing for Felix, Electra, Rufio and Clara to sit together on those last couple of days in the city of the Goddess Athena, for though they truly enjoyed each other's company, the day of departure loomed like a Titan's shadow over their conversations.

They paid one last visit to the Taberna Thesias, walked the agora and made offerings to Athena Parthenos one last time in her shining temple on the Acropolis. Apart from their offerings to the goddess, it all felt half-hearted.

Rufio had also stopped by the great library to see Phemius one last time, but their discussion of Terentius had been brief, for a group of young men from the Academia had arrived and had pulled the librarian away with their questions about Archimedes' texts.

As Phemius was drawn away by the eager students, he turned to wave one last time to Rufio. "Come back to Athenae soon, Rufio Pagano!" he called out.

But Rufio knew that was unlikely as he waved back politely.

That evening, the nostalgia was thick, like a fog on a still sea, and as Felix, Rufio, and Clara reminisced and relayed the tales of their Etrurian youths to Electra, they all wondered at the lives their own children would have. It was difficult not to recall the melancholy and worry displayed by Publius Leander and Delphina for their eldest daughter. As they watched the children play upon the ground in their midst in the peristylium garden, the future seemed both exciting and terrifying all at once.

"Felicia will have some semblance of a normal life in Etruria," Electra was saying, "but what about our Thespis? Are we to drag him from city to city, never really spending time at home in Ephesus? And what kind of home is Ephesus anyway?"

Felix glanced at Rufio and Clara, for now it seemed that Electra had donned the mantle of panic which he had so recently shed. He got up from his couch and went to sit with his wife, his arm about her. "We don't have to remain in Ephesus if that is not what you want. We can go anywhere."

"I just want Thespis to grow up safe and strong."

"So long as I have anything to do with it, Electra, he will be safe." Felix reached down to stroke his son's head. "Look how he sits and plays already!"

They looked at Thespis who bobbed and smiled a little before falling backward onto Peli's neck.

Felix helped him sit up again.

"Electra," Clara said. "You can always come to Etruria if Ephesus is no longer safe."

"Thank you, Clara, but what would we do for a theatre? Is there one on your latifundium? Should we entertain the peasants for a bag of bronze asses?"

"There are quite nice theatres in Volaterrae and Florentia," Rufio offered. "They're less than a day's ride from our home."

Electra gave him a strained smile that betrayed her doubt. "Maybe this *was* meant to be our last show, as Felix suspected…"

"I was wrong," Felix said. "Absolutely. We are…my love…" Felix took both his wife's hands. "We are meant to bring joy and laughter to the people of this empire, to make them think, and weep, and cherish the lives that they have. It is the purpose for which the Gods have brought us all together. We cannot shun the gifts we have been given, that purpose for which The Etrurian Players exist. Can we?"

Electra closed her eyes and grew calm again. "You are right," she sighed with relief and nodded. "I cannot possibly deny the people the thrill of seeing me upon the pulpitum."

Felix grinned and kissed her hands. "And what would our son say if, some day, he discovers that we gave up our glories too young, or that I denied the people the chance to glimpse their Hercules!"

Rufio rolled his eyes and looked to Clara who was looking down at their daughter, trying not to laugh.

"We're going to miss you lot," Rufio said to Felix and Electra, and he meant it.

"So shall we," Electra's eyes glistened.

"I can't believe we're all leaving," Clara added. "There is something about Athenae…and being here with all of you."

"Well," Felix said, getting to his feet. "If it is the Gods' will, we shall be together again soon."

"To that end," Electra declared, "Thespis and I shall make

an offering in the lararium."

"Good idea," Felix said. "We are recently victorious, and so the Gods' ears are more attuned to our words in this moment."

"Is that how it works?" Rufio asked with an arched eyebrow.

"Felicia and I will join you, Electra," Clara declared as she picked up her daughter.

Just then, in perfect concert, the children flatulated so loudly that Peli jumped to his feet and barked.

"Ach!" Clara gasped. "First a change of bracae, I think."

"Yes," Electra held her son out and looked at his relieved face. "Thespis, one cannot go before the Gods to offer prayers with soiled bracae."

"MA-MA!" Thespis shouted.

Electra's eyes lit up, and she turned to look at Felix. "Did you hear that, *The* Felix Modestus?"

"I did," Felix said proudly as Electra followed Clara to the second storey, both of them holding their smiling, stinking children. When they were gone, Felix turned to Rufio and whispered. "Thespis actually said 'Modestus' to me yesterday, but I didn't tell Electra that."

"Best not," Rufio laughed.

Felix poured them both some watered wine and handed Rufio a cup. "To our success!"

"Which one? There are so many! Do you mean arriving here in Athenae safely, delivering your own child, or keeping our children alive?" Rufio drank. "Or do you mean our defeat of The Rome Antics, not getting hanged, or putting on the most brilliant smart-funny play this polis has ever seen? Honestly, Felix, if one counts them all, there are too many victories to be grateful for."

"I meant the play, of course, but you're right about all of it. We should celebrate all of our daily victories, large and small, and not take them for granted."

"What the Gods grant, the Gods can take away."

Felix frowned. "I think I heard a Christian say something like that in Ephesus."

"It makes sense."

They were silent for a minute before Felix spoke again. "It was magnificent though, wasn't it? When the audience finally gave us their applause. And to see Cassius and his troupe leading the charge…" Felix shook his head in disbelief. "That alone shows me that the Gods are watching!"

"And that they have a sense of humour," Rufio said.

"Yes!" Felix drained his cup and filled it again. "I had a moment though, when I thought we were done for."

"I'd say we've all had a few *moments* this time around."

"And we are better off for having had them," Felix declared as he refilled Rufio's cup. When he sat down again, he was quiet, his jovial mood much tempered. He looked at Rufio. "Have you seen him since?"

"Seen who?"

"*Him…*" Felix looked around to make sure no one was listening. "Terentius," he hissed.

Rufio looked into his wine cup and shook his head slowly. "No. I haven't."

"Do you think it worked?" Felix asked. "Do you think we helped him? I mean, he did appear to thank us during the ovation. But where did he go from there?"

"I just don't know," Rufio replied, and there was sadness in his voice.

They drank in silence again.

The truth was that Rufio had been unable to think of much else since the play's end. While Clara and Felicia and the rest of the domus had slept fitfully each night, satiated with wine, food, and some with lovemaking, Rufio had lain in bed, eyes wide, staring at the shifting shadows displayed by the moon and trees outside.

That night, again, Rufio wondered if Terentius still wandered in the woods outside the villa walls, side by side with the forest nymphs and satyrs who teased the shades trapped there.

He breathed deeply and rolled over to try and sleep, comforted by the breathing of his wife and child in the room with him.

SLEEP DID NOT LAST LONG FOR RUFIO, AND THE MOMENT THE first dove uttered a mournful note, even before the sun had risen and the cicadas began their chorus, he was awake.

Rufio opened his eyes to find Peli's snout resting on the bed beside him. He stared at Rufio, eagerly awaiting his attention. "What do you want?"

Peli whined, his tail beginning to wag hesitantly.

"What?"

Peli lashed his face with his tongue and nuzzled Rufio.

"Oh, all right. I can't sleep anyway," he whispered. "Just don't piss in here. Hold it."

Peli went to wait by the door while Rufio sat up on the edge of the bed, rubbing his face. He slid his indigo tunica over his head, belted it sloppily, and tied up his sandals.

"Where are you going?" Clara said groggily from beneath the bed coverings.

"Just taking Peli for a morning walk. I'll be back shortly." Rufio walked over to Clara and kissed her forehead. On a whim he grabbed his satchel before heading to the door where Peli waited.

One never knew when Apollo and the Muses would fill one with inspiration and, when they did, Rufio wanted to be ready.

After a quick stop in the triclinium for a cup of water and a crust of bread, Rufio made his way to the first courtyard where he roused the servant there to open the gate.

"It's still early," the servant grumbled, only just beating the villa's cockerel to its utterance.

"Not according to the cock, it isn't," Rufio said as the man got to his feet and opened the gate.

Once Rufio and Peli were outside, he closed the gate again and lay back down in the dirt. "Farmers..." he grumbled.

THE EARLY MORNING AIR OF AUGUSTUS WAS DAMP AND FRESH, perfumed with mountain pine, oleander and wild thyme which sprouted along the roadside. An owl hooted from an oak tree in the forest on Rufio's left, and he wondered if it was Athena's own sentry, keeping watch over all who tread the pathways about her beautiful city.

And it was beautiful. Over the past weeks, Rufio had come to admire Athenae in a way that he could never feel about Rome. The light was brighter in Athena's city, the colours more brilliant, the air somehow sweeter. There was a sense of antiquity and tradition that he found quite remarkable, and he could understand why so many students and truth-seekers flocked there, like bees to an apiary, or animals to water. The draw to Athenae was unmistakable, and the impression it left was, Rufio had to admit, undeniable. The temples of the Gods, the theatres, the sacred groves...the libraries... Rufio loved all of it, and had been drawn to it from the moment their gaudy wagon had approached the city's long walls.

However, as he walked past the great Panathenaic stadium on his left, and looked to the Parthenon shining on the Acropolis as the very first rays of morning sunlight shone upon it, Rufio knew that, were he forced to choose, he would pick his farm in Etruria over any other place in Rome's great empire. He smiled at the thought of Errol's voice croaking at the workers about their villa rustica in the early morning hours. He longed for the orderly rows of the vineyards, and the vast groves of olive trees sloping away from the villa, their silver-green bows lit by a million fireflies at dusk. He missed the lazy voices of his sheep and goats, and the happy braying of his donkey, Stella, who would come running to him when he emerged in the morning.

"Hopefully, Stella has repelled her would-be husband!" Rufio said aloud to Peli who trotted happily alongside him as they approached the bridge over the Ilissos River. "Salve, Arcas!" Rufio called out to the guard who stepped forward.

"Kalimera, Rufio Pagano!" Arcas replied.

Surprised by the warm greeting, Rufio asked, "Don't you ever go home?"

"It is an honour to guard the gates of Athena's polis. Besides, it is easier to sleep here than at home where my new-born daughter wails all night."

"I understand," Rufio laughed. "Trust me, it gets better soon."

"I am glad to hear it," Arcas said, nodding toward Peli who sat down beside Rufio's leg. "He seems to have calmed down."

Rufio pat Peli. "I think he's had quite enough excitement." He looked up at Arcas. "But before long, I'm guessing that you'll see more than a few mischievous black and white canines running around Athenae's streets."

Arcas pursed his lips. "May the Gods prevent it! The howling alone will drive my men to insanity!" He laughed. "Are you going to the agora?"

"No. Just walking this one along the Ilissos."

"I see. Well, I wish you well, Rufio Pagano, and I congratulate you on your performance."

"Were you there at the odeon for it?" Rufio did not remember seeing Arcas in the audience.

"No. I was not. But I have heard people speak of nothing else… The Etrurian Players this, and Hercules that! It seems that you conquered the city after all!"

"Well, their hearts and minds at least," Rufio conceded.

"Do you return to Rome then?"

Rufio shook his head. "To Etruria and the peace of my farm."

"A wise man works the land."

"Quite true."

"Do your servants do it for you?" Arcas asked with a smile.

"I'll have you know that both dirt and ink stain my fingers!" Rufio laughed.

"A wise man indeed," Arcas said. "May the Gods warm your back on your way home, Rufio Pagano."

"Thank you, Arcas," Rufio said before stepping off the road and into the forest along the river.

At once, Peli darted off into the trees.

THE EARLY-MORNING WORLD OF THE SHRINES TO THE GODS along the Ilissos was hushed but for the river's caress along the grass and rock banks, and the serenade of one nightingale to another in the branches of the plane and willow trees.

Rufio walked slowly along the pathway, his eyes seeking Peli's darting form ahead among the stone-faced statues of gods, heroes, and philosophers. He passed the temples of Chronos and Rhea which looked ancient and somewhat angry in the dark of the wood, and beyond them, adjacent to the shut-up Panhellenion, the temple of Apollo Delphinios emerged from the morning mist, inviting him in.

"Peli!" Rufio called out, suddenly worried that he had gone to harass the guardian serpent of the temple. "Peli, come here! I don't feel like extricating you from that thing's jaws." Rufio shuddered involuntarily, and turned quickly to see Peli where he was barking on his way to the river for a drink. "That dog," Rufio grumbled as he followed after him.

He heard a voice then, and it was not Peli's.

Rufio walked slowly, pushing his satchel back to free his arms should he need to defend himself. "Whoever's there, you best leave my dog alone or he'll piss in your face!" Rufio stepped around a statue of the muse, Thalia, her hand outstretched and holding a comic mask. "You?" he gasped, and his heart sank. "It can't be!"

Sitting upon the ground, leaning against the trunk of a broad plane tree, Terentius turned his head to look at the mortal man approaching him. He held his endless scroll in his hands and was rolling it up slowly.

"Peli, come here," Rufio hissed, but Peli wagged his tail and allowed the shade to run his hand over his furry head.

"Always good to have a bit with a dog," Terentius said with a smile.

"What?"

"You would not have come if he had not brought you here, would you?" The shade continued rolling his scroll.

Rufio noted the satchel on the ground beside him, out of which jut many more scrolls. "You mean you wanted me to come here?" Rufio certainly was not sure how he felt about that, but after wrestling with his initial discomfort, he realized that he too had been hoping to meet Terentius one last time, to know if The Etrurian Players had helped or hindered the shade's suffering.

"I wanted to thank you, Rufio Pagano."

Rufio stepped closer and as he did so, the shade stood to face him, his hands still working at rolling up the scroll. "You disappeared at the play's end. I wasn't sure if…well…you know…"

Terentius nodded. "I know. Your company succeeded in doing what I could not… You won over the Athenians. You helped them to feel what I was trying to say."

"Which is what, exactly?"

"That kindness and understanding matter. That the affairs

of men should matter to us all. That parents have a duty to love, protect, and let go of their children."

Rufio nodded. "Is that all?" *Terentius is speaking to me…* Rufio thought. *This is momentous.*

"Of course it is," Terentius replied.

"Oh, don't start that," Rufio said, but with a smile.

The shade returned the smile. "Also…"

"Yes?"

"I had to wait for a long time for my words to be understood and appreciated. It is a long and lonesome road at times, to do what we do."

"You're the writer, and I'm the farmer."

Terentius' wild hair fell about his face as he shook his head. "The two are not mutually exclusive, and certainly not in you. Your time is coming, Rufio Pagano."

"Do you think so?"

"I do. But remember that the road to all that you envision, hope for, and seek is long and punctuated with great indignities. Learn to laugh at and honour those moments, to live comfortably with them. The Gods will love you for it."

"Oh, trust me," Rufio said. "I've had my share of indignities."

"And you will have many more."

"Great."

Terentius smiled, finished rolling his final scroll, and tucked it into his satchel with a sigh.

"Are you leaving Athenae then?" Rufio asked. "Are you able to?"

"Yes." Terentius looked around at the trees where morning sunlight dappled the canopy above them. "At last."

"If you like, you can sail back to Italy with us."

The shade opened his eyes and stared at Rufio. "I have another boat to take…" He then opened his pale palm to show an obol with the owl of Athena upon it. "I've been saving this for a long time."

Rufio shuddered, but he could see that it was what the shade wanted.

When Rufio did not speak, the shade placed his hand over his still heart. "Thank you, Rufio Pagano…for freeing me."

"You're welcome."

"I have left something in the temple for you," Terentius said. "Apollo commanded it of me, and I wanted to do it." He looked at Rufio's satchel and smiled. "Do not give up. Remember, words gain credibility by deed."

"I understand. Thank you." Rufio did not know what else to say, for the emotion that wrung his heart at that moment was overwhelming.

A sound rang out then, a ghostly horn that felt somehow nearby, but not of that place or time.

Terentius looked up. "I must go now." He smiled one last time, his face relaxed and at peace. He began to walk along the riverbank, away from Rufio and Peli. Then, he turned back one more time. "Farewell," the shade said and, with a bow, he was gone.

Rufio stood there, still, his heart racing, and reached up to wipe the tears from his eyes.

Peli whined beside him and jumped up, his paws upon him.

"Good boy," Rufio said, rubbing Peli's face and neck. He then turned to look at the temple of Apollo. "Come."

They walked slowly toward the temple, and mounted the steps beneath the pediment to look into the fire-lit interior. After looking for the serpent, Rufio walked in, approaching the altar before the statue of Apollo.

The altar was empty.

"He said he left something for me here," Rufio said, immediately noting the strangeness of what he was saying and doing. "What was I expecting? Presents from shades?"

Peli sat down, his mismatched eyes searching the dark recesses of the temple, his body not daring to explore.

Rufio looked up at Apollo's face and bowed his head. "Thank you, Lord. Thank you for bringing us all together here to help Terentius." He found himself at a loss for words then, the great swirl of his emotions being what he had to offer. "Oh, Apollo… May we all be together again soon, my family and The Etrurian Players."

Rufio then opened his satchel and pulled out the olive crown which the people of Athenae had given him at the play's end. He held it up to Apollo. "Please accept this, Apollo. Thank you for the success of our performance… I will build the temple I promised to you when we return to Etruria. Please bless our journey…" He set the olive crown upon the cold marble of the altar and closed his eyes for a few moments, his mind going over all that had happened over the past weeks during that momentous sojourn in Athenae.

When Rufio looked up again, the crown was gone and, in its place, was an ancient bronze stylus. Its surface was worn, polished to a brilliant sheen from much use, but the tip remained sharp and ink-stained, ready for more toil and tales.

He picked the stylus up and held it in his right hand. "Thank you."

Rufio looked to the temple doors and the growing light outside. He then turned back to Apollo and bowed his head.

"Words gain credibility by deed…" he repeated Terentius' parting advice. Rufio smiled with amusement. "Quoting himself… Come, Peli," he said. "Better get back."

Rufio and Peli exited the temple to a brilliant summer's day bursting with colour, and life, and nature's song. With a last glimpse about the shrines of Ilissos, they set off for the villa, their family, and their friends, Terentius' stylus tucked safely in Rufio's satchel.

No one will ever believe me, Rufio thought.

XXII

THE SAILING OF SHIPS

The day of departure from Athenae arrived at last, but it was a bittersweet occasion. The Etrurian Players were excited to go to Alexandria, especially after being newly-crowned in Athenae, and Rufio and Clara were keen to return to Etruria for the harvest and the calm, rustic peace of their home. But it all came at the cost of separation, a thing that was much more difficult after the trials they had endured together.

The long procession of wagons passed through the Atticus villa's gates, leaving the servants with a mixture of exhausted relief and sadness.

"Life won't be the same without The Etrurian Players!" the man at the gate said to Atticus as they watched the wagons drive away accompanied by the sound of singing.

"No, it definitely won't," Atticus replied, astonished at how sad he was to see them go.

"Farewell, Atticus!" The Etrurian Players called out, their arms waving like olive branches in the hot wind.

Atticus raised his hand to wave and then turned to go back into the villa. His dominus had new guests arriving for the festival of Eleusinia, and there was much to do. He sighed as he began going over his lists in the tablinum, the sound of sweeping and silence echoing in the peristylium outside.

Atticus stopped to look down at the silver armilla which Felix Modestus had given him in thanks. He smiled to himself.

In his mind, no other guests would ever measure up to The Etrurian Players.

DOWN IN THE NORTHERN HARBOUR OF CANTHAROS AT PIRAEUS, the sunlight glittered upon the surface of the sea, as though Helios had cast great fistfuls of diamonds into the blue depths.

At the far end of the harbour, where Romans usually made berth, the Hippocampus was moored, the cargo of Attic wine, oil, and honey which Rufio and Clara had purchased being loaded into the hold. Captain Memnon strode about the deck, ordering his men to secure everything.

"Nice corbita!" Felix said to Clara and Rufio as the wagons came to a stop at that end of the harbour first.

"She is beautiful," Clara replied as she got down out of the wagon and reached up to take Felicia from Rufio.

"Where is yours?" Rufio asked as he jumped down and held out his hand to Electra.

"Oh, we don't make berth at this end," Electra smiled. "The Priapus is down there in the middle of the harbour."

"I'm sorry…" Rufio laughed. "The 'Priapus'?" He looked to where a crowd waited for a last glimpse of the victorious theatrical troupe. Above a display of colourful banners, and a brightly-painted hull, there hovered over the quarterdeck a great winged phallus. Rufio turned to Felix. "Your idea?"

"One cannot have enough good luck!" Felix said. "Besides, everyone will know we're coming."

"I should say!" Clara added, hoisting Felicia in her arms as she reached out for Thespis who was in Electra's.

The rest of The Etrurian Players jumped down out of the wagons which then turned around and made for the Priapus to begin the process of unloading all of their possessions and props into the hold.

The company lined up in front of Rufio and Clara to say their hurried farewells, for the people of Alexandria awaited them.

"Well, everyone," Rufio said. "It has been another adventure."

"You sure you won't come with us to Aegyptus, Rufio?" Fausto asked. "We'll have a lot of fun!"

"He's got to bring in his harvest, Fausto," Pollux said. "The olives aren't going to pick themselves!"

"No, they won't," Rufio replied. "But we'll miss all of you very much."

Castor bent down to pat Peli who was walking in front of all of them. "I'm going to miss this one as well."

"Perhaps you can all come to Etruria some day?" Clara said, smiling at Beatrice and Julius.

"We would like that," Beatrice replied, trying not to weep.

"Come on. We'll see them again," Fausto said to her.

Peli went to each of the others, and finally came to a stop before Domela who was making eyes at Felicia. He lifted his leg then, and wet the hem of her tunica.

"Oh, Gods! Oh dear!" Domela cried out. "Is it a bad omen?"

Julius took her hand and kissed it. "I believe it means he has accepted you."

"Oh," she said with a more relaxed but slightly disgusted expression. "I suppose."

The others snickered.

"Why don't the rest of you go and help with the unloading?" Felix said. "Electra and I will be along shortly."

Hugs were given all around, and when that was done, Castor and Pollux, Julius and Domela, Beatrice, Fausto and

Damon turned and made their way through the crowded harbour toward the bobbing knob of the Priapus.

When they were gone, Felix turned to his friends. "First Sextus and Martia leave, and now you two. Time robs us, my friends."

"Well," Clara said, "if you ever need to slow things down, come and stay with us." She took Electra's hand and squeezed it.

"I doubt that we'll ever slow down," Felix laughed, "but that would be nice someday. For now, though, we have places to go, and audiences to impress!"

Electra was quiet then.

As Clara comforted her and they held the children together for their own farewell, Felix took Rufio aside.

"I've been looking for him everywhere," Felix said. "I haven't seen him."

"Who?"

"You know!" Felix looked at the women before turning back to Rufio. "The shade…Terentius!" he whispered.

"Oh, him."

"Yes!" Felix's previously bright and confident face grew anxious then. "I need to know for sure, Rufio. Did we succeed? Did we fulfill Apollo's command?"

Rufio nodded. He could see that Felix would not relax, that he would not be free of the worries he had buried in the strong box of his mind. "I *did* see him."

"You did? Where?"

"Yesterday, when I went to the Ilissos shrines in the morning."

"Why didn't you tell me?"

"I didn't have the chance with everyone around."

Felix gripped Rufio's shoulders. "Tell me, Rufio! What did he say?"

"Terentius is free, Felix."

"You're sure?"

"I am. He told me himself. He was packed and ready to board the ship."

"What ship?"

"*The* ship."

"Oh." Felix lowered his hands, his shoulders hunched. "I don't know why, but the thought of that makes me sad."

Rufio looked at his dear friend. In truth, he did not know when they would meet again, how many months or years it would be before they laughed together. He could see that Felix was distraught, remembered all that Felix had gone through during their time in Athenae. An idea came to Rufio then, and with a little smile, he now put his hands on Felix's bulky shoulders. "Terentius did ask me to tell you something before he disappeared."

"A message from the shade? For me?"

"Yes."

"What is it? What did he say?"

"He said 'Please thank Felix Modestus for all that he has done for me. Tell him that he is the greatest of performers and that he must continue to perform, so long as he has joy for it in his heart.'"

Felix nodded, moved by the words. "That sounds like something he would say."

Rufio pat him. "There is no greater endorsement."

"Of course...he is right," Felix said. "He's quite an astute shade, isn't he?"

"I suppose," Rufio smiled.

"He's smart, *and* funny. Just like his work!" Felix clapped his hands. Peli barked at him and Felix bent down to pat him. "And of course, we had our bit with a dog at the very end." He ruffled the canine's neck. "Good boy!"

"All is ready, Domina!" Captain Memnon called out from the deck of the Hippocampus.

"Thank you, Captain!" Clara called back before turning to Electra and hugging her one last time. "We love you. Take care of yourselves."

"We shall," Electra said, her dark eyes glassy in the midday sun. She then turned to Rufio who reached up to shake Thespis' tiny hand. "Thank you, Rufio Pagano."

"For what?"

"You know."

Rufio nodded. No words were required. "May Janus and Hermes guide you safely to Alexandria."

"And you to Etruria," Electra replied, kissing his cheek and turning to wait for Felix.

"Goodbye, Felicia," Felix said. "You keep them busy for me, will you?" he said.

Felicia let out a high-pitched squeal at that.

Felix's eyes widened. "Did you hear that?" he asked the others. "What a range!" He turned back to Felicia. "We'll make a singer of you yet!"

"She'll be too busy running the latifundium!" Rufio countered.

"She can do both, can't she?" Clara asked.

Rufio and Felix looked at each other and smiled.

Felix took Rufio up in a big hug. "Safe journey my friend. Thank you for everything." His voice shuddered.

Rufio felt his throat tighten. "You too."

Felix smiled and took his son in one arm, and his wife in the other. "We'd better go. Our public awaits!" Felix declared. He winked at his friends and then turned with Electra and his son to wade into the cheering crowd that formed a path to their ship.

"You all right?" Clara asked Rufio.

"Yes. Sad...but I'm fine. You?"

"Me too. I don't know when we'll see them again."

"Hopefully it won't be too long," Rufio sighed.

"Let's go home, my love," Clara said, taking his hand.

Rufio nodded and followed her to the gang plank. "Peli, you coming?"

Peli barked and charged up ahead of them.

"Welcome aboard, Domina!"

"Thank you, Captain," Clara replied.

"All of your things are loaded into your cabin." He turned to Rufio. "You survived the Athenians then?"

"We did, Captain," Rufio replied. "Just."

"Glad to hear it."

"Now if I can just survive the sea voyage home!" Rufio laughed.

"Should be fine, Rufio Pagano." Captain Memnon looked up at the sky. "The Gods have blessed us with fine weather."

"That's a relief!" Rufio replied.

"Ready, Captain!" one of the sailors shouted.

"Excuse me," Captain Memnon said as he went to give the orders.

"Rufio come," Clara said. "Let's wave to them."

Rufio climbed up onto the quarter deck to where Clara stood with Felicia at the railing.

The Priapus was rowed backward, out of the row of ships, and began to turn slowly, its colourful banners billowing in the late summer wind. Cheers erupted from the docks and The Etrurian Players sang out, Damon's flute like a flock of seabirds, and Beatrice's tambourine like the waves splashing against the painted hull.

"It's like Cleopatra leaving Tarsus for Alexandria," Rufio mused.

"Except Anthony is going with her," Clara said with a smile. "Good Gods!"

"Well that's something you don't normally see on a corbita!" Rufio laughed.

When the Priapus was fully turned, the crowd cheered at

the enormous wooden bollocks adjoined to the winged phallus at the stern.

A great hooting followed them from the docks, whistles, and songs for *The* Felix Modestus.

When the adulation peaked, the Priapus' sail unfurled to reveal a titanic olive wreath with 'The Etrurian Players' in the centre.

"Of course," Rufio said as they waved.

"Do you like it?" Felix shouted from far off.

"YES!" Rufio shouted back.

"The Etrurian Players are coming!" the entire company shouted from the deck. "Brace yourselves!"

ON THE DECK OF THE PRIAPUS, AMID THE SUN-DRENCHED singing and dancing, Felix, Electra, and Thespis watched as the Hippocampus backed out and prepared to sail, their own ship already pulling away quickly, leaving Athenae's great port.

"We shouldn't have to say goodbye like this," Felix said. "Rufio and Clara have both changed so much."

"So have you," Electra said, turning to kiss his cheek.

Felix returned the gesture, but was thoughtful for a moment as the other corbita's sail unfurled. There was a sting of sadness as he thought of the adventures of the past weeks, but then he looked at Electra beside him, holding their strong, healthy boy, and he knew then that as long as he was with them, all was well with the world. "You know what?"

"What, my love?" Electra said as she wiped her eyes one last time, her tears spent.

"I used to care so much for what others thought... But now, I do believe I'm free of that."

"You are?" Electra said, most doubtfully, amused that he should think so.

"I am. And it feels good. All I need is you and Thespis. Truly."

"And a good review or two, maybe?" she added.

Felix shrugged. "Well…that is always nice."

Electra laughed. "Since I met you, Felix Modestus, life has certainly been an odyssey of our own making, with victories and joys, humiliations and all manner of chaos." She turned to face him. "And I love it."

They kissed while Thespis' tiny hands grabbed at their hair.

Felix laughed. "Life can be an altar of indignities at times… But, it is our life, and I wouldn't change that for all the praise in the world!"

The Felix Modestus is back! Electra thought, rejoicing inside.

The Priapus broke free of Piraeus' great harbour walls and set off into the open sea.

As the ship began to rise and fall more drastically upon the waves, Electra handed Thespis to Felix and went down to the lower deck.

Before joining her, Felix Modestus looked out to sea, his son in his arms, a great smile upon his face. "Thank you, Apollo… Thank you."

EPILOGUS

It was good to be back in Etruria. The familiar sounds, the crisp smells, and the sight of soft green hills stretching into the distance was all the fanfare that Rufio Pagano needed on their three-day journey from the port of Pisae to their home. As their wagons pulled onto the long drive leading to the main villa of their latifundium, Clara and Felicia settled beside Rufio on the driver's bench of the lead wagon. Peli bounced around excitedly in the back, whimpering with excitement, his snout almost as thrilled to smell home as Rufio's nose was.

"I can't believe we're back," Rufio said. "Feels like years!"

"We've had quite an adventure," Clara said, holding Felicia on her lap. "Do you recognize home, my girl?"

Felicia, whose wild blonde curls bounced up and down in Clara's face, pointed. "Donkey!"

"Yes! There's Stella!" Clara said. "I'm surprised she remembers," Clara said to Rufio.

"Who could forget Stella?" Rufio said, feeling emotional as the donkey came charging down the dirt road, her braying echoing over the entire farm. "Stella!" Rufio called.

Unable to contain himself any longer, Peli jumped out of the wagon bed and ran to meet Stella, barking and wagging his tail furiously.

The two animals circled each other at a happy run before Stella came to the side of the wagon, braying with her head tilted up to Rufio, Clara, and Felicia.

"I missed you too, girl!" Rufio said, reaching down to pat her head as she fell in step beside the wagon.

"Salvete!" Clara called to the men and women at work in the fields to either side of the road. "Good to see you all!"

"Welcome back, domini!" some of the workers called out.

"I don't see Errol." Clara shielded her eyes from the sun to peer ahead.

"I hope he hasn't died on us!" Rufio said with a sudden panic. "He's grumpy…but I do love the old goat."

There was some shouting and barking up ahead as Peli tore through the orchard, nipping excitedly at the workers, one of whom dropped the full basket of apples which he had just harvested.

"The crops are thriving, thank the Gods," Rufio said as he observed the laden apple and plum trees to one side, beneath which the sheep and goats grazed.

"Looks like the olives are nearly there too," Clara said. "And the grape vines are heavy with fruit!" Clara smiled. "We'll have a healthy harvest!"

"Ahh!" Rufio sighed. "I can't wait for a plate of warm chestnuts, fresh apples, and our own cheese!" He licked his lips.

Clara laughed. "It doesn't take much to make you happy, does it?"

"Not if I have the two of you," he said, turning to kiss her.

The wagons pulled up in front of the villa, in a circle about the well.

Rufio closed his eyes and listened for a few seconds. The sound of the rooster by the stables, the singing of the birds upon the rooftop, and the murmur of their small force of farm hands approaching all served as a reminder of how fortunate he truly was.

"Errol!" Felicia piped up suddenly, pointing at the old man who came walking out of the main doors of the villa.

"Sweetheart!" the old man called, his wrinkled old face clearly emotional. "Look how big you are!"

Clara looked at Rufio as she navigated the step down with Felicia. "See, *not* dead," she whispered.

"Domina," Errol said as she got down. "Thank the Gods you're home safe!"

"Safe, and victorious, Errol!" Rufio said from the other side of the wagon. "We were the glory of Athenae's stage!"

Clara shot him a doubtful look.

"Pah!" Errol said, still smiling at Felicia. "Well done, then."

"Thank you, Errol," Rufio said proudly.

"Now, if you're done nancing about Greek pulpita, we've got a harvest to bring in!"

"Good to see you too, you old goat," Rufio muttered. But his annoyance abated as Stella came rushing up to him, nuzzling him and leaning into him most desperately. "I missed you too, girl!" Rufio said as he rubbed her long, furry ears and stroked her neck and cheeks. "Where is…" Rufio looked around, and then turned to Errol. "Where is that farm hand who was chasing after Stella when we left?"

"Oh, he's gone."

"Where is he?" Rufio asked, feeling a great wave of relief.

"Well that's a story!" Errol said. "A few days after you left for Graecia, he got a little too persistent in his attentions. Stella wouldn't have any of it, and so she kicked him."

"In the head? Is he dead?" Rufio asked.

"Not dead," Errol continued. "She got him lower down. Planted both her back hooves into his figs!"

"Gods," Rufio gulped.

Errol nodded. "Lad couldn't walk let alone work with his hurt feelings and figs and all. So, I sent him back to his parents."

"Maybe we should send them an amphora of oil," Rufio mused, before chuckling and patting Stella. "Good girl. Serves him right."

"Rufio," Clara said.

Peli rushed up to Errol then, tail wagging, jumping up on the old man.

"All right, you!" Errol said, swatting at Peli. "I see he joined you then?"

"He did," Clara said. "Peli leapt into the sea and chased after the ship!"

"He did, eh?" Errol eyed Peli and knelt stiffly to pat him. "You did as I asked then, did you?" he whispered. "Good boy!"

Peli turned round three times, licked Errol's face, and then pissed on him.

The old man was too slow to react and got a wet shoulder for it. "Ahh! I see his manners haven't improved," Errol said to Clara.

"Not really, I'm afraid. Peli put on quite a show for the people of Athenae!"

"I didn't mean Peli," Errol said, eyeing Rufio who could hardly contain his laughter as he pulled his satchel out of the wagon bed.

"Oh, Errol!" Rufio said, as he came around the wagon and hugged the old man, uncaring of the wet stink on his arm. "It's so good to see you!"

"Aye..." the old man replied. "It's good to see you!"

"Really?" Rufio turned back to him from the doorway.

"Not you! Your wife and child, you bookish ninny!" Errol barked back. He then turned to the workers gathered about the wagons. "What are you all waiting for? Start unloading!"

Clara and Felicia joined Rufio at the threshold of their home and looked out at the thriving, fertile land and soft hills that were getting back to green after a hot summer.

"Welcome home, my love," Rufio said to Clara, kissing her there before they went inside to get settled.

From among the wagons, watching them go in, Errol smiled to himself.

That night, Rufio, Clara, Felicia and Errol sat in the triclinium together for the cena, enjoying a meal of boiled vegetables, olives, bread, roasted boar's meat, and wine, all of it from the latifundium.

Sitting with Felicia on his lap, Errol watched Rufio sigh, eating with is eyes closed as he savoured the tastes of home. He looked to Clara. "Didn't they feed him in Athenae? I thought the Greeks were famed for their hospitality?"

"Oh, they fed him," Clara said with a smile as she sipped her wine. "Mostly fish."

"Fish?" Errol cried. "No wonder he's half-starved!" Errol turned to Rufio who had opened his eyes again. "Don't you worry, lad, we'll have meat aplenty! A family of boar have been terrorizing the area. We'll have them caught and cooked in no time! Fish?" the old man grumbled. "Disgusting."

"Oh, I don't know, Errol," Clara said. "It can be quite nice."

"I don't believe it."

Felicia reached up and grabbed Errol's chin, wrenching a smile from the old man. "I can't believe how grown you are, little one!" He bounced her and she giggled. "So tell me…" Errol began. "What did you get up to in Athenae? Was it quite boring?"

Rufio and Clara shot each other an amused look.

"It was quite busy actually," Clara said. "Rufio got arrested and thrown in jail."

"In jail?" Errol turned quickly to Rufio. "You?"

"They caused quite the scene. A riot in fact!" Clara added.

"I don't believe it! I didn't think you had it in you, lad!" Errol scoffed. "I'm sure your father would have been proud."

"Do you think so?" Rufio asked, the adolescent in him somewhat hopeful.

"No!" Errol grumbled across the table. "He would have lashed the bracae from off your bottom!"

"Or at the least, given me a round of applause," Rufio said.

Errol couldn't help but laugh then, his shock now vanished

at the thought. "Aye, he probably would do that! Ha!" Errol handed Felicia back to Clara when she started to squirm. He then turned to Rufio. "And the play? Was Felix Modestus pleased?"

"We got off to a rough start but, in the end, it went very well," Rufio said.

"I should like to see you perform one day," Errol said quite suddenly as he slurped from his wine cup.

Rufio and Clara looked at him, their eyes wide.

"Really?" Clara asked.

"Why not? I'd like to see what all the fuss is about."

"Oh! That reminds me!" Rufio snapped his fingers.

"Of what?"

"We're building a temple to Apollo."

"Where?" Errol asked.

"I was thinking beyond the orchard." Rufio scratched his beard. "Just at the edge of the forest."

"Could do, yes," Errol said. "But why Apollo? Why not Mars, or Ceres, so that they can look after our crops properly? What's Apollo done for you except drag you across the sea to be jailed in Athenae?"

"Oh, Errol," Rufio said with a smile. "You have no idea."

As twilight faded into dusk, and night's mantle filled the sky outside their bedroom window on the upper floor of the villa, Rufio and Clara lay entwined in bed, gazing out at the flickering stars.

"I love Athenae," Clara said to him, her finger tracing the line of his shoulder, "but it is good to be home."

"Yes," Rufio sighed and kissed her head. "Our own domus, with our own food and our own bed. Hard to beat."

"Do you miss them?" Clara asked suddenly.

Rufio did not answer right away. "Of course I do."

"Me too."

"Who knows? Maybe someday, The Etrurian Players will actually return to Etruria?"

"Wouldn't that be something!" Clara laughed at the thought.

"If Clinia returned home from the wars, why not *The* Felix Modestus?"

As Felicia dozed softly in the far corner of their cubiculum, with Peli at the foot of her bed, Rufio and Clara made love to the sounds of the night and then fell asleep, grateful for each other's loving arms.

But Rufio Pagano had an uneasy sleep that night, for his mind drew him back to Athenae and that quiet world of the sacred shrines along the river Ilissos' banks. In his dreams, he wandered there, happy, quiet and contemplative.

It was as if he waited for something, or something was expected of him. He walked until he came to the temple of Apollo Delphinios, and looked into the temple's cella. No one was there, but a voice echoed all around him as the branches of the trees outside shivered in the breeze, and flames suddenly burst to life in the bowl of the temple's altar.

Words gain credibility by deed…

The voice was familiar to Rufio, but he knew not how to respond as he stood there.

Suddenly, he was back in his bed, in Etruria, on his farm, gazing out the window as the early morning sun began to light the eastern horizon with a faint red glow.

Rufio turned to look at Clara sleeping, and he kissed her forehead.

She murmured something incoherent and turned over to carry on sleeping.

Right, he thought. *It's time.*

Rufio put on a tunica and slid on his sandals. Quietly then, he went out of the cubiculum and found his way downstairs to his tablinum where his satchel sat upon the large desk that looked out over the land. He lit the lamps, poured a cup of water, and then sat down.

"Words gain credibility by deed," he repeated to himself, shaking his head. "Can't even sleep in on my first morning back." But he smiled and shrugged. "I guess I don't really want to."

Rufio Pagano unrolled a clean sheet of papyrus upon the tabletop, placing rocks at each corner. He then reached into his satchel and took out the linen bundle with the ancient stylus in it, hefting the implement in his hand.

His heart beat quickly as he contemplated what he was about to begin, but he knew it was time. His mind had been turning it over for so long, and now it was time to put ink to papyrus. He looked out his window at the rich, dewy, and blessed land of his home, and smiled to himself.

"Apollo… Thank you for bringing me to this beginning," Rufio prayed. "Guide me in this tale…"

Rufio dipped the stylus into the ink pot, his hand poised over the papyrus.

The ink dripped once, twice, three times, and then he began to write… *The Joy Seeker.*

THE END

Thank you for reading!

Did you enjoy *An Altar of Indignities*? Here is what you can do next.

If you enjoyed this dramatic, romantic comedy of ancient Rome and Athens, and if you have a minute to spare, please post a short review on the web page where you purchased the book, or on the Eagles and Dragons Publishing website.

Reviews are a wonderful way for new readers to find this book and your help in spreading the word is greatly appreciated.

The Etrurian Players will be back, and more Eagles and Dragons Publishing novels will be coming out soon, so be sure to sign-up for e-mail updates at:

https://eaglesanddragonspublishing.com/newsletter-join-the-legions/

Newsletter subscribers get a FREE BOOK, and first access to new releases, special offers, and much more!

To read more about the history, people and places featured in this book, check out *The World of An Altar of Indignities* blog series at the following link:

https://eaglesanddragonspublishing.com/the-world-of-an-altar-of-indignities/

Become a Patron of Eagles and Dragons Publishing!

If you enjoy the books that Eagles and Dragons Publishing puts out, our blogs about history, mythology, and archaeology, our video tours of historic sites and more, then you should consider becoming an official patron.

We love our regular visitors to the website, and of course our wonderful newsletter subscribers, but we want to offer more to our 'super fans', those readers and history-lovers who enjoy everything we do and create.

You can become a patron for as little as $1 per month. For your support, you can also get fantastic rewards as tokens of our appreciation.

If you are interested, just visit the website below to watch the introductory video and check out the patronage levels and exciting rewards.

https://www.patreon.com/EaglesandDragonsPublishing

Join us for an exciting future as we bring the past to life!

When I typed 'The End' on *An Altar of Indignities*, it was only then that it really struck me how much I enjoyed writing it, but also how great a challenge it had been for me. After the success of *Sincerity is a Goddess*, which garnered a few awards and a feature in Times Square, New York, the bar seemed to be set unbelievably high. To be honest, this book took me over a year to write, and that has not happened to me since the beginning of my writing career.

I had to learn to let go in writing this story, to not take things too seriously. And that meshed perfectly with the story I was trying to tell, and the themes I was trying to highlight.

This book, however, had to be born! After all, in the final lines of *Sincerity is a Goddess*, Rufio and Electra do indeed receive an invitation from Felix Modestus to come to Athens for the Panathenaic festival. While writing that first novel, I had been unsure whether I would write a sequel, but having reached the end with this troupe of characters, I knew that I could not leave them behind. I found that Rufio and Clara, Felix, Electra and all the others had become my literary *familia* in a way.

An Altar of Indignities had taken root and sprouted even before I decided to write it.

Before I began writing, I knew that the novel would be set in early third-century Roman Athens, but I did not know which play I wanted The Etrurian Players to perform. I knew it had to be a Roman comedic play, of course, for the thought of a Roman (sorry, Etrurian) theatre company putting on a play in Athens, the birthplace of theatre, was too tempting a prospect. In the previous novel I had used Plautus, and so I thought it only fitting that I go to the other master of ancient

Roman comedy, Publius Terentius Afer, or Terence as we know him.

Terence, though much lauded as perhaps the greatest Roman comedic playwright, only authored six plays in his short lifetime. Where Plautus' plays were more laugh-out-loud funny or even slapstick, Terence's work was more thoughtful and subtle. When I was researching his plays and their plots, I read that *Heautontimorumenos* (also written as *Heauton Timorumenos*), '*The Self-Tormentor*', was thought by some to be his greatest, most thought-provoking work. I also read that it is often overlooked by performers and scholars due to its complexity.

Not being one to shun a literary or historical challenge, I decided to go with *Heautontimorumenos*.

However, I had not fully realized what I was getting myself into. Terence's play has a complex plot with many layers, so much so that I had to read and re-read it seven times to make sure that I fully grasped it and how it would fit into the lives of The Etrurian Players.

It is indeed a 'smart-funny' play as Rufio points out in the story. It is not raucous or bawdy in the Roman sense. It is a very heartfelt and human story, and the sentiments it explores remain relevant to this day.

The play is referred to by ancient writers like Cicero and St. Augustine who admired Terence's astute views in lines such as "I am a man, and nothing that concerns a man do I deem a matter of indifference to me." And there are several such observances in the play that are said to have garnered applause from audiences over time.

In a review of the play that was published in *The Spectator* in the eighteenth century, Sir Richard Steele wrote that the play was "from beginning to end a perfect picture of human life, but I did not observe in the whole one passage that could raise a laugh. How well-disposed must that people be, who could be entertained with satisfaction by so sober and polite mirth!"

Smart-funny indeed. *Heautontimorumenos* seemed, to me at least, to be the perfect play for The Etrurian Players to perform for the haughty and discerning Athenian theatre crowd.

The fact that Terence is thought to have died in Athens, or on his way there, added an extra dimension to the story and, for Rufio and Felix, no small amount of pressure.

Readers will notice that I have quoted extensively from the play. The reason I did so is because Terence's dialogue is so rich, so difficult to summarize without losing something in the process, that I thought readers would be missing out if I did not. I wanted to give a full experience when it came to this wonderful play, for it is as much a character as Felix and his company.

For those who are interested, the version of the play which I used can be found in *The Comedies of Terence*, translated by Henry Thomas Riley, B.A., and published in 1896. It is available for free on the Project Gutenberg website. As far as other sources I have quoted from for this book, *The Iliad*, the Homeric Hymns, Euripides, and Pindar are all available from Project Gutenberg.

When it came to the setting of *An Altar of Indignities*, I was in familiar territory. Athens is my second home, and when I am there, I find my way around the city not by the modern street names, but rather by using the ancient monuments as my markers. These same monuments loom large in the story.

Roman Athens in the early third century would have been a magnificent place, especially since the city had so recently been graced with new monuments built by Emperor Hadrian, as well as other rich patrons of Athens and the arts, like Herodes Atticus. One can not walk around Athens without seeing the mark of these men upon it, including the great library, the temple of Olympian Zeus, and the magnificent odeon of Herodes Atticus which is still in use to this day. While Rome's initial interactions with the Greeks and Athens included such things as the sack of Corinth and Sulla's destruction of Athens, men like Emperor Hadrian and Herodes Atticus more than made up for it in later years.

The villa of Atticus where the company stays in the story, and which is meant to belong to the family of Herodes Atticus, is something of my own creation and is meant to be located in the area of the modern neighbourhood of Pangrati where we live whenever we are in Athens. It is just up the hill from the Panathenaic Stadium and the ruins of the temple of Artemis Agrotera. History is everywhere in the Goddess Athena's city!

For more information about the archaeology and history of the places and monuments mentioned in the book, readers can check out *The World of An Altar of Indignities* blog series.

The major event at the centre of the story is the Greater Panathenaea, that ancient festival of Athens which was put on every four years from 566 B.C.E. until about 410 C.E. I really wanted to try and bring this most important of Athenian festivals to life in the book. One can imagine that the atmosphere, though deeply religious, was also chaotic and supremely exciting. I would have liked for The Etrurian Players to be a part of the competitions, but non-Greeks were not permitted to compete in the Panathenaea. The festival did indeed include musical and rhapsodic contests, athletic competitions, equestrian and naval events and more, and the prizes for victors included fortunes in coin and an immense supply of precious olive oil in the ornate red and black Panathenaic *amphorae* that adorn so many museum shelves today. A winner in the chariot race, for example, would take home not only a fortune in money, but also one-hundred-and-forty *amphorae* of olive oil!

I tried to stick to the order of the Greater Panathenaea's events as much as possible, but I did diverge on one important point for the sake of the story. Traditionally, the Panathenaic procession from the Dipylon Gate to the Acropolis took place on the sixth day of the festival, after the night of the Pannychis, and just before the *hecatomb* sacrifices and subsequent public feast. However, in *An Altar of Indignities*, the Panathenaic procession, which is beautifully portrayed on the Parthenon Frieze, is used to begin the festival. I made this change so that the Panathenaea could make a grand start in the story. It is an event of which The Etrurian Players are keen observers, though they certainly are not the centre of everyone's attention. There was a bit of indignity there, I suppose. At any rate, I hope that readers and purists will forgive this somewhat drastic change to the order of the Panathenaic festivities. You can read more about the Panathenaea in *The World of An Altar of Indignities*.

At the outset of some of my novels, nailing down a solid theme has sometimes been a challenge. Such was not the case with this particular book. If our own lives are altars before which we stand, offering various intentions, words, and actions throughout our lives, a whole range of indignities are, inevitably, going to be a part of that. Many of us (myself included!) tend to take life, and ourselves, far too seriously, much like Felix Modestus. If we don't let go of our self-imposed struggles, our egos, life or the Gods will find a way of forcing us to do so. And parenthood can - as Felix, Rufio, Clara, and Electra discover - be one of the most joyous, challenging, terrifying, humbling, and sometimes humiliating roles one can undertake. It is amazing how so wonderful an experience can be so replete with indignities, poop, pee, and all!

It seemed only right that the new parents in our story, so victorious in other areas of their lives, be brought back down to earth by their newborn babes, something which Terence surely contemplated as he developed *Heautontimorumenos*.

Some readers may find a few of the incidents in the book to be a bit off-putting, or over-the-top. Once again, however, we should remember that Roman comedy was indeed bawdy. The new theatre company, The Rome Antics, is intended to represent this raunchy aspect of Roman theatre, a distinct contrast to the more professional, almost sophisticated persona which Felix Modestus wishes to portray, and almost manages, for The Etrurian Players. I truly did enjoy pitting these two companies against each other, including the dog, Peli, and the monkey, Momo.

Speaking of Peli the dog, some of the incidents in this novel are not entirely fictional. Once again, I'll leave it at that.

For those of you who have enjoyed *An Altar of Indignities*, and who have become as attached to this colourful cast as much as I have, you will be glad to know that we are not yet finished with The Etrurian Players.

Just as Rufio and Clara are sad and reluctant to bid farewell to Felix and the others, so too am I reticent to see them go. For that reason, The Etrurian Players will indeed return in the third book in the series, *A Muse for All Seasons*.

Brace yourselves. The Etrurian Players will be back!

Thank you for reading.

Adam Alexander Haviaras
Stratford, Ontario
April 2024

GLOSSARY

adyton – the innermost sanctuary or shrine in the cella of a Greek or Roman temple

aedes – a temple; sometimes a room

aedile – an elected Roman official responsible for public buildings and public festivals

aedituus – a keeper of a temple

aestivus – relating to summer; a summer camp or pasture

agora – Greek word for the central gathering place of a city or settlement

amita – an aunt

amphitheatre – an oval or round arena where people enjoyed gladiatorial combat and other spectacles

apodyterium – the changing room of a bath house

ara – an altar

archimima – a rare 'leading lady' of the ancient theatre world

argentarius – (plur. *argentarii*) a banker, usually for the wealthy

armaria – closed, wooden shelves or cupboards where scrolls were kept in ancient libraries

assarius – (also *as*) lower denomination bronze coin, later minted in copper

athlothetai – high-ranking priestesses of Athens who played a large role in the Panathenaic Games

augur – a priest who observes natural occurrences to determine if omens are good or bad; a soothsayer

aulaeum – the curtain that was raised out of the floor before the stage of a Roman theatre

aureus – a Roman gold coin; worth twenty-five silver *denarii*

auriga – a charioteer

avia – grandmother

avus – grandfather

bibliostasion – part of an ancient library complex where the books were kept in *armaria*
bireme – a galley with two banks of oars on either side
boule – the citizen council of ancient Athens; consisted of up to five hundred citizens
bouleuterion – council house where the *boule* council of citizens met
bracae – knee or full-length breeches originally worn by barbarians but adopted by the Romans

caldarium – the 'hot' room of a bath house; from the Latin *calidus*
caligae – military shoes or boots with or without hobnail soles
cardo – a hinge-point or central, north-south thoroughfare in a fort or settlement, the *cardo maximus*
cavia – the seating in the auditorium of a Roman theatre
celebritas – fame or renown
cella – the inner chamber of a Greek or Roman temple
cena – the principal, afternoon meal of the Romans
cetus – (plur. *ceti*) a whale
chiton – a long woollen tunic of Greek fashion; also could be short, to mid-thigh for young men
chlamys – a short cloak worn by men in Ancient Greece
chryselephantine – ancient Greek sculptural medium using gold and ivory; used for cult statues
cinaedus – (plur. *cinaedi*) the 'receiver' in a homoerotic relationship
civica – relating to 'civic'; the civic crown was awarded to one who saved a Roman citizen in war
civitas – a settlement or commonwealth; an administrative centre in tribal areas of the empire

clepsydra – a water clock

cognomen – the surname of a Roman which distinguished the branch of a gens

collegia – an association or guild; e.g. *collegium pontificum* means 'college of priests'

colonia – a colony; also used for a farm or estate

consul – an honorary position in the Empire; during the Republic they presided over the Senate

corbita – a large, Roman merchant ship capable of carrying very large cargoes

cornicen – the horn blower in a legion

cornu – a curved military horn

cornucopia – the horn of plenty

corona – a crown; often used as a military decoration

cubiculum – a bedchamber

curule – refers to the chair upon which Roman magistrates would sit (e.g. *curule aedile*)

cythara – ancient harp used by Apollo

decumanus – refers to the tenth; the *decumanus maximus* ran east to west in a Roman fort or city

dediticii – a class of persons who were neither slaves, Latin allies, or Roman citizens

demos – (plur. *deme*) neighbourhood of the people or administrative area of ancient Athens; root of 'democracy'

denarius – a Roman silver coin; worth one hundred brass *sestertii*

depositum – the deposit of a very large sum of money, usually with an *argentarius*

desmoterion - a prison in the agora of Athens

dignitas – a Roman's worth, honour and reputation

domus – a home or house

doru – (plur. dorata) the cornel or ash-wood spear that was

the primary weapon of a hoplite soldier; about three meters (ten feet) long

drachma – (plur. *drachmae*) a silver coin of Ancient Greece, similar to the Roman *denarius*

dupondius – bronze Roman coin worth two asses

eques – a horseman or rider

equites – cavalry; of the order of knights in ancient Rome

fabrica – a workshop

fabula – an untrue or mythical story; a play or drama

falcata – curved, single-edged blade capable of delivering extremely heavy blows

familia – a Roman's household, including slaves

flammeum – a flame-coloured bridal veil

forum – an open square or marketplace; also a place of public business (e.g. the *Forum Romanum*)

frigidarium – the 'cold room' of a bath house; a cold plunge pool

fullo – a launderer

funeraticia – from *funereus* for funeral; the *collegia funeraticia* assured all received decent burial

futuere – literally 'get fucked!'

garum – a fish sauce that was very popular in the Roman world

gladius – a Roman short sword

gorgon – a terrifying visage of a woman with snakes for hair; also known as Medusa

greaves – armoured shin and knee guards worn by high-ranking officers

groma – a surveying instrument; used for accurately marking out towns, marching camps and forts etc.

hasta – a spear or javelin

hecatomb – a sacrifice of one hundred cattle

hieropoioi – high-ranking priests of Athens involved in the Panathenaic Games

horologion – a timekeeping device or station that included a sundial or water clock

horreum – a granary

hydraulis – a water organ

hypocaust – area beneath a floor in a home or bath house that is heated by a furnace

ientaculum – breakfast in ancient Rome, which was a small meal often consisting of *puls* (porridge), or bread dipped in honey or olive oil

imperator – a commander or leader; commander-in-chief

insula – a block of flats leased to the poor; also means 'island'

itinere – a road or itinerary; the journey

kenephoroi – young Athenian girls who were charged with carrying the sacred *peplos* of Athena, and leading the sacrificial animals in the Panathenaic procession

lanista – a gladiator trainer

landica – literally 'clitoris', a very big insult in Latin

lares – (singular *lar*) guardian spirits or deities in Roman religion

lararium – the household shrine to the *lares* and other gods

latifundium – (plur. *latifundia*) a large agricultural estate, typically worked by slaves

lemure – a ghost

lena – (masc. *leno*) a madam or pimp

libellus – a little book or diary

lituus – the curved staff or wand of an augur; also a cavalry trumpet

lorica – body armour; can be made of mail, scales or metal strips; can also refer to a cuirass

lotium – literally 'urine', sometimes used as an insult

lupa – a prostitute (literally a 'she-wolf')

lustratio – a ritual purification, usually involving a sacrifice

manica – handcuffs; also refers to the long sleeves of a tunic

marita – wife

maritus – husband

matertera – a maternal aunt

mati - the 'evil eye'

maximus – meaning great or 'of greatness'

metics – resident non-Greeks of Athens, or 'resident aliens'

mina – (plur. *minae*) the equivalent of one hundred *drachmae*, or fifty *shekels* in the East

mortarium – wide Roman kitchen vessel used for grounding, mixing and pounding food

mundus stercoris – literally 'a universe of shit' as a curse

murmillo – a heavily armed gladiator with a helmet, shield and sword

nomen – the gens of a family (as opposed to *cognomen* which was the specific branch of a wider gens)

nones – the fifth day of every month in the Roman calendar

novendialis – refers to the ninth day

numina – a spirit in Roman religion

nutrix – a wet-nurse or foster mother

nymphaeum – a pool, fountain or other monument dedicated to the nymphs officium – an official employment; also a sense of duty or respect

onager – a powerful catapult used by the Romans; named after a wild ass because of its kick

oneirocritica – an ancient manual or guide for the interpretation of dreams

palaestra – the open space of a gymnasium where wrestling, boxing and other such events were practiced

palliatus – indicating someone clad in a *pallium*, a cloak

parentalis – of parents or ancestors; (e.g. *Parentalia* was a festival in honour of the dead)

pater – a father

pax – peace; a state of peace as opposed to war

peplos – (plur. *peploi*) main piece of clothing for women in Ancient Greece; usually a long, pleated garment tied and folded over at the waist

peregrinus – a strange or foreign person or thing

peristylum – a peristyle; a colonnade around a building; can be inside or outside of a building or home

plebeius – of the plebeian class or the people

pompa funebris – a funeral procession

ponos – the toil or struggle that is a part of, and essential to, one's life

pontifex – a Roman high priest

popa – a junior priest or temple servant

posca – watered vinegar (poor man's wine)

pronaos – the porch or entrance to a building such as a temple

propylon – (plur. *propylaea*) a monumental entrance or gateway

protome – an adornment on a work of art, usually a frontal view of an animal

pugio – a dagger

pulpitum – the raised stage or dais on which actors performed

quadriga – a four-horse chariot

quadrans – smallest coin denomination used until c. A.D. 301

quinqueremis – a ship with five banks of oars

retiarius – a gladiator who fights with a net and trident

rosemarinus – the herb rosemary

rusticus – of the country; e.g. a *villa rustica* was a country villa

sacrum – sacred or holy; e.g. the *via sacra* or 'sacred way'

scaena frons – the stage background of an ancient theatre

schola – a place of learning and learned discussion

sestertius – a Roman silver coin worth a quarter *denarius*

sica – a type of dagger

sistrum – (plur. *sistra*) instrument made up of a handle with metal discs that one shook

skamma – the sand where fighting took place in athletic competition, or in the *gymnasium* or *palaestra*

skene – the theatrical backdrop of an ancient Greek theatre

spina – the ornamented, central median in stadiums such as the Circus Maximus in Rome

stadium – a measure of length approximately 607 feet; also refers to a race course

stibium – *antimony*, which was used by women for dyeing eyebrows in the ancient world

stoa – a columned, public walkway or portico for public use; often used by merchants to sell their wares

stola – a long outer garment worn by Roman women

strigilis – a curved scraper used at the baths to remove oil and grime from the skin taberna – (plur. *tabernae*) an inn or tavern

tabula – a Roman board game similar to backgammon; also a writing-tablet for keeping records

tabulae – the books or codices in which an *argentarius* would record the details of transactions

talent – the heaviest unit of weight in Ancient Greece; used to measure amounts of gold, silver, or copper coin (e.g. a talent of silver was equal to about six thousand Roman *denarii*)

tepidarium – the 'warm room' of a bath house

tessera – a piece of mosaic paving; a die for playing; also a small wooden plaque

thermae – public baths

thymele – altar to Dionysus set in the middle of the orchestra of a Greek *odeon*

titulus – a title of honour or honourable designation

torques – also 'torc'; a neck band worn by Celtic peoples and adopted by Rome as a military decoration

trepidatio – trepidation, anxiety or alarm

tribunus – a senior officer in an imperial legion; there were six per legion, each commanding a cohort

triclinium – a dining room

tunica – a sleeved garment worn by both men and women

ustrinum – the site of a funeral pyre

vallum – an earthen wall or rampart with a palisade

velarium – (plur. *velaria*) awnings that extended over the seats of a theatre or amphitheatre to provide shade for spectators

venator – (plur. *venatores*) a hunter

veterinarius – a veterinary surgeon in the Roman army

vicus – a settlement of civilians living outside a Roman fort

vigiles – Roman firemen; literally 'watchmen'

vitis – the twisted 'vinerod' of a Roman centurion; a centurion's emblem of office

vittae – a ribbon or band

vomitorium - (plur. *vomitoria*) passageways in and out of a theatre, circus, or amphitheatre to ease the flow of pedestrian traffic

xenos - (plur. *xenoi*) a foreigner or outsider; non-Greek

ACKNOWLEDGMENTS

It is always something of a task when it comes to acknowledging the many people who have helped me to complete a particular novel, no matter how large or small their conscious, or unconscious, contribution has been. From someone familiar who regularly gives input to someone unknown who offers a friendly smile at the store, every interaction can have an impact on the creative process and, depending on the day, can slow or speed that process.

In writing *An Altar of Indignities*, there have been many who have come in and out of the frame of my consciousness. Some of those people have lingered, while others have raced through, but all have left an impression of the world, and of the nature of mortals. And that is good, for this story is one that strives to look at the nature of humans and how they interact with each other.

Before thanking the living, it is important to thank others.

First and foremost, to Apollo and the Muses, I offer my undying appreciation for the path I was set upon so very long ago, for every act of creativity is both a toil and a joy from which I manage to learn something new and gain further wisdom. This book is no different. I am grateful for the creative force that drives me to get up at 5 a.m. every morning to do what I am meant to do. I have much gratitude for those golden hours and, though I am not a traditionally religious person, I certainly have faith and believe that there are forces of good that are far beyond our understanding. And that is a mystery I am happy to live with.

I would be remiss if I did not give some credit to the shade of Terence for his subtle genius, especially when it comes to his *Heautontimorumenos*. For so young a man (it is believed he died at around 25 years old) to have written so thoughtful a work about life, and fathers and sons, guilt and joy…well…it is awe-inspiring. Wherever he is on the other side of the river, I offer him my thanks. I hope he doesn't mind being a part of this story.

Likewise, I am grateful to the spirit of Henry Thomas Riley whose English translation of Terence's play is accessible and entertaining. I'm not sure if he knew that the work he toiled over in the mid-nineteenth century would be so helpful and enjoyable today, but I do hope that he can take some pleasure in the thought of his legacy.

I would also like to express my gratitude to the shades of my departed grandparents, Policarpos and Ploumi Haviaras who, so long ago, made their way across the war-torn world of the 1940s from the island of Chios to Detroit, Michigan to start a new life for their family. Journeys are a part of every story, and theirs was certainly epic. They passed away all too soon, but their kindness resonates across the years. Thankfully, they were not fishmongers.

Now for the living…

I would like to thank all of the fans of *Sincerity is a Goddess*, the first book in *The Etrurian Players* series, for all of their supportive and encouraging messages over the last year and a half. All of the positivity that emanated like sunshine from my readers for that first book helped me to push on through to the end of *An Altar of Indignities*. Writing can be a very lonely endeavour and, when a book is released into the world, authors do not know who reads it and if they enjoyed it. To all those fans who took the time to leave a review, or send me a message, I am grateful for the encouragement that helped me to keep going.

Once again, it befalls me to present my gratitude to all of my fellow historians, romanophiles, and philhellenes in the various Facebook groups who have provided information related to the history and settings of this book, particularly

Roman Athens. I am always grateful to the online community of history-lovers whose members are, more often than not, just happy to share their enthusiasm for ancient history.

As with all of my books, I am deeply thankful to my wonderful patrons on Patreon whose generous support and faith in my work, and that of Eagles and Dragons Publishing, continues to astonish me. I am grateful to these amazing patrons at the time of publication: Edwin K. Gwaltney, Greg Hancock, John Meyers, and Bonnie Miller. Thank you to all of you!

To my amazing editor, A. Diassiti, at Beautiful Ink Editing, I must express my deep thanks and admiration for her professionalism and attention to detail that has helped bring this book to full fruition. As one editorial review stated of her work "the editing…is top-notch in this book, making for a smooth reading experience." I couldn't agree more.

I wish to acknowledge my dear friends, Jean-Francois and Heather Lamontagne who are the most dedicated and selfless parents I have ever known. Their sacrifice and courage is inspiring and truly Spartan.

I also want to thank my in-laws, Lena and Costis Diassiti in Pangrati, Athens, for their love and support whenever we are blessed enough to visit Athena's ancient city. The atmosphere of laughter, food, and family chaos at our Athenian home is a constant source of inspiration, as well as a blessing. Life at the villa with The Etrurian Players is in no small part a reflection of the reality of our family visits and though the goat was fictional, the dog will long be remembered! For these reasons, and much more, I have dedicated this book to them.

With all my heart, I would like to thank my daughters, Alexandra and Athena. To be a parent is, I now know, one of the most joyous, challenging, terrifying, humbling, and sometimes humiliating experiences of life. From the day that they were born, I have been in awe of my daughters, how they have grown from babes-in-arms into young adults with opinions and reasoning that would challenge the mightiest of philosophers, let alone their doting father. I am grateful for the love and support they constantly show me - which I endeavour to return in kind - and for their patience with me at every stage as I stumble my way through the trials of parenthood like an agoraphobe in the streets of Athens. Thank you for all that you are and do, my girls. I wouldn't change a thing.

Lastly, to my wife, Angelina, I offer my undying gratitude for all of her support for this novel, all those that have gone before, and all of those yet to come. She is, without question, my greatest inspiration and has a direct impact on all of my work. She doesn't complain when I wake her as I stumble out of bed in the wee hours before dawn, nor does she chide me when I don't hear what she is saying due to the 'voices' in my head, as I'm constantly formulating the next plot point or story. No author can find true satisfaction or success without support at home and in the heart. If the Muses drive me to be a story-teller every day I draw breath, Angelina drives me to be the very best version of myself and to see the beauty that is all around us.

Adam Alexander Haviaras
Stratford, Ontario
April 2024

ABOUT THE AUTHOR

Adam Alexander Haviaras is a best-selling and award-winning author and historian who has studied ancient and medieval history and archaeology in Canada and the United Kingdom. He currently resides in Stratford, Ontario with his wife and children where he is continuing his research and writing other works of historical fantasy.

Historical Fiction/Fantasy Titles

The Eagles and Dragons Series

The Dragon: Genesis (Prequel)
A Dragon among the Eagles (Prequel)
Children of Apollo (Book I)
Killing the Hydra (Book II)
Warriors of Epona (Book III)
Isle of the Blessed (Book IV)
The Stolen Throne (Book V)
The Blood Road (Book VI)
The Eagles and Dragons Legionary Box Set (Books 0-I-II)
The Eagles and Dragons Tribune Box Set (Books III-IV-V)

The Carpathian Interlude Series

The Carpathian Interlude - Complete Trilogy Box Set
Immortui (Part I)
Lykoi (Part II)
Thanatos (Part III)

The Mythologia Series
Chariot of the Son: The Story of Phaethon
Wheels of Fate: The Story of Pelops and Hippodameia
A Song for the Underworld: The Story of Orpheus and Eurydice
The Reluctant Hero: The Story of Bellerophon and the Chimera
Mythologia: First Omnibus Edition

Heart of Fire: A Novel of the Ancient Olympics

Saturnalia: A Tale of Wickedness and Redemption in Ancient Rome

The Etrurian Players
Sincerity is a Goddess (Book I)
An Altar of Indignities (Book II)

Novels of Alexander the Great
The Asp of Saqqara (Book I)

Titles in the Historia Non-fiction Series
Historia I: Celtic Literary Archetypes in *The Mabinogion*: A Study of the Ancient Tale of *Pwyll, Lord of Dyved*
Historia II: Arthurian Romance and the Knightly Ideal: A study of Medieval Romantic Literature and its Effect upon Warrior Culture in Europe
Historia III: *Y Gododdin*: The Last Stand of Three Hundred Britons - Understanding People and Events during Britain's Heroic Age
Historia IV: Camelot: The Historical, Archaeological and Toponymic Considerations for South Cadbury Castle as King Arthur's Capital

Eagles and Dragons Publishing Guides
Writing the Past: The Eagles and Dragons Publishing Guide
to Researching, Writing, Publishing and Marketing Historical
Fiction and Historical Fantasy

Stay Connected

To connect with Adam and learn more about the ancient world visit www.eaglesanddragonspublishing.com

Sign up for the Eagles and Dragons Publishing Newsletter at www.eaglesanddragonspublishing.com/newsletter-join-the-legions/ to receive a **FREE BOOK**, first access to new releases and posts on ancient history, special offers, and much more!

Readers can also connect with Adam on Twitter @AdamHaviaras and Instagram @ adam_haviaras

On Facebook you can 'Like' the Eagles and Dragons page to get regular updates on new historical fiction and non-fiction from Eagles and Dragons Publishing.

To watch Eagles and Dragons Publishing's mini documentaries and other fun videos, be sure to follow us on TikTok and subscribe to our channels on YouTube or Rumble.

More from

EAGLES AND DRAGONS PUBLISHING

Step into the world of Ancient Rome with the Etrurian Players!

Sincerity is a Goddess is a heartwarming story of friendship and love that takes you on a bawdy and hilarious journey through the world of ancient Rome.

If you like dramatic and romantic stories about second chances, misunderstandings, and a bit with a dog, then you will love *Sincerity is a Goddess*!

Read this book today for a theatrical adventure that will have you cringing, laughing, crying, and realizing that there is indeed hope for everyone. Well, almost everyone…

The Etrurian Players are coming! Brace yourselves!

Step into the world of the ancient Olympic Games!

A Mercenary… A Spartan Princess… And Olympic Glory…

Heart of Fire is a book for all those who struggle to make their dreams come true.

Start your adventure today and set off on a gritty, mysterious, and emotional journey into the heart of Ancient Greece.

Available from all major retailers and public libraries in e-book, paperback, and hardcover editions, or direct from Eagles and Dragons Publishing at:

www.eaglesanddragonspublishing.com

Enjoy some Roman Holiday reading with *Saturnalia: A Tale of Wickedness and Redemption in Ancient Rome*

Long before Ebenezer Scrooge, there was Catus Pompilius, the meanest man in Rome.

Saturnalia is an exciting retelling of Charles Dickens' classic tale. It is also a story for fans of ancient Rome, of tales of gods and men, and stories that make one examine the quality of the life we lead as mortals.

If you are a fan of *A Christmas Carol*, stories about life and redemption against all odds, then you will love *Saturnalia*!

Available in audiobook, e-book, paperback, and hardcover editions from all major book retailers and public libraries.

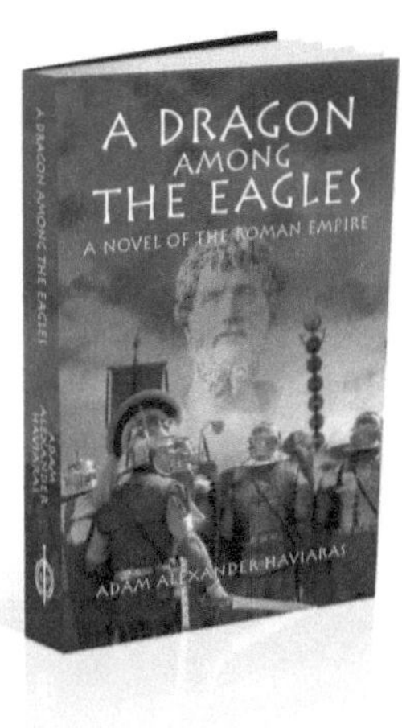

EAGLES AND DRAGONS LEGIONARY BOX SET

BOOKS O - I - II

Begin your adventure in the Roman Empire with a great deal!

Get the Eagles and Dragons series Legionary Box Set today.

This digital box set includes the #1 best-selling prequel novel, *A Dragon among the Eagles*, as well as Book I, *Children of Apollo*, and Book II, *Killing the Hydra*.

The Eagles and Dragons Legionary Box Set is available from all major on-line e-book retailers, public libraries, or direct from Eagles and Dragons Publishing at:

www.eaglesanddragonspublishing.com

EAGLES AND DRAGONS TRIBUNE BOX SET

BOOKS III - IV - V

Continue your adventure in the Roman Empire with another great deal!

Get the Eagles and Dragons series Tribune Box Set today.

This digital box set includes the reader-acclaimed novels *Warriors of Epona*, *Isle of the Blessed*, and *The Stolen Throne*.

The Eagles and Dragons Tribune Box Set is available from all major on-line e-book retailers, public libraries, or direct from Eagles and Dragons Publishing at:

www.eaglesanddragonspublishing.com

DISCOVER THE *MYTHOLOGIA* SERIES TODAY!

Long ago, when gods and heroes walked the earth in triumph and tragedy, true love and epic deeds were set among the stars...

Do you love Greek and Roman Mythology?

If so, then you will love Eagles and Dragons Publishing's newest series!

In this unique, ground-breaking fantasy series suitable for all ages, you will discover a world of Titans, Gods and Heroes.

Start the series the First Omnibus Edition of the *Mythologia* series and escape into unique retellings of the poignant and epic myths of Phaethon, Pelops and Hippodameia, and of Orpheus and Eurydice.

New books are being added all the time, so you will never run out of adventures!

Begin the *Mythologia* series today and embark on an epic adventure with the Gods and Heroes of ancient Greece!

Available from all major retailers and public libraries in e-book, paperback, and hardcover editions, or direct from Eagles and Dragons Publishing at:

www.eaglesanddragonspublishing.com

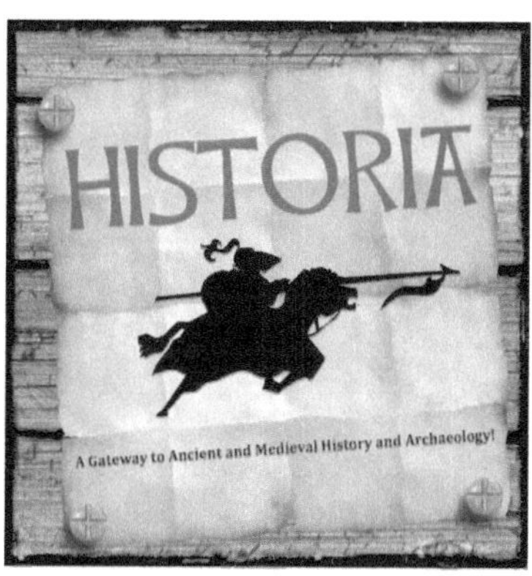

HISTORIA

A Gateway to Ancient and Medieval History and Archaeology!

Do you find ancient and medieval history and archaeology fascinating?

If so, then you will love Eagles and Dragons Publishing's *Historia* non-fiction series of books!

In this series, author and historian, Adam Haviaras will take you through such topics as Celtic mythology, medieval knighthood, and the search for the historical King Arthur and Camelot.

If you are interested in ancient and medieval history, and Arthurian studies, then you will want to check out the *Historia* non-fiction series.

Available from all major on-line e-book retailers or direct from Eagles and Dragons Publishing.

Do you love ancient and medieval history and mythology?

Visit 'EDPublishingAgora' on Etsy today to check out our array of vintage, used, new and handmade items including clothing, prints and stationary, jewelry, various collectibles, ceramics and, of course, new and used books, including signed and/or inscribed copies of our own titles.

Check out Eagles and Dragons Publishing's AGORA on Etsy at the following link:

https://www.etsy.com/ca/shop/EDPublishingAgora

See you in the AGORA, the marketplace for history-themed gifts and books!

Planning a vacation in Europe or the British Isles?

Visit Ancient World Travel for a wide range or helpful articles, travel tips, travel resources, and amazing deals on everything from airfare and accommodation, to car rentals, museum passes, and behind-the-scenes tours of the world's greatest historical sites.

Check out Ancient World Travel today at:

https://www.ancientworldtravel.net/

*Ancient World Travel© is a subsidiary of Eagles and Dragons Publishing©.

www.ingramcontent.com/pod-product-compliance
Lightning Source LLC
Chambersburg PA
CBHW022248310726
48973CB00001B/3